The Childs Conundrum

The Childs Conundrum

G.K. Sutton

Copyright © 2009 by G.K. Sutton.

Library of Congress Control Number: 2009911708
ISBN: Hardcover 978-1-4415-9696-3
Softcover 978-1-4415-9695-6

All rights reserved. No part of this book may be reproduced or transmitted in any form or by any means, electronic or mechanical, including photocopying, recording, or by any information storage and retrieval system, without permission in writing from the copyright owner.

This is a work of fiction. Names, characters, places and incidents either are the product of the author's imagination or are used fictitiously, and any resemblance to any actual persons, living or dead, events, or locales is entirely coincidental.

The cover photograph depicts the Grace Church & St. Stephen's Parish Episcopal Church in Colorado Springs, Colorado, home of a rare 1928 Welte (New York) four-manual organ (IV/61). Photograph is by William van Pelt and is used with permission.

The author's photograph depicts the console of the Mander chancel organ (IV/135, 2002) at Peachtree Road United Methodist Church, Atlanta, Georgia. Photograph is by J. O. Love and is used with permission.

This book was printed in the United States of America.

To order additional copies of this book, contact:
Xlibris Corporation
1-888-795-4274
www.Xlibris.com
Orders@Xlibris.com
70072

DEDICATION

Rise up, my love, my fair one, and come with me,
for lo, the winter is past, the rain is over and gone,
the flowers appear upon the earth;
the time of the singing of the birds is come.

Song of Solomon 2: 10-12
preferably to the tune of the anthem by Healey Willan
(1880-1968)

O taste and see how gracious the Lord is:
blest is the man that trusteth in him.

Psalm 34: 8
preferably to the tune of the motet by Ralph Vaughan Williams
(1872-1958)

Foreword

Yes, it is that time again, where I ramble on (how I do go on!) about the evils of the first few pages we call a foreword (you would not believe how many times people mangle that word); apologize to the readers therefor (another misunderstood legal term that others think I've misspelled, along with 'situate' and 'personalty'; by the way, 'aka' stands for 'also known as', just to help you out); thank a bunch of saintly souls who took pity upon me and helped me through this latest attempt at literacy (it surely ain't literature); and pontificate (my favorite part).

I need to start with a *caveat*. This is a sequel to my first novel, *The Witherspoon Legacy*, and the action picks up where that book left off. I'm not trying to bilk you out of money for another book. However, there are parts of this one that may not make sense unless you have read the first volume. I did not regurgitate those events, but plunged right in with the plots, subplots, splots, whatever, that make up this tome. I tried to fill in some blanks, but many of the characters and underlying events in this book have already been fleshed out in the first one, and I am just building on those.

Secondly, it is LONG. I have developed this pattern: I seem to get to the point of 80K words, like the novel pretty well but realize I need to start filling in some blanks. Then it just takes off. This one apparently was a runaway horse.

Thirdly, I must apologize. Chapter 1 starts out with sex. I was so proud in the beginning stages of writing this novel, because I had kept all the steaminess confined to one chapter at a turning point in the plot. So the revelation of the affair was a shock to me, too. You know, you hear a whisper here and there, but you think, "There's just no way . . . ."

I attempted to make this vignette a flashback later in the book, but the whole affair acted as a backdrop for much of the motivations in subsequent scenes of the book. Besides, it was nigh impossible to create a workable flashback that lasts three chapters. My writing is confusing enough for the reader without creating more obstacles to comprehension.

And then, to make matters worse, in this novel other characters started appearing, just to get killed off, and they began dropping like flies. At some point I had to consider the future of humanity and just stop writing, solve it already. I mean, this is Florida, not Texas, and we don't kill them just because they need it. Otherwise, my books' death tolls might rival Tolstoy's in *War and Peace*.

This book, although action-ridden, deals with all Amanda Childs' angst and demons that have been resurrected. Marjorie's death and the events of the first novel have left her alone to do battle with old feelings, now complicated by new discoveries. Frankly I left some of the subplots purposefully obscure and/or unresolved, because in real life we don't always solve all the puzzles. And the sequel to this one is already in the works and rough-written, possessing a whole new set of challenges.

People to thank? This part always scares me, because I know there are so many I will forget to acknowledge. I'm always thrilled when people tell me they read and enjoy my writing, and that inflames me to write more. So those are always my first loves, and the most expedient to blame for these new novels.

The first name that comes to mind is Fred Swann. I cannot believe that a short e-mail inquiry about his recital program some twenty years ago spawned such a friendship and collaboration, for he has been so much help and encouragement to me. You in the organ world know what a great personage he is, as well as a fabulous musician, and those of you who don't, well, you don't know what you've been missing. He has read the thing and found errors and made suggestions on all sorts of topics. Some of these suggestions took me quite by surprise, but all were valuable. I'm engaging him to collaborate with the organ consultant on designing this new organ for the church, and he has been diligent in developing a marvelous stoplist for Amanda. She for one hopes that building a new organ will be safer than some of the activities in which she has heretofore engaged.

As a digression (I do that a lot), I must confess to you that the mistakes still found in my novels are wholly my fault. As I alluded to in the foreword to *Witherspoon*, I cannot leave a manuscript alone, so it gets extensively 'diddled with', even while others are proofing. Fred has found errors for me in the finished version of *Kreiser*, but those were added during and after his initial proofing.

Peter Storandt is a true friend who has suffered my cooking a time or two and my prose for several years now, and even ended up at a redneck cookout with me once. (I think the latter discouraged his visiting again! It certainly scared me; the transition from a rickety tracker organ in a historic church to a bunch of geetars was jarring. You have to admit, though: the venue was one heck of an antebellum house, a real beauty in its heyday.) Peter suggested one of the D.C. churches I used in *Kreiser*. He kindly consented to proof this novel. His help was sorely appreciated, for he discovered many of my redundancies, mistakes I was too myopic to spot myself.

Then there is my good friend Mark Quarmby, from Sydney, who tried to give some helpful advice about Aussie idioms for Ian Callander, who had such a small part in this play. Of course, after the advent of Australian clichés in our movies and television commercials, I just could not bring myself to have him say "G'day, mate." Mark also steered me away from impaling an organist on the pipes at one of the large Sydney organ venues, persuading me that would be a difficult feat logistically. And crucifixion would have been impossible for this murderer to accomplish acting alone. I would otherwise have found a way to fly over and try it, only for the purpose of book research, of course. There were interesting discussions one night at the Organ Historical Society Convention in Cleveland about stuffing bodies inside 32' pipes, and I have taken that under advisement for a future whodunit.

I wish to thank one of my old friends from my college English days, Angela Broxson Sanders, who proofed my work as well. I apologize: I acknowledge that I didn't take all her excellent advice. By golly, I made As in every English course I took, and I like my rules better than those of the *Chicago Manual of Style*. Because I am a lawyer I have naturally found justification for every one, and as a last resort there's a gun around here somewhere. In the middle of all these improbable plots (see below) are myriads of grammar and punctuation rules that I have apparently consigned to the landfill. English teachers nowadays take exception to my use of dashes and quotation marks (and sometimes commas). But my style books from my high school and college days tell me I'm doing it right, and if the rules have changed, they are just wrong.

I am extremely fortunate to have many friends of overwhelming talent who actually acknowledge me and are kind to me. One of these, William van Pelt, again a great name in the organ world, has been of inestimable assistance in submitting several stunning specimens for consideration as a cover photograph. The one that grabbed me and was eventually chosen depicts Grace Church & St. Stephen's Parish Episcopal Church in Colorado Springs, Colorado, home of a rare 1928 Welte four-manual organ. And Bill and I have engaged in several conversations regarding appropriate organs, stoplists and church settings that might approximate Amanda's present church instrument. Therefore, I thank him heartily for his generosity of talent and time.

There are many people who have become dear to me for their championing the cause of my writings. Just to name a few, in addition to Fred and Mark, I must again applaud J.O. Love. His photo of me is apparently the only one I like. There are many discarded attempts by others I have saved in case I ever break up a vegetable garden again. I will need them to scare off the varmints. A huge thanks to Sheri Hundley, with whom I work, for causing a public scene and shaming a local bookstore for not carrying my books. Stephen Best, an organist and professor with whom I've had the pleasure of corresponding over the last few years, wrote a glowing review of the last book for both the online bookstore sites and the organ e-mail chat lists, and his prose made me so much want to meet the author! Sue Goddard in Atlanta, a true Southern belle and grace personified, as well as one heck of an organist, not only was a source of useful information for *The Kreiser Affair*, but has been so kind as to promote my books on several occasions in the Atlanta area. Louise Peters, who I watched grow up and whose family I have known all my life (her father and I both being Baptists converted to Episcopalianism), has graciously sold my books in her local shop.

I am blessed to have friends all over the world that spread the word. In fact, so far the only advertisement has been by word of mouth and internet/e-mail, but I'm always astounded and grateful to hear from someone halfway across the country or world that took the time to read my work and liked it.

There is someone I wish to thank, whose name I don't even know. She, some alleged author in New York City, was given my first novel by a friend. Of course, I am always amused by the left-handed compliments from Manhattanites, natives and imports, but mostly the latter (who cover their inferiority complexes because not 'born' in New York City; of course, I think the only people actually born in Manhattan just happened to arrive at the wrong time and place). She informed my friend that it was 'OK for a first book attempt', but 'the plot was so improbable'. I started thinking back over the scenes in the book, and every one was based loosely on events I had personally experienced, seen or read about. In other words, I know stuff like this happens, attested to by anecdotes from my work, the courthouses, CNN, NPR, church coffee hours, the local greasy spoon. Then I looked at the *New York Times'* bestseller list and thought, yeah, there's a slough of improbable plots. People must really like that. Hmm. As well-bred Southerners say, "That's nice."

That being said, I will again inform the reader that all people and events are the product of my overactive imagination, spurred on by the craziness which comprises real life. I feel I must repeat this, because I had lunch not long ago with someone who had read the first book and informed me that everyone in my home-town community (I guess she meant those half-dozen who actually found the book, bought it and read it) was trying to determine who were in actuality my subjects. I take great pains to avoid writing about 'real people'. Yes, sometimes similar events have occurred in my own life; they always say to write about what you know. My characters are amalgams of my experiences and exposure to various media, which I wrap and mold into fictional persons. All the judges I know can rest assured they are not being described herein.

My brother for one (and who is and always has been older than I, as I constantly remind him when he starts spouting about my approaching middle age) is convinced that I am writing some rosy view of my ideal life as an heiress abducted by gypsies, because yes, as children we had a dog named Bozo, yes, my maiden name was Andrews, and yes, we have a cousin named Charlie Petrino. But I LIKE those names, even the name Audsley, which I thought would work for my organ consultant. I am making no implied statements by doing so. I decided I'd rather use those names than peruse the telephone book for other names for my characters. At the rate I go through these people, I may have to resort to that as well before long.

I'm not Amanda or Charlotte. I'm ugly and fat and dangerously close to being middle-aged (as opposed to my brother, who *is* middle-aged). Some person of the male persuasion with whom I used to work asked me how I knew so much about sex to write the love scenes. Of course I stared him down like Amanda did Clarence during the doctor's first appearance, and his name went on the list of possible future victims. Apparently thirty plus years of marriage are not qualification enough. I admit I am in the fourth stage of marriage, and have probably forgotten some of the steps (when Alzheimer's threatens, one has to skip a few and cut to the chase). But I read a lot.

Pet sermon for the day: So many people who write books about the South cast their characters with an awful accented redneck dialect. As far as the South goes nowadays, there are more imports than natives, and one is not as likely to encounter those speaking with my thick South-Alabama drawl, honed over many years attempting to get it right. I get somewhat incensed at Yankees and Southerners alike who patronizingly try to emulate the Southern accent in print, and I don't engage in it myself. Besides, there is a myriad of localized dialects that only clued-in Southerners and linguists can distinguish, so one cannot generalize about the subject without revealing his ignorance.

Furthermore, there is much value in my accent (something I didn't possess until after the age of twelve, when my Southern lineage was denigrated by an English teacher because I possessed no accent back then; this is yet another example how teachers can unwittingly inflict damage upon their students by careless remarks). Like one of my favorite judges, now deceased, I have had the pleasure of mopping the floor with those who mistook the drawl and my Southern graciousness for stupidity. And I find that juries are more likely to trust someone who can talk turkey with them.

Speaking of which, I wish to close by remembering someone who meant a great deal to me in my formative years as a lawyer. His name was Robert Meredith Tippins, who we affectionately called Tip. I met him while interning with the public defender's office my second summer in law school, and I later ended up working in the same office for a few years, during which time I handled everything but first-chair capital murder cases (my first would-be murder client opted for a 'real' lawyer instead, and her grandparents mortgaged their house for him to cop her a plea to second-degree murder, something she could have gotten for free, but I again digress).

Tip taught me so much about the day-to-day practice of law, and helped me lose the horror and panic of appearing in court and trying cases. He made practicing law, and life itself, practical and fun. My best war stories always include Tip. He was a true mentor and friend, and bought me my first four martinis (payment for my closing a very old estate for him and saving him from a contempt of court charge; that final accounting balanced on the first try, thereby proving the value of good gin). I shake my head in disbelief at some of our escapades during those days of unreal caseloads, taking investigative jaunts to crime scenes, second-chairing each other's trials, and happy hours and holidays with our public defender family. Oh, and that damning videotape.

Tip would laugh heartily if he knew I was writing novels, and probably contribute anecdotes. I am convinced he is representing St. Peter against all those lawsuits by people not making it into heaven (if he isn't representing them), and throwing something on the counsel's table in theatrical disgust. I miss you, man.

Prologue

"Find the medical examiner and see what he has. Let's move on this."

The ruddy balding man nodded, acknowledging the whispered charge given him by the tall, spare, severe looking man sitting in the pew. The former straightened up and disappeared, melting into a sea of black suits.

The large Baptist church was well lit, and the morning sunlight through the lightly colored stained glass windows competed with the sheen provided by the creamy walls above the darkly paneled wainscoting. The huge wooden decorative rafters at regular intervals along the room met at points in dramatic fashion along the apex of the symmetrical open A-frame high ceiling, the latest in popular standard architectural features over the last twenty years of construction. Between the beams the ceiling was punctuated by large pendant light fixtures, the ambience enhanced by indirect track lighting focusing front and center. The effect was an aesthetically pleasing open and airy space for Protestant worship.

The room was thronged with somber-faced people dressed in black and dark tones. At the end of the long center aisle a white coffin stood open, supporting a substantial drape of red roses and white calla lilies, and was situate just before the elevated carved large wooden pulpit. The scene was framed by an enormous stage, empty choir loft and baptistery with a large stained wooden cross suspended above it. People milled around in a half-hearted queue before the bier, viewing the corpse and speaking in hushed tones, many eyes darting from the coffin to the bowed figure sitting in the front pew. The inevitable crimson carpet spilled from the raised dais, flooded down the aisle, and was staunched only partially by the massive gushing groupings of flower wreaths and potted plants sent by well-meaning friends of the family.

The Honorable Lawrence Kilmer, Circuit Judge, sat two pews back from the front, replete in navy suit, separating himself from the pallbearers dressed in black in the front pew ahead of him. He tried to maintain a sober demeanor while curiously looking around him at the sanctuary rapidly filling up with humanity. He was burning to know just which of the who's who in the community was making an appearance for the funeral service of the doctor's wife.

He glanced over at the coffin, open for visitation prior to the service, and thought with a start the old cliché, 'She looks really peaceful.' For a murder victim, that is, he added to himself.

Then Kilmer turned his eyes over to the left row of pews, toward the vista of the widowed doctor on the front sitting with his father and sister, his young twin boys sitting still and wide-eyed beside him. Other family members flanked him like a personal guard detail as he replied stoically to the throng of mourners encircling him, now and again wiping his eyes with a handkerchief in sorrow for his dead wife.

Poor sod, the judge thought sardonically, he'll have plenty to cry about soon. Right now he's clueless as to how much trouble he's in. Of course, who wouldn't give his eyeteeth to be surrounded all day long by all his sweet young nurses. Guess he will miss that.

Judge Kilmer was making a reluctant but obligatory appearance in partial concession to his mother, because of her lifelong friendship with the Young family, particularly the elder patriarch Dr. Young, the area's family dentist for many years. That relationship had thrown the judge and doctor together at social events from time to time, even though they were about eleven years apart in age, the judge being older.

Particularly after his appointment to the judiciary, Kilmer made sure his personal contacts with the Youngs were few and far between, inasmuch as he had determined long ago that the Young clan was beneath the Kilmer patriarchal line in social status. He took great pride in the fact that he was the only child of a former president of the Florida Senate; his father, who had died several years earlier, was a life-long politician who also served as lieutenant governor. His great-grandfather had been elected governor of the state, a fact of which Kilmer was inordinately smug.

However, his mother had asked him as a special favor to make an appearance. He had initially refused, citing professional reasons, but saw the stubborn line of her jaw. He knew that her ire boded ill for his plans to modify some of the investments from his father's testamentary trust, an act which required her consent. Therefore, he agreed to accompany her to the funeral, where he sat in sullen silence, maintaining an icy dignity he thought befitting a judge, not deigning to mingle with others come to pay their respects.

The judge sat seething, his druthers being making a dramatic entrance where all eyes were on him. His mother had insisted, however, that they be early. Curious, he stiffly turned in the pew to look behind him, and noticed more than a few dignitaries in attendance, some of whom he acknowledged with a nod. He caught the eye of one of his young judicial clerks, the latest in his string of damsels in distress to whom he gave counsel during work hours. She waved timidly at him, and he nodded at her, turning back in his seat. Thankful his wife chose not to attend this service, he thought, 'There's at least one person to flirt with after the service,' and he was momentarily satisfied.

The anticipation withered as he caught the eye of a stunning auburn-haired woman, dressed in a clingy black dress which stopped above her knees and hugged her attractively petite figure, who had come up to the bereaved doctor and had clasped his hand possessively, clinging to it and speaking softly to him. The judge's mother, Elizabeth Kilmer, an elderly woman, slender and patrician, impeccably dressed in expensive black crepe and with carefully coiffed white hair, quietly took her seat beside her son, saw the woman and hissed under her breath, "What is that hussy doing here?"

Kilmer frowned, not deigning to answer. He glanced at his mother and saw hatred and a touch of fear in her features. He was taken aback by her reaction, wondering how the woman's presence would be able to ruffle his mother's normally serene and controlled demeanor. An idea flitted through his mind, leaving him in momentary disquietude, but he shrugged it off.

Why does my mother have to entangle us with the Young family? he railed inwardly, as he had many times before. He could not fathom the tie that seemed to bind his mother to the doctor's clan.

Looking at the red-haired beauty still insinuating herself with the doctor, he thought, That particular sweet thing is deadly. She will be Alan Young's undoing. As though she had divined the judge's thoughts, the woman straightened up from kissing the doctor's cheek and wiped the remaining lipstick she had smeared there. She looked over at the judge and smiled, as the doctor awkwardly disentangled himself from her grasp. Kilmer inclined his head slightly toward the woman, stiffly, suddenly wary, and darted his eyes around surreptitiously to see if anyone had noticed the exchange of looks.

The coffin was closed by the funeral home staff, and the large church seemed to flow with mourners as soft organ music began filtering through the room, cascading from the hidden pipes housed in the overhead chambers flanking the baptistery and choir loft. The music acted to deaden the conversations of those around him to whispers, and to cause others to drift toward the remaining available seats. The sanctuary was filled to capacity, and people were standing lining the back wall, there to show their respects.

The judge, startled at the advent of the music, turned to look up at the console above him to the right of the pulpit on the dais and noted the female organist, who nodded at him briefly in recognition before turning her attention back to the music. He recognized her at once as Amanda Childs, an attorney in town and the organist of St. Catherine's Episcopal Church.

Feeling somewhat unsettled and irritated after making eye contact with the beautiful red-haired woman, he wondered irrelevantly, What is Amanda Childs doing here? Of course, he knew that in such a small town, it was likely that she knew the Youngs. In fact, she and Alan Young were about the same age. In any event, Kilmer never expected to see her here, playing for a service at the Baptist church, although as he recalled her parents had been Baptists. Listening to a few bars of the music, he found it unfamiliar and fumed, Why doesn't she just play 'Amazing Grace' or 'What a friend we have in Jesus'?

He noted that Dr. Young looked up at the organist, a look of mute gratefulness on his face. She met his look with a sad smile. Momentarily and irrationally angry, the judge was outraged that she had smiled thusly at the doctor but not at him. A hush fell over the room as the music solemnly wove its pattern, before being replaced by other quiet music.

As the music ended, two men entered from a far door and made their way onto the raised platform. One took his place beside the organ and sang an arrangement of 'Blessed assurance' in a strong baritone voice. Then the second man, the minister in professional gown, took the podium, reading the obituary and delivering a reading from scripture. A short homily and eulogy followed. The baritone then sang 'O God, our help in ages past'.

The judge sat back, his face a stone, his mind formulating his plans, oblivious to the encomiums heaped upon the deceased and family and the muffled sobs by mourners. He finally came to himself as the beginning strains of music were heard, the motif of the hymn woven into a fugue. Gradually the throngs of people exited the church, until just the family and pallbearers remained and the church was quiet. Kilmer started to leave as well, but his mother halted his progress, her hand on his arm. Kilmer hesitated.

As Alan Young paused, his hand on the closed casket, Kilmer observed as he gazed across the room and called softly, "Amanda." Amanda Childs, who had been standing in the far aisle, walked up to him and they embraced.

"Thanks so much for playing," he spoke hoarsely.

Amanda whispered something to him, squeezed his hand, and stooped to hug and speak briefly to the two solemn-eyed boys, who clung to her a few moments. Then the doctor's father led him off down the aisle, the two boys following, escorted out of the church by a pretty dark-haired woman holding them by the hand. Amanda looked on in pity as the rest of the family followed suit. Kilmer noted that the Chief of Police, Charles Petrino, who had served as an honorary pallbearer, was standing in the back of the church, and nodded at Amanda solemnly before disappearing.

Again Amanda's and the judge's eyes locked briefly, and she said quietly, "Hello, Judge Kilmer." He nodded and spoke an acknowledgement.

He wondered briefly at the nature of the relationship between Young and Amanda Childs as he reached the main door of the church. So they are more than mere acquaintances, he concluded. He sensed a pang of disquiet. Her friendship with Young could pose unforeseen complications. Her prowess as an attorney was well known.

He had heard a rumor that Childs, a widow for the last five years, was now dating someone. The current story circulating was that she had just become engaged, which might occupy her energies and keep her at bay. However, if her law partner Ralph Carmichael, another much sought-after and aggressive criminal defense attorney, became involved . . . .

Kilmer continued to think about the doctor in the back of the family's large black Lincoln sedan on the way to the graveside service with his mother, and even afterward, as he remained in the background and received hugs from a former secretary and the young clerk, weathering the frown of disapproval from his mother from across the cemetery. He looked around for Amanda Childs, but did not observe her. He sighed with relief.

A hand touched his shoulder. Looking around, he tensed as a familiar voice with an unusual accent stated quietly, "Hallo, Judge."

Turning, he saw the beautiful red-haired woman gazing at him. She licked her lips suggestively. "How have you been, Larry?" she whispered huskily as she reached up and kissed his cheek.

He swallowed as he felt color suffuse his face, and she wiped a smudge of her lipstick from his cheek. "I'm fine, Evie," he stated nervously, his eyes darting to see who might have noticed the exchange. "And you?" he asked politely.

She replied throatily, sudden tears in her eyes, "Oh, it's just so sad for Alan, you know, losing his beloved wife. But," her volume dropped dramatically, "I intend to take very good care of him. And I'm sure I can call on you for help, for old time's sake."

A touch of terror crossed Judge Kilmer's face before he masked it, murmured some excuse, quickly turned on his heel and fled as gracefully as he could. Seeing the balding man, Chief Assistant State Attorney Clarence Banks, to whom he had given the whispered task earlier, he walked up to the man and pulled him aside where they could not be overheard.

"What do you have, Clarence?" the judge asked urgently.

The prosecutor stated, "Medical examiner's findings are inconclusive. He refuses to submit a report until he receives toxicology results and reviews the medical file."

The judge squeezed his arm tightly but unobtrusively, and Clarence winced. "Sounds as if you need a 'come to Jesus' meeting with the medical examiner. I can't wait—I want to see an arrest warrant on the SOB on my desk tomorrow. You can hunt for evidence on the way to trial. And take care of it yourself. I don't want anyone else screwing this up."

"Doris, I need that amended itinerary now," the measured tones held a tinge of irritation.

Richard Dover, senior aide to U.S. Senator Thomas Whitmore, was speaking into a Bluetooth headset as he loped quickly down the plushly carpeted hallway. The man, of medium height and slight build, with youthful if chronically serious face, was dressed in a dapper Brooks Brothers suit. His tread bespoke a man on a mission, brooking no nonsense.

He stopped to speak briefly to a dark suited security officer standing stiffly outside a set of double doors. "Have we coordinated with the local law enforcement on security?" His voice was clipped, business-like.

"Yes, sir. We've been assured of their cooperation. I took care of the arrangements myself. Everything is in place."

Dover nodded as the officer opened the door for him. The senator was completing his final review of a speech with an assistant. He nodded at Dover and stood, pulling on his suit jacket.

"We are ready to roll, sir," Dover spoke respectfully.

"My itinerary?" the senator inquired.

The documents appeared in Dover's hand before the words were out of Whitmore's mouth. He gave the secretary a sharp look as he handed a copy over to the senator for review. Whitmore grimaced. "And this is styled as a weekend getaway?"

Thomas Whitmore scanned the pages, finally nodding his approval. He handed it to a pretty young assistant and turned to Dover. "Let's go."

The two men and the small entourage swept out, the security detail acting as advance guard with one officer behind, the members communicating with each other via their small wireless two-way headsets. Finally, as they made it outside and settled themselves into the limousine, Whitmore turned to Dover.

"The timing of Knox's news could not be worse," Whitmore muttered.

"Senator, it's best that we sit tight and say nothing. I'm working on that situation, so I should be able to provide you alternative resolutions shortly."

"Alternative resolutions?" the senator echoed disbelievingly. "I would think there is only one: disclosure before exposure."

"Only as a last resort," Dover replied soothingly. "For all we know, this story will not break. There are a myriad of possible scenarios. Let's do nothing for now."

Whitmore stared at him woodenly, choosing not to respond. At that point a small signal erupted in Dover's ear. "Excuse me, Senator," Dover spoke as he took the call. "Dover here."

"You know that glitch in the hardware we've been working on?" the unidentified voice spoke. "It's been taken care of."

Dover allowed himself the briefest of smiles.

PART I

Four Years Previously

Chapter 1

"Charlie, Amanda is gone." Charles Petrino heard the distraught voice of Marjorie Witherspoon over the phone line.

"What do you mean, gone?" he demanded.

"She has disappeared. Amanda told Sheila that she wasn't coming in tomorrow, and to cancel all her appointments. Amanda left all upset, with Sheila trying to stop her. That's not like her. She's never just walked out of work."

"Maybe she just went home to the farm to be alone," Charlie suggested gently. "She's been looking tired lately."

"I've checked with Fred. She's not at the farm. He hasn't seen her there in over three weeks. I don't even know where she's been sleeping at night."

Marjy's voice broke. "Charlie, there's more. Sheila said two men from the FBI showed up at the office this afternoon, and gave Amanda Andy's badge and some commendation plaque. Sheila said Amanda got quite irate with them, loudly insisted on knowing the circumstances behind his death, and demanded that his service revolver be returned."

"What?" Charlie croaked, suddenly alert. "How long ago?"

"Sheila said the men left hurriedly, and she walked in to find Amanda crumpled at her desk sobbing. Sheila tried to call you at the sheriff's department when they showed up, and was told you were out. She called me to come ASAP. When I got here, Amanda had already left." There was a muffled question, then Marjorie came back on the line. "She's been gone about twenty minutes."

Charlie was livid. "Why dispatch did not contact me I don't know."

Marjorie interrupted. "I'm still at her office. She left her purse here, her wallet, her driver's license, her money, all on her desk. Charlie, she would never go anywhere without those."

"Oh, God," Charlie groaned under his breath.

"I'm frightened. I thought she was better, that she was beginning to accept—things. I had hoped she was turning a corner. You've got to find her."

"I'll do my best," Charlie promised hoarsely.

Amanda Childs was a home-town girl turned attorney, having her own successful solo practice in Mainville. She and Charlie had been childhood friends, along with their best friends Monica Witherspoon and Billy Barnes, and the four had spent much of their adolescent years in the others' company.

Amanda, Charlie and Billy all completed college at Florida State University; then she was accepted into law school there, while Charlie took a job with the Florida Department of Law Enforcement in Tallahassee and toyed with the idea of an FBI career, and Billy obtained his law degrees at the University of Alabama. Upon graduation, Amanda spent three years with a private law firm in Orlando. Then just a few years ago she had moved back home and taken a job with the public defender's office, about the same time that Charlie had come back and accepted a job as chief investigator with the local sheriff's department.

Amanda cared for her mother until the latter's death from cancer, and planned her wedding to Andrew Childs, an FBI agent she had met when she was still in college. She had opened her own office a couple years ago, and was doing well.

One of Amanda's best friends was Marjorie Witherspoon, a wealthy woman several years her elder, who kept Amanda busily involved in community and church projects. Marjorie was the mother of Amanda's friend Monica, who had been killed, while in college, in an automobile accident several years before, along with her father and Marjorie's husband Jerrod Witherspoon.

Amanda's happiness had been shattered last year when Andrew was found murdered during an investigation into an international drug ring and money-laundering scheme. Suddenly she was alone, and could obtain no answers to the questions as to why Andy was killed. The Bureau had refused to disclose any details about the case.

Charlie still remembered the day she was told about Andy's death. Charlie had accompanied the sheriff who broke the news, and she had become hysterical and collapsed. She had withdrawn from all social activities, and it had taken much coaxing and effort by Marjorie Witherspoon and Dr. Malcolm Howells to pull Amanda out of her shell.

Charlie, concerned about his long-time friend, visited her regularly. As Marjorie stated, Amanda had seemed to be gradually accepting Andy's death, and was becoming more involved in church, community and other social activities, largely at Marjorie's insistence. But Amanda was only a shadow of her former self.

Now, out of the blue, the Bureau had apparently decided to descend upon Amanda. He too was worried. Where would she go, if not to the farm where she and Andy had lived?

He suddenly recalled a conversation from years ago. Oh, no, he thought, snatching up his car keys and striding out of the office.

It was a summer afternoon when they had just graduated from high school and were about to leave for college. Amanda and Charlie, along with Monica and Bill, had spent the entire afternoon down at the gulf at Billy's family's beach house, swimming in the pool, diving in the gulf for sand dollars, walking the beach shallows desultorily looking for crabs.

After a while in the pool, Billy started flirting outrageously with Monica. Charlie, thinking to get scarce, hauled himself out of the pool and threw on a shirt, intending to take a walk on the beach. He then noticed that Amanda was missing. Geez, Billy has embarrassed her again, he thought, disgusted.

Concerned, he traversed the house interior quickly, checking the rooms, but not finding her. He jogged up the outside staircase up to the widow's walk, and found her sitting in a deck chair, book in hand, but not reading. She was staring out at the azure Gulf of Mexico against the white sands.

"Why did you take off?" he asked her, sitting down on the ottoman at the foot of the chair, facing her. "You have to ignore Billy's vulgarity."

Amanda didn't meet his gaze. "Have you ever wondered about people who commit suicide?" she asked absently. She stared past him to the beach. "Not necessarily why they do it, but how they choose their means?"

Taken aback, he had laughed uneasily. "From where do you get this stuff? You're not suicidal, are you?"

She smiled pensively. "No, but I just wondered. If you were going to do it, how would you?"

He shook his head. Even back then she prodded him, provoked him, worried him. "Mandy, I can't imagine doing it. There's so much living to do, and death comes on its own soon enough without our help." He paused, looking at her concernedly. "You've apparently given this some thought."

"Not really, but I was just thinking if I was ever driven to it, I would walk into the gulf and keep going." She looked past him to the beach.

Charlie took hold of her wrists, gently dragging her up from her lounging position on the chair to sit facing him. He saw her troubled features and sensed that she was battling to keep from allowing tears to fall.

His face only inches from hers, he said softly, "Don't cry, baby. I can't handle that, Mandy."

He cupped her face in his hands, his gaze intent on her, tenderly wiping a tear off her cheek with his thumb. "You're not going to let Billy win that easily, are you?"

He felt her stiffen slightly at his touch. "What—what do you mean?" she blinked, looking at him guilelessly.

"The way to get his attention is to make him jealous as hell. And you do it quite easily," Charlie laughed.

"Where do you get this stuff?" she parroted him. "Why would I want to do that? He's Monica's guy," Amanda smiled, her sudden brightness forced.

"Just because you can," Charlie whispered knowingly. "Let's test my theory. I hear them coming up the stairs. Just follow my lead."

He had placed his hand at the small of her back, and quickly drew her to him. Before she could protest, he had pressed her to him and his mouth lowered to hers.

Charlie felt her tense against him, but then Monica had exclaimed, "Whoa! Are we interrupting something?" He knew Amanda had glanced up and observed Bill's face, suddenly hard and flushing with irritation.

Immediately she had relaxed against Charlie and returned the kiss, her arms around Charlie's neck, holding him tightly. Charlie was surprised at her response, but took advantage of the moment. They remained entwined for a moment, until Amanda pulled away. They were alone. Monica and Bill had disappeared.

He had laughed at the expression on her face. "See, baby?"

She crimsoned, unsuccessfully trying to cover her embarrassment. "Every time you call me 'baby' I'm calling you 'Pete'."

He roared, shaking with laughter. "You're priceless. You just do that, but make it real sexy, and see how Billy reacts. It'll piss him off and make me happy at the same time."

She had laughed then, shaking her head. "You're as bad as he is. I can see you had an ulterior motive."

Charlie smirked. "Whatever it takes. You know, you need a bit more practice," he added slyly.

He kissed her again, and she didn't protest. As his kisses became deeper, his hand started moving down her throat and started stroking her breast through her swimsuit.

Amanda pulled away, breathless. "As Monica said, 'Whoa'." Her voice was husky.

"You don't like it?" he had asked, not releasing her, his hand still on her breast.

"I like it, but if you leave hickies on me, my dad will beat us both," she whispered, removing his hand.

He burst out laughing, and she did too.

"Your dad likes me," Charlie grinned. "And he damn sure doesn't like Billy."

"Where do you get that idea?" she asked, trying to withdraw, but Charlie kept his arm firmly around her.

"Because you wouldn't get to come along on these excursions except for the pact between your dad and mine that I will keep anything from happening to you," he murmured as he played with her hair. "My ass is on the line every time we come down here to the beach."

She blushed. "I didn't know that."

"Yeah, your dad and mine are pretty tight," Charlie chuckled. "There's a secret handshake between church deacons." Charlie tucked a strand of her hair behind her ear. "You know, baby, I could make you forget Billy."

"Pete," she blushed as she practiced the name on her tongue, "you have somehow gotten the wrong idea about me. I'm not interested in Billy."

"The hell you ain't," he growled. "Don't you think I can read it in your eyes when you look at him?"

"I would never allow myself to—feel something for my best friend's boyfriend," she insisted. She pushed against him, and he released her. "Besides, why are you hanging around me? You're the big football star, every cheerleader's dream. I hear the stories about you. You know Jacquie Williams is two doors down at their place, and she's just waiting for you to give her a thrill."

"Yeah, right," he rejoined disdainfully. "Like I want Billy's leftovers."

She looked at him with surprise. "Leftovers?" she echoed, her voice dropped to a whisper. "But Monica—"

"Monica and you are good girls, the type one marries and lives with happily ever after," Charlie replied smoothly. "Billy was raised by his dad to think sex and marriage seldom mix, and one marries for enhancing one's position in life but gets one's fun elsewhere."

She looked shocked. Charlie added, taking one of her hands in his, "I thought you knew this." He watched her intently.

"No," she breathed. "That's not how I was raised. Monica will be so hurt if she finds out."

"No," he explained patiently. "Unlike you, my sweet Mandy, Monica knows what's going on. And as much as Billy flirts with her, he's not going to cross the line, because he doesn't want to incur the wrath of Marjy and Jerrod Witherspoon. His future is mapped out by his dad; marriage to Monica after college is pretty much a done deal."

He smiled at her. "You're actually in more danger from Billy than Monica is."

"Why?" she gazed wide-eyed at Charlie.

"Because as well-known and respected as your parents are, they aren't rich," Charlie whispered. At her stunned look, he cupped her face in his hand. "But Billy isn't going to cross Tom Andrews either, although he might be tempted. Your dad may be a church deacon and upstanding citizen, but he wouldn't stand on ceremony—he'd thrash Billy to within an inch of his life. And Billy knows it—your father informed him of the fact."

"He did?" Amanda was startled. "But I'm not on his list," Amanda protested.

"Baby, you'd be surprised," he gazed down at her form. "I mean, you look good enough to ravish. I'd be willing to incur both our dads' ire over you."

She blushed as she pulled her cover around her tightly, embarrassed.

"Why are you such a big flirt with me?" She pushed against his chest teasingly. She tried to stand, but he was in her way. "You know I'm not your type, nor Billy's. And you certainly have plenty of girls who wouldn't mind accommodating you."

"Because they're not you," Charlie guffawed. "You give me a run for the money, always with a come-back to whatever I say." He stood and held out his hand, helping her stand. "Besides, I'm not Billy. You're the girl I want to marry, and once I do, you'll be my only one," he winked, leaning and kissing her again.

She laughed as she extricated herself. "Enough teasing. I'm hungry, Casanova." The tense moment passed.

The memory, pleasant as it was, brought to mind her words about suicide. A chill ran down Charlie's spine. Please let me be wrong, he thought.

He called Bruce Williams, his first lieutenant at the sheriff department's investigations unit, where Petrino was still working as chief investigator while waiting to see if he would get the appointment as Chief of Police.

"Bruce, Amanda Childs can't be located. It may be nothing, but I need you to call Sheila at her office, try to determine the places Mandy hangs and check them out. Check out the park, Jack's, St. Catherine's. Make it discreet. I'll check with Fred at the farm. You know Marjy Witherspoon doesn't want a public fuss."

"Why? What do you think has happened?" Bruce was immediately suspicious.

"I'm hoping she just went off to be alone," Petrino asserted, the picture of her reaction the day she received word of Andy's murder flashing through his head.

"Where are you?" Bruce inquired.

"I'm following a hunch, to see if she maybe went down to the beach to some of the places we used to frequent as kids. I'll stay in touch."

Charlie rang off.

He left the sheriff's department vehicle behind, choosing instead his vintage 1967 Pontiac GTO, figuring he could make better time. He took off, accelerating out onto the highway. Plopping a blue light on the dash, he squeezed on the accelerator and the car responded smoothly, skimming the ribbon of road leading down to the Barnes' beach house.

It was September, and the tourist traffic had lessened considerably. Still the distance yawned before him. Mandy wouldn't actually take her life, would she? he wondered anxiously.

He had made it a point to check on her regularly since the news of Andrew's death. Ever since the day she was informed of her husband's murder, Charlie could not rid himself of the picture of her, her utter despair. Since then she had become thinner and paler, her smile rare, her eyes hollow. Neither could he erase the memory of Andy's corpse hanging in the warehouse that early morning, and the rage surged through him anew.

He was aware that Amanda had battled the Bureau for the last eleven months to find out the circumstances behind Andy's murder and to obtain any sliver of reason behind the loss of her husband. The FBI had ordered no information to be released, not even to the man's widow, so she found no answers.

"Eleven months, hell," he said aloud, looking at the date indicator on his watch. It was the one-year anniversary of Andrew's murder. He floored the accelerator.

How asinine that the agency sent out men today, of all days, to deliver Andy's badge to her, just as she might be on the road to acceptance. Charlie resolved to raise some hell with them, but he had to first make sure Amanda did not lose her head and do something rash.

After what seemed like forever, he arrived at the Barnes' beach house, the spot on the beach they spent most of their summers in their youth. Amanda's car, a BMW coupe, was parked beside the driveway. OK, so she's here somewhere, he sighed. He noticed without surprise that there was no sign of life at the house. Billy was on a trip to Monaco with his wife Celeste.

Charlie's first act was to check her car. The hood was still warm. The keys were left in the ignition. That's not like her, he thought, his heartbeat quickening.

Alarmed, he turned toward the gulf and started striding to the beach, the sun low in the sky. He surveyed the shallows, looking for anything. How would I find her if she did indeed walk into the sea? he thought despairingly. But he found no evidence of anything or anybody in the water, no one on the beach, and no sign of footprints on the white sand. He took that for a good sign.

The sun was setting, and he was at a loss, when he looked back at the house. There on the widow's walk he thought he saw a dark figure. Maybe she went inside, he thought. Hoping against hope that it was not some mirage, he made his way back to the house. Picking up the doormat, he found the key and let himself in, putting the key back.

"Mandy?" he called, the sound echoing through the empty rooms. He checked the rooms quickly on his way out to the stairwell leading to the widow's walk.

Sprinting up the steps, he made it to the top. He held his breath. There on the deck chair was Amanda. She was leaning back in the deck chair, very still. He swallowed.

"Mandy?" he called softly. "Are you OK?"

Walking up to her, he was relieved to see her alive, conscious, staring out at the gulf, a full bottle of Crown Royal in one hand, a glass in the other.

He touched her on the shoulder. "Mandy?"

She gazed up at him. "Hi, Pete. Have a drink?" she offered casually, although he could see the signs of recent crying.

"Sure," he replied, equally casually, taking the bottle and glass out of her hand. "Did you start without me?" He was curious, as he broke the seal on the new bottle, poured a large amount of liquid in the glass and drank deeply, observing her closely.

"No, just contemplating the pretty bottle," she maintained, reaching for the glass, taking it from his hand and finishing the contents. She held out the glass, and he obliged, pouring more amber liquid into the glass. She sipped the whiskey.

"I have been trying to screw up my courage to get drunk and walk out into the sea. But I started thinking, true to my Baptist upbringing, what if Andy is in heaven? If I kill myself, I'll go to hell. So it's a bust either way."

He took the glass from her, finished the contents, set the bottle and glass down on a table beside the chair, knelt down beside the chair and took her hand. "I'm glad you didn't," he whispered. "I would have been heartbroken."

She closed her eyes. "Then I couldn't get drunk in the car, or I'd pass out and be found and arrested for DUI. So I came up here, and have been arguing with myself. Life is hell, and I can't kill myself," she laughed mirthlessly.

She turned her eyes on Charlie as he stared back at her. "I need to call Marjy and Bruce, and call off the search for you," he said huskily.

He pulled out his phone, and punched a button. "Bruce, do me a favor. I found her, and she is OK. Call Marjy and tell her she's fine, and that she's with me. I appreciate it."

He hung up, and reached for her, took her by the wrists, raising her to her feet, one hand around her waist.

She looked at him, blinking. "You have plans for tonight?"

He met her gaze, his eyes wide. "No, baby. I'm free."

She looked briefly back to the gulf, then took his hand, entwining his fingers in hers. "Let's go inside. It's getting chilly. Bring the Crown."

"You get the glass," he quipped.

She dragged him after her down the steps and through the French doors into the house. He reached for a light switch, but she whispered, "No lights."

He followed her willingly as she continued through the rooms, down a hallway, into a guest room with rustic white furnishings tastefully decorating the room.

She placed the glass on a glass-topped bedside table adjacent to the four-poster bed. She took the bottle from him, and poured some more alcohol in the glass. She drank some, then offered the glass to him. He tipped the glass and emptied the contents, then placed the glass beside the bottle on the table.

In the shadow cast by the setting sun, she turned and wrapped her arms around his neck. "Let's make Billy really jealous," she whispered provocatively.

Surprised but needing no second invitation, he ran his fingers through her hair, captured her head in one hand, and found her mouth with his, as she clung to him. "I want to do much more than that," he mumbled against her mouth, as he hauled her to him, the other hand moving up under her blouse to cup her breast under her bra.

"Me too," she sighed. She reached down and tugged at his belt, loosening it and his fly, pulling his shirt to loosen it from his pants waist, unbuttoning it and reaching inside.

He gazed at her questioningly. She beseeched him, "I can't be alone any longer, Pete. The pain is smothering me. I want you, badly."

"Is it me, or Andy, or will just anyone do?" he asked against her ear. His tongue ran down her jawline to her throat and he reached behind her back to undo her bra. "No, don't answer that. I don't want to know."

His mouth became more insistent, as his hand trailed down and unzipped her skirt, and slid to her bare skin caressing down her back, pulling the fabric down and letting it fall to the floor. He pulled her top off over her head, closing his lips over her breast as she moaned and strained toward him, and his hands ran down her torso.

Naked, she unbuttoned his shirt. "You, Pete. I want to drown in you instead."

He shrugged out of the shirt and his pants, and she drew him toward her and onto the bed on top of her. "I always wanted to know what the girls found so irresistible about you," she blushed, "but I was too afraid to ask."

"I've always wanted to show you, baby." His voice was husky as his hands and mouth moved down her body.

Hours later, she stirred next to him in bed. He awoke, immediately alert, always a light sleeper. He opened his eyes and gazed at her, her back to him. The moonlight cast a faint glow over her. He snuggled to her, and she sighed and nestled closer, still asleep. He nuzzled her neck and ran his hands lightly over her arms and down her spine, enjoying the feel of her skin. She moved in response, making a small whimper, her body quivering lightly.

He teased her into wakefulness, stroking her until her body tensed and she stretched languorously, arousing him even more. She turned toward him, smiling sleepily, and he tangled her hair in his hand as he brought her to meet him, devouring her mouth. Her hands reached out for him as desire was stoked again.

She gazed at him. "You're the best sex I've ever had, Charlie," she sighed, her breathing quickened by his hands on her.

"We're just getting started," he informed her smilingly.

"I'm not sure I have the strength to do it again," she moaned, aroused, as he pulled the covers away from her and his hands parted her legs, his fingers lightly kneading up the inside of her thighs.

He chuckled. "And just what other experience have you had, other than Andy and me?"

Suddenly awake, she blushed, blinked and looked away. He divined the answer.

"You were a virgin when you married?" he smiled tenderly.

"What do you think?" she mumbled, embarrassed.

"What about you and Billy? Are you telling me you managed to resist Bill's advances throughout college? How?" he teased her, tracing her lips with his finger lightly.

She frowned. "There was never any me and Billy." She tried to pull away.

Charlie held her, not releasing her. "He had every intention of correcting that situation."

"I decided Billy wasn't what I wanted," she mumbled as his lips trailed down her throat.

"But you carried a torch for him all those years. Why not?"

"Maybe I did. But Charlie, Billy is much too needy for my taste."

"Needy?" Charlie stopped and stared at her, surprised.

"Yes. He craves attention and affection, generally from the highest social stratum he can score. His ego needs constant stroking."

"No shit?" Charlie laughed in agreement.

"Don't you ever notice that we are on some sort of hierarchy for him? Sometimes our name comes up, then we're cast aside for someone more important, higher on his list."

"I never thought of it that way," Charlie conceded thoughtfully.

Amanda smiled. "In college, I was Billy's fallback date on those few occasions when he was without anyone better. And I guess I represent the wall he hasn't breached, some unconquered territory, a perennial challenge," she blushed.

Amanda ran her fingers up Charlie's chest to his lips. "I'm so thankful he married Celeste and is off my back."

"Me, too," Charlie continued teasing her, and her breathing quickened. "I always hoped you'd see through him."

"I always wondered what it would be like with you," she offered shyly. "But all you did was flirt back then."

She gasped as his fingers slid inside her, and she arched toward him. "I'll try to make up for lost time now," he whispered.

"Oh," she cried, one hand clutching the sheets desperately, as he moved down her body.

He crooned, "Mandy, I've always loved you. I can't believe you're here."

"You loved me?" she echoed, her mind trying to grasp his words as the sensations he was creating crowded out rational thought. "Yeah, right," she started to retort, but swallowed a cry of intense pleasure.

"I want defense counsel to beg," he murmured over her, his hands and mouth wreaking havoc with her senses.

"I'll beg right now," she panted, writhing as her fingers ran along his back and she strained to draw closer to him.

"No, I want an involuntary, impassioned plea. But don't worry, you will enjoy every minute of it."

He continued to tantalize her and she became lost, stroking him mindlessly. The tension built in her like a body of water pushing against a dam, until her eyes glazed over, she screamed, and the dam burst, enveloping her like a huge cramp and shudder, and time slowed.

Still reeling, she was carried by the tide, as he grasped her hips and entered her and she wrapped herself around him. Time fled, as he brought her again and again, until they fell together, a free fall in slow motion.

Chapter 2

Amanda awoke with the sun streaming into the window, the fall breeze billowing the white sheer curtains. She felt chilly. She pulled the covers up tightly to her, trying to shut out the thoughts that crowded her mind.

Petrino walked through the door, dressed only in swim trunks, carrying a tray. He smiled at her. "Good morning, baby." His voice was low, musical. "Could you use a little breakfast?"

She smiled back shyly. "How wonderful. Thanks."

Amanda sat up with the covers wrapped around her as Charlie set the tray before her. She reached up and drew him down to her and kissed him. He returned her kiss warmly, then sat down beside her.

"Well, you have the day off," he remarked conversationally. "What would you like to do with it?"

She reached for the glass of orange juice on the tray, then stopped. "That's right, I do," she grinned. "I probably should go in to work, but I don't want to."

"How about we don't go back?" Charlie sipped a cup a coffee, looking at her over it.

"What about you? I have trouble believing the sheriff's department can run without its chief investigator."

"It's Friday, and nothing much is going on," he shrugged. "Nothing that Bruce can't handle without me. I could take off if given the appropriate incentive."

She looked at him and winked. "What do you suggest?"

"Hiding out with you sounds awfully good," he reached over and touched her cheek.

"Here?" she waved her arm around the room. "You know we're trespassing." She stuffed a bite of toast in her mouth.

"Not exactly," Petrino chuckled. "Billy allows me to crash here from time to time, if no one else in the family is using the place. His secretary keeps a log. I already called first thing and made sure the place was open for the entire weekend. In fact, I spend a lot of my free weekends off-season here, when I can get away. Mr. Barnes employs staff that keep it clean and stocked with staples."

"Ah, your babe lair?" she teased.

She suddenly looked apprehensive. "You don't think anybody will find out that—that we . . ." she stammered.

He ran his fingers through her hair. "No, baby," he discerned her concern. "There are very few locals down here this time of year. If you want to keep—us—this—a secret, it's no problem."

"Don't you?" her eyes were wide with fear.

Charlie frowned. He took her hand and brought it to his lips. "No, Mandy, I don't want to keep you a secret. Not at all. But I respect your decision if you want to keep it from being disclosed. I understand your need for discretion."

Amanda surveyed the tray nervously, not meeting his eyes. "I just—I mean there's no obligation on your part. Just because you slept with me doesn't—it doesn't mean you're engaged to me. If it was just a casual thing, I mean, no one needs to know, do they?"

"Shit, Mandy." He jerked the tray up and set it on the floor, turning back to her. Sitting on the bed, he drew her to him, stroking her back as he explored her lips. She responded, pulling him toward her as she leaned back against the pillows.

"I can't believe you came on to me last night. I love you, dammit," he whispered to her. "I've always loved you. I want you. But I'm having a helluva time trying to figure out what you want."

He touched her cheek. "I know you've been through hell, and if you want to take it slow, or if you want us to run off and elope, whatever, that's what I want too. So however you want to handle this—us—" He didn't finish, as he pulled the covers down to her waist and began stroking her, his thumbs caressing her nipples.

"Oh, I'm sorry," he spoke, a wicked smile playing around his lips. "You were saying?" he nibbled her earlobe.

"Forget it," she sighed. "I don't give a damn right now."

Suddenly he hauled her out of the bed, naked, and strode through the house with her. "What are you doing?" she cried, as he carried her through the house and out the French doors to the deck.

Walking to the pool, he dumped her unceremoniously into it, jumping in after her.

They spent the day swimming, walking the beach, taking a ride and exploring their old childhood beach haunts. Late that afternoon they returned to the beach house, a carryout pizza and bottle of wine in hand. After eating and imbibing, they fell asleep together on the sofa, the CD player playing Robin Trower ballads.

As the shadows fell, Charlie woke up and watched her sleeping in the crook of his arm, her body draped over his. She awoke suddenly, startled, looking at him, at first frightened, then smiling as she recognized him.

He bent his head and kissed her. "What are our plans for tomorrow?" he asked softly as she stretched.

"I don't know about your plans, but I have to go back. I have an important interview tomorrow."

"But tomorrow's Saturday," he protested, stroking her back. "I thought about taking you to St. George Island shell hunting."

"Andy and I were always going to spend a weekend there, but it never came to pass," she ruminated, then stopped, embarrassed that she had spoken aloud. She tried to cover her chagrin. "Marjorie and I have been a couple of times. It's beautiful."

She suddenly kissed him and gushed, "But you'll never guess who might come back to Mainville and work with me at the office," Amanda's eyes sparkled.

"Ralph Carmichael?" he asked, arching his eyebrows, inwardly thrilled at the momentary joy in her face. It had been so long since he had seen her smile like that. Ralph Carmichael, one of their fellow childhood friends and classmates, had gone off to Duke after high school on a basketball scholarship, then on to law school. He was currently a prosecutor in south Florida.

"How did you know?" she cried. "How is it you know everything before anyone else?"

"I have excellent sources," he replied drily, watching her face avidly.

"I told him not to tell anyone until we were sure," she lamented. "But he has to go back to Tampa on Sunday. It will be fun having you all around again."

She sat up, and he joined her. "Why don't you come back, have lunch with us? Then you could—maybe—" she faltered, blushing, "spend the night."

"Where?" he smiled, running his fingers down her arm.

"I've been spending the nights at the apartment above the office," she looked away. "That way I can work late, stay busy. There—there are too many ghosts at the farm," she added, her voice small.

"What do you intend to tell Ralph about—us? Marjy?" he asked softly.

"We'll let them know when it's time." Amanda pulled away, standing.

Charlie clasped her hand, detaining her. "And are you going to keep it a secret from me until it's time?"

She giggled. "Perhaps," she replied wickedly, shaking free and walking away. At the doorway she stopped and turned, looking at him. "Well, are you coming or not?"

The next morning, Amanda rose early, gently disentangling herself from Charlie, who was sleeping unusually soundly from the dancing and wine they shared the previous night between lovemaking. She quietly went down the hall to take a shower without awakening him, dressed and made coffee.

When Charlie awoke, he was alone. "Mandy?" he called, but there was no answer. He quickly pulled on his shorts and walked through the house, looking for her. He found a note propped up by the coffee pot:

> I've gone to the office to meet Ralph. Please let me know if you will join us. Amanda

He shook his head. No word of endearment. Why should he be surprised? In fact, thinking back over the last thirty-six hours or so they had shared, she had never once committed herself to pronouncing any feelings whatsoever, except for the fear he read in her eyes when they first discussed the possibility of discovery.

For the first time in my life I'm out of my depth, he thought. I've always been in control; I've always known when matters with a woman were getting too serious and when to break it off. I've never let a woman worm her way into my heart.

But he was no fool; he had always known there was something about Amanda that was different, a part of him that acknowledged that he had felt something for her for years. He had always just explained away his feeling to himself that she was a special friend and perhaps the sister he didn't have, and he had always been protective of her. That was the reason he had been so willing to be her escort on outings with Billy and Monica.

Although he had secretly harbored those feelings, he never dreamed that the opportunity would arise for him to be with Amanda. He had always assumed during their college days that she still nursed a crush for Billy Barnes. Then she married Andrew Childs, and had seemed blissfully happy until his untimely death. Charlie was never conscious until last night just how much he wanted her, wanted her to want him. It was a new and exhilarating experience for him.

He suddenly realized he was on the receiving end of his own tried and true strategy with women, and that he was apprehensive about her feelings for him. The last two nights had been so delicious for him, and he could still feel and taste her. She had been free and giving in bed, her appetite matching his, her movements igniting the fire in him like no other woman had. She had been everything he had dreamed of and more. He loved her hopelessly, and every time he looked at her or touched her he was more tightly drawn into her web. How did I let this happen to me? he wondered.

But he was assailed by doubts. Was Amanda ready to try again at a relationship? Could she bury the past? Was she capable of taking the risk again so soon, to love someone, to love Charlie?

She had said very little about Andrew. But he had watched her struggle over the last year to overcome her loss. Charlie had seen the bond between Andrew and Amanda. Since his death, Charlie could sense that there was something inside that Amanda dared not give away, that she did not share, a deep pain that she had not relinquished. She let slip the veneer at times, and he at those moments had stared at the locked door in her mind, knowing there was no key except the one she held and guarded jealously.

"I don't care. I'll be happy with whatever she gives me," he said aloud.

So he showered and dressed, locking up the beach house and driving back to Mainville. He called her cell phone on the way.

"Hello?" she spoke, her voice neutral.

He smiled to himself. "Charlie here. That invitation to lunch still good?"

"Charlie. Hi, good to hear from you. What are you doing for lunch?" He was gratified by the flood of warmth in her voice. "Ralph is here, and we're thinking about lunch at Betty's. Ralph wants some fried mullet. How about 11:30? We'll beat the crowd."

Charlie laughed at her. "Sounds good. See you there."

He stopped off at his own apartment to change clothes, choosing some dressy pants and a striped button-down shirt of blue oxford cloth, then headed to the restaurant. He soon pulled into the parking lot of a nondescript low-slung concrete-block building, a local eatery. As he stepped out of his car, Amanda's BMW pulled alongside.

A tall handsome black man jumped out of the passenger seat, dressed in dark suit, sans jacket, tie loosened. He smirked at the 1967 GTO as Charlie disembarked. "Well, I see you're stuck in the sixties. Nice wheels. Couldn't you afford a new car?" he joked.

Charlie held out his hand. "My God, but you clean up well," he rejoined, as Ralph ignored his hand, hugged him and patted him on the back. "You had to dress up for this interview?"

"Geez, man, I had to impress her, show her how suave and debonair I have become," Ralph retorted, grinning. "She drives a hard bargain." He laughed. "You know Amanda—her standards are high."

He gave Charlie the once-over. "You haven't changed. Amanda says you might be appointed Chief of Police."

"Without a dream the people perish," Charlie remarked drily. "So is it official? Are you coming home?"

"Well, Amanda has certainly made it tempting," Ralph replied as Amanda walked around the car to meet them. Charlie appraised her approvingly. She was dressed in a pair of khaki trousers with matching jacket, a light-weight sleeveless V-necked sweater underneath. A colorful silk scarf fluttered around her throat. She noted his eyes on her and flushed slightly.

"Guys, I know it's cooler than August, but it's still hot out here. Let's go in," she pointed to the door.

They seated themselves at a table, as Betty herself came bustling up to the table. "Well, if this isn't a sight, to see you all here at one time," she exclaimed. "Ralph Carmichael, what have you been doing with yourself?"

"I'm a prosecutor in Tampa, but," he glanced at Amanda, who beamed, "I'm making plans to come back home and hang up my shingle here with Mandy."

"Oh, that's wonderful," Betty kissed his cheek, patting Amanda on the back and winking at Charlie. "And your wife?"

"Wife?" Charlie echoed disbelievingly.

"Don't get the cart before the horse," Ralph pursed his lips. "She's only a girlfriend right now. But she's fine, very fine," he grinned. "She's thinking of relocating here too."

Betty took their orders and disappeared.

"Has Claire met your family?" Amanda asked slyly.

"Well . . ." Ralph drawled, and Amanda and Charlie both gawked at him.

"She came up with me, and yes, she's met Mom, Louise, Danny and their kids."

Betty brought them all sweetened ice tea as Amanda bit back a grin and Charlie noted, "That sounds pretty serious to me."

"What about you, man?" Ralph turned to Charlie. "I think it's past time you settled down. You've certainly sown enough wild oats for yourself and half of the Florida Panhandle, perhaps the whole tri-state area."

Charlie didn't look at Amanda as he advised, "I'm giving it a bit of thought."

"Who is she?" Ralph asked excitedly.

Amanda interposed wryly, "Charlie is just pulling your leg, Ralph. Do you think he'll settle for one woman?"

Charlie looked over at Amanda, and their eyes met briefly. She was smiling, but he didn't return the smile.

Ralph didn't notice. He was saying, "I could get us all tickets for the FSU game next weekend, if you two would drive over for it. Claire has a FAMU band reunion, so we'll be back up this way." He suggested jestingly, "Surely you couldn't get in too much trouble riding in the same car a couple hours together?"

"I'll have to see." Amanda was noncommittal.

They talked about people and places from the past, and Ralph regaled them with some of his courtroom dramas. Charlie smiled and provided repartee, but his eyes drifted to Amanda from time to time, despite his efforts not to stare at her.

After lunch, they all walked back to the cars. Charlie clapped Ralph on the back. "OK, so when are you moving back?"

"I have to give them a month's notice, because I have a couple of nasty trials I want to do myself before leaving. But I should be here very shortly afterward, that is, if the boss will give me enough time to move my stuff up here," he winked at Amanda.

"I'm anxious for you to start, now that we've sealed the deal," she spoke warmly.

As Ralph got into Amanda's car, she brushed past Petrino. "Call me this afternoon," she whispered, surreptitiously squeezing his hand.

His heart leaped. "How soon?" he inquired, a slight smile on his lips.

"Give me an hour," she winked.

At 4:00 that afternoon, Charlie still hadn't called. Amanda, upstairs in her apartment, was nervous. OK, so the last two nights were just a fling, she told herself. It meant nothing. Charlie got a call from another girl, found something better to do. Something detained him. He decided it was better to just cut her loose. All the different scenarios played in her head. She was pacing. I just cannot do this, she thought, aggravated with herself.

An image of Andrew, unbidden, suddenly flooded her mind. She was suddenly paralyzed with longing and remorse. What am I doing? she asked herself, burying her head in her hand.

Her phone rang. She picked it up, breathless. "Hello?"

"Why don't you let me in?" Charlie whispered.

"Where are you?"

"At the back door, silly," he retorted.

She ran down the stairs and unlocked the door. He stood there, a paper grocery bag in his arms. He walked past her, pulled out the contents, and stood there with a bottle of champagne and roses in his hands. She pulled him in quickly and shut the door.

"Where's your car?" she looked out the window anxiously.

"I left it at the police station and walked," he grinned broadly. "It was damned sure hard to hide this stuff in a paper bag and look nonchalant walking down the block."

"What—?" she looked at him confusedly.

Charlie noted her breathlessness. "Are you excited to see me?" he asked wickedly, his eyebrows raised.

Amanda flushed. "Just worried about you," she muttered.

"I'm sorry," he was suddenly contrite. "You're looking at the new Chief of Police."

"Oh, my God," she cried, wrapping her arms around his neck and kissing him impulsively. "That is so great. I can't believe it."

"Whoa, watch the flowers," Charlie warned as he returned the kiss, and she released him. "I was detained, of course, and couldn't tell the commission delegation I needed to call my girlfriend. I mean," he chuckled mischievously, "I got the impression at lunchtime you wanted us to keep it secret."

"I'm sorry," she was rueful. "I am just not sure yet how to deal with all this."

"Well, then," he looked about him, "unless you want me to announce it publicly, maybe we should adjourn upstairs before someone looks in the window and sees me." His eyes twinkled as he turned back to her.

"I want to hear all about it," she crooned enthusiastically, as she took his hand and dragged him through the hall and upstairs.

He looked around with admiration at the apartment. "Wow, this looks pretty nice. I've never been up here before."

He walked into the kitchen area and found two glasses.

"It was a shock," he told her. "I went by the police station just to kill time until I could call you, and suddenly there was the mayor. A moment later, two more commissioners appeared, and I was ushered into the office, and asked if I still wanted the job."

"Just like that? After all that sweating over it?" Amanda found a vase and arranged the roses, placing the bouquet on the table.

"Just like that," he echoed. "I really had almost given up, and certainly didn't expect it today, on a Saturday. The city council meeting is Monday, but that's just a formality. So I'm sorry to be late getting back with you."

He expertly opened the champagne bottle, and poured some in the glasses, then noticed Amanda was not there.

"Mandy?" he called.

"Right here," she responded. He turned. She was standing in the doorway wearing nothing but a black strappy lacy silk camisole and matching high-cut tap pants. "I'm sorry," she said, walking up to him, taking one glass and downing it. "I'm not sure I can wait much longer. You can tell me the rest in bed."

Charlie's face broke into a big grin. "Right away," he downed his champagne, then set down the glass and picked her up in his arms. "Which way?" he asked.

She pointed through the doorway.

"You're insatiable. I need to take you out to celebrate your new position," she mumbled breathlessly two hours later, between kisses. "Your public awaits."

"I thought we were celebrating," he retorted as he touched her and she went rigid, whimpering, then crying out with pleasure. "My public can wait. And you're pretty damned insatiable yourself. If I remember correctly, you started this," he replied as he entered her and she cried out, clutching at him.

After several hours of lovemaking, they both slept, exhausted, entangled in each other. Charlie shifted sleepily, feeling for her, running his hands down her torso and gently pulling her closer to him.

"Oh, Andy," she sighed in her sleep.

Charlie awakened, suddenly alert. He held her and watched her sleep, his mind troubled.

After a while he drifted back to sleep, relinquishing his hold on her.

Chapter 3

Charlie awoke early. Amanda was already up, dressing for church. He raised himself up on one arm and admired her profile and fluid movements as she slipped on hosiery.

"I love your legs," he informed her.

She started. "I didn't realize you were awake," she mumbled.

"I want to make breakfast for you," he murmured.

"No, don't bother. I always go in to church early on Sundays for one more run-through." She would not look at him.

"Could I come to church and watch you play?" he teased her.

"No." Amanda was adamant, cool, as she stood. "You need to go to the Baptist church and be congratulated by your fellow church members and constituents. The word will be out by now. You're an important man now. You'll have to stand election next term."

"But I've sinned all weekend, and I'm not repentant," Charlie smiled. He reached out and caught her hand. "Perhaps I need to convert to Episcopalianism."

"You think that will get you off?" she retorted, shaking him off distractedly. "There are more Baptists in town than Episcopalians anyway, and they would not approve."

"I think they just might," he remarked.

He sat up, feeling something was amiss. He noted the worried look on her face. "What is it, baby?"

"Nothing," she said shortly, turning her back to him.

"Mandy, talk to me," he insisted, taking her hand and pulling her back around to face him. She would not meet his gaze.

"I've got to face Marjy this morning at church after running off Thursday. I haven't talked to her. I know she is going to ask me where I've been. I don't know what I'm going to say." She pulled away, slipped into her dress and zipped it up.

"Why not tell her the truth?" he asked gently, staring after her.

She moved to the doorway, stepping into high heels. "And what is that? That I've gone crazy and become one of your wanton women? That I've thrown my widow's weeds away in favor of becoming a notch on your bedpost?"

He stood, reaching for his boxers, his jaw clenched. "Is that all you think this is?" He was suddenly angry.

"Charlie, you've never been serious about a woman in your whole life. And I'm still in mourning for Andy. So I'm supposed to believe that we've suddenly 'found each other' and will be each other's endless love?"

Charlie towered over her. "Yes. God damn it, yes. Amanda Andrews, I have loved you all my life. Yes, I've been a reprobate up until now, but you never let me near. I'm willing to renounce all before God and the world, and love you and only you for the rest of my days. I want to sign on the dotted line. I want to marry you. It's you who are backing up, afraid to give up your widow's weeds, scared to try again."

She stalked out of the bedroom without answering him.

"Don't walk out on this conversation, baby," he countered.

He followed her as she gained the kitchen. He reached for her arm to halt her retreat. It was then that he saw the badge and framed commendation on the kitchen table.

He stared down at them, stunned, speechless. She must have brought them upstairs while I was asleep, he thought irrelevantly.

Amanda collapsed into a chair by the table, trembling, her eyes glued to them.

"Oh, my God," she broke into tears, weeping piteously. "I'm so scared. I cannot remember his voice, his touch," she sobbed, her face hidden in her hands. "He was my very life and breath. Now his memory is getting fainter. What am I to do?"

Shaken, Charlie went to her and knelt before her. "Oh, baby, I'm so sorry." He tried to remove her hands. But she kept rocking and crying.

"He was so wonderful. And he's gone, and I don't even know why or what for," she mumbled. "I mustn't forget him, cannot let that memory fade to nothingness. It's all that's left of him. And here I am, being unfaithful, just throwing myself at you like some slut."

"No, Mandy, no," he pulled her to stand and put his arm around her, rocking her. "You are not being unfaithful. Andy would not want you to sit the rest of your life holding a candle for him. You haven't forgotten him by trying to find happiness for yourself."

"But don't you see? I have forgotten him. I can't do this." She was beside herself, quivering violently, her eyes wild, pushing him away. "I just can't," she became hysterical, her voice raised. "Andy didn't deserve this."

Charlie was suddenly afraid for her. He clasped her arms. "Mandy, I love you. We can work through this. It will take time, but it will all be OK."

"Can't we just be friends?" she muttered, not looking at him. "Right now you can just blow this off as a pleasant weekend. But later . . . I don't want us to hurt each other. I cannot take the chance of losing you as a friend if I fail at being your lover."

"No, Mandy," breathed Charlie, embracing her, kissing her cheek. "I'm not going to let you fail."

She pushed him away roughly. "You need to go. Don't make this any harder for me," her voice was barely audible.

"I'm not leaving you, particularly like this," he stared at her, surprised.

She transformed before him, her anger icy. "For God's sake, go! Leave!" she shouted. "You want me to call the cops to you before you even start your job as Chief of Police?"

Charlie gaped at her. She turned away, shaking. She walked out of the room, and he followed her. "Please, Mandy, stop and talk to me."

She walked to the front door, her hand on the knob. "Please go. I'm asking nicely. I've got to get to church. I can't deal with this right now."

"Please listen to me," he pleaded. She refused to look at him.

"Please," she whispered, gripping the knob.

He touched her arm, but she pushed him away violently. "Don't touch me. Just go." Her voice was hoarse.

He turned and walked to the bedroom. A moment later, he came striding out, fully dressed. Amanda was sitting in a chair in the small open sitting room, her eyes down, her body tense.

Charlie laid a hand on her shoulder. She didn't respond.

A few seconds later she heard the door of the apartment shut.

A couple hours later, she completed her final practice before church, and headed for the choir room to robe. As she started out, she came face to face with Dr. Malcolm Howells in the doorway. Malcolm had practiced medicine in Mainville for over thirty years. He had been Amanda's family doctor, and a surrogate father to Amanda since the death of her own father when she was in law school.

He peered at her face as he asked, "How are you, my dear?" He took her hand and squeezed it solicitously.

She smiled wanly, pretending a brightness she did not feel. "Just a tad tired," she said, knowing that he could see the pallor she had tried to cover with makeup.

"You're pale as a ghost," Howells observed, his eyes intent upon her. "You've made yourself scarce this weekend. Marjy told me about the incident Thursday."

"Yes," Amanda answered carefully. "I just had to get away and be by myself a little while."

Howells stared at her dubiously. "It was the anniversary of Andy's death, wasn't it?" he was direct.

She blinked but nodded, a tremor going through her body. She couldn't look at him. She felt faint, her blood singing in her ears.

Her hand in his quivered, and she tried to still the trembling. "Amanda, I'm worried about you. You are not well," he spoke, his voice low. "Charlie called me this morning, said he was worried about you too."

"He what?" Amanda screamed, suddenly shaking hysterically. "He had no right." She felt the walls closing in on her, and swayed. "How dare he!" she exclaimed weakly, as the room whirled.

Howells quickly guided her to a chair and made her sit down. "I don't know what is going on, but he said he was concerned and wanted me to check on you at church this morning. Your response just now tells me something else, something much more troubling, dear." She felt his eyes boring through her.

"Doc, I have to go," she stirred desperately. "The choir members will be here any minute. It will soon be time for the prelude." Amanda tried to stand, but Howells put his hand on her shoulder, stilling her. She was still shaking.

A young man walked in. Howells turned to him. "Steve, could you fetch me a glass of water, please?"

"Sure, Doc." The man hurried away.

The doctor pulled out a pill bottle and opened it. "You know how I feel about drugs, Amanda Katharine, particularly in your case, but I know you are not yourself. In fact, you are scaring me. I also know you won't go to the hospital or home. So I want you to take two of these now, and one again if you feel any panic or anxiety."

Amanda looked at him in surprise, and started to protest.

Howells held up his hand, silencing her, and smiled reassuringly. "I assure you it won't hurt you, as long as you don't take the whole bottle at one time. And I limited you to only six."

Steve brought him the cup of water, and Howells thanked him. He handed the cup to her. "Take it, now," he ordered.

She obeyed reluctantly. Oh, God, let me get a grip, she prayed. She stood unsteadily. "Please don't let anyone see me like this," she whispered pleadingly.

Howells took her arm and steered her next door into an empty Sunday School classroom, closing the door, and forcing her to sit down.

"Now," he continued, sitting beside her and putting his arm around her, "after church I'm taking you to Marjorie's."

"I'm just fine," she insisted weakly.

"No, you're not. We'll sit here just a minute. Hopefully you will begin to feel better. You need to eat." His tone brooked no discussion. "You're going to spend the night at Marjorie's. I know you will go to work in the morning, even if I order you not to. But I want you to be where I know you are safe, where I can check on you. And you need to try to get some rest."

They sat there silently several minutes, Amanda with her eyes closed and Howells with his arm around her. As they heard the sounds of the choir warming up, he smiled. "Better?"

She nodded, standing. The trembling had subsided.

"Will you make it through church?" he stood with her, concerned.

"Yes, sir," she nodded again, taking a deep breath.

"Good. I told Charlie I would take care of you, and for him not to contact you, to let you have a little time to deal with your demons. I think you should reciprocate."

She stared at him wordlessly.

"Time for church," Howells quipped.

For a couple of months Amanda shunned extensive contact with Charlie, which was not hard to do, because he was thrown into the transition of assuming his duties as Chief of Police, and she was busy with the advent of Ralph's joining the law firm. It was impossible to avoid all contact, but Charlie did not press her, acknowledging her briefly at public functions before excusing himself. She felt the lingering pressure of his hand when they met, could feel his eyes on her, and could see the unspoken question in his eyes. She felt miserable, wanting him, wanting to say something, but remaining silent.

One day Ralph asked her to join him and Charlie for lunch, but she demurred. He held up his hand, stopping her in mid-sentence.

"What is going on between you and Charlie?"

"What do you mean?" she asked, feigning innocence.

"You two have barely spoken since I've made it back. We've attended the two get-togethers, the reception for him and the coming-home party for me, and you two remained on the opposite sides of the room. And you keep making excuses for not joining us for lunch. I ask him what's up, and he just says you are probably busy. But something isn't ringing true here."

"Nothing is wrong," she protested. "It is just a busy time for both of us, and I've had a lot on my mind. I'm trying to get some practice in at the church during lunchtime."

"Well, I think you could forego one practice to eat with us," Ralph insisted. "Whatever it is, we're all friends, and you need to kiss and make up."

"But there's nothing—" she started, but Ralph shoved her purse into her hands and took her by the arm.

"C'mon," he said, pulling her out of the office with him. "My treat."

She didn't see any way to refuse. They walked down the street to the deli, ordered their food, and took a seat at a corner table. Charlie walked in, saw Amanda, and nodded, smiling slightly. She tensed, but knew Ralph was eying her.

Charlie gave his order, then joined them at the table. "Long time no see," he said conversationally to Amanda, sitting down beside her.

"Yes, I've been busy trying to make room for Ralph at the office," she tried to sound casual.

Ralph chimed in, "As if I'm that much trouble. But I at least got her to update the décor in the office."

"It needed it," Amanda agreed. "I was letting things go. But it was all Marjy's idea. She said the place needed to look more like a real law office. And she has good taste, a flair for decorating."

She looked at Charlie. "I imagine your plate has been full at the police department."

"Yeah. I enjoy it, but there's a lot of work to do, whipping everything and everybody into shape. Everything had gotten lax." He smiled at the young woman who brought their food, and she winked at him.

Amanda noted the exchange and smirked. "I'm sure you will do just fine. I have no doubt of your abilities."

"Thanks for the vote of support," he retorted, catching her tone and gazing at her reproachfully. "I'm generally very good at what I do," he added meaningfully, and she looked away.

They ate their lunch, Ralph cajoling them both into talking about past anecdotes, and Amanda teasing him about his girlfriend.

As they were finishing, Ralph suddenly stood. "There's the clerk of court. I was supposed to get her an answer to a question, as a personal favor. I'll be right back."

He walked off, and Amanda was left sitting alone with Charlie. "Well," she tried to cover her nervousness, "our godchildren's birthday party is Saturday. Are you coming?"

"I plan to make an appearance. You?" he asked, his eyes on her.

"Yes," she colored under his scrutiny, fingering her napkin. "Charlie—" she faltered.

"Yes?" He did not break his gaze.

"Listen," she stammered, her voice low, fierce, "I'm so sorry about—about—my actions were unexcusable. I wasn't myself, but that's no reason for what I did. I lost my head and threw myself at you."

He leaned closer. "So you're telling me you were just horny?" he asked, so low that only she could hear him.

She looked down at her plate, blinking. "Yeah, I guess so," she muttered shortly.

"Look at me, Mandy," he commanded quietly, surreptitiously covering her hand with his.

She found it difficult to meet his gaze. When she did so, he took her hand, stroking it between his thumb and fingers. Her breath quickened, and she closed her eyes at his touch.

Charlie continued, his voice soft, "See? I know you better than that, and I don't believe it for a second. There's not a casual bone in your body. You're lying, but your body isn't."

She glanced at him, her face showing her surprise.

He bent closer. "There's nothing impulsive in your nature. Your mind constantly calculates, processes. You don't know how to go about having an affair. You feel things too deeply."

She held her breath, willing herself not to show any reaction. He continued, "I love you, Mandy. You feel it too. I haven't said that to any woman, ever. I'm risking all by baring my soul to you. I would wait, forever if necessary, for you. It's your call."

His eyes pleaded with her. "I can't make you love me back, or make you acknowledge it if you do. If you're not ready, need more time, that's fine. If you want to hide behind Andrew's memory, that's fine. If you want us to work it out, I want to more than anything. I'm here for you, no matter how little or how much you want." He paused. "But if you've convinced yourself it was simply a fling, just know it wasn't for me."

"It's irrelevant," she whispered.

He stared at her disbelievingly.

"How can you say that?" he demanded.

"I—I can't let go, Pete," she unconsciously used the nickname. Her resolve wavered. Overwhelmed at her feelings, at his touch, she opened her mouth.

Then she thought of Andrew, and swallowed convulsively, as if coming to a decision. She pulled away. "I mean—I mean, it wasn't meant to be serious. I feel so badly if you think otherwise. If we could just forget it happened and remain friends . . . ."

A mask fell over his features. "Whatever you say," he stood abruptly. "See you Saturday." He turned and walked out.

Amanda watched him leave, her heart breaking. He's hurt, and it's my fault, she thought. I need to stop him, apologize, tell him. But, she stopped herself, I can't just use him and allow him to hope.

Ralph returned to the table, and saw her face. "What happened? Where is he going?"

"Exactly where we should be going," she said, her tone cool and business-like as she stood. "Back to work."

After that, she and Charlie tried to act as though nothing had happened. They called a silent truce and entered into easy banter around others, but avoided being alone with each other.

So Charlie was surprised when he received a call at the office one day several months later. "Amanda Childs on line 2."

He picked up the receiver and pushed the button. "Petrino here," he spoke, his voice business-like.

"Charlie?" she said breathlessly. "Amanda here."

At the sound of her voice he closed his eyes. "Amanda. How are you?"

"Fine. Is business booming?"

"Crushing crime is a full-time job," he quipped. "What can I do for you?"

"I was just wondering if you might be free for dinner," she sounded hesitant.

He was taken aback. "When?" he found himself asking.

"Tonight," she responded. "I know it's short notice—"

"What time?"

"Say 7:30? Jack's?"

"I'll be there."

What is up? he wondered. Was Amanda rethinking her position about the two of them? He felt his spirits lifting at the thought.

He looked at his calendar, and it suddenly hit him. It was again the anniversary of Andy's death. Just two years ago, Andy had been alive. And just one year ago . . . .

He tried to squelch the rush of memories of his time with Amanda. I mustn't read too much into this, he considered. She could just be lonely and trying to make it through the day. But he couldn't help but hope that perhaps Amanda had made a decision she was ready for a relationship.

On impulse he picked up the phone and called Felicia Brown, who owned a florist shop in town, and he ordered an arrangement of flowers sent to Amanda.

Felicia asked, "What do you want on the card, Chief?"

He thought a moment. "Just 'Charlie'," he decided.

"What's the occasion?" Felicia pried.

Again he thought a moment. "Just something to help her through a bad day," he said.

"Oh," Felicia understood. "I had forgotten. It is that day, isn't it? It's still hard for her without Andrew. That's thoughtful of you."

He rang off.

That evening he spent some time trying to decide what to wear, and finally decided on gray slacks and a navy blazer.

He made his way to Jack's, anticipating seeing Amanda. As he walked into the tastefully furnished restaurant, a waiter recognized him. "Good evening, Chief Petrino. I'll seat you. They're already here," he said, leading the way.

They? he thought, but had no time to dwell on it. Suddenly he was at the table, and Amanda was standing there to greet him, dressed in a beautiful form-fitting green silk jacquard dress that complemented her eyes. He smiled broadly at her, then his eyes looked down to note a pretty young woman sitting at the table.

"Thanks so much for the flowers, Charlie," Amanda greeted him warmly, clasping his hands as he kissed her cheek. "It meant a lot to me."

He looked inquiringly at her. She introduced the woman. "Charlie Petrino, this is Jill Frazier. Jill is a new arrival in town, teaching at Westside Elementary. She was at Florida State with us. She and I had classes together."

He smiled politely, "How do you do?" He took Jill's hand. "Very nice to meet you."

"I'm happy to meet you too." Jill's smile transformed her into a beautiful woman. She was demurely dressed in a deep blue dress, fitted at the waist and ending right at the knee. "I remember you were a football hero. You dated my sorority sister briefly."

"Please have a seat," Amanda pointed to the chair next to Jill. He looked at Amanda, a question in his eyes, before seating himself.

"Really? Who?" he asked genially.

"Brittany West," Jill spoke shyly.

"Oh, yes," he replied politely, although he couldn't remember the name.

Amanda noted his bemusement and bit back a smirk. "Charlie, as I've been saying, is our chief of police now," Amanda interjected, coming to his rescue. "He's really the best law enforcement officer we've had, even better than his dad, who was the sheriff for years," she teased.

Jill smiled, her eyes deep brown. She's pretty, Charlie thought, before turning to Amanda. "So what is the occasion?" he asked, the smile not quite reaching his eyes.

"I thought this would be a perfect time just to have some dinner together and catch up, and I wanted Jill to meet some of the important people in town. And I couldn't think of anyone more important than you."

He suddenly understood what was happening. Amanda wasn't trying to rekindle a relationship with him. She was trying to play matchmaker, to offer him a consolation prize.

"I don't know about that," he murmured. "What grade are you teaching?" he asked Jill. He was pleasant, but inwardly seething at Amanda.

"Kindergarten, at least this year," Jill smiled. "And Amanda has already talked so much about you. I feel I know you."

I'll just bet she has, he telegraphed to Amanda in his steely glance to her.

"I would love to hear about you," he smiled winningly at Jill. I will give Amanda what she wants, he thought, turning his attention to the beautiful young woman and exuding his charm.

He found her lively and witty and was gratified. At least Amanda has good taste and chose someone pretty and interesting, he thought, although he was still angry.

Amanda kept the conversation flowing, but at times he noted her sitting back, a frozen wistful smile on her face. She seemed far away. He discerned she was thinking of Andrew and missing him, and he was pricked with remorse at being angry with her.

The dinner was enjoyable, and he was surprised when the waiter appeared and asked if anyone wanted dessert. After they made their orders, Jill excused herself to go to the restroom, leaving Amanda and Charlie alone.

Amanda leaned forward, her eyes dancing. "Well, what do you think?" she was excited. "She is so great."

Charlie hissed, "I can find my own girlfriends, thank you very much."

Amanda blinked. "I really didn't mean for you to get that impression," she blurted. Trying to swallow her hurt, she retorted, "I have no doubt of your prowess, but you apparently can't find a wife. And it's time you did."

Charlie, his jaw set at her words, just stared at her. "Am I that big a threat to you?" he sneered, his voice low. "Did you buy the ring and set the wedding date too? I mean, it would save me a lot of trouble."

She flushed and looked down at her plate, struggling for words. "I see no reason in both of us being miserable, Charlie," she whispered, her voice tremulous. "I love you and want you to be happy. I don't know any other way to accomplish that."

"Yes, you do," he retorted hotly, then relented as he saw the raw hurt reflected in her features.

Contrite, he whispered, "I'm sorry, baby. Don't cry." His anger was deflated. He reached across the table and took her hand momentarily. "Was it bad today?" he asked tenderly.

"It was the worst," she admitted, trying to smile, her eyes luminous. "Now it is two anniversaries in one. I think about both Andy and you." She blushed, embarrassed at having revealed too much. "Oh, Pete, I'm sorry. I just want to make it all right, and all I do is make things worse."

"It doesn't have to be this way, Mandy," he murmured.

She looked away, swallowing convulsively, then shook her head.

Saddened by her response, he leaned back in his chair. "She's really nice," Charlie asserted, trying to lighten the mood. "And kind of sexy, in a school teacher sort of way. I wonder if she has a ruler at home, and what she's wearing under that dress."

Amanda, piqued, suddenly flared, "Why don't you just ask?"

"Are we jealous?" Charlie met her eyes, and she looked quickly away.

"I'm sorry I asked you here tonight," she muttered sullenly.

"I'm not. It's the most you've talked to me in months," Charlie rejoined, his eyes on her. "And I will seriously consider your offering of a prospective bride."

He looked up and saw Jill returning. He stood and took her hand, helping seat her. Dessert was served, and he was assiduous in his attention to Jill.

As the dinner drew to a close, he asked, "Did you drive here?"

Jill smiled, surprised at his question. "I came with Amanda," she offered shyly.

Good girl, he telegraphed to Amanda, winking. "Could I see you home?"

Jill looked at Amanda, who bit her lip. "Last I checked, both of you are adults. Charlie will probably behave like a gentleman," she added jokingly.

"That might be nice," Jill smiled again, and again Charlie was struck by her loveliness.

"Thank you, Charlie," Amanda smiled politely.

Charlie stood and assisted Jill to stand, holding her hand a bit longer. Amanda stood also.

"Thank you for joining us this evening," Amanda said to Charlie.

"No, thank you for introducing me to Miss Frazier," he winked at Amanda, who was ready to strike him.

They walked out together, and Amanda watched the two walking to Charlie's car, her heart heavy. She turned back and went inside.

Later that night, Amanda was still sitting at the almost empty bar, nursing a drink. Some stranger, a man in a business suit, the only other customer, accosted her.

"You look lonely," he remarked, sitting on the barstool beside her.

She downed her drink, then nodded to the bartender. "Another, please, Bob," she ordered. She turned to the man. "Just hungry," she said, her voice enticing.

"Really?" he moved closer, emboldened by her response. "I might be able to help. Could I buy you dinner?"

"No, thanks, I just ate," she replied.

Confused, his brow knitted into a frown. "My name is George," he smiled pleasantly. "I'm a pharmaceutical distributor, and was just here for the day." He placed his hand over hers on the bar. "What's your name? What do you do?"

"Just call me Katy," Amanda purred. "I'm a lawyer by day, a serial killer by night," she replied casually, nodding her thanks to the bartender as he provided her another drink and took away the empty glass. She faced her companion, licking her lips suggestively.

George laughed, picking up her hand and kissing it. "Pleased to meet you, Katy."

"Could I buy you a drink?" she smiled sweetly, moving closer, reaching past him to snag a maraschino cherry with a small plastic skewer.

"Whatever the lady is having," he told the bartender, his eyes not leaving Amanda. She pulled the cherry off the skewer and placed the cherry in her mouth, slowly pulling the stem off, watching him all the while.

George moved closer, placing his arm on the back of her stool, his fingers lightly touching her back, moving slightly back and forth along her spine through the silk of her dress. "I like you already. Just how do you do your victims in?"

The bartender looked questioningly at Amanda as he placed the drink before the man, and the man took a deep draught. She downed her drink again quickly and gestured to the bartender to refill it. She turned back to the man and smiling engagingly, her knee brushing against his leg, her fingers playing with the small plastic trident she had dropped on the bar.

"I first get Bob here to add a concoction to their drink to make them groggy, then I carve out their organs with a fork," she gazed soulfully at George. "Good for the organ transplant business around here. And how do you think Jack gets the ingredients for his fabulous entrees?"

She straightened up as Bob refreshed her drink, and looked George up and down critically. "I might need the butcher knife for this one," she winked at the bartender.

The man laughed uneasily, as Bob looked at him and nodded, a slight smile on his face. "Jack sharpened it just this afternoon," he remarked, turning away and polishing a glass.

"Do you ever seduce them first?" George inquired, leaning forward, his hand reaching out and tucking a strand of her hair behind her ear, allowing his hand to brush down her cheek and neck lightly. She took a sip of her drink, her eyes not leaving his.

"Naw," she drawled, reaching out and straightening his tie, her fingers resting lightly on his chest. "I pick out strangers who won't be quickly missed."

She too leaned forward, until her face was only inches from his. Her voice was sexy. She ran her fingers up and down the shirt under his tie. "Take you, for example. I would never have sex with you, because I don't know where you've been. But once you've been carved up, tested and approved by the FDA, you'll be OK in a béarnaise sauce."

"I was thinking a red wine reduction in some of Jack's rue," a dry voice interrupted.

She turned, and Dr. Malcolm Howells was standing staring at her, his face a mask. He was dressed in a dark suit, and looked younger than his years.

Howells took one look at the man, and jerked his head toward the door. "Everything she told you is true. I think you should absent yourself now and be grateful I was in time to stop her."

George, his eyes wide, grabbed his drink and stalked off. Howells took his place at the bar.

"What are you doing here, Amanda?" His voice was low. Bob looked at him inquiringly, but Howells just shook his head.

"I'm a grown up girl, Doc," Amanda smiled tightly as she turned back to the bar and downed the drink before her. "I'm just enjoying myself. A little fun never hurt anyone. Didn't he look good enough to eat?"

She smiled at the bartender. "Another, please," but Howells shook his head in the negative.

"I countermand that order," he said. He took her arm. "I know why you're doing this, what day it is."

"What, did Marjy send you to save me?" she asked bitterly, refusing to look at Howells.

"No, Charlie did," Howells replied quietly.

"Ah, he was too busy to come himself," she spat, her hand trembling slightly.

Howells whispered. "He said he had dinner with you earlier. You fixed him up with someone. He saw your car still parked outside and was concerned. He had your well-being at heart. How would it look for you if the chief of police showed up and had to drag you home? Tongues would wag for weeks about poor pitiful drunken Amanda, drowning her sorrows and making a fool of herself, having to be escorted home by the police."

Amanda looked down, chastened, mute.

"Amanda Katharine," Howells pleaded, taking her hand, "please come with me. I'm not leaving without you."

The next morning, she walked into the office thirty minutes late, rubbing her forehead.

Sheila looked at her concernedly. "I was worried about you," she remarked.

"Do we have any aspirin?" Amanda spoke, blinking a few times. She looked up, and Charlie stood in the doorway to the kitchen area.

She stiffened reflexively. Ralph walked out of his office, file in hand. "If you can't make it on time, just come in when you can," he teased her. "I gotta get to court. Charlie, there's a bottle of aspirin in the cabinet over the coffeemaker."

Without replying she walked into her office, sitting down at her desk. Charlie came in momentarily, with a cup of coffee and two aspirin. "Here," he shoved them unceremoniously before her.

She took the aspirin and swallowed some coffee, as he turned and shut the door to her office. "Late night last night?" He was grim.

"I could ask you the same thing," she muttered.

He glared at her. "Jill is the type of girl one marries. No, I didn't make out with her on the first date."

Amanda flushed, her anger not abated. "Oh, by the way, thanks for sending the posse to rescue me last night. I'm so glad I didn't inconvenience you personally."

"Is that what you wanted, for me to show up personally?" he demanded.

She tensed, embarrassed, not responding.

"Where did you spend the night?" he asked, his voice softening.

"What do you care?" she was venomous. "With my keeper, of course."

"I knew you weren't at the farm, and you didn't show up at the apartment."

"You—you checked up on me?" her voice caught in her throat.

He towered over her exasperatedly. "Mandy, I didn't come into the bar for you last night because I didn't want to embarrass you. People would talk if law enforcement had to take you home, particularly if it was me. And we both know how you feel about being discreet."

His remark was not lost on her. He paused, gazing down at her, as she refused to look at him. His voice softened. "But there was an even more important, personal reason. If I had appeared and taken you home, I would not have been responsible for my actions. As angry as I was with you last night for 'fixing me up' I would have spent the night, stayed with you, loved you until you screamed that you loved me too. It would have been broadcast on the news this morning."

His look was dangerous, and she was silent. "And no amount of cops or restraining orders would have induced me to leave you."

He turned, his back to her. "Mandy, I thought I could settle for anything with you, just be happy with whatever you gave. But I've suddenly become very greedy. I don't want just a bite at the apple, a slice of the pie. I don't want to share you, not even with Andy's ghost."

She looked down, tears pooling in her eyes, grasping her desk. "I wish I could . . ." she whispered helplessly.

He faced her. "For the first time in my life I want the whole thing, dammit: love, marriage, babies, growing old together. With you, Mandy. And you've made it clear that's not going to happen, baby, not with us."

She looked at him, willing him to take her in his arms, to love her.

He looked back at her, his eyes understanding, pleading. "God, how I want to. I will, baby, if you say the word." His look hardened. "But when I do, it's not going to be a secret any more. I might wait long enough to get you upstairs to your bed. But Sheila and Ralph will know. The rest of the world will know."

He took one step toward her. "I'm not going to take that look in your eyes for granted. I gotta hear you say that it's what you want."

She looked away miserably, mutely, closing her eyes.

"I just can't," she finally whispered despairingly. "Jill will make you a good wife," she breathed.

He sighed dejectedly. "That's what I thought." He strode out.

PART II

The Present—Week 1

Chapter 4

Amanda Childs tried to ignore it. She had thought it was over, and had breathed a sigh of relief. But the loud pounding suddenly resumed, even more insistently. If I make no noise, maybe he'll give up and go away, she thought.

She sat tensely at her desk, not moving, staring unseeingly at the computer screen before her, the pleading she was typing forgotten, her mind frozen. She held her head in her hands, her elbows propped up on the computer credenza. The monitor and a desk lamp in the room provided the only light in the dark building. She glanced apprehensively at the closed slatted shutters covering the window of her office.

She stood and nervously started pacing in front of her desk. Resolutely she tried to shut out the sound. Please go away, she willed the unwelcome intrusion. Haven't I had enough?

Suddenly there was a familiar male voice at the window. "Amanda. I know you're in there. Let me in."

"Go away," she said loudly.

"Or what? You'll call the police? I am the police, dammit. I'm not leaving here until I talk to you. Do you want me to break down the door?"

"Damn," she muttered, sighing deeply. She wiped her brow on the towel draped around her neck. Then, the decision made, she walked out of the room, turned on the hall light, and padded to the back door of the law office, cutting on the outdoor and indoor lights. She unlatched the deadbolt and lock and opened the door.

Charles Petrino strode in angrily. He was still dressed in a tuxedo, his bow tie undone and flapping. His large muscular frame towered over her, as he ran his hands through his dark wavy hair in agitation. "Just what the hell do you think you're doing?" he hissed.

He looked past her, noting the light from the computer monitor screen in her office. "Working tonight, a Saturday night after midnight? We just saw Ralph and Claire off on their honeymoon. What's wrong with you?"

He stared at her disbelievingly. She was dressed simply in cotton tank top and loose-fitting shorts, athletic shoes on. The towel was still draped across her shoulder, and her blonde hair was damp and curling, framing her solemn features. Her face was still flushed, and it deepened under his scrutiny. He could see the signs of crying as she glared at him sullenly.

"What? You couldn't wait for the newlyweds to leave town before you peeled off your glad rags and stepped on the treadmill?" Charlie was thunderstruck. "What has gotten into you?"

Amanda muttered, "OK, you've seen me. I'm alive and well. Can you just go now? I'm not in the mood for chit-chat, Charlie."

He glared back at her, unaffected by her cold reception. Amanda stared back at him a moment.

"Suit yourself," she muttered crossly, then locked the door behind him, pushing past him back to her office without a word. He followed her. At the door he reached out and grabbed her arm, halting her progress.

"Mandy? What is it?" He turned her to face him.

Her face was devoid of expression. He could tell she was trying to keep a tight rein on her feelings. "I can't talk about it."

"Jon is beside himself with worry about you. He told me he tried calling you, knocked on the door here for almost an hour, then went back to the farm, hoping you had decided to go home," Petrino insisted. "Why aren't you there?"

"I can't face Jon right now," she responded, her teeth clenched, her eyes flashing fire.

"Why not? Just a few hours ago you were ecstatic, wearing his ring."

"It's just not going to work," she spouted. "Real life gets in the way every time."

"What?" he demanded vexedly. "You and Jon? Why do you say that?"

She shook her head vigorously, words failing her, and stalked into her office. She cut on a floor lamp in the room, then moved fluidly to a bottle of Jameson's sitting on the shelf of a beautifully carved mahogany armoire standing open. She poured a generous measure of amber liquid into a crystal tumbler. She carried her libation with her to the desk, slumping down into her brown leather executive chair, sipping it, staring at the wall mutely.

Charlie regarded her soberly, then walked over to the armoire. Reaching past the bottle she had chosen, he pulled out a bottle of Jack Daniel's Single Barrel, helping himself to a drink as well. "You and your fancy foreign crap.

Thank God Ralph has better taste," he muttered, loud enough for her to hear. She chose not to rise to the bait.

Looking around the tastefully appointed office, he saw a Duke University pennant pinned to her wall over a Florida State one.

"What's this?" he pointed, in an attempt to lighten the mood. He sipped his whiskey.

"What do you think?" she retorted. "Ralph is lording it over me that Florida State didn't even make it in the NCAA tourney, and Duke is in the Final Four. But I get the last laugh. He'll be in Europe and will probably miss seeing the championship game. I'm waiting for him to call and beg me to record it for him."

Charlie seated himself in one of the comfortable chairs facing her desk. "Some things never change. Remember all those basketball games I dragged you to when we were in college?"

Amanda nodded, her mood still dark. "Yeah. And Ralph would want us to cheer for him when Duke came to Tallahassee to play. He understood nothing about our perhaps feeling some loyalty to our alma mater."

They were both silent a moment, Amanda staring down at the liquid in her glass, Charlie nursing his. He finally spoke. "I never asked you. What was up about the senior prom business? I couldn't believe you hesitated when I asked you, told me you'd 'think about it'," he ruminated. "Hell, I wasn't exactly chopped liver."

"You're still stewing over that?" she rejoined. "I was surprised you asked me. You had your pick of girls, and you were just too damned sure of yourself. I wanted you to sweat. But you ended up my date anyway, thanks to—to . . ." she stammered and left the sentence unfinished, turning away in her chair.

"Bill had nothing to do with it," he protested. "I was afraid you were going to go with that nerdy guy in the senior play. I had to stake a claim quickly to beat him out."

He shook his head, sensing her prickly mood and determined to cajole her out of it. "Somehow we all ended up right back here," Petrino chuckled. "Go figure. Those were the best times. Those days at Bill's beach house, you in a swimsuit . . . ." His voice trailed off.

She said nothing. They both sipped their whiskey, Charlie regarding her gravely.

He asked her, "Did you ever imagine that you and Ralph would be law partners back then?"

"No," she replied, her mood relenting. "I really didn't expect Ralph to come back home. He was on the fast track to success. Basketball scholarship, fellowship to law school—he could have gone anywhere he wanted. He was smart and charming as hell, a born politician."

She turned her gaze on Petrino. "Did you really think you'd come back here to be chief of police?"

Charlie smiled slightly. "I always knew it," he declared emphatically. "I thought I might retire from the FBI or FDLE first, then come back and run for chief or sheriff. But I've always wanted to be sheriff."

"Because your dad was sheriff?" she queried.

"Because I watched him and knew that's what I wanted to do," Petrino shot back congenially. "I grew up riding with deputies and seeing how they did things. It just seemed like a natural extension of me."

"You're certainly good at it," Amanda conceded.

He sipped his drink. "Would you have married me instead of Andy had I played basketball instead of football? If I had taken a job elsewhere?"

"Hell, no," Amanda swung around to face him, propping her feet in front of her on her desk and leaning back in her chair. "Charlie, I always knew you were going to be a cop somewhere."

"But you ended up marrying a cop," Charlie reminded her.

"Yeah, and see how that turned out," she retorted, a mask falling over her features. "Besides, this town is too small for the two of us as it is." She stared at him, her face furrowed into a frown. "You weren't ever seriously interested in me anyway."

Charlie took another taste of his drink, his eyes averted. "You know better than that. I wasn't on your radar, girl, just someone to drag you away from your books every now and then. But there was a moment . . ." his voice trailed away.

Suddenly serious, she looked at her shoes. "Why are you talking like this, Pete?" she whispered hoarsely.

He flushed at her use of the nickname. "You are actually the only one I've ever allowed to call me that." He stared at her solemnly.

"You are the only one that got away with calling me 'baby'," she rejoined quietly.

"I'm aware of that. I remember the day you slapped the crap out of Billy for calling you that. You said, let's see, you said you weren't anyone's baby, and that he should never forget it."

She shifted uncomfortably. "You're stirring up a lot of nostalgia. As it is, I found you the best wife in the world." Amanda wadded up a piece of paper from the legal pad on her desk and threw it at him, hitting him upside the head.

"Yes, after you made it clear that no one could compete with Andrew, even dead," Charlie looked at her pointedly. "You did everything but push me into her bed."

"I'm sorry," she whispered. She flushed, her features suddenly sad. "Andy always thought the world of you, Charlie," she said softly.

"And you?"

The question hung heavily in the air. "You know the answer to that."

"No, I don't." His face darkened. "I guess I never have. I just know I let him and you down by not being there for him that night. I still can't forgive myself for all your pain. Maybe you'd still be happy."

Amanda shook her head sadly. "Please don't think that way. We'll never know why Andy did what he did. That's the hell of it." She downed the rest of her drink in one gulp, her hand trembling slightly.

Charlie paused, his eyes on her. "You know, I always liked your legs."

She threw another wadded piece of paper at him, but missed. "Why are you bothering me tonight? Why aren't you at home harassing Jill instead?"

"She sent me to help Jon find you." Charlie would not meet her eyes. "I don't know what happened between you two. But it is going to work out."

She was silent. He pressed her. "What is it? Can't I help?"

"No." She stood suddenly, restlessly.

He gaped at her. "You don't trust me?"

"It's not that," she muttered. She sauntered back to the armoire.

"Say it. You didn't trust me, Mandy," he said softly. "I saw your eyes that day the sheriff announced to you that Andy was murdered. It was my fault. You even said as much."

He walked back to the armoire and reached past her, grabbing the bottle and pouring himself another drink. "Then you led me on, just to blow me off." He stood just behind her, his voice hoarse. "That hurt like hell.

"If that wasn't enough, then not so long ago you suspected me of being in league with Claude Brown. After growing up together, hanging together all those years, after—everything . . ." he faltered, "I would have gone to hell to protect you from that slime. I did it once before. I hoped we were at least friends."

She turned on him, her eyes dilated, her voice raised. "I did too. What was I supposed to think? When I found out Claude was at large, escaped from prison, I knew you had to be aware of that fact. You knew I was supposed to be notified, but I wasn't. And you didn't tell me. How else could I possibly explain that at the time?

"And you knew about how Andy was killed. I was left in the dark about that, too." Her tone was bitter. "Maybe I deserved it, for what I did to you. I don't know. I only know I felt betrayed, by one from whom I didn't expect it. By you." The last words were like a slap.

"I'll always regret that, but the Bureau had everyone gagged," Petrino mumbled over her shoulder. "I know I should have said to hell with them."

She turned and looked straight at him.

"I'm sorry, Mandy," he pleaded. "But I do have your best interests at heart. I always have. I want to make it up to you, somehow."

She reached out and clasped his hand. She said softly, "It's over now." She looked at him fiercely as she added, "Just don't let it happen again, Bureau or no Bureau."

"Promise," he replied, his voice low, as she released him and turned away, as though embarrassed.

"And where Andy was concerned, Charlie, I never blamed you. I'm sorry if I ever gave you that impression. Andy was his own worst enemy. How could you stop that?" The rage burned in her eyes momentarily, then was gone.

"Besides," she tried to smile, "I'm in your debt after you saved my life, twice," she swallowed, averting her eyes. "But it's still hard to trust anyone, after—after—Bill." He sensed her tensing, as her hands clenched into fists, as she said the name.

"Mandy, don't beat yourself up about Bill," he placed his hand on her arm. "How were you supposed to know? We can't change the past. But you're safe now. He can't hurt you any more. It will take time, but all this too shall pass."

"You killed your best friend for me," she whispered. "That had to hurt."

As she turned and faced him, she saw Charlie's jaw tighten. "Like you, I thought he was my friend," he growled. "Guess he fooled me too."

They stared at each other silently for several minutes, before Amanda looked down. "I never thanked you for—for being there, for finding me that night, Pete." The last words were barely audible, but her use of the name again was deliberate. He understood. He clenched his hands at his sides.

"Don't mention it," he said, his voice low. "I'd do it all over again."

She blushed. "I'm so sorry. I would not have hurt you for anything."

Tears filled her eyes. Petrino smothered an oath, put his arm around her, his hand to the small of her back, enfolded her to him, took her chin in his hand and forced her to look at him. "Don't cry, baby. You know I'm a sucker for you when you cry."

She buried her head on his shoulder, closed her eyes and shuddered, and Charlie held her. "Oh, Mandy," he breathed, kissing her hair.

She clung to him a moment, opened her eyes, and pulled away. She mumbled, "I'm sorry. I shouldn't do that. Neither of us is free."

Charlie cleared his throat and released her. "Now tell me what is going on with you and Connor. It just can't be that bad." He stepped back, his hands at his sides.

She turned back to the armoire, picking up the bottle to refill her glass. He reached over and took it from her, placing it back on the shelf. "Enough. Talk to me."

She stared down at her glass. "It's just that—I should have known it was too good to be true. I'm mad with myself for succumbing to a feeling so quickly. I've been acting like some desperate schoolgirl, oblivious to the consequences."

"God, it's only been over five years since Andy was killed," Charlie exclaimed impatiently. "I wouldn't call that quick. You've grieved long enough. It's time."

"Time to make a fool of myself again?" she whispered, her voice bitter.

"No, you haven't made a fool of yourself. The man is crazy about you. Can't you see that?"

"That's irrelevant," she snapped, sounding like she was making an objection in court.

"Why? My God, baby, why can't you just let someone love you?" he remonstrated, his voice a roar, his anger boiling over.

"You're right." She wiped her eyes then, her lower lip quivering. He noted it.

"Damn it, Mandy, I'm sorry." He stepped toward her, but she held up her hand, stopping him.

"Don't," she warned, swallowing convulsively. "You should go home now, Charlie."

He spoke reluctantly, his voice husky, "Why don't you let me drive you home to the farm?"

"No. Jon is there. He can stay at the farm. I'll sleep here. This office has been as much home to me as anywhere else. I've spent many nights upstairs."

"I remember," Charlie mumbled meaningfully, and she blushed again.

He turned and walked away, putting space between them. "Jon wants to see you. He's worried about you," Charlie said softly. "Won't you talk to him? At least call him."

"Talking doesn't solve the problem between us."

"Do you mind if I at least assure him that you're OK?"

Amanda nodded mutely.

Charlie demanded suddenly, "You're running scared. You love this guy, don't you?"

She hung her head. "I don't want to," she confessed, her voice breaking. "And I can't afford to, not—not now. You know that."

"Why?" he pressed her, frowning.

"It's not over yet," she muttered angrily.

He looked at her and shook his head, sighing but saying nothing.

"Will it ever be over?" she cried, clenching her fists.

She shuddered slightly, suddenly cold. "Besides, I know next to nothing about Jon. And my dad's not around to vet him and give his approval, like he did with you."

"Jon is a great guy," Petrino assured her. "Top notch. Tom would approve. And you deserve the very best."

"Charlie, I love you," Amanda mumbled, tears forming, "but you are not helping the situation."

"Damn it, please talk to me," he insisted, concerned.

But she again just shook her head. "Go home."

"I don't want to leave you alone like this."

"I'm a big girl." She was stubborn. "I'll be fine."

He stared at her sadly and shrugged, defeated. "I'll go then. Come lock up behind me. Get some sleep, Amanda."

He took her hand and dragged her behind him. She unlocked the deadbolt.

He turned and drew her to him, kissed her on the cheek, then brushed her lips with his, lingering just a second. "This conversation is not over," he warned as he released her, abruptly opened the door and took his leave.

When he walked out to his car, Connor was there sitting on the hood. He jumped off when Charlie approached.

"You take directions really well," Charlie shook his head irritably. "I thought I told you to stay at the house."

"Well?" Jon demanded impatiently, ignoring the remark.

"No's the word," Charlie shook his head. "She doesn't want to see you; she refuses to talk about it. I pushed as hard as I dared. She won't listen. She's spending the night here, says you can stay at the farmhouse."

Jon's face fell. "This can't be happening. I'll break down the door. I will make her see reason."

He started toward the door to the office, but Charlie grabbed his arm. "Leave her alone," Petrino growled as he stopped Jon's forward movement. "Don't you think she's hurting enough?"

"But—" Jon started, trying to jerk free.

"But," Charlie jerked back, forcing Jon to face him, "she is loyal as a St. Bernard, Jon. For better or worse, your buddy, Mr. U.S. Attorney himself, reminded her of her loyalties tonight."

Jon stared at him confusedly.

"Andy has held number one slot for years now," Charlie explained, his features softening in sympathy. "His death did nothing to change that. Her heart has been nothing but a huge shrine to his memory, leaving no room for anyone else."

He dropped his hand. "She's finally beginning to let go. But she is within sight of bringing his killers to justice, or at least that's the way she sees it. Do you think this close to the end she is just going to shrug her shoulders and walk away into the sunset with you?"

"Did she tell you that?" Jon countered hotly.

"She didn't have to," Charlie replied gravely, turning his face away.

Jon stared at the darkened office dazedly. "So she doesn't love me?" he mumbled.

"Amanda does love you. I saw her face tonight at the reception. I had not seen her look like that since . . ." his voice trailed off. Clearing his throat, he continued, "But she's scared shitless. And she is not about to risk messing up this prosecution just because of it."

Jon rubbed his forehead irritably. "So what do you suggest I do? I'm not going to just give up. I love her, Charlie."

Charlie gazed at him sadly. "I know it, man. And I'd think a lot less of you if you said anything else. But I can tell you one thing—you can't manhandle her into submission. And once she is committed to a cause, you have a battle royale trying to change her mind."

"Don't I know it?" Jon grumbled.

"Didn't the prosecutor say trial was scheduled right around the corner?" Charlie interjected. "Surely you can hold out that long. Once it's over, maybe she'll finally be free, and consider her debt to Andy paid in full. I think she really wants some closure. And she's let you get closer than anyone else."

He clapped Jon on the shoulder. "Go get some sleep, man. Tomorrow will be better."

Chapter 5

Sunday morning Amanda awoke early, after only a couple hours of sleep. She thrashed about in the bed restlessly, her mind on Jon. I cannot do this, she told herself. I ran this play before, with disastrous consequences. She thought of Charlie. God, don't let me make another mistake or hurt anyone else, she prayed.

She finally decided to give up on sleep and get up. She padded to the shower, hoping to wash away her turmoil.

While in the shower she had a thought. That's a good idea, she concluded. So after she dried off, while looking in the closet to see what clothes she had left in the law office apartment, she dialed the phone.

"Good morning, Amanda Katharine," the voice greeted her warmly.

"Morning, Doc Howells," she spoke brightly. "I knew you were always up with the chickens, or I wouldn't have called so early. Have you finished your morning rounds?"

"As a matter of fact, I have," he said jovially. "Why—do I need to make a house call?"

"I was thinking, if you would not be too offended at the idea of playing hooky from church, that I might take you away from all this to the beach. I'll cook for you."

"The beach?" he echoed. "You know how I feel about missing church."

She held her breath, steeling herself for the lecture. But she was in for a surprise. "But you're cooking? Hmmm. Sure. I'll be a renegade with you. Where are we going?"

Whew, Amanda thought with relief. "I rented a place on the gulf, a nice spot. How about 9:00? I need to check with the cleaning crews to make sure all the wedding stuff made it back where it belongs."

"Don't go to the grocery store without me," Howells ordered. "We'll stop at Seb's."

So promptly at 9:00 Amanda pulled up to Howells' brick Georgian two-story home, and he was ready for her, toting a cooler out of the garage to her trunk. At her questioning look, he smirked. "Just a few necessary items that may not be available at your beach house."

"You'll be surprised," she countered enigmatically, as she popped open the trunk. He bit back a retort as he saw a cooler already in her trunk. "I'm prepared as well," she winked.

She took off, the spring breeze whipping through the open sunroof. Howells looked at her. "So how are you doing, Amanda Katharine?"

"Busy," she replied, her eyes on the road. "With Ralph gone, there's plenty of business. And Malachi keeps my head spinning with all the decision-making generated from Marjy's estate. There are barely bathroom breaks in my life right now."

Howells interjected. "Amanda, I'm talking about you."

She was careful not to look at him. "I really don't know how to answer that, Doc. There are times when I think I need to call Marjy, or wonder if she'd like to go to dinner. Then it hits me that she's not there. There's been no time to grieve." She took a deep breath. "And I try not to think about the other . . . ."

"That Marjy was your mother?" Howells hit the nail on the head.

Amanda sighed. "I don't know how I feel about that. Sometimes I miss her so badly, the longing to talk to her overwhelms me. All the things we did together, all her projects, her efforts to help me forget Andy, crowd my mind. Sometimes I'm angry and feel like she betrayed me by not telling me, by letting me believe a lie. Other times I'm grateful to her for the childhood I had. But then I'm faced with the fact that Mom and Dad weren't my mom and dad."

Howells said softly, "Dear, they were every bit your parents. At first they were very protective, jealous of Marjorie's inquiries as to your health. They wanted to do everything for you, to make you theirs. They refused any assistance, particularly financial. Marjorie respected that and kept her distance. I was your family doctor, so Marjorie knew you were in good hands and trusted your parents to take care of you."

Amanda was silent. Howells continued. "Can I tell you a story? When you were three, you came down with influenza. You were hospitalized, and were running a high temperature. We were doing anything we could think of to try to break the fever.

"I had come in to check on you, because you were at a critical point. I found Tom, Mary and Marjorie all hugged up together beside your bed, praying and crying. Poor Jeffrey was fast asleep on the other bed in the room. They were so afraid they were about to lose you.

"You know, after you pulled through, they shared everything about you. Even Tom would pick up the phone and call Marjorie to tell her something. And Marjorie was allowed to take you home to play with Monica, and Monica was allowed to come home with you."

Howells chuckled. "They were apparently successful in keeping you from knowing all this, but they were all so solicitous of you, very sheltering. I know you chafed at that strictness. When you became sixteen, Tom finally relented and allowed you to go to the beach with Billy, Monica and Charlie. But he and Sheriff Petrino made a deal that Charlie would protect you, and Tom threatened Billy in order to make him keep his hands off you."

Amanda flushed. Howells continued. "Marjorie was so determined that you have a normal childhood with loving parents, and that you never suspect the ugly fact of your conception. She loved you from the distance of mere friendship, and that was her gift to you. And Tom and Mary adored you to distraction."

Amanda bit her lip. "I keep telling myself that, but with the impending trial and all the publicity that will be generated, has already been generated, I feel exposed. And lost. I know all these questions will surface, and I have no answers, and don't know how to deal with them."

They were silent a moment. Amanda finally blurted, "But I miss her, despite all my confusion. I wish she were here so I could talk to her about it all."

"I miss her too. I'm there any time you need me," Howells clasped her hand on the gear shift lever briefly.

"I know," she smiled tremulously. "And I really wanted us to just get away and have some time together without all these distractions."

They drove down to the south end of the county, stopping at a small community grocery store which doubled as a seafood and produce market. Howells and Amanda sauntered in and were greeted by the owner of the establishment.

"What are you doing here on a Sunday?" Amanda asked Seb.

"Hard to find good help these days," he smiled. "My better half is laid low with the flu, and Jamie caught it also. That left only me."

"I completed those new rental agreements you wanted. Sheila put them in the mail last week."

"I got them Friday. Thanks, Amanda." He pointed to the display cooler. "I got some pretty stuff came in off the boat just this morning."

Amanda admired some grouper and jumbo shrimp, while Howells' attention was drawn to the oysters. Seb noted his interest. "My grandson brought those last night straight from Apalachicola."

Howells looked over at Amanda, who wrinkled her nose. "I'll take a couple dozen of those," he ordered.

Amanda picked out some fish and shrimp. While Seb was wrapping up their purchases, Amanda walked down the produce aisle and selected some early peas, new potatoes, and some fresh greens. She also chose a package of fresh baguettes and some coffee flavored ice cream.

They paid for their items, and Amanda placed them in the cooler in the trunk. She waved goodbye to Seb as they pulled out from the store's parking lot.

A few minutes later, they pulled into the driveway of a two-story rambling wooden lapped siding home with wraparound porches and a gazebo widow walk on top with an outside staircase leading to it. The back opened to the beach.

Howells looked at her in surprise. "Why are we stopping at Bill Barnes' beach house?"

Amanda opened the door and stepped out, quipping, "It's my rental."

She shut her door and moved to the trunk. Howells joined her, and took her arm. "Your rental?"

She was careful not to look at him. "I took a lease last week on the place, with an option to buy. Just had it cleaned and the pool scrubbed and gleaming."

She grabbed her cooler and started to the door with it. Howells took the other cooler and followed her. She felt the unspoken question. "Barnes needed the money to pay his legal fees," she offered over her shoulder.

As she stopped to unlock the door, he asked, "Does Barnes know you're the tenant?"

She opened the door and lugged the cooler in. "Well, probably not yet. Malachi Feinstein set up a corporation for me, and negotiated the lease. But of course I have no reason to hide it. Once the lease was in stone, I signed the check and sent it to his agent."

She took a breath. "I just decided I might like a beach house and wanted to try it. Marjy always hated the beach. This was available, and the place holds a lot of memories for me."

She moved through the house to the kitchen with Howells following. They both set down their coolers. "So you're now helping out Barnes' legal defense fund?"

"Hardly," she laughed mirthlessly. "Malachi got an excellent deal. It was a steal. I knew it would piss Mr. Barnes off when he found out, but he can't do anything about it."

"Why would you do that, Amanda?" Howells was dumbfounded, his tone hinting at displeasure.

"Has the man not screwed up my life and enjoyed doing it?" she flared. "Why not? Payback is hell," she muttered.

Howells said nothing, but Amanda could feel his disapproval. "It's not just revenge." She was defensive.

"You sure?"

Amanda sighed and faced the doctor. "Doc, let's not mar our time together by fighting."

He relented. "OK, but you know we'll come back to this."

He retrieved an apron from the top of his cooler and donned it. Amanda looked at him in surprise. "I thought I was cooking for you."

"Do you think you can do Oysters Rockefeller better than I?"

She shook her head, grinning. "You got me there."

"We got spirits?" Howells queried.

"But of course. The bar is stocked." She gestured toward the door.

"Well, go put on your swimsuit and let me check out the kitchen."

Amanda complied, coming back a few minutes later wearing a one-piece suit and a gauzy coverup. She could smell the scent of lemons, and observed Howells shucking oysters and carefully placing the open shells on two trays. One tray was already prepared and the oven was preheating. Over the other tray he was squeezing some fresh lemon juice.

"I'm glad you have Coronas and limes, an essential accessory for these," he remarked.

He turned to a couple of covered plastic bowls. "I mixed up the oyster sauce and some of my cocktail sauce this morning. And Seb carries the best horseradish in the world."

Amanda smiled. "So you were extremely busy before I picked you up. You have taken care of the aperitif. When do you want to eat?"

"I say we put these out and we can wait for the other. Pleasure before business."

Amanda laughed. "That's never been your policy before."

"No work on Sunday," he winked. "I want to try out the pool."

"Have at it," she replied. "Take your oysters, and I will get the beers.'"

She heard a buzzing and glanced in her purse. She noticed the number on her cell phone. Jon. He left a message. She listened.

"I've gone back to Pensacola, so you can feel safe to return to the farm. But I love you, Amanda. I'm not giving up."

She closed her eyes and bit her lip. She stared at the phone and noted a second call, this one from Ralph.

She opened a couple of Coronas and quickly cut a lime into wedges, sticking one in the mouth of each bottle. She grabbed them in one hand and the cell phone in the other, and made her way out to the deck.

She punched the speed dial on the phone. "Hey there," she spoke warmly as Ralph answered. "How was the flight?"

"We've just retrieved our luggage and are on our way to the hotel." She could hear the tired elation in his voice. "It's exciting. I love marriage so far, although we've had little sleep. Do you know how hard it is to make out on a plane?"

She laughed. "Trust you to figure it all out."

"Where are you?"

"You'd never believe it if I told you. I've kidnapped Doc Howells and we are at the beach."

"I wondered why you weren't playing at church."

Amanda giggled. "As hard as I worked getting you married, I felt I deserved the day off. And I knew Ken could use the spending money, so I let him sub."

"Glad to hear it. Is Jon there? I want to give him some advice."

"N-no," she stammered. "He wasn't invited to this party."

"Why not?" Ralph wanted to know.

She joked, "I'm getting old, and can only handle one man at a time."

Howells walked past her, dressed in swimming trunks, and dove cleanly into the pool. "And Doc has just beat me into the pool," she added.

"Well, we're beat, and I gotta show my wife who's boss," he countered wickedly.

She could hear Claire's voice in the background. "Amanda already knows the answer to that one."

Amanda chuckled. "Give Claire my love."

She hung up and watched Howells swimming laps, his breast stroke strong and clean, belying his age.

Amanda stepped down the steps into the pool and followed his lead, choosing a butterfly stroke.

After a few minutes, Howells paused and watched her lithe movements admiringly. She did several more laps, then stopped.

"Giving up?" she called breathlessly.

"Just enjoying the view," he replied.

She splashed him playfully. He dove under the water and grabbed her feet, pulling her under. She surfaced sputtering.

"Now I'm ready for my beer," he smiled, as he made it to the end and stepped out.

Amanda shrugged and did a few more laps, before joining him at the deck chairs.

Howells went inside and soon brought out the tray of Rockefellers, nicely done. He placed the tray on the table, then sampled one of the raw oysters. "Very good," he intoned. "Best oysters in the world. Here, try one."

Amanda grimaced. "You know I'm not fond of oysters."

"That's because you've never had them prepared the way I do them," Howells admonished her gently. "I'm sure when you were a kid they were served on a Saltine cracker doused with ketchup or hot sauce." He picked up one of the raw oysters in the shell, and plopped a tiny amount of horseradish on it, handing it to her.

Take it," he ordered. "I'm going to show you how it's done. Just one," he coaxed, as she looked distastefully at it.

"OK," she agreed reluctantly. He took one for himself.

"You do them pretty much like drinking tequila. The order is a little different."

"I didn't know you were familiar with doing tequila shots," she laughed.

"Watch me."

He downed the oyster from the shell, sucked the lime wedge from the top of the beer, then swigged the beer.

She gazed at him a moment, then followed suit.

"Yeowch!" she cried.

Howells laughed at her. "Was it that bad?"

She coughed, fanning her mouth with her hand. "Not too bad, after you get past the burn," she confessed. "The horseradish and lime together seem overkill." She laughed, tears in her eyes. "Clears the sinuses."

"Makes you forget that raw oyster. Another?"

"Just one more." She took the challenge. His smile broadened.

"A little of that cocktail sauce, please," Amanda ordered.

She downed it, then shook her head in the negative as he pointed to the tray. "Enough for now."

"OK, but in two minutes you have to try the cooked ones," he warned.

He disappeared and came back with small serving plates and little forks.

They sat down at the table, and he served a couple on her plate. She watched him as he helped himself, and emulated him. He watched for her reaction. "Umm," she nodded. "I like these better. They have an actual texture. And that sauce, oh, man . . . ."

He laughed as she ate three, then waved him off when he offered more. "OK, I've done the oyster thing for today."

She seated herself on a chaise, rubbing some sunscreen on. He remained in his chair by the table, helping himself to some more oysters. She leaned back and closed her eyes.

"So tell me—why am I here instead of your fiancé?"

She didn't move. She knew Malcolm would ask sooner or later.

"Can't I just spend a day with my best guy without the third degree?" She turned her head, and met his gaze staring at her, his lips drawn in a thin line.

Amanda sighed. "Please, Doc, just let it go."

But he was not deterred. "I take it, knowing you as I do, that this is more than a lovers' spat?"

Amanda bit her lip. "I broke it off." Sensing his response, she continued quickly, "Doc, it's just too big an obstacle to the resolution of the Barnes case. That is my focus. I don't have the time to tackle anything else."

"So you don't love Jon?"

She caught her breath. "I think so. But—"

"I mean," he retorted, "this is not a decision of whether you are going to get a puppy or take a pottery class. Shouldn't you make the time to explore an opportunity at love? Don't you think it's time you moved on?"

"Not as long as Andy's death is unavenged," she raised her voice, spitting the words. "I am not doing anything, including falling in love, particularly falling in love, if it jeopardizes this case."

She settled back in the chaise. Howells said nothing, but Amanda could feel his eyes boring through her.

"I mean," she continued, her voice softening, "Andy gave his life, and Jon has devoted a great deal of his career, to the solving of this case. How does it look if the initial prime suspect is dating the case officer, and the star prosecution witness exonerating her is her long-lost father?"

"That's a valid point," Howells replied gravely, his voice low.

Amanda turned again and gazed at him. "You mean you aren't going to argue the point?" she was astounded.

"Amanda Katharine, you are an extraordinarily intelligent woman. Why would I disagree with your undeniable logic?"

"Thank you," Amanda reached out and clasped his hand gratefully.

He squeezed her hand, but wasn't finished. "So you've thrown Jon Connor over?"

She shrunk away but he refused to relinquish her hand. "I don't know," she whispered. "I haven't thought that far."

"Is Jon going to go the way of Charlie Petrino?" he asked her bluntly.

She flushed. "What has Charlie got to do with this?" she was suddenly irate. "What did he tell you?"

"Don't take that tone with me, young lady," Howells was stern as he pulled her to face him. "You think I don't know?"

"Know what?" she challenged him, her eyes flashing. Amanda pulled away, standing up. "I think it's time I started dinner," she stated flatly, stalking away to the kitchen.

She stopped at the bar and reached for the bottle of bourbon to pour a drink. She looked around the familiar room, sighing deeply. The idea of taking this place was probably a mistake, she thought. Ghosts everywhere.

She noted that her hand was trembling. She downed the bourbon in her glass quickly, then mixed another to take with her to the kitchen.

She tried to banish Howells' words as she began preparing the vegetables, but his statement lingered, an accusation, bothering her, churning inside her.

She washed the peas and drained them in the colander, did the same with the greens and scrubbed the potatoes. She located a broiling pan for the fish.

As she placed the potatoes and peas in a pot, Howells walked back into the kitchen.

"Amanda Katharine, I'm sorry," he said earnestly.

"Why? You are absolutely right," she interrupted, her voice unsteady. "I can't argue with your undeniable logic," she echoed.

He stared at her, shocked.

"I know what a screwup I've made, and how I've hurt others, including Charlie," she turned her back to him, clasping the counter. "That's why I really don't want to make that mistake twice."

Howells went to her and turned her around to face him. She was crying. "I mean, I didn't really hurt him, did I? He's married and happy, isn't he? Charlie was never serious about anyone in his whole life. It was a pleasant diversion for him. He moved on."

Howells held her as she cried. "You didn't move on after Andy. You think it's somehow easier for a guy to do so? Do you really think Charlie saw you as only a momentary fling? That he took advantage of your vulnerability for a quick flirtation? You've known Charlie all your life. Yes, he has been a ladies' man, but not to you. Surely you are not oblivious to what's been going on all these years." His voice was momentarily stern. "Is that all you meant it to be?"

"No," she blubbered. "I tried, Doc. I really tried. I wanted to forget Andy so badly. I wanted to start over. I love Charlie."

"But—" he prodded her.

"But I just couldn't do it," she mumbled into his shoulder. "The guilt over the thought of loving someone else was overwhelming. I needed to keep Andy's memory alive.

"I didn't ever think that Charlie could be hurt, certainly not by me. He's always had the capacity to never miss a step. I never imagined he would ever be serious. I was scared when he said he loved me. I couldn't handle that."

"You don't notice how he looks at you, even now?" Howells pushed her away, holding her arms and shaking her gently. "Marjy and I always assumed you two would marry sooner or later. He always loved you."

She said nothing, remembering Charlie's brief kiss just the night before. "Oh, God," she whispered. "But what can I do? He's married to Jill. I introduced them, for God's sake. I pushed them together. I can't fix that, Doc."

"Just like you can't fix Andy's death," Howells was sober, his hands still gripping her arms. "But you've got to break this cycle, girl. I know you don't believe this, but you have a devastating effect on men. Billy Barnes, Andrew Childs, Charlie Petrino. And now Jon Connor is in love with you. It's time you took that next step."

"Billy?" Amanda's voice failed her, and she croaked. "I was just a means to an end for Billy." A wave of rage rolled over her at the memory of Bill's assault on her in the warehouse.

"You were an obsession to Billy. Billy had never been taught anything about love," Howells' voice was grave. "Even as a child when his mother was alive. Bill Barnes molded Billy into what he was. Billy was shoved at Monica Witherspoon by his father, who was determined to link the two families. But you were as close to love as Billy ever got. It's a sad statement that Billy never knew what love is and what to do with it. He read the feeling as a need to conquer, to possess.

"William Barnes devastated the life of Billy, and through him, Andy and you. And by exerting his influence over Stephen Marks, Bill destroyed him as well." Howells paused. "And I tried to warn the authorities that Celeste's death was not accidental. But I had no proof."

Noticing that Amanda was trembling, he paused. She covered her eyes with her hands. He pushed her into the next room and guided her to a chair.

"I guess I'll never be able to erase that night from my mind," she whispered, shuddering. "I still have nightmares of Billy holding me while his dad came toward me with the syringe."

She paused, trying to pull herself together. "Doc, I know Andy's not coming back. I'm trying. I want Jon. I think I love him."

"The way you wanted Charlie?"

"No," she insisted wildly. "No. I knew—no," she thrashed about for the words, "I love Charlie, Doc, I really do. But I knew I couldn't give him what he was wanting. I wasn't expecting—I mean—it was never meant to be—to be serious," she finished lamely, knowing that Howells surmised she was lying.

"Speak for yourself," Howells peered at her sadly.

"What do I do?" She looked down, rocking back and forth nervously in tiny motions.

"You need to make your peace with him."

"With Andy or Charlie?" she asked dully.

"Both, my dear. You can't erase what happened with Charlie, and you can't bring Andy back by dwelling on his memory, by denying yourself the rest of your life."

"But doesn't Andy deserve to be remembered by someone?" she argued desperately.

"Yes, and he will always be remembered by everyone whose life he touched, including you. Nothing will change that, even your learning to love again."

Howells kissed her forehead and released her. "Just think about it, dear. Let's get dinner on the road, so we can go swimming again before it's done."

Chapter 6

Friday morning Amanda made it to the office and greeted Sheila at her desk. "How much longer before Ralph gets back?" she groaned good-naturedly. "What a wild week. I cannot remember from one minute to the next whether I'm supposed to be in court, meeting with a client, or drafting something. I must have been out of my mind to agree for him to be gone on a honeymoon."

Sheila grinned. "I don't remember his giving you a say in the matter."

"If Claire didn't deserve it so much for marrying his sorry butt, I'd have vetoed that idea," Amanda grumbled.

"We've handled this office by ourselves before," Sheila smiled. "And with a heavier calendar than this. But right now next week's schedule isn't quite as loaded."

"And it's nice not having Ralph around bossing us," Amanda laughed. "But I have a feeling I'm going to miss him terribly before he gets back, much as I will try not to admit it."

"You already miss him," Sheila replied, shaking her head.

"You're right." Amanda disappeared into her office, and a few minutes later reappeared, file in hand. "I'm off to the courthouse to handle this pre-trial and to pick up my certified copies for the Webster case. They'll probably have those deeds recorded by now for Mrs. Blount. I'll pick them up as well. It shouldn't take long."

"Famous last words," Sheila smirked.

Later that morning, close to noon, Amanda returned. "I thought I was never getting out of court. All that effort working out a pre-trial stipulation, and then having to cool our heels for the judge to get around to us. And it's old home week, with all the attorneys in two counties standing around waiting their turn. At least I caught up on the gossip. And I set that motion to dismiss on Thomas for hearing. Barney's representing him, and was gloating over his new Blackberry calendar software. Here's the date and time."

"Not everyone has the memory to carry around their appointment books in their heads like you do," Sheila laughed.

"Yeah, but thanks to you I have the old-fashioned crutch of the little black book which you religiously keep up to date," Amanda held up the small planner.

Sheila handed her messages as Amanda handed her the file and copies. Amanda perused the messages. "Pamela Young Bates," she said aloud. "'Important—call ASAP.' Wonder what that's about."

"I know the answer to that," a voice interrupted behind her. Startled, she turned. Charlie Petrino was standing in the doorway. She suddenly tensed, remembering their encounter Saturday night, and her conversation with Howells on Sunday.

"You startled me. I didn't hear you come in," she stammered. Then the grim look on his face registered with her. "What is it, Charlie?"

"I think you should sit down," he replied gravely.

Attuned to the urgency in his voice, she suggested, "Come on in to my office."

She led the way, and gained the safety of being behind her desk, as Charlie shut the door then turned back to face her.

As she seated herself, he announced without preamble, "Shelby Young died this morning."

She turned white. "Oh, my God," she murmured. "What—how?" She found she couldn't say any more.

He crossed over to the armoire, opened it, and quickly poured her a splash of whiskey in a glass, and handed it to her. "Take this," he instructed.

She downed the whiskey, coughing, as tears formed. "Oh, my God. Alan must be beside himself. What happened?"

"He apparently found her collapsed at home last night, and rushed her to the hospital. Dr. Cardet brought her back, but she died this morning." Charlie turned back to the armoire, pouring himself a whiskey and downing it in one gulp.

"What caused it? Does anyone know?" Amanda reached for a tissue from the holder on her desk, standing and moving toward Charlie.

He shook his head, his back to her. "No. An autopsy will be done."

"We need to go over there," she spoke. "The kids, Alan—oh, my. This is such a shock."

"I sent Jill on over. Alan asked me to make sure you knew."

Amanda touched his arm impulsively. "Thank you, Charlie."

"You can go with me." He was careful not to look at her, as he took her arm and gently pushed her ahead of him toward the door.

She stopped by Sheila's desk, glancing at the calendar. "Sheila, see if you can reschedule today's and Monday's appointments," she told the surprised assistant. "Charlie and I need to go to Alan's right away."

"What happened?" Sheila's eyes were wide.

"Shelby Young died this morning." Amanda's eyes were still on the calendar, as she blinked back tears.

Sheila gasped. "Oh, Amanda, I'm so sorry. How?"

Charlie answered for her, "We don't know yet."

Amanda spoke calmly, although her heart was heavy. "Please explain that it could not be helped. Ask them if you can call them Monday to reschedule, because we'll know about the funeral arrangements by then. And Sheila, please call Felicia and order—oh, I hate funeral flowers—a large bouquet of flowers to send to Alan's house, and a black wreath for our office door. She knows what I like."

"Tell Felicia to check first, but I think the family is over at Alan's dad's house for now," Charlie chimed in. "Let's go."

Amanda noted the anxiety in his voice, and knew he was anxious to find out what was happening, so she complied.

Alan Young was a physician in town, a life-long friend and schoolmate of Amanda and Charlie. He and his wife Shelby had twin boys, eight years old, and Amanda and Charlie were godparents to the children. Alan's father Benjamin Young had been the town dentist for over thirty years. Alan's eldest brother Ben, having followed in his father's footsteps, now ran the dental office. And Alan's older sister Pamela and her husband Mike had just recently moved back to Mainville to help care for their aging father.

In the car on the way over, Amanda turned to Charlie. "What do you know?" she demanded crisply.

"Not much more than what I've told you," he admitted, never surprised by her mood change. "It just happened this morning, and Alan was completely distraught when he called. He sent me here to collect you; he didn't want you to find out by accident."

"Have the boys been told?" she thought aloud.

"That's why I sent Jill over," he said softly. "I figured she could help there, inasmuch as she deals with children every day."

"They adore her," Amanda smiled sadly. "She would make a much better godmother than I am."

"You're great with the boys. They love you. But Jill is so fond of them." He paused, swallowing. "I think Jill is anxious to start a family."

"And you aren't?" Amanda asked, looking at him, surprised.

"I don't know." He stared at the road. "I love Joshua and Caleb, and we always have a great time fishing or swimming or hanging out. I'm happy to be their godfather and to shower them with gifts and attention. They and Alan like camping and doing 'guy things'. But I realize, from watching Alan, what a huge responsibility being a parent is."

"But you'll make a great father," Amanda replied warmly. "If you think you enjoy your godchildren, just wait until you have some of your own."

"I guess so," he was noncommittal.

"Is anything wrong?" she touched his arm. "I mean, is there something going on between you and Jill? I mean—" she colored, "it's none of my business."

"It's nothing," he muttered. "Like you, I have some unfinished business."

She flushed and fell into silence.

They said nothing else until they pulled up to the sprawling two-story framed home of Dr. Young, Alan's father.

As Amanda got out of the car, the two children spied her and ran out the front door to meet her. She knelt and reciprocated as they engulfed her in a big hug. "Hey, my boys," she said as she tried to smile brightly.

"Miss Jill just told us Mommy is gone to heaven." Joshua was clearly agitated. "I don't want her to go."

Caleb clung to her, saying nothing, but his face was tear-streaked. Amanda's heart went out to them, as Jill walked up to her. "Alan and I tried," she submitted, her voice low, "but they haven't completely grasped it."

"It's OK," Amanda crooned, shushing Josh's crying and holding Caleb. Gently disentangling herself, she took their hands. "We need to be really strong for your dad," she urged quietly.

"But I don't want to be strong," Caleb spoke up, looking at her.

"I don't either," Amanda admitted sympathetically. "But we also have to eat our English peas when we don't want to, because it's good for us." She bent down and ruffled their hair. "If Daddy is trying to be strong for us, we gotta do the same for him."

"Come on." Jill held out her hands to the boys, and they reluctantly relinquished Amanda. "I'll be right behind you," Amanda told them, nodding at Jill.

Just inside the foyer, Amanda met Alan's brother Ben and sister Pamela. She hugged each of them. "Is there anything I can do, help notify family, make any arrangements?"

Ben looked somber, and Pamela answered. "Alan will want you to play for the service, I'm sure, that is, if you can. We've notified most of the family, and others are helping get the word out to the church and community."

An elderly man, attractively tanned with white hair, came up and put his hand around Amanda's waist. She kissed his cheek. "How are you, Doc Young?"

"Old Doctor Young to you," his eyes twinkled at her. "How are your teeth lately?"

She put her arm around him. "Great, thanks to you. You're still at it, I see. I guess you are never going to retire?"

"When the Good Lord takes me," he replied. "But Ben is head honcho at the office now. And I get to spend time on the boat these days. Too many Dr. Youngs in this family."

"It is hard to keep up with which Dr. Young one is addressing nowadays," she agreed.

"Alan has been asking for you," the elder Dr. Young's face was suddenly solemn. "This came out of the blue for us. We're all stunned." He pointed through the door. "He's in there."

Charlie had gone in before them, and was standing in the living room with Alan when Amanda walked in. Alan stopped talking in mid-sentence and crossed over to her. She embraced him.

"Oh, Mandy, this is unreal," he whispered as he hugged her back. She nodded.

"I can't believe this, Alan," she agreed, her voice low. "Do you know anything—?"

"Bob said there was something unusual in the blood they drew when she came into the ER. I don't know what he meant." Alan was wide-eyed, beside himself. "Oh, God, Amanda. What am I going to do without her?"

"Shh, we're going to make it through this," she tried to reassure him. She gently led him into the front parlor away from the others. "Alan, what happened?"

"I found her last night collapsed at the house. She was unresponsive, so I picked her up and raced to the emergency room with her." Alan's eyes filled with tears. "She coded on me right there, and Bob brought her back. But this morning she was gone."

"I don't like the sound of this," she was grave, thoughtful, her eyes on Alan.

"What?" he looked at her in alarm.

"It may be nothing, but say nothing more about the facts for right now," Amanda warned him.

"What do you mean?" he became agitated.

"You know that a death under any suspicious circumstances will be investigated. You said Dr. Cardet felt there was something unusual. Let's just err on the side of caution," she kept her voice low so that only he could hear her.

Alan stared at her and nodded mutely. She added, "Not even Charlie."

"Why not?" he was shocked.

"Because Charlie is a sworn law enforcement officer, dear," she replied matter-of-factly. Seeing the stunned look on his face, she took his hand and pulled him down to the sofa to sit beside her. "You know how paranoid I am, and this could all be nothing. But just humor me for now," she tried to soothe him.

Alan nodded, still dazed. "Amanda, I've known you and your instincts for a long time. I trust them too much to discount anything you say."

Charlie and the boys walked into the room. The funeral director, dressed in black suit, also appeared in the doorway. Noting that, Amanda squeezed Alan's hand tightly. "I think I can do more good right now keeping the boys occupied so that you can speak to the director."

He nodded as the twins came up to them. She turned to the boys, stood and took each one by the hand. "Let's go upstairs to your room a little while and let the grownups do their thing," she suggested, her eyes meeting Charlie's briefly. They trooped out together.

She kept the twins occupied with a board game for a while, then noticed how tired they seemed. She suggested they lie down to relax a few minutes. They were asleep almost instantly. Amanda sat on the edge of one bed and watched them, lost in thought. Why Shelby? she asked God silently. These little boys need their mom.

Jill slipped in and laid her hand on Amanda's shoulder. "They're so cherubic," Jill whispered as she gazed at the sleeping forms.

"Only when they're asleep," Amanda laughed softly.

"Where's your engagement ring?" Jill asked suddenly.

Amanda started. "I—I broke it off," she whispered.

"Why? Jon adores you," Jill squeezed her shoulder. "I have such high hopes that you will find Mr. Right."

"I have to get past this trial," Amanda contended, more to herself. "I owe it to Andy."

"You keep trying to close that door, and it keeps opening back up," Jill asserted knowingly. "It's like a recurring nightmare."

Amanda peered at her and nodded. "Yes," she said simply. Amanda glanced at her sleeping godsons. "I just can't hurt anyone else until I can leave this behind."

Jill hugged her. "It will happen."

Amanda embraced her back. "Hope springs eternal. I was just worrying about what these boys are going to do without their mother."

"It will not be easy, but they have the love of many friends and family, and God will make a way," Jill replied gravely. "But it's so hard to believe."

"I told Charlie on the way over here that you'd make a much better godmother than I do."

"Nonsense. Besides, that was before I was on the scene." Jill added wistfully, "I sometimes wish I had had the opportunity to grow up with such close friends like you are with Charlie and Alan and Ralph."

Amanda nodded soberly. "I am blessed," she conceded. "They are my family. And now you are part of it." She squeezed Jill's hand. "I will try never to let you down."

"I know," Jill smiled. Amanda felt guilt rising inside her as she looked away. "I thank you for introducing Charlie and me."

"Are you happy?" Amanda asked earnestly, standing and gazing at her friend.

"Yes, I think so," Jill smiled broadly. "I know Charlie is the best thing that ever happened to me. We're still learning about each other."

"I'm so glad," Amanda breathed. "It means a lot to me that you and he are happy together."

"Did you love him?" Jill asked suddenly.

Amanda caught her breath, surprised by the question. "Who?"

"Charlie," Jill lowered her voice.

Amanda was stunned.

Jill observed her closely as Amanda blinked. "I know about you two. It's all right."

"But," Amanda caught herself, "of course. It makes sense that you two would share everything."

"Not everything," Jill looked away, at the boys. "Charlie does not discuss you. But I know him well enough now to read him. He still cares for you. He wants to protect you."

Amanda shook her head sadly. "Charlie and I are only friends, Jill." She swallowed. "I owe him a lot. He saved my life. I can't repay that." And I hurt him, she thought but did not say.

"What about Jon?" Jill squeezed her hand sympathetically.

"I don't know. I know I just can't commit until I've closed the door on Andy for good." Amanda bowed her head. "That's the problem. I have not been able to do that, after all this time."

She clasped Jill's hands in hers. "Charlie needs you, Jill. You're good for him."

Jill inclined her head. "I hope so. I feel lucky. I'm sorry for your troubles, Amanda. I always pray for you, that you will find a love of your own."

Amanda closed her eyes, trying to squelch tears.

Jill squeezed her hand again then released it. "Why don't you go downstairs a bit? I'll watch the boys. Besides, I'm better at this than at socializing with strangers."

"If you're sure," Amanda stood. "I do need to see if I'm going to be needed for the service and if I can do anything else to help."

She let herself out quietly, walking quickly down the hall. Turning the corner, she ran into Charlie. He caught her in his arms.

"I'm sorry," she said breathlessly, as his arms lingered around her and she awkwardly extricated herself.

"You OK?" he asked, his hand still gripping her arm.

"Yes," she affirmed shakily. "Jill is with the boys. She would probably appreciate your company."

Turning, Amanda fled down the stairs.

Chapter 7

The next morning Amanda was over at the Young household early. It had been decided that Alan and the twins would spend the night again at his dad's house, to avoid the children's facing the scene where their mother collapsed until they had more time to accept her death.

When Amanda arrived, she observed that the kitchen and dining area were overflowing with food brought by the ladies of the Baptist church and the community. Alan was looking at the mounds of serving bowls and cakes, pies and other items with trepidation, as the housekeeper bustled around him tutting over the chaos.

Amanda had laughed despite the seriousness of the situation. "Trust the church ladies to make sure you are fed."

She looked critically at the items brought and tried to make a list of condiments, drinks, plates, cups, ice, utensils and other foodstuffs, so that Pamela could respond to inquiries from neighbors and friends offering assistance. She looked around for the twins.

Pamela answered the unspoken question. "They are outside playing with the cousins. Ben is trying to watch them, but they are a handful when the six get together."

Amanda nodded. "Maybe I can help with that." She pulled out her cell phone.

"Fred, you know your offer this morning? Is it still open? I may marshal the kids and bring them out, if you're still game."

She hung up. "What if Ben and I take the kids to the farm fishing? Ben is a great dentist, but he's out of his element here. It will get them out of your hair for the morning, and that way Alan and you all can finish making arrangements."

Pamela's look of gratitude matched her sudden embrace of Amanda. "You are such a dear," she said, tears in her eyes. "Alan has been beside himself, and he is overwrought about the boys. That will relieve his mind for a bit. I can get Mike to help as well."

So in the end Amanda and Ben took the twins, and Mike, Pamela's husband, and the other children and two teenagers followed in Mike's SUV to the farm.

When they arrived at the gate, Fred was already there, with rods, tackle, bait and necessary gear in the back of his pickup. He smiled at Amanda. "Don't worry. We'll keep these whippersnappers occupied and wear them down a while fishing around the pond."

He took charge and soon had all the kids and adults equipped and ensconced around the pond fishing.

Amanda remained busy providing sunscreen, mosquito repellant, folding chairs, baseball caps, and a cooler with drinks and snacks for everyone. She sat in a folding chair and watched as the kids enjoyed themselves, allowing herself to think.

I have avoided Jon all week, she thought with a start. She realized how much she missed him. I really should call him. No, she reprimanded herself, I mustn't encourage him to hope. Look how I messed things up before.

Caleb started yelling as his cane pole bent in an arc. Fred headed toward him, and Amanda made her way to him as well, as it appeared that whatever was on the other end of the line might drag the child in. Just as the two adults made it there, the boy triumphantly pulled the line close enough to grasp.

Fred helped him, reached down and captured a catfish carefully in the mouth, avoiding the barbs as he lifted it out of the water. Caleb's eyes grew wide as he admired his catch. "Aunt Mandy, lookie!"

"My heavens, dear," she exclaimed. "It is almost as big as you. That one could eat Momma Cat."

Joshua ran up to examine the fish as Fred carefully disentangled the hook from the fish's mouth. "That's a good three pounder," Fred stated critically. "Good eating."

"You're gonna eat him?" Caleb asked wonderingly. "I want to keep him."

"In what?" Amanda laughed. We don't have an aquarium big enough. So you have to release him, or else let Fred kill and clean him to eat."

Caleb studied the fish seriously. Josh started jumping up and down. "Kill and eat! Kill and eat!"

Caleb turned to Fred. "Let him go," he begged the man.

Fred turned to Amanda and mumbled good-naturedly, "Guess if we were depending on him for food, we'd starve to death."

Amanda laughed at him and turned to the boys. "OK, gotta bait the hook again. Or do you want to spare the worms?"

Caleb grimaced, "They're slimy."

Amanda grinned. "Give him here. Geez, where is a good man when you need him? I even gotta bait your hook for you."

Fred had released the catfish back into the pond, and turned back to her. "I'll do that," he said, nodding behind her.

She turned, and Charlie and Jill were coming toward her. "Are you here to help your godsons bait their hooks?" she smiled.

Charlie did not return the smile, but took her by the arm. "Excuse us, boys," he told the twins as he steered her back up the bank. "I'll see you back at Dr. Young's house," he smiled at Jill.

"What is it?" Amanda stopped, concerned.

"I was almost here when Bruce called. The state attorney's office has obtained a search warrant of Alan's house. Law enforcement are on the way there now. I asked Bruce to wait until we got there."

"Does Alan know?" her anxiety showed.

"Yes. Let's go."

She turned to Jill and Ben. "They don't need to be out more than another hour, then they need to get back to your dad's house to wash up for lunch." She smiled grimly. "I promised Alan they'd be there to help eat up that mass of food the church ladies brought. And watch the sunscreen."

Jill pushed her gently. "Go on."

"We'll take my car," Charlie suggested. "Give Jill your keys."

"Can you drive stick shift?" Amanda asked Jill.

Ben spoke up. "I can. We'll take care of things here."

Amanda strode up the hill, trying to keep up with Charlie's quick tread. He opened the passenger door for her, then shut her in and strode to the driver's side. She saw the set of his jaw and knew he was worried.

He spun off, the GTO stirring dust as he took the road quickly. Amanda held on as he spun around a turn. "The Beemer takes curves better than this antique," she tried to lighten his mood. "And I could probably take you in a race."

"But I'm driving, and I can outdrive you any day," muttered Charlie grimly.

"Typical chauvinism, with no basis in fact," she retorted. "You men in your muscle cars."

She gritted her teeth as he hit a bump on the dirt road. "Damn," he swore under his breath. "I'd think you and Fred could keep this road in better shape. I'll have to have a realignment."

"What do you know about this warrant?" she diverted his attention to the subject at hand.

"The State had it done and signed before anyone knew about it. That's all I know for now. I'm afraid Alan will go off like a bomb if we're not there," Charlie responded, reaching the paved road and shifting gears as he accelerated.

"Wouldn't the police department be doing the investigation?" she queried.

"I have a conflict of interest." His jaw jutted with irritation. "I can't run the criminal investigation because of my relationship with Alan and the family."

"I'm sorry." Amanda did not look over at the speedometer. She decided that she was better off not knowing.

Charlie noticed her tension and covered her hand with his briefly. "Trust me."

She nodded mutely as he turned his attention back to the road. She closed her eyes. Please, God, she prayed, take care of Alan. This situation is unreal.

They arrived at Alan's home just as Alan was getting out of his Land Rover, his father with him. Law enforcement cars were already there, and Bruce Williams, Chief Investigator for the sheriff's office, was at the door with several investigators and deputies. Amanda jumped out and ran to Alan as he started to push past Bruce.

"No, Alan," she took his arm. "Just a minute, OK?" she said to Bruce.

Bruce nodded, and she dragged Alan away, as Charlie intercepted the senior Dr. Young.

"They're now invading my home," Alan spat at Amanda. "It's not enough that Shelby is dead. I'm now a suspect."

"OK, Alan," she pulled him just out of hearing. "Keep your voice down and talk to me. Do you know of anything they would find that would point to you?"

Alan looked at her, startled. "Are you on my side or theirs?"

"Yours, of course," Amanda tried to soothe him. "Just answer my question. I need to know whether there's something I need to be objecting to, if I can."

His eyes filled with tears. "No, Amanda, other than I don't want the bastards putting their hands all over her stuff."

Amanda breathed a sigh of relief. "Then there's no reason to object, is there?" she pointed out. "Now, I want you and your father to turn around and go back to the house," she ordered. "Charlie and I will stay here and take care of the situation."

"But—" Alan began.

"Honey," Amanda's fingers bit into his arm as her voice became low and controlled. "Remember our talk yesterday? I do not want law enforcement even hearing your breathing right now, much less any statements of any kind. Please listen to me," she pleaded with him. "I will want you to walk me through everything after they are gone."

Amanda thought he would refuse, but he looked at her and nodded. She took his hand in hers and they walked back to Charlie and Dr. Young. "You two are going back home for now, and Charlie and I will stay and report to you later."

Charlie nodded his assent. Dr. Young kissed her hand. "Thank you, Amanda, dear," he said gratefully. "Come on, son, let's go."

Amanda watched them pull out of the driveway, then strode up to Bruce, with Charlie behind her.

Bruce introduced a man with an FDLE jacket on. "This is Joe Betts with DLE. He will supervise the gathering of evidence."

The man spoke up. "Nice to meet you, but I don't want civilians on my crime scene."

Charlie bristled, but Amanda laid a hand on his arm, silencing him. Bruce shrugged. "You know I can do this and make you both stay outside. I don't have to share any of this with you. The judge has signed the warrant."

"But you're not going to do that," Amanda smiled winningly. "I've saved you from the good doctor's wrath, and you're going to let us stay. Besides, later on you're most likely going to appreciate having a witness, because you know the hell I can raise in court over anything you find."

Bruce looked past her to Charlie. "She's good," he intoned. He turned to Betts. "I'll vouch for them. Let's get 'er done. I don't want to be here either, particularly on a Saturday."

"Do you need all these law enforcement officers?" Amanda insisted.

"We can do it Bruce's way, or we can be here all day," Charlie explained, his voice low. "Let's get started," he growled to Bruce and Betts.

"You know the drill," Bruce commanded. "Don't touch anything. Stay out of our way."

Betts gave instructions to the officers and divided up the house, made sure they all had gloves, evidence bags, cameras and equipment. "I want one investigator to be the go-to man for evidence in your area," he ordered.

They opened the door. The foyer was an area of small chaos, with the console and a large plant turned over. Bruce snorted, "Guess we have to start here." He pointed to an officer. "Slip through and let these guys in the back door."

The remaining officers combed the area until they were able to divide up and go their separate ways. Charlie looked at Amanda as an investigator headed up the stairwell.

"Go with him," she whispered. "I'll stay here."

Bruce and Betts, along with another investigator, were carefully examining the foyer, Bruce superintending the front rooms as well. Bruce countered, "I guess you're not going to tell me whether this was where she was found?"

"I can't tell you for sure because I wasn't here," Amanda was matter-of-fact. "But that would be my guess."

"Mine too," Bruce concurred. "The ER records reflect that the doctor said he found her in the hallway, picked her up and toted her to his car and raced to the hospital with her." He turned to the officer. "Print the table."

As the investigator complied, Betts glanced at Amanda. "Has anyone been back in the home since the deceased was found?"

"She wasn't deceased at the time," Amanda flared. She took a deep breath, calming herself. "But not to my knowledge," Amanda shared the information. "Alan and the boys have been at his dad's house, because Alan didn't want the boys to see the place like this. The boys spent Thursday night with their grandfather after Alan found Shelby and took her to the hospital."

Bruce carefully examined the floor of the foyer, gingerly lifting the fallen plant with a gloved hand after photos had been taken. "Here," he directed, as he motioned for an officer to come forward and take pictures. Then he carefully picked up a small object with tweezers and placed it in an evidence bag, placing a numbered piece of paper at the spot.

Amanda stepped forward, but Bruce stopped her. "Stay there. I'll let you see it."

As he started toward her, Betts, kneeling on the floor, spoke up. "Hold up a minute," as he took some tweezers and picked up something off the floor, placing a small placard where he had found the item.

Bruce showed her the object visible through the plastic bag. It was a small vial labeled as lidocaine. "We'll have FDLE print this. What did you find, Joe?"

"Several red hairs," the officer stated. "Don't know what to make of that."

Amanda spoke without thinking, "No one in the family has red hair."

"Thank you for that observation," Bruce smirked.

"Do they have any pets?" Betts asked, still kneeling.

"No, other than a turtle every now and then," Amanda replied. "The boys are allergic to pet dander."

Betts picked up some hairs and dropped them into a bag, leaving another numbered placard as he wrote on the bag.

The officer in the living area stopped in the doorway. "All clear here and in the parlor."

Amanda moved cautiously into the kitchen and watched the officers meticulously go through the cabinets. Charlie came back downstairs with an officer, the latter with a bag in hand.

"They collected all her medications," he informed Amanda.

"Did you get a list?" she asked sadly.

"Bruce promised us one."

The men filed out, as Bruce and Betts took photographs of the foyer with the numbered placards scattered about.

"We tried not to leave a mess," Bruce was apologetic to Amanda.

"That's good. The boys live here. It's already tough on them," Amanda muttered darkly.

"Just doing my job," Bruce was defensive.

"Thanks," Charlie clapped him on the back.

"Sorry about all this," Bruce said over his shoulder as he left.

Amanda sank to a chair in the foyer, bereft, staring at the floor. "I need to get Alan to walk me through the events here," she spoke absently, to herself. Tears filled her eyes. "I can't believe she's gone."

Charlie placed his hand on her shoulder, squeezing it gently. "It's hard to accept," he spoke quietly.

"Guess we'll be called on to shoulder our godparent duties in earnest now," she sniffed. "Poor babies. But we're going to have to rescue Alan first. They found a vial of lidocaine on the floor."

Charlie looked at her sharply. "Lidocaine? I don't understand."

"Dr. Cardet said labs showed something suspicious in Shelby's system. I don't know yet if that's important or not. I'm guessing it is, particularly if a vial was found here," Amanda informed him.

His eyes widened. "The autopsy will tell us," Charlie was grim.

She looked around the room and shuddered. "Let's get out of here."

She stood and took a step forward, tears blinding her eyes, and stumbled. Charlie caught her and pulled her toward him, righting her. Before she knew what was happening, she was in his arms, his mouth found hers and she responded, her hands in his hair as he crushed her to him, moving a hand down her back as she kissed him back fiercely, blindly.

"I still can't stand to see you cry, baby," he whispered against her mouth.

She came to herself. "Oh, God, Charlie," she pulled away, horrified. She stammered, "I'm so sorry for—for kissing you like that." She covered her mouth with her hand. "I don't know what came over me." He could feel her quivering. "I don't want to break Jill's trust in me, in us."

"I'm sorry, too," he released her. "You're absolutely right. I was out of line." He stepped back. "It's still hard, Mandy."

He started to walk away, but she put her hand on his arm, stilling him. "Charlie, I want to answer your question from the other day. I have to be honest with you. You asked how I felt about you."

She swallowed. "I thought you could help me forget Andy, and I wanted that. When you said you loved me, I thought I loved you too, and it scared the hell out of me. I couldn't handle it. I backed away," she confessed. "With every breath I felt I was being unfaithful to Andy. I know that's silly, but I so wanted to cling to every bit of what was left of him. I just want you to know I'm sorry for what I put you through."

"I know," he murmured. "My love wasn't enough. So you introduced me to my wife. And you're still fighting Andy's memory."

She nodded mutely. He turned to her, took her chin in his hand and stared into her gold green eyes. "But I'm still betting on you to win. Don't give up."

He released her, turning away. "You know, if I had had any sign at all that you felt something for me, I would have waited." His voice held a tinge of bitterness.

"I know," she said sadly. "But Charlie, as much as I wanted you, I just couldn't use you and let you hope for something I couldn't promise you. I couldn't stand to kill our friendship and watch you grow unhappy with me. You deserve so much better. And you have it with Jill."

"I realize that now, but there are times when it doesn't help knowing that." He gazed at her. "I want you to find that happiness again, Mandy. If I wasn't the one, maybe Jon is."

"Maybe," she echoed.

He suddenly grinned, attempting a joke. "You caught and released me. Don't let Jon get away. He's good enough to stuff and hang on the wall."

She started giggling, and he joined in, putting his arm around her shoulders and hugging her briefly. "Let's get out of here."

PART III

Week 2

Chapter 8

Sunday morning Jon Connor, dressed in dark suit and tie, stood on the deck of his parents' vacation townhouse in Panama City overlooking the Gulf of Mexico. Although it was not located on 'the strip' of U.S. Highway 98, the neighborhood, relatively quiet most of the time, was still the victim of some rowdiness during the early spring weeks when college students from all over the country descended upon the beaches. Thankfully, the gated community was largely populated by permanent residents.

Nevertheless, he had little sleep, and couldn't even fault the faint strains of party music from down the road that played all night. He could not still his thoughts.

He stared out over the gulf, whipped into some wave action by the stiff winds blowing in an early shower. It was too early for most of the Northern spring-break visitors to be out on the beach; they were still sleeping off their Saturday night hangovers.

Jon was sipping a cup of coffee and contemplating his dilemma. He had been so sure that a future with Amanda Childs was within reach. But the events of the last few days had shaken his hopes.

He thought back to Ralph's and Claire's wedding reception only a week ago. Everything had seemed so perfect and he had Amanda in his arms, his engagement ring twinkling on her finger. They were dancing, and she was glowing.

He had looked down at her, drinking in the sight of her, dressed in a pale yellow satin fitted bridesmaid gown with tiny spaghetti straps drawing attention to her slim shoulders. "I really like you in yellow," he whispered.

"Thanks," she had beamed up at him.

"I missed you last night," he murmured beside her ear. "But Ralph got stinking drunk, and put in telling me and Charlie his life story, then your life story. I didn't realize you and Charlie used to date."

Amanda blushed. "Not actually." She was defensive. "Charlie was drafted into being my date a lot of the time by—by Billy Barnes." She looked down.

Jon took her chin in his hand and kissed her cheek. "No sad memories today," he ordered tenderly. "Anyway, Charlie was driven home by one of his officers about 3:00, but I was quite afraid to leave Ralph alone. He started crying over the fact that he almost lost Claire, and you brought them back together. And when he passed out a little later and I finally got back to the farm around 6:00, you were gone."

She smiled. "I was at Claire's for the bridal shower until about 2:00 myself. I was so anxious to get back home but tried not to let it show. And then we had to meet early for last-minute fitting, floral consultation, and hair and nails and all that girl stuff. I'm sorry I missed you, too."

He pulled her tighter. "I'm glad to hear it. That makes tonight even more special. I hope you manage to stay awake for me." He brushed his lips against hers. Her mouth parted, and he took advantage of that moment, cradling her head in his hands as he kissed her deeply and she returned his kiss.

Suddenly there was a tap on his arm. Expecting some rival for his dance partner's hand or someone offering congratulations for their engagement, he was surprised by Greg Boyer's stern face. "I need to talk to both of you," he said curtly.

Jon frowned. "Now?" he queried, as Amanda looked questioningly at the stranger.

Jon introduced the two. "Amanda Childs, this is Greg Boyer, the Assistant U.S. Attorney on the Barnes case and my temporary roommate."

Boyer nodded shortly at her. "Now, please," he repeated as he stepped between them, took each one by the arm and manfully steered them away from the dance floor. He pushed them roughly out of the room and into an empty antechamber.

Closing the door, he announced without preamble, "William Barnes has demanded speedy trial, and the judge has set it within this month."

Amanda froze, her eyes wide with shock, relinquishing Jon's hand.

Jon noticed her change in demeanor. He upbraided Greg. "How long have you known this?"

"Last week. You've not been easy to find," Greg added accusingly. "All negotiations failed. Yesterday I received word from the judge's office setting the motion to suppress for hearing."

Amanda, stricken, walked apart from Jon and sat down in a nearby chair, her hand massaging her temple. Boyer continued harshly, "It's pretty obvious that Ms. Childs here will be the main course for the defense, with you running a close second. And you two are here making moon eyes at each other in public, oblivious that you're screwing with my case."

"What is it with you two? Don't you realize the defense will mop the floor with both of you? I can hear it now. Haven't you heard of cold showers and pick-up bars? Did you have to choose each other?"

Jon remonstrated, "Now just a damned minute, Greg. You have no right talking to Amanda like that."

Jon continued in his diatribe against Boyer. Amanda, at first preoccupied, was shaken out of her reverie and interrupted, standing and grabbing Jon's arm.

"He's right, Jon," she whispered. "This looks terrible. What was I thinking?"

As Jon looked at her, thunderstruck at her reaction, she twisted the ring off her finger and handed it to him.

"No," he winced, his eyes wide with disbelief, "don't do this."

"I will not jeopardize this case, Jon, not even for us." She turned to Boyer. "I'm sorry. How utterly stupid of me. I cannot believe I didn't think of this. You're absolutely right."

"Hell, no, he's not," Jon swore savagely. "Amanda . . . ."

She swallowed convulsively, interrupting Jon, careful not to look at him. "Now if you will excuse me, I must attend to my friends' wedding." She turned on her heel and walked out.

Jon had run after her, wanting to dissuade her, and afraid if he stayed he would kill Boyer. He stopped her in the hallway, holding her by the shoulders. "Amanda, please," he whispered to her, his eyes pleading.

She had refused to look at him; the shutters were down, her heart closed to him. "I can't do this, Jon. It's just too important to me." She took a deep breath. "Not a word of this to anyone," she muttered coldly. "I will not have Ralph's and Claire's big day ruined. We will pretend nothing has happened. I believe you and I have responsibilities to attend to."

She shrugged him off during the remainder of the reception, attending to guests, remaining busy and inaccessible and refusing to discuss the matter further with him. She disappeared after the reception, and although he waited for her she never returned home that evening and did not answer his calls.

He searched for her, with Petrino's help, until Petrino found her at the law office. She had refused to discuss the matter with Charlie, and refused to see or talk to Jon. Charlie was apologetic when he relayed the conversation with Amanda to Jon, to say that Amanda was not returning to the farmhouse that evening.

Morose and impotent with anger, Jon had tried to make contact the next day, but Amanda had made arrangements for Ken to take the service and had absented herself. Not able to locate her and finally admitting defeat, he packed up and returned to Pensacola. He avoided Boyer, livid about the latter's interference.

Since then Amanda had remained distant, resisting his attempts to see her and not returning his messages. His meetings with Boyer to provide information and to rehash the facts of the case for trial were cold, Jon controlling himself with difficulty and refusing to discuss Amanda with him.

Discouraged, Jon had finally called Charlie on Friday evening. Charlie answered, his voice gruff.

"What's wrong?" Jon asked, immediately concerned.

"An old friend and classmate lost his wife suddenly. It just happened today. I've been dealing with it all day. Amanda is also here," Charlie volunteered.

"Amanda?" Jon was alert. "How is she?"

"Shelby's sudden death has been a shock for all of us. Amanda and I are godparents for the twins. She is very close to Alan, Shelby and the boys."

"I remember meeting them once. We had dinner together," Jon murmured. "I'm so sorry." He paused. "I didn't know. Amanda hasn't returned any of my calls."

Charlie was instantly sympathetic. "I'm sorry, man. I've not had much contact with her since Saturday night myself, until today. Give her a little time, Jon. She'll come around."

Jon had finally decided to spend the weekend at Panama City, and drove down early Saturday morning. But today he was going to Mainville to see her at church, where she couldn't hide herself away from him. He hoped to make her see reason, that the prosecution of Bill Barnes, Sr., would not be compromised by their engagement.

He looked at his watch. *I have time to get there before the service and try to make contact with her*, he thought.

Just then his cell phone buzzed. Frowning, he answered. "Connor here."

"Where are you right now?" a voice demanded.

"Good morning to you, too, Kimball," Jon replied. "I was on my way out the door. Why?"

"Simpson's orders—whatever plans you have, cancel them."

"Why?" Jon demanded hotly.

"Because you are tagged to brief Senator Thomas Whitmore on the William Barnes case."

"*The* Senator Whitmore? Why? And why not you?" Jon wanted to know.

"Actually, he asked for you by name, as the official case officer. The Bureau has agreed that he is cleared for certain information."

Jon sighed. "What? Is there some sort of congressional interest in this case? Why does the venerable senator from New Jersey want to know?"

"Actually, his staff has been tight-lipped about the reason. But the clearance came from the highest channels."

"The Director?" Jon was surprised. "OK, so when?"

"This morning. He happens to be in Panama City visiting with an old hunting and fishing buddy of his, retired Senator Ernest Keely. Nine o'clock sharp."

Jon glanced at his watch. "Thanks for the advance warning," he quipped sarcastically. "I'll need directions."

"No need. Swing by the office. Simpson said he and I were going with you."

"You're in town?" Jon was dumbfounded.

"Yep. We'll meet you there. Twenty minutes."

Jon hung up, scowling. So much for his plans to see Amanda. He grabbed up his keys and headed toward the door.

On the way, Simpson advised Jon regarding the extent of clearance the Senator was to be given. They arrived at the posh gated community and flashed their identification to the officer at the gate, receiving directions to the home. Again they exhibited badges to the men in black at the front entryway outside the spacious, rambling stucco estate.

As they were shown in the large atrium foyer, a man in tailored suit approached. Simpson introduced Jon. "Senior Special Agent Jon Connor, this is Mr. Richard Dover, Senator Whitmore's Chief Aide."

"How do you do, Mr. Dover?" Jon was polite as he appraised Dover.

Dover shook hands with him, his eyes cold. "The Senator is expecting you, Agent Connor. He will see you momentarily."

As he spoke, one of the double doors behind him opened and out strode a trim man with carefully coiffed white hair, in the latest Hugo Boss casual wear. He was instantly recognizable.

"Senior Special Agent Connor?" he asked, his voice authoritative, crisp, business-like.

"Yes, sir," Jon confirmed as the Senator offered his hand and Jon shook it.

"I'm Thomas Whitmore. Please come in." Whitmore gestured toward the door from which he had just exited.

Simpson started to follow, but Dover raised his hand. "The Senator wants to speak to Agent Connor alone."

"But—" sputtered Simpson, flustered. "I'm his superior," he finished lamely.

"It is my understanding the Bureau has agreed to cooperate. Are you going to deny the Senator?" Dover asked, his voice cold.

Simpson's eyes narrowed and he stepped back. "No, our orders were to provide cooperation as long as it doesn't interfere with the prosecution. However, even the Senator is not cleared for the top-level confidential information."

"I'll keep that in mind," the Senator quipped as he turned, motioning for Jon to follow him into the room, Dover following and closing the door behind them.

Jon gazed around the room curiously. It was a large study, with paneled wooden walls and massive windows looking out over a courtyard studded with rosebushes.

Suddenly he looked around and saw the Senator's cold blue eyes on him, appraising him. The senior legislator from the state of New Jersey spoke. "Please have a seat, Agent Connor."

Jon patiently waited until the Senator seated himself before sitting down on a sofa facing Whitmore. Without preamble, Whitmore demanded, "You are here to brief me on the case against William Barnes, Sr. I've been told you are the primary case officer."

Connor carefully countered, "May I inquire the reason for your curiosity?"

The Senator's eyes flashed. "Why do you think you need to know the reason?"

"Because," Jon smiled his most charming, "your reason has a lot to do with how much information you are entitled to, Senator Whitmore. The Bureau's instructions were clear that release of confidential information was on a 'need to know' basis. I'm merely trying to determine to what extent you need to know. Is this a formal inquiry, the type that would more properly be developed by subpoenaed testimony at a committee hearing?"

Whitmore seemed to pale at his last words. Whitmore leaned forward confidentially.

Dover interrupted. "Senator—" he began, walking up to the Senator and engaging in a hurried, whispered dialogue. The Senator rose and took the aide by the arm, pulling him to a corner of the room where they huddled for a moment.

Whitmore finally raised his hand, silencing his aide. He spoke, his voice low so that only Dover could hear, "Richard, I'm going with Plan B for now. That's my compromise with you, and I need to be consistent with what I've already said to Bob to arrange getting this information. I still don't like lying."

Whitmore returned to his seat across from Jon. "I apologize, Agent Connor, for my rudeness." He glanced back at Dover, who was frowning. "This is totally off the record, a confidential inquiry which will not leave this room. I'm trying to discreetly determine the circumstances surrounding my son's murder and the prosecution of his killers."

"Your son?" Jon's brow furrowed. "I was unaware you had a son, Senator, and fail to see the connection to this case."

"It is my understanding you knew him well," Whitmore replied, his words measured. "Andrew Childs was my son."

Jon stared at him. "That cannot be," he finally said, the shock registering on his face.

"It is true," Whitmore responded gravely. "I have evidence that supports that statement." He handed some documents to Jon.

Jon studied the papers handed him. "How did you obtain these?"

"That remains confidential at this time," Whitmore said stiffly. "My people are still trying to verify this information." He paused, frowning at Dover, who was intent upon his words.

Dover again interrupted. "Senator, I don't think it advisable to disclose any more until we've had a chance—"

"Richard, the damage was done a long time ago," the Senator silenced him. "I need to mitigate that damage as best I can."

He leaned forward, his eyes brilliant blue as they regarded Jon. "Agent Connor, all of a sudden I'm faced with—" he paused as if groping for words, "disclosure of the news I have—uh, had—a son. I—" he paused again, obviously uncomfortable, "I know it's much too late to have a relationship with Andrew. But I'm vitally interested in seeing his killers brought to justice." He looked up and met Jon's eyes, his face impassive. "So I'd appreciate anything you can tell me."

Jon swallowed his surprise, nodded, and began briefing the senator on the beginning investigation, the different facets covered by himself and Andrew, and how the investigations converged into one. Whitmore nodded, seemingly unsurprised by the revelations.

"And how did my son die?" Whitmore asked.

Jon met his eyes. "He walked into an ambush by Claude Brown intended apparently for his wife Amanda. For some reason we have never been able to determine, he went in alone, without backup. Later investigation revealed that Claude Brown had shot him, and that Billy Barnes finished the job."

"His wife?" the senator interposed. "Wasn't she a suspect in the investigation?"

"Later, yes, as to the embezzlement scheme, but she has been cleared," Jon replied smoothly.

"The woman to whom you're now engaged?" Whitmore inserted casually.

Jon started. "I was, but she has broken it off," he was short. "And her name is Amanda, sir."

"How convenient," Whitmore looked at Connor and smiled thinly.

"Senator Whitmore, I take it you've not been briefed on Amanda Childs." Jon's voice was even, although he was angered. "Amanda loved Andrew dearly. She has never gotten over his murder, even now. Her number one concern has been bringing the conspirators to justice."

"As is mine, Agent Connor," Whitmore replied coolly.

"Please call me Jon, sir. And I really think if you want to know more about Andy, you should meet Amanda. She is a phenomenal woman."

"I'm sure she is," Whitmore watched him closely. "Have you slept with her?"

Jon's eyes narrowed. "Not that it's any of your business, but no, sir," he admitted, his face flushing. "But I did ask her to marry me just last week, since you seem interested."

"So you are engaged?" the senator appraised him.

"No, we are not," Jon replied, his voice clipped.

"So how do you know she wasn't part of the conspiracy?"

Jon summarized the investigation and the evidence that had exonerated Amanda. Whitmore listened gravely without comment. When Jon had finished, Whitmore queried, "Are you sure your excluding her wasn't just wishful thinking on your part?"

Jon stood, his eyes flashing. "I'm sure, sir. I'm as sure of her as your son was. And, if I may be so blunt, she loved Andy and knew him so much better than you will ever be able to."

"Touché, Jon," Whitmore said softly, the hint of a smile playing around the corners of his mouth. "I'm intrigued. I think I should interview Mrs. Childs myself."

"Interview?" Jon echoed disbelievingly. "Why don't you just talk to her, Senator?"

Whitmore stared at Jon, his eyes suddenly cold. "Perhaps I shall. Thank you for your time, Agent Connor. I will contact you should I need any additional information."

As Jon turned to leave, the Senator added, "My aide shall accompany you to inform Mrs. Childs of this news. I think she should at least be informed before she hears about it from the newspapers."

"You are right. It would be better if she didn't hear it from any stranger," Jon conceded, his jaw still clenched.

"That's why I'm certain you will want to be there. Good day, Jon. I'll be in touch," Whitmore replied dismissively. "Richard, I'll want you to follow Agent Connor and handle this personally," Whitmore turned to Dover, who had been quietly talking on his Blue Tooth.

"Senator, I still think this is premature," Dover interposed smoothly. He obviously wanted to say more, but held his tongue, glancing at Jon.

Whitmore asserted quietly, "Some disclosure will be inevitable, Richard, despite your theories. I owe Andrew's widow some advance notice."

"But the itinerary?" Dover spoke up.

"I can handle the driving range, and probably even the afternoon cocktail party, without you," Whitmore advised wryly. "I want Mrs. Childs notified today before something should happen to break this story."

"Yes, sir," Dover was obsequious, following Jon out.

After Dover and Connor had left, Ernest Keely walked into the study. "Tom, there's something on the news I think you should see."

"Has it been vetted by Richard first?" Whitmore retorted, a trace of bitterness in his voice.

Keely opened an armoire where a large television was tucked, and wielded the remote. There was a network news story about the most recent developments regarding the investigation of a car explosion in Washington.

Whitmore listened, his voice grave. "So it wasn't Knox in the car? I knew Walter Norton. A good man." He listened a moment. "There is no explanation?"

"Not at this time," Keely replied. "Could be a terrorist reprisal for the last series of articles he released. Who knows? Burton will know sooner or later."

Whitmore turned away, sadness and disgust warring in him and showing on his face. "Walter had no close family. This is bad. What about Knox's whereabouts?"

"No one seems to know where he is." Keely cut the television off. "Enough. Let's head out to the driving range with your security entourage. Shall I provide clubs for them, too?"

Whitmore turned to follow Keely. "That's not even funny."

Keely grinned. "You'd better get used to it if you're seeking a Presidential nomination."

"That is in question now," Whitmore shook his head pensively.

Chapter 9

Amanda pushed the general cancel button after her Sunday postlude and slid off the organ bench, amid the clamor and applause by a myriad of elementary school children.

She absently ran her fingers through her golden hair as she quickly stepped out of her organ shoes and donned pumps, answering questions of the children all talking at once. A little boy in a bow tie came up and asked, "When are you going to play the guy with the bonnet again?"

"His name is Bonnet," Amanda explained patiently. "Miss Amanda needs a little more practice time than I have had the last couple of weeks," she apologized. "That one is tricky if you're not playing every day."

"Can you do it next Sunday?" he asked, his eyes pleading.

"We'll see," she laughed.

As she turned to take the steps down from the chancel to the ambulatory, she spied a man standing there. He was slim, dressed in a tailored dark suit, his dark hair carefully groomed. He was amusedly studying her entourage that ran off around them.

"Your fan club today is rather young," he remarked, grinning.

"The organ needs all the fans it can get," she retorted amicably.

He stuck out his hand. "Mrs. Childs, you apparently don't recognize me. I'm Stephen Audsley."

She was surprised. "Mr. Audsley, how nice to see you again. It's been a while. I'm sorry. I wasn't expecting you until tomorrow."

"I know, but I had a last-minute cancellation of plans, and wanted to hear this instrument in a service," he smiled engagingly. "This old organ is a nice fit to the room. But I can see the limitations you face. What wonderful use you make of it—a lovely service."

"Thank you so much. Marjorie was proud of it, but was insistent that the time would come when we needed more. She has made that provision now."

"And that prelude by Marco Enrico Bossi—I am not sure I've heard that before. It was gorgeous, with almost an Oriental flavor. And was that two different time signatures, one in the right and one in the left?"

She blushed slightly. "Yes. That was a piece Marjorie loved. I had to be a bit creative on the registration. I had not played it since before she died. And the postlude—well, I was fulfilling a promising to the kids today."

She paused. "Thanks so much for doing this. Marjorie was very pleased with your father's consulting on this organ, and wanted to use him again. I'm very sorry about your father's death."

He nodded. "I am, too. I can only hope I remember all he taught me and be half as good as he was."

Amanda laughed. "I'm sure you will be. In fact, I am already aware of your work product, Mr. Audsley."

Audsley smiled back. "Please call me Steve, remember? You were less formal when we visited here before."

"And I'm Amanda," she rejoined pleasantly. "I don't recall you being dressed up as nicely during the installation process. You clean up well." They both laughed. "Since you are here, do you have lunch plans?"

"I was hoping you might be free." He gazed at her. "I know it is short notice, but you could fill me in on the job."

"Actually, I am," she decided, nodding. "It will be harder for me to give you my undivided attention tomorrow. Let me change out of this gear," she gestured toward her surplice.

"That's fine. I'd like to take just a minute or two and walk around the room, if you don't mind."

"So I'll meet you back here," Amanda acquiesced.

She made her way to the choir room, almost empty of people. She rid herself of her robes, hanging them up carefully, then looked up as a good-looking man in his forties approached her.

"Hi, Arnold," she spoke warmly. "Thanks for the good job today. With Gerald absent, you had to carry the ball for the basses."

Arnold Freeman smiled. "You know, singing in the choir has been one of the best decisions I ever made. I had given it up for some time, and since I started back a few years ago I have enjoyed it so much." His eyes bathed her in a warm glow. "I think it has a lot to do with the director/organist."

Amanda grinned. "I know you have certainly made my life easier. You are a godsend to the choir, and a good soloist too. Taking the baritone lead in 'A Spotless Rose' at Christmas—no one could have done it better. We wouldn't have made it through today's anthem without you. I'm glad to have you on board."

"That's good to know," Freeman stared at her. "I know that has not always been the case between us."

Amanda's face became solemn, as she bowed her head. "I'm sorry. It wasn't your fault. That was a bad time for me."

"Don't apologize, Amanda. Ms. Witherspoon warned me back then that sessions with you might not go far, and that you would see me only as a 'necessary evil' for you to endure in the wake of Andrew's death. I just hope in some small way I was of help to you in getting through that time."

Amanda did not meet his gaze. "I'm sorry. I was resistant to help. I wanted to cling to Andy, to deny the truth that he was gone and wasn't coming back." She smiled sadly, looking at him. "It doesn't mean you're not a great psychologist."

He chuckled. "I'm glad to hear that. You know I'm there if you need me."

She paused, her brow troubled. "Actually, Arnold, I'm not sure but what I could use someone to talk to. I'm surrounded by well-meaning friends, but I know they don't understand why I still have trouble letting go, and they are impatient with me at times. I'm impatient with myself."

Arnold nodded. "I've noticed at choir practice and even today you have been preoccupied. And the last few weeks you seemed so happy, like you had made some breakthrough."

Amanda stared at him thoughtfully. "I thought I had. But circumstances changed, and I realized I had not thought it all through carefully. And just as I think I've made the break, all of a sudden I'm back where I started with my doubts about Andy."

"Doubts?" Freeman echoed.

"That's not the right term," Amanda, flustered, blurted out defensively.

"Amanda, I'll be glad to make time for you," he spoke solemnly as he scanned her face concernedly. "How about this week?"

They set a date to meet later that week. Amanda clasped his hand thankfully and made her way back to the sanctuary.

As she walked by the church office, Father Anselm saw her and called to her. She turned back to him.

"My dear, that was absolutely stunning this morning," he clasped her arms as he gushed. "Marjorie would have enjoyed that. I am so thankful that God has put you here."

"And I'm thankful that you are here, Father," she rejoined affectionately.

"Where is our Jonathan this morning?"

"I—I don't really know," she stammered uncomfortably.

Anselm regarded her sympathetically. "I will check on him this week," he answered carefully. "How are Alan and the boys holding up?"

She was solemn. "It's hard, Father, such a shock."

"I am remembering them in prayer, and I'll make contact with them after the funeral, when the crowds have dispersed."

"They will appreciate that." Amanda squeezed his hand gratefully.

"And I am praying for you and Jonathan as well."

Amanda, trying to cover her embarrassment, changed the subject. "Father, I'm going to lunch with Stephen Audsley, the organ consultant. Would you care to join us?"

"Thanks, my dear, but I'll have to decline today. I'm doing a little consulting myself this afternoon, meeting a couple here for their pre-marital counseling. I'll see you tomorrow, then?"

"Yes, sir, I will be here for our planning meeting," Amanda tried to smile.

She hurriedly made her way down the ambulatory. Wherever Jon was, his absence was her fault. She had rebuffed him and avoided him, and he had moved on. It's better this way, she told herself. I'm not good at holding onto a man, she thought ruefully.

Walking into the nave, at first she did not see Audsley anywhere. "Steve?" she called.

"Up here," was the answer, and he peered at her over the balcony railing of the back gallery. "I'll be right down."

She stood in the center of the nave, and soon he joined her, his eyes sparkling. "I've been trying to determine all the options at our disposal for the new organ," he provided. "And I really think we should not dismantle the current instrument. If you don't need two in here, then you're going to have to build a chapel for it."

She guffawed. "You're a chip off the old block, that's for sure. Your father was insistent that we find a home for this instrument, but he also wanted something else for this space."

"I know. He told me several times, and sketched out a few ideas himself when he was last here," Steve said with a grin. "He warned me to be prepared for the phone call. Besides, he really liked you."

"I liked him too. But remember, the vestry has the final say, even if Marjorie is footing the bill," Amanda shook her head good-naturedly. "So let's not get carried away. Come on, I'm hungry. We can discuss this over lunch."

Steve noted Amanda's preoccupation, and cajoled her into cheerfulness with anecdotes of some of his recent jobs. Lunch was a light-hearted affair, with much witty repartee mixed with some serious discussion about the prospect of a new organ for the church.

After lunch, while they were sipping coffee and Steve was drawing and making notes on a sketchpad, Amanda's mind wandered. She thought of Jon.

I guess I successfully drove him away, she concluded. She realized that she missed him, but tried to put all thought of Jon Connor out of her head. It's not productive to think of him right now, she concluded.

"Come back to me, my Amanda," Steve snapped her out of her reverie. "Have you given thought to what you're looking for? What period instrument, what builders you like?"

She giggled. "I of course want it big enough for Fred Swann to play anything his heart desires," she remarked playfully.

"Ah, I may get to retire after this job," Steve smirked. "What did he think of the present instrument?"

Amanda shook her head, a sly look on her face. "He was a perfect gentleman, and said nothing untoward about the lady."

"Yeah, but what did he think?" Steve insisted, laughing.

"He thought you had done a good job on it. But Fred is happy about the prospect of the new instrument tailored to the room."

"So back to my original question—what kind of instrument?"

She smiled. "To paraphrase former Supreme Court Justice Potter Stewart on his view of obscenity: I know it when I hear it."

He ticked off several organbuilders, and she responded to each name with her impressions, as he drew her into a discussion of the pros and cons of various installations she had experienced. From there they discussed favorite instruments, and what periods of literature she favored.

"Let's talk turkey a minute, as you Southerners say. How much space do I have to work with? Layout? Position in the room?" he inquired, arching his eyebrows.

"That could be the sticking point for the vestry," Amanda replied gravely. "They like the current arrangement. And to an extent I'm like them. We get comfortable with the status quo, set in our ways."

"What would they think of having the organ console in the back gallery?" Steve asked.

"That presents a problem, because they really like the English style with the organ and choir in the chancel. And I direct the choir most of the time, at least until we hire the new church musician, so it would be problematic to have us apart. I don't know if the church members would go for not seeing the choir and organist. We do a pretty mean English Evensong once per month, well attended; people will drive an hour or more from neighboring communities for it. And of course placement will militate on tracker versus electro-pneumatic action to some extent."

Steve nodded. "I would tend to agree, particularly with your style of worship, that the current placement seems a good one. Do you have a preference on the action?"

"Unlike many organists, I try not to develop a preference, as long as the instrument is a good one. The bigger the organ, the less I favor tracker action, for obvious reasons. But we all need our exercise," she laughed. "And an AGO pedalboard does make it more predictable."

Steve grinned. "I know that vestries are creatures with their own sets of ideas. Perhaps I need to gather as much information as I can, get some measurements, rough up a few sketches, and maybe let's schedule an informal discussion with them?"

"They would appreciate it very much," Amanda said gratefully. "I really do not want to exclude the church from this decision process. I know that creates more complications, and we cannot please everyone. But this is a tight-knit community of believers, and we are family. And the vestry would rather spread the blame, so to speak."

"Well, then, let's make it happen," Steve laughed. "Give me some dates that are good, and I'll schedule myself to be here."

"But you're so busy up in New York," Amanda protested. "And I know you have work all over the country. Shouldn't you tell me what dates are good for you, and let me set it around your schedule?"

He looked at her intently. "I consider working with you the best incentive to make it down here." He smiled slightly. "I think I'm in love."

Amanda flushed under his scrutiny, laughing uncomfortably. "You certainly move fast, Steve."

He placed his hand over hers. "That is, if you're free," he added, his voice low.

"You're not serious?" she murmured, amazed.

His gaze made her blush. "Like a heart attack."

She stared at his hand over hers, and gently withdrew hers. "Steve, I'll make the time for you and this project," she responded slowly. "But I'm somewhat of a mess personally. I don't think I can offer you anything more."

"You're seeing someone?" he asked her pointedly as he sipped his coffee.

"Yes, I mean, I—I was seeing someone," she faltered. "But—but it's off, at—at least for now," she added confusedly. "I can't really think about that right now—too many complications." *I have unfinished business with Andy's killers*, she thought, but did not say.

"I know what happened to your husband," Steve responded quietly. "But that was several years ago, wasn't it? It's time you got out a little."

She looked away. He smiled at her. "I'm excited about this project, Amanda, and hope you will choose me for it. As for the other, I'm sorry if I startled you. I certainly don't mean to scare you."

She suddenly hooted with laughter, doubling over. "You sly dog."

"What is it?" he demanded, concerned.

"I cannot believe I just swallowed that."

"What are you talking about?" he smiled confusedly.

"You had me going, Steve. I really had forgotten what a blatant flirt you are," she sputtered, laughing and holding her sides.

"Do you think I'm kidding?" he asked with mock indignation.

"Of course you are—your lips are moving," she laughed at him heartily.

His face broke into a wide grin. "I'm always serious about women," he drawled.

"I do want you," Amanda assured him, tears forming from her mirth.

"Glad to hear it," Steve interrupted, chuckling.

"No," she tried to regain her composure, "what I mean is I have followed some of your other consulting jobs, and am impressed with the final results."

"I never thought I'd see you at a loss for words," he chuckled again. "Fair enough," Steve nodded encouragingly. "So I can still meet with you tomorrow? I can make some sketches and take some measurements on my own, but would like to run through some ideas with you at the church. Besides," he grinned, "it's another chance to see you."

"You're incorrigible," Amanda smirked. "I should have remembered what a terrible tease you are. Yes, you may have access to the church any time during the day, and we can still meet tomorrow afternoon."

"Good," Steve agreed.

She sobered. "I will be occupied most of the day until then. I'm playing for a dear friend's funeral."

"I'm sorry," he murmured. "Anything I can do?"

"No, thanks," she smiled. "You have made me forget my troubles for an hour. It has been great fun, and I thank you."

She rose, and he followed suit, trailing behind her. She drove them back to the church.

As they pulled up to the church parking lot, she saw Jon's Mercedes parked in the parking lot not far from Steve's rental car. Next to it was a long shiny black limousine. Curious, she pulled up, and they both alighted.

As she turned to say her goodbye to Audsley, she noticed that Jon and another man were getting out of the limousine. The man had dark well-groomed hair and was dressed sharply in an expensively cut suit with blue striped shirt and navy tie. Two men in dark suits, apparently bodyguards, flanked the other man.

"Until tomorrow." Audsley smiled at her, took her hand in his, lifted it to his lips and kissed it.

Amanda blushed. "Around 5:00."

She watched Audsley get in his car and pull off, then turned to face Jon as he and the other man approached her. The two bodyguards were given terse instructions, and took posts where they could watch without being within hearing. She saw a frown on Jon's face, his eyes steely as he gazed at her.

Still flushed, aware he must have seen Audsley kissing her hand, she spoke. "Hello, Jon. Father was asking about you after the service today," she looked quizzically at the other man, who was regarding her intently.

"Mrs. Childs?" he spoke, his voice commanding, his eyes piercing.

"Yes?" she smiled tentatively.

Jon made the introduction. "Amanda, this is Richard Dover, senior aide to U.S. Senator Thomas Whitmore."

She extended her hand. "How do you do?" Amanda looked at him curiously.

"I take it you are familiar with the Senator?" His voice was almost arrogant, as he quickly shook her hand.

"It would be hard not to be," she smiled quizzically. "His name is a household term these days, since he is the senior ranking member and former chair of Appropriations and Armed Services committees as well as previously serving on Judiciary and Intelligence. Word is he is throwing his name into the hat for the Presidential nomination next term." She paused. "That Senator Whitmore?"

"The same," the man studied her gravely. "He has sent me. I have some business to discuss with you, Mrs. Childs," the aide spoke.

"Me?" she started. "I don't understand." She glanced from him to Jon, question in her eyes.

"Is there somewhere less public we might speak?" Dover looked around him uncomfortably.

"We could adjourn to the church," Amanda suggested, still uncertain.

"That would be great," Jon inserted smoothly, as he gestured toward the door.

Amanda retrieved the key from her purse and led the way, the two men following her, the two guards trailing behind them.

Jon caught up to her and took her arm, applying pressure as his step matched hers. "Who was the Casanova?" he asked quietly.

Amanda's eyes met his, and she noted the glint of his eye. Nothing gets past him, she decided. "The organ consultant Stephen Audsley showed up unexpectedly today at church. I—I took him to lunch." His hand at her elbow made her aware of his nearness. "Where were you this morning?" she asked lightly, looking away.

"I planned on being here, but was unexpectedly detained by the senator's staff," he answered, his voice low. "Perhaps it's just as well." Their eyes met again momentarily. "Old boyfriend of yours?"

She smiled sweetly. "Jealous? No, Steve and his father were the consultants on the present organ." Her heart lurched as her eyes met Jon's, and she was surprised to see tenderness there.

"What is this about, Jon?" she whispered.

He didn't answer her, as the key turned in the lock and Jon grasped the handle of the large door.

Entering the darkened narthex, she led the way into the church. As the guards fanned out, Dover looked about him, taking in the lovely old wood paneled walls and layout of the nave lit only by the sunlight through the stained glass windows.

He pointed to a pew. "Please sit down, Mrs. Childs. I'm afraid what I have to say may be a shock."

Chapter 10

Amanda faced him as he stepped into the row in front of her. "What would we have to talk about, Mr. Dover? I don't understand."

Jon took her arm and drew her down to sit as the aide stood before her, his eyes coolly appraising her.

"It seems that the senator and you are related, in one sense of the word," he replied reluctantly, his voice low, his eyes locked upon hers.

"How?" Amanda looked at him confusedly, then at Jon. "Is this something to do with Marjy? Stephen Marks?" She turned her gaze back upon Dover. "Don't talk in riddles, please," she ordered, her eyes glinting as she tried to quell her irritation.

Dover continued as if she had not spoken. "Senator Whitmore happens to be your father-in-law."

She stared at him as if he was mad. "I'm sorry. I'm sure I didn't hear you correctly."

"Andrew Childs was the illegitimate son of Senator Whitmore."

She stood, her eyes wide with shock. "You are quite mistaken, Mr. Dover. Andy's father died when he was a child. I have no idea where you would have obtained your information."

Jon also stood and turned her to face him. "It's apparently true, Amanda."

She reeled as if he had struck her. "No," she stuttered. "That can't be. Andy would not lie about that." She shook free of him. "How do you know this, Jon? What is your involvement in this?" Her voice rose in anger, her tone accusing.

He tried to reassure her, "I just found out about this today. It was a shock to me too. I met with the senator myself. He was briefed as to the investigation and Andrew's murder."

"It's not true," she insisted dazedly. "Andy told me himself. He was raised by his aunt and mother, and never knew his father. He lived with his aunt and uncle until he went to college."

"What exactly did your husband tell you about his father?" Dover broke into the conversation, suddenly interested.

Again Jon pressed her to sit down in the pew. Dover leaned against the back of the pew behind him and regarded her intently.

Hazily she tried to recollect his words. "He said his father had abandoned his mother when he found out she was pregnant. Andy never knew his father. His aunt informed him that his father died in Vietnam when he was small." She paused. "Andy never wanted to speak of him, would change the subject if anyone asked a question. I avoided asking because I knew how badly it upset him, but I never knew why."

"From where did you hear his father was dead?" Dover asked eagerly.

"From—from Andy when—when my mother . . ."

She was overcome, and found she couldn't go on. The event played itself in her mind as though it was yesterday, Andrew holding her as she cried when Dr. Howells informed her of her mother's death, his taking her home and comforting her, his telling her about his own mother's death, about the father he never knew. She remembered his kissing her into silence as she asked him for details about his parents.

"It's none of your damned business," she cried, suddenly enraged. "You're wrong. There's no way that . . . ."

She stood and turned to walk out, but Jon took her arm. She shook him off, irate. "How dare you!" she muttered, her eyes flashing fire. "Andy would never have lied to me."

She took two steps toward the exit, but Jon's voice echoed in the room. "I talked to the Senator, looked at his evidence. I believe Whitmore. Why would he make this up?"

She froze. She stared unseeingly at the room. "How?" she asked hollowly. "And why now? Why would he keep it from me? Why would his father show up now?"

"I can answer some of those questions," Dover's voice cut through her spoken thoughts.

She paused, and Dover thought she was going to leave, then she turned back to face him, strode back and sat down in the pew before him. "I'm all ears, Mr. Dover."

Dover inquired, intent upon her face, "Did you ever see any evidence in your husband's personal effects or papers that would lead you to believe his father was alive, or that he in actuality knew his father's identity?"

"N-no, of course not," Amanda shook her head vigorously, her mind casting about desperately, trying to remember. "There was nothing."

Dover took a breath, his eyes flickering to the side. "No evidence has come to light that your husband knew. Therefore, we don't know if your husband was ever aware that the senator was his father. There was never any known attempt by Andrew Childs to contact the senator." Dover paused. "Senator Whitmore himself had no idea until just recently that he had a son."

"How could that be?" Amanda demanded, her mind in turmoil.

"Back then he was a young U.S. Representative, just in his second term, and married to a wealthy socialite. But he had an affair with his assistant, a young woman named Emily Childs. She broke it off with him, left his employ, and disappeared. He didn't know where she went. He never saw her again."

Amanda looked at him stonily. "So from where did this revelation about a long-lost son originate?"

"The information was actually delivered to him by an investigative reporter just recently," Dover acknowledged reluctantly. Amanda's eyes narrowed at this information. "The senator didn't believe it, either, and thought it was a scam aimed to blackmail him or discredit him."

"So this came to light about the time he leaked to the press his presidential aspirations?" Amanda countered drily.

"Mrs. Childs, he did not 'leak' any such information. He has been approached by party members and asked to consider running for the nomination. If you wish to cast it in that light, yes, it transpired about the same time," Dover replied loftily.

"So this is just a nasty piece of embarrassment for him?" Amanda flared. Jon caught his breath as he saw Amanda's eyes glow with the fire of her anger. He was so mesmerized that he could not tear his eyes away from her, could not intervene, even though he felt the situation escalating out of control.

"Based on my research into your history, I was afraid this might be your reaction, and cautioned the Senator against a face-to-face meeting with you. He was insistent that you be informed before the information could be released publicly. I requested that I be the advance party to disclose the information and judge your reaction."

Jon's eyes narrowed thoughtfully at Dover's statement.

"Just what of my 'history' did you research, Mr. Dover?" Amanda's jaw tightened as she faced the man, her eyes flashing. "Yes, for heaven's sake, let's not cause the good senator any embarrassment," Amanda hissed, beside herself with emotion. "The man who of course knew nothing until now—we're supposed to believe that—has come forward all concerned about his long-lost son five years after his murder. Don't worry—you can tell him no one will hear it from me. We don't have to acknowledge each other."

Jon turned her to face him and took the unwilling woman into his arms. "Stop this, Amanda," he pleaded with her, his voice low. "I know this hurts like hell and the timing is bad, but we'll get through this."

She clung to Jon momentarily. All too quickly she pushed away. "OK, so what does Whitmore want?"

"He's very interested in the investigation and upcoming trial, and is following it closely," Dover replied briskly, ruffled at her impertinence. "I'm sure we will schedule time to interview you, take a statement."

"Interview?" Amanda's eyebrow shot up. "Me? I see no reason to provide you anything at this moment. In fact, I believe you can obtain what information you need from the prosecutor."

"Senator Whitmore can subpoena you," Dover warned, his voice supercilious.

"If he wishes to do so, that's his prerogative," Amanda retorted icily. "Are you sure he wants a public airing of the questions about his absence from his son's life all these years?"

Dover flushed and started to respond, but Jon intervened, stepping between the two of them. "That's enough," he replied, his voice hard, his fingers tightening around her arm, silencing her. He towered over Dover, his bearing obviating objection. "I think you've asked quite enough of Amanda for one day. This is a lot for her to swallow. Give her some time to digest this."

Dover stared at her then nodded his head. "We will speak again," he spoke coolly. He turned on his heel.

"Good day," he said as he left.

Amanda dazedly saw the men out, locking the church door and heading quickly toward her car. Jon followed her, standing beside the car door as she reached for the handle.

"Amanda," he began, but Amanda cut him off.

"Jon, I can't talk right now," she croaked, hoarse with emotion. "This is more than I can believe. I need some time alone." She looked up at him, her eyes brilliant. She took a breath. "I'm sorry."

"I want to be here for you." He reached for her, but she stepped back. He looked sadly at her and dropped his arms.

Amanda turned away from him. "Jon, I think I'm in love with you. But I made a commitment some time ago to a man who I thought was everything to me. I have to see that through, even though it could be that he lied to me about something so personal as his parentage. I don't know why he would do that, and it makes me scared to trust anyone. I just have to be able to resolve this, lay it to rest, before I am free to commit again. And I'm not going to rest until I've seen Barnes punished for his crimes. I hold him ultimately to blame for Andy's death."

She closed her eyes. "I didn't need this," she mumbled. "Every time I think I'm making some progress, I get hit in the stomach again. I told you once before that I'm damaged goods. I understand if you don't think you can wait for me."

Jon put his hand on her shoulder. "I've waited a long time for you, Amanda, and I'll keep waiting until you're ready. Just try not to drive me utterly mad, like you are doing right now."

She turned and smiled. His heart lurched, and he smiled back. He asked her tenderly, "Are you sure you want to be alone right now?"

"No, but I really do have some things to do," she replied firmly, still smiling.

She shrugged free of him and gained her car, inserting the key and pushing the ignition button. She smiled goodbye to Jon. I need to check on Alan and the boys, she thought suddenly.

She went by Dr. Young's home and spent a little time with the family. She was having trouble focusing on what others were saying, preoccupied with the news she had just received.

Jill noted it and urged, "Why don't you go home and get some rest? Tomorrow will be a stressful day."

Charlie walked up behind Jill. "I agree," he said quietly. "You look all in. There's nothing for you to do here."

She sighed distractedly. "I think I will." She squeezed Jill's hand, said her goodbyes and walked out.

She made it to her car and pulled out, heading for home. Her mind was whirling.

Was it true that Andy did not know his real father? That the senator was Andy's biological father? And if so, why now was the man suddenly taking an interest in his deceased son? What were his motives? She could not fathom the dilemma.

But for some reason the thought that Andy might have lied to her bothered her the most. She might understand his harboring such a secret if he was angry at his father's rejection, but would he keep it from her? They had shared so much together—she thought everything—about their personal lives. The thought that he might have kept this knowledge from her had shaken her to the core.

She suddenly thought with horror: when the media gets this news, the whole ordeal regarding Barnes's criminal enterprise and my alleged involvement will be splashed across the front pages all over the country. The paparazzi will eagerly devour any information related to Senator Whitmore, and in their quest would cover every iota of Andy's life, his death, and the investigation and trial now pending. Nothing was safe—they would also uncover the story of Amanda's illegitimate birth and true parentage.

"No," she breathed despairingly. "Nothing will be sacred."

It dawned on her the senator's true motives: to contain the damage as much as possible, so as to salvage his career from the impending doom that loomed by the release of such a story. And she realized that to a certain extent she shared the senator's motive. She wanted to protect those she had loved and lost, so that their memory was not sullied by a voracious press.

Could Whitmore and she find a common ground, she wondered? Or would the senator in his zeal to distance himself try to wash his hands of the situation, leaving her in even worse circumstances than she had faced before his appearance on the scene?

She surmised that she had to tread carefully, for she did not trust a politician to protect anyone but himself. She realized that she might have to play his game in order to prevent becoming a pawn in his own struggle.

"I need to play politics?" she asked aloud. No, her mind answered. Surely not. Yes, she argued with herself. Unless she had some leverage, the power monger could easily crush her under his momentum.

She suddenly became aware that she was being followed. At first she dismissed the idea, aware that the sudden revelation about Andrew's parentage would naturally stimulate her paranoia. But after checking several times in her mirror, she was sure that a black sedan was behind her.

Suddenly angry, she thought, I am not going to be under a microscope, shadowed, tailed because of this man.

She turned onto the dirt road leading home. After a few minutes, she pulled up in front of Fred Vaughan's farm. Getting out, she looked behind her. She could not see the automobile, but the dust swirling in the distance told her that there was another vehicle on the road.

She walked over to the barn, which was open. "Fred?" she called, as a black and white cat came up purring and encircling her legs. She picked up the cat, carrying her and rubbing her head as she looked vainly for Fred.

She turned around, and Fred was standing right behind her. She gave a startled cry. "Damn, don't sneak up on me," she laughed shakily, as the cat lithely leaped from her arms onto the ground.

He was direct. "Who's that following you up the trail?"

She was surprised that he already knew. "I don't know. Fred, the car followed me here. I just met Senator Whitmore's aide."

Fred's jaw tightened reflexively. "What for?" he gazed at her steadily, a mask falling over his features.

"It seems that the senator is under the impression that Andy was his son," Amanda replied lightly. "Some sudden discovery. I guess he is here to check it out." She attempted a small laugh. "What do you think about that?"

Fred turned away from her, stepping into a small tack room. "It doesn't matter what I think. What do you think it's about?"

Amanda stared at his back. "Fred, do you know anything about this? Did—did Andy ever say anything to you?"

She gasped as he suddenly whirled around, a shotgun in his hands. "I need to get rid of some varmints," he said shortly, and strode out of the barn.

She looked on in dazed fascination as he strode up to the black car that had appeared before the house. There were two men in the car, who quickly got out and pulled sidearms when they spied Fred approaching fast.

One of the men held up a badge and said, "Federal agents, sir. Put the weapon down."

"So am I," growled Fred, "and I outrank you. I can fell you where you stand and no one will ever come asking for you." Leveling the shotgun at the man's head, he added tersely, "State your business."

"You surely don't think you can take both of us, do you?" the man laughed uneasily.

"Maybe, maybe not," asserted Vaughan forbiddingly. "But your mother will be sonless if you try."

The man held up his hands in surrender, then replaced his gun in his holster, gesturing to the other to do the same. "We're here as a protection detail to Mrs. Childs. Is this where she lives?"

"Maybe it is, and maybe it isn't," Fred responded, not lowering his gun. "She doesn't need protecting by you, and you are trespassing on private property."

"But we are federal agents," the man protested.

"And when you bring a warrant, the story may change," Fred warned. "Until then you are trespassers on a private road at a private dwelling. Now get in your car and proceed back the way you came."

"But the Senator—" started the other man.

"The last time I checked, no senator had the authority to allow you on my property."

"OK, OK," the man nodded to his partner. "We're leaving."

They quickly got into the car and pulled out, doubling back over the dirt road.

Fred stood and watched them out of sight. Amanda came up to him.

"Thanks, Fred, but you took an awful risk," she said.

"That's not the end of it," he frowned. "I told you some time back you needed a security system, in case someone came in through the woods on you. I chased some men away today at the house."

"My house?" Amanda was aghast. "No," she replied, suddenly white hot with fury.

"At least my motion detectors went off, but they can only do so much."

"Motion detectors?" Amanda queried confusedly.

Fred continued as if she had not spoken. "Bruce Williams and one of his investigators are up there now waiting for you so that you can do a walk-through, see if anything is missing."

Fred's gaze was steely. "You go on up to the house, and I'll be right behind you with some equipment," Fred told her. "I'm not taking any chances."

In the limousine on its way back to Panama City, Dover's Bluetooth buzzed. He answered. "Dover here."

"We checked out the premises—found nothing. But we were surprised by the appearance of some guy with a shotgun, barely got out. Almost hit my man. Place must have some kind of delayed alarm system we didn't find."

"That's OK. It's obvious the widow knows nothing. If there are documents, she's unaware of them."

"You sure?"

"I saw it on her face. She was in shock. We need to be focusing on the first target." Dover paused. "And we need to eliminate the proof as well as the source. Don't screw this up."

Chapter 11

Amanda quickly made it home, spooked by Fred's conversation and the appearance of the men, and upset at the news of the burglary of her home. A sheriff's car was parked in front of the house, and on the porch were Bruce Williams and another officer.

"Hi, Bruce," she spoke, taking a deep breath.

"Howdy," he drawled. "Fred is having to shoot at possible suitors now?"

She jumped as behind her Fred responded, "Don't know if they made it in the house or not. When the alarm went off, I was out of range, didn't hear it. But they weren't carrying off anything noticeable."

"The front door was jimmied. No other sign on the outside. Nothing looks disturbed, but only you'd know that. Will you do the honors?" Bruce held the screen door open.

Amanda walked in before him, gazing around her. She went straight to her desk and checked. "Someone looked through the papers, but it appears they were careful about disturbing anything." She methodically looked through the drawers and the papers on the desk. "I don't see anything missing."

She wandered through the rooms, checking jewelry cases and drawers. "Nothing so far," she replied to Bruce's unspoken question.

She finished checking the downstairs and moved upstairs, Bruce behind her. After a moment or two, she shook her head. "Nothing appears to be missing, but—oh, I can't tell, Bruce. Things aren't exactly where they should be."

"Whoever was searching didn't want you to know the search had been made," Bruce suggested.

"Perhaps." She snapped her fingers. "The attic! Andy's things."

She marched outside to the hallway and pulled a cord, which brought down the stairwell to the attic. She bounded up the steps with Bruce following.

She cut on the light and looked around her. She looked at the floor. "Footprints," she noted, pointing to the floor. "I haven't been up here in a while, so it hasn't been dusted."

Bruce pulled a small digital camera out of his shirt pocket, and took some pictures, then took out a tape measure and stretched it out beside one, taking more pictures. Amanda carefully made her way around the room.

"The boxes have not been moved," she observed. "But . . ." she lifted the lid of the top box, "someone has looked through these."

"How can you tell?" Bruce asked her curiously.

"These were boxes Andy packed," she spoke as she stared into the box. "He was very organized, and these items are just a little mussed, out of place." She could not tear her eyes away.

"Can you tell if anything is missing?" Bruce inquired.

"I—I haven't gone through all of these," she stammered and turned her head away. She picked up the top box, and looked inside the one under it. "This one does not appear disturbed. Whoever it was must have been interrupted."

"Do you have any idea what they'd be looking for?" Bruce questioned.

"No," she shook her head. He could see her jaw tighten.

"What is it?" Bruce demanded.

"I don't like being violated," she muttered.

"Well, it could have been worse. You might have walked in on them."

They left the attic. Amanda queried, "You gonna look for fingerprints?"

Bruce smirked. "Why do you think Jake is here?" Turning to his man, he ordered, "Focus on the attic boxes and the desk down here."

He turned to Amanda. "Go make some coffee or tea or something. We'll be out of your hair soon."

She walked into the kitchen where Fred was busy at the back door with a screwdriver, installing a box. She put on some tea to brew and sat down at the table, contemplating. *So the senator's men are looking for something. Obviously to see if she possessed some sort of proof that Andrew knew his father's identity.*

She was still steaming as she strained up the tea. Bruce and Jake walked into the kitchen. "Got a few prints, but we'll have to run them. Could be yours. I have a feeling that whoever went through the stuff wore gloves."

Jake grinned at Amanda, who was scowling at him. "I cleaned up behind myself—no mess."

"Can we do anything for you, Amanda?" Bruce was solicitous.

"I'll take care of her," Fred growled as he straightened up from his work. "No one else will be breaking in on her."

Bruce winked at Amanda. "And I believe him. What about the front door?"

"The lock will be changed before dark," Fred offered.

Amanda asked, "Would you like some iced tea?"

"No, thanks," Bruce signaled his investigator. "It's Sunday, and I'll have to pay this joker overtime. We'll be in touch."

Amanda followed them out, then returned. She quickly went around checking the windows and doors to ensure they were locked, and the closets and rooms to make sure no one was lurking. Satisfying herself, she went to a closet in the guest room. She rummaged through neatly stacked boxes, but did not find what she sought. Where would that box be? she asked herself.

She walked back into the kitchen. "What are you doing, Fred?"

"I'm installing a security system for you, and some lights around here with motion detectors," he announced. "Can't be too careful."

"But Fred," Amanda protested, "I don't want lights going on all the time, every time I walk out to the dock or a deer grazes in the yard."

"Don't worry, you won't even realize they are there, unless someone is breaking in on you. I can adjust the sensitivity," Fred assured her, although Amanda looked dubious.

"What about all the wiring? I don't want wires all over the place that I accidentally cut or have to cover up."

Fred looked at her patronizingly. "You're behind the times, my girl. This will mostly be wireless, with cell phone technology to call for help if the phone lines get cut."

Amanda shook her head, knowing it was useless to argue. Fred set himself to working again, as Amanda excused herself and made it upstairs. She quickly changed into denims and a loose-fitting white shirt. That done, she then turned and caught her reflection in the mirror. Staring at herself, she let her mind wander.

She recalled coming home early one afternoon, only a few weeks before Andy's death, anticipating Andrew's arrival for a few stolen days together. She discovered that he had made it there before her. She rushed to their bedroom, only to find him poring over documents and old photographs on the bed.

"Dearest!" she cried, so happy to see him that she paid no attention to what he was doing. She had flung herself into his arms and kissed him. He had responded, but with less ardor than she. She peered at him, and he seemed troubled.

She released him, and glanced down at the items on the bed. "What are these?" she picked up some old photographs, noting one of a young man not unlike Andrew.

"This is—nothing," he replied, as he snatched the photos out of her hands, and hurriedly gathered up the remaining documents, placing them in a small wooden chest.

"What is it? What don't you want me to see?" Amanda had demanded, shocked at his reaction.

"It is a—a case, Amanda," he turned his back to her and closed the chest. "Top secret. I was reviewing some research entrusted to me. I—I just wasn't expecting you so soon."

Amanda gaped at him long and hard. "Is there something you aren't telling me, Andrew Childs?" She used his full name.

He carefully placed the box under the bed and pulled her to him. "Nothing, dearest," he murmured as he kissed her and they fell on top of the covers together.

A week later, she was cleaning out closets and came across the box again. Curious, she just stared at it.

After that she saw the chest no more. But I'm wondering if it is still around, if he hid it somewhere here in the house, she thought. It had been long forgotten until now, and she suddenly wondered if perhaps he had kept family papers or other secrets there. She had trusted him so completely that she had never thought to question him further. But now the disclosures about Andrew's alleged paternity made her ponder. Was there something he had been keeping from her? Was that what the men were looking for?

She went downstairs to get a bottled water. "Do you want anything?" she asked Fred, who was busy at the front door.

"No, thanks," he replied, not looking up. "Jon Connor called and asked if you made it home OK. He wants you to call him."

She was suddenly torn. She wanted to talk to Jon, to see Jon, to be with Jon, but the news about the senator had ignited the ambivalent feelings she still harbored about Andrew.

"Fred, I've got to run back to the attic a minute," she informed him, and retraced her steps back upstairs. Retrieving the cord, she pulled down the stairwell again and gingerly made her way up, groping for the light switch and flooding the dark dusty room with light.

She had not been in the attic in a while until today. Her last trip had been to put away some things from the renovation, including some photos and keepsakes of Andy. She gazed around the room, where storage boxes were neatly stacked back in place, apparently by Jake. She had organized and packed away items neatly one day in a fit of depression not long after Andy's death. She smiled grimly; she and Andrew had made a pact to keep the attic neat, but Andy was better at it than she.

She studied the row of plastic storage containers that Andrew had stored and labeled. After his death, she had never had the courage to open more than the top one. The contents had filled her with such a longing for him that she could not go on. So she had left the boxes untouched all this time.

You mustn't look at everything now, she reminded herself sternly. This is not the time. Just see if the box can be found.

She gingerly set down the top box and lifted the lid, steeling herself. She forced herself not to peruse the items, but only to check to see if the box was inside. No, she concluded. So she carefully set the first box aside.

She did the same with the next two boxes, with the same results. These weren't disturbed, she thought to herself. Just as Andy left them. She closed her eyes a moment, willing herself to continue. She couldn't help but linger over several items, and felt herself more and more overwhelmed.

She came to the next to last box, and hesitated. She willed herself to open the lid. There on top was a framed photo of her and Andrew together on their wedding day. She stiffened. I can't do this, she thought, suddenly overcome. But I must do this, she reprimanded herself.

She picked up the photo, studying it. Something fell out of the bottom of the frame, clinking on the wooden floor. She bent down and picked it up. It was a shiny brass door key. She stared at it, spellbound. It had apparently been taped to the back of the photo, but the tape had given way. What does this unlock? she wondered.

She heard Fred calling her, and she went to the head of the stairs. "I'll be right there."

Amanda checked the last container, but found no chest. She carefully put everything away as she found it, clasping the key in her palm, then made her way downstairs, closing up the attic. Fred looked at her from the foot of the stairs.

"I was worried. Couldn't hear any noise up there." He regarded her critically. "Once I set this up, do you mind if I find a corner somewhere up there to set up the command center and cell phone hookup?"

"That will be fine. Thanks, Fred," she replied.

She made her way to her bedroom. Where do I put this? she considered, gazing at the key. Until I find the lock for this, I don't want anyone to accidentally find it.

She remembered having some duct tape in the hall closet and found it, tearing off a small piece. She walked into her bathroom and knelt in front of the lavatory. She opened the cabinet doors, reached up and taped the key to the back side of the false drawer face of the vanity.

The phone rang, startling her. She closed the cabinet doors quickly, stood up and moved to the bedside table, picking up a cordless receiver. "Hello?" she said tentatively.

"We need to talk," Jon's voice answered tersely. "I'm coming over."

"Jon, I—" she began.

He cut her off. "Amanda, this is a serious matter. We need to discuss the best way for you to deal with this news. There will be media all over this story, and all over you."

She sighed. "I know, Jon. I don't know if I can handle . . ." her voice trailed off.

"I'm not taking no for an answer. I will be there soon," she heard him say. The receiver clicked; he had hung up.

She felt the tension smothering her. Stepping out of the bedroom to the top of the stairs, she called, "Fred, I need to take a quick shower. I'll be down soon. Jon is coming over."

She quickly showered and changed clothes, choosing a pale blue casual cotton sundress, applying just a hint of makeup and leaving her hair curling around her face. Just as she was smoothing on some lipstick, she heard a voice behind her.

"Good enough to eat," Jon drawled, as, startled, she turned to face him.

"You scared me," she smiled nervously.

He looked around the room admiringly. "Never been up here," he said softly. "Is this where you and Andy—" he left the sentence unfinished.

"No," she answered, clearing her throat. "This was a spare room. I moved up here when I returned to the farm." She attempted a smile. "I wanted to change everything around, to make the farm less filled with memories."

He approached her and took her into his arms. "You smell nice," he whispered before kissing her.

She relaxed against him, returning his kiss, wrapping her arms around his neck. The kiss deepened as he pulled her even closer and she responded. I want him so badly, she realized.

Suddenly the image of her and Andrew from the wedding photo flooded her mind. She stiffened and pulled away.

"What's wrong?" he asked, still holding her.

"Please," she cried, wrenching herself away, and putting distance between them. "This is so hard," she moaned, flushed with embarrassment.

Jon looked at her and nodded, his face grave. "I know," he concurred. "This is one more complication you didn't need."

"Exactly," she mumbled. "I don't want to meet this man, Jon. I don't want to have anything to do with him. Why now? After this struggle to get over

Andy, now his long-lost father shows up, a famous senator? What could be worse? I want to put this all behind me. I'm tired of living with a ghost."

"It will be over soon," Jon tried to reassure her.

"Will it?" she muttered tiredly. "Will it ever be over? Everywhere I turn, Andy's there, but he's not there."

Jon looked away, a mask falling over his features. "I know."

"Do you? I'm scared to love again," she turned to him, her voice almost pleading. "If getting over him is this hard, what would I do if something happened to you? I cannot go through this again. I don't know if I will survive Andy as it is."

"I'm not going to let anything happen to us," Jon said softly.

"Can you keep such a promise?" Amanda implored.

"I'm damned sure going to try," he stared back at her. He held out his hand to her. "Come on," he countered tenderly. "If we don't leave this room I won't be responsible for the consequences."

He took her hand and drew her out of the bedroom and down the stairs. She led the way into the kitchen, where Fred was putting tools back into his box.

"Did you tell him about the break-in?" Fred asked casually.

Amanda frowned as Jon's face creased with concern. "Break in?" he echoed, turning to her.

"I scared two guys off from the place today, and then two more followed Amanda to my place," Fred offered before Amanda could say anything.

Amanda flushed as Jon registered this information. "The senator?" he surmised, his jaw tightening in anger.

"Who else?" she mumbled. "Why would anyone else be breaking in to my house?"

"Why?" he asked hotly.

"Looking for evidence is my guess," she retorted. "I want his ass," she hissed impetuously.

"I'll finish this up in the morning," Fred regarded them expectantly. "You two have matters to discuss."

"Is it a good idea for us to be alone?" Amanda asked, looking from one man to the other. "Fred, I think you ought to stay."

"Hell, he's not gonna bite you," Fred retorted, winking at Connor as he strode to the front door. "I'll keep watch—ain't no one gonna sneak up on you again."

She watched silently as Fred walked out. Left alone with Connor, she was suddenly jittery. His nearness again made her aware of how much she desired him. "Shall I prepare something to eat? Are you hungry?" She moved restlessly away from him toward the refrigerator.

Jon took her hand and pulled her back to him. "Only for you," he murmured.

He was not prepared for her reaction. She suddenly kissed him desperately, her hands moving down the front of his torso, her touch searing him through his shirt like a bolt of lightning. "I want you," she whispered against his lips.

"Oh, Amanda," he groaned, his hands running down her back to her waist as he molded her to him. He could feel her trembling as she strained next to him. Smothering an oath, he picked her up bodily and carried her into the living room, gently depositing her on the couch before joining her, towering over her, his hips moving seductively against hers, as he leaned over her and claimed her mouth.

She whimpered as her breaths became shallower, and he trailed kisses down her throat, as he unbuttoned the front of her dress. "I've wanted this for so very long," he murmured, his mouth reaching the cleft of her breasts. She sighed as his hands moved up her thighs.

She suddenly went still. Jon noted it and hesitated. "What is it, darling?"

She shifted away from him and moaned, "I'm sorry. I can't do this, Jon, no matter how much I want to, and I do, so very much. But I cannot give Barnes ammunition to discredit you in court." She choked despairingly, "We mustn't lose this case."

She silently burst into tears, her body wracked with sobs as she tried not to give voice to them.

Jon swallowed his desire with difficulty, moving off her, sitting beside her and pulling her to him. He rocked her as she continued crying, trying embarrassedly to regain her composure. "I'm so sorry," she kept gasping between sobs.

"I understand, Amanda," he whispered, surprising himself. "It's OK, dear," he crooned to her, as she leaned against him and he smoothed her tresses.

It dawned on him that Charlie Petrino had been right. Amanda had indeed made this trial her number one priority, subsuming everything, even her desires and future happiness, into what in her mind was some form of vindication for Andrew Childs' murder. Jon knew he had experienced first-hand the violent conflict within her, because he was convinced that she truly wanted him, and even now could feel her body rigid with passion as she struggled to deny herself.

After a few minutes she was again calmed. "I don't mean to lead you on," she whispered against his shoulder.

He kissed her hair. "You are truly a vixen," he retorted playfully. "You're going to drive me to drinking." He pulled her away from him and looked in her eyes. "Amanda, we are going to get through this. Now go wash your face, because we need to talk about it."

She gazed at him with apology in her eyes, as he urged her to go.

While she was gone, Jon was somber. Why would anyone, even the senator, have people breaking into Amanda's home? What would they expect to find? It was obvious from her reaction to Dover's news earlier today that she was shocked, so she obviously wasn't harboring any evidence.

But he was even more worried about Amanda's reaction to him, and her comments. Can we survive Andy? he echoed Amanda's question. The appearance of the senator on the scene had thrown a wrench into an already complicated situation, catapulting into relief the investigation and trial that was already fraught with the probability of unwelcome publicity.

Meanwhile Amanda, bathing her face in cold water in the bathroom, was lost in thought. She had to keep her urges in check. This trial had to be won, and Barnes convicted and sent to prison for a long time. She could not let Andrew and his memory down. But she realized just now how difficult that would be when she was in Jon's presence.

Her thoughts turned to Andrew and the newest dilemma. She acknowledged that Andrew might have been in the dark regarding his father. He could have been misled by his mother as to the identity of his father. But the doubts still lingered. What if he knew or suspected that Whitmore was his father? He apparently made no attempt to contact the man. There was no evidence that either was aware of the other at the time.

And now this Whitmore is invading my life, searching my house, having me followed. Why?

She returned to the living room, but Connor was not there. Surprised, she sauntered into the kitchen, where Jon was busy at the counter. Her eyes widened when she saw that he was preparing two sandwiches, placing them on plates. He turned to her.

"This will keep our strength up, and preoccupy us from wandering into—other activities," he smirked.

She smiled. "Would you like a drink?"

"Just some of your iced tea," he turned and placed the two plates on the kitchen table. "We need to keep our wits about us," he joked.

She busied herself with glasses and ice as he rummaged for napkins, and soon they were seated at the table as she poured tea. She took Jon's hand briefly and said grace, as he gazed surprisedly at her.

"OK," she spoke in her best business-like tone, "what did the senator say?"

Chapter 12

Jon marveled at the lightning change in her demeanor. She was again Amanda Childs the litigator, her tone crisp and business-like.

"He was officious as hell," Jon replied, a hint of anger in his voice as he recalled the interview. "The Bureau had agreed to cooperate with his inquiry under the circumstances, and I briefed him on the case." He paused. "He wanted to know the extent of your involvement."

"Me?" Amanda's eyes grew wide. "Why? What did he say?"

"He wanted to know if my feelings for you had clouded my conclusion that you were innocent," he remarked, his voice tight.

"That is what I'm so afraid of, Jon," Amanda rested her head in her hand, her elbow on the table. She rubbed her temples distractedly. "If the senator thinks that, the defense can plant the idea in the jury's mind as well."

"I think you underestimate Greg Boyer," Jon said quietly. "He takes his cases seriously. He may be an ass, but he is not the U.S. Attorney's golden boy for nothing. As he made painfully clear the other night, he has already considered that possibility and is planning to combat it."

"But we're not helping his case by being together," Amanda murmured.

Jon took her hand. "Amanda, I respect your feelings and your great desire to see this through. But I also take pride in my work, and I am meticulous when investigating a case. The evidence will hold."

They sat there silently, Jon prodding her to eat. She picked at her sandwich. He noticed the emotions flitting across her face.

She finally looked up at him, embarrassed, noting his eyes on her.

"What were you thinking?" he asked softly.

"About whether Andy knew or suspected that Whitmore was his father," Amanda confessed. "Did he ever mention his father to you, Jon?"

"I've been wracking my brain to try to remember anything," Jon rejoined. "He was reticent about his family and childhood. He did relate once that his parents were both deceased during his childhood. I never knew whether he had any living relatives. It seemed to be a subject he avoided."

Amanda nodded. "With me as well. I didn't push the subject, because I could tell it was painful. I felt he would tell me when he was ready." She looked at her plate.

Jon squeezed her hand. "Andy loved you better than life itself."

Amanda muttered, "Did he? I thought we had no secrets, at least of a personal nature. Now I just don't know."

"Never doubt it," Jon spoke sternly. "If he kept it from you, there had to be an awfully good reason."

"Is there a good reason to lie to your loved one?" Amanda wondered aloud. He could read the anguish in her eyes.

"I cannot answer that for him. He's gone, and you mustn't give in to these doubts about him. Andy can't defend himself," Jon reminded her.

Of course, I lied to Charlie, she suddenly thought, and sent him to the arms of Jill. The thought was sobering.

Amanda's eyes glittered and she disentangled her hand from Jon's. "What was the senator's explanation for his long absence?"

"He states that he only recently was confronted with this information, and was given some documentation purporting to prove it. He would not reveal his sources, but I did see a copy of a letter, allegedly from Andrew's mother, stating the facts of her affair with Whitmore and the resulting conception of Andy. There was another letter from Andy's aunt confirming the facts, and a birth certificate. The father named was a Smithson."

"But how do we know this is authentic?" she questioned.

"The senator stated that his people are trying to verify the information. But he apparently is not denying that the affair occurred, and seems convinced that Andrew is his son."

Amanda stood and took her plate to the sink. Jon broached the subject. "You know that the media will discover this. In fact, if an investigative reporter was the one giving the information to Senator Whitmore, I'm surprised the story hasn't broken yet."

"I know," she concurred, her voice barely above a whisper.

"You must be prepared for them when they come knocking on your door," Jon watched her back. "You must be careful what you say to them."

"I don't intend to say anything," she retorted, as she washed the plate and placed it in the dish drainer. "But I'm afraid of what Senator Whitmore might do that could affect the Barnes trial."

The statement hung heavily in the air. Jon replied, "I'll make sure Greg Boyer knows about the situation. He'll take whatever steps are necessary to keep anyone from tampering with his case."

He stood and brought his plate and glass over to Amanda. He spoke over her shoulder. "You know, sooner or later you are going to have to deal with Whitmore personally."

"Not if I have anything to say about it," she muttered. "I see no reason to give Whitmore the time of day." She turned toward Jon. "Jon, I have to believe that Andy told me the truth, unless or until someone provides me evidence otherwise. Right now I cannot accept another alternative." Her eyes pleaded with him.

He nodded. "I don't believe he would lie to you. He loved you too much."

Amanda looked at him, suddenly vulnerable, her eyes wide. "Tell me about Andy."

Jon was surprised. She took his hand. "I need to know about the other Andrew, the one he didn't let me see."

Jon took her hand and led her into the living room. Sitting on the couch, he pulled her down to sit beside him, cradling her in his arms. "What do you want to know?" he asked tenderly.

"Whatever you will tell me," she mumbled, not looking at him, her hand on his chest.

He kissed her hair. "Andy was a brilliant agent. He was methodical and very thorough. He would follow every theory down to its possible conclusions. I was always surprised by his ideas, and how he left no stone unturned. He made meticulous notes. I was amazed at his sketching ability and his quality of writing. He was always level-headed, never seemed to get overly excited.

"Except when it came to you," he added, and noted her surprise as she glanced up at his face. "When he was getting ready to come home to you, suddenly he was in a frenzy to have everything just so, to put it away and focus on the time he was going to have with you. The job suddenly became like some uniform he couldn't wait to shed."

"Did he ever talk about me?" she asked, embarrassed.

Jon sensed her need to connect, to understand the husband about whom she suddenly faced serious doubts. "Generally not during work. He kept that part of his life very private. But on those times we were off duty and he couldn't come home, he would sometimes open up. He would talk about how he would forget his train of thought when you looked at him, about how much he missed being near you. Every now and then he shared some anecdote, like the time you gave him a black eye while you were asleep."

The corners of her mouth curved into a smile. He pulled her tighter. "He once told me he had made a big mistake marrying you."

Amanda sat up, shocked. "Why?" she croaked.

"Because he was worried that he was doing you a disservice, by being gone so much, not being there for you. He told me you deserved so much more, that you should have someone there to hold and protect you all the time. He knew that you were outwardly tough and didn't complain, but he said there was a frightened little girl locked inside you that he had lost his heart to, that he wanted to shield from the rest of the world."

He felt her gasp of pain. "I'm sorry," he pulled her to him and kissed her as the tears fell. "We shouldn't talk of this. It's too painful."

"No, I need to hear it right now," her voice was muffled against his lips. "Since this afternoon, I have been so scared that all those years were wasted, that he was not the man I fell in love with, that I was obsessed with someone who wasn't really real. I was afraid I had just dreamed him up."

"No, Mandy," Jon crooned, pulling her head to his shoulder and rocking her. "You mustn't think that. Andy told me he found it increasingly harder each time to leave you to come back, and that all he lived for were those moments with you."

She was silent, but he could feel her trembling. He cupped her chin in his hand, and could see pain in her eyes. "Did his work suffer near the last?" she whispered fearfully.

He was surprised by the question. "His work was always impeccable, but his concentration seemed to waver. Just before he dropped me off at the airport for me to fly up to New York, he seemed troubled. He told me to have a good time, but to hurry back, because he felt Claude Brown was close. He was obsessed with catching the man."

"Tell me again what happened," she whispered brokenly.

"Are you sure?" he was concerned.

She nodded. "Please."

He took a deep breath. "I was about to board the plane at Kennedy for Atlanta, and Andy called. He said that Claude was in the area, and had sent a note to you for you to meet him. Claude had threatened you, warned you to come alone. Andy intercepted the note, and was going to make the rendezvous. He asked how soon could I be there. I told him I'd be there in about four hours, and for him not to go without me."

Jon swallowed. "He seemed not at all like himself. I asked where were Petrino and his usual back-up. He said Charlie was out of town with an old girlfriend, and Fred was overseas."

He felt Amanda pulling away, and she took his hand, gripping it tightly, not looking at him. "Please go on," she whispered.

"I had a bad feeling then. He told me where the rendezvous was to be. Andy was afraid that even though you didn't know about the note, Claude might try to contact you by another means. I asked him to meet me at the airport. I told him I would call my contacts, and they'd go in with us. I again told him not to go alone. I assured him we'd catch Claude, that nothing would happen to you."

He leaned forward, his elbows on his knees, his hands in front of him, not looking at her.

"But he did," she said simply.

"But he did," Jon repeated. "I called George and Zeke and asked them to meet us in Pensacola. Zeke alerted local law enforcement when Andy didn't appear as scheduled. When I got there, they were there, but no Andy. We raced to the warehouse." His voice broke. "That's when we found him."

They were silent several minutes, not touching. He finally broke the quiet. "I'm so sorry, Amanda."

"No," her hand touched his arm reassuringly. "I'm sorry I made you relive it."

"I don't know why Andy didn't tell you about his father. But there is no doubt in my mind of the depth of his love for you. And I now feel what he felt." He turned to her. "I want to love you, to enfold you, to protect you, to be with you night and day. I don't want you to go through that again."

She stood and walked away from him. "I want that too, Jon. It has been hard to be strong and tough all the time. With Andy I had a glimpse of paradise, but I had to cut the switch on and off, on and off. And then—" she sighed, "then he was gone. Now I'm beginning to feel that feeling again, with you. It's been so long. I'm so tired."

She walked over to the mantel, staring at the photograph depicting Andrew and Jon on the fishing boat. "Part of me wants to tell Barnes to go to hell and let the prosecution do what it will with me. If you kissed me right now, I would not have the strength to say no to you. I would give you everything I have left in me. None of it would matter, if I could have that moment and feel truly free."

Jon stood. He knew it would be so easy to walk over to her and enfold her, to take her, to make love to her, to make her forget the hurt, if only momentarily. But he also realized the recrimination she would feel tomorrow, and the very real danger of losing her to those feelings that still held her in thrall.

She walked to him and put her arms around him, pulling him down to her hungrily. He gave in momentarily, his hands running down her body, hauling her to him. He kissed her fervently, then pushed her gently away, stroking her hair, staring at her.

"I want you so badly. But Amanda, I don't want just a moment with you. I want forever with you. And I intend to have it, when you are ready for it.

I'm not going to squander it tonight, when I know the remorse you will feel afterward.

"And I'm not Andy. I can't be Andy. I think I can give you that love which you crave, and I want to more than anything. And I think we can find out how to disable that on-off switch."

She gazed at him, then laughed. He laughed with her.

"So quit coming on to me like this, until you're ready to stand me a long, long time." He kissed her again. "Because that is the package I'm offering, and I'm not settling for less. When I take you to my bed, you're not getting away."

He released her and stepped away. Changing the subject, he asked casually, "What is this Fred was saying about the burglary, and your being followed home by G-men?"

Amanda responded, "When I arrived at Fred's, the men were behind me. Fred chased them away with a shotgun. But one of them acknowledged they were federal officers, there at the behest of the senator. Fred had just chased two men away from the house here. He called the sheriff's department, and Bruce Williams and his investigator have been out gathering evidence."

"Had you ever seen any of these agents?" Jon inquired.

"No," she shook her head.

"I know of no agents here guarding the senator," Jon said slowly. "I will check on that."

"Fred thinks I need protecting, so he was here installing a security system."

"I happen to agree," he murmured. "I could stay here," he suggested. "I could sleep on the couch or in the guest room," he added quickly, the corners of his mouth turning into a smile.

"Jon, you are too great a temptation." She tried to sound casual, but she realized how much she wanted him to stay. No, she told herself with the old resolve, this is not going to happen.

"So what do we do?" he asked simply.

"We take each day as it comes," Amanda answered. "I'm vulnerable around you right now."

"You need protection," Jon remonstrated. "I can keep my hands off you."

She walked up to him and put her arms around his neck. "Can you?" she purred. "What if I don't keep my hands off you?"

She kissed him, and he responded. "You have a point," he chuckled, pulling her closer.

"And it doesn't matter whether we do anything or not," she reminded him. "We're together, so in the minds of the jury we're sleeping together, even if we aren't."

He pulled away, staring at her solemnly. "Mandy, I'm not going to lie to them. If asked the question, I'm going to shout to the world I want to take you to my bed yesterday, that I love you madly, that I want you to marry me, but that has nothing to do with your innocence."

"You've been calling me Mandy all night," she giggled.

"So I have," he smiled down at her. "So it's settled, and I get to stay?" he teased her.

She withdrew from his arms. "No, Jon Connor. You need to go. I think the senator's men won't be back, at least at the farm. My guess is that Fred frightened them off pretty effectively."

"I'll take my leave then." He was reluctant. "But Amanda, don't think this is the end of the matter." He reached over and quickly kissed her on the cheek. "I love you. Please be careful. You don't need to go out alone. Lock up behind me."

Then he was gone. Amanda felt bereft. This is all for the best, she told herself yet again, as she again checked the doors.

The phone rang, startling her. She walked to the desk and answered it.

"Mrs. Childs?" an unfamiliar male voice inquired.

"Yes," she confirmed. "Who is this?"

"My name is Michael Knox, with the *Washington Post*. I think you might have heard of me."

So it begins, she thought. "I have heard of you, Mr. Knox. What may I do for you?" Her heart sank.

"Mrs. Childs, I have certain information that I think you might be interested in. And something tells me you are aware of why I'm calling."

"Mr. Knox," she responded carefully, "I am not sure what you are talking about. And I am not in a position to give you any information."

"You misunderstand me," she heard him reply. "I'm not seeking information, but hoping for some confirmation. I have information regarding your husband that I think you would like to see before it becomes public."

Amanda felt her ire rising. "So you think I'm ripe for some sort of blackmail?"

"No, ma'am," the voice quickly denied. "All I want is an opportunity to meet with you and show you what I have. You're entitled to know this before it becomes public. I think you have already discovered the senator's news. There is more to it than his staff would like revealed." He continued quickly, as if afraid she would hang up on him. "I would just like to meet with you."

"You may call my office in the morning and make an appointment," she replied crisply. "No recording devices, no pictures."

"Mrs. Childs, they are watching you," the voice warned.

She started. "Who?" she asked, suddenly afraid.

"You had a taste of it today, didn't you?"

"How do you know this?" she demanded.

"Just check me out. Google me—I'm on the up and up. I will contact you. And, Mrs. Childs? Please keep this between us." The line went dead.

She stared at the telephone receiver, dazed. This was sliding from bad to worse, she thought. Why was the *Washington Post* contacting her? Of course, how did she know this man was actually a reporter from the *Post*?

It was possible that the media might have already sniffed out the story regarding the newsworthy Senator Whitmore and was only trying to get an inside scoop from her. But what did this man think he had that she needed to see? Or was that just a ruse to obtain access?

Why was the senator so eager to determine her involvement in the case? If he was Andrew's father, why didn't he just introduce himself and ask her? She realized that wasn't the Washington way of doing things. But did Whitmore seriously suspect her of being a conspirator?

She concluded that he must be trying to maneuver himself very carefully around the subject, and to keep her at a distance where she was less likely to cause him negative publicity, if he did think her capable of such a terrible crime. But would he then turn the media's attention away from him and toward her, re-igniting the suspicions of the Bureau or others against her?

"He mustn't," she said aloud. "He mustn't screw up the prosecution of Barnes. Oh, God, please don't let that happen. Barnes must be punished. He doesn't deserve to live."

She was shocked that she had voiced a prayer asking for such. She was instantly ashamed. Please forgive me, God, she mouthed silently. I'm becoming a monster.

"Our contact with the phone company said the location was a pay phone in a rural area about ten miles away. I've sent two out there to try to locate and intercept him."

"He's already gone. But keep an eye out. He might decide to use that phone again."

Meanwhile, Jon broke with his moratorium on speaking to Greg Boyer, calling the man on his cell phone.

"Hello?" he heard the familiar voice.

"Jon here," Jon was curt.

"Man, am I glad to hear from you," the voice said with obvious relief. "I'm so sorry . . ."

"Never mind that," Jon interrupted. "Just listen."

He summarized the day's events and the senator's inquiry regarding the case against Barnes. As he relayed the senator's questions about Amanda's involvement, Boyer broke in excitedly.

"Damn the Bureau!" he exclaimed. "Senator or no senator, I don't want him messing with my case. It's bad enough trying to combat the defense's expected attacks, without some brainless elected civil servant sticking his nose in it and turning it upside down."

"That's not all, Greg. Someone broke into Amanda's home, and she was being followed today. She won't admit it, but I'm sure she's afraid. Can you do anything about it, stop him from causing any more damage? She needs some protection. Her neighbor is worth four good agents, but he can't do it 24/7," Jon implored. "And she won't let me."

"I will certainly try," Boyer promised. "But the damage may be done. I will do what I can in the morning. But Jon, would Whitmore go to those lengths? I mean, he is pretty influential, and a very public figure. That just doesn't seem to be his mode of operation."

"I just don't have any other explanation at this moment," Jon replied.

Greg continued, suddenly contrite. "How are you, Jon?"

"Just great, thanks for asking," Jon's tone was sarcastic. "Later." He hung up, Boyer's voice protesting in his ear.

His next call was to Kimball. "Jon here." He summarized the day's events to Kimball. "I'm just not comfortable with Amanda being out at the farm without protection, particularly after this break-in and with the impending trial."

"I don't have a problem with you keeping an eye out on our witness. But Jon, you know the more you see her, the stronger the defense's claim of bias," Kimball responded soberly. "I can't tell you what to do. I don't really have anyone to spare at the moment to assist. This is more a matter for local law enforcement." He paused. "I'll make contact with the locals to see if we can't garner some help in some surveillance."

"Thanks. I can also ask Petrino to check for us." Jon rang off.

He pulled up to the gate by Fred Vaughan's house. To his surprise, Vaughan showed up out of nowhere and opened it. Jon drove through and stopped, getting out.

"Well?" Fred asked.

"Well, what?" Jon shrugged his shoulders.

"You left her alone?" Fred contended, his voice matter-of-fact.

"She refused to let me stay," Jon retorted flatly.

"Figured as much, when I heard the car coming," Vaughan turned away. "Good thing I have set up some countermeasures to protect her."

"Countermeasures?" Jon echoed.

"What you don't know won't hurt you," Vaughan retorted.

"I could stay, spell you, sleep in my car," Jon offered.

"No need. If someone messes with her, he will be hurt, or worse. That might not look so good on your resume."

Jon looked hard at Fred, believing he meant what he said. "Do you think I care about that? It's Amanda we're talking about."

"She already rejected your offer. That's why what you don't know won't hurt you," Vaughan repeated stubbornly. "If she finds out, you won't be blamed. Damn, you're dense."

"OK, so tell me what you know about Andrew's father," Jon countered.

"Where would you get the idea I know anything?" Fred's face became hard.

Jon stared at him. "Because if Andy told anyone, it was you."

"You think he would tell me and not Amanda?" Vaughan did not meet Jon's eyes.

"Yes," Jon said shortly.

"What you don't know—"

"Won't hurt me, yeah, yeah. I got that part. But it might hurt Amanda," Jon glowered. "This Senator Whitmore is raising questions again as to her involvement in the Barnes' conspiracy."

"Once a bastard, always a bastard," Vaughan muttered. "If you lie down with dogs, you'll get up with fleas."

"Skip the homespun and answer my question," Jon's temper flared.

"Let me give you one more," Fred spoke up. "If the Senator stirs shit, the smell is going to settle on him." He then looked at Jon. "I promise. So why all this today, with the break in and guys following Amanda? You're smart. Isn't that a bit too obvious, even for the senator?"

Jon shook his head. "I have no idea."

Fred continued. "You should ask yourself why the senator is on the scene, why he is suddenly so interested in this investigation."

"I have. If you have any ideas, I'd sure like to hear them," Jon raised his eyebrows.

"If he's running so hard, someone must be chasing him. Or maybe the acts only appear to point to the senator."

Jon exploded. "Can you forget the riddles, Fred?"

"One name—Michael Knox."

"*The* Michael Knox? Of the *Washington Post*?" Jon was incredulous.

"The same. You might want to check him out." Vaughan started off toward the house, waving at Connor. "Have a safe trip back to Pensacola."

"But Amanda—" Jon called.

"Amanda will be safe. I'll see to that."

"You can't protect her all by yourself."

Fred stopped and turned back. "The hell I can't. But Petrino is out there somewhere, keeping watch. And I'm sure he has twisted Bruce's arm to lend a deputy, maybe two, to patrol the area after this break-in."

"Charlie? How did he find out? Why would he be out there?"

Fred just shook his head. "You'll have to ask him that. But Bruce Williams and Charlie are tight. Charlie's network runs deep and wide."

Jon asked coldly, "Where is he now?"

Fred shrugged, and pulled out his push-to-talk phone and activated the button.

"Yeah," Petrino's voice was heard.

"The boyfriend wants to see you," Fred looked at Connor.

"I saw him leaving. Send him back this way. I'll find him," the voice came back.

Fred pointed back the way Jon came. "He'll be up the road there."

Jon jumped in his Mercedes and turned around, speeding back up the trail. Just before making it back to Amanda's he noted a figure in the road. Jon pulled to a stop and sprang out.

"Cut your lights," a voice said. Jon complied.

"Back already?" Petrino quipped, walking up to Connor.

"She wouldn't let me stay, but she'll allow you protect her?" Jon was livid.

"What she doesn't know won't hurt her," Charlie smiled knowingly.

Jon grit his teeth. "She's my fiancée, Charlie."

"You've got a lot to learn about her, man," Charlie retorted. "She's a lawyer. It's better to ask forgiveness than ask permission, particularly if you already know she's not going to agree to what you want."

Jon leaned against the driver's door. "She doesn't let me get close," he threw out, still angry.

"Jon, she hasn't let anyone close since Andy," Charlie remarked. "She's a beautiful woman. Don't you think others have tried?"

"What about you, Charlie?" Jon was direct. "Have you tried?"

Charlie turned away. "What do you think?" he answered harshly. "I was in love with Mandy since second grade. There was a brief time when I thought maybe I had a chance."

He turned and faced Jon. "But until now she's never been able to exorcise Andy's memory. Did you ever notice his clothes were still in the closet until just recently, after you came on the scene? Why do you think I feel so badly about not being there to help prevent Andy's death?

"Now she knows the reason behind Andy's murder. That's why she's attached so much importance to this trial. Did Bill Barnes, Sr., kill Andy? No. But his conviction represents vindication, closure to her. She can let go and begin living again."

Jon surveyed Charlie impassively. Charlie continued, "And you know what? I've found Amanda generally gets what she wants. She makes prosecutors and judges dance her tune. She got Billy off her back for a while, married to Celeste. She's got Ralph and me both married off. And she wants you something terrible. That's a very good sign."

Jon studied him. "I don't want to compete with you, Charlie."

"Don't worry. She rejected me. So I've taken myself out of the running," Charlie replied lightly. "But protecting her is ingrained in me. I promised her dad and mine years ago I wouldn't let anything happen to her." He smiled grimly. "Tom Andrews may be dead, but my dad isn't, and he wouldn't hesitate to beat my ass if I break that promise, even now."

He walked up to Jon and put his hand on Jon's shoulder. "I'm going to have to hand this task off to you sooner or later. Jill is a saint, but she is getting jealous."

"So am I," Jon admitted unsmilingly.

"That's a good sign, too," Charlie laughed shortly. "So let's hope Amanda finds her closure soon." He surveyed Jon. "I just want her to look happy again like she did in your arms at Ralph's wedding."

Jon's face softened at the memory. "Me, too."

Charlie dropped his hand and turned away. "So if you want first shift, be my guest."

"I do."

"Good. I'll go home a few hours and then spell you. Shelby's funeral is in the morning, and I will keep watch during the day tomorrow." Charlie shook his head thoughtfully. "I really think they were after something in the house, and won't be back."

Charlie pulled out a slip of paper from his shirt pocket. "Here," he thrust the paper in Jon's hand. "I anticipated your wanting to hang around. Here are Fred's, Bruce's and my cell numbers." He smirked. "Fred doesn't sleep much. He'll come running if you need cavalry."

Chapter 13

Tuesday morning Charles Petrino let himself in the back service entrance of Childs & Carmichael, Attorneys at Law. Waving at Sheila, he greeted her and they chatted quietly about the events of the past weekend and the weather forecast as together they headed for the kitchen and the coffee pot.

A few moments later, he stood in the doorway of Amanda's office, coffee cup in hand. He quietly watched as Amanda sat at the computer, her back to him, the morning sun filtering through the window and dancing on her golden hair as she busily typed, a large case file in her lap. Every moment or so she stopped to check a pleading, statute or case law books open in front of her and stacked on the credenza. She was so engrossed that she did not notice Petrino. After a while she sat back, unconsciously pulling her hair out of her face.

"I see you're earning your pay this morning," he said.

Startled, she gave a small cry and dropped the massive file onto the floor. "Geez, Charlie, don't sneak up on me," Amanda censured him, reaching to pick up the crumpled mass of papers at her feet.

"Sorry, didn't mean to startle you, especially after the weekend you've had," he replied, closing her door and sidling up to the comfortable chairs facing her desk.

"You know?" her eyes grew wide. "But of course, I forget. Charles Petrino knows all things."

"I do what I can," he quipped. "You got a minute?"

"Looks like I do now," Amanda scowled as she plopped the sheaf of papers on her desk and turned to click the "save" button on her work. "I'm in court before Judge Farley in Pensacola on Friday for Ralph, and the Friday after that on one of my cases. I have to get this memorandum of law out before close of business today. He's a stickler for procedure."

Buzzing Sheila, she quickly relayed, "I just finished the draft. Do you mind pulling it up on your screen, proofing it and cleaning up the certificate of service for me to sign? Don't worry about my citations. I've already checked them. Thanks, Sheila."

She turned to see Petrino staring at her. "How are Alan and the boys this morning?" she inquired.

"Exhausted. I think they're still in shock," Petrino was grave. "They always say that it's after the funeral and after all the friends and family have gone that reality sets in with a vengeance. Until now it's been surreal; now comes the hard part for them."

"I'm sorry I couldn't be there this morning. I knew this had to go out, and came in early. I hope to make it there at lunchtime. I ordered lunch to be delivered, and hope to sit down with them a little, now that the crowds have thinned out."

Petrino frowned. "Are you OK? I've been worried about you," he demanded.

"It has been busy with Ralph gone, but that's good," Amanda responded, her cheerfulness forced. "I like to be busy, and I'm glad for the chance to prove to Ralph I can still run a law office single-handedly."

"Not the practice, Mandy. I mean all this hullabaloo happening to you," he frowned. "The wedding, the breakup with Jon, Shelby's death, the news about Senator Whitmore, then the break-in. They've all slammed you at one time. You're past due for a nervous breakdown at this rate."

"You know about all that?" She pursed her lips, shaking her head in disbelief. "I'm OK," she mumbled, not meeting his gaze.

As he settled himself into the chair Charlie asked casually, "Have you heard from Ralph and Claire?"

"Yes, late last night. They're 'lost in Provence' as we speak. I told Ralph not to get too comfy over there. They're due back home early next week, but who's counting, other than I and all his clients."

She looked suspiciously at him. "What's on your mind, Charlie? You're not here to talk about Jon again, are you?"

Charlie shook his head. "Mandy, I'm still worried about you and Jon. But no, that is, unless you want to."

She shook her head, averting her eyes.

He went straight to the point. "You know they're still eyeballing Alan over Shelby's death?"

Amanda drew her breath in sharply before releasing it slowly, cautiously gauging her response. "I had hoped that would die a natural death," she remarked, flushing when she realized the double meaning of her statement.

"I talked to Alan." She looked sharply at Petrino. "You know I advised him not to talk to anyone, including you, without a lawyer present."

"Just as I told him myself," Petrino rejoined smoothly. "Hell, Mandy, Josh and Caleb are our godchildren. Do you think I want to see anything happen to Alan?" He sighed. "I'm worried about the direction this investigation is heading."

"Are you involved?" Amanda asked quickly.

"Only peripherally. The state prosecutor insisted this be investigated, and is pushing it unmercifully. Because of my relationship with Alan I had to call in the state and county guys for the investigation. But of course, I'm still in the loop somewhat, because Bruce tells me what he can."

"So what do you want me to do?" Amanda responded.

"Are you going to represent Alan?" Charlie was direct, his frank eyes meeting hers.

"It's gone this far?" Amanda was incredulous. "Well, Charlie, that depends. I haven't been asked. You know Ralph normally takes the lead in criminal defense cases nowadays—that's our agreement—but I don't know if Alan wants us."

"You know the answer to that question. And this is off the record—he's going to need you."

Amanda rocked back in her chair, turned her back on Petrino and looked out the window, sighing. She knew that Charlie was generally the first in the community to know any news, and his contacts spread far and wide. "Well, you've not brightened my day. But neither you nor I have any business soliciting business or borrowing trouble."

Charlie leaned forward, his voice barely above a whisper. "I have it on good authority that the medical examiner's report is inconclusive, but that an arrest is to be made anyway."

"Why would the State do something so foolish?" Amanda quizzed.

"Perhaps because someone else is pulling the strings over there," Charlie met her eyes.

Amanda's eyes widened in disbelief. "Isn't there any way to stop this?"

"I can't stop the State Attorney," Charlie growled.

Just then her intercom buzzed. Amanda said, "Excuse me," and picked up the receiver. She listened impassively for a moment. "I'll take it."

She pushed a button. "Good morning, Dr. Young. What may I do for you?"

She listened several minutes, her jaw tightening in anger. "Where is he?" she asked tightly, then listened. "It will be all right," she murmured soothingly, then added, "I'm on my way there now."

Amanda stood, Charlie following her lead. "Charlie, you must be clairvoyant. That was Alan's dad. Law enforcement showed up at the house and has hauled Alan in for questioning."

She suddenly shook, livid with rage. "The sons of bitches!" she cursed loudly. Petrino was shocked, as she slammed a statute book on the desk violently. "Only by the grace of God were the boys spared the sight of Alan being handcuffed and snatched out of the house. They were upstairs getting dressed. Someone will pay for this," she muttered, angrier than Petrino had ever seen her.

"Are the boys all right? What have they done with Alan?"

"The boys have been told their dad had to run to the office. Alan is apparently being taken to the sheriff's department. Give me just a minute."

She picked up the telephone and quickly dialed a number. After giving her name, she waited only a moment. "Hi, Gerald, how are you? I missed your voice in choir yesterday. You're my best baritone. Yes, Arnold did a great job."

A pause ensued. "Doc, you know I don't normally interrupt your work or ask you about your findings before your report is out, but it's urgent. The state has dragged Alan Young in over his wife's death. His dad has just called me. Yes, this morning. I know—that's crass. Yes, the kids were there, but thankfully didn't see it.

"I'm out the door to the sheriff's department now. Can you divulge whether you have a cause of death yet?"

There was a short pause, and even Petrino could hear the coroner's voice raised in anger. She nodded to Petrino. "You told Clarence this already? So there's no reason on your end for them to be proceeding with an arrest at this time?"

She listened a moment. "So I take it you haven't signed any reports or affidavits? No, I don't know, but I'm going to try to find out. If I need to, can I quote you, call on you? Thanks bunches—I'll see you Sunday. No, Wednesday night choir rehearsal has been cancelled."

Replacing the receiver, she turned back to Petrino. "You're right. The ME has no clear cause of death at this time. He said that Shelby died of heart failure, and that there were traces of what he thought was lidocaine in her blood. Gerald doesn't have toxicology back yet to confirm that. He does not know at this time whether it was prescribed, or whether it was lethal. He's not sure why lidocaine would be prescribed, and has ordered the medical records. Cardet said he didn't prescribe it.

"Gerald is to review the records this morning and complete his findings, and informed the prosecutor of all this yesterday. Clarence went off like firecrackers. I guess he has decided to insinuate himself and handle this case personally. I can understand the desire to question Alan, but the state seems to be in an awful hurry to pin this on him."

She grabbed her criminal rules book and a legal pad, shoving both into her attaché. Charlie piped up, "May I tag along?"

"You sure you want to be seen in close company with the enemy?" she asked, preoccupied.

"If you don't mind being seen with me. There's no monopoly on justice."

"Let's go, then. I'll drive," Amanda answered, pulling on her blazer and grabbing her purse and attaché.

"You sure? You're pretty upset," Charlie countered, trying to control his own ire with difficulty.

"Don't start," Amanda warned, as she strode out rapidly, Charlie at her heels.

They left the building and headed for her car. As she pulled out of the driveway, Charlie noticed her long slim ringless fingers. "You're still not wearing your engagement ring?" he wanted to know, trying to divert her from her obvious frenzy.

"That was off before we even got started," she subconsciously gripped the wheel tighter.

He flushed. "I thought you and Jon would have worked it all out by now."

"It's not going to happen," she insisted, her eyes on the road.

"Why not?" Petrino demanded. "What's happened?"

"William Barnes, Sr., happened," she hissed angrily. "The U.S. Attorney showed up at Ralph's and Claire's wedding reception to let us know that the old man has demanded speedy trial, and it's been scheduled in two weeks. But you knew all that. Jon told you, even before you showed up at the office Saturday night after the wedding. So don't pretend ignorance."

Charlie, surprised that she knew, replied sympathetically, "What has that got to do with your engagement?"

"There is no engagement," Amanda stated flatly, turning a corner sharply, causing Charlie to grab the dash. "Charlie, just think a minute about what an incestuous case it is. The main evidence is the confession of a conspirator that just happens to be the initial prime suspect's real father. He ends up damning Barnes and incidentally exonerating his long-lost daughter. The other co-conspirators are dead. Now the main FBI case officer is dating and engaged to that same former suspect? As old Judge Williams, may he rest in peace, would have said, 'That dog won't hunt with me.' The U.S. Attorney was even less tactful about the matter."

Charlie said softly, "You didn't used to be so concerned about appearances, Mandy."

She slammed on brakes suddenly as a light turned yellow, throwing Charlie forward. "I'm not concerned with appearances, Charlie!" she shouted furiously. "I don't give a damn about what people think of me. I'm worried about a jury believing the truth and sending William Barnes away for the rest of his life. I don't want all this work of Andy's and Jon's to be for naught, and the old man to walk."

"I'm sorry," Charlie whispered. "Calm down. You're absolutely right. Barnes needs to go down."

"And to further create a flap, now Senator Thomas Whitmore is on the scene, asking questions. Seems he thinks Andy was his son."

Petrino looked at her closely. "Why does the Presidential hopeful show up now if he's Andy's father?" he asked.

Amanda glanced over at him. "I guess I shouldn't be surprised that you already knew about this too. Why now, indeed? I don't know it all yet," she shook her head, aggravated. "And he is apparently convinced I'm the wicked witch of the west."

"But you were cleared," Charlie's voice rose.

"Go figure," she bit back an oath.

"What about Jon's resignation? How does he feel about this?"

"Jon, as case officer, is in Pensacola on temporary assignment there, and at the beck and call of the U.S. Attorney. He tendered his thirty-day notice, and it was rejected pending disposition of this case."

Petrino spoke savagely. "They can't do that. The feds have no right to screw with your life any more, Amanda."

"They can and they have," she spat venomously. "But the U.S. Attorney is right. I realize that no matter what, Barnes' defense will be pointing the finger at me. I will end up being the one on trial. William Barnes, Sr., destroyed my husband, as well as his own son. I'm next on the list. I can't let him get away with it, and I don't intend to give him more ammunition."

Charlie said quietly, "Mandy, Billy created his own means of destruction. It is not your responsibility to avenge him or Andy."

"I'm not avenging Billy," Amanda quarreled bitterly. "But I must be a poor judge of character. I thought I knew Bill better than that." And I might have even married him not so long ago, she thought silently, shuddering.

"Whoa, remember to watch the road," Charlie reached out and touched her arm comfortingly. "Mandy, we all were in the dark about Billy and just how far he would go," Petrino almost whispered.

He could tell that Amanda was struggling with her emotions; the tension was flowing out of her. "But nothing changes my opinion that Andy's life and death, and Jon's work in solving the crime, cannot be in vain. I won't let Barnes walk away. And I lay Bill's fall to the blame of his father, who I want to see punished. I cannot help myself—I want to see him pay dearly.

"If my having a relationship with Jon allows the old man to walk, would not the U.S. Attorney look for an indictment against me? That's a big case—someone needs to go down for it. What would that do to Jon's career?

"Besides, Jon and I don't really know much about each other. How do I know that he's not just feeling sorry and a passing infatuation for his best friend's widow?"

She pulled into a parking space in the lot between the sheriff's administrative offices and the courthouse and cut off the ignition, staring ahead of her, her anger spent. "Sorry, you didn't ask for that. I'm still upset about it all. And I've got bigger fish to fry in there; I need to be worrying about Alan." She nodded toward the sheriff's office.

"This is bad, Charlie." She closed her eyes a moment, gripping the steering wheel tightly. "I've got to keep my temper under control and handle this with a cool head, and I don't know if I can. It's Alan. We've known him all our lives. I have to win, for the babies' sake. I really want to hurt someone right now. With all that's happening, I feel like I'm losing control."

"Stop just a minute. Just take a deep breath. One thing at a time." Charlie touched her arm again, momentarily halting her exit from the car. "I know life is complicated right now, baby," he spoke comfortingly. "But I'm sure Jon loves you, Amanda—as you, not Andy's widow. I think you may be selling that love short."

"Just like I sold yours short?" she whispered, her eyes looking straight ahead.

"Yes," Charlie's answer surprised her. "Just like. Are you going to keep throwing Andy up as a barrier to your future happiness? Furthermore, you don't owe anybody anything, least of all an explanation. You must decide what you want and take it. Maybe what you choose is a mistake, but you never know unless you try. Life keeps ticking away, and it leaves us in the dust."

Amanda opened the car door. "I'll keep that in mind. Meanwhile, let's see what we can do for Alan." She glanced at him and squeezed his hand gratefully. "I'm glad you're here, Charlie, the voice of reason. Please keep me from killing someone today."

They made it to the sheriff's department, where they were made to cool their heels in the lobby for several minutes, Petrino refusing to sit and Amanda pacing angrily, until Bruce Williams, the Chief Investigator himself, showed up.

"What the hell do you think you are doing?" Amanda accused the officer hotly.

Bruce held up his hands in surrender. "I had nothing to do with this. I just found out. I will dress down the deputy myself. He doesn't work for the state attorney," he added under his breath testily. "Right this way."

Williams escorted them down a long hallway to an interrogation room. Entering the room, Amanda was surprised to see Clarence Banks, the chief prosecutor, already in the room with a deputy. Quizzically she looked at the two men and her client, dressed in casual clothes but with handcuffs on.

"Slow day at the office, Clarence? I'm not used to seeing you here," Amanda remarked to the prosecutor coolly, but her outrage was unmistakeable, just below the surface. Nodding at her client, she asked Young, "Have you made any statement to these men?"

Alan shook his head, his face a picture of worry, but his jaw set arrogantly. "I told them I would say nothing without you present."

Amanda turned to the men as they straightened up and the deputy turned off a recording device. "I am assuming my client demanded his attorney immediately upon being taken into custody, so may I ask why you were starting without me?"

Clarence flushed. "We weren't, and Dr. Young is not in custody."

"Then pray tell why was the recorder on, and why is he shackled? Why was he snatched out of his father's home this morning?" Amanda demanded authoritatively.

Clarence blustered, "I don't have to take this from you, Childs. The officer here has done the paperwork to arrest the doctor for murder. The judge's assistant just buzzed to say the judge is free and can see us as soon as we get there. Bruce, let's go—Dr. Young can face first appearance right now."

Amanda countered argumentatively, "So he is in custody. Are you sure you want to do that?"

Clarence, enraged, knocked his chair over as he marched out of the room. Bruce Williams just shrugged at Amanda and Petrino and spoke to Young apologetically. "Sorry, Doctor. Come on, let's go."

Alan's eyes grew wide with fear, but Amanda patted him on the shoulder, exuding more confidence than she felt, as she and Petrino turned and followed them next door to the courthouse.

Arriving upstairs to the judge's anteroom, Amanda pulled on Young's arm.

Alan breathed, "Thank you so much, Amanda. I'm sorry to bother you, but—"

"Alan, say no more. You know I'll do whatever I can for you. And Ralph will be back next week."

As she steered him out of earshot, the deputy put out a hand to stop her. She turned to him, fire flashing in her eyes. "Don't even think about it," she warned between clenched teeth. "As Dr. Young's attorney, I have the right to speak to him confidentially."

Amanda and Young walked to the other end of the room. Amanda told Alan, "You know, we are at the mercy of how the State chooses to charge you. When they picked you up, was anything said?"

Alan squinted as he tried to remember. "Nothing more than 'an open count of murder'. What does that mean?"

"That means that they are waiting for a grand jury to convene to determine the exact charge. The State cannot charge you with first degree premeditated murder without a grand jury indictment in this state. But because the State holds all the cards in a grand jury proceeding, depending on the evidence, that may or may not be hard to do. Do you know what law enforcement may have on you?"

"No. Gerald told me yesterday that Shelby's autopsy was inconclusive. But they found something suspicious and have sent off samples to toxicology." He grasped Amanda's arm desperately. "Amanda, you know I didn't kill her. I loved her with all my heart. She was the mother of my children. I wouldn't hurt her ever. I don't know what I'm going to do without her." His eyes filled with tears.

"Alan, it's OK. I believe you," Amanda assured him. "You need to be strong for this moment. Let's just see what happens."

A bailiff came up to Amanda. "Judge Latimer is ready," he said solemnly.

"Where's Judge Kilmer?" Amanda asked in surprise.

"He had some mandatory capital certification course he had to take in Jacksonville," the bailiff replied as he led the way to the judge's chambers. "He apparently had forgotten about it until late yesterday."

As Amanda turned to follow her client in the room, the judicial assistant spoke. "Just a minute, Mrs. Childs," she hurriedly shoved a fax into Amanda's hand.

Amanda dazedly thanked her and glanced at the sheet.

When Amanda and Young walked in, the chief prosecutor and investigator were already present, Clarence looking as surprised as she at the identity of the judge. A deputy clerk of court turned on a recording device as the proceedings began. Amanda and her client took a seat at the table facing the prosecutor and case officer, the judge sitting at the head of a large desk adjoining the table, and Bruce standing just behind her client.

Judge Latimer looked down his nose above his half-glasses and greeted Amanda. "Good morning, Counselor. Good to see you again, but for the circumstances."

"Yes, Your Honor," she murmured.

"It's unusual to have defense counsel at a first appearance. But then it's not every day we have an arrest for murder."

"Yes, Your Honor," nodded Amanda politely.

"The warrant lists the charge as an open count of murder, but the probable cause statement alleges premeditation. Ms. Childs, will you be making formal appearance for the defendant in this and subsequent proceedings?"

Amanda paused, looking at her client, who nodded. "Yes, Your Honor."

"Do you have anything you wish the Court to consider at this time? You, I'm sure, are aware this is only a probable cause proceeding."

"Yes, sir, but the Court at this hearing must determine whether there is probable cause to believe a crime has been committed, and that Dr. Young committed it. Although I have not yet seen the probable cause affidavit before you, I am unaware that a cause of death has been established. In fact, I have just been in touch with the medical examiner's office, and he has made no conclusions. That would be a fatal flaw to my client's arrest at this time.

"If I am mistaken, I apologize to the Court—I do not intend any fraud upon the Court. But I am concerned whether there is indeed sufficient evidence to support probable cause before my client is charged and his liberty infringed."

The judge frowned, rifling the papers before him. "I don't see a medical examiner's report or affidavit in the probable cause packet. Does the State happen to have one for me?"

The prosecutor, his face scarlet, perfunctorily reviewed the papers in his file. "Your Honor, I'm sure we had an affidavit from the ME. I don't know where it is at this time. The examiner has not completed his testing, and of course is awaiting toxicology results. But he opined that he felt foul play must be involved."

Amanda watched the State Attorney intently. He did not seem to be looking all that hard for the allegedly lost document. Why would he be lying? she concluded.

She responded quickly, "Judge, I move to strike that last remark. It is hornbook law that the state must provide probable cause by sworn statement. Without the medical examiner present or his sworn statement, the Court cannot take the prosecutor's word for what evidence he might have, particularly on a case of this magnitude and in light of the conflicting information I have just proffered to the Court regarding my conversation with the ME. He is on standby if needed for testimony, and he has just faxed over a sworn statement that his report has not been completed." She held up the sheet of paper.

Clarence, his face turning a shade redder, blustered, "Are you calling me a liar?"

Of course I am, you ass, her eyes telegraphed to him, but she bit her lip, her hand tightening into a fist. "No, Your Honor," said Amanda, addressing the judge and not the prosecutor, but her eyes sliced Clarence to shreds. "I am not calling the prosecutor anything. He knows me better than that."

The judge sighed, rubbing his forehead as he regarded the probable cause packet before him. "Clarence, you know she's right," he addressed Clarence sternly. "I've known you for twenty years. You know better than this. You have nothing here but the deputy's speculation. I'm disappointed in you. But I see from the calendar that a grand jury is to be convened week after next. Maybe you'll have time to get it together by then."

Turning to Amanda and her client, he stated, "I find no probable cause, so I'm dismissing it without prejudice. Officers, release the defendant, with the admonition that the next time you might not be so lucky, so you might as well not make any travel plans right now."

As Amanda and Young stood, she took Alan's arm and propelled him gently toward the door. Clarence and she met face to face at the door of the judge's anteroom. Her eyes steely, she leaned over close to Banks and rebuked him very quietly, "I don't know what you are thinking, Clarence. But you never know when Dr. Young will be meeting you in court in a suit for unlawful arrest. And you know what? I'm going to advise him to do just that. It will be fun to kick your ass for old times' sake."

The State Attorney looked at her, his face ashen, his jaw set angrily. She reached out and smilingly straightened his tie, her voice even softer. "Your only saving grace was having first appearance this morning. If Dr. Young had spent the night in jail, I'd have had your job on a platter by the end of the week, chief prosecutor or not. I'm sure my petition for writ would generate a bar grievance. And a suit for intentional infliction of emotional distress would not be out of the question. Please share that with whoever is pulling your strings these days."

His face turned another shade of scarlet, as Charlie came forward and took her arm.

"Come on, Mandy," he coaxed her quietly.

"I'm done here," she smiled saccharinely at Clarence, as she turned on her heel and left the room with her client.

As Dr. Young's cuffs were removed by Bruce Williams in the hallway, Amanda spoke to Alan quietly. "You need to come with me over to my office right now. We need to consummate the sacred relationship and get started planning our defense. This was only Round One. I don't understand why the State jumped the gun, but we need to get busy. I need to know everything you can tell me."

Chapter 14

Amanda pulled up to the law office with her two passengers. They all disembarked from her vehicle.

"You should be glad there was a cop in the car. You should have been stopped and issued several traffic citations," Petrino tried to dispel the passengers' funereal mood. He winked at Alan. "When Mandy reached over to straighten Clarence's tie, I just knew she was going to make good her threat and kill him in cold blood, with the judge looking on."

Alan broke into a tight smile too, nodding distractedly.

She looked thoughtfully at Alan, then turned and spoke briefly to Petrino. "Sorry I can't invite you in for this," she informed him.

"It's fine. I know the drill. Take care of him, OK?" Charlie squeezed her hand and clapped Alan on the back. "I'll check in with you later about that other matter," he added meaningfully to Amanda before taking his leave.

Amanda took a shell-shocked Alan Young by the arm and led him into the building and down the hallway to her office. She showed Alan a seat. Sheila came in briefly, and Amanda signed the forgotten memorandum and certificate of service, giving quick instructions to Sheila.

"And Sheila, please call Dr. Young's residence and let Alan's family know he is OK and at my office. There's no need for them to be worrying about him."

Sheila smiled encouragingly at Alan, as he looked at her with gratitude, before letting herself out and shutting the door of Amanda's office behind her.

"Can I get you some coffee? Soft drink? Anything?" Amanda asked him. "Have you even had breakfast?"

Young replied, "I'm fine. I need to call my office to let them know where I am."

Amanda indicated the telephone, picking up the receiver and dialing the number for him. She excused herself, going into the kitchen for a soft drink.

She returned as Alan was hanging up the receiver. She settled back in her seat.

"Everything OK?" she asked.

"I'm short two nurses right now. My P.A. is going to see what patients he can see for me. It's so hard to believe that in the midst of all this turmoil life is going on as normal."

"Two nurses?" Amanda queried, surprised.

"Edna is on an extended European cruise and is about to retire on me. And Eve has flitted away again. She doesn't need to work anyway."

"Again?" Amanda repeated.

"Yes. She married some big money overseas and is a wealthy widow. It's just as well. She was openly flirting with me, and I didn't know exactly how to rid myself of her advances."

"Eve? Evie Brown?" Amanda was incredulous. "You know, I thought I saw her with—well, a well-known public official out of town a little while back. But that was about a year ago or so. Oh, well, never mind. Are you sure she was after you?"

"Pretty sure," Alan had relaxed momentarily. "Only about three weeks ago, after office hours. She came up to me. She kissed me and was wanting me to—well, you know," he stammered. "I was not expecting it. I was shocked. I told her I was sorry if she got any signals that I was interested in her like that, that I was a happily married man." Alan took a deep breath. "She stormed out and gave her notice the next day, leaving at the end of the week."

"I saw her at the funeral," Amanda murmured.

"Yeah, she was hanging on to me there too. It was too embarrassing." He shook his head. "Edna had told me Eve might turn into trouble, but she was a good nurse, and I needed the help. But Eve has never been dependable. Just as I begin to count on her, she's off and gone. Just shows how good Edna is—a woman who knows all things, and keeps her finger on the pulse, keeping my office running like a well-oiled machine. I miss her and am still trying to talk her into staying."

Alan took a deep tremulous breath. "Amanda, you know the board will suspend my license to practice medicine if I'm under suspicion for murder."

"Yes," she nodded somberly, "but only if you are formally charged or a grievance filed and probable cause determination made. Don't worry—I will fight the board if that happens." She smiled encouragingly. "Alan, one thing at a time. We'll cross that bridge when we need to."

"You're a good friend," Alan smiled, then shuddered at the enormity of the ordeal they had just endured. Looking at the wall and the Duke pennant still hanging there, he smiled briefly. "Ralph and Claire still off on their honeymoon?"

"Yes," Amanda nodded. "I—I haven't told them the bad news about Shelby yet. OK, let's start at the beginning," Amanda, sensing that he was mentally thrashing about, still in shock, gently steered him back to the subject. "Tell me about Shelby. Why would she collapse?"

Alan frowned. "That's just it. I'm not sure what brought all this on. You know she had breast cancer."

Amanda glanced up from a notepad where she had begun taking notes to herself. "But I thought that was in remission?"

"Yes, it was," Alan agreed. "Shelby always thought that meant that the worst was not averted, only delayed. We talked about it at some length, but I could never dispel her underlying feeling of doom. I guess that was some impression she had developed from her days as a hospice nurse. And it's true that it seems most women who've had breast cancer end up relapsing, with the cancer showing up in other areas, and mostly fatal. And there's no cure. However, she just had her annual checkup, and passed with flying colors. We were ecstatic, and I got to say, 'I told you so'."

He covered his face with his hands. "Then I came home late from the ER last Thursday evening, and found her collapsed in the front hallway. She had apparently fallen over the console in the foyer. Everything was in disarray. She wasn't responsive, and her pulse was barely perceptible. I was distraught.

"Dad had taken the boys to their ballgame, and I was supposed to meet everyone there. But I had an emergency in ER and knew I had missed most of it, so came on home. Thought I would surprise them and start supper. That's when I found her."

Amanda looked at him with concern. "What did you do?"

Alan looked down at his hands. "I bundled her up, put her in my car and drove her to the ER myself. I didn't want to wait for the ambulance." He swallowed. "I called ahead and Bob Cardet was there checking on a patient, and he did the workup. I was a basket case."

Amanda made a note on her pad. Alan looked up. "God, Amanda, she coded right in front of me in the ER. Bob pushed me out of the way and brought her back. I know," he caught his breath, trying to stem the tears, "I'm not using medical terminology, but it's Shelby we're talking about. She's not just any patient."

"It's OK," Amanda said soothingly. "Take your time."

"I was frozen. Do you know how awful it is to see the procedure happening before you when it is someone you love lying there?" he mumbled.

Amanda's heart went out to him. She moved across to the chair beside him and took his hand in hers. "Dear Alan, I'm so sorry," she murmured, as he broke down and sobbed.

She allowed him to release the spent tension, saying nothing, holding his hand comfortingly.

"It's been such a nightmare, and I just keep thinking I will wake up and it will all be over, everything will be back to normal, and she will be here," he stuttered. "I don't know what I'm going to do with her gone." He buried his head in his hands.

At those words Amanda closed her eyes, and suddenly she was back in time. It was in this very office, she recalled, that she was first informed of Andrew's murder. She remembered that some nameless, faceless man in a suit flashing an FBI badge had accompanied Charles Petrino, then chief investigator at the sheriff's department, and the sheriff that day, and Sheila had let them in without announcement.

Her eyes had opened wide with surprise as she stood and laid down her dictaphone microphone to greet them. She was arrested by Charlie's ashen countenance as he gazed at her before looking away, walking up to her and taking her hand. She had taken a step back, bumping into her executive chair.

"This can't be good," she had smiled politely. "Three law enforcement officers at one time. What may I do for you, gentlemen?"

They did not answer her. Then it suddenly hit her, and her eyes dilated. "Andy. Something has happened. Where is he?"

The sheriff and FBI agent looked at her, then at Petrino. He cleared his throat. "Mandy," he began, squeezing her hand comfortably.

She had suddenly felt claustrophobic, like the room was too small. She sat heavily in her chair, gasping, leaning forward and grasping the desk drawer for her purse. "I need to go to him. Is he hurt? It's bad, isn't it?" she managed.

"Amanda, dear, Andrew is—something terrible has happened. Dear, I'm afraid he—he is dead," Sheriff Watson finally stammered, his voice tinged in sorrow. "I'm so sorry to be the bearer of such horrible news, my dear."

"He was killed during an investigation," the nameless person spoke. "He died in the service of his country," he added, his voice sounding pompous.

Amanda stared at them. She couldn't breathe. "You must be mistaken. How? It's not possible," she mumbled, her voice sounding far away. "He told me he would have to work late, and might not be home last night. That's normal."

"Did he tell you why? What he was working on?" the nameless one asked, his eyes intent upon her.

She shook her head. "What?" she suddenly demanded, standing. "What is he working on?" She stood, pushing Charlie away from her as she faced the man across the desk. "Tell me," she croaked desperately.

"That is classified information," the man stated, his eyes boring through Petrino, whose face became a mask.

She turned to Petrino. "Tell me, Charlie. What's happened? Where is Andy? Take me to him," she demanded.

Charlie shook his head sadly.

"He can't be—dead?" she cried, the last word almost inaudible. "You wouldn't let that happen, would you?"

Charlie swallowed hard at her words and the accusation therein. He tenderly grasped her by her arms as she started trembling and the full enormity of what was said hit her full force. She had stared at him, reading the awful truth in his eyes. "No," she muttered dully, shaking her head.

Petrino whispered, "Mandy, I'm sorry. Oh, God, Mandy, I'm so sorry."

"No." She had struggled as he gripped her arms, supporting her. She felt as though she was slipping down a deep crevasse. Amanda beat Charlie's chest with her fists, until he finally enfolded her and hugged her tightly to him, rocking her as she had screamed Andy's name over and over, shushing her as her happy world fled forever.

Amanda suddenly realized that she could remember very little else of that fateful meeting, and was brought back to the present as Alan squeezed her hand and she handed him some tissues from a holder on the edge of her desk.

"Are you OK?" Alan asked her. "You seemed far away for a moment."

"I'm sorry," she smiled pensively. "Your words brought back sad memories for me. I know exactly how you feel, Alan."

He nodded. "Shelby was so upset at Andy's memorial service." Amanda was surprised that he had guessed the reason for her preoccupation. "She said she hoped neither of us would ever have to face what you did with the loss of Andy. And here I sit. Oh, my God."

Amanda was touched, and the tears started. "Oh, dear, I'm so sorry," she murmured, as they held hands and cried.

After a moment she was able to pull herself back together, and patted Alan's hand as she wiped her eyes with a tissue. "OK, let's see if we can make any more progress. Cardet brought Shelby back?"

Alan nodded, sniffling. "Yes. But she was not able to speak to me. She kept trying to tell me something. I could tell she was agitated. She kept squeezing my hand, mouthing words, but we couldn't figure out what she was trying to say. Bob finally told me that he needed to give Shelby something to calm her so as to reduce the shock her heart had already sustained. I stayed with her all night. I wanted to be there when she awakened again."

Amanda nodded. "Then what happened?"

"Bob finally convinced me to go home and get some rest, and said he would call me the minute there was any change in her condition. So I went to check on the twins, and got there just in time to get them ready for school, let them know about their mother."

He closed his eyes. "I should never have left. I never got to speak to her again. I took Josh and Caleb to school and had just started back to the hospital, when I got the call." He sobbed, "It was too late."

"Did Cardet give you any reasons, any theories as to what caused this?"

"None," Alan frowned. "He said he didn't know, and that the autopsy was necessary. Oh, Amanda," he gushed, "I can't function without her, and Josh and Caleb are just lost, cannot understand that Mommy is gone. And now this—being accused of her murder. What am I to do?"

"We're going to make it through," Amanda reassured him. "Alan, can you think of any reason why someone would want to hurt or kill Shelby?"

"Murder?" he was wide-eyed, gazing at her uncomprehendingly. "No, that just can't be," he was solemn. "Everyone loved her, from her Sunday School students to the people at the nursing home where she volunteered her time."

Amanda gazed at him sorrowfully. "What about you? Is there anyone who would want to hurt you in some way?"

"Me?" he laughed hollowly. "Why would someone do that? No, Amanda, I cannot think of any reason for foul play." He stared at her. "You don't really think so, do you?"

"Why would there be lidocaine in Shelby's system? And why would there be a vial of lidocaine on the floor in your house?"

He was shocked. "In the house? Where?" He stared at her, stricken.

"In the foyer," Amanda replied, watching him.

"That can't be," he echoed, beside himself. "There's no reason for her to—for there to be lidocaine. I mean—why? Oh, Mandy," the realization hit him, "surely no one would kill Shelby? Lidocaine? Why lidocaine? That would not be indicated for anything—oh, my God." He started shaking. "The symptoms, the heart failure. Why would anyone do that? To Shelby?"

Amanda took his hand. "Alan, you've got to get a grip. This is just the beginning, and we've got a long way to go. I'm just saying you need to be thinking back, making notes to yourself of anything unusual that has happened recently, anything that could lead us to a motive and a person if Gerald rules this a homicide," Amanda informed him. "And talk to no one, NO ONE, about this matter, not even Cardet or Gerald. Tell them I said so if they press. Anything you say, no matter how innocently, may come back to haunt us. So say nothing. Send them to me."

Alan nodded, dazed. "I know the drill also," he smiled bitterly. "Never thought I'd be asking advice from a lawyer on a criminal matter," he tried to joke. "This is worse than any nightmare."

"You doctors give us a bad rap, but you need lawyers too," Amanda assured him. "Stay in touch. Call me if anything comes to mind. If you need anything at all, even babysitting, call me. We're going to make it through this."

They stood and she hugged him.

"Thank you, Amanda," he whispered.

She walked him out, where his sister Pamela was waiting. She squeezed Amanda's hand. "I don't know what we would have done if you hadn't been there this morning."

After he had gone, Amanda resumed her seat in her office, leaning back in her chair and staring at the ceiling. She tried to banish the thoughts from her mind, but the memory of her being informed of Andy's death played over and over in her head.

On that day Sheila had, unknown to any of them, immediately guessed the reason for the men's sudden appearance at Amanda's office, and called Marjorie Witherspoon. Marjy in turn had called Dr. Howells and had him meet her at the law office only moments after Amanda's outburst, where they found her still clinging to Petrino and screaming. Marjorie had Sheila usher out the law enforcement officers and took charge of the shaken and incoherent Amanda. Because of her hysteria, Howells had immediately given her a sedative, and Marjorie had enlisted Charlie and Howells to assist her in transporting Amanda to Marjorie's own home to watch over her. Amanda had collapsed, withdrew into herself, and cocooned herself against all the condolences pouring in, shutting down, her heart in denial.

Although it had been over five years, the suddenness of remembering about that day left her breathless, the memory as fresh as if it was yesterday.

She recalled their telephone conversation the afternoon before his death. Because his trip home was unexpected and he informed her he could only spend the night, he had asked if they could meet and stay at the apartment above the law office. He had called her just as she had seen Sheila out for the day.

"How was your day?" his voice had greeted her.

"Pretty hard, but I've consoled myself all day with the thought of having you to myself tonight," she had purred. "Where are you? I thought you would be here already."

"I planned on it, but something has come up," Andy's voice was suddenly tense. "Amanda, darling, I love you."

"That means you're not going to be here tonight," she laughed softly, a hint of reproach in her voice, even as she tried to cover her disappointment.

"I'm sorry, darling." She could sense a barricade being thrown up, the way it always did when his work intervened. "This can't be helped, and I have to take care of it, tonight."

"Guess I'll go home to the farm then," she murmured.

"No." She was surprised by the vehemence in his voice. "Promise me you'll stay there," he demanded angrily. "Please do something for me—go check all the windows and doors, and set the alarm. I want you locked up safe and tight. I'll wait for you to do it."

"What is wrong?" she was suddenly nervous.

"Nothing. I just heard an alert that there's an escaped convict out on the loose, thought to be in this area. I hate not being there, and I want to know you are safe," he had insisted, his voice edgy. "Besides," his voice softened, "I may be able to swing by if I finish this early."

She had placated him by doing as he asked. When she returned to the phone and assured him she had all the locks and deadbolts fastened and the alarm set, he had murmured, "Thank you, my dearest. Please stay in tonight. I want to know you are safe," he repeated distractedly. "I will try my best to make it back just as soon as I take care of this matter. Forgive me."

"I'll have to think about it," she had replied resentfully. "It's hard being married to you and yet being the 'other woman', playing second fiddle to your job."

"Please don't think that of me, Amanda," he spoke earnestly. "I have to go. I love you more than anything."

Then, before she could respond, he was gone.

She shook her head, marveling how at the most inopportune times she was transported back to that time of intense pain and suffering. She knew now the circumstances behind his absence that night, that he was answering Claude Brown's summons in her stead, and that he died horribly that night at the hands of Billy Barnes while trying to protect her.

"Oh, my dearest Andrew," she whispered. "I never got to tell you goodbye, that I loved you. Will I ever get over you?"

Chapter 15

Tuesday evening Jon decided to make a visit to St. Catherine's. He hesitated before knocking on the rector's door. He heard, "Come in," and turned the knob.

Father Anselm was sitting at his desk, peering at a computer monitor. He squinted, then rose and greeted Connor warmly with an outstretched hand.

"Jonathan, how good to see you," he stated heartily. "Please come in. I'm getting addicted to these machines. They make typing sermons a lot easier. And Amanda has been trying to teach me how to Google for information, research, texts." He grinned. "I missed you last Sunday. I've been thinking about you, my dear man."

"And I you, sir," declared Jon, smiling as he shook hands with the rector and took the chair indicated. "Hope it was good."

"I have heard some fabulous news through the grapevine, and wanted to congratulate you. You could not find a more wonderful girl than our Amanda."

Jon frowned. "Thank you, but your congratulations may be premature, if not totally misplaced."

Anselm paused, concern written on his face. "I'm sorry. I was afraid on Sunday that something was amiss, from Amanda's troubled countenance when I asked about you. I did not mean to spread unfounded rumors."

Jon hastened to reassure him. "No, it is true that I proposed to Amanda. However, certain circumstances have occurred that have placed our engagement on hold, if not nixed it altogether."

Anselm was all sympathy. "I'm sorry, my boy. Is it something you feel comfortable talking about with me?"

Jon looked at him soberly. "That's why I am here. I'm not one to share my troubles, but I'm not sure what to do or who to turn to.

"You see, after I gave Amanda the ring, we found out that William Barnes, Sr., is demanding an expedited trial on his federal charges. The hearing on the motion to suppress the wiretap and listening device evidence was moved up, and is scheduled for hearing next week.

"Upon hearing the news, Amanda immediately handed me back the ring that night during the reception and said that we could not do anything that might jeopardize the case. She fears she will become the main feature of the defense, and does not want me or the case 'tainted' by a relationship with her."

"And how do you feel about it?" Anselm asked quietly.

"Father, I worked hard on this case and have as much incentive as anybody to see the conspirators brought to justice. I think the evidence will hold. If so, not only will Barnes be convicted on the current charges, but he is also looking at prosecution and two life sentences just for the murders of Celeste Barnes and Claude Brown, not to mention the murder conspiracy counts and other charges. We're still looking into another count of murder from years ago."

He paused. "Andy was my best friend, Father. His murder angered me, shook my faith in God, but spurred me on to find his killer. I had to somehow see this case through to the end.

"And now I've fallen for Amanda. I love her. I feel so guilty because she was my best friend's wife. But he's gone and I can't bring him back for her. I love her so much that I would if I could."

Father Anselm looked on, nodding. Jon plunged on, as though afraid to stop. "I want her so badly it hurts. I want to wipe away her pain-filled past and assure her she can trust me, that I will do everything in my power to make her happy. I can respect her views and her concern for me and the case, but I'm worried that this case is just fertilizing doubts in her mind about us."

"Have you talked to her about your fears?"

"I pressed her the day of Ralph's and Claire's wedding to talk to me. But she kept finding excuses and running away, cleaning up the aftermath of the wedding, handling Ralph's caseload while he's away. It's so hard to corner her, to talk to her. She says she loves me too, but she has shut me out."

Father nodded slowly. "I too have noticed her preoccupation and bustling around. She's frightened, Jon, and she's covering it up."

"Don't I know that?" Jon replied, his frustration evident. "But I don't want our lives on hold any longer. And I don't know what to do to reassure her. You've known her longer than I have. What can I do?" he asked gruffly.

Father was silent for several minutes, deep in thought. Finally he broke the silence. "Jon, my advice is two-fold, and the two points are contradictory.

If you know she is the one, you must fight for her. You must never give up. Amanda is worth whatever it takes to win her.

"But you are going to have to give her some time and space. The stronger one's faith, the larger the demons one has to battle. Amanda's experience with love has been traumatic for her."

Jon interposed, "And now there is the added complication of Senator Whitmore's appearance on the scene, and the allegations that Andrew was his son. Now she wonders whether Andy was truthful with her about his parentage."

Anselm was surprised. Jon continued, "It hasn't hit the papers yet, but will at any time. This has complicated Amanda's life even more."

"I'm so sorry to hear this. She did not need any more stressors," Anselm gazed on Jon sympathetically. "Jon, I truly believe that Amanda loves you. She has made great strides this last year in ridding herself of that stranglehold that Andrew's memory has held over her life. This is not the first time she has used Andrew as a shield, a reason to avoid a chance at happiness."

Jon's eyes narrowed at his statement. Anselm continued. "It took her a very long time, but I have seen her shed much of the past, step out of her shell and again take her place among the living. I worried about the effect of Marjorie's passing on Amanda, and whether it would set back her progress. I see how she looks at you and it gladdens my heart.

"However, deep inside I feel that Amanda thinks you are too good to be true, and, more troubling, she does not believe she is entitled to love with someone else." He smiled slightly. "I've noticed that attorneys are a bit on the superstitious side. I feel Amanda is afraid that any relationship she has is bound to end badly. In fact, she made the comment once to me that her loving someone else puts them in danger."

Jon nodded. "I think I know what you're talking about."

"And Amanda, although she is completely innocent, and will never breathe a word about it, and even though she is as outwardly loyal to Marjorie as the day is long, is quite ashamed of the facts now coming to light about her conception and parentage, the advent of media publicity that may occur as a result of the case, and the shadow cast on her integrity by the rumors of her involvement in the embezzlement of funds."

Jon nodded again, deep in thought at the vicar's words. "Yes, she has acknowledged that to me."

Anselm continued gently. "My dear boy, Amanda has discovered that her best friend was actually her biological mother, that Stephen Marks is really her father, and that her childhood friend Bill Barnes was capable of brutally violating her and killing her. It is quite an understatement to say that Amanda may need some persuading to trust anyone again."

Anselm paused, a slight smile on his face. "Doc and I consult often about our dear Amanda. We want her to again find a degree of happiness this side of heaven." He laughed softly. "We've been hoping you're the ticket. Don't give up on her. She is a priceless gem."

In the distance they could hear the strains of the organ. Jon listened a few seconds, then asked, "Is that—"

"Amanda? Yes, she's a little late this evening—it was an unusually hard day for her today."

They both paused, listening. Anselm watched Connor intently, noting the passing emotions flitting over his features. Connor, finally aware of Anselm's scrutiny, colored uncomfortably.

Anselm finally broke the silence. "Why don't you go listen awhile? There's no telling what you might discover."

Jon stood and shook the older man's hand gravely. "Thanks for listening, Father. I'll try to take your words to heart."

Jon quietly left the rector's office and followed the hallway to the ambulatory and around to the chancel. Quietly he followed the far aisle to the back of the church. He found a seat in the shadows where he could watch Amanda undetected.

She was playing an improvisation to a hymn tune he remembered, 'All creatures of our God and King'. Ever so often she would stop and write some notes to herself on a score, then back up and continue. Then she began a harmonization of another hymn he recalled, 'All things bright and beautiful'.

She completed it, pulled out a score, set some pistons, and began a quiet and ethereal piece, something impressionistic, he guessed. She would stop at times to re-set a piston or make a marking on the manuscript. When she finished, she ran through a row of buttons, pushing each and examining the stops that drew on. Satisfied, she made further notes to herself.

Then she pulled out what appeared to be a bulletin, and worked through methodically each piece in order: prelude, hymns, gradual, service music, anthems, communion and a fiery postlude. Jon was mesmerized by her absorption, attention to detail, and musicianship.

Completing her job and leaving the console, Amanda was unaware that Jon was present. He made his way to the front until he was at the foot of the steps leading to the console. She was changing into her street shoes.

She gasped at his sudden appearance, then recognized Jon. She breathed, "Oh, you startled me." Then she gave him a dazzling smile. "Hi there."

"Hi, yourself," he said huskily, clearing his voice. "What was that you were playing just before you ran through the service?"

She caught her breath. "You've been here all this time?"

"Yes. I didn't want to disturb your work. What was it?"

Amanda smiled at his persistence. "Louis Vierne wrote an organ fantaisie he called *Clair de Lune*. Yes, same name as the piano piece by Debussy."

"Are you going to play that for a service?"

"In a couple of Sundays. The sixth Sunday of the Easter season has traditionally been designated a Rogation Sunday, where special emphasis is placed on praising God for the season, nature, the planting of the crops and God's bounty. So I've chosen hymns that speak to that theme. Also, historically people have looked to the moon and its phases for guidance in planting, transplanting, harvesting. So *Clair de Lune* didn't seem all that far out. And I like to keep introducing classical literature to my congregation when it fits the theme of worship."

Connor laughed. "I like the way you think, Amanda Childs."

She smiled pensively in return. He continued, "I called to check on you yesterday, but there was no answer at the office." He chose not to disclose that he had again assisted in staking out the farm the previous evening, and that he had observed her leaving early for work.

She looked down, the smile fading. "The office was closed. Yesterday was Shelby's funeral. I played for it, and tried to keep the twins occupied afterward. I had to meet with the organ consultant yesterday afternoon briefly." She paused. "It was a hard day."

"I'm sorry," he was sympathetic. "I went by your office a little while ago, but missed you again."

Amanda turned away. "I had an emergency hearing this morning, then an appointment after work."

"What kind of appointment?" he asked curiously.

"A doctor's appointment," she replied vaguely.

"That late? Are you all right?" Jon demanded concernedly.

"Yes, everything is fine." She was suddenly irritable. As he approached her, he sensed a sudden wariness in her features, and she shrank back.

Jon pleaded helplessly, "Amanda, don't close yourself off to me."

She turned her back on him. "It's best this way. It's just hard for me when you are so near."

He gazed at her golden hair. "I'm right here. I want you more than anything. It's you pushing me away."

She turned, flashing angry golden green eyes. "It's called self-preservation, Jon. You should try it. Messing with me can tarnish your whole career with the Bureau. You need to distance yourself from me and make sure your case against Barnes is as watertight as possible. Because I can assure you his lawyer will be going after me and why I should be the one charged, not his client.

"And if he walks, the U.S. Attorney will be licking his wounds and probably seeking a grand jury indictment against me, as the next best defendant. You don't need to be along for that ride. You'll have enough questions to answer as it is, particularly with Senator Whitmore's new-found interest in this case."

Jon reached out to touch her arm, but she jerked away. He said defensively, "We have a strong case against Barnes."

"You have little without the wiretap and bugs. The defense will attack that with gusto."

"The probable cause for the wiretap/eavesdrop warrants will hold. We legitimately excluded you as a suspect."

Amanda turned, her eyes cold with fury. "Are you so sure? How do you really know I wasn't the culprit all along, Jonathan Connor?" Mimicking the defense attorney, she asked him, "And just what evidence do you have that exonerates Mrs. Childs? Isn't it true that you and she have been seeing each other? Agent Connor, have you slept with the suspect? Haven't you let your emotions cloud your judgment in this case?

"Jon, perhaps I charmed you into discounting me, or perhaps for the sake of your old friend Andy Childs you're just blinded by his poor lonely widow—"

"Stop it, damn it," Jon commanded quietly, his eyes boring through her.

Turning from him again, she continued, her voice a whisper, as though talking to herself. "Mr. Barnes hated me all these years. I still don't understand it—the racial and class prejudice all around me in this little town. But after all this time, I think it would be easier to just give in to the anger, to blindly hate him back, to imagine and relish an eternal hell for the Barnes family for all the times they robbed me, stood between me and love, trashed my years of trying to live a life of integrity. It's just too much. Not only would they take Andy away and destroy me, but now you too, just as I have found you."

He was startled by her vehemence. "No," Jon breathed, reaching out to her, turning her to face him and embracing her. She struggled against him, but he held her fast, whispering, "No, Amanda, don't do this to yourself."

She ceased her resistance as he enfolded her, passive and silent, to his breast. He rocked her back and forth. "Do not give in to that rage. Don't let it fester. Remember what the Apostle Paul said: 'My grace is sufficient for you, for my strength is made perfect in weakness.'"

She mumbled against his shirt, "I'm really scared now. You're quoting the Bible to me."

"Don't be too impressed. I can quote Dylan Thomas too. No, Amanda. I'm not a stranger to faith," Jon mumbled, his lips against her hair. "I just took a sabbatical from the Church. I was bitter too. I could not understand why God allowed Andrew to be killed. But being around you has made me miss it, to understand the value of faith, to want to believe again."

"Well, maybe your meeting me hasn't been entirely in vain," she laughed weakly, looking up at him.

"Not at all," Jonathan stared back at her, his mouth descending on hers.

She gasped with pleasure, returning his kiss hungrily. But then she pulled away from him.

"What now?" he demanded, not relinquishing his hold on her.

"No matter how modern the Church has gotten, it's still not proper to make out here," she smiled at him.

"Then let me take you home," his heart leaped as he pleaded with her, pulled her to him and nuzzled her neck.

Amanda shook her head vigorously. "No, I can't." Her voice was tremulous.

"Why not?" he asked huskily, cupping her chin in his hand.

"Because it's been a hard day and I just don't have the strength left in me to resist you," she replied frankly.

"But I don't want you to resist me," he chuckled and kissed her again, holding her mouth hostage with his.

She felt the almost irresistible urge to give in, to enjoy being lost in the feeling of being with him. Wasn't it time? How long did she have to wait? Why could she not say 'go to hell' to the world and just let her emotions have sway? She savored the moment before reluctantly pulling away, finally extricating herself from his arms.

"No, Jon. I meet with your buddy Boyer, U.S. Attorney extraordinaire, on Friday, to go over the case and what he will need from me. I have to see what he thinks about the case."

"Why?" Connor was nonplussed. "You know it's not as if Greg will give his blessing to our seeing each other, Amanda."

"But it's his case, and he has every motive for winning it," Amanda retorted firmly. "And so do I, if it will resolve this matter once and for all and free both of us."

She turned from him and cut off the organ blower, as Connor silently regarded her.

They walked out together. As she pushed the button on her keychain to unlock her car, he attempted to catch her hand. She shook him off. "I tell you what," she avoided looking at him. "I'll cook an early dinner Sunday afternoon at the farm for you, if you can make it. Come out about three."

His hopes were raised. She was inviting him to dinner? "If you let me come home with you tonight, I'll cook you breakfast in the morning," he teased her.

Smilingly she shook her head.

"If that's the best I can do, so be it," he accepted resignedly. "Guess I will drive back to Pensacola tonight and spend the night alone."

She smiled wickedly. "As Jake would say, *Pobrecito! Que lastima! Que se mejore pronto.*"

He did not return the smile. "Don't tempt me, woman."

Seeing the dangerous look in his eyes as he moved toward her, she quickly got into her car, waving goodbye as she pushed the ignition button and the engine sprang to life. He watched her out of sight before tucking himself into his own Mercedes.

He called Petrino. "I saw her at church just now. She is on her way home."

"Couldn't you wangle an invitation to spend the night?" Petrino queried.

"I did what I could," Jon was morose. "It's just as well, I guess. I have to make an appearance at the Pensacola office early tomorrow morning."

"It's fine. We have it covered tonight. Don't worry about her, Jon. It will work out."

Connor reluctantly pulled away, heading toward Pensacola. Unknown to him, Charlie Petrino sat in his car a block from the church and watched the car out of sight. He shook his head, brooding. Amanda, he thought, can't you just give in? The man is dying for you. Charlie cranked his car and u-turned back toward Amanda's farm.

Meanwhile, Jon was deep in thought. The interstate highway stretched before him, cold and dark, as he felt his frustration growing. He turned to a classical music radio station, trying to listen, but his mind wandered. Now that he had found the woman with whom he wanted to spend the rest of his life, the obstacles between them seemed to mount, piling higher and higher.

Jon finally pulled up outside the apartment he shared with Boyer, noting Boyer's car parked in front of the apartment. Aware that he had whipped himself into a black mood and taking a deep breath, he let himself in.

Boyer was in the living area, watching the evening news. He cut off the television, approaching Connor warily.

"Jon," he began earnestly, "it's good to see you. I've wanted so badly to just talk to you, to say how sorry I am."

"No shit," Connor snarled. "How could you be so crass, Greg? I had just proposed to her the day before the wedding. That was the happiest day of my life."

"Jon, I didn't know that. You didn't tell me you were that serious."

"Why should I? I knew you wouldn't approve."

Boyer frowned. "Jon, I hate it for you, and I admit I handled it all wrongly. But she is a principal witness, she was the principal suspect, she is our informant's and co-defendant's daughter, and she is Andrew Childs' widow, don't forget. Don't you want to protect her and yourself? Why are you suddenly hell-bent to throw this case away?"

"There's no way for me to forget who she is, and I'm not any less committed to seeing this case through to a successful conviction of Barnes. I've spent years of my career to nail this case and catch Andy's killer. You lay off Amanda." Jon's voice lowered. "I love her—don't you understand?"

"Are you sleeping with her?"

"That's none of your God damned business!" Jon slammed out of the room, leaving Boyer alone as he stamped upstairs.

Later, in a cool shower, Jon thought back. His anger had subsided somewhat, but he felt bereft and hollow. *I have to do something to occupy myself. Maybe I can get her to see reason when we have dinner Sunday.* The thought of seeing Amanda again filled him with renewed hope.

Chapter 16

"What a long day," Amanda muttered, as she walked in the door of the law office from court Wednesday afternoon. "Thank God choir practice tonight was cancelled. I am beat."

"Greg Boyer is on the line," Sheila informed Amanda.

Amanda hesitated. "OK," she replied, as she crossed over to her office, shut the door, and dumped her file and volume of *Ehrhardt's Evidence* on the desk.

She picked up the receiver. "Amanda Childs; may I help you?" she responded automatically, although her gut was churning.

"Mrs. Childs? Greg Boyer here," the voice came through, brisk and business-like.

"Mr. Boyer, what may I do for you?" Amanda tried to exude polite charm but tensed, wondering why the call, inasmuch as there was already an appointment with Boyer scheduled later in the week. "Is our appointment still on?"

"Yes," he assured her, "but Senator Whitmore's interference has proved to be troublesome, to say the least. I've been involved with wrangling with his staff to leave my case alone."

Amanda interposed, "I hope the trial is not put off or compromised. I'm really anxious for it to be over."

"So am I," Greg stated fervently. "What is the situation between you—and Jon?" he was direct.

"The engagement is still off," Amanda was brisk. "I have seen him once or twice, but mainly in conjunction with the advent of the Senator's inquiry."

He cleared his throat. "That's why I am calling. I have voiced my strong objection to their interviewing my witnesses, and spelled out the dangers posed by that while the criminal case is pending. But," he paused, "you know that this inquiry by the senator could lead to the defense's claim that new evidence has been uncovered, and a demand for any *Brady* material."

"I am aware of that danger," Amanda replied quietly. "And not only would that cause another complication, but a continuance also, as well as fertilizing the chances for the jury to find reasonable doubt."

"Exactly," Greg breathed. "Mrs. Childs," he hesitated. "Senator Whitmore stated he does not want to pose any obstacles to the prosecution, and is willing to defer any further inquiry until after the trial. However, he has asked to speak to you. Alone."

Amanda was silent. The voice asked, "Are you there?"

"Yes," she replied. "When?"

"His office is going to coordinate with you on a time. Mrs. Childs," he hesitated, "I hate to ask you to do this, but . . . ."

The unspoken question hung in the air. Amanda did not speak.

"Mrs. Childs?"

"I'm here," she stated shortly. "Yes, I will meet with him. Anything to keep this case on schedule."

"Are you sure? If you want, I can accompany you. I can insist that it be recorded."

"No. It's all right. I can handle it." She was rigid. What did Whitmore want?

"Please keep me in the loop and contact me after the meeting," Boyer's voice sounded as though he was pleading.

She rang off. Almost immediately the intercom buzzed. "A Mr. Knox is on the phone, said you knew him."

"I'll take it," Amanda replied as she picked up the receiver and pushed the button. "Amanda Childs. What is this about, Mr. Knox?"

"Are you alone?" the voice asked.

"Yes. Answer my question," she demanded.

"I have just faxed you some documents to show you my good faith. We need to talk."

Sheila peeked in the door, papers in hand. Amanda nodded, and Sheila quietly brought her the papers and quickly left. "I've just received them," she replied, glancing at the papers. "What are these? Lab results?" she quizzed him.

"HLA results, what was used years ago for paternity testing, prior to perfection of DNA testing."

"Human leukocyte antigen. Yes, I am aware of that. Where did you get this?"

"Not over the phone. Follow the instructions."

The line went dead.

She hung up, sitting in her chair to read the pages in her hand. On one sheet was scrawled an unsigned message:

Tonight at 8:00 in front of the Godwin General Store. Alone, please. Both my safety and yours could depend on your discretion. The fewer who know this right now, the better.

The next few pages contained lab results with comparison of genetic markers, and photographs showing a young woman, a baby of about a year old, and a young man. The man's name was listed as 'Thomas Smithson', and the fax of the photo was dark, but Amanda saw the striking resemblance to Senator Whitmore. The results showed that there was a 99.4% chance that 'Smithson' was the father. Looking at the blurred picture of the baby and the mother, Amanda realized she had never seen any baby pictures of Andrew, and only the one framed photograph of his mother, a lovely woman in her thirties who resembled the young woman's photo on the faxed page.

She sat back, her mind whirring. So Dover's story about the senator's just recently knowing of Andrew's existence might not be true. Obviously the testing could not have been done without the father's participation. But was it Whitmore? And why? From where did Knox get this? Why would Knox or she be in danger?

"I don't have time for this," she said aloud. With Ralph still on his honeymoon and their business in full swing, she was carrying a double caseload. Furthermore, Barnes' trial loomed large, and she did not relish what was coming. Not only would the trial and her testimony be taxing, but the advent of the publicity surrounding the case and the disclosures about her unwitting involvement and history were frightening.

Now she was also dealing with the high probability that her childhood friend Alan Young would be charged with homicide because of the untimely death of his wife.

The disclosure about Andrew's paternity was almost overwhelming, because it raised in her mind questions about whether Andrew had kept matters from her. Oh, Andy, she cried silently, did you know about your father? Was it Whitmore? Why didn't you tell me?

Now this unknown person, ostensibly a reporter, had set an appointment for her to meet him tonight, and cautioning her to keep silent about his revelations. I'm so afraid of making a misstep, she thought. But she knew that it was dangerous for her to keep such an appointment alone, without anyone's knowledge of where she was.

She shook herself mentally. I've got to concentrate. There's so much to do. She busied herself making a list of things to do and prioritizing them. She remembered her resolve to check on Alan Young.

She picked up the phone and dialed a number. "Alan? Amanda here," she said.

"Amanda! I was just thinking of you," the voice responded. "I am on my way home. I had to run into the office for a little while. Danny is doing all he can, but he is overwhelmed. And Dr. Howells has been so good to pull duty for me at the hospital during all this. You don't know how grateful I am for the presents you sent the boys. And we were glad to spend the time with you at lunch yesterday."

"I was happy to do that. I know it's a difficult time," Amanda was sober. "How are you, Alan?"

"Well, I keep looking over my shoulder, expecting to see Shelby there any minute, then it hits me all over again that she's—she's gone. Then I worry about the police coming to get me, arresting me in front of my patients, or worse, in the presence of Josh and Caleb."

Amanda interposed, "Do not worry about the latter. I've already made arrangements with Sheriff Watson and Bruce. If worse comes to worst and another warrant comes down the pike, they are to contact me, and you can turn yourself in." She smiled grimly. "Clarence won't be pulling shenanigans like that again. A memo went out to the deputies about chain of command. And I'm going to do all I can to try to keep it from happening, Alan."

"Thank you." She could hear the relief in Alan's voice. "I know you have so much on your hands right now. I hope it doesn't come to that, but after what we've already been through—"

"I know, dear," Amanda soothed him.

"I'm grateful to you for your efforts, Amanda. One good thing, if anything can be good, that has come out of this is that so many friends and church members have rallied around us, making sure the boys are busy and taken care of, bringing food and checking on us. Charlie and Jill have been great."

"I think Jill has already adopted the boys," laughed Amanda. "She needs to have one of her own."

Alan rejoined, "Don't rush them. They haven't been married but a couple of years. That's what I keep telling them. But Jill is anxious."

He paused. "How about you, Amanda? I had hoped by now that you would be making a nest of your own. What about that guy Jon?"

Amanda was silent a moment. "That's on hold right now. I've got to get through this trial, and there are several other matters pressing right now."

"You know, you can stay busy with all these 'pressing matters' until life passes you by," Alan's voice was gentle. "Every day I berate myself that I didn't spend more time with Shelby."

"I know, Alan," Amanda was sympathetic.

"So don't let that happen to you," Alan choked. "And come to dinner one night. It makes the nights less lonely for us when your smiling face graces us. I'll even cook."

"I will. Take care."

She rang off. Poor Alan, she thought. What a blow for him. At moments when she was reminded of Alan's troubles, all the pain of losing Andy washed over her afresh.

"There's no time to dwell on that," she said aloud, looking at her watch and realizing that it was 5:30. My heavens, she thought. She got up and walked out into the spacious work room where Sheila was still typing, her headset on.

Amanda went up and put her hand on Sheila. Sheila started, then looked up at Amanda and smiled, pausing the dictation machine and removing her headset.

"Sheila, I know nothing is more fun than working here, but you should have gone home already," Amanda joked.

"I just know that you are doing so much with Ralph gone, and I want to help you all I can," Sheila spoke.

"But we have to rest some time. And you've ploughed through so much today." Amanda looked at the empty inbox and the neat stack of documents awaiting her review and signature. "Ralph will be back next week, and we'll make him pay dearly," she added, a broad smile on her face. "Go home," she admonished Sheila gently. "It will be waiting for us tomorrow, I promise you."

"What about you?" Sheila looked at her boss concernedly.

"I have a couple of phone calls to make, then I will also be out of here," Amanda promised her.

Amanda and Sheila made the rounds, locking the doors and checking the windows. Sheila let herself out.

Just as Amanda turned to go back to her office, she heard voices outside the door, and it opened again. "Sheila, have you forgotten some—" she began as she turned toward the sound, then stopped as she saw Charles Petrino standing there.

"Come on in, Charlie, and lock the door," she called as she made her way back to her office.

He followed her into the room. She waved her hand toward the armoire. "Make yourself at home," she said as she regained her chair.

"No, I'm just off duty."

"We're going to have to quit meeting like this. People will talk."

"Been there, done that, got the t-shirt," Petrino quipped, as she blushed. "Actually, I'm here with a message from Jon. He asked me to check on you and send his regrets. He wanted to surprise you, show up and take you to dinner, but he was surprised at work himself with a task tonight."

"It's just as well, except that I needed a bodyguard for tonight," Amanda murmured.

"What for?" Charlie was curious.

"Oh, nothing," Amanda said quickly. Now who will I tell about my rendezvous tonight?

"Out with it, Mandy," Petrino commanded, his eyes on her.

"It's just—just that—" she stopped. Knox was reluctant to talk on the phone, and seemed concerned for his safety and hers. What if her office was bugged? Surely not, she thought.

Picking up her purse she said loudly, "I'll walk you to your car. I saw a weed I want to pull up in the flower bed."

Charlie stared at her amazedly, as she grabbed her purse, took his arm and steered him out of the office around to the back parking lot.

"Charlie, I was contacted by a man identifying himself on the phone as Michael Knox with the *Washington Post*," she began, her voice low. "He wanted me to meet him tonight at the Godwin General Store to show me some material he has about Andrew."

"Andrew?" Petrino started, but Amanda put her finger to her lips quickly.

"What, do you think someone is listening in?" he asked her.

"I don't know, but this guy faxed me this," she pointed to the papers folded and in her purse. "Not here," she whispered as he made as if to reach for them.

"What are they?"

"HLA blood testing results showing some guy looking a lot like Senator Thomas Whitmore as the father of Andrew. If so, he would just about have to know back then about Andrew's being his son."

Charlie looked thunderstruck. "You're kidding?" He glanced down at his watch. "Listen, come home with me. Jill has dinner ready. You can tell me there."

Amanda demurred, but he insisted. "What time were you to meet him?"

"Eight o'clock."

"We have time. You don't think I'm going to let you go off alone to meet some stranger, when you don't even have any verification he's who he says he is? Follow me home." His tone brooked no discussion.

He walked her to her car, then followed her in his. She drove for several blocks, finally pulling up to the curb in front of a cheerful Victorian home, freshly painted. As she disembarked, Jill walked out on the porch.

"Amanda! Please come in," she held out her hands to Amanda, who took them and squeezed them gratefully.

"Jill. I'm so sorry to crash like this," Amanda began, "particularly with it being your first night home together after all this with Shelby."

But Jill interrupted her, "I'm glad Charlie was able to drag you over. I was just telling Charlie you work too hard, and we need to have you and Jon over for dinner."

Amanda smiled, but the reference to Jon made her wince inside. Will we ever be a couple, socializing with other couples, taking for granted our being together? she thought. It seemed more and more incredible.

Jill drew Amanda inside, chattering all the while, Amanda smiling and entering into her small talk. Jill and she walked into the bright kitchen, and Jill set another place at the table.

Soon they were all seated at the table. Jill made Amanda feel at home, and they talked about people in the community and current events. Jill kept the conversation light, trying to avoid the subject of Shelby's death. Charlie joined in, but his eyes were intent on Amanda, concern written on his face.

As Jill was clearing dishes away, Charlie asked Amanda, "Do we need to talk in private?"

"Charlie, I'm not going to ask you to come with me. I just want someone to know where I am," Amanda said quietly.

"I'm not letting you go alone," Charlie said, equally quietly. "So why don't you tell me what's going on?"

Jill turned back to the table, facing them. "Do I need to leave?"

"No," Amanda replied firmly. "I don't think spouses should have secrets from each other." She looked down at her hands. "So if I tell Charlie, you're entitled to know."

She summarized for them the events of the last few days, about the revelation regarding Andrew's paternity, and the two phone calls and facsimile. She pulled the papers out of her purse to show them.

"Why would this man call me twice, send me this and want to meet with me? If he isn't on the up and up, would he go to such elaborate lengths? I don't know."

Charlie studied the sheets. "You're right. None of this makes sense."

"He said to come alone," Amanda recalled. "For his safety and mine."

"Well, that ain't gonna happen," Charlie stood up. "I'll go and see this guy."

"No," Amanda replied forcefully. "I don't want to chase him off before we find out what he's up to, and how and where he got this. If he has this information, he has other information about Andy. I'm going to keep this appointment."

"She's right," Jill spoke up. They both looked at her. "I feel deep down this person means her no harm. Otherwise why go to that trouble? But you're right, too," she turned to Charlie. "You need to go with her."

Amanda stood, protesting. "No," but Jill laid her hand on Charlie's arm.

"Amanda, you don't need to go alone. Be careful, dear," she reached up and kissed Charlie's cheek. "I promised to check in on Alan and the kids anyway."

"I'll be back," he assured her tenderly. "Let's go."

Shrugging, Amanda followed him out of the kitchen toward the front door. "We'll take my car. If he's done research on me, he'll know what I'm driving," she explained.

Charlie nodded. "I'll drive."

"No," Amanda objected. "He'll expect to see me driving. You need to be in the back. We don't want to scare him."

"I'm not going to let you chauffeur me," Charlie sputtered. "I'll get in the back when we're almost there."

Amanda shrugged again, and walked out the door with him.

Chapter 17

"I really don't want to take you away from your time with Jill. You don't need to go with me. I can just check in with you later," Amanda protested as she reached for her seat belt.

"Shut up," Charlie admonished her. "There's no way you're going alone. I couldn't face Jon if something happened to you. Just drive."

She pushed the ignition button and the car sprang to life. She pulled out from the driveway, checking her mirrors, as Charlie checked his handgun. "Just in case," he quipped.

They were silent as she maneuvered through the streets of the town. Charlie kept directing her until she stopped at a stop sign and turned to him balefully.

"I know how to get where we're going," she spoke through clenched teeth.

"Mandy, I'm just trying to make sure no one is following us," Charlie rejoined quietly, looking out her rearview mirror.

"So am I," she countered, her rancor subsiding.

Soon they were on the ribbon of road heading south toward the beaches. Neither said anything, but they were both remembering past days when as teenagers they, along with Bill and Monica, would travel down to the beach in Bill's convertible to Bill's father's house on the gulf. They'd spend the day swimming, sunning, playing volleyball, crabbing and boiling their catch in a huge stock pot with corn on the cob, onions, shrimp, potatoes and whatever else. Bill would invite all his buddies for a party, and she and Monica were not allowed to stay for the rowdy evening festivities, by edict of their parents. Several times Charlie would volunteer to take them home.

Charlie glanced over at Amanda, and saw the pain in her eyes. He said softly, "Don't think about it."

"It's hard not to," she confessed, trying to smile. "My whole childhood was wrapped up with Monica and—and Bill," she sighed. "And you were always there, Charlie," she blushed. "How do you swallow that, ignore it, go on?"

"Amidst the pain are a bunch of great memories," Charlie spoke, looking out the windshield at the black road. "It takes time, Mandy, but one day we'll be able to sort those out. They are part of who we are. You can't just shove them all in the trash."

Amanda nodded. "Yeah, you and I might not have been friends but for those days and Bill's always pairing us up."

Charlie shook his head irritably. "Damn it, Mandy. Do you always take such a dim view of yourself? Bill had nothing to do with it. Sure, we were thrown together a lot because of Bill, but I volunteered most of the time. I was determined to know you since we were in second grade together."

He smiled. "I went home and told my dad about you that first day of school, that I was going to marry you. Dad thought you were the prettiest girl he had ever seen, and after that he teased me about you constantly. Every year after the first day of school he'd ask if you were in any of my classes."

"Sorry I was a source of ribbing from your dad," Amanda blushed.

"Hell, I had a crush on you throughout elementary school," Charlie laughed. "But you only had eyes for Bill. Then puberty hit, and I became too shy to act on those feelings."

"There was nothing shy about you, as I recall. You always had a bevy of girls giggling over you and flirting with you."

It was Charlie's turn to blush. Amanda continued, "I was surprised you had time to stand in as my date when Bill asked you. They were all jealous, and oh, the catty things they said. All true, of course—like you'd look twice at me with all those cheerleaders and majorettes surrounding you."

"I never knew that," Charlie was nonplussed.

"You guys are always oblivious," Amanda countered wryly. "You have no idea the manipulation we women pull to get you to dance our tunes."

"What? Like the prom?" Charlie chuckled.

"Exactly," Amanda grinned. "Except I was trying to be fair, stalling, giving you every opportunity to escape. There was a line of girls that wanted you to ask them."

"That was mean," Charlie exclaimed. "I didn't want to escape."

"How was I to know that? I just figured Bill put you up to it, the way he always did things," Amanda retorted.

"Why were you considering marrying Billy last year, after you rejected me?" Charlie asked suddenly.

Amanda, her eyes wide, sputtered, "Where would you get that idea? I was never committed to the idea of marrying Bill." She was defensive.

"But you thought about it," Charlie persisted.

Amanda was silent, staring at the road. Finally she replied, "I knew there was no danger of losing my heart to Billy."

"And you could have with me?" he was dubious.

"Yes," she surprised him. "Yes, Pete. I was drowning again. Andy was dead, Marjorie was gone so I couldn't cry on her shoulder, and I couldn't turn to you. So I guess Billy presented a possibility."

She paused, taking a deep breath. "He wanted to elope, kept pushing me to get married just—just before . . . ." Her voice trailed off. She cleared her throat. "I didn't understand his urgency then. Now I do." She shuddered. "But I couldn't give in to him in college, and I couldn't do it last—last year, thank God," she stammered.

"Not even—?" Charlie let the question hang.

"Not even," she refused to look at him.

"Thank God," he repeated fervently. She repressed another shudder at the thought that she had entertained the idea of a match with Billy.

They were again silent. He cleared his voice, breaking the silence. "When you set me up with Jill, that sent the message loud and clear that there was no reason for me to hope for you."

"Don't you love Jill?" Amanda exclaimed, surprised.

"I adore her. I'm grateful to you for introducing us. She means the world to me. I can't imagine living without her. But—"

"But nothing," Amanda contended fiercely. "I was in your words 'fucked up'. I can't even let myself have a meaningful relationship since Andy died."

"Not even with Jon?" Charlie demanded, his tone noncommittal.

"Especially with Jon," she replied desperately. "Don't you think I want that? That I crave what you and Jill are building? A simple trusting relationship, a sharing of myself with someone who is physically there. But as long as Andrew's memory haunts me, I—" she paused, unable to finish the sentence. She took a deep breath. "I pray that this trial will lay some of that to rest, that I will feel that Andy's death was not in vain, that it had meaning, that he is vindicated."

"Avenged, you mean," Charlie almost whispered.

Suddenly wrathful, she lashed out. "Yes, maybe I do. Is that so wrong?"

"What if, after all this anguish, it doesn't turn out as you wish? Or it does, but does not bring peace? You have pinned a lot on this trial, Mandy. It is just a trial. Barnes is ruined, no matter what happens." His voice lowered. "Andy is dead, no matter what happens."

"I know," she said wearily. "But Jon needs to win. Andy needs to win. I need my integrity back. I need to be free."

"Is that going to make everything OK?" Charlie rebutted gently.

Amanda had no answer for him. They both fell silent.

After several minutes, he asked her, "Have you checked this guy out?"

"If he *is* Michael Knox, he is a nationally known investigative reporter and has won some prestigious awards. I don't understand why he would necessarily be covering this story. It doesn't seem to be his type of news."

"IF he is Michael Knox," Charlie repeated. "Did he tell you at all why he's skulking around, why he is worried about safety?"

"No. But I think it would be worrisome to possibly expose an extremely influential public servant, a senator, no less, of conduct unbecoming him. If you believe Robert Ludlum and Tom Clancy, men have been killed for just that."

Charlie's jaw was set grimly. "Well, we are almost there. You need to pull over and let me slip into the back seat."

She nodded. At a gas station in a nearby community, she pulled in. The station was still open, but the area was quiet with only light traffic.

They pulled off again, Charlie in the back. Charlie asked, "What do you hope to find out?"

"Well, I want to know what he knows and see his proof. I want to know the truth, but I'm more interested in knowing how he knows, where he found this. I guess, "Amanda paused, "I guess I want to know if there's any indication Andy knew of all this and kept it from me . . ." she faltered, suddenly ashamed of her admission.

"Do you really think Andy would do that?" Charlie asked her. She could feel his eyes boring through her back.

"Charlie, I don't know any more," she sighed. "You know, we could turn around. We could go back. I can wait for the story to break in the newspapers."

"Do you want to?" he stared at her.

"No," she admitted. "I have to know."

A few minutes later, even though it seemed longer, they arrived at the general store, which was closed. There was no sign of life. Amanda looked at her clock. "It's 7:51. So we're on time. I guess we wait."

"There is a full moon. Cut the car off and douse the lights," Charlie suggested. "It's not hot yet so we can stand it without the AC."

She did as he suggested. They sat there a while in the darkness. There was no activity on the country road.

"Do you love him, baby?" Charlie's voice broke the stillness.

"Yes, Pete, I do," she whispered. "But I'm scared."

"Like you were with me?"

"Yes," she nodded, her voice small.

"Give me your hand," he whispered.

She turned around and placed her hand in his. He clasped it. "Jon is not going to be content for you to fix him up with someone else."

She smiled. "What, you think I'll need to use a gun this time?"

Charlie did not smile back. "Mandy, do not keep chasing love away," he implored her.

Charlie's cell phone buzzed. He relinquished her hand and looked at the number. He told Amanda quietly, "It's Jon."

Charlie answered the phone. "What are you doing?" she could hear Jon's voice through the line.

"I'm on a detail. What about you?"

"Is Amanda with you?"

Charlie looked at Amanda. She nodded her head. "Yes."

"Stay there. I'm coming to you."

Before Charlie could ask any questions, the line was dead.

"Something's up," Amanda spoke aloud. She unlocked the car door and opened it.

Charlie reached over the seat and touched her shoulder. "What do you think you're doing?"

"Investigating," she replied, shaking loose.

Pulling a small flashlight out of the pocket in the car door, she stepped out, Charlie following suit. She walked slowly around the loose gravel and sand making up the parking area for the store. At a pay phone she stopped.

"Look at this," she pointed. There was the sign of a vehicle spinning off, but only one tread.

"Motorcycle?" Charlie mused.

"This Knox fellow is a connoisseur of motorcycles. I did my research," Amanda responded.

"That doesn't mean anything," Charlie pointed out.

"But this does." Amanda bent down and picked up a small object lying on the ground half buried in the gravel. "He's been here. He left his calling card."

She studied it then handed it to Charlie, who took her flashlight. "A Virginia driver's license issued to Michael Knox," he observed.

"Something has happened," Amanda stared out into the night. "He left that for me to find, part of his 'good faith'."

"We need to call in the Bureau if he's missing," Charlie countered, but Amanda shook her head, taking the driver's license back from Charlie.

"I'll keep this. Something tells me the Bureau already knows," her voice was grave. "Jon didn't ask where we were. How does he know where to find us?"

Charlie stared at her and nodded. "You're right."

"Someone's coming," she noted, seeing headlights approaching rapidly along the road. "Let me handle this," she ordered Petrino.

"But I'm the law here," he reminded her.

"You're here only at my behest," she retorted.

The big black sedan pulled up to them, and Jon stepped out of the passenger side. Kimball opened the driver's door, but Jon said tersely, "You stay there."

He strode over to Amanda and Charlie. "What are you two doing here?" he demanded, his eyes glittering as he looked at her. Although his voice was calm and authoritative, she could sense that he was barely controlling his temper.

"I could ask you the same thing," she smiled sweetly. "Charlie and I were just looking for a place to go parking," she added flippantly.

He took her arm and steered her toward her car. "I was looking for you," his eyes looked from her to Charlie and back.

"How did you know where to find us?" she refuted, her eyes meeting his coldly.

"I have my ways," he smiled grimly. "Amanda, you shouldn't be here," he squeezed her arm gently.

"Answer my question," she shook free of him, her eyes not leaving his.

"You know I can't do that," his eyes beseeched her.

"Is Michael Knox safe? Is he OK?" she demanded, her voice so low only Jon could hear her.

He looked over at Charlie, who was staring at both of them. He nodded.

"Please take her home, Charlie," he spoke to Petrino.

Turning to her, Jon added reproachfully, "Amanda, you have no business being out here, even with Charlie to protect you. We need to talk but now is not the time. It will all be OK. I promise you."

She allowed him to lead her to the car. "Please," he whispered. "For both your sakes."

She thought, Michael Knox must be in protective custody. Jon knows where he is.

"Charlie, let's go home," she said aloud, her jaw set arrogantly. "We're not going to learn anything tonight."

"I'll drive this time," Charlie walked up between her and Jon and took the keys out of her hand, his eyes silently sizing up Jon.

Jon said simply, "Thanks, Charlie," as he stepped back, taking Amanda's arm and guiding her to the passenger side.

He opened the door for her. She whispered, "I need to know, Jon."

He pulled her into his arms and kissed her, a lingering kiss.

"Don't patronize me," she warned ominously. "I can't be kissed into submission, Jon."

"Later," he promised, his lips against her mouth.

She got into the car and Charlie pushed the ignition and pulled out, leaving Jon and Kimball behind.

"So what was that about?" Charlie demanded, his eyes on the road.

Amanda reached over and turned the radio on, choosing a 70s rock station and turning up the volume. She leaned over and said in Petrino's ear, "I think they have Michael Knox."

"Why do you think that?" he whispered back, looking at her momentarily, before turning his eyes back on the road.

"Trust me," she said before settling back into her seat.

She turned the volume down. "Well, what do you want to do now? Go lie on the beach in the moonlight?"

He shook his head. "As tempting as that might be, I'm taking you home."

"We'll drop you off at your house and I'll go home from there," Amanda closed her eyes and leaned back.

"No, too much strange stuff is going on. I'm going to make sure you are safe. In fact, I don't like the idea of you at the farm alone. Why don't you spend the night with us?"

Amanda stared at him. "That's crazy. Why wouldn't I go home? Fred is installing a new security system. It's safe."

"No," Charlie was adamant. "I'll check with Fred tomorrow to see if he's finished. You need to stay in town tonight."

Amanda flushed, and he could tell she was not happy being ordered about. "No. If it makes you happier, I'll stay at the office," she countered. "I have clothes there, and can sleep and get a shower there."

He started to object, but she put a hand on his arm. "It has a security system. I'll be fine."

"I can see why Ralph is so aggravated around you," he muttered. "Damn it. You don't listen to anybody."

"You rejected my plan, I rejected your plan, I offered an alternative," she retorted. "It's called compromise, Charlie. You should try it sometime with Jill."

"Hell, I just let her win rather than fight," he laughed then. "I know we men can't win."

"Could you do me a favor tomorrow?" Amanda suddenly asked.

"What?" he countered, surprised.

"Do you have some equipment that can check for bugs, eavesdropping, electronic surveillance, that sort of thing?"

"Bruce does," Charlie looked at her.

"I want the office, the car and the house checked out, if it's not too much trouble," Amanda was careful not to look at him.

He studied her a moment. "No problem."

Moments later they pulled up to Charlie's house. He said, "I'll follow you to the office."

"OK, Charlie, that's just plain silly," she remonstrated, aggravated. "I can drive myself there, and I'll call you as soon as I get there and lock myself in."

He stared at her long and hard, then shrugged. "I'll give you ten minutes. One of my officers will be patrolling that area by the time you get there."

"OK," Amanda jumped out and ran around the car as Petrino let himself out. "Thank Jill for dinner."

She pulled off before he could pose further objection, and made her way to the office. Geez, she thought. I'm surrounded by bossy, chauvinistic males.

Moments later she pulled into the back parking lot. She noted that the street light was out. Damn, she thought. She grabbed the door key in her right hand. She was suddenly nervous. It's just all this cloak and dagger stuff, she told herself.

She got out, pushing the button to lock the car, and quickly made her way to the back door. Finding the lock, she stuck the key in and turned the lock.

As she pushed open the door, quickly cut off the alarm and groped inside for the light, a voice behind her said softly, "Don't do that."

She started to scream, but a hand was placed over her mouth, and she was roughly pushed inside.

Chapter 18

Jon Connor watched the car bearing Charlie and Amanda until it was out of sight, then rejoined Kimball in the black car.

"How did that go?"

Jon frowned. "Not good. First Knox isn't exactly happy with our timing now that we're providing him protection, then we find out he was scheduled to meet tonight with Amanda. This just gets worse."

"Trouble in paradise?" Kimball asked.

"She's hell bent that this case against Barnes not be compromised."

Kimball was sympathetic. "I'm sorry, man. But you know the Bureau supports her view. Are you sure you want to be a part of this debriefing with the reporter?"

"Yes, I'm very interested," Jon replied. "Evidence that Andrew Childs was Senator Whitmore's son? This I've got to hear."

"Well, we're stashing him at a rental house owned by one of the local sheriff's friends. It's not far." Kimball glanced over at Jon. "You sure you don't need to be mending fences?"

"Let's go," Jon was terse. "I'll do that later."

Amanda, caught off guard, struggled against her attacker as he forced her into the office and closed the door. She could see nothing.

"Amanda Childs?" he asked against her ear, his voice beseeching, his hand still against her mouth. "I'm sorry. Didn't mean to startle or manhandle you, but it was necessary. I'm Mike Knox."

Her eyes went wide.

"Please don't scream. A police car just went by," he begged, his voice a whisper. "I have evidence that Senator Whitmore has known from the beginning about Andy's being his son. I promised I would inform you before I released this. Will you please not scream?"

She nodded, and he let her go.

She turned, facing him, and gasped. "Why are you hiding out here?"

He took off his motorcycle helmet. "I had to hide my bike in the bushes a couple blocks away and make it here on foot. I just escaped from the FBI guys providing me 'protection'." He smiled wryly. "I made you a promise, and I mean to keep it."

She walked over to the desk and turned on a lamp. She peered at him in the sudden dim light. "OK, I believe you're who you say you are," she said quietly. "Why did you have to scare me? And why did you escape?"

"I could not be sure whether I was trusting the right people. It's hard to tell—all feds end up looking alike." He gave her a boyish grin. "You sure you can trust me?"

"I did my homework." Despite her scare, she couldn't help but smile back. "What you have to tell me must be awfully important," she murmured.

Just then a cop car drove through the parking lot. She quickly doused the light, speaking in a whisper. "Mike, you can't stay here, you know. I just left the chief of police, and I'm supposed to call him to tell him I made here all right. He has cruisers patrolling."

Mike's smile faded. "Well, I guess several agencies will be looking for me now."

"Shhh," she warned. She could see the cop talking into his radio, no doubt reporting that her car was at the office, but no lights were on.

She moved closer to Mike. "I may be just overdramatic, but I don't know but what the office is bugged," she whispered. "So we can't safely talk here, and if someone is listening we have to get you out quick. But I must call Charlie and give him the head's up, or the cops AND the feds will be crawling this place any minute."

He looked at her suspiciously, then nodded.

She picked up the office phone and dialed a number. "Charlie?" she spoke. "Amanda. I'm here, and fine. I think I will go ahead and turn in tonight. Talk to you tomorrow." She paused. "Yes, a cop just went by checking the premises. I'm fine," she repeated. "I left the lights off. Yes, the alarm is on."

She hung up. "OK, Mike," she whispered, "we have to get you out of here. I've got to figure out where."

"I mailed some documents to your law partner's home address," Mike supplied, also whispering.

"Ralph? How did you know—never mind. You're a reporter," Amanda replied. "We've been leaving the mail on his kitchen table. He's still on his honeymoon. So I guess that's where we go."

She looked out the blinds over the window in the back door to see if the coast was clear. She nodded. As they stepped out, he handed his helmet to her. "Leave your car here—less questions."

Minutes later, they had trekked to where he had hidden his motorcycle. She looked on in admiration. "An Indian Chief? Cool. You must have a cast-iron butt."

He grinned. "It's an interest of mine. How far to your partner's house?"

"Not far," she said, putting the helmet on her head and strapping it on.

"Point the way," he straddled the machine. "Need help getting on?"

"I can figure it out," she climbed on and settled behind him.

She pointed out the direction to him, and they were off. Amanda grabbed on to Knox as he took off at a high rate of speed.

Just within sight of where Jon left his car, Kimball's cell phone went off. He answered it. "Kimball." He listened a few minutes. "Shit! You sure? How far a head start? You don't know? We'll be right there."

Jon asked, "What is it?"

"The guys just showed Knox in the house, and he said he needed to get some papers from his saddlebag. Instead he just disappeared, took his bike and hauled ass. No one even saw him leave, so we don't know how long he's been gone."

"Zeke is slipping." Jon stared at him. The realization dawned on him. "Amanda. He was mad that we foiled his attempt to make contact with her. That's where he is heading. Drop me off at my car. I'm going to Mainville."

In just a few minutes, Amanda and Michael Knox pulled into the driveway to Ralph's house. As a precaution she had Knox round the block, so that they could assure themselves they were not being followed. Once in the driveway Amanda pushed a button, and the garage door opened. Knox slowly cruised in, and Amanda hit the button to close the door.

Knox parked, hopped off and held his hand out to Amanda, helping her off. He grabbed a small duffle bag out of one of the saddlebags, and set the helmet handed to him by Amanda on the seat.

He admired the black Lexus sports car sitting beside them. "A bachelor's car," he noted.

"His bachelor days are over," quipped Amanda. "He's sporting a SUV now. If I know Claire, I have a feeling that after the honeymoon this will be for sale. This way."

She unlocked the door and beckoned him to follow her. "Careful," she called. "I don't want to cut lights on until we get to the study."

"I could really use something cold to drink. I'm parched," he suggested.

He gingerly followed her through the murky darkness lit only by shafts of moonlight intermittently shining through windows. She stopped suddenly, and he almost bumped into her. She opened a refrigerator, and pointed inside.

"Help yourself," she offered.

He grabbed a soft drink and reached over to the counter, snagging an apple in a bowl.

He followed her. She cut on a light over a table where mail was piled up.

"Quickly," she said. "Do you recognize any of these as your package?"

He looked through the various envelopes on the table and finally grabbed one, nodding at her. She cut the light off. "Follow me."

They arrived at the study, where she turned on a lamp and quickly checked to make sure the blinds and shutters were closed. She walked around cutting on other lamps in the room, illuminating the comfortable room lined with bookcases, with a desk, leather chairs and a sofa.

Amanda took the envelope from Knox and seated herself at the desk, indicating he should sit.

"Now, Mr. Knox, tell me why we needed to meet," she inquired, tearing open the envelope and pulling out the papers therein.

Jon was heedless of the speed limit, angry that the Bureau had botched up such a simple plan. He knew he was to blame, and needed to salvage the situation. He also worried that Amanda was possibly in danger, if the reporter was being watched.

He mentally retraced their steps, reviewing the recent events leading up to the present. After locating and tailing the reporter, it had been determined that others were apparently looking for him as well. It was decided, after Knox's editor made a call to Kimball personally, that he should be approached that evening to inform him of that fact and to offer 'protective custody' in exchange for information from him. Kimball had called Jon to make up part of the intercept team.

Jon had met up with Kimball, and quickly climbed into Kimball's car. "He's just ahead—don't want to lose him," Kimball said urgently, as he sped off.

They carefully tailed the man, who was driving a vintage motorcycle.

"You sure this is the guy?" Jon was incredulous.

"Yes. We made a positive ID earlier today, and have had him under surveillance since then. He's big into motorcycles."

Kimball followed at a distance for several miles. Suddenly Knox ended up stopping at the little general store in the small isolated community. Kimball quickly pulled off beside the road and extinguished the lights. They watched as the rider sat placidly in the parking lot, not far from a pay telephone out in the open.

Kimball looked at his watch. "You know, we may not have a better opportunity than right now, with him stopped."

"It appears he is waiting for someone," Jon pointed out. "Don't you want to find out who his contact is?"

Kimball snorted. "In a perfect world, yes, but we need to drop the net while there are no witnesses. That will be hard enough to accomplish. We don't need any additional complications. We really need to leave no trace." He smirked. "Did you ever think you would be doing U.S. Marshal's work?"

"It's not too bad," Jon retorted. "I've worked closely with some of them."

Kimball watched for a moment. "What do you think? Now?"

Jon shrugged. "No time like the present."

Knox just sat in the parking lot, his helmet still on, apparently waiting for someone or something. Kimball eased back onto the road and cruised up to the parking lot, suddenly pulling in and up alongside him. Jon stepped out. "Michael Knox?"

He stiffened, and quickly cranked the cycle as if to flee. But Jon stepped in front of the bike, his badge out, putting his hand on the gear handle. "FBI. We just want to talk."

Knox tried to jerk away, but Jon held firm and killed the switch. Defiant, Knox raised the visor on his helmet. "I don't know what you want. I'm not guilty of anything. I'm just waiting for a friend," he was wary.

"Did you realize you're being watched?" Jon asked curiously.

"Since when does the FBI work for Congress?" Knox, unblinking, met his question with a question.

"We don't," Jon grinned. "But your boss was concerned enough about your safety to call in a favor and have us look you up."

"Yeah, right."

"No, he's telling the truth," Kimball walked up beside Knox. "Jim Talbot has friends in high places too. He's a good man."

"You know my editor?" Knox was skeptical.

"Yes. He says you've crossed swords with some big guns lately. And he hasn't heard from you in a couple of days."

"Maybe, maybe not," the reporter was cautious, appraising the two men. "What's it to you?"

"Nothing much, unless you would like some protection."

"You think I need protecting?" Knox looked at Connor suspiciously.

"Don't you?" Jon stared back.

There was a small silence. Knox nodded, and pulled off his helmet. "But I have something I have to do first. I made a promise to someone. Can't I check in with you later tonight?"

Kimball said brusquely, "Now or never. As it is, our ass is hanging out here in public. Bad for business. Not good for either of us. What's it gonna be?"

Knox frowned, as another dark sedan pulled up. "Shit," he whispered. "OK, I'll follow you."

Jon laughed. "No way we're going to leave you out as a target. Zeke," he gestured to the officer walking up, "will drive the Indian back behind us."

"Hell, man, I don't let just anyone sit the Chief," Knox protested. "This is my baby."

Zeke looked admiringly at the low-slung carriage of the motorcycle. "She's a beaut. I'll take good care of her. It's not far."

Knox shrugged and handed his helmet to the officer, getting off the bike. Jon escorted him to Kimball's car.

Jon had found the young reporter to be chatty on the way to the location where he was to be housed. He introduced himself to Knox, who looked at him with interest.

"You were in charge of the final investigation that netted the Barnes fellow, weren't you?"

Jon was surprised Knox had recognized his name, but acknowledged the fact.

"You and Andrew Childs were colleagues?"

"Yes," Jon acknowledged.

"Friends?"

Jon hesitated, again surprised. "Yes."

Knox grinned. "Is it true that you and Amanda Childs are an item?"

Jon, again startled, was momentarily speechless. But Knox smiled. "It's OK. I have done my homework."

"No, we are not an 'item', as you put it," Jon said icily. "She is an extraordinary woman who loved her husband dearly."

"And you are now in love with her, and she broke off the engagement," Knox inserted smoothly.

As Jon flushed, Knox continued, "Agent Connor, I'm not trying to piss you off. But I'm very good at creating a network and working it, milking it for necessary information. Anything going on between you and Mrs. Childs is only incidental to my inquiry, and I'm not interested in reporting that."

Jon, somewhat mollified, asked, "Why are you so forthcoming with me? Aren't you suspicious of me? I'm a fed, and you don't know me."

Knox gazed at him. "Andy told me you could be trusted."

"Andy told you?" Jon was stunned. "How did you know Andy?"

"Long story. What say we wait until we get there? I could use something cold to drink."

Jon stared at him. "Why were you so against coming with us tonight at first?"

"Because I had an appointment with Amanda Childs," Knox answered him truthfully. "I had promised to provide information to her before it became public, and you interrupted my accomplishing that."

"Tonight? You were going to meet Amanda? Where?"

"Right where you picked me up," Knox replied, looking at him. "At the general store. At 8:00. I guess she didn't tell you."

Jon looked at his watch. It was almost 8:15. "Damn!" he muttered. "Alone?"

"Yes," Knox responded. "It was safer for both of us, or so I thought until you guys showed up. If you had tabs on me, others might have tabs on her."

It was at that point that Jon realized his mistake. In his concern for Amanda, he had left the reporter in the care of the other agents to escort Knox to the safe house, while he and Kimball raced back to the general store. On a hunch he called Petrino, and found to his relief that he was with Amanda. *At least she's not alone*, Jon thought. But in the meantime Knox decided to make good his escape, ostensibly to accomplish his mission.

Now Jon was racing to Mainville, hoping to intercept her and Knox. *I let my feelings for Amanda and my concern for her safety cloud my judgment*, he berated himself, as he noted how fast he was driving. *Why didn't she call me?* he fumed. And now Knox was again out there, vulnerable, and probably on his way to rendezvous with Amanda, recklessly putting her at risk as well.

Jon headed straight to the farm, surmising that Amanda would be home. As he pulled up to the gate at Fred's property, Vaughan was outside waiting for him.

"Amanda at home?" Jon asked.

Vaughan shook his head, concern written on his face. "She has not made it. I'm worried. I was waiting for her because there was—something at the farm I wanted her to see."

"She's not home?" Jon's heart lurched. He pulled out his cell phone and called Petrino.

After a few rings, Charlie's voice came on the line. "Where's Amanda?" Jon plunged in, skipping the preliminaries.

Petrino, suddenly alert, replied, "She insisted she was spending the night at the law office. I talked her out of going home to the farm, but she didn't want to stay with us. We compromised. I hadn't called Fred yet."

"Are you sure?" Jon asked anxiously.

"I had a cop patrolling the area, and she just called me a little while ago to tell me she had arrived safely, that she was going to bed. Her car is in the parking lot. Why?" Charlie was suddenly suspicious.

"She was to meet Michael Knox tonight, wasn't she?" Jon asked excitedly.

"Yes," Petrino affirmed. "Do you know where he is?"

"We did, but he has given us the slip. He made a comment that we prevented his fulfilling a 'promise' to meet with her." Jon took a breath. "Charlie, I think he's on his way to find her. And Charlie, someone's tried to off the guy twice. He's trying to hide out from someone, but we don't know whom and if he's being watched right now."

"Where are you now?" Petrino wanted to know.

"At Fred's. I'm on my way to the office now."

"I'll have a unit there immediately. I will try to raise her, make sure she is OK."

Jon hung up. Fred stared at him. "Is she in danger?"

"I don't think she's in danger from this Knox fellow, but I'm worried about who may be watching him. I'm concerned that whoever that is may not want him to divulge his information."

"What can I do?" Fred wanted to know.

"Just keep an eye out, in case he or she shows up here," Jon replied tersely. "I'll call you when I know something."

He u-turned and started to town. He pulled out his cell phone and tried Amanda's number. There was no answer. Her voice mail came on. "Amanda, it's Jon. Call me, please. It's urgent."

It was late, and Dover was standing on a balcony in D.C., smoking a cigarette. It was one of his rare indulgences, and generally saved for times when he needed to think, to sort through problems.

His cell rang, and he answered it. "Yes?"

"We were about to acquire the target, and some black cars picked him up."

"I should have known your guys would fail. Bureau?" Dover asked.

"Yes."

Dover smiled. "An added complication, but I'll handle it. Federal agencies can't keep a secret. My man will lead us to the prey."

Chapter 19

"Andy told me a lot about you. I'm glad we finally get to talk. I feel as though I already know you."

Amanda's eyes narrowed as she gazed at Mike Knox. "Andy? How did you know Andy?"

He looked at her quizzically. "You don't remember me, do you?"

"We've met?" Amanda frowned.

"Andy and I grew up together," Knox met her gaze. "We lived down the street from each other, went to school together, played ball, were best buddies. We always got together when he was in D.C."

Amanda, exhausted, laid the papers on the desk unexamined, and leaned back in the leather chair. "Mr. Knox, I have trouble believing that. You're not exactly unknown."

As the words left her mouth, a picture came unbidden into her head, of Andy and she on the porch swing with the newspaper, Andy's head resting on her lap as she read the cover story to him, something about an international disarmament conference, written by Knox. At one of his biting double entendres, Andy had laughed. "That sounds just like Mikey."

It suddenly hit her why he seemed so familiar. "I now remember you, from the wedding." She flushed. "You stood in as best man. Andy introduced you, but I honestly did not make the connection or remember you until just now. You didn't work for the *Post* then."

"I'm hurt," Knox laughed. "I thought I had made a favorable impression on Andy's girl."

"I'm sorry for not recognizing you earlier, Mr. Knox," murmured Amanda, embarrassed, "but a lot has happened since those days."

"Call me Mike," Knox leaned forward. "Did Andy ever tell you anything about his childhood? About where he grew up? About his family?"

As Amanda looked away, he nodded. "I thought not. He told me he didn't want anyone to know much about that past."

"Even his wife?" Amanda asked coldly.

"Especially you," Knox's tone was sympathetic.

"Why should I believe you? How could you even prove it to me?" Amanda demanded, as she pulled the papers toward her.

"Let me tell you the story, then the papers will make sense."

"I'm waiting," she looked up at him expectantly.

"We grew up in a small town, really a community, outside Chapel Hill, North Carolina. Sort of like Mayberry. However, real life is not as whimsical. Andy was raised by an aunt and uncle." Knox paused, his face sad. "His mother had been diagnosed with what today would be called a schizo-affective disorder, and was in and out of the state mental hospital."

"Oh, my," Amanda breathed.

At Amanda's sorrowful look, he nodded. "Yes. She had apparently left home right out of high school, got a job working for the local congressman as a secretary, then worked in New Jersey for some lobbyist, and met the senator while he was running for re-election to the House. He was so impressed he took her with him to Washington and gave her a job as his personal aide."

He leaned forward, his tone confidential. "Things got too personal, then she became pregnant. At that point she apparently had a breakdown. Rumor is that she tried to kill the senator—attacked him with a knife—and he had her committed. Turned out he was married to some old money that was backing his political aspirations.

"She came back home to her sister, who took care of her. Andy was born. Apparently Emily Childs was never the same. Aunt Chlothilde—Chloe—tried to keep as much of this from Andy as possible, but of course as he got older he learned bits of the story. Even though Chloe and Hank raised him just like he was theirs, his mom would get better and be released from the hospital, come home for short periods, and when she'd decompensate, she'd tell him his father was very important, famous, and going to show up and take them away one day."

Amanda stared at him, fascinated. Suddenly her phone beeped. She pulled it out of her purse, frowning.

"Just a minute." She looked at the numbers. "Charlie and Jon. That means they are looking for you."

She listened to the messages, and her frown increased. "They know you're missing. They're converging on the office, ostensibly to protect me."

She pushed a speed dial button and waited. Charlie's voice came on. "What is it?" she tried to sound casual, yawning as she spoke.

"Apparently Mr. Knox, your reporter friend, has disappeared, and Jon thinks he is on his way to meet you. Jon is on his way as well."

"Charlie, I was fast asleep," Amanda lied. "I'm so tired, and the place is locked up tight. No one's here and the alarm is on. Please call Jon off." She paused. "I'm just not up to talking to him tonight. I'm still mad at him." She listened a minute. "Please, Charlie. I promise to call you before unlocking the office door in the morning, and I'll call Jon in the morning. Just let me sleep." She listened a minute, irritated. "I'll call him myself, then." She hung up.

She hit another button, waiting while the phone rang. "Jon. Charlie said you're on your way here. I was asleep. I don't want to see you."

She paused. "No. I'm not letting you in. We can talk tomorrow."

Another pause. "Not tonight. If not for you, I'd know what Knox wanted. If you break in, I will sue the Bureau. I'll have your job. That won't do either of us any good. You know I'll do it too." She hung up.

"I have no idea if that will work, but hopefully I bought us just a little more time. Otherwise, they're going to find out I'm not at the office, and there will be a manhunt for both of us."

"You talk to your fiancé that way?" Knox was awed.

"He's not my fiancé, at least not right now," she retorted angrily. She turned back to Knox. "Please continue. How did you know all this, if Andy's aunt tried to keep it from him?"

"My mom and Chloe were best friends. And I was always a curious kid," he smiled briefly. "Eavesdropped a lot. Did lots of sleuthing. Andy and I were always 'investigating' something."

"Did Andy ever know or suspect that Senator Whitmore was his father?" Amanda was direct, staring at Knox.

Knox looked down at his hands, silent. Amanda prodded him. "I need to know. This is the reason I agreed to see you at all."

"Not until just a few weeks before he was killed," Knox responded sadly. "His mother died when he was ten, overdosed. His aunt would not tell him anything, told him no one there knew his father, and that his father died in the Vietnam War.

"Andy was bitter when his mom died. He hated his father, who he was convinced had abandoned them both, despite Chloe's stories to the contrary. He once told me if his dad was alive and he ever met the man he would kill him."

Amanda's eyes clouded with tears. "He would never talk of his father to me. I could tell it was a terribly painful subject."

"He adored his Uncle Hank, who was like a father to him. But then Hank had a massive heart attack and died during our senior year in high school. Chloe made Andy promise to go on to college, and he got a scholarship to Duke. I was accepted at UNC.

"Andy thought Chloe was paying for college with his mom's life insurance proceeds, but it was apparently money put away, sent by his real father over the years. Andy knew nothing about it.

"When Chloe died, she had kept papers about Andy's paternity and his parents stowed away in a little wooden chest. She meant for him to have them after her death, but her daughter Esther just packed everything away in the attic of the farmhouse."

He paused. "Then one day Esther cleaned out the attic and she found the chest. Andy was off on assignment somewhere, and she didn't know how to reach him. But she knew that the two of us stayed in contact, so she entrusted the box and papers to me.

"Well, I was curious, and read through the materials. I knew I shouldn't, but it blew my mind. It was just too fantastic. I kept them until one day Andy was in D.C. and called me to meet him for drinks.

"I showed him the box, and he was stunned. He took the box and studied the items for several days. Then one day he called me and gave me some of the originals of the documents."

"Why?"

"He told me that he wanted to keep some of the items and photos, that he was going to have to tell you about it, and he dreaded it. He was shook up about it. He was having trouble accepting it himself and was pretty upset. But he said there was so much going on, that his investigation at the Bureau was reaching a critical point, and he just didn't have the time or strength to deal with all this about his father right then.

"He told me that if anything happened, if Whitmore ran for President, to use my best judgment about divulging this information." He leaned forward again, his eyes intent upon hers. "Amanda, that was less than two weeks before he was found dead."

Amanda closed her eyes, heedless of the tears streaking down her face. "Yet you've done nothing with this information for five years," she whispered.

Knox shook his head sadly. "There were two reasons for that. Firstly, he was adamant that as long as Whitmore maintained the status quo, he didn't want the information divulged, at least until he decided what he wanted to do with it. I respected that. Whitmore didn't announce the possibility of his seeking the Presidency until just recently. That's when I made the tough decision and sent word to Whitmore that I had information about the Senator's past indiscretion."

Amanda opened her eyes and stared unseeingly at the papers on the desk. "And the other reason?"

"Andy kept some of the papers, as I said. I didn't have all the proof, particularly bank records showing deposits into the special trust account set aside for Andy. That shows the Senator knew about his son much longer than I think he'll try to let on. I tried to check in the places I thought Andy might secrete the papers." He paused. "I finally concluded he must have left them somewhere for you to find."

Amanda shook her head, overcome. They were both silent. She finally offered, "I came home one afternoon, and found him perusing some documents and photos from an old chest. He did not let me see them, said they were part of a 'case' he was investigating." She swallowed. "I looked around for that chest the other day when I was given the news about Whitmore—did not find anything."

Knox nodded. "I know. He told me he had lied to you about the box, because he was having such a hard time believing it himself. He hated that he had done that. He had, however, made up his mind to tell you all, feeling that talking to you about it would help him make the right decision about what to do." He looked at her sympathetically. "I take it he never had the opportunity to do that."

"No," she whispered, choking back a sob.

He reached over and covered her hand with his. "Amanda, I'm so sorry," he said feelingly. "When I heard the news of his murder, I was in shock. I just couldn't believe Andy was gone. We both always thought we were indestructible.

"I was at the funeral, and even spoke to you briefly. But you looked so dazed, so lost." He paused. "I just couldn't bring myself to tell you all this then. And I had decided it should die a natural death until about a month ago."

"At least you thought more of Andy than his own father, who didn't acknowledge him or even show up for the funeral," Amanda spoke bitterly.

"You're wrong," Mike said softly.

She looked at him sharply.

"Whitmore was there. Very discreet and in the background, and not recognized by anyone, but he was there."

"You're sure?" she was amazed, catching her breath.

"Yes," he nodded solemnly. "What's more, he knew I recognized him."

Amanda closed her eyes and leaned back in the chair. "Why did you decide to tell me this?"

"Andy was adamant, and I felt I owed it to Andy to tell you before it became public. I also felt like perhaps you should have a say in the use of this information." He observed her profile as she turned sideways to stare at the bookcased wall. "But I'm afraid I may have unwittingly put you in danger."

"How?" Amanda countered dully.

"In the last month I have had two brushes with death," his voice was muted. "Some mighty coincidental accidents. I told my editor about them, and he apparently called in a favor with a buddy of his at the FBI. They picked me up tonight just before our appointed meeting."

She gazed at Knox. He continued. "I told Jon Connor tonight about our aborted meeting. Andy said they were friends and that Jon could be trusted. So when I absconded, that's why he made the mad dash up here to find you. He guessed what I was up to."

"Do you really think the Senator would involve himself in trying to cover this up, in killing you?" she whispered.

"Someone tried," Knox affirmed, staring at her.

She reached for the documents on the desk. "What are these?"

"The original document with the photos, Andy's birth certificate and baptism certificate. And a note."

She gazed at the HLA results, then the pictures. "I've seen this—this picture before."

"Where?"

"I—I don't remember," she faltered. She suddenly thought back to the day she caught Andrew in the bedroom and picked up the photo of the man, glancing at it before he snatched it away. She closed her eyes. "That day, the day I caught Andy going through the items." The memory seared her brain.

The birth certificate yielded no additional information, but the baptism record showed the illegibly written signature on the line indicated as 'father'. Amanda examined it critically. "How do we know this is the father's actual signature?"

"We don't," Knox replied. "The priest is deceased, and those who would have been there are gone as well. But why would there be a signature at all? Who else would sign? And this matches the signature on the church registry."

"And," he moved the certificate to the side and revealed the document under it, "do you see any resemblance to this signature?"

She stared. "Where did you get this?"

"One of the Senator's autographed photos sent to a loyal constituent," Knox smiled slyly. "And note the similarity to this," he pulled out yet another piece of paper, an old faded note on expensive note card stationery. On it was scrawled, "He is beautiful. I love you," and initials looking similar to the two signatures.

She was fascinated. "My heavens, Mike," she exclaimed. "Did you tell the Senator you had this?"

"I sent copies of some of it, although not the HLA testing results," Knox spoke solemnly. "Apparently the senator wanted confirmation that Andrew was his?" he mused aloud.

He leaned forward. "Amanda, do you have any idea where Andy would have stashed the other documents? Those bank records show deposits being made from birth through the time he completed college. I traced the latter deposits to a shell corporation held by the senator's wife's family.

"However, I need the original documents that Andy kept. They prove that the senator knew before he claimed to know, that he had secretly paid monies all those years for the support of his son. He didn't just find out when I spilled the information, Amanda."

"Tell me about these 'accidents'."

Knox frowned. "The first incident occurred about a week after I sent Whitmore the copies. A car almost ran me over while I was crossing the road in D.C. There was no tag, no identifying information." His face was grave. "I had taken the precaution of first sending the originals to a safe place until I provided where they should be forwarded. As you see, I requested they be sent here because I didn't know any other way to get them to you that someone else wouldn't be watching."

"And there was a second incident?" Amanda whispered.

"Yes," Michael swallowed, his face pale. "I allowed one of my colleagues to borrow my car." He paused.

"What happened?" Amanda stared at him.

He looked at his hands, mutely.

"Mike, what is it?" she was anxious.

"There was an explosion. My car blew up, and my friend in it. It was meant for me."

Chapter 20

Jon strode up to Petrino, standing in the parking lot outside Amanda's law office. "Would she speak to you?" he demanded, his voice low.

"She said she had been fast asleep when I called, that she was not going to talk to you tonight. She said the place was locked up, the security system on, and that no one, including Michael Knox, was getting in. She was pissed."

"But why?" Jon argued. "Why would she be so angry?"

"Because you thwarted her in her attempt to get information about Andy from this reporter," Charlie replied matter-of-factly. "And now neither of you are any the wiser for the Bureau's interference, and this Knox is at large."

"But we're trying to protect him." Jon was obviously aggravated, trying to rein in his emotions. "Apparently there have been one, maybe two attempts on his life. His editor and Kimball go way back."

He looked up at the dark upstairs windows. "She threatened to have my job if I tried to gain access. I tried to call her back, and she won't answer."

"I did too," Charlie was grim.

"You don't think he made contact, that he is in there?"

"We haven't found any sign of his motorcycle in the area," Charlie supplied. "He didn't have that much time to hoof it here from very far away."

"So what do we do?"

"I suggest you leave her alone tonight and try again tomorrow."

Jon slumped, leaning against his car.

"Things aren't going any better with Amanda?" Charlie surmised.

"It's like I can't make a right move with her. Now she's angry at me."

Charlie smiled. "I think you'll find that Mandy doesn't hold grudges. She quickly gets over being mad most of the time. But where Andrew is concerned, she is like a bulldog. She doesn't let go."

Jon nodded. "I'm beginning to realize that."

"Have you noticed that there is more than one Amanda in that head of hers?"

Jon stared at him. "I have. When she changes tack, it takes my breath away. I don't know what to expect." He chuckled. "Kind of sexy."

"Guess that's what makes her such a good attorney—she keeps 'em guessing." Charlie smirked. "Don't let her scare you. You'll get used to it. But steer clear of her when she's mad. Give her a wide berth and let her cool off."

"Guess you do know her well," Jon submitted, his eyes on Charlie.

"A lifetime of personal experience. I've been on the other side of that anger a few times," Charlie grunted.

"So what now?" Jon stared up at the windows.

"I'm going to put a man on the building to look out, in case Knox or someone else should try anything. Then I'm going home and getting some sleep. I'll be here early in the morning. We'll try again."

He turned away. "Your guys had better be looking for this Knox fellow. Something tells me he'll end up needing your help."

"He gave the FBI the slip," the voice complained bitterly. "No one knows where he is."

"This is getting out of hand," Dover remarked coldly. "The longer he is out there, the more dangerous this becomes."

"I think it may already be too late," the voice proffered. "I think this idea of getting you appointed to the appellate bench is too much trouble for the family."

"No evidence has surfaced, other than what Knox has," Dover replied calmly. "That is our top priority. If it's gone, everything else will fall into place. Without proof, anything about his death is pure speculation."

His voice rose in anger. "A lot is riding on this plan. You know the Man said we have to spread our information and influence base. This insider job with the Senator opens lots of doors, and that appointment will smooth the way for some favorable business as well. While this is keeping my man preoccupied so that I can get our business done, we damn sure don't need the senator under any public scrutiny right now." He paused significantly. "If you can't do the job, I can."

Dover took a breath, stilling his anger with difficulty. "Park your men watching Childs. That has to be whom he was waiting for. He apparently feels some need to tell her all before going to print. So that may buy us enough time to find him before he and she meet. But be careful—the feds are already watching her. I will arrange to call off the senator's surveillance."

"Will do," the voice replied.

"Don't let the two of them make contact, or she'll have to go too. That will be harder to clean up."

Amanda sat stunned, as Michael Knox looked down at his hands, tears in his eyes. She finally found her voice.

"Someone special to you?"

"A dear friend and colleague, one of my first mentors. Walter Norton."

"Walter Norton? The international correspondent?" Amanda was startled.

"He was back stateside, his car was in the shop, and I loaned him mine so he could run an errand. The car blew up with him in it."

Amanda was stricken. "Oh, my heavens," she whispered, horrified.

He leaned forward. "I was supposed to pick up my sister from the airport that day, but she had called that morning and told me her plans had changed. But for that, she and I would have died instead. As it is, I'm minus a good friend, and the paper a great newsman. And I was informed by Talbot that my apartment was a shambles."

"Are the police investigating this?" Amanda asked hotly.

"Yes, but you know nothing definitive is going to come of that, if it is the hand of the powers that be," Knox spoke angrily.

They were both silent.

Amanda stood and started pacing. "This could not have come at a worse time," she whispered.

"Why?" Knox stared at her.

"Because the trial of the man behind the conspiracy that led to Andy's murder is coming up week after next," Amanda said. "The release of this information will cause quite an uproar, and probably cause the defense to obtain a continuance, claiming this news may lead to 'new evidence'." She sighed. "I don't know if I can take that."

Knox stood up and stilled her, taking her hand. "I don't want to do anything to prevent the punishment of those who caused Andy's death." He paused. "You understand that?"

She nodded. "But if someone is after you to keep the story from going public, time is of the essence. You may not be able to wait."

She looked at her watch. It was almost one a.m.

"What do we do now?" Knox asked.

"I need to think. I need a drink. You want anything?"

"I could use a bourbon right now," he smiled tentatively.

She stalked out of the room and headed in the darkness toward the kitchen. Mike followed her. She cut on a small lamp in the room next to the kitchen, walked inside the kitchen and reached into a cabinet, retrieving out two highball glasses and a bottle of Wild Turkey. She poured some into both glasses.

"Want anything in it?" she raised her eyebrows.

"It's fine just like that," he remarked, reaching for the glass.

She handed it to him, then opened the freezer, grabbing a couple ice cubes that she dropped into her glass, and then the fridge, where she retrieved a can of soft drink, which she added to the mix.

She reviewed the contents of the refrigerator critically. "When was the last time you ate anything, Mike?"

"I'm fine," he shook his head. "I had a large cheeseburger with fries this afternoon. It's not something I do often because it requires an extra mile running for a week to pay for it."

She closed the door and reached for a banana in the fruit bowl. "We have to decide what to do with you. There aren't too many places to hide you."

She sipped her drink in the dark, as Mike downed his. "We can keep you here for a day or so. Ralph and Claire will be back Monday or Tuesday. No one will think of looking for you here, as long as I can keep those following me at bay, and it will buy us time to figure out what to do next. The guest room is just across the hall from the study."

"What about you?" Mike asked anxiously.

"I have a hearing in the morning. I have to go in. Besides, they'll be looking for me if I don't. As it is, I will lay odds that Charlie or Jon is camping outside the law office. I'll wait until about 5:00, then either jog to my office or call Sheila to pick me up on her way to work. I'll sack out on the couch here."

"Amanda, I really need those documents. Do you have any ideas where Andy would hide them? He always said you were his home, his refuge. So my guess is somewhere at your home is where he hid the proof."

Amanda turned away. "I've looked. So did someone else, just the other day."

"What?" Mike's eyes grew wide.

"The day I heard about the senator's news, someone broke into my house. But I could find nothing missing. I feel certain it's not there, or at least where someone could easily find it."

Mike touched her arm. "This is dangerous, Amanda. I'm afraid you're involved whether or not you want to be."

Amanda shook her head. "I also have well-placed friends who are apparently watching out for me." She smiled grimly. "When I get back to the farm, I'll see what I can find. Mike, you need to get some rest."

He was still gazing at her. "Did you actually go out to the general store tonight?"

"Yes, of course," she answered quizzically.

"Alone?"

She looked away. "Not exactly," she admitted. "Charlie wasn't going to allow me to go alone."

"Who exactly is Charlie?" Mike asked, anxiety on his face.

"Charles Petrino, Mainville Chief of Police," she answered. "He's one of the good guys, Mike." She spoke confidently. "I trust him." She surprised herself. Yes, I do trust him, she thought. Why did I ever doubt him?

"Are you going to tell him about my being here?" Mike waved his hand around the room.

"Not unless or until we need him," Amanda smiled reassuringly. "The fewer who know your whereabouts, the better for now."

Knox's look was grateful. "I know you've had to swallow a lot tonight, and I appreciate your believing in me."

"Don't thank me yet. We've still got to decide where we go from here."

Jon's phone rang. "Connor here," he said abruptly.

"Kimball. Where are you now?"

"I'm still outside Amanda's office."

"Any luck?"

"No. No sign of him. And she's not letting us in. She says she's mad that we thwarted her meeting with Knox."

"We need to find him. Talbot's madder than hell that Knox ran off. He said that his senior international correspondent was killed the other day." Kimball paused. Jon could tell his ire was near the surface. "He was driving Knox's car at the time."

"Any evidence it wasn't accidental?"

"An explosion with C-4 residue? Don't think so." Kimball was infuriated. "ATF is on it, but our guys up there are looking into it also. So this has escalated into something more serious. They're wanting us to pick Knox up for questioning."

"Yeah, if we can find him," Jon agreed glumly. "But I'm convinced he will probably stick around this area. I believed him when he said he had a promise to keep. He's going to look for an opportunity to contact Amanda."

"So you need to keep a close eye on your fiancée, so that she can lead you to him before something happens," Kimball was cross.

"I'm not letting her become bait," Jon answered sourly.

"She already is. So you might as well use this as an opportunity to stick to her like glue."

Amanda stretched out on the couch in Ralph's living room. She was tired, but still questions assailed her. Why is the senator so interested in this case? Would he go so far to squelch the allegations about his fathering Andrew that he would attempt to snuff out Michael Knox? If so, why would he voluntarily acknowledge paternity to Jon?

She set the alarm on her wristwatch, thankful that she had for some reason chosen this watch when she got dressed the previous morning.

She must have dozed, because the next thing she remembered was the tiny alarm insistent in her ear. She pushed the button stilling it and sat up, trying to clear her head. It was still dark. OK, I need a plan for getting back into my office.

She went into the kitchen and made some coffee. She wandered into the master bedroom and into Ralph's closet. On a shelf she found some woman's sweats, clean and neatly folded. Ah-hah, she thought, smiling broadly, Claire has apparently been spending time here, something I can tease Ralph about.

She examined the clothes. Yes, she could cinch them tightly and make them work. Now what for shoes? She looked under the clothes and found a pair. Only a half-size too large—that's perfect, she thought.

She quickly changed into the clothes, borrowing a pair of Ralph's thick sports socks. She gazed at herself critically in the mirrored closet doors. A little sloppy, but not bad for a jogger out on an early morning run.

She walked out of the bedroom, and straight into the arms of Mike Knox, who had seen her but not in time to avoid her. "Sorry," she laughed, embarrassed, as she pulled away. "You're up?"

"Yes," he grinned. "Can't sleep. Heard you moving around. What's the game plan?"

"I've made coffee. You're staying here. You need to lay low, not making anyone suspect you are here. I'll get you something to eat and some clothes." She looked him up and down. "Ralph's clothes would swallow you whole."

"I have a change in my bag," he smiled.

"Good. Make yourself at home. There's a treadmill in the den. Keep the noise, lights, activity down to a minimum. Thank goodness Ralph has a large yard, no close neighbors."

She moved down the hallway. "Mike, do you need to get word to anyone that you're OK?"

"Just my editor Jim Talbot," he spoke behind her. "But I've been afraid to use my phone. And I don't know but what his work number is tapped."

"I can call him. What do I tell him?"

"Tell him that the story is on its way. I have only one more confirmation to go." He pressed a piece of paper in her hand. "This is his home number. Unlisted—no one much knows it. Leave a message."

As they entered the living room, he put a hand on her shoulder. "And Amanda," he was solemn, "be careful. At the first sign of danger, you tell that boyfriend of yours everything. Andy would not want anything to happen to you over this."

Amanda bit her lip, swallowing the retort. "As soon as I can get away from work, I'll look again for the documents," Amanda promised. She looked through her purse, taking her keys and her cell phone with her.

She looked out the window, trying to determine whether anyone suspicious was lurking outside. "Well, wish me luck," she said lightly. "I'll be in touch. Mike, I'll probably be sending someone out with some supplies, so lie low and don't scare them. I won't be able to sneak back here until after dark at the earliest. Lock the deadbolt behind me."

She carefully let herself out then casually looked both ways, jogging down to the sidewalk and turning in the direction of her office. She was careful to watch her surroundings in anticipation that she might be followed, but saw no one.

She decided to take a less direct route to the office, and jogged down a couple blocks to the park surrounding the lake in town, running the length of the park then doubling back. As she rounded a corner only a block from her office, a police car drew up alongside her. She knew without looking who it was.

"Morning, Charlie," she spoke brightly.

"Get in," he ordered.

"I'm doing my morning run and am almost done," she pointed to the office just in sight.

"Bullshit," he growled. "Don't you think I know you didn't spend the night at your office as promised?"

"I don't know what you're talking about," she mumbled, continuing her run, as his car crawled alongside her.

"You can either get in with me, or face the FBI by yourself when you get there," he nodded in the direction of the office.

She stopped, sighing. Shrugging, she walked around and let herself into the cruiser.

"OK, so where were you?"

"Does Jon know?" she asked.

"Not yet, but when I show up with you in tow, I think he'll put two and two together. Answer my question."

"I was with Mike Knox," she stared straight ahead. She gave a brief summary of the information he had imparted. Charlie listened impassively.

"Where is he? Why doesn't he turn himself in?" Charlie demanded.

"He's safe for the moment. I can think of several reasons why he would hesitate," Amanda's jaw jutted stubbornly. "Why would he trust any feds right now? How does he know they are not in cahoots with the senator? And he is probably afraid that his story will get deep-sixed if he allows himself to be taken into protective custody."

"He might get deep-sixed if he stays out there," Charlie retorted. "And now he has involved you."

"How could I avoid getting involved?" Amanda countered angrily.

"Is that the answer you're going to give Jon?" Charlie glanced at her. "What are you going to tell him?"

"I don't know yet," Amanda admitted. "I was hoping you would help me, Charlie, to buy some time."

"You want me to lie to the FBI?" Charlie was incredulous.

"You lied to me for them," Amanda responded, her anger just below the surface. "Are you going to tell me this is any different?"

"That was a low blow, Mandy," Charlie countered reproachfully.

"I know, but I need your help. Just keep all this under your hat for twenty-four hours." She was pleading, placing her hand over his on the steering wheel. "Then you can spill all. In fact, I'll do it myself."

As they approached the office, she could see a black sedan and Jon's Mercedes in the back parking lot. Her mind was whirring.

"They're advertising their presence to keep anyone scared away," Charlie observed thoughtfully. If they were just looking for Knox, they wouldn't be so obvious, he thought but did not say. "What are you going to tell them?"

"I'll come up with something. Just follow my lead."

Chapter 21

As they drove into the parking lot, Amanda sighed. "I dread this. I don't want to lie to Jon. But I already have once."

She got out of the car and Petrino followed. Jon was sitting on the steps outside the back door. When he saw her, he stood, his eyes wide, his face unsmiling. She could sense that a slow boil was in progress. She took a deep breath.

"Good morning, Jon," she smiled, going up to him. Disobeying her own rule about not showing intimacy in public, she reached up and kissed him on the lips. She could feel the tension in his body as he did not return her kiss, but gently gripped her arms and pulled her away, his eyes meeting hers accusatorily.

"So you didn't spend the night here after all?" he asked icily. "Where have you been?"

Kimball walked up at that moment. "Good morning, Agent Kimball," Amanda smiled at him as he scowled back at her. She shook free of Jon's grip. "Of course I have been here. I just decided on an early morning run."

They looked at her dubiously. She waved her hand toward Charlie. "Then the Chief stopped me and demanded that I accompany him back here."

"Jon's been here all night, and I've been here over an hour. Just how would you leave here without our knowledge?" Kimball demanded hoarsely.

Amanda turned to Kimball, avoiding Jon's intent gaze. "I saw Jon's car out my window. I am still angry at your interference last night, and at being under the equivalent of house arrest. I had to be alone and think. I decided a jog this morning might clear my head. So I was able to sneak right past you all. You think Ralph and I don't have a secret exit to escape unwanted visitors?"

"Where is Knox?" Jon charged quietly.

"I wouldn't know," she answered, not looking at him.

"Did you know there have been two attempts on his life?" Jon persisted.

She turned away from the men, fishing her keys out of her pocket. "Is that supposed to change my answer? You don't believe me?" she argued, a hint of anger in her voice.

She unlocked the door and punched some numbers on the keypad just inside the door, disabling the delayed alarm. Jon followed her, taking her by the arm, and turning her to face him. "He needs our protection," Jon stared at her as Kimball and Charlie entered behind them.

"And if I have the opportunity to make contact with him again, I will try to convince him of that," she spoke, her jaw set stubbornly.

"We can arrest you for being an accessory," Kimball spoke up, bristling.

"An accessory to what?" she looked at Kimball coldly, then Jon. "Just what have I done? What has Knox done, for that matter?" she demanded, her gaze slicing them. "Don't threaten me unless you have the wherewithal to carry it out."

"Amanda . . ." Jon said, his voice low.

"And I'm not a schoolgirl for you to dress down with that patronizing tone," she hissed, her fury coming to the fore. "I didn't appreciate it last night, and I don't now. You'd do well to remember that, Senior Special Agent Connor."

Jon, taken aback by her response, released her arm. Amanda looked at him then, her eyes relenting. "If he contacts me, I promise I will let you know. It's the best I can do."

She turned away. "Now I need a shower because I have a juvenile delinquency pre-trial at nine. Judge Kilmer is nothing if not punctual. With Ralph gone, I am hopping busy. Sorry I can't offer you all breakfast. Charlie, will you lock the door behind you when you've seen these men out?"

She walked quickly down the hall, jogging up the stairs to the living quarters upstairs. She let herself into the bedroom, locking the door behind her. She leaned against the door. God, forgive me for lying, she prayed quickly.

About forty minutes later, she came downstairs, dressed in a fitted black suit. She walked into the kitchen area to make coffee, but was surprised to find the coffee already made. She opened the cabinet door for a cup and poured herself some. She felt a presence behind her.

"Want some?" she asked evenly.

"We need to talk," Jon's voice cut through her.

She didn't turn around. "You first," she murmured.

"Amanda, I don't—want it to be this way," he offered hesitantly. "I don't want all these—complications. I want to be open and honest with you."

"But you can't. It's your job," she finished for him. "I understand. I have lived with the Bureau before."

"That's why I want to leave," he sighed. "I don't want anything coming between us."

"But can you live without it? The excitement, the chase, the authority?" she asked, going over to the refrigerator for cream then slamming the refrigerator door. She poured the cream and sugar into the coffee and stirred it vigorously. "Andy couldn't. And it killed him."

"I can't live without you," Jon murmured.

Her heart constricted. "Jon—" she paused, "you need to go. Please."

He made no move. She turned and faced him. "I keep my promises. All of them. And I will keep the one I made to you this morning. Call your men off, Jon."

She walked up to him and put her arms around his neck. She reached up and kissed him. He pulled her to him, returning the kiss fervently. As his kiss trailed down her neck, she whispered in his ear. "I met with Knox last night. He's safe for the moment. His story is almost ready. I'm going to try to talk him into turning himself over to you. But he has every right to be afraid right now."

He froze. She pulled away resolutely. "That's the best I can do, Jon," she whispered. "Now, please let me get to work. I have so much to do today."

"How do you know he's safe?" Jon whispered.

"It's as safe a place as you could provide," she replied softly.

Jon stared at her for a minute, willing her to say more. She smiled pensively and shook her head.

He nodded reluctantly. "When can I see you again?"

"Do you think that's wise, at least until after the trial?"

"You're going to have to keep fending me off," he warned.

"Get out of here," she said lightly. "How can I pay the bills with you constantly bothering me?"

He reached over and kissed her once more before disappearing through the door. She looked after him, sad to see him go.

She walked into the hallway, to see Sheila walking in. "Good morning," she greeted her. Sheila looked perturbed, gazing at Jon's retreating form, then her boss.

"Long story," Amanda said. "I need the Sanchez file for this morning."

Within seconds the file was handed to her, and she walked into her office to face the morning's agenda, glancing through the file and her notes, before striding out the door to her car.

On the way to the courthouse, she stopped off at the public library. She walked into the librarian's office. A beautiful black woman rose. "Hi, Amanda," she greeted Amanda, her voice musical.

"Good morning, Louise. How are you?"

"Still reeling that my baby brother has actually taken the plunge and got married, and to a wonderful woman at that. How about you?"

"I'm well." Amanda shut the door. "Louise, I never thanked you for all the work you did helping me renovate the farm and box things up. I couldn't have done it by myself. And thank Danny for carting everything off and disposing of it." Amanda paused solemnly. "It was something I should have done long ago."

Louise reached out and placed her hand on Amanda's arm. "That's always hard to go through. We were happy to do it. Does the place feel more like home now?"

"Yes," Amanda smiled. "Less like a mausoleum. I feel like it's my space now, and I can keep the ghosts at bay."

"But that's not why you are here this morning?" Louise was perceptive.

"You're right," Amanda agreed. "I need to ask two favors."

"Of course."

"I have a celebrity of sorts hidden out at Ralph's guest room for a day or two," Amanda spoke carefully, her voice low. "His appearance was unexpected last night, and I couldn't think of anywhere else. He needs to lie low until the paparazzi looking for him die down." She laid some bills on the desk. "Would you mind taking him out a few groceries and something from the deli around lunch time?"

Louise looked at her quizzically. "Sure thing. Celeb, huh?"

"Well, you might recognize him, but don't tell anyone, please."

"What's the second favor?"

"I need to borrow your phone for a few minutes," Amanda said confidentially. "It's something I don't need anyone overhearing."

Louise looked at her questioningly. "OK," Louise shook her head. "If it was anyone else, I'd wonder. But anything for you."

"Thank you so much," Amanda said. "I would take the stuff out myself, but am afraid I may be under surveillance."

"What for?" Louise was alarmed.

"Some people are looking for this guy, and I'm afraid I may unwittingly lead them to him. This is only until I can make other arrangements."

Louise smiled. "Don't worry about it. It's taken care of."

Amanda squeezed her hand thankfully. "You do not know how much I appreciate this."

"I will leave you alone to make your call." Louise left the room. Amanda quickly picked up the receiver and dialed the number given her by Knox. She received a voice message. "You don't know me, and I'm calling from a phone I borrowed because I know it isn't being bugged. But I'm passing on word that Michael Knox is safe for the moment. He said to tell you the story is almost finished, and he only has one more confirmation. I will try to contact you later if there's any change."

Satisfied, she left the office, waving at Louise as she left the library.

She made her way to the courthouse and completed her hearing. As she entered the elevator to go downstairs, she saw out of the corner of her eye a man, in dark suit, carrying a file folder. Don't know him, she thought.

She made it to the car and pulled out heading back to the office. About a block from the office she looked in her rearview mirror, and was surprised to see the same man in a white Impala behind her. This is not happening, she fumed.

She pulled up to a stop sign, put the gear in neutral and applied the emergency brake, and stepped out of her car, walking purposefully toward the man in the oncoming car. He saw her and stopped suddenly several feet away. She saw the confusion in the driver's eyes, as he hurriedly backed up, u-turned and sped away.

Still peeved, she returned to the office. She walked in and handed the file to Sheila, then looked at the calendar book. Sheila handed her a message.

"Fred Vaughan called and said it was important that he see you," Sheila said uncertainly.

"Fred? Did he say why?" Amanda mused aloud.

"No, but he wanted me to impress upon you that you need to come. Something about the cat being sick."

Suddenly alert, Amanda again looked at the calendar. "OK. I'm going out there right now. I'll be back this afternoon. When Hank comes in, make my apologies for not being here and let him review the deeds and power of attorney. If he's happy, we can set up the closing for early next week."

She was concerned. It was unlike Fred to call unless it was urgent. She generally saw him once or twice per day coming and going from the farm. She felt the statement about the cat was a subterfuge. So she drove a little faster, but always checking her mirrors to make sure she was not being followed, the memory of the senator's men and the incident this morning making her cautious.

She pulled out her cell phone and tried Vaughan's number. "Hello?" she heard him respond.

"Amanda here. I got your message, and I'm on my way. Is there anything wrong?"

"I'll be waiting by the gate when you get here," he replied tersely, hanging up.

Amanda was nervous. What would be wrong that would make Fred so mysterious? She accelerated, no longer caring about being stopped for speeding.

After what seemed a lifetime she arrived at Vaughan's, where he was waiting as promised. He got in beside her.

She looked at him with anxiety. "What is it, Fred?"

"I'll show you when we get to the house," he pointed down the trail.

She took off at a high rate of speed. He put out his hand and touched her arm. "Slow down," he said. "The barn won't burn down before we get there."

Clearing his throat, he said, his voice low, "I just found something that I thought you should see. I felt it might be important."

She glanced over at him, bewildered.

Several minutes later, they appeared at the house. She flung herself out of the car, Fred following. As she bounded up the front steps, he called, "Wait a minute. You don't know how to disengage the alarm."

"Alarm?" she was uncomprehending.

"The security system," he explained, as he pushed past her and pointed to the small box on the wall beside the front door.

He handed her a key. "You put the key in and turn it to the right, then to the left, then punch in the code, see?" He punched in five digits. She heard the lock click open. "Now."

She entered with him following. He locked the door back, punching a code in the box on the inside wall beside the door. He handed her the key. "You can also program it to open with code only, without the key. I want to show you some other command features. But now is not the time." He took her hand. "Come with me."

He pulled her up the stairs, then grabbed the cord bringing the attic stairwell down. "Go on," he commanded. As she hesitated, he urged her. "I've dusted so you won't mess up your suit too bad."

She made her way up the steps to the attic, with Fred behind her. Clicking on the light, she saw that the boxes had been restacked and a wall was bare.

"OK, so what is it?" she was confused.

Vaughan bent down beside the wall and beckoned her to come closer. He pointed to the bottom left corner of the wall near the floor. "Do you have a key that fits that?" he asked.

She bent down and peered, as Fred illuminated the area with a flashlight. It was barely visible. "A deadbolt?" she was amazed. "To what?"

With the flashlight beam Vaughan followed a small almost imperceptible demarcation up the wall, across a seam between wooden beams in the wall, and back down near the corner of the wall. "This is a hidden door to something," he replied.

"To what?" she laughed. "Outside?"

"Your powers of perception are slipping," Vaughan reprimanded her. "If you look closely, there is a good six feet here before one would reach the exterior wall."

"What are you saying, Fred? That someone built an alcove in the attic?" Amanda shook her head, her mind not following his train of thought. "This is not an old house. You know that. Andy and I designed and had it built."

"Precisely," Fred stared at her. "I don't know if you were aware or not, but Andy was very good at carpentry and woodworking. So what was to keep Andy from designing a secret room?"

Their eyes met, Amanda's disbelieving, Fred's willing her to comprehend.

Suddenly she jumped up. "Just a minute," she said, running across the attic and bounding down the stairs. She made her way to her bathroom.

Kneeling down before the open vanity, she reached up and retrieved the piece of duct tape with the key secured to it. Ripping the tape off, she closed the vanity and raced back up the stairs to the attic.

Breathlessly, she handed Fred the key. "Let's see if it works," she panted.

Fred looked at it and her, then placed it in the lock. He turned it and the wall sprang open just a bit.

"Hmm," he mumbled, running his finger along the slight exposed edge and finding a niche and a latch. Pulling it, he ordered, "Move back."

The wall moved with him, and Amanda looked on in fascination. He stepped back and they stared at the dark corner. He illuminated the alcove with the flashlight, finding an old-fashioned light switch. He turned it and a light bulb hanging from a cord from the ceiling came on.

Amanda stared at the small area. There was a simple wooden desk, with a laptop computer and a notebook sitting on it. She walked slowly toward the desk, mesmerized. She looked at the notebook and saw some notes in Andrew's handwriting.

Her voice caught in her throat. She read aloud, "Amanda dearest, if you find this, you must get this box to my old friend Mike Knox of the *Post*. He'll know what to do. Here's his private cell number. I love you with all my heart."

Her heart felt as if it would break. She touched the notepad lovingly, tears blinding her. Oh, Andy, her heart constricted.

Fred pointed past her. "What is that?"

She blinked several times, looked where he was indicating, and gasped. There in the corner of the tiny space was a wooden box, the box she remembered.

Chapter 22

"Take a deep breath, Amanda," Fred, alarmed, reminded her, as she stared, transfixed.

"Fred, this is the box," she rasped. "The box Andy had that day not long before he was killed. I think he kept information about his father in it."

She gingerly picked it up and set it on the desk. She opened the lid slowly. Inside were some papers and photos. She carefully took them out and laid them on the desk, examining each one, Vaughan by her side.

"Who are these people?" she wondered aloud. There were old children's drawn pictures in crayon, small trinkets, a few school papers and report cards, photos of a young solemn-eyed dark-haired boy and a taller girl standing beside him, family scenes, another of him with a man and woman in Sunday best. There was one of a small baby in the arms of a lovely young woman.

"Do you think these are Andy?" she choked. "And perhaps this is his mother, and his aunt and uncle?"

She scanned through the stack, but shook her head. "There are no bank statements here," she muttered.

"What? Bank statements?" Vaughan echoed.

She summarized the events leading up to her meeting with Knox and his revelations. "He said that the bank statements proved that a corporation associated with the senator made regular payments to an account on behalf of Andrew."

Inside the velvet-lined interior on the inside cover of the box was a small brass plate bearing an engraved inscription: "Happy birthday, Aunt Chloe. Andy." There was also a photograph of the boy, a little older, standing at a table saw with the man, other woodworking equipment in the background, the boy holding the box and smiling into the camera.

She touched the wood lovingly. "He must have made this for her," she murmured.

"Good job," Fred remarked. "Always wondered where he learned to use a scroll saw."

"Scroll saw? You knew he could do this?" Amanda was incredulous.

"Yes," Fred acknowledged cryptically. "He told me once his uncle was a cabinet and furniture maker."

She admired the box exterior. "Such a lovely job, so smooth. The finish is well done. His uncle must have been very good."

She closed the box and studied the inlay on the top. "Is this hard to do?"

Fred studied the design. "Yes, intricate work."

"And these carvings along the edges of the box?"

"Yes," he nodded. "A little rough, but exceptionally done. The work of a young but talented apprentice."

She ran her finger along a top corner, noticing that a spot seemed rougher and more pronounced than the other corners. She absently pressed with her thumb, and heard a small click.

"What was that?" she asked, surprised.

Fred reached around her and opened the lid of the box. Her eyes grew wide as she saw that the lid to the box had slipped. Running her fingernail along the slit that had formed, she removed the lid. "A hidden compartment," she whispered, as several documents and photographs dropped out.

"Where are you?" Charlie's voice inquired over the phone.

"I sacked out at a local hotel for a couple hours' sleep," Jon yawned. "Just had a shower. Why?"

"You're still in town?"

"Yes, I am still on the lookout for Michael Knox," Jon replied drily. "Didn't you get the memo?"

"Oh, those faxes and e-mails sent out by the feds every time they fail to do their job?" Charlie gibed. "Yeah, we hang them on the bulletin board for dart practice." He paused. "Amanda didn't offer you accommodations?" Charlie prodded.

"Don't go there," Jon warned ominously. "I'm not on her short list of favorites right now."

"Sorry about that. I left you at her office to kiss and make up."

"Yeah, thanks. Wish it would have worked."

"How about meeting me for a bite to eat? We can talk about it."

Jon paused. He had known Charlie long enough to know he was not proposing a casual social encounter. "Sure," he responded cheerfully. "Where?"

"There's a little hot dog joint just around the corner from the police station, on 9th. We can grab a few."

"Mainville *haute cuisine*? I'm game," Jon chuckled.

"See you there in ten?"

"OK."

Fred sat down beside Amanda on an old trunk in the corner as she inspected the documents. There was a photo of the young man holding the baby in a church, the same man and baby depicted in the photographs in Knox's possession. "Whitmore?" she asked. "Looks a lot like him to me."

Fred nodded. "Me too, and I remember pictures of him from back then."

She studied the statements and several uncashed checks. "Mike said this was a company owned by his wife's family," she pointed to the recurring name of the depositor and the name on the checks. "This is what Mike was looking for as verification. He told me he had seen this before, but Andy kept the originals."

"What are you going to do with this?" Fred looked at her.

She leaned back and closed her eyes. "Andy apparently wanted Mike to have this proof," she said slowly.

"But Andy's gone. What will exposure of the senator accomplish, other than focus more attention on you, and possibly create danger for you?"

Amanda shook her head tiredly, a hint of irritation in her voice. "Fred, I didn't ask for any of this. All this couldn't have come at a worse time. Why did the senator suddenly show up after all this time? Why has all this past suddenly come to light? Just because Andy's buddy wants an exclusive news story?

"But I don't want anything to mess up this prosecution of Barnes, either," she stared at the box and the items in her hands. "I don't know what to do, Fred. Andy did not want the senator to get off scot free, I guess. And I don't think he should get away with the lie that he didn't know about his son."

She sorted through the papers idly, noting a folded group of papers she had not noticed before. "What's this?" she opened it.

She froze. Fred noted it. "What is it?" he asked concernedly.

She didn't answer. Looking over her shoulder, he immediately saw the reason for her reaction, recognizing Andrew's handwriting on the top page. She gasped when she noted the date was only a day before his death. She caught her breath, full of sorrow, as she read:

Mike,

This is a letter that Esther found and sent me from Aunt Chloe's personal effects. It spells out her knowledge of Whitmore's involvement. There's also a letter written by Mom, and the statements. Hope it doesn't come to the point you actually use this information, but if you are reading this instead of hearing it from me, then the odds are that you had to find it yourself, or Amanda has found this and is handing it over, not I.

Things are heating up in my case, and the danger has become very personal. Therefore, this note and my hiding the proof are part of the necessary protections I am putting in place, just in case.

Mikey, you have to make sure that Mandy knows how much I love her and wanted to share all this with her myself. As I told you before, it's the price of your using this information.

One more thing. As much as I want to blame him for my mother's illness and death and for abandoning us, living with Amanda and seeing her faith in God have taught me the value of forgiveness. She has taught me there is more to life than hate, rage and vengeance, more than justice and righteousness, and that I have spent a lifetime missing that larger picture. I'm hoping to change all that. She is quite wonderful in her stubborn devotion, and through her I realized being a Christian requires a much deeper examination and commitment than I had realized.

Therefore, you must give Whitmore the chance to come clean publicly before breaking the story. Even my father needs a shot at redemption.

You know he is a powerful man, and you must be careful, because you don't know how he will react to the possibility of disclosure. Take care, and please make sure Mandy is safe. Do not put her in danger. She means more than life to me.

Yours,

Andy

Amanda swallowed, her heart in her throat, tears close to the surface. She closed her eyes. My God, the idea washed over her, he wrote this shortly before going out to his fateful meeting with Claude Brown. Did he have a premonition he was not coming back?

Jon walked out to his car, letting himself in and gunning the engine. The Bureau might as well open a branch office here in Mainville, he thought ruefully. Of course, I wouldn't mind manning it.

His thoughts turned to Amanda, remembering the fire in her eyes as she lashed out at him in her office. He rather enjoyed ruffling her feathers, he decided. But I need to tone down some of my chivalric, or as she calls them, 'chauvinistic' gestures, at least if I value my limbs, he smiled to himself. He could sense that being on the receiving end of her rage could be far less than pleasant than what he had experienced so far.

After a moment or two he pulled up before the establishment described by Charlie. It was just a tiny shot-gun one-room clapboard building with a bar running the length, and bar stools down one side, thronged with people. On the other side were a man and young teenaged girl in front of a long grill, busily engaged in taking orders and serving up dogs and burgers.

Charlie sidled up beside Jon. "Take your pick," he offered between boisterous greetings with the people in the crowded room. "It's all good. My treat today."

Jon placed an order as Petrino dropped coins into a soft drink machine and retrieved bottled drinks, and soon the chief was handed several small brown paper bags with food, which he exchanged for some bills, waving at the girl at the cash register as he and Jon left the building.

Charlie pointed to a group of picnic tables across the street in a shady area of the park with a view of the lake. "I got my man over there saving us one."

Jon followed Charlie to a table, where a man in deputy uniform was waiting for them. He stood as they arrived.

Charlie said gruffly, "Seek and ye shall find. Jon, meet my newest deputy."

Jon looked into the eyes of Michael Knox.

Amanda, overwhelmed by the enormity of the discovery, felt Fred's hand press comfortingly on her shoulder. Blindly she stood, dropping the sheaf of papers, and turned, and he enfolded her in his arms as she quietly erupted into silent sobs.

He said nothing and allowed her to cry. After a few minutes, she mumbled, "Oh, Fred, he wrote this just before going out to try to catch Claude. It may have been the last thing he wrote."

"He was still trying to protect you to the last," Fred replied quietly. "The letter shows he meant for you to know about this, and just didn't have the chance to tell you." He patted her back clumsily. "He loved you."

She was silent, trying to pull herself together. He added, "Maybe there's some good in this. Maybe you can lay to rest your doubts about Andy."

"Doubts?" she was amazed, pulling back and staring at Fred. "How—how did you know?"

Fred dropped his hands and stepped back, looking down. He was silent for so long Amanda had to prompt him. "Fred?"

Fred peered at her sadly. "Andy himself knew you were plagued by doubts about whether he loved you more than his work. He agonized over it. He was afraid you might not ever understand that mindset, the way a good agent compartmentalizes everything to keep one aspect from spilling over into another. He talked to me about that, and how he wanted to protect you from that other life, how shutting you out of that life was necessary for him to do his job."

"You never said anything," she breathed, stung.

"The time has never been right," Fred replied, turning away. "He told me that once he completed this investigation he was getting out, that life was too short, and his time with you even shorter. He was tired—the job held no excitement for him anymore. He told me all he lived for were the times he was home with you."

Fred gazed at her. "He wanted to resign from the Bureau and build furniture and cabinets like his uncle, work as a local deputy, or just do anything, so that he could be home. With you. All the time."

Amanda, numb, just sat back down in the chair, too spent to cry any more. She closed her eyes, swallowing convulsively. Fred turned away. "How could I ever tell you that after his murder? It seemed just too cruel."

Amanda held her head in her hands. "Maybe that's why he's dead. Perhaps the threat to me upset the equilibrium, his insight. Maybe he wasn't thinking clearly when he went after Claude."

"Perhaps he was so anxious for an end to the case, so he could leave, that he threw caution to the winds," Fred said quietly. "We'll never know. I wish I had been home," he added angrily. "It never would have happened."

They were silent for several minutes.

Finally Amanda opened her eyes and stared at his back. "Did he tell you he suspected that Whitmore was his father?" Amanda was pained.

"In a roundabout way," Fred nodded. "He never named Whitmore, only said that he had been told his father was a very powerful man who abandoned his family. But we had a little discussion of politics only a week before—before his death," Fred swallowed, "and for some reason Whitmore's name popped up. I could sense Andy's immediate antipathy toward the man. It was obvious he had deep personal feelings about the man that had nothing to do with his politics. There was a simmering rage, the same rage I had seen once when he mentioned his father. I put two and two together. Then when you informed me the day the men followed you home, it confirmed my suspicions."

"That bastard Whitmore," Amanda whispered brokenly.

"But do you know the whole story?" Fred confronted her gently.

"The whole story?" she echoed disbelievingly.

"You've heard one side. What about Whitmore's side?"

"What? You think there is some reasonable explanation behind Whitmore's abandoning his lover and son?" Amanda laughed bitterly, turning away.

"Apparently Andrew was willing to give him the chance to prove it, even after all that time," Fred reminded her.

"Even if the senator is trying to kill to keep the information from becoming public?" she cried.

"What do you mean?" he was concerned.

She summarized Mike's relating about the attempts on his life. Fred was somber.

"And now he has compromised you, done the very thing Andy most wanted to prevent." Fred replied unhappily.

Amanda countered with asperity, "What was Mike supposed to do, Fred? As it is, he did exactly what Andy asked, which was nothing until the man announced his aspirations for higher office. No other reporter would do that; the scent of a story like that would override any restraint. He came to me to fulfil his promise to tell me, and to obtain the rest of the evidence as Andy wanted."

"I don't give a good goddamn about him, the story or Whitmore," Fred responded with quiet vehemence. "Andy wanted you above all safe and happy. Right now you're neither. All this does nothing for Andy—he's gone. All this revelation has done is entangle you more deeply with the past, when what you need is to free yourself from it."

"So that I can entangle myself with Jon Connor?" she stood and retorted fiercely.

"So that you are free from the memory of Andrew, to live, to love again. You had come so far, and you were beginning to be happy again. Now this comes along." Although his voice remained low, she could feel his anger.

Realizing that he had strayed farther than he intended, he maneuvered the subject back to the issue at hand. "Do you realize what a man in Whitmore's position might do to keep this under wraps?"

"Or what he has already done?" she added, flushed with cold resolve.

"The question is what do you do with this now?" he asked her.

She sat back down in the chair, shaking her head.

"There has to be a way to get Mike and this information out safely," she mumbled.

"You know if they suspect you know where he is and/or have this proof, you are not safe," Fred pointed out. "And if they should see this letter, it will confirm suspicions that you have the documents."

Amanda looked down at her watch. "I have to do something in the meantime. I've got to get back to the office for afternoon appointments."

"I think you should stay home until we can come up with a plan. I also believe you need to involve Jon in this."

Amanda shook her head. "Fred, all that will do is alert anyone watching me that something has happened, that I've probably found the incriminating evidence. And," she faltered, "I need to keep my distance from Jon right now." She fell silent, suddenly embarrassed.

"If you don't call Jon, I'm calling Charlie," Fred warned, his eyes boring through hers.

"Charlie?" Amanda stopped. "Why Charlie?"

"Because he can be trusted, and he knows every inch of this territory and who is where," Fred answered. "And he doesn't have a federal boss with conflicting interests to dictate his actions."

"Yet another person I don't need to entangle myself with any more than I am already," she muttered.

Fred laid a hand on her shoulder. "This isn't a game, girl. This is the big league. There are suddenly some bad elements hanging around town. I think it has something to do with this business with the senator. I'd feel better if we have someone with a badge and gun on your side."

"For what?" Amanda demanded. "How is that going to help?"

He went on as if she hadn't spoken. "Let's lock this all back up for now. I'll call Charlie. Invite him out night fishing."

"Night fishing?" Amanda echoed confusedly.

"It's our code," Fred smiled enigmatically. "But I'm not allowing you out there alone."

"Fred, I just can't afford to hide out right now," Amanda's voice was weary. "Despite the cloak-and-dagger shenanigans going on, I have to make a living."

"I thought you were an heiress," Fred countered.

"I have a job and people depending upon me, deadlines to meet," she retorted, irritated. She took a breath. "I'm sorry, Fred. I don't mean to snap at you. I know you are trying to look out for me. I promise to be careful and to watch out for people following me." Her voice softened. "Let's think about this before involving anyone else in the mess."

She shook her head, as if to clear her mind of all the questions. "Fred, I have to get back to work. Maybe you're right, and Charlie can help us figure this out tonight. Just don't tell him too much."

They put back all the papers, returned everything back as they found it and locked the room back. Fred pulled some stacks of boxes in front of the wall obscuring the lock from view.

Satisfied, she turned to leave the attic, Fred behind her. He closed up the attic stairwell as she went on down the stairs. Before she made it to the door, he called out, "Just a minute."

She paused in her tracks. Fred brushed past her and motioned that she follow him. He quickly showed her the codes for setting and disabling the alarm, and handed her a key.

He looked at her, disapproval in his eyes. "Put this on your car keychain. I still think I should follow you."

"No," she was firm. "I am already overwhelmed with gratitude for your protection, Fred. If you will do me the favor of keeping an eye out on the place until we can decide where to go next . . . ."

He nodded. She reached up and kissed him on the cheek and squeezed his hand warmly. "Thank you," she mumbled. "I'll be back in a little while."

Jon swallowed his shock. Mike stuck out his hand. "Nice to meet you again, Special Agent Connor."

"Please sit down," Charlie said, his voice low. Jon did, and Mike and Charlie followed suit.

Mike quickly took charge, looking through the paper bags of food. "I'm starving," he smiled. "So while I'm wanting you to take me into custody and all that jazz, I'm more interested in eating right this minute."

Jon looked at Charlie. Charlie shrugged. "He called me, said he was willing to turn himself in to you. Made me promise to take good care of his Indian."

Connor shook his head. "OK, so what was so important you had to talk to Amanda Childs before the feds?"

Mike swallowed a mouthful of a chili cheese dog. "Hell, I hope there's a treadmill where you're hiding me out. These things are evil, artery-clogging good." He grinned at Jon, aware that Jon was keeping a tight rein over his temper.

"Here's the scoop," Knox suddenly became serious. "Andy's charge was for me to make sure Amanda knew about Whitmore, and how Andy came to find out, before any public disclosure. All this time I'm sure she was upset, thinking Andy had kept from her this pertinent information about his past."

Mike took a sip of the cherry soda. "And I was right. Andy never had a chance to tell her before he was killed. She knew nothing."

He brought both of them up to speed on the information he had imparted to Amanda. "But when we finally made contact last night, Amanda recognized me from the wedding. I showed her the proof Andy had entrusted to me, and told her there was more hidden somewhere."

"What more?" Charlie asked.

"Banking records that showed that Whitmore had been sending money for Andy from birth through his college years. Whitmore knew the whole time he had a son. And there were some pretty damning photos and letters."

"You've seen these?"

"Yes," Mike nodded. "But Andy wanted to show them to Amanda, so he kept those items." He looked disappointed. "She said she had seen some of the pictures before, but did not know where Andy might have hidden them, and she had looked through the house for them before."

"Where else would Andy have hidden them? A safe deposit box?" Jon wanted to know.

"I don't know," Mike admitted. "But they exist, and he put them somewhere safe. I have enough to file my story, but I wanted the confirmation to show that Whitmore hasn't just found out he had a son."

"How did you get involved? How did this all happen?" Jon put a hand on Mike's arm to halt the next bite of food from making it to Mike's mouth.

Mike stopped and put down his hotdog. He looked around to determine whether there was anyone else around. He explained to Jon and Charlie the history of his childhood with Andy and all he had told Amanda the evening before.

"How did Andy take the news?" Jon asked softly.

"At first he was in shock, then angrier than I've ever seen him," Mike acknowledged. "Aunt Chloe had tried to feed Andy the line about his dad dying in Vietnam, but he always knew his father had abandoned him and his mother. And his mom didn't help matters any. Every time she went downhill and the paranoia hit, she was always telling Andy something about his famous father." Mike took a deep breath. "Andy had hated his father, so finding out the man's identity brought all that back. And apparently at the worst possible time for him, in the middle of the case that killed him."

"I know," Jon muttered. "And Amanda?" Jon couldn't help asking.

Charlie shot a look at Jon as Mike answered, "I really think she was relieved. It was as though she had been holding her breath. When I told her that Andy always meant to tell her and apparently just didn't get the chance, you could see it in her eyes, a burden lifting."

"And your proof?"

"In a safe place," Mike grinned. "I have copies, but am smart enough not to carry around the originals."

"You know we could protect the originals for you," Jon smiled.

"Yeah, sure," Mike laughed. "Like I would trust any federal government employee right now, with the sword of Damocles over my head? The only reason I am trusting you, Jon Connor, is because Andy told me I could. Andy and I went way back. He told me if ever in a jam, I was to look you up, and you would do the right thing."

"You know they're going to want to question you about the attempts on your life? There is an investigation."

"I'll only talk to whomever you clear," Mike looked at him directly.

"Where did you spend last night?" Jon asked casually.

"With your girlfriend," Mike grinned. "But don't worry. She only has eyes for you." At Jon's smoldering look, he shook his head. "No, I'm not telling you. I might need that hiding spot again sometime. But it wasn't her place."

Jon looked at Charlie. "Why the getup?" he jerked his head toward Mike's uniform.

Charlie shrugged. "It was all I could think of at the time. As it is, we've put out that his motorcycle was found abandoned and we've impounded it, with no evidence of his whereabouts."

Jon looked at Mike. "OK, I need to get you to the safe house so you can be debriefed and hunkered down."

"You are going to protect me?" Mike stared at Jon.

"That's the plan coming from on high. Your editor has some big guns at his disposal."

"If you like, I figured I'd have him ride out with me and we'd patrol a little farther than my jurisdiction," Charlie interposed.

"What happens when you come back without a deputy?"

"I just dropped him off at his home," Charlie shrugged. "As I told you before, I'm better at avoiding detection than you government guys. I can get him there without anyone knowing."

Jon thought a moment, then nodded. "OK." He shook hands with Mike. "I'll be seeing you."

"Where are you off to?" Mike asked.

"As the old guy at the fish market said earlier this week, 'I'm frying more than one fish at a time,'" Jon grinned as he stood and moved away.

Mike turned to Charlie, his voice low so that Jon could not overhear. "Amanda's going to be either scared or pissed when she doesn't find me. You gotta clean up that mess and set her mind at ease."

Charlie nodded, as Jon's brows knit into a frown, noting their whispered conversation.

"What was that?" Jon asked.

"Just about my bike," Mike answered with a smile.

Chapter 23

Later Jon called Kimball to make sure Knox made it safely to the safe house. "ATF is wanting to interview our man now about the explosion. The FBI has claimed the right to be included in the investigation. Knox is not talking to anyone without your OK. But the Director is stalling on access to Knox anyway," Kimball relayed over the phone, a secure land line installed at the house.

"The Director?" Jon was surprised. "Why?"

"I'm guessing that just as our senator has pulled some strings in order to be briefed on the Barnes criminal case, Jim Talbot has made some noise in high places to protect his reporter. He's afraid now that we've got him in protective custody, it wouldn't be hard for the right hand to find out what the left hand is doing, and for Knox's location to be revealed to the wrong person, putting him in danger all over again."

"So he doesn't trust G-men as a group?" Jon snickered. "Of course, neither do any of us. But I agree—the fewer people who know where Knox is, the better."

"There's more," Kimball interjected. "There's a mole somewhere. Apparently within the Bureau or ATF, per Washington's sources. And we're on the lookout for some mafia henchmen right now, allegedly combing this area for Knox, and perhaps even your girl."

"She needs protection," Jon raised his voice.

"Damn it, I'm doing all I can," Kimball retorted. "And I certainly can't hogtie her."

"I know," Jon was sober. "Did our boy offer to share his proof regarding the senator's past?"

"He has copies but states he has stashed the originals in a safe place and provided copies to his editor. He also knows there is additional evidence, but says he doesn't know where. So you tell me," Kimball was enigmatic.

"I have no idea," Jon was bemused.

"You know this guy was childhood friends with Andrew Childs? That they remained buddies and maintained contact?"

"Yes," Jon acknowledged. "He made a comment the other night about Andy's having said he could trust me, but that's when he disclosed he was to meet Amanda and I never got to follow up on that statement. But when he turned himself in to me, he told me the story."

"Do you know where the guy was found?"

"No," Jon admitted. "And Charlie said Knox called him and met him, and Charlie wouldn't say where. Knox said he'd prefer to keep the location private."

"Ah," Kimball said significantly.

"Ah?" Jon echoed.

"Your newfound friend Knox met somewhere with your girlfriend, just as he planned. And she knows, or he thinks she knows, where the rest of the evidence is hidden."

Jon was silent so long that Kimball prompted him. "Jon, are you there?"

"I'm here," he replied. He mused, "Do we have a right to demand this evidence? Has any crime been committed?"

"Man, I don't really care, but if whoever is gunning for Knox comes up with the same conclusion, your girlfriend could become a target."

"Her name is Amanda," Jon muttered irritably. "Do you think that's why the attempts on Knox?"

"He does, says that he has not been working on anything else that would generate an attempt on his life. And he told us he sent copies of his proof to Senator Whitmore only a week before the two attempts."

"Yeah, he told me the same thing."

"Why? Why would he send the proof to the man before breaking the story?"

Jon replied, "Most reporters confront the subject to allow the opportunity for rebuttal. And he states that Andy told him to give the man a chance to come clean before going to press. I could believe that."

"That's white of him," Kimball remarked drily, "but sounds like Andy. Why so long before all this came to light?"

"Andy was killed right after he found out this information. Andy had said to leave things as they were until he figured out how he felt about the news and had a chance to tell Amanda." Jon paused. "He didn't get the opportunity. And he had told Knox no movement on the info unless Whitmore decided to move up the ladder. Knox tried to respect Andy's wishes. And then the news broke that Whitmore was eying the presidency."

Kimball interposed, "You need to have a talk with your girlfriend."

"Her name is Amanda," Jon reiterated, annoyed. "Why?"

"Because she keeps slipping away from our surveillance teams. It's hard to keep an eye on her. She confronted one of our guys today, halted at a stop sign, jumped out of her car and started walking toward him."

"You're following her now?" Jon asked.

"Knox insists that she needs protecting. I can't just pick her up. She's too high profile in this community. Her absence would be noted, particularly by others who may be watching her." Kimball's voice hardened. "And she knows she is being watched."

Kimball added, "You're not to tell Amanda we have Knox."

"Why not?" Jon demanded. "If she has been hiding him out, she's going to know something's up the minute she finds him gone."

"Simpson said need to know basis only, and she doesn't need to know. Besides, Simpson feels your fiancée has been disloyal to the Bureau."

Jon choked. "You have got to be kidding."

"No joke," Kimball's voice was grave. "But Knox is making his own demands. He wants Amanda in the loop and wants to talk to her himself. And I believe it won't be long before Knox's contacts trump Simpson's edicts."

"I hate being told to lie to Amanda," Jon muttered.

Jon's call waiting beeped. He looked at the number. "I don't know who this is, but let me take this. Not that many people have my number. I'll call you back."

Answering the line, he heard a hesitant voice. "Senior Agent Connor?"

"Yes, sir," Jon replied, immediately recognizing the voice as that of Senator Whitmore. "What may I do for you?"

"I'd rather you not use my name over the phone," the voice said. Jon was surprised at how shaky the senator sounded. "I'm calling from a pay phone." He paused. "I'm alone. Can we meet?"

"Of course, sir," Jon replied, his intuition humming. "Tell me where and I'm on my way."

"Do you know someone named Colin?"

Jon's memory locked into gear. "Yes," he answered.

"I've been invited to tour his facility."

"I'll be there."

Jon hit the speed dial button. "Kimball?"

"Yes?"

"I may be about to find out another piece of the puzzle. I'll let you know."

Amanda left quickly, Fred stopping to set the alarm as she made it to her car. She pulled onto the trail toward the highway.

Pulling out her cell phone, she called Sheila. When Sheila answered, she cut in. "Amanda here. I'm sorry for the delay, but I am on my way back," she explained.

"Well, your afternoon appointment with the new client was cancelled."

"Any explanation?" Amanda was surprised.

"No. But Father Anselm called here just a few minutes ago and said he needed to see you. He said it was an emergency, a vestry crisis, and for you to drop by the parish house as soon as you can."

"What's that about?" Amanda wondered out loud. All these emergencies are wearing me thin, she thought.

"And you got several messages," Sheila informed her.

"Those can wait," Amanda announced abruptly. "I'll be at the office as soon as I see what is up with Father."

She accelerated, looking at her watch. Ralph will eat me alive if I let a new client get away, she thought irrelevantly. I'll need to personally follow up on that. I wanted to have a whole list of new retainers when he returned. And I'm not accomplishing any billable hours today with all this personal stuff going on. There's that mountain of paperwork to sign in my inbox. I need to practice at the church. And I'm tired, she thought; the lack of sleep is catching up with me.

She watched her rearview mirror, trying to determine whether anyone might be following her. Once in town, she drove in a circuitous route to the priest's home.

She thought about her dilemma. How can I smuggle these documents and Mikey, as Andy called him, out of town and to safety? She thought about Mike's editor, or Feinstein's law firm in New York City. But the key is to figure out how to prevent others from finding and intercepting them, she concluded.

She studied the problem without coming to a clear answer, until she pulled up into the driveway of Father's Anselm's home.

She parked next to a shiny new white Cadillac Sedan deVille in the driveway. Wonder who that is, she thought. My timing is bad, but I'm not going to leave until I see what Father wants.

She walked up to the front and knocked on the door. Father Anselm opened the door almost immediately. "Amanda," he said with relief, motioning for her to come in.

She walked in past him and he quickly shut the door. "Father, I'm so sorry for the delay. I was tied up with something. What can I—" her voice trailed off as she looked behind the priest, her eyes widened in surprise.

Behind the priest was Jonathan Connor, his eyes on her, his face impassive. But she was not prepared for the further shock.

In the doorway to the parlor stood a man, with a surprisingly familiar face, but whom she had never before met. Senator Thomas Whitmore.

"Mrs. Childs, we finally meet," a low musical voice greeted her.

Suddenly frightened and angry, she hissed at Jon. "What are you doing, Jon? Just whose side are you on?"

Before he could answer her, she turned to Anselm. "Have you been threatened in any way, Father?" she asked him anxiously, casting her eyes suspiciously at Whitmore.

"No, no," the priest, surprised, took her arm and assured her. "Everything is fine, my dear. Jon asked if it was possible for me to arrange this meeting secretly, for the senator's benefit."

"I'm your 3:00 appointment, recently cancelled," the senator spoke behind her, his voice exuding authority.

She was nervous, and suddenly distrustful of Connor's motives. No one but Sheila knew she was here. Why did the senator want to see her, and in secret?

"Mrs. Childs," he noted her anxiety, and his voice softened. "I am here alone, no coercion, no aides, no witnesses, just us." He smiled hesitantly, holding his hands out, palms up. "No tricks. I needed to meet you. My staff has been adamant that that not happen, that it is not in my best interest. So I have defied them. I asked Agent Connor to arrange this secretly. No one knows I am here."

Amanda looked at him dumbly, her mind whirring, poised as if to flee.

He paused. "I assume that you have met my chief assistant Richard Dover, and that he has briefed you on the situation."

"I know only that you are apparently Andrew's father," she spoke evenly, although she was inwardly shaking.

"Yes, I am afraid it is true," he assented.

"Afraid?" she echoed balefully, suddenly wrathful. She was surprised at her own antipathy toward the man.

He flushed. "Mrs. Childs. May I call you Amanda?"

She took a deep breath, trying to steady her nerves. "Please," she acceded.

"Amanda, please come in and sit down," Anselm placidly gestured toward the parlor. "You're pale. I think perhaps a seat and a glass of brandy might be in order."

"Please, Amanda," Jon stepped forward, tenderly took her arm and drew her with him into the parlor.

She allowed herself to be led to a sofa, and she sat down, Jon joining her. Whitmore sat across from her in a wing chair, and Anselm walked over to a tea trolley in the corner of the room.

"Senator?" he inquired.

The senator gazed at Amanda. "A whiskey if you have it, Father."

Father Anselm nodded.

"The same for me," Amanda added, her eyes not leaving Whitmore.

Anselm looked over at Jon. "Nothing for me, thanks," Jon replied.

They were silent as Anselm prepared and handed them their drinks. "I will now excuse myself so that you can converse in private."

Jon stood. "Thank you, Father," he replied feelingly.

Whitmore also stood. "I appreciate your allowing us to inconvenience you this way."

Anselm nodded pleasantly. After Anselm had gone, Jon and the senator returned to their seats. Whitmore cleared his voice. "I couldn't think of a way to ditch my staff for this meeting. Ernie Keely is covering for me at the moment. I drove into town to—to see where Andrew's remains are reposed." He took a shaky breath. "I met Father Anselm and this plan came together."

He looked at Amanda, resolve in his voice. "I realize this is an especially difficult time. I want to assure you that I want justice done for the conspirators involved in my son's murder." His eyes bored into hers.

"You have certainly embraced Andy quickly enough," Amanda observed coldly, setting down her glass untouched. "Why the sudden paternal instinct after all this time?"

Whitmore flushed, trying to control his sudden temper. He had never before allowed someone to speak to him that way.

Jon warningly squeezed her arm.

She ignored Jon's touch. Whitmore countered coolly, "It's my understanding that you are also under suspicion as a co-conspirator?"

It was Amanda's turn to blush. "I was," she admitted, her eyes shooting daggers.

Jon intervened. "Senator, as I told you, the investigation was very thorough and she was excluded as a suspect. She was almost killed by the conspirators."

Whitmore gazed at Jon. "And you're sure Amanda was not involved?"

Amanda interposed petulantly, "I'm sitting right here."

Jon took her hand in his reassuringly. "Yes, I'm sure," he replied shortly, his eyes flashing as well, swallowing his ire.

Smiling saccharinely, Amanda went on the offensive. "How long have you had the information that you are Andrew's father?"

Whitmore frowned, and she thought she had silenced him.

He finally answered, "It's apparent that you and I are starting out with a lack of trust in each other. I forget my manners, Amanda. I apologize for antagonizing you. I'd like to start over." He smiled beguilingly. "I'm here to try to correct any misinformation."

"What misinformation?" she echoed.

Whitmore's voice lowered. "Amanda, I am here because this matter threatens to become an explosive public issue. I am trying to contain the damage that could occur from an—indiscretion of mine in my younger years, a situation I have allowed to get out of hand." He leaned forward, his gaze upon her. "I think you join me in not wishing that to happen, for your own reasons?"

She also leaned forward, her eyes intent upon him. "Senator, I know the truth. All of it."

The color drained from his face. "Did this information come from a certain reporter from the *Post*?"

"Some, but not all," her voice was controlled. "I have proof from Andrew himself and his family that you knew that you were Andy's father from the very first."

He flushed, and Jon looked at her curiously. Amanda continued, deciding to try her hand at bluffing. "It is in a very safe place, and enough people have been made aware of it and have been furnished copies to make you an automatic suspect if anything should happen to Mike Knox. In fact, I believe two attempts have already been made on his life."

Whitmore's eyes widened in shock. Amanda noted it, before his jaw jutted out stubbornly and his eyes flashed. In that moment Amanda caught her breath. Andrew had looked exactly like that when angered. She had wondered why the senator seemed so familiar. She suddenly recognized the resemblance between father and son.

"How did you know this?" he demanded shakily. "I assure you I have had nothing to do with any alleged 'attempts' on Mr. Knox' life," he countered testily.

"But someone has," Connor interposed quietly. Both Whitmore and Amanda turned their gaze upon him, Whitmore's mouth open in surprise.

Chapter 24

"How do you know this wasn't something made up by Knox?" Whitmore demanded, standing. He paced the floor, but Amanda noticed a slight tremor in his hands.

"Because someone was killed in an explosion while using Knox's car, and Alcohol, Tobacco and Firearms is investigating. The Bureau has stepped in as well," Connor answered.

Whitmore sank back into his chair, the color having drained from his face. He suddenly seemed older, tired. "I saw the story on the television news. I had nothing to do with it," he whispered, visibly shaken, his eyes enormous. "Mike Knox was my son's friend," he spoke, more to himself. "I would never do anything to hurt him."

"What about your staff? Someone else in your family?" Jon couldn't help himself.

"No," he said, at first vehement, then as the enormity of the situation dawned on him, he shook his head confusedly. "I don't know; surely not." He took a deep breath. "I have no other living family, just Althea's father, who is in the final stages of lung cancer and under constant nursing care. As far as staff...."

Jon noted his hesitation, his sudden apprehension. "What is it, Senator Whitmore?" He leaned forward. "There's something you know. What is it?"

Whitmore was hesitant, his confidence vanished. "I—I have had some suspicions recently regarding Richard," his voice was reduced to almost a whisper. "He is very ambitious, and that's no crime. Got me where I am today," he added, almost apologetically.

"But I was recently approached secretly by Burton, and asked point-blank if I was aware of some of my aide's associates."

"Burton?" Amanda interposed curiously.

Jon answered for the senator, "Burton Holt, the Bureau's Director."

"Burton and I have been friends a long time," the senator smiled slightly. "We were college roommates at Princeton."

Amanda sat there, still as a stone. Jon prompted him, "Associates?"

"It appears that Dover has close ties with some major organized crime elements in my home state," the senator admitted, looking down at his feet. "This was a major shock to me, something that did not show up on any background checks. I wanted to do something about it immediately. But Burton told me the Bureau would like to follow the matter and see if surveillance would net some of the big fish. I told him not to wait too long—it was killing me to pretend ignorance to this man who was playing fast and loose with my career.

"When I received the documents from Knox, I wasn't shocked. I guessed it was coming sooner or later. I hated myself for not breaking it, but once Andrew was—was gone, I could see no good in disclosure.

"But Richard became rabid, wanting no acknowledgment, no disclosure. He kept saying he would handle it. When I told him I wanted to go public, he vetoed the idea, and said at worst we could put a spin on it that I was just confronted with this evidence and didn't know."

"Were you OK with that?" Amanda questioned, her chest heaving sorrowfully.

"No, Amanda, I was not," Whitmore answered her sadly. "But Burton's guys were telling me to play along just a little longer.

"I saw on the news about Walter Norton's death, the explosion. I knew Walter well. I knew Knox was missing. I wondered. But until today I had no idea . . ." he swallowed. "This is terrible."

"So you're telling me the Bureau is already involved in an investigation on Dover?" Jon was dubious.

"Only at the highest levels. I pledged my cooperation to Burton," Whitmore replied. "And by the way, Burton knew about—about Andrew. When my—my son applied to Quantico, Burton followed his progress, and told me." He looked grave. "Andrew excelled and was tagged for promotion, was selected for several special details. I was very proud of him."

Whitmore fell silent, as though exhausted by the effort.

"Senator Whitmore, we of course would like your cooperation in the investigation," Jon spoke quietly.

"Yes, of course," he nodded distractedly. "I never thought—" his voice trailed off as he rubbed his forehead with his hand. Amanda again caught her breath; it was the same gesture Andy used when he was frustrated. It was as though she was seeing an older version of Andrew before her.

Whitmore looked over at Amanda and sighed. "This secret has been an enormous burden on me. I wanted to come clean years ago, but my wife Althea was adamant that she and her family would not be humiliated by the public disclosure that I was unfaithful and fathered a child by another woman." He paused. "So all these years I kept silent. I realized there was not much of a life with Emily, even though I loved her. Her sister Chloe read me the riot act dispelling that pipe dream.

"I asked if it were possible that they would allow me to take Andrew; Althea wanted a child but couldn't have any. But both Althea and Chloe objected. Althea said she didn't know if she could stand looking at the child and being reminded daily of my 'sin', as she put it. And Chloe said I wouldn't get him without a fight." He looked up and met Amanda's eyes. "Back in those days, it was bad enough that Andrew was fatherless; to publicly bastardize him was worse than the lie Chloe was floating. Neither of the women in my life would allow me to work it out to raise him as my own.

"I kept in touch with Emily and her sister, and through them was able to follow Andrew. I supported him, set up a trust for him, provided a college fund, all secretly.

"I thought Althea might relent once Andrew became an adult. But she was jealous, jealous of my desire to acknowledge him. I wanted it so badly, I admit. Althea died a couple years ago. By then it was too late—Andrew was also dead. I saw no reason to disclose this until—"

"Until Mike sent you copies of his proof," Amanda countered quietly.

His eyes became pleading. "What good would disclosure have done then? I swear to you, Amanda, that I have not at any time done anything to put Mr. Knox or anyone else in danger. And I loved my son." He paused, looking down at his hands. "He was my only child. I loved Emily, madly. By the time I met her I was already deeply enmeshed in my marriage, and could not hurt my wife." He paused, the pain filling his features. "I was honest with Althea and told her I would not fight a divorce if she chose that route. She chose not to."

He buried his face in his hands. "Many times I rued not publicly acknowledging Andrew. But Emily was so sick. Chloe was unmoving. And Althea had stood by me in tough times. I could not repay that devotion and—love—by destroying her, making it public. I guess that makes me a weak man."

She stared at him, struck by the change in him from an arrogant, self-important man to the humble person before her, and she suddenly believed him. "Senator Whitmore, I have no desire that you be subjected to media scrutiny for the past. I personally don't see what good it will do. However, Andy left strict instructions which seem to indicate his feelings were otherwise." Amanda took a breath. "He hated his unknown father for abandoning him."

She observed the look of raw hurt that flitted across Whitmore's face. "But his last known instructions, once discovering your identity, were to give you the chance to come clean before the story broke."

"So he did know?" Whitmore croaked, his face white.

"Not until just before he was killed," Amanda answered gently. Jon stared at her. "He was going to tell me, but never got the chance."

Jon whispered to her, "How long have you known this?"

She looked over at Whitmore, who was staring at the coffee table. She just shook her head and mouthed, "Not now."

She took a deep breath and continued. "My overwhelming concern is for this upcoming trial. I realize you don't know me," she faltered, her cold veneer slipping. "But you have intimated that you believe me capable of conspiring against the very man I have loved with all my heart, the man I have struggled to live without for the past five years. More importantly, this sudden inquiry of yours threatens to jeopardize the criminal prosecution of the very man who has ultimately been responsible for taking Andy from me, for creating this hell."

Her voice became very controlled. "Senator, I'm not into making threats. I have no idea whether the story about you will break or not. I have little control over that at this point. But I am committed to the punishment of the one who took my husband and to vindicating Andy's efforts to crack this case. I am also committed to the safety of Michael Knox, his friend."

Her eyes became steely. "I'm not blackmailing you. But if you end up mucking up this case, you can count on me to personally call the press conference and share the evidence."

Jon was stunned. "Amanda," he breathed.

But the senator held up his hand, silencing Jon. To Amanda's surprise, he nodded. "I understand perfectly. And I intend to make a public pronouncement of my own, if that makes you feel better. I want the truth to be known. I'm just sorry I didn't do the right thing years ago."

He was solemn. "I don't want to 'muck up this case', as you so succinctly put it. So I would like to wait until after the trial. And of course if my silence a little while longer nets the arrest of some major crime figures, I would like it to mean something."

Amanda was too surprised to respond. But Jon interposed, "Have you told anyone on your staff that you intend to reveal this news?"

"No. I have been struggling with this decision alone." He paused, swallowing. "I have not shared that with Richard, for obvious reasons."

Whitmore stared at Jon, who stared back at him. "If Dover and/or someone else on your staff are behind the incidents against Knox, you may not be safe if that person realizes there is an investigation, or that you are about to publicly announce this. You need to keep this close to your chest. Trust no staff right now."

Whitmore pursed his lips. Amanda shook her head—there again the resemblance to Andrew was strong. He finally nodded. "OK."

Whitmore took a breath, turned toward Amanda and smiled slightly. "And I reviewed the Bureau's investigation, and know that no stone was left unturned. I happen to believe Agent Connor's conclusion that you are innocent of wrongdoing, Amanda Childs. But I felt I had to goad you into responding, to test your reaction." He shrugged. "It's what I do. I had to reassure myself."

He downed his whiskey, then stood. "Agent Connor, I am concerned about the allegations that Mr. Knox has been the victim of attempts on his life. I obviously have an interest in not being made a suspect in criminal wrongdoing," his face was grave. "I would appreciate it if the Bureau could resolve this matter quickly."

Jon also stood. "We will do our best, Senator."

Whitmore nodded, his demeanor uneasy. "I intend to inform Burton of my revelation to you, and the information we have shared. I would ask that the two of you also maintain this as confidential for now."

Whitmore's eyes softened. "What is the status of your engagement to my daughter-in-law?"

Amanda drew in her breath sharply, surprised that Whitmore knew. Jon, looking at Amanda, spoke softly, "Sir, the engagement is still off, against my wishes and despite my efforts to make it otherwise."

Amanda said stiffly, "I want nothing to interfere with this prosecution. Andy deserves no less."

"Hopefully it will be over soon and your life can go on," Whitmore replied sympathetically. He reached out his hand toward Amanda. Amanda hesitated a second before standing and taking it.

"Again I'm sorry for sounding so mercenary." He squeezed her hand gratefully. "In my line of work, one doesn't always know who to trust, and posturing is necessary."

Whitmore suddenly glanced at his watch anxiously. "I must go. It is extremely difficult to shake off all my staff, and they are by now wondering where I am and discussing a manhunt. I had to borrow Ernie's daughter's car so that I could slip out as it was." He frowned. "And Richard will be suspicious. So I'll have to lie and say it was a rendezvous with a woman or something. Which in a sense it was." He smiled pensively.

Amanda countered, "Senator Whitmore, I don't appreciate being followed, tailed and eavesdropped upon. Are you doing that?" She paused as he turned to her, his face a mask. "If so, I would appreciate it if you'd withdraw the surveillance."

He looked at her thoughtfully. "I'll see what I can do. Mind you, if someone else is out there also watching you, I have no control over that. And you must be extremely careful, Amanda. I don't know how broad this net of Dover's is."

He strode to the doorway, but turned back. "Amanda, when this is over, do you think it is possible for you and I to meet and—to talk about my son?" He looked uncomfortable. "I would like to hear more about Andrew."

Amanda nodded solemnly. "I'd like that."

He smiled then, and again she was reminded of Andrew. "Then it's a date. I'll be in touch. No, don't bother to see me out," he waved away Jon, who had started to follow him.

"But, Senator," Jon started, but the senator interrupted him.

"Agent Connor, I'm a grown man, and just because I have all this staff running when I snap my fingers does not mean I can't do things for myself. I will talk to you again."

Amanda watched him leave, careful not to look at Jon. Jon turned to Amanda as the front door was heard closing. "OK, so when were you going to share all this about Knox? And this information, this proof you have given to everyone but the Bureau?" his eyes searched hers accusingly.

She gazed at him, her eyes large and framing her pale face. She replied evenly, "Hopefully very soon."

"Amanda, you're playing a dangerous game," Jon whispered, concerned.

"It's no game," she rejoined. "And I don't want to be involved in it, but I am. If I had my say, I'd turn it all over to you and be done with it. But there are others to consider."

"Knox?" he asked.

"Yes. And Andy apparently had some very definite thoughts about the circumstances behind disclosure of this information," Amanda turned away, sighing. "Could I trust the Bureau with this proof? Why should I?"

He walked up behind her and placed his hands on her shoulders, his thumbs gently stroking her neck, his hands kneading her shoulders. "Please trust me. Let me protect you, Amanda. This could get nasty. If someone is gunning for Knox, why not you as well, if you are in possession of the evidence?"

"You know I can't think straight when you're touching me," she murmured.

"Just say yes, my love," he whispered, as his arms encircled her and he trailed kisses down her neck.

"Don't you think I want to?" she closed her eyes and leaned against him.

They heard the sound of footsteps, and she quickly disentangled herself from him as Anselm cleared his throat and tentatively walked into the room.

"Am I interrupting anything?" he looked at them with mock innocence.

"No, Father," Amanda smiled, blushing. "I really need to get back to the office. Thank you so much for allowing us to meet here in your home."

"Anything for you, my dear," he spoke warmly.

"But—" Jon started.

"Later, Jon," she spoke hurriedly, as she fled from the home as gracefully as she could.

Chapter 25

Amanda pulled out of Anselm's driveway heading back toward her office. She mulled over the situation in her mind. She could not understand what was behind Whitmore's sudden appearance or his statements to her just now. She was still not sure whether to trust the senator, particularly in view of the revelation by Knox of his brushes with death.

Was Whitmore sincere? Could she trust him? Or was he lulling her into a false sense of security? Was he actually the one behind the incidents threatening Knox's life? Was he a master of spinning tales to cover himself? Or was it indeed a staff member and/or the mob?

And why was Jon involved? Because, of course, she concluded, the Bureau would be called upon to dance attendance upon the powerful senator, or to react to him in some way. The thought made her sad. I guess the Bureau will always be in my life. I need to add them to the Christmas card list.

Well, at least I don't have to chase down the client who cancelled the appointment, she smiled grimly. That mystery is solved.

She pulled into the parking lot of the law office and let herself out. She pushed the ignition key button locking her car and made her way into the office.

Sheila smiled with relief when she walked in. "It's been busier than a beehive here," she announced. "Chief Petrino and Bruce Williams checked the office for bugs. He said you had asked for it. They found nothing."

"That's good," Amanda nodded.

"There is a stack of messages." She handed Amanda the small sheaf of pink slips. "Two were from Louise at the library."

Amanda's eyes narrowed as she scanned the messages. "It's nearly quitting time, and I have not accomplished much work today," she asserted distractedly.

"And your absence has allowed me to catch up to you," Sheila laughed. "Your inbox is full, and everything else has been filed and mailed out."

Amanda looked down at the woman admiringly. "I don't know what I'd do without you," she spoke fervently.

Sheila beamed briefly. "Like you, I want to show Ralph that we girls can handle the office just fine without him."

Amanda laughed heartily. "Am I that obvious?"

Sheila joined in the laughter. "I haven't worked for you all this time without figuring out a few things about you."

"Lock up and get out of here," Amanda ordered good-naturedly. "I will promise not to clean out my inbox tonight. I'm beat."

Amanda walked to her office, messages in hand. I am tired, she thought again.

She continued to review the slips of paper as she closed her office door and walked to her chair. When she got to the message left by Louise her eyes grew wide. "Elvis has left the building."

What on earth does she mean? Amanda wondered. As the possible meaning dawned on her, she picked up the phone and dialed the library.

"Is Louise still there?" she asked breathlessly.

"Just a moment," the receptionist replied and put her on hold.

Surely not, Amanda kept saying to herself as she pulled some of the papers from her inbox toward her and started reviewing and signing letters and pleadings.

Finally, she heard the familiar voice. "Louise here. May I help you?"

"It's Amanda," she broke in. "I have just gotten back from—from a meeting. Does the message think what I think it means?"

"Brad Pitt was not playing at the theatre where you said he'd be. No sign of him," Louise confirmed. "Wasn't that movie supposed to be in town a while?"

"I don't know; I thought so," Amanda responded, suddenly anxious but inwardly smiling at Louise's coded message. "Thanks so much, Louise. I will keep you posted."

Amanda hung up, resting her head in her hands. What now? she wondered. Where is Mike Knox? Where would he go? Had someone discovered him?

Sheila stuck her head in the door, a collection of mail in her hand. "I had just gotten back from the post office. I'm going to run to the courthouse before it closes, then take Ralph's mail from the post office box to his house."

Amanda jumped up so quickly she startled Sheila. If Sheila saw anything out of order at Ralph's house, she'd call the cops. "I'll take the mail," she interjected quickly. "I just remembered I forgot to water Ralph's schefflera plant. I need to check on it because he will kill me if I let it die."

"But," Sheila began, but Amanda shook her head.

"I insist," she smiled brightly. "I could kick myself for forgetting. You know how he is."

Sheila looked at her skeptically. "OK. I will make the courthouse run."

"Thanks. Let's lock up, because I may grab a bite to eat. I don't know if I'll come back after all. I didn't sleep much last night."

They made the rounds, Amanda stuffed the contents of her inbox in her briefcase to take with her, and they locked up, Amanda trying to mask her desire to hurry. Then Amanda followed Sheila out of the office.

She tried to walk nonchalantly to her car, but felt herself trembling. What if something happened to Mike? The evidence he had? She should have insisted that he turn himself in to Jon. But would he have been safe?

She pulled out, looking both ways for traffic, intent on spying anything unusual. She realized that despite her request to the senator not to continue to have her followed, she did not know but what she was under scrutiny. The recent events of the criminal investigation involving her were fresh in her mind, especially the revelation that she had been a focus of the Bureau's probe. Jon once intimated that she might have even been the subject of electronic surveillance at her home and business, and she had not at the time followed up with questions. But she remembered the sudden uneasiness she had felt, that someone might be watching, listening to her.

Now that she had become embroiled in befriending the reporter and had actually spied others tailing her right after the advent of the news about Whitmore's paternity, she was more vigilant, ever mindful of the possibility of eyes upon her.

So on the way to Ralph's house, she watched to see if she might be followed. Although she was anxious to get there, she forced herself to maintain a casual speed.

Arriving at the house, she pushed the remote button, opening the garage door. Ralph's car was still in its customary spot, but the motorcycle was no longer there. She drove in, closing the garage door behind her.

She jumped out quickly and let herself into the house. As it was not quite dusk, she made her way easily through the house, not turning on any lights.

She went through all the rooms, satisfying herself that Knox was indeed gone. She saw nothing out of order. She dropped the mail onto the kitchen table and walked into the study. She looked around, but there was no evidence of the documents that Knox had mailed to Ralph and that she had reviewed the prior evening. There was no evidence to suggest Knox had ever been there. She checked the guest room. The bed was made up and there was nothing amiss, nothing left behind.

She retraced her steps to the kitchen, going through the mail methodically. In the middle of the envelopes and packages was the manila envelope Knox had mailed to Ralph. Opening the little metal tab to check the contents, she saw that the documents were all there, along with a folded piece of paper with a handwritten note:

> Amanda, I'm leaving these in your care for now. Gotta check the landscape first. Keep them safe. It's time I look up your boyfriend.
> MK

She immediately took the envelope and made her way back to the study. She pushed a hidden button and carefully pulled back the bookcase, which slid easily from the wall, revealing a safe. She placed the envelope in Ralph's safe, putting everything back as it was.

Did Knox leave on his own or at the behest, or coercion, of someone else? If he left voluntarily, why didn't he take the papers with him? There was nothing indicating forced entry or struggle.

She absently walked to the refrigerator to pull out a bottled water. She started to close the refrigerator door, when something on the floor caught her eye. She reached over and turned the light over the sink on, and leaned down to examine it.

It was a glass, and it was broken. The shards were scattered across the floor. And there were blotches of blood.

"This isn't good," she whispered, suddenly frightened.

As she straightened up, there was a sudden sound. She jumped and cried out. The sound repeated itself, a knocking on the kitchen window. A muffled voice said, "For God's sake, Amanda, let me in."

She looked out the kitchen window and saw Charles Petrino's face looking back at her. He pointed toward the French doors from the nearby salon to the deck outside.

She quickly went to the door and unlocked it. He slipped in past her, locking the door behind him.

"What are you doing here?" she demanded shakily.

"Trying to catch a burglar," he answered shortly, gazing at her.

She sank to the sofa. "I'm not a burglar," she retorted. "I came to—to water the plant and drop off the mail."

"Like hell," he muttered, standing over her. "Your reporter friend isn't here."

"You—you knew?" she managed, the shock evident on her face.

"He called me, wanted to get in touch with Jon, turn himself in. Said you told him I was one of the good guys."

"But—" Amanda stuttered.

"But nothing," Charlie said shortly. "He told me it was bad enough that he had possibly put you in danger. He wasn't going to let that continue. He had discharged his promise to Andy to tell you before anything happened."

"So where is he?"

"Somewhere safe for now." He stepped into the kitchen. "I apparently scared him like I did you. Cut his hand when he tried to pick it up, and bled like a stuck pig. He told me I needed to clean up his mess before you saw it and got scared."

"Too late," she followed Charlie, going to the counter and pulling off some paper towels to hand him and going to the pantry and retrieving a broom and dustpan. "I really was frightened."

"I'm sorry," he remarked earnestly as he bent down and tried to wipe up some of the blood and glass.

Together they quickly cleaned the floor and put everything away.

"When did this happen?" she asked casually.

"This morning."

"Does Jon know?"

Charlie stopped and turned his gaze on her. "Yes, Amanda. Jon, Knox and I all had lunch together."

"Why the hell couldn't he tell me that?" she cursed, vexed.

Charlie's brows knit into a frown. "He didn't tell you?"

"I just came from seeing Jon. No, he didn't tell me that Mike was now in federal custody."

She turned away, ran some water into a pitcher and disappeared a moment. Returning, she offered in response to Charlie's unspoken question, "I had to water the plant. If it dies, it is a capital offense to Ralph."

"No shit," he laughed.

"Seriously. I killed one when he was gone on vacation last year, and he raised such a ruckus I thought I'd never hear the end of it."

She looked around, still peeved. "I'm going to get the housekeeping service to clean everything for Ralph's and Claire's return home," she remarked absently, trying to divert attention from her anger at Jon.

"Not too much longer," Charlie nodded. "How did the meeting with the senator go?"

"How—never mind," Amanda, surprised, shook her head. "I will never know how you and Fred know everything around here. The senator has agreed to withdraw his inquiry until the trial is over, and says he believes in my innocence. He even states he is going to make the information public. But I just have trouble believing him."

"So what are we going to do about the proof you found?"

Amanda stared at him. "How did you know that?"

He snorted. "How do you think? For all your smarts . . . Fred called me, and I went out to check on the water temperature for fishing." He smiled briefly. "I checked the house for bugs. You're clean. Fred is on guard with a shotgun and his new-fangled alarm system."

She looked away. "I guess the Bureau will be demanding that next."

"I want it miles away from you, as soon as possible," he replied vehemently.

Amanda looked at him in surprise. "I agree. But I'm afraid of tipping off some voyeur that I have it."

"Chances are they already know. Problem is how to get it out." He paused. "We could just call the FBI," he spoke wryly.

"And take the chance on trusting the Bureau?" she was incredulous. "They'll probably deep-six this information, and the world will never see it."

"Might not be a bad idea," Charlie muttered.

Amanda faced him, her face pale in the light of the kitchen, her voice raised. "I'll be damned if I just turn anything over to the FBI *carte blanche*. What about my history with the Bureau makes you think that is a remote possibility?"

Charlie's eyes grew wide. "Excuse me. I thought you were thinking of marrying one of them," he murmured sardonically.

"Not when I cannot trust him to tell me the truth," she muttered.

Amanda, trying to mask her irritation, turned away, laughed shortly and retorted, "I should have married you when I had the chance. Lately you're spending more time with me than with Jill."

When he didn't respond, she turned around. Charlie was staring out the kitchen window. "I don't think that is fucking funny," he whispered.

Amanda crimsoned. "I'm so sorry, Charlie," she reached out to touch his arm, but he shook her off gruffly.

"Let's get the hell out of here."

She shrugged, reached over and cut off the kitchen light. He followed her through the door to the garage. "Where's your car?" she tried to make her question light.

"Down the street," he spoke. "I didn't want to tip anyone off. I walked up."

"You want a lift?"

"I can walk," he was short. "Where are you staying the night?"

"I'm going back to the farm," she answered. "I'm going to take Fred something to eat. It's the least I can do."

"You might want to call him first. I think he is cooking for you."

At her surprised look, he added, "He said you were too thin, that someone needs to fatten you up. I'll follow you to the gate at Fred's." Charlie's tone brooked no opposition.

"If you like." Amanda decided not to engage him in battle. "What about our dilemma with the proof?"

"I'll collect it when you say the word and deliver it wherever you want," he replied, not looking at her. "Tonight, preferably."

She started to say something, then thought better of it. "I'll drop you off," she spoke, clicking the button twice on her key to unlock the doors.

She got into her car, leaving Charlie scowling. "Coming?" she called, putting the key in the ignition.

He climbed in. She hit the garage door opener and backed out. "Which way?"

"Right," he pointed.

A moment later she pulled up to his unmarked sedan.

"Don't speed," he warned as he stepped out. "I'm right behind you. Don't think I won't pull you over."

She revved her engine for his benefit, but waited until he cranked his car before pulling out.

She drove more slowly than usual, trying to determine what CD she should shove into the player. "Christopher Herrick, Saliva, Bela Fleck or Kissin?" she asked aloud. Pretty soon the sounds of hard rock guitars and driving bass assaulted her ears. "Yeah," she nodded. "Sounds like my day."

She tried to clear her mind of all the questions that whirled in her head. But when she did that, a picture of Jon's face floated to the fore. Lying sack of shit, she dubbed him, suddenly livid. She tried to banish all thought of him as well, concentrating on the music and the road.

She thought of what still lay unspoken between her and Charlie. I have to close that chapter somehow, she told herself, for both our sakes.

She finally turned onto the trail leading to the gate. It was almost dark as she climbed out to open the gate, Charlie's car pulling up behind hers.

She walked up to him as he debarked from his vehicle. She put her hand on his arm. "Charlie, go home," she commanded softly.

He just stared at her. She continued, "At what point do we let go, Pete? The past is just that—in the past. We can't change any of it. Go home to your wife."

"But the documents—" he looked at her, suddenly earnest.

She shook her head. "I'll figure it out and let you know. I mean it. I know what you're thinking, what you are trying to do. You can't hold on to me, and I can't hold on to Andy any more." She swallowed. "And Charlie, the feelings I harbored for you, and the guilt that I let you go, and the hurt I've caused between us, threaten to destroy what we have left." She looked away. "I can't live with that, can't live without your friendship. But I can live with you being happy with someone else."

He was silent. She felt his eyes on her. He finally whispered, "I will always love you, Mandy. I can't help that."

"I will always love you too, Pete. But I screwed up and let the golden opportunity for us slip away. It's gone. And you and I are not going to hurt the others we love." She continued, her voice small. "We can't change any of it," she repeated. "So stop it."

She grabbed his arms and shook him. "Didn't you once tell me that I needed to quit drowning in the memory of Andrew and 'what might have been'?"

"My advice didn't seem to have gone far with you," he retorted.

"But it has, finally. Too late, but better than never," she responded intently, dropping her hands. "And you need to start living in the present and planning for the future. I am, as of right now." She held out her hand. "Shake on it."

He stared at her, then shook his head, and started laughing. She did too, as they shook hands.

"You know, if Jon isn't good to you I will thrash him," he muttered good-naturedly.

"I know," she smiled. "Now lock the gate behind me, go home and give Jill a night to remember, maybe even a baby," she pushed him playfully.

She walked to her car and pulled through the gate, heading home. She felt remorse over her botched relationship with Charlie, but knew she had done the right thing. *It's time for both of us to start over,* she decided.

After a few minutes she pulled up to the house. She looked at the home, with the lights already glowing through the windows in the gathering dark. She smiled and thought, *This is what home feels like. I had forgotten. I can't wait until this trial is over.*

She grabbed her briefcase and let herself out of the car. As she walked up the steps to the porch, the screen door opened, and Fred stood there. "I wondered if my food was going to get cold," he spoke accusingly.

"I'm sorry," Amanda was contrite. "If it makes you feel better, I'm famished and grateful to you."

He looked behind her. "Charlie didn't follow you?"

"I sent him home to his wife."

Fred looked at her and nodded. "Best place for him."

"I know," Amanda smiled. "Let's eat."

She set down her briefcase on the desk and led the way into the kitchen, where Fred had already set the table. She went over to the stove and lifted the lid of the large frying pan. "Umm, swiss steak and gravy." She turned toward Fred. "You didn't? Mashed potatoes too? Home made biscuits? And your own home-grown early peas? And it's not even my birthday."

"When was the last time you ate a real meal?" Fred countered. "Not since Ralph's been gone on his honeymoon, I know. You've been walking around hollow-eyed."

He pushed her toward the table. "Sit down while I serve this up."

She was obedient, and sat in a chair while he opened a bottle of wine and poured her a glass. Within minutes he had put the food on the table before her, and sat down himself.

"Say grace," he ordered. They bowed their heads while Amanda prayed.

They passed the bowls around in a comfortable silence. Amanda split open a biscuit and ladled gravy on it, as Fred grinned. "As Dad always said, acid test for both the gravy and the biscuit," she quipped.

As Amanda cut and tasted the steak, Fred watched her.

"Oh, my God," she mumbled, her mouth full. Chewing it and swallowing, she took another sip of wine. "That is a slice of paradise. I'm in love. My heavens, Fred, someone should have snapped you up and married you a long time ago."

"Someone did," he murmured.

Amanda looked at him in shock. "You were married?"

"Still am," he replied, taking a bite of potatoes.

Amanda was stupefied. "Fred, I never knew this."

"Well, it's not a very pretty story."

"I'd like to hear it," she said quietly.

"Some time maybe I'll tell you. But suffice it to say, she was mentally ill, a very sick woman. I didn't know it until later. She left me."

Amanda gazed at him sympathetically. "No divorce?"

"No," Fred buttered a piece of bread. "If she had wanted one, I would not have stopped her. But I couldn't abandon her, even if she was crazy. She's still out there somewhere. Every now and then I get word about her. I worry about her."

"I'm so sorry," Amanda looked at him, stricken.

"Don't be. Life goes on," Fred responded tersely. "You need to remember that."

"I know," she nodded somberly. "I'm doing something about it."

"Marrying Jon?" he quipped.

"Maybe, when the trial is over," she smiled enigmatically.

"Amanda, I've been thinking about those papers upstairs," Fred changed the subject.

He fell silent a moment. Amanda prompted him. "And?"

"And I have a possible hiding place, very safe, known only to me, here on the farm."

"Why didn't you say so earlier?" Amanda demanded, another bite of steak on its way to her mouth.

"Well, I thought you were hell bent on getting these papers to that reporter right away. But if you want to store them away until needed . . . ."

Amanda chewed thoughtfully. "Actually, that is an excellent game plan. Mike is in protective custody, and it's not—convenient," she faltered, "for him to have the papers right now."

"After dinner, I can show you the place," Fred offered.

"Actually," Amanda paused, "maybe it's better I don't know where this spot is, at least right now. That way, I won't be lying if that question is asked."

Fred concurred, "I thought the same thing, but didn't want to broach the subject. I would have to leave information of the location somewhere, in case something should ever happen to me."

"That's true," Amanda agreed. "We just need to make copies, so I can forward them to several people for safekeeping."

"Fine. If you agree, I'll take care of the matter," Fred concluded with a quick rare smile.

Amanda raised her glass. "To Fred, my knight in shining armor."

"She's aware she's being followed," the voice stated. "It's hard to keep her under surveillance. But something interesting. She apparently had some sort of rendezvous with the chief of police at a private home this evening. One of my men caught her leaving the place with the guy. She let him out, and he followed her to her home out in the woods. They've been spending a lot of time together."

"Did you check the place?" Dover was anxious.

"Made it in without even breaking a door. Security system was off. No sign of your reporter. I checked thoroughly—nothing else in the house."

Dover sighed. "Knox has turned himself in to federal custody. The Bureau. He has no documents on him, just some copies. Due to the bungling of your people, I don't know yet if he made contact with Childs or not."

He was agitated. "And the senator disappeared this afternoon. He has just reappeared. He says he had a rendezvous with a woman. I have no idea whether he trusts me or not."

"This plan of yours has gone south," the voice insisted. "I'm going to have to handle the situation by another means."

"No," Dover controlled himself with difficulty. "I can force a meeting between Knox and the senator. We can eliminate both of them, if it comes to that. I can force Knox to reveal where the documents are. But if we go with Plan B, finding the documents will be moot. I can still make this work."

"You are on a short leash. I can't wait much longer. Make it so."

Chapter 26

"Mrs. Childs is here," the secretary reminded Greg Boyer of his appointment, although he had been feverishly preparing himself for it all morning.

"Send her on in," he replied without looking up from the papers on his desk. "And, Jeannie, hold all my calls." Despite his disdain for impressing people, he found himself straightening his tie and rolling down and buttoning the sleeves of his dress shirt. He stood and quickly donned his suit jacket.

Amanda Childs entered the office, impeccably dressed in a pale peach colored tweed suit. She appeared tense, but extended her hand to him cheerfully. He could understand Connor's fascination with her. Her smile was instantly disarming, her green eyes mesmerizing.

"How was court this morning?" he asked her conversationally.

"It went well. Judge Farley was in an uncharacteristically good mood," she replied.

"Did you win?"

Amanda's eyes bored through his. "You know it's not whether you win or lose, but how you play the game," she said softly.

"So you didn't win?" his eyebrows shot up.

"Actually, I did win," she laughed, a pleasant sound. "And a very gratifying win for my client, for by winning at summary judgment he saved a lot of money not having to go to trial. We were both happy."

"Please sit down, Mrs. Childs. Can I get you anything to drink—coffee, water, soft drink?" he asked gruffly. Graciousness was not one of his strong suits, but he found himself wanting to put her at ease.

"Nothing, thanks," she responded politely, surveying the bare office as she seated herself stiffly in the leather chair, her purse clutched tightly in her hands on her lap.

"Not much to it," he answered the unspoken question. "I'm just borrowing it. Because they're short-handed on prosecutors, and because of the potential publicity and high profile of this case, they called me in." He shrugged modestly. "I travel around trying the more complex cases. It's what I do. So these are temporary quarters."

He came around the desk and seated himself in the second chair beside her, startling her. He sensed her immediate withdrawal. Turning to face her, hesitantly he proffered, "I got off on the wrong foot with you at the wedding reception, and I need to apologize. I do come off like a bull in a china shop, and I am prone to take my cases too seriously. But it was no time to spring the news on you about the trial. And Jon has already given me the cold shoulder about it."

Amanda met his gaze unblinkingly. "That's fine, Mr. Boyer. I understand perfectly what you're up against in this case, and in your position I might have done the same, who knows? An attorney always hopes that his witnesses won't be the cause of further complications after the event."

Boyer stared. "So you and Jon—"

"Were seeing each other occasionally," she filled in the blanks. "If it helps, only after the arrest was made. I actually never met Jon until after Marjorie's death, and we never saw each other socially until after Marks and Barnes were—arrested," she stammered momentarily, her face somber. "However, Jon had asked me to marry him the day before your debut and announcement at the wedding reception."

Boyer slumped, an angry flush on his face at the confirmation of his suspicions. "I'm sorry. Jon refused to talk about it, said it was none of my damned business. He forbade me to talk to you of it. But—"

"It's certainly relevant information, and you're entitled to know and be prepared for any claim of bias put forth by the defense. And Jon knows better than to withhold the information. But the engagement is off," Amanda interrupted him.

"Still?" stuttered Boyer. "But—"

Amanda again cut him off. "Just like you, I am unwavering in my desire to see justice done in this case. I realize that the defense will try to create a case of bias if he can, and there seem to be several promising fronts to interject that argument. What better case than when the star witness is a co-conspirator who is providing the prosecutor substantial assistance, and whose daughter happened to be the prime suspect and ended up dating and engaged to the chief case officer?"

Greg sighed. "Exactly," he replied resignedly, stunned that her assessment matched his.

Amanda continued, "My husband died at the hands of these men, Mr. Boyer. Andy, as well as Jon, spent much time and effort to crack this case." She swallowed, her face grave. "Andy gave his life to protect me from these men. So, you see, something precious was stolen from me. I cannot allow Barnes to go free, no matter whether Jon has feelings for me."

"Or you for him?" Greg countered softly.

"Or me for him," Amanda repeated solemnly.

Boyer flushed uncomfortably. "I'm so sorry."

"Since meeting Jon I haven't been thinking too clearly. But I guess I wanted so badly for the nightmare to be over that I never imagined that Mr. Barnes might fight the charges. Foolish of me, I know, after knowing the man all these years. It's well known that he's always relished a fight. And I'm sure he sees me as the cause of Billy's death." Her jaw clenched momentarily. "Mr. Barnes has never taken responsibility for his own actions.

"But I pledge my support and assistance. I will endeavor to create no more complications. It's just that—"

"You're in love with Jon?" Barnes interrupted her perceptively.

Amanda looked down at her hands. "It's complicated," she stammered. "Andy was my life, and life has been so empty without him. But since—since Jon and I have been—well, seeing each other, I've been delirious, like a schoolgirl. At least until the day of Ralph's wedding."

Greg grimaced. "I'm sorry, Amanda."

"If it helps you any, we've not slept together, although if you hadn't interrupted with your news at the wedding reception, I am not sure I would still be able to say that."

"Not even the night before?" Greg demanded gently.

"No. We were both hauled off after the rehearsal dinner, he to a bachelor party, and me to a bridal shower. We—we never connected again until the wedding."

"I'm sorry," Greg's face reddened as he repeated himself.

There was an embarrassed silence. She finally broke it. "So I'm here to provide whatever testimony and assistance you need. It is my hope that I have not compromised this case too badly."

"Well, I only know that whatever you managed to do, Senator Whitmore has backed off on his demands, and is letting the trial proceed unmolested. What exactly did you do?"

Amanda smiled knowingly. "The senator and I called a temporary truce, so that justice could be done."

"I appreciate that. You know, you enjoy an excellent reputation as an attorney. Everyone says you are tough but honest." He hesitated. "You know, there's a lot of interest being generated in this case. Your life will be under a media microscope."

Amanda frowned. "I dread that the most. So far, I've managed to avoid most of the reporters. I have been grateful for that. I know that will not last.

In fact, I've been worried that the senator's appearance would fuel new interest by the paparazzi. With the trial approaching, I'm expecting the worst. I'm trying not to read the papers."

She paused. "I've met with the vestry and my choirs at St. Catherine's, to disclose the facts of—of my—conception, and to give them a highlight of this—case," she stuttered, taking a deep breath. "I wanted them to know before the worst hits the news."

She smiled sadly. "I have spent my career being plain old Amanda Andrews, trying to be the best I can be, while maintaining my integrity and ethics. So it hurts being in the spotlight and allowing the defense to take potshots at my credibility, to have it smeared in front of a jury and the public. And I'm frankly scared about how the rest of the community will take the news about my being the illegitimate daughter of Marjorie Witherspoon and—and Stephen Marks. I hate for Marjy's name to be sullied in any way."

She took a deep breath, almost overcome. Boyer waited patiently for her to compose herself. "But to have Jon face that is even harder, for some reason."

"You fear for Jon?" Barnes queried, surprised.

"Yes. The Bureau is his life." She met his gaze then, smiling pensively.

"Well, I can tell you that he is one of the finest field officers I know. I and others have tried for years to get him to take a U.S. Attorney position, but he always preferred the field work and he had a mission to find your husband's killer. Jon is meticulous, and his record is unblemished. Mrs. Childs—"

"Call me Amanda, please," interrupted Amanda, "and I don't want to be the cause of any spot on his record."

"And call me Greg. Amanda, you know as a lawyer we have to take our cases as we find them. I have every confidence we'll make it through, and we're going to give it the Boy Scout try.

"And now I really need to ask you some questions, to prepare you for what to expect at trial. We might not have another opportunity to go through the evidence before then," he finished briskly.

The lawyer side of him reasserted itself, and he returned to the other side of the desk. Facing her, he started firing questions at her, listening to her responses, making notes to himself, and interrupting her from time to time to discuss points of her testimony. Amanda was impressed with his uncanny ability to leave no stone unturned in fleshing out possible weaknesses, hammering out all the details, and hitting her with possible cross-examination questions.

A couple hours later, he sat back in his chair. "Whew! Lawyers generally make the very worst witnesses, but I must say you came through with flying colors," he smiled.

Amanda smiled tightly too. "And were my answers about Jon and me satisfactory?" she asked anxiously.

"You'll do just fine," he added, with more than a hint of admiration in his voice. "There is the hearing on the motion to suppress next week, then trial has been moved up to two weeks after that. You will not be called as a witness at the motion hearing, but Jon will. He'll be the major player, along with Stephen Marks' statement. Depending on the outcome of the motion, there may be a continuance of the trial. The judge on the case does not like to continue cases. I'm all for going ahead, although I'm not sure whether I'll be able to survive a directed verdict without that eavesdropping and wiretap evidence if we lose the motion."

Amanda asserted quietly, "I understand. You know how to reach me, should you need anything."

"Actually, there is something," Greg surprised her, coming back around the desk and sitting on the edge, facing her. She looked at him expectantly, questioningly.

"I have a special request. You don't have to do this, and I understand perfectly if you decline. I have little to offer Stephen Marks for all his cooperation, except perhaps a good word for him at a future parole hearing. And he asks about you all the time, is very keen to know that you are all right. I think he is truly concerned about you. His health is not the best."

She paled, looking away, biting her lip.

"He is being housed at the federal prison facility in Bayview. He has already been sentenced, but may be eligible for earlier parole depending on his substantial assistance in this case." Boyer paused, clearly uncomfortable.

"Amanda, this trial is going to bring up some very unwelcome questions, and I have no doubt the defense will try to push your buttons, particularly when it comes to your feelings about Barnes and Marks.

"Would you consider going out to the prison to see Stephen, talk to him?"

She recoiled as if slapped, her shock evident. Before she could reply, Boyer continued hastily, "Don't give me an answer. You are under no obligation. Just think about it. Despite our preparation today, I don't know what the defense might try. I want you to be emotionally prepared."

"What am I supposed to do?" she snapped, her eyes brilliant. Taken aback, Boyer felt the sudden anger boiling from her. "Act the part of the doting daughter? Tell him I love him for all he's done for me? In spite of all he's done to me?"

She took a deep breath before continuing, her voice icy. "Acknowledging him at all is a betrayal of the people who raised and sheltered me. What's going to happen when the community finds out the whole sordid truth? When the media spills it all, and all those I have loved—still love—are exposed to public ridicule? I am helpless to protect them, and they are not here to defend themselves. Don't you know how hard this is for me, how this man destroyed everything I held dear? Because of him, my whole life has been a lie."

Boyer saw her pain as she struggled to regain her composure. Sympathizing with her, he commented quietly, "He has no one other than Adam Brownlee, who goes out there once or twice a week bringing him communion. Like I said, just think about it. I understand your feelings, and for that matter, I think he does too. I just don't want those unresolved issues to become a problem for you on the stand. Better to deal with them now."

Amanda rose to leave. As she reached for the door handle, Boyer warned softly, "Amanda, if you should falter in your resolve regarding Jon, it's OK with me. All I ask is that you let me know. I don't want to be surprised with the information by defense counsel in court. I want to best defend you and him."

Amanda looked at him woodenly. He gazed back at her. "Contrary to what you might have heard about my cold-bloodedness, I've been in love. You and Jon are human, and you could do a lot worse. He's crazy about you."

"Good day, Mr. Boyer," Amanda's response was brisk as she left.

Whew, he thought to himself as he stared at the closing door. He thought, Remind me not to meet her in a dark alley. Jon has met his match.

PART III

Week 3

Chapter 27

Jon stood at the screen door, in chinos and a polo shirt, with a bottle of wine in one hand, a DVD in the other. As he hesitated, rearranging his cargo to knock, Amanda appeared before him, a slight flush to her cheeks, dressed in denim bermuda shorts and yellow pullover tank shirt.

"Hi, there," she opened the door for him. "The roast just came out of the oven, so your timing is excellent. How are you at carving?"

Walking in past her, handing her the DVD, setting down the bottle of wine and slipping an arm around her waist, he murmured, "I'm much better at kissing," as he pulled her to him and his mouth found hers.

She kissed him back before whispering, "There you go again, seducing me."

He released her mouth, continuing to hold her and replacing a wayward strand of her hair as he mused lightly, "I'm glad I brought a cabernet. What else do you have for me?"

She ignored the double entendre as she replied, "Let's see, a Southern feast—salad, roast, carrots, onions and potatoes, asparagus, some of Fred's early peas, your choice of homemade cranberry and orange compote, Seb's horseradish, gravy, and hollandaise, just in case you have to cover your green vegetables with sauce, a loaf of fresh crusty French bread, with fruit, cheese and banana pudding for dessert. What did you bring me?"

Her pulse quickened as he released her and replied casually, "Oh, just me. And a DVD of *Tosca*—Domingo is singing. You told me once how you always cry when you hear him sing *E lucevan e stelle*, so I guess that makes this a chick flick."

Amanda peered at him. "You really are too good to be true."

"Not as good as I'd like to be," he suggested, stalking her as she playfully fended off his advances and fled to the kitchen. Following her, he found that the table was set, with gleaming china, crystal, candles, and damask linens on the French country table.

Transfixed, he opined, "Wow, Mrs. Childs, you set an impressive table."

"Thank you, Mr. Connor." She turned to face him. "How is Mike Knox?"

"He is fine for the moment. Wanted me to thank you for the copies of the documents and to give you his love when I saw him." He frowned. "What is that about?"

"Oh, nothing. Probably just the night he and I spent together," she smiled wickedly.

"You vixen!" Jon exclaimed good-naturedly, moving toward her.

Amanda took refuge behind a chair at the kitchen table. Her face was suddenly solemn. "I only wish you felt you could tell me after the meeting with Whitmore that Mike was in the Bureau's custody."

Jon flushed. "I'm sorry—"

She waved away his response. "Please don't explain. Do you think I've not been there before? Many times." The last words held a tinge of bitterness.

She turned away, changing the subject. "I know we're a little early, but I hate for good food to get cold. Why don't we set it all on the table and pig out?"

Jon thought, I feel like such a heel. There's nothing I want more than to tell her everything, all the time.

But he entered into her light banter as he presided over the electric knife, carving the roast. She disappeared, returning momentarily with a highball glass of scotch on ice for him. He murmured his thanks as she busied herself with the remaining dishes.

They finally seated themselves at the table. Amanda said grace. He uncorked the wine and poured some into their glasses. As she passed the platter of meat to him, he quizzed, "Anything going on between you and the guy in your choir? I noticed you two deep in conversation after church today."

She looked at him, flushing. "You mean Dr. Freeman? No. He just had some material for me on depression for—for a client."

"Doctor?" he repeated questioningly.

"He's a psychologist," Amanda supplied evenly. "Why do you ask?" she was defensive.

"No reason, just wondering," Jon gazed at her intently as she looked away, reaching for the vegetables to pass to him. So there's something she doesn't want me to know. That's cool, he thought. She's just trying to preserve the attorney-client privilege.

But it wasn't cool at all, he realized. He remembered the other evening when she disclosed she had a doctor's appointment. Was she the one suffering from depression? Was he part of the problem? Were the upcoming trial and the advent of Senator Whitmore's news, with the resurrection of all the memories of Andrew, contributing to her stress and sadness to the point that she needed counseling? She had every right to feel overwhelmed. God, he prayed, let me be there for her.

"Would it spoil a beautiful afternoon to talk about your meeting with Greg Boyer on Friday?"

She frowned. "Well, it is not my pick of topics, but there's no use avoiding it. Let's get it over with. I have good news and bad news."

"Let's have it," Connor stated quietly as he accepted another serving plate from her.

"The prosecutor is not going to need me for the motion to suppress, but that pretty much stands to reason."

"Greg mentioned that," confirmed Jon solemnly. "But my testimony will be critical there. We've worked on my listing of our steps of establishing probable cause and eliminating you as a suspect. One really good point is that we had not ruled you out at the time we got the bugs at the warehouse. But to your credit we had previously bugged your home and did phone tolls on the home and office without obtaining anything incriminating."

"You did?" Amanda breathed sharply.

"Even after Stephen Marks made his statement, we used the information of your name listed as the CEO of WWAC, Inc., in the probable cause statement to obtain our bugs. The Bureau had not ruled you out and was still trying to obtain evidence against you, and did obtain what evidence we needed to make the case, just against the real culprits." He hesitated. "So what's the bad news?"

"Well, there are several facets, one of which you have just touched on. You will end up being the feature of the motion to suppress hearing. The defense will try to discredit your informant Stephen Marks. Greg Boyer confirmed my fears that I will probably be the focus of the defense at both the motion hearing and trial. He told me to be prepared for questions about the recital series, Bill Barnes, my feelings about Marks, and—and us."

Connor, sensing her anxiety, covered her hand with his. "Amanda, all I care about is you, us. What I feel for you is going to last after this trial is over and long forgotten. If only I could make you believe that."

"But that is not enough," she suddenly flared. "Barnes must go down for his actions," she cried, turning away from him. "Andy must not have died in vain. He has to be avenged."

Jon looked at her amazedly as she covered her face with both hands.

"I'm sorry," she whispered. "I've prayed so hard that I could give up this desire for revenge. Oh, heavens, if this trial isn't over soon, I'm afraid what a monster I will become."

He reached over and gently pulled her hands away from her face. "My dearest," he murmured as she refused to meet his gaze, "you misunderstand me. I don't for a moment intend that this case be lost."

He stood and pulled her out of her chair to him, embracing her. "I love you dearly, Amanda, but please believe that my resolve is as strong as yours. I am not the enemy here. I fully intend that Andy's killers and your persecutors pay. I admit that I too will find justice extremely sweet, and there's nothing wrong with that. I just don't think we have to wait until the goal is accomplished to be together."

She was silent and passive. "I'm sorry, Jon," she whispered. "It's not that I don't love you and want to be with you more than anything. It's just that I don't want to keep looking over my shoulder, to feel this burden hanging over me, between us."

He held her close. "I know. I feel it too."

She exhaled deeply. "It's been such a hard week, what with Shelby's funeral and fighting the prosecutor over Alan's arrest, then all this about the Senator, and the upcoming trial," she finished, her voice tired.

Jon kissed her. "My Amanda, I hate for you to face all this alone. You don't have to. Please know I want to be there for you, with you, when you are ready. Any time."

He released her, pushing her gently back into her chair. "Now you need to eat before your fabulous dinner gets cold."

She smiled tremulously as he returned to his seat beside her. He added lightly, "And I no longer have any doubts about your taking care of yourself. The interview with the senator amazed me. I'm recommending the Bureau hire you as an enforcer."

Amanda, realizing that any conversation that involved the Bureau was a potential minefield, briskly changed the subject. "Is there not anything else we can talk about? Surely we have a lot to find out about each other. I realize I know very little about you. Mom would have had a fit if she was alive and knew I had accepted a ring from you without a full *curriculum vitae* and criminal, family and credit history on you."

"OK, so what do you want to know?" Connor conceded, stuffing his mouth with roast.

"Tell me about your family," solicited Amanda as she sipped wine.

"Let's see. Not much to tell. I have a mother and a father, a younger brother and sister."

"Where do they all live and what do they do?"

"Mother was a stay-at-home mom for us, and is a children's book author and executive wife, flitting around doing her charity work and the like. She's active in politics, a wheeler-dealer."

"What about your father?"

Connor reached for his wine glass. "Dad made his money in the computer software design business. They live outside the Denver area, where we grew up."

"And the siblings?"

"Kelly has followed in Dad's footsteps, and is a vice-president of the company. She's got a few copyrighted products of her own, and she's a part-time free spirit and daredevil, big skier, hot-dogger, stuff like that. She's impulsive. Colorado fits her to a 'T'. Then there's David, who's a rake and a reprobate."

"David? What does he do?"

"He is only two years my junior. He finished med school, passed his boards, and mainly plays around the hot spots. He has received his certification as a plastic surgeon, mostly elective. He can't decide where he wants to settle down, so he hops from L.A. to Miami to Aspen."

"Sounds like a total overachiever family. Way out of my league."

Jon caught her hand and kissed her fingertips. "Never." He smiled self-deprecatingly. "I have a confession to make. I've told my sister about you, but I've been hesitant to subject you to the others just yet."

"Why?" Amanda demanded, plopping a bite of bread in her mouth.

"Because they are a little intense, and I think I love them more from a few thousand miles away," Jon countered with a wry smile. "My mother can be overbearing at times. Besides, my brother would be seducing you. He's made a play for every girl I've ever dated. I couldn't handle that with you. I like having you to myself and don't want to scare you away. I surmised you would meet them all soon enough."

"Jon! You wouldn't want me to meet your family? Or," Amanda paused, as another thought hit her, "are you more worried about their meeting me?"

"I'm not worried about showing you off to anyone, dear," Jon assured her.

"'Dear'—I like the sound of that," Amanda grinned.

"OK, so what about your family?" he gazed at her. "I want to know about the relatives who might show up at our door unannounced."

"Not many there, I'm afraid," she replied. "Actually, my dad—" she suddenly paused, coloring, embarrassed.

Jon, divining her thoughts, murmured, "They were your mom and dad, Amanda. Don't ever forget that."

She squeezed his hand gratefully. "Dad was a late baby, and his brothers and sisters had all predeceased him before I was old enough to remember them. My mother still has a living brother and sister, but they don't live nearby anymore, and I don't hear from them except for the annual Christmas card exchange. My brother, Jeffrey, is a mechanical engineer and lives just outside Philadelphia now. He and his wife Phyllis have a little girl, Desiree, now eight. They come down Memorial Day weekend to the beach, and I try to make it up there for Thanksgiving. We talk on the phone about every other week."

She paused. "We love each other, but we're not demonstrative. It's like we want to keep it a secret from everyone else," she laughed softly. "And Ralph, Marjorie and Doc have been as much my family here, particularly since Dad and Mom are gone. Then there are Alan, Shelby and the boys.

"And Charlie," Jon inserted smoothly.

"And Charlie." She sobered, her manner subdued.

"I'm sorry about Shelby. I know that must be hard."

"I spent some time with Alan and the boys yesterday, took them to the mall just to get out a little. It's like there's nothing anyone can do. And I feel his pain. It brings back memories of my own loss." She looked down.

She steered the conversation away to more pleasant topics. They finished lunch lightheartedly, then together put away the food and tucked the dishes in the dishwasher. As Jon turned to her, he inquired lightly, "What now? How about the video?"

"I have a better idea," Amanda countered. "Let's sit on the back porch and enjoy the spring day."

Together they placed everything on a tray, and Connor carried it out as Amanda led the way out the French doors to the screened porch. Outside the sun warmed the air as bees buzzed around the beds of riotous spring flowers. Amanda paused at an oversized porch swing, the seat covered with a blue and yellow chintz cushion and pillows.

Connor whistled when he saw it. "Wow! I've not seen one this big. Did Andy make it?"

"No. This is a Fred Vaughan original," Amanda replied proudly. "Long enough to seat an army or take a nap."

"Has it been tested for other activities?" Connor watched her amusedly.

Amanda turned her back so that he could not see her blush, as she pointed out a side table on which he could set the tray and settled herself on one side of the swing. As he moved to join her, he spied an old battered book on the seat. Picking it up, he read the cover and rifled through the pages idly.

"*The Norton Anthology of Poetry*," he read aloud. "Is this part of your plan?"

"You didn't think I'd take your word for it that you could quote Dylan Thomas?" she winked, a smile peeking from around the corners of her mouth. "I thought a pop quiz might be in order."

"Mom made us learn and recite poetry during summers off from school, to keep us out of trouble, or for punishment," he chuckled.

Jon sat beside her, glancing quickly through the tome before placing the book on a matching ottoman in front of them, taking her hand and reciting 'The force that through the green fuse drives the flower', as she listened.

He smiled. "Or how about some Andrew Marvell's 'To his coy mistress'? I know—Yeats. I noticed that you have the section of his poems dog-eared. Much more sensuous, don't you think?"

He recited the first stanza of 'Leda and the Swan'. She stood suddenly and moved away, finding herself embarrassed by the words and his nearness. Noticing her retreat, he frowned. "Are you afraid of me?"

"I'm afraid of myself and how you stir me," she affirmed frankly.

Jon relented. "Woman, I'm ready for dessert and coffee. While you serve it up, do you mind if I find us some music?"

She laughed nervously as she bent over the tray. "The stereo is just inside the French doors there."

She spooned dessert into cups and poured coffee, as he disappeared indoors. Soon strains of Heifetz playing a Beethoven violin concerto were heard, as he reappeared. He was saying, "What a great collection of music."

"Yes. Those old LPs are Marjorie's. I couldn't bear to part with them, even though a few have made it into CD form."

As he retook his seat she handed him dessert, placing coffee on the ottoman in front of him. "Black, right?"

He nodded. She then picked up a cup of coffee and walked across to an Adirondack chair. She blushed at his scrutiny of her.

"I'm sorry, Jonathan, but when you're so close, I can't think straight."

He stared at her glumly. "You drive me utterly crazy, Amanda. I'm hoping against hope that one day you'll want me so much that you'll come to me, no reservations, no fears, no anxiety about the consequences. Until then I will try to wait. But don't think I won't keep trying to gnaw away at those barriers."

"Is that the purpose of the DVD?" she countered lightly.

"I am found out," he grinned. He devoured his pudding, then stretched his full length on the swing, using the pillows to cradle his head. "No use wasting such a wonderful swing. Read to me."

Amanda, placing her coffee cup on the ottoman, stood up and reached over for the book, but he took her hand and pulled her down to kiss her, before abruptly letting her go.

Surprisingly bereft, she realized that she didn't want him to stop. But she retrieved the book, settling herself back in the chair and reading aloud passages as he identified the author. Then he began to doze as she continued reading. She stopped to observe him sleeping, before settling back in her chair to continue her reverie alone, the strains of Beethoven still wafting pleasantly through the air.

The early spring warmth was inviting, and the lazy buzz of the insects enticed her to slumber. She also succumbed, drowsing as the sun asserted its dominance in the sky.

She didn't know how long she was asleep, but suddenly her senses were assaulted by the sound of loud knocking and someone calling, "Amanda, Amanda, are you there?" followed by the words, "I hope they're decent."

As Amanda's eyes opened and she took in the words, two figures burst onto the porch, laughing. "Amanda!" a familiar voice called.

Connor sat up sheepishly, as Amanda, galvanized, stood, and cried, "Ralph! Claire! You're back! I wasn't expecting you until tomorrow or Tuesday."

Claire's face mirrored her concern as she took in Connor's presence. "Oh, I'm so sorry. We shouldn't have intruded. I told Ralph we should have called ahead," as she looked from Amanda to Jon, embarrassed.

"Don't be absurd," cried Jon, as he walked over and slapped Ralph on the shoulder and Amanda kissed Claire. "We were both snoozing after Amanda's dinner."

Ralph gazed at both of them slyly. "Sorry if we interrupted something important," he grinned mischievously.

"Nothing doing," Amanda laughed heartily. "When did you get in?"

"We just drove in from the airport," Claire replied, still hesitant. "We thought we could use an extra day to set up housekeeping. Ralph insisted that we come straight here first."

"And I'm glad you did," insisted Amanda. "The housekeeper has cleaned Ralph's house from top to bottom. I had ordered dinner and flowers for your first evening home, but wasn't expecting you so soon. Are you hungry now?"

Ralph laughed. "You bet. Did Jon leave any leftovers?"

"Yes. Come on in the kitchen and we'll set you up."

Chapter 28

Soon they were all sitting around the kitchen table while Ralph and Claire helped themselves to the tempting array of food placed before them. Amanda poured herself and Connor each a cup of coffee and sat down, as Ralph, stuffing food into his mouth, began describing their trip.

"One could spend weeks just at the Louvre. And I thought of you every time we walked into a church or cathedral."

Claire chimed in. "Ralph was going to bribe the titulaire at Notre Dame to offer you an organ recital, but Ralph's French is so awful, the organist thought that Ralph was making a major contribution to the organ, and got really friendly. I had to intervene quickly."

Amanda laughed. "Thank God you were there. There's no telling what trouble Ralph could get into all by himself."

"So is the law practice a shambles?" Ralph demanded.

Amanda looked at him in mock disgust. "Dearest, Sheila and I did just fine without you. In fact, I think we accomplished more work and made more money with you gone."

"Bull—I mean no way," Ralph grinned. "Claire is trying to get me to clean up my language."

"Way," Amanda rejoined in her best teen lingo. "And all your clients said they liked me better," she added mischievously.

"You really need to quit smoking that weed," Ralph joked. "It has addled your brain."

He continued. "This roast is really good. You are a fabulous cook. So have we set the date? When are we repeating the performance for the two of you?" Ralph demanded.

Connor looked at Amanda, who flushed.

"The engagement is off," she announced.

A bite of buttered bread was on its way to Ralph's mouth, as he stopped and stared at them. "Why?" he asked hotly.

Jon stood up, his eyes meeting Amanda's. "I think I need a walk." He stalked out of the kitchen.

Claire looked over at Amanda, who was staring at her coffee cup. "What's going on?"

Amanda felt tears stinging her eyes, but blinked and willed herself to stop. "Mr. Barnes, Sr., is moving to suppress the evidence obtained by the eavesdrop warrant, and is demanding speedy trial." She took a deep breath. "I just felt that Jon's having a relationship with me was just one more nasty complication in an already messy case, and I gave back his ring. I've had a long discussion with the U.S. Attorney Greg Boyer, who agrees with me."

"Damn it all—" Ralph started to protest, but Claire squeezed his arm painfully to silence him. Leaning over and taking Amanda's hand, she inquired softly, "Are you sure that's what you want to do? What's best for you?"

"No," whispered Amanda, the strain beginning to show. "But there are a lot more important things at stake here than what I want."

"But Mandy—" began Ralph, but a voice behind him cut him off.

"You know better than to argue with her, Ralph," Jon had walked back into the kitchen, setting his empty coffee cup on the counter. "She's made up her mind. But with God and these two as my witnesses, I want to say this."

He knelt before her and took her hand. Into her upturned palm he placed the engagement ring and closed her hand around it. "I understand what you're trying to do, but I don't agree with you. I don't need your protection, Amanda, and we will prevail—you'll see.

"Keep this in a safe place. I don't want it back. It's yours, and I hope you will wear it if or when you decide you are ready for me. Remember—no reservations."

Standing up, he kissed her on the ear, whispering, "I love you, Amanda." Then he straightened up and cleared the huskiness from his throat. "I hate to run, but I just got a call. All hell is breaking loose on a case in Panama City, and I volunteered my assistance to Bubba."

Seeing her stricken face, he added softly, "I don't want to leave. But I have to do something or I'll lose my mind. I'll be down at my parents' condo for a few days. I'll have my cell phone with me."

Pausing at the kitchen door, he said, "I'll see you all later. Amanda, call me. I at least want to hear your voice." And he was gone.

Claire and Ralph looked at Amanda, who was staring intently at the empty doorway. She then looked at them and asked, struggling to keep her voice even, "Can I get you some dessert?"

Ralph looked at her angrily, then shrugged. "Women," he muttered irritably. Then getting up from his chair, he turned to Claire. "You talk to her," he ordered as he quickly left the room, following in Connor's wake.

Amanda looked ashen, and Claire went to her. Taking Amanda's hands in her own, she pulled her up. "Let's go down to the dock and sit."

Amanda absently began picking up dishes to place in the sink, but Claire took the dishes from her and returned them to the table. "This can wait."

Amanda numbly followed Claire as she led Amanda by the hand out of the house and down the trail to the dock, where two old Adirondack chairs stared out at the water before them. She sat down in one, patting the other for Amanda. Amanda complied dazedly.

Claire murmured, "That all this turmoil was going on—I'm sorry we weren't here for you."

Amanda turned to Claire. "No, I'm sorry that you came home from a wonderful honeymoon to bad news like this. I spoiled it all for you. I don't know how it is I cannot get my life in order, get something right for a change . . ."

"Amanda, dear, this isn't your fault. You didn't ask for this. Men don't see progressions of events like we women do. They're more immediate-minded and worry about the justification later. Women are the long-range planners."

"I know I'm crazy for turning Jon away, but I loved Andy so much. I cannot allow his killers to squirm out of this. What happened is a direct result of William Barnes, Sr., no matter who pulled the trigger, damn it." The last words were a whisper.

"How do you feel about Jon?" Claire whispered, leaning toward Amanda.

"Claire, I want him. He's constantly in my thoughts; it's so hard to concentrate on anything else. Is that wrong? I desired no one but Andy for so long. I've never been able to make the break. I don't know how to deal with this feeling."

"Andy is gone, and he would want you to find happiness with someone else."

Amanda was silent. Claire prodded, "You aren't sure about Jon?"

Amanda blurted out, "Jon says he loves me, but can I be sure he would feel the same after Barnes' defense lawyer tore him and me to shreds in court? How could he not feel betrayed, like his life's work so far has been for naught? That's not what I want for him, and I love him too much to risk it because of some sentimental stirring in my loins."

"So you do love him."

"It's been a long time. Is that what I'm feeling?" Amanda's voice was barely audible.

Claire leaned forward and squeezed her hand tightly. "Amanda, I understand what a terrible sacrifice you're making for a worthy cause. But I can't help but wonder if the cost isn't too high. None of this is going to bring Andy back. His ghost isn't hanging around waiting for you to bring the bad guys to justice. You do realize this? How much more can you take? How long do you keep putting off a chance at happiness?"

Amanda hesitated, then slowly began talking, rambling to keep from breaking down. "I always felt that it was heretical to ask God why he did things. After all, he is God, and my God needed to be omnipotent and omniscient, or he wouldn't be of much use to me. I embraced the old 1801 Articles of Religion, and that's where I fell out of step with main-line Episcopalians, who seem to recreate God in their images as often as necessary, and to divide and subtract from Holy Writ when it suits the current political agenda.

"Of course, at the other extreme are the ultra-fundamentalists, who are on first-name basis with God and act as though He's on their speed dial. They are always at the right hand of the Almighty, everything is black and white, and therefore all other views or positions regarding social justice are largely blasphemous and damnable. So I've tiptoed around all these groups trying to be nonjudgmental and unquestioning".

Her voice trembled. "But, Claire, it is so numbing to not allow yourself to ask 'why' at times, because one becomes fatalistic in mindset. I sometimes find it hard to pray, particularly for others, because I wonder if the paths of the future are set in stone. It doesn't matter what we want, because He is in charge and has foreordained it all. Just accept it and go on. The other alternative, that we and our free will are in charge, is frightening beyond belief.

"But underneath it all is this simmering anger of which I try to remain in denial. Just as I think I have a handle on it and have accepted that Andy's gone, the rage hits me again without warning. But without questioning it's too easy to become content with Thomas Hardy's 'immutable will', 'Hap', or fate, whatever you want to call it. So I'm damned if I do ask why, and damned if I don't."

She closed her eyes, sighing, and began rocking back and forth. "I keep reminding myself that I am no better or more deserving of God's grace than anyone else, and others have suffered greater tribulations. And I try to remain grateful daily for the comparative smallness of my troubles and for all the good things that have occurred.

"In the final analysis there's so much we don't know about God, and for good reason. That's to keep us humble, open-minded, and free from judgmental self-righteousness. The only way to hear the still, small voice is to be quiet and listen, and even then accept that some answers to the 'why' won't be revealed in our lifetime."

She turned to Claire, her eyes wide. "I tell myself all this, over and over, every day. But will I ever quit wanting to know the 'why'? Will the rage over Andy ever leave me? I have to keep hoping that I can make peace with Andy's memory and make a life without him; otherwise, the anger and hate will wash me away. Some days I wonder what of me is left under it all." She laughed mirthlessly. "With all the revelations about my true origins, I'm not even sure what is 'me' anymore."

"Well, that's my sermon for the evening," she finished lamely, looking out unseeingly at the lake. "I'm spouting a lot of drivel to you, trying to cover up my true feelings. I want to lash out, to scream 'why?' I want to be selfish. I want Jon so much. I even want to see Barnes dead. But the cost to Jon is too dear. I cannot take the chance."

"Even if Jon is willing to pay that cost?" Claire asked her softly.

"He says that now. What about later, when all hell breaks loose?" Amanda closed her eyes. "I cannot open myself up again to loving a man and then losing him. Been there, done that, and I'm afraid I cannot survive that again," Amanda insisted, her eyes opening and resting on the water beyond them.

They were silent for several minutes. Claire finally broke the silence. "OK, what now?"

"Life goes on," Amanda finished wearily. "It's not like I don't have plenty of work to do."

Claire whispered, "Don't look now, but Ralph is on his way down here."

Ralph soon joined them, leaning down and kissing his wife. Amanda, eager to change the subject, said, "I've got you a really big high-profile murder case while you were gone."

"Oh, yeah?" Ralph rejoined. "Who did you kill?"

"Not me. Shelby Young died while you were gone, and they're about to bring charges against Alan for it."

Ralph whistled lowly, shock registering on his face. "Alan? That's just too incredible. I cannot believe this. You didn't say anything about it," he accused her.

"I didn't want to create a cloud over your honeymoon," Amanda reasoned.

"We can't leave you people alone without all sorts of trouble happening. Has the sacred attorney-client relationship been consummated?"

"Yep, a substantial retainer. He insisted on it. You know I'd do it for free. And I've already managed to avoid Alan's going to jail once. It is such a blow to him and the boys."

Ralph nodded sympathetically. "That's too bad. They were a great couple."

"He is going through his own personal hell right now, being without her, he and the boys in shock, and the fact that they had had a few minor squabbles the week before her collapse and death. And now this criminal investigation."

"Tell me what you know," he insisted.

"But you're technically still on honeymoon," Amanda retorted.

"This is Alan and Shelby we're talking about," he countered stubbornly.

So she brought him up to speed on the events, as he and Claire listened gravely.

They were silent a moment when she finished, sober at the thought of looming serious charges against their friend.

Ralph finally asked, "Are you going to be OK, Mandy? I hate all this is happening to you and Jon."

"You know me. I'll survive."

"Well, I am glad that I finally realized that I can't go it alone. This woman is my lifeline," he said, grabbing Claire's hand and squeezing it. "It feels good."

"You two need to leave before you start slurping all over each other and making me sick," Amanda laughed.

Claire looked anxiously at her. "I hate to leave you alone."

"Don't be silly. I'm fine. Enjoy your time off together, because Ralph is double-booked with clients when he gets back."

"What a slave-driver," Ralph grumbled good-naturedly, as they stood.

"Oh, and one more thing," Amanda said quietly. "There is an envelope in your safe. I needed some quick place no one would think of to stash it. Please tell no one about it."

"Not even Jon?" Ralph teased, but his smile died when he glimpsed Amanda's countenance. "Shit, ouch," he started when Claire pinched him for cursing, "is it that confidential?"

"The less you know, the better for now," Amanda remarked. "It's a long story."

The three walked up the hill together. At the front sidewalk they each kissed Amanda. She watched them drive away, then returned inside to clean up, engage the security system, turn on the dishwasher and settle down alone to watch the DVD.

"Well, Placido, looks like it's just you and me," she told the television ruefully.

Chapter 29

Jon made it to Panama City just as the sun's light was fading over the waters of the gulf. He was discouraged. *I'm getting nowhere with Amanda,* he thought. *And this case is sucking the life out of both of us. It's been the longest couple of weeks in my life. When will it end?*

He reviewed his long friendship with Andrew Childs. He mulled over the same questions over and over regarding his longtime comrade. Andy spoke to Jon occasionally of his life with Amanda, and at rare intervals he confided in Connor his feelings of gratefulness for the moments stolen away and shared with his wife. Before his death Andrew admitted his desire to leave the Bureau and find another job that would allow him to be with Amanda all the time. The revelation had surprised Jon.

Andrew once described the guilt at his inability to share with her that part of him that devoted itself to service to the Bureau. "It's as if I'm torn in two, two different people," Andrew had confessed. "And I would gladly give up my former life, yet . . ." he did not finish the sentence.

He didn't have to. Jon knew of what he was speaking. For years he had thrown himself wholeheartedly into his work, enjoying the search for clues, the constant challenge, the everchanging landscape, the solving of puzzles. He liked the authority he had, the camaraderie of his colleagues, the sense of accomplishment of a job well done, the traps laid and the criminals caught.

But all that was before Andrew's untimely death. Just before that fateful day, Jon had sensed in Andrew a restlessness, a dissatisfaction with the job. Jon had dismissed it and Andy's words as simply a sign that Andrew needed to take a vacation. However, now Jon had found the excitement of his own career waning, and an ever-present sense of something missing in his life. He had expended his energies in trying to break the case on which Andrew was working when the latter met his demise. Then Jon's money laundering investigation ended up converging into Andy's international-flung drug distribution ring probe.

That was when Jon's path crossed that of Amanda Childs. Although friends with Andrew, he had never met Andy's wife until several years after Andy's brutal death, when she became a suspect in the case.

After the arrests were made in the case and she was exonerated, he realized he had fallen for Amanda. He too had tasted the exhilaration of wanting to share the rest of his life with someone. But it seemed the closer he got, the further he had still to go to experience that life.

When his thoughts turned to Andrew, he found himself ruminating about Andy's death again. Why did Andy seek out Claude Brown alone that night? Why didn't he wait for backup before taking on the fugitive alone? Which part of Andrew made that decision? Was it his love for Amanda and desire to protect her? Was it his overwhelming need to see Claude vanquished, to see his enterprise shut down, to bring the case to a successful close? Was there some other reason?

In any event, Andrew had failed. Andy was dead, and Amanda was left alone and vulnerable, stripped of all defenses. And she had almost become a victim, the culprits pinning blame on her for the embezzlement conspiracy.

Since she had lost Andy she had woven an armor to shield her weakness from scrutiny. Jon sensed her reticence, her great fear of revealing her vulnerability to anyone. He felt that her love for Andrew Childs still held sway over her, and that she felt an overwhelming need for the closure that she hoped this trial would bring.

Despite his great allegiance to his friend and desire to see Andrew's death avenged and his work accomplished, during the investigation Jon had felt more and more drawn to Andy's widow. He was in love with Amanda Childs, and instead of his love becoming a liberating force, he felt increasingly crushed in the maelstrom of circumstances beyond his control. He realized how Andy, dead though he was, still stood between Jon and Amanda, and that until the criminal matter was finally resolved Jon might never be able to win her. Even then, could she truly let go of Andy's memory? And given the trauma she had endured, would she ever risk giving herself to someone else?

And now all this mess had surfaced with Senator Whitmore, not only the revelation about Andrew's paternity, but also the secret investigation into the possible shenanigans involving the senator's staff and the attempts on the reporter's life. Although Michael Knox was currently safe, he was chafing at his imprisonment at the safe house. Amanda had forwarded copies of the additional documents for Mike, which he had shared only with Kimball, selected Bureau officials and his editor. Knox had completed his report, but the Bureau had prevailed upon the editor to hold back the story for just a while longer in light of the pending investigation.

Jon was not able to entice Amanda to divulge the whereabouts of the originals. Nor did he particularly want to. But he worried about protecting her from possible harm from others who might be seeking to destroy them.

His phone rang. He noted it was Kimball. "Connor here. How's the babysitting job going?"

"Now that we've moved Knox to a safer spot, I am breathing easier. I'm hoping it's drawing to a close," Kimball replied. "There is actually a meeting set up between the senator and Knox. The Bureau has identified the mole, and is feeding him some misinformation, hoping to draw out the players and bring this matter to a head. In fact, although I'm not in the loop, I believe a sting may already be in progress. Whitmore is anxious, and I think they're worried about his holding matters together much longer."

"Do you need help?"

"Yeah, and I would sure love to have you, but I can call for reinforcements. Meanwhile, we're short-handed where you are. Simpson has answered Bubba's call for help and blessed your presence there, at least until this trial is over."

Kimball continued. "I'm actually calling because Knox is wanting to know from the horse's mouth how Amanda Childs is. He's worried about her. And he now has the clout to get what he wants, because the feds smell larger fish to be caught if Knox and Whitmore cooperate."

"And I'm supposed to know the answer to that question?"

"If you don't know the answer, lie," Kimball laughed. "The man is driving me crazy. He wants to talk to her personally, but I told him the Barnes' trial is too soon now to chance some major secret meeting, particularly with everything else blowing up."

"Tell him she is OK. I just left her house, had dinner with her."

"You haven't married her yet? His words, not mine."

"That's her call," Jon retorted. "Tell him to find his own woman. Later."

Jon pulled up to the condo and shook his head, trying to clear his thoughts. He got out and pulled his bag from the back seat. Letting himself into the apartment, he pulled out his cell phone and hit a button.

"Yo," he heard a familiar voice.

"Well, I'm here," Jon tried to make his voice cheerful, even though his heart was heavy. "What's my assignment? Where's the stakeout? Do you need me to start tonight?"

"Whoa," George Cramer drawled. "The excitement for today is over. We got word that the subject had been sighted, and we were hoping to close the net. However, it was a false alarm." His voice held a hint of defeat. "I really hoped we had the end in sight.

"I've set up a meeting for you with the case officer first thing tomorrow, and I'll brief you then. The case of the red-headed vixen serial killer," Bubba intoned ominously.

"Wow," laughed Jon. "I'm in."

"Wanna go grab a bite, hit a club, check out the spring break gals?" Bubba asked.

"I think not. I'm saving myself," Jon remarked, a picture of Amanda flitting through his thoughts.

"Are you sure? You used to be fun. I mean, Amanda Childs has turned out to be more trouble than you ever counted on."

"Bubba, don't go there," Jon warned ominously.

"Do you think you can handle taking this on?" George persisted. "So much has been blowing up in your own case."

Jon's voice hardened. "I'll let you know if I feel it's beyond me."

"OK, OK," Bubba backed off. "Just asking."

Jon relented. "My assistance is not currently needed on the other aspects of the case. Simpson has responded to your call for assistance. So yes, I'm free to help you."

"OK. Tomorrow at eight."

Dressed in a gray suit, Jon Connor was at the office promptly at 7:55. Knowing from past experience he would make it to the office before Bubba, he had stopped for coffee for both of them.

The receptionist was already at her desk. When Jon identified himself, she stood. "Right this way, sir," she smiled sunnily, and showed him into Bubba's small office.

"Special Agent Cramer said for you to make yourself at home and to feel free to read that stack there," as she indicated a pile of papers on the corner of his desk. "He just called, said you would already be here, and to tell you he is stuck on the Hathaway Bridge."

She left him alone, and he perched on the chair in front of Bubba's desk and began a perusal of the documents.

About halfway through his review, George Cramer, alias "Bubba", strode in, straightening his tie, with a jacket over his arm. He nodded to Connor. "Glad you remembered," he acknowledged the cup of coffee on the desk. "Hadn't seen as much of you lately. Heard you were trying to leave the Bureau."

Jon didn't look up, but the corners of his mouth turned into a slight smile. "Same old Bubba. Always a font of information. Nothing gets past you."

"Why would you want to leave? I thought you loved us," George lowered his voice as he turned around and closed the door. "All over a woman. You're not one to lose your head over a girl. Not even that fox Lauren Mallory who so wanted to eat you alive. Remember her? And geez—wasn't Amanda Childs the chief suspect in our case?"

"Tell me about this particular red-head, why don't you?" Jon retorted, trying to steer Bubba away from the subject.

But Bubba was not deterred. He sat down in his chair and pulled up to the desk, facing Jon. "Talk to me, man," Bubba pleaded. "Is she making you quit the Bureau?"

Hell, no," Jon looked up, his eyes flashing, meeting George's. "She's thrown me over entirely. Will barely talk to me. Gave my ring back. Says we are not jeopardizing this case just because we might be in love."

"Smart girl," Bubba muttered under his breath.

Jon's eyes became cold. "My resignation has been rejected, but you knew that too, didn't you?"

Bubba leaned back in his chair. "Yeah, I knew that. I also knew you would go nuts being cooped up sitting around waiting for Barnes' trial. And Kimball couldn't keep you hopping, since he's now full-time liaison on the senator's saga. So I asked Simpson for your help here. He was enthusiastic, because he thought that might keep you away from the Childs woman and prevent your screwing up the case."

Her name is Amanda," Jon said curtly. "And I'm not screwing up the case, damn it," his voice rose angrily as he stood and struck the sheaf of papers with his fist.

George stood also, leaned over and placed his hand on Jon's shoulder. "I know," he replied quietly. "We've worked together a long time. We've got a tight case against Barnes. I trust you, Jon. You won't mess it up." He frowned. "And I'm really sorry about you and Amanda."

He straightened up, suddenly all business. "What do you think so far?" he pointed to the papers under Jon's fist.

"Pretty interesting," Jon replied evenly, taking a deep breath.

"Good, because unless I miss my guess, here is our Aussie policeman himself."

"What about Interpol?"

"This cop from down under wanted to come over himself. And Interpol is now dealing with French police, who think they may want in on this action because of a similar murder over there."

Jon looked up and saw through the window a guy with sandy hair and medium build approaching Bubba's office.

George opened the door for him. C'mon in, Ian. This is Jon Connor, the guy I was telling you about. Jon, this is Sergeant Ian Callander of the New South Wales Police Service. Ian has a hard-on for this sweet thing you've been reading about."

Ian raised his eyebrows, frowning at Bubba's remark. Jon shook his head. "Never mind. Better to just ignore his colloquialisms," he smiled as he shook hands with the officer, also dressed in a suit.

"This room is a little small. Why don't we use the conference room? I'll let the boss man know where we are in case he wants to join us." George bustled out.

They all moved down the hall to a larger room with a table and several chairs. Bubba placed the stack of documents in front of Jon as another man, his well-groomed hair peppered with white, joined them.

"Jon, you remember Craig Walker? He's the honcho here."

"Yes. How are you?" Jon shook hands with the guy. "We most certainly appreciate George's help with the Barnes arrest. I hate to praise him too much," Jon winked at Bubba, "but we couldn't have made the case without him. I'm sure he is gotten his subpoena for trial as well."

"Glad to be of service. It was certainly peaceful with him gone," Walker responded, smirking. "I was halfway sorry to see the arrest made."

"OK," George interrupted testily. "I don't need for the two of you to get chummy and swap war stories about me. Here are the highlights. I told Ian this is the South, and we're all comfortable with first names and not overly enamored with rank and job title. Take it away, Ian."

Ian nodded, taking a seat across from Jon. "Evelyn Abermarle is the name, or one of the names, for this woman," he pointed to the picture on top of the documents. "American, early thirties, states on her passport 30, but we're not sure that's accurate."

"She was over in my country for two, almost three years on a work visa until a couple of years ago. She returned to the States for about a year. Then she came back apparently for about six months, and left again. While over in my jurisdiction the first time she apparently married a wealthy chap over there, hence the name Abermarle."

"Maiden name?" Jon was again reviewing papers as he listened.

"Listed as Smithlee on the marriage certificate. But my team thinks that is an alias—dead end so far."

"So you have evidence she murdered this Abermarle guy, her husband?"

"His family had suspected foul play, but he was much older with a heart problem, and the autopsy, while suspicious, didn't net us enough when he died over two years ago. At first we took it as sour grapes by the family because he had a will, authenticated by his long-time lawyer, leaving everything to

Evelyn except for a few trust funds scattered around for the adult children, grandchildren and various charities.

"However, some new legal documents came to light that cast some doubt on whether his death was from natural causes. And the lawyer was indicted on several major fraud cases, where evidence came to light that he was in league with this Evelyn. She had threatened to have him pushing up daisies, and once arrested he decided to sing to the police. Body was exhumed, and *voila!*"

"You don't sound Aussie," Jon quipped, not looking up.

Ian guffawed. "Perceptive. My parents are Australian, but moved here when I was a small child. I went to school here in the States, on the West Coast. But the surfing is much better down under," he grinned, "so I emigrated back."

He continued, "To get back to business, in the meantime this Evelyn had come back to the U.S. for a while, but returned to Australia for a short time. Her time back in the Sydney area coincided with another homicide. This time it was the dean of the Anglican cathedral, one Matthew Bicknell, found dead right in front of the altar. The choirmaster was apparently left for dead only a few feet away."

"You said 'left for dead'. He survived?" Jon posited.

"He survived. For a while we deemed him the prime suspect, but he has recovered and has 'turned state's evidence', as you Yanks say. Seems he and this Abermarle woman had an affair, which lasted a couple or three months. He said she was pretty loony, kept eating some kind of pills all the time.

"She apparently was angry at the dean because he and the head musician butted heads on several issues. He would laugh at her tirades, gratified that she took his side when he related the arguments to her.

"He said after Matins one morning, the Dean had asked him to stay behind. Evelyn showed up, and confronted the Dean, injecting him with something."

"I read about this, the dean offed right in the cathedral," Jon interrupted, his eyes narrowing.

"It made quite a stir over there, a bit of a scandal. When this Mattingly fellow, the choirmaster, tried to wrestle her away from the Dean, she knocked him down. Apparently she popped him with some of the same stuff, expecting him to go the way of the Dean."

"OK, so why do you think she's in this area?"

"Some correspondence has recently come to light. No return addresses—she was careful to destroy that evidence, or so we have surmised. But postmarks were right here in Panama City. There were letters addressed to her from an Adam without return address, as well as a couple of letters with return addresses left at her last known address, from people here in Panama City. From the context of the letters, it appears she was applying for jobs in this area. We've scoured the tri-state area here—haven't found an Evelyn Abermarle."

"No other leads?" Jon asked.

"No other leads," Ian echoed. "George has helped me check with the Panama City contacts. One hadn't heard from her in a while, but one said she had helped Evelyn secure an interview with a hospital in the area."

"Hospital?" Jon asked excitedly.

"She was looking for an administrative job, per the source. She'd worked in this area before, but the woman couldn't remember any references. We have checked the prior place of employment given by this woman, but the doctor has passed away."

"Murdered?" Walker's eyes shot up.

"He was in his eighties," Bubba remarked with a smile. "There's no evidence that foul play was involved. And she was overseas when he kicked."

"At what hospital was she applying?" Jon asked.

"Here at Bay Memorial," Ian checked his notes.

Bubba intervened. "We checked. She never showed for the interview. We've been checking the references she listed on the resume."

"So it was someone there that tipped you off that she was spotted yesterday?" Jon inquired.

"Yes," George nodded. "That didn't yield anything. But the person thought she might have worked there before. There's no record of an Evelyn Abermarle or Smithlee on the employee list. So this is where you come in."

Walker spoke up. "I'm short-handed here, because we have a re-opened murder investigation, a task force operation involving a civil service employee found dead at the air force base three years ago. George," he waved toward Cramer, "was involved in the original joint investigation with the case officer, and will be called upon again. So I'm hoping you can take the lead on this."

"And I'll help when I'm not otherwise tied up," Bubba finished.

"Of course I want to lend my assistance," Ian added. "I'm very interested in this case. I am only down here for probably no more than a week or two, depending on how things are going, before I need to get back." He grinned. "I offered to take leave, particularly when I heard there might be a few waves around here. If we make some progress, I may get to stay longer."

"I believe you must have a thing for this Evelyn," Jon asserted quietly.

Ian flushed. "Never laid eyes on her. But the diocesan office, as well as the Abermarle family and the government, are putting pressure on the police to solve this case and find the one responsible."

He allowed himself a smile. "This woman is a looker. Striking, great figure, gorgeous red hair. The family provided a whole album of pictures the old man had taken of her."

"I'm in love," Bubba sighed dramatically. "I told this hospital administrator to expect your call," he turned to Jon. "Name's Nelson Henderson." He handed over a business card. "Here are his numbers. He's pledged his cooperation, will get you into records, lend his staff's assistance in pulling whatever you need and calling people in for interviews if you desire."

"No time like the present, if you're ready," Jon took the documents and looked at Ian, who nodded. "If you don't mind, let's scan through the rest of this stack, then we'll pay a call to Mr. Henderson."

Chapter 30

It was very early Tuesday morning. Amanda sat on the dock sipping the coffee in her mug and staring out across the lake. It was dawn, and she was tired, but had been unable to sleep since around four o'clock. So she had finally given it up, thrown on some sweats, made coffee and wandered to the dock so that she could watch the sun rise and herald the new day. The mist rose off the water in a lazy steam, 'meandering in a mazy motion', Amanda thought, borrowing from Samuel Taylor Coleridge.

But life had been no Xanadu for her. Her mind was in turmoil, and she tried vainly to push away the memories and questions chronically crowding in. The morning was quiet, punctuated only by the sound of a stalwart ensemble of crickets and frogs singing matins as the gray sky lifted, the dull darkness losing the battle, retreating until time to advance again.

She longed to clear her head. I want to just not think any more, she thought. Thinking hurts. She had spent many sleepless hours trying to analyze the persistent issues for which she sought answers.

Her labyrinthine cogitations turned to Billy Barnes. Why had her childhood friend turned bad? Why had he abused their friendship, framing her for embezzlement and money laundering? Why had a man she trusted and contemplated marrying been willing to ultimately sacrifice her in another vain and ultimately fatal attempt to please his evil father? How could she have ended up trusting the man who had killed her husband and was about to kill her as well? Was it predestined that Billy would turn out to be such a villain? How was it that she did not divine Billy's true nature, instead of being duped by him?

She thought of Claude Brown: what within him steered him to a life of criminal enterprise? He was raised in a good family, and his siblings had turned out so differently. What had made him what he was? What caused him to despise her, his former attorney, so much, and to conspire in a scheme to destroy her life by ensnaring her husband and framing her for embezzlement and drug distribution?

During these times of reflection, her thoughts often turned to Andrew. As much as she tried to convince herself that her husband had loved her, he could not tear himself away from the Bureau. Even in their brief respites alone together, she always sensed there was a part of him that was distant, closed off, reserved for that aspect of his life. He never wanted to speak of work when they were together, but it was there, unspoken. She reciprocated, because there was so much about their respective professions that was confidential, privileged, unshareable. She was merely happy to greedily lap up those stolen moments when they were together, before their lives interrupted them again. She respected his dedication to his chosen profession, but wondered about that locked compartment inside him. What was the cost to him for the double life he led?

In light of the recent revelations, she had discovered that there was so much about Andrew about which she had been in the dark, a whole cauldron of pathos he had endured alone without sharing with her. She was suddenly faced with the realization that she didn't know much about the man to whom she had been married, only the compartment to which he had allowed her access.

She concluded that since Andy's death she had made him into a demi-god, and was now rudely reminded that he was only human, and that he was gone forever from her, no matter how much she kept her heart as a shrine to him. Amanda felt sadness that Andrew did not realize his goal of solving the case, of leaving the Bureau and finding another avenue of contentment.

Unknown to her, her thoughts followed the same path as Jon's thoughts earlier. She wondered what caused Andrew to throw caution to the winds that fateful night and go after Claude Brown alone, without backup. Why would he be so precipitous, so reckless? The Andrew she knew was methodical, organized, by the book, and thorough, never jumping the gun. Was it his love for her and his wish to protect her, or was it some foolhardy sense of invincibility, some latent machismo? Was it frantic desperation that the culprit was about to escape his clutches once again? Was he so anxious to complete the case and leave the Bureau that he became careless? She knew she should let go of these questions, because the answers were perhaps never forthcoming.

She had discussed some of the questions regarding Andrew with Arnold Freeman the preceding Tuesday evening. Freeman did not interrupt her, but allowed her to talk, to give voice to her thoughts. Amanda surprised herself: she found herself eager to pour forth her issues about Andy to Freeman, a disinterested professional. She carefully avoided discussion about her own newly discovered parentage, about which she found she could still not voice her feelings.

When she finally ran out of steam, she just stared at him.

"Well, tell me," she whispered. "What's wrong with me?"

Freeman had laughed shortly. "You know, Amanda, there is no diagnostic checklist, where I listen to you then label you." He smiled at her engagingly. "There's nothing wrong with you."

"But I can't escape the past, all these questions that keep slapping me in the face."

"Amanda, that's not entirely your fault. With all that has been happening, I think the past is wrapping itself tightly around you, strangling you."

"But it's been five years since Andy's murder," she insisted. "Why can't I turn loose? Can't you throw fairy dust on me, or pronounce like Christ, 'Your sins are forgiven; go, and sin no more'?"

She leaned forward, facing him over the coffee table in his office, her features earnest.

"Arnold, I know we could engage in some lengthy Socratic dialectic where I come to some sort of 'epiphany'. But I just don't have the energy for that." She looked down at her hands. "I relive this every night, every morning. I just want some understanding, if not a cure. I want to shed this skin and start anew, because I fear I'll never find the answers." She gave a short laugh. "Isn't this classic obsessive-compulsive behavior?"

Freeman leaned forward too. "Amanda, I won't deny that you most certainly have a strong obsessive-compulsive streak. I think it would be an easy way out for me to just diagnose you and be done with it. But with the stress you've suffered the last few years, I would be surprised if you didn't show some symptoms. You are a surprisingly strong person in many ways. Many would not be able to stand up to that pressure and still function as well as you do.

"I think this obsessive behavior is a coping mechanism, something you do to deal with grief and depression over the man you thought was your lifetime soul mate. And I wonder if it isn't some form of security blanket in which you've wrapped yourself to avoid finding yourself in that predicament again."

"So I am depressed?" Amanda had smiled tightly.

"Most definitely," Freeman concurred, surprising Amanda. "But before you start wearing the label, let me throw out a theory." He smiled reassuringly. "You have all this time harbored this fear that Andy didn't love you as much as you loved him. I also wonder if you haven't mixed in some guilt, that perhaps if he had loved you more, if you had loved him more, he wouldn't have been killed, and he would still be here.

"Coupled with that is the knowledge that he went out that night in response to a threat to you. You are consumed with the guilt that maybe he loved you too much, and it clouded his judgment. Then there's always the possibility of the guilt on top of the guilt, for thinking those thoughts." He paused. "Can you tell me that is not the case? No, don't answer that now. Think about it. We'll talk about it more later."

As she stood to leave, he stopped her. "And Amanda, it's not unusual for someone to suffer these feelings for a loved one, particularly as deeply as you loved Andrew. There's nothing wrong with you for going through this struggle, and for it taking this long."

"Yeah, right," she muttered.

"No," Arnold took her hand, shaking his head. "Remember that. There's no rule book that says after so many hours, weeks, months, it will all go away. As long as you recognize it, are working through it, trying to come to grips and move on, that's a form of progress. But you must not give up trying. You mustn't hide behind it."

She had remembered, and still struggled with those thoughts. But nothing seemed to help.

Then there was Jon. Jon. Him she didn't want to think of most of all. She had allowed herself to become vulnerable again, to feel the momentary cascading rush of delirium described by many as love. But was it, or was it some infatuation born of her self-isolation and his attentions?

She had shut off her feelings after Andrew's murder. Freeman was right: she had never wanted to risk opening herself to love and loss again. She had pushed Charlie away because of it. Only the chaos of the last several months had stripped away her defenses. Were her feelings for Jon just a desperate thrashing around for sexual release? Was she latching on to him because she feared being alone? Was it simply lust?

She had always secretly worried that her attraction to Charlie might have been born only of sexual frustration, particularly when she was unable to rid herself of the ties to Andy in order to pursue a relationship with Charlie.

There were many aspects of the Jon she had met that reminded her of Andrew: the rugged masculinity he exuded, the steely determination, the meticulous attention to detail, his no-nonsense attitude. Charlie had exhibited those traits as well. Was it those similarities to Andy that had drawn her to Charlie, and now attracted her to Jon?

However, Connor possessed a certain charming chivalrous nature, and she was not sure but whether it was a cover for guile. In fact, the Bureau and its insistence on secrets had stood between her and Jon on more than one occasion just in the last weeks, and she knew she and he had both resorted to subterfuge recently with each other.

Something about Andy that endeared him to her, and that he found a handicap, was his raw honesty, his lack of a poker face. And she recalled Andy's great sensitivity, which he managed to hide from his colleagues but not from her. The evening her mother finally succumbed to cancer he had taken her home, held her and described the events leading up to losing his own mother to lingering illness as a child of ten. The pathos of his boyhood suffering reached out to her even as he comforted her.

Although Andy never spoke of his father other than to state flatly that he was dead, she sensed his simmering anger for the man who was not there for the child and his mother, and the wall he had built to contain that rage. She closed her eyes, and could still feel how he made love to her after their discussion, how he had seemed to be exorcising those memories and attempting to pour himself into her, to make them physically one, even as he consoled her and brought her to release.

The memory of his anguish over his first kill came back to her. Andrew was sent home on administrative leave for a few days after the incident. Even through his tough outer shell, she could tell he was badly shaken, and she recalled his hours of silent, agonized soul-searching and recrimination.

But then, she argued with herself again, did she really ever know Andrew Childs?

Sometimes she wondered if Jon would have reacted the same way as Andrew in that situation. She realized that she also knew little about Jonathan Connor. Amanda felt extremely attracted to him. But did he, like Andrew, possess that same fanatical drive for the job, the thrill for the chase? Did he also, unlike Andy, have a taste for the kill?

Although during the aftermath of Bill Barnes' death and the arrest of his father they had talked briefly about that night and what had transpired, he was careful not to discuss his part in Bill's death. She had always assumed that he was trying to spare her feelings about reliving the betrayal of her friend.

However, Jon had never spoken much of his job to her, always seeming to steer the subject away to other matters. That reticence reminded her of Andrew. Yes, she was drawn to Jonathan Connor, but that aspect of his life he kept carefully closed off. Yet she knew that the Bureau constituted a large measure of his life, as it had Andrew's.

Could Jon actually walk away from his career with the FBI without a backward glance? Did she want him to? Could he be the one to provide the love she desperately craved? If not, was she willing to settle for less with him? Although he professed his love to her often and wooed her assiduously, Jon always kept himself in check, his emotions tightly under control, never giving anything of himself away, never seeming to need anything or anyone. Was she able to penetrate those barriers?

But, she mentally shook herself, what did it matter? At least as long as this case continued, there was no future for her with him. She was resolved that she would see through to the end justice for those who ended Andrew's life and changed hers forever. Amanda had carried this burning burden inside her for over five years, and was not going to throw it away so close to resolution. She was so determined to assuage her loss that she wondered if she would ever be free again.

Amanda was troubled with her decision. Was it revenge she sought? Sometimes she frightened herself, the rage at Bill Barnes and his son, her childhood friend, rising to the surface and overwhelming her. She felt sometimes as though she was capable of killing Barnes herself, coldly ending his existence, watching him die.

She thought back to her outburst to Jon at the church after her practice. Did she want Billy and his father 'consigned to hell' for their part in robbing her of happiness? Was she wrong, un-Christian, in wanting to see justice done? Or perhaps she was secretly concerned with preserving her own good name from the besmirching the defense would exact at trial, painting her black with the truth behind her conception, the family secrets uncovered for all to see, her integrity tainted by the alleged complicity in the scheme of which she had been accused, and by her having a relationship with the primary case officer. She could not fathom her true motives.

And if these dilemmas did not tax her Christian conscience sufficiently, she was suddenly faced with a father, a former bishop of the Episcopal Church, whom she neither needed nor wanted. Her secure history was suddenly swept aside, and now she was a stranger to herself. Her presumed parentage was a lie, and instead she found she was the product of a lurid, violent and ugly union between a woman she had thought her best friend and a man she had assumed from his actions an enemy, although she had not known why until recently.

When she was alone with her thoughts, she was assaulted by a myriad of conflicting emotions: sadness at the cruel tearing away of the curtain; love and sympathy for Marjorie Witherspoon and what she suffered; confusion over her feelings toward her long-time friend, now discovered to be her mother; ambivalence toward Marjorie for keeping the secret from her; rage for the perpetrator Stephen Marks; helpless anxiety because of the years she lived in ignorance of the truth; and fear at the consequences of public disclosure, both for her friend's and family's memories and for herself. She tried desperately not to open the door to those feelings.

Now she was faced with news that Andrew also had a father he never knew. All the stress from dealing with this information, of finding the proof, of trying to make sure Mike Knox was safe, of wondering why Andy kept the information from her, made for extra icing on the cake. She felt drained, empty.

And the bottom line is that I cannot just take all this change in stride, she thought. I have to sift and weigh and ponder, over and over, and it's driving me crazy. Yes, I crave the simple, tender marriage that Ralph and Claire are weaving, that Charlie and Jill seem to share. To see their devotion to each other, their trust and easy banter, the melding of their lives, makes me miss what I had once, even if I grasped it for only moments at a time with Andy. And my trust and self-esteem are in shreds now. I have no one. I can't do this the rest of my life, she suddenly realized.

I want so badly that life. Is it possible? Can I find it with Jon? Will I ever find it?

Sighing, she stood, suddenly wrathful with herself for her thoughts. All this gets me nowhere, she chided herself. She abandoned her vigil as the sun finally preened in its early glory over the eastern horizon. She trekked back to the house so that she could spend her allotted sentence on the treadmill before preparing for work.

Later, having completed her workout, she was choosing her suit for the day as the phone rang. Picking it up, she heard a familiar voice saying, "Had we but world enough, and time, this coyness, lady, were no crime.'"

"Good morning, Jon," Amanda smiled.

"And to you, milady," he responded. "I hope I didn't wake you."

"Not at all. I could not sleep, and watched the sun rise on the dock."

"I wish I could have been there with you," he stated fervently. "You know, I have a cure for insomnia."

"I bet you do," she laughed.

"I know what I'm thinking would cure mine," he chuckled wickedly. "I, too, am having sleepless nights, thinking of you."

"What are you doing?" she turned the subject away.

"I'm on the treadmill and watching CNN. Can't you hear me breathing hard? And you?"

"I've just finished the treadmill and am about to hit the shower," she smiled.

"I'll be right there," he teased her.

"What do you have planned today?" she ignored the bait.

"There is much work down here, many more criminals on the beach than one would suppose."

"I'm glad you are earning your pay," she teased him back.

"When can I see you?" he asked her.

"I'll have to consult my calendar. I'm a busy girl, you know."

"Try to fit me in somewhere," he growled good-naturedly. "I miss you. And Amanda?"

"Yes?"

"I know you're full of doubts, but know that I truly love you," Jon said simply.

Her heart caught. "Jon, I need to go."

"I know. Goodbye, my love."

She hung up, swallowing hard. I cannot do this, she said to herself. My heart is not free to give away yet. But how much longer? she argued with herself.

She showered and prepared herself for work, resolutely shutting out all thought of Jon. Finally making it to the office, she walked in to the shrill ringing of the telephone.

Sheila answered the phone, and waved good morning to her, as Amanda spoke a greeting and made her way across to her office. Turning on her computer, booting it up and waiting for the software to load, she finally was able to scan her calendar.

Ralph walked in, and she grunted as he cheerily said good morning. He walked into his office. "My God!" he exclaimed.

Amanda and Sheila followed him in, grinning. A banner and balloons were strung across the wall facing his desk, welcoming him home. A cake and gifts were on the conference table.

"Did you think we weren't going to celebrate your first day back at work?" Amanda demanded, her eyes dancing.

"You both acted like you didn't even care when I walked in," he lamented. "I was afraid you didn't miss me at all."

Amanda engulfed him in a hug. "Of course we did, silly. It was the longest couple of weeks I ever spent," she responded fervently. "You can never leave again. No more honeymoons, no vacations."

"Yeah," he replied. "All hell breaks loose when I am away."

She sobered. "Yes."

He kissed her forehead. "Alan and the twins met Claire and me for breakfast at Betty's this morning. They still look lost."

Trying to lighten the mood, he looked around. "Where is that mountain of work and double-booking you promised?"

Sheila smiled at Amanda and replied, "We took pity on you. We tried to get as much work done before you made it back, and spaced out your appointments so that you still have a little time to be a newlywed."

"That's unheard of in the law business," Ralph smiled gratefully. "Thank you both."

Amanda turned away. "OK, enough bonding. Let's get to work," she quipped.

She had finished an appointment and dictated some interrogatories on a case, when Sheila buzzed her.

"Dr. Young is on the phone for you. He said it is urgent."

Amanda picked up the line. "Amanda Childs; can I help you?" she said automatically.

"Amanda, it's Alan. Do you have a minute to run over to the ER? I found something I want to show you."

"What is it?" Amanda was suddenly interested.

"Not over the phone," he said quickly, mysteriously, his voice low. "I'm calling the Sheriff's Department, but wanted you to advise me first."

She quickly looked at her calendar. "I have an appointment at 11:00, but sure. I'll be right there."

"Thanks, Amanda. Trixie at the desk will ring you through. And please hurry." He rang off.

Amanda picked up her purse and headed out of her office. "Sheila, I've got to run a quick errand. I'll be back in time for the next appointment."

"What's up?" Ralph walked out of his office.

"Alan Young just called and wanted me to meet him at the ER. Said it was important."

Ralph looked at the book. "New client at 11:00. I'll handle it if you're not back."

"Thanks, Ralph," she said gratefully.

She was at the hospital in minutes, and walked through the public entrance to the emergency room/admitting wing of the hospital. Walking up to the window beside the locked double doors, she came face to face with a young woman, not much more than a girl.

"Hi, Trixie," Amanda spoke warmly. "It's great that the hospital hired you. How do you like it?"

"I really enjoy it so far," the girl smiled. "Dr. Young twisted an arm or two for me. He's really a nice man."

"He is," Amanda agreed.

"He said for you to go right in and around the corner from the counter to the pharmacy. He's already there."

Thanking her, Amanda waited for the buzzer, then walked through the doors to the empty emergency room suite. It was unusually quiet as she made her way past the counter. "Alan?" she called. "Is anyone here?"

She heard a noise, and followed it around the corner. Seeing a white-coated figure walking rapidly away and around another corner, she started to follow, but then stopped in horror. In the doorway to the small pharmacy closet was Alan Young, crumpled on the floor.

Chapter 31

"Oh, my God," she cried. "Help!"

She ran after the figure, but it had disappeared. She ran back and knelt over Alan. Noticing a syringe stuck in his arm, she snatched it out hurriedly, noting that it was almost empty. He was unconscious, and she smelled a vague sickly sweet fragrance.

"Alan! Alan!" she pleaded, slapping his face. She felt at his neck, looking for a pulse. It was there, but it seemed slow to her. She happened to look up, and noticed that the shelves were empty.

An orderly walked in the ambulance doors toward her, then halted, surprised. "Call for any doctor in the hospital!" she ordered tersely. "See if Dr. Howells is on the premises. Call 9-1-1, and ask for Charlie Petrino and Bruce Williams to be notified. Quickly," she commanded, as she stood and snatched a pillow from an outside gurney and placed it under his head.

The man obeyed, scurrying off. Amanda dropped to her knees. "Please, Alan," she begged the unconscious man helplessly.

Within seconds there were persons scurrying around. Dr. Howells pushed his way through. "Move back, Amanda," he pulled her away.

Howells knelt over Alan, checking his pulse, trying to get him to respond, doing a cursory examination. He signaled to the orderly and a nurse to assist him, and they gingerly picked him up and placed him on the nearby gurney. Howells listened to his heart.

"He's in defib. Let's get him in a cubicle stat. Gotta act quickly. Raise Dr. Cardet."

As they wheeled the unconscious man away quickly, he turned to Amanda, grabbing her arm. "What did you see?"

"He was on the floor, and someone in doctor garb was leaving in a hurry. I snatched that out of him." She pointed to the syringe on the floor.

"No vial around?" Howells asked hopefully.

"Just as you see here."

"Stay here. I want the lab to test that immediately and see if they can tell me what's in the syringe."

He ran off after the gurney. Amanda could see that the paddles were being prepared. She looked on, stunned, until someone pulled the curtain closed.

A man in lab coat carrying a tray showed up at her side. "Doc said there was something I needed to test right away," he offered excitedly.

Amanda pointed to the syringe. "That's it, Mike," she recognized the guy. "But handle it with gloves, and be careful. That's evidence, and needs to be checked for latents. It's already got mine on it."

"I'll be careful," the man's eyes were wide. "How's Dr. Young?"

"It's bad," Amanda whispered. "Please hurry."

"You bet," he replied, hurrying off.

Dr. Cardet walked by her, hardly noticing her as he joined the group behind the curtain. She was rooted to the spot, in shock, not knowing what to do, but determined to guard the pharmacy so that evidence could be gathered.

She listened intently, and could hear Dr. Howells' instructions and the murmur of voices. The commands "clear" and "again" filled her with dread. "Oh, please, God, don't let Alan die," she prayed aloud fervently. "The babies cannot handle losing both mother and father."

She saw Mike the lab tech slip into the room. As the curtain was open, she saw him talk quietly to the doctors, but could not hear what he said. Then he hurried off again.

As EMTs walked in the emergency doors, Bruce Williams strode in, diverting her attention. He saw Amanda and headed to her. "I got the message and was in the neighborhood," he announced. "What has happened?"

She described the events as Bruce questioned her.

"Sure it wasn't a suicide attempt?" he glanced to see her reaction.

"Alan would not have summoned me here to witness his suicide. No," she was determined. "You need to comb this room for evidence. There was someone leaving quickly as I got here, someone in a white coat and surgical cap."

"Any better description?" he inquired.

"It was so quick, and all I got was a glimpse. When I saw Alan, I cried for help, and tried to hunt the person down, but whoever it was disappeared. I—I thought there was red hair peeking out from the cap."

"See a face?"

"No," she frowned. "Slight build."

"Gender?" he asked hopefully.

"Can't tell you—could be either one. My best guess is female."

"Anything else?"

Amanda paused. "The person was carrying a black bag, kind of like a big duffel bag."

"Why are you so insistent it's not a suicide?" Bruce persisted.

"Well, look around you, Mr. Eagle-Eyes Investigator," Amanda's tone became icy. "Do you notice anything unusual?"

He looked at the shelves. "They look a little dusty, being empty."

"Bingo," she said, annoyed. "The shelves are cleaned of drugs and supplies. Where are they? This is the ER pharmacy, Mr. Investigator."

"OK, I get your drift," he held up his hand. "Don't be a smart-ass. We have a major theft. But this is locked up. The question is who had access?"

"Yes, a theft. And Alan said he wanted to call the Sheriff's Department, but wanted me to see something first," Amanda disclosed. "I don't think he'd have gone to the trouble for a suicide. He was not suicidal, Bruce."

She thought aloud, "He wouldn't have called me out here to see a burgled pharmacy, either. He'd have automatically called law enforcement first. So what's up?"

"I believe you, I believe you. Just covering the angles." Bruce pulled out his cell phone. "Get me Hendrix." He paused, looking at her as she gazed anxiously toward the curtained alcove.

"Hendrix, we need a couple of crime scene techs over here. FDLE is there? Fabulous. Della? From FDLE? Well, she's too pushy for my taste, but yeah, see if she'll head over. If you tell her it involves Dr. Young, she'll come running."

He rang off, and watched Amanda's troubled features as she continued to stare at the curtain. "He's going to be OK, isn't he?" Bruce asked softly.

"He's in defib," she whispered. "That's generally bad. They were using the paddles on him." Her eyes filled with tears.

Bruce's voice was husky. "Buck up, Amanda. I don't want to be seen comforting defense counsel."

"That would be frightening," she attempted a weak smile. "It's just that Alan and I were in elementary school together. We both grew up Baptist, and were in church and Bible School together, along with Charlie. He was so smart, and could have made his ticket anywhere. But he came back here and threw himself into his home community with a vengeance."

"I know," Bruce squeezed her arm. "He is a good man. Saved me from bleeding to death once. I'm really sorry for all his trouble."

"I promise not to tell anyone about your soft side."

"Well, don't expect to see me that way often," he smirked briefly.

"What was all that about the other day?" she asked suddenly. "Why did you jump the gun?"

"I didn't. Clarence was hell bent that we needed to go forward. He kept mentioning 'the judge' wanted an arrest made quickly. I had made an appointment with the doctor for questioning that morning, and the next thing I know Clarence had already dragged him in the office, handcuffed no less, and into the department interrogation room before I even arrived. Young immediately bristled and lawyered up, and I silently cursed Clarence for screwing up what might have been a chance to uncover some real information to help my case. So I slipped out quietly to let you in before more damage was done.

"Clarence apparently had this deputy working on warrants all weekend. I knew I didn't have evidence to make an arrest yet and told him so, and I was pissed that he was mucking with my investigation behind my back. But with Sheriff Watson out doing chemo, and he is not doing well, Amanda, I just didn't want to call him with this. I knew what the Big Man would do to Clarence if he was well, but I also knew that if I did that, I would stir up all kinds of stress for him that he doesn't need right now. So I just sucked it up. Bad decision, I know. But it all happened so quickly."

"So Sheriff Watson is not well?" Amanda echoed, knowing that Bruce was fond of the man.

"He is not going to last much longer," Bruce was somber.

"We're going to need a good sheriff, Bruce," she peered at him.

"I don't want that headache," he asserted seriously. "I'm hoping Petrino is going to be the next sheriff."

"Charlie?" she was surprised. "You sure you don't have aspirations?"

"Maybe ten or even five years ago, but no. I've had to do much of the job since the Big Man got so sick, and dealing with the public and politics takes me away from what I enjoy—the investigation of crime."

Howells came out from behind the curtain and walked toward them. Amanda informed Bruce, "When I found Alan, there was a syringe in his arm. I snatched it out, so it's going to have my fingerprints. The lab tech took it to test the contents, but I told him to preserve it as best he could for evidence."

Bruce nodded at the information. "What's the verdict, Doc?"

"He's back with a weak sinus rhythm. Cardet is trying to undo the damage. All we can do now is pray."

As the emergency doors opened again, a crew of law enforcement came in, and Bruce waved them over. "That's my cue to get to work," he excused himself.

Howells took Amanda's arm and steered her away.

"But I want to be here in case Alan needs me," she protested.

"You're not any good to him right now."

"But if the person who did this is dressed as hospital personnel—" she argued.

Bruce overheard her comment. "I'll keep an eye on things, Amanda. Don't worry."

Howells insisted. "Let's go get some coffee. Let's allow Bruce and his men to do their job here."

"I've got to call Charlie," she suddenly thought out loud.

Bruce called, "I've already done so. He's on his way."

Reluctantly she walked with the doctor to the cafeteria. Howells looked tired, she noticed.

They walked through the line and Howells ordered them each a cup of coffee. The man behind the counter smiled. "Got a fresh pot just for you, Doc," and poured two cups.

They sat down at a table in the corner of the cafeteria. "Do you think Alan is going to make it?" she demanded.

"Cardet is the best. If anyone can pull Alan through, it's him," Howells remarked. "I trust him with my life," he added.

"You?" Amanda was thunderstruck. "You have heart trouble?"

"Nothing too bad," Howells noted her concern. "It's all under control," he added, placing his hand over hers.

"You never told me," she accused him quietly.

"I can take care of myself. You forget, I am a doctor and I have lots of doctor friends," he grinned briefly. "But getting back to the subject of Alan. Tell me everything that happened."

She started at the beginning, relaying the information to him while he listened gravely. When she noted that the pharmacy had been emptied, he started.

"I personally ordered it restocked yesterday because we were low on certain items. I thought it odd that so much lidocaine would be missing, because we don't use a lot of that as a rule, at least as much as it appeared was missing. And Alan and I have discussed that pain meds also seem to be disappearing, and we had developed a second logging system to track where they're going."

"Lidocaine?" Amanda asked, interested.

"A local anesthetic," Dr. Howells explained. "It has other uses, too, but it slows the heart down, and could cause heart arrest. In fact, that's what was found in the syringe you said you found in Alan's arm."

"But why would someone inject Alan? And how?"

"Gerald found lidocaine in Shelby's blood during the autopsy," Howells told her quietly.

Amanda leaned forward. "You don't think Alan would commit suicide, do you?"

"No," Howells said, his voice very low. "He has been depressed after Shelby's death, but he is devoted to Joshua and Caleb. And he was crazy about Shelby."

"What do you know about his office staff? Hospital staff who worked with him?" Amanda wanted to know.

"Everyone had nothing but high praise for him. When he first became a doctor here, someone filed a malpractice claim against him with the state board. But I was on the committee that investigated, and he did everything just as I would have done. It was dismissed with no probable cause. His career has otherwise been exemplary."

"What about staff? Disgruntled patients? Any scuttlebutt?" Amanda demanded, her voice low.

"There have been whisperings that some of his office staff were sweet on him, and that is often a peril in a doctor's office. But Alan hired Edna, one of my former nurses, as his chief, and he is careful to see patients with her in tow. She runs a pretty tight ship, and generally deals with the personnel. Lately she has been gone on her vacation and he has had to struggle somewhat with staff problems, something he is not accustomed to doing. He asks my advice. It's funny how serious he is, but I admire his attention to detail and his ethics.

"And he was never out in public without Shelby by his side or the kids there. He adored his family."

"I know. I hate all this has happened, and I'm worried about the suspicion that has fallen on him," Amanda replied. "Shelby's death is such a blow to him and the kids. You know that Clarence Banks hauled him in for murder?"

"I had heard a rumor," Howells' face was enigmatic. "We doctors have a network too. You gained more than a few brownie points in the medical community, winning a case at first appearance." He smiled. "The other doctors think highly of Alan, so they were silently cheering. And you moved up the notch from just 'one of those damned lawyers'."

"I am sure the first time I have to depose one again, I will be back to my old status," Amanda smiled faintly.

He took her hand. "Speaking of doctors, what is this about another doctor you saw?" he quizzed her.

"I don't know if it was a doctor, but it was a person in a white coat and surgical cap with a black duffel bag. I tried to run after this person, but with no luck."

"There wasn't anyone else assigned today. We were short-handed at the ER today, and Alan was covering with our best nurse John and an extra orderly. But it has been quiet all morning. I will check to see if anyone else saw this person. And I'm going to check with the pharmacist about the status of the inventory."

He stopped as if about to say something else.

Amanda paused. She finally spoke. "Out with it. What is it? I know you."

"What would you say," he began slowly, "if I told you I'm seeing someone?"

Amanda's eyes grew wide, and she smiled broadly. "You sly dog," she accused good-naturedly. "Who is it? Do I know her?"

"Yes, you do," he responded. "Gwen Bradley, the physical therapist."

"Gwen?" Amanda laughed. "You two have certainly kept it a secret."

"Well, we're both set in our ways, and a little stubborn," he smiled. "We weren't sure dating each other was a good idea. But we actually enjoy each other's company."

"She's in my choir," Amanda reminded him. "Sounds like a good excuse for you to come back—lots of opportunity to steal a look here, socialize together," she added with a mischievous grin.

"It's nothing serious, yet. I just wanted to know how you feel about it. You're the daughter I never had. You know I count on your opinion."

"I'm thrilled for you," Amanda assured him. "But I'm jealous that my best guy has been stolen."

"It was my understanding that my best girl was engaged to someone else for awhile," he remarked quietly.

She colored and looked away. "Not any more," she stated flatly.

"So you haven't kissed and made up with Jon? Colin said he had hopes after you and he had dinner together Sunday."

"What—am I the talk of the town?" she muttered darkly.

"Amanda Katharine, a great deal of people care deeply for you," Howells rebuked her gently.

She said nothing, fingering her empty coffee cup. He took her chin and made her look at him. "I want to hear it from you—what's going on?"

"Nothing new. The trial will be over soon, I hope."

"You have to follow the course you feel best," he reaffirmed, "even if it hurts. But you also mustn't use these circumstances as an excuse to keep you from happiness, Amanda. I understand your reasons, and they are valid. But I really like Jon, and from what I've seen he cares deeply for you. I think he could be the one for you.

"The timing is bad, I agree. It may be that you both need to wait and test that resolve, and the Barnes' trial may be part of that test. But, Amanda, make sure that you don't use it as a subterfuge to deny yourself the happiness you deserve. When you know it's right, act on it."

Amanda started to speak, but he held up his hand. "Listen to me, the older and wiser one, for a second. You were raised Baptist, and your dad Tom Andrews was a Calvinist adherent if ever I saw one."

"He wasn't my dad," Amanda said under her breath, her eyes closing to block out sudden tears.

"Amanda, I've told you not to ever say that," Howells admonished her sternly. "Tom was your dad in every sense of the word. He adored you, and could not have loved you more had you come from his loins.

"I admired him immensely, because I think if more of the world saw things as more black and white like he did, society would be the better for it. We are too permissive and promiscuous, and we forget the two greatest commandments, which are mirror images of each other and dictate the rest of the commandments."

Amanda looked down at her hands. Howells sighed. "You know I am old-school 1801 Articles of Religion Episcopalian, and embrace a much more defined stance on the doctrines of faith than most of our fellow parishioners."

Amanda smiled slightly. "I know. You taught my catechism class."

"And you were my best student," Howells squeezed her hand affectionately.

"I was your oldest student at the time," she retorted. "I was the only adult in there with a bunch of teenagers."

"Anyway, back to my homily," Howells was not deterred. "I agreed with Tom on many points. However, the entire world is not black and white. We see results of people's actions and jump to conclusions, and are quick to judge, when there are other equally rational explanations, which gray up the world. People do all sorts of things for the most altruistic of reasons. God's will is not always clearly black and white to us. And even if what people do is not from pure motives, the heart is not a rational thing.

"But I digress. I have a theory about you. You have somehow come up with some world view that happiness on this earth must be an evil thing, fraught with danger of hell fire. Heaven knows that you have had more troubles than some, and I can understand where you might arrive at that conclusion. But Tom would be appalled if he knew that his training went so far astray with you.

"I will concede that St. Paul said that for someone who is convinced that an action is sinful, it is a sin to him. But it is simply not true that happiness for you is a sin. God wants you to be happy. These trials are lessons for us, so that we recognize and appreciate the happy times when we experience them, and for us to find a deeper joy in the midst of the bad."

He stared her down, his eyes tender. "Amanda, you've always felt things much too deeply for your own good, looking for meaning where there very well may be none. You need to accept those moments when you have them, and let them go when they are gone."

Amanda noticed that Bruce Williams had walked in, accompanied by Charlie Petrino. Howells noticed too, as the men saw them and came striding toward them. He concluded, "If you decide that being with Jon is right, you two can work through the defense's questions and insinuations in this case. If you decide that it's more prudent to wait, that's fine. But don't make the decision because you think you don't deserve to be happy."

Williams and Petrino arrived at the table. "Are we interrupting?" Petrino asked, his eyes on Amanda.

Howells responded briskly, "No. Please sit down. I was just leaving."

Amanda interposed, "Did they find anything?"

"The FDLE operative over here on the Shelby Young investigation is in there. She has found some hair and fibers she's taking back to the lab. And we collected the syringe for latents, and will do some of our own toxicology tests on the residue."

"I am going to check with the pharmacist on the drugs on stock in the pharmacy this morning, and to see if any of the staff saw another doctor or anything unusual," Howells stood. "And I will check on Alan's condition."

Bruce also stood. "If you don't mind, Doc, I'd like to accompany you."

"Be my guest," Howells responded. He turned to Amanda. "Go back to work, Amanda. I'll let you know if there's any change in Alan's condition, and when you might see him. And think about what I said."

Amanda stood and looked at Bruce. "Don't let anything happen to him," she ordered tersely. "And you are not to talk to him without me present, Clarence or no Clarence. I'll have you and Clarence both hanging with bloody stumps if you do."

Bruce held up his right hand. "I promise."

She turned to Charlie. "We're going to have to notify the family."

Charlie nodded. "What if I meet you there?"

"I really don't relish breaking this to the boys," Amanda was sober. "Do you think Jill could get away and help?"

"I'll see," he walked away, pulling out his cell phone.

The large man sat at a table, motioning the waitress to bring another drink. The nondescript bar, situated just outside Mainville, was dark and dank, far from the country club environment to which he was accustomed. But then again it had been a while since he had been summoned to do drudge work for the company. He knew it was a test, a jostling in the family for an adjustment in position, and he had failed.

Known only as 'Bo', he handed the girl a large bill. "A bottle this time," he ordered, a trace of a New Jersey accent in his tone. She smiled suggestively. As she walked away, he stared at her butt. Too bony, but it would do in a pinch, he decided.

It was Thursday night. He had already grown tired of watching what he determined was the small club of stellar members of the redneck race watching NASCAR on the flat-screen television. He had decided to get drunk. His job was pretty much done here. Apparently his boys had already botched the job, the subjects were out of reach, and he had missed the last opportunity to eliminate them. The critical documents, the destruction of which was of high importance, were already in the hands of the authorities.

He realized with unhappiness that tomorrow he would face the Man and try to explain his failure. In olden days he might have been frightened, but he had married the Boss' stepdaughter as a personal favor, and didn't worry so much about ending up in a dumpster himself. He knew the reprisal would be in his pocketbook and his status.

The waitress returned with the bottle and a clean glass. Behind her appeared a beautiful woman with flaming red hair. "Would you mind some company?" she asked, her voice low and flirtatious with a trace of a foreign accent.

I'm not drunk enough to have this dream, Bo thought.

She did not wait for an invitation, but sat down in the chair nearest him.

"What's your name?" he pushed the clean glass toward her and opened the bottle, pouring some for her.

"Does it matter?" she laughed throatily.

"I don't guess so," he conceded. "Any reason in particular why someone as pretty as you would be sitting in this bar tonight?"

She leaned forward, stroking his hand resting on the table. "I heard you've been making inquiries around town about Amanda Childs."

Oh, shit, he thought. She's probably an undercover cop. "You have the wrong man," he spoke carefully, pouring his glass half full and downing it.

"What if I told you I could take care of the lovely Mrs. Childs, and it wouldn't cost you a dime?" she whispered, smiling conspiratorially.

"I'd want to know why and what your name is," he muttered.

She took the glass out of his hand, and stood. "Just call me Evie," she winked. "Are you coming or not?"

"Where?" he looked at her blearily.

"To your room. Bring the bottle. I'll explain when we get there."

Chapter 32

"Did you hear me?" she heard Greg Boyer demanding over the line. "We won—the motion to suppress was denied."

"That is great news," she breathed, relieved. "Congratulations. I'm so thrilled. Is Barnes going to plead, or are we still on for trial?"

She could hear Boyer's enthusiasm temper at the question. "It's too soon to know. His attorney gave no indication after the judge ruled." He continued excitedly, "This is a major victory, Amanda, but we may still have the war ahead of us."

"I know," she replied soberly. "I guess Jon is elated—he 'done good', as we say around here."

"Actually, Jon doesn't know yet. He was called out at the beginning of our arguments, after the testimony was in. Yes, he did a fabulous job, and was meticulous in detail, as I've come to expect from him. And he fielded the questions about the two of you up front and very professionally, so the Court did not allow the defense to venture far down that trail." Boyer took a breath. "I'll call Jon next to give him the news, but I just wanted you to know first."

"Thanks," Amanda was touched. "I'm so glad," she added fervently.

"Have you seen Jon lately?" Boyer wanted to know.

There was a strained silence on the line. "Yes," Amanda finally admitted. "But largely in relation to Senator Whitmore and that—complication," she finished uncomfortably. "I had him over to early dinner last Sunday after church." She paused. "Since then it's been a busy week for both of us," she ended lamely, as she opened her center desk drawer and pulled out a ring box.

"He took the assignment in Panama City. I'm afraid he's still mad at me," Boyer rejoined glumly. "When he left here that Sunday morning, he had a bag packed, and he told me he had offered his assistance to the Panama City office. His parting shot was he was going to see his girl, and to spend some time away from me. He was cold with me during our meeting to prep his testimony, and short and to the point with me before taking the stand." There was a pause. "I'm sorry, Amanda."

Amanda opened the box and stared at the contents, Jon's ring he had left with her the past Sunday. She swallowed hard and changed the subject. "Well, if it makes you feel any better, Greg, I have an appointment at the prison to meet with Stephen Marks this afternoon. I surmised it was probably time."

Amanda could sense Greg's relief. "I think that's best, Amanda, particularly in view of the fact that jury selection is still scheduled for Monday after next for now. I have to assume the worst, and am calling all my witnesses to be prepared to appear. I feel that you and Marks may face questioning at trial better if you've confronted each other face to face. I'm always amazed at how a person's unresolved issues assert themselves on the witness stand, usually with unfavorable results."

"I know," Amanda agreed. "And, Greg, I intend to be ready for trial." Her voice had a touch of asperity, and Boyer had no doubt regarding her resolve. "Congratulations again on winning round one."

"I'm so sorry to be the cause of the trouble between you and Jon," Greg breathed remorsefully.

"It's not your fault," she murmured.

"Amanda, don't forget what I said. Jon is a great guy, and he is crazy for you."

Amanda hung up and stared at the ring, lost in reverie. Sheila silently regarded her while picking up the signed documents from Amanda's outbox. Amanda finally snapped the box closed and returned it to her drawer, picked up her purse and file, spoke to Sheila briefly with instructions, and headed to her car. She remembered Ralph's words yesterday when she discussed with him that she was going to visit Marks: "Just remember—don't let him get to you. You can always walk away."

Later, as she finished her hearing in Pensacola and was driving back to the federal correctional facility, she almost talked herself out of stopping. But she remembered her resolution to Boyer.

She pulled out her cell phone and dialed a number. "Dr. Howells speaking," a voice greeted her.

"Hi. It's Amanda," she responded. "I just finished a hearing in Pensacola, and I'm on my way to see—" she paused and swallowed, "Stephen Marks."

"You're still sure you want to do this, Amanda Katharine?" She could hear the concern in Howells' voice.

"I think it's best before I face defense counsel at Barnes' trial," she replied, her voice small. Changing the subject, she asked, "How is Alan today?"

"He is still in a coma," Howells reported gravely. "His vitals look improved. Cardet is optimistic, but I'm definitely worried." He paused. "The kids were allowed to see him last night."

"I know," Amanda's voice was low. "I was over at Dr. Young's house last night after their visit, and stayed with the boys until they fell asleep. Ralph and Claire have been spending a lot of time with them. I think Charlie and Jill are going to accompany them to Josh's game tonight, in case Ralph and Claire don't make it back from Tallahassee in time."

She paused. "You know, I should be there . . ." she started.

But Howells interrupted, his voice stern. "No, Amanda. You can do nothing here, and Alan and his family are being looked after by friends, church and community members. I will make sure you are the first to know when Alan regains consciousness."

Amanda found herself unable to reply. His voice softened. "My dear, I agree that you need to do this, confront Stephen, talk to him. I would do anything to keep you from suffering this alone, but I think you've got to face him, and now is better than later." He paused. "Do you want me to meet you there? I'll be glad to leave now and drive over, go in with you."

"No," Amanda was touched. "Doc, you've been more father to me than he could ever be. Thank you for offering, but I think I need to be able to do this on my own."

She smiled. "Besides, you have a hot date tonight with Gwen. The New York City Opera at the Saenger, huh? I'm jealous."

"You know I'd throw her over for you in a New York minute," Howells informed her teasingly. "Here, let me call her right now and tell her I've given her ticket to you."

"Naw," Amanda drawled. "You two have fun, and give me a blow-by-blow account Sunday after church."

She rang off, concentrating on her driving, trying to steady her nerves and steel herself against the upcoming interview.

Parking in the visitor's lot at the prison, she made her way to the main entrance, signing in. As instructed, she sat tensely in the lobby for several minutes until her name was called. Coming forward, she met a large muscular man with crew cut, in corrections uniform, stripes on his sleeves. Although he initially appeared menacing, he smiled and made her feel at ease.

"Ms. Childs, I am Sergeant Wolfson. I will escort you to visitor's quarters, but first you will need to check your purse and any metal objects. We will collect your items and place them in our safe."

Amanda followed him into an office, where she surrendered her purse to him and was frisked and checked by a female officer. Moments later she was following Wolfson down a long windowless hallway to a large cafeteria-styled room. He instructed her to sit at a metal picnic table. Left alone, she sat quietly, trying to calm her fluttering nerves as she waited.

Several minutes later, the door at the far end opened, and in walked the living remains of Stephen Marks, in dark prison coveralls. She was taken aback by how thin and frail he looked, although he still walked with a regal bearing. She sat frozen, fixed somewhere between fascination and revulsion, as he approached her.

"Hello, Amanda. I'm glad to see you," a surprisingly strong voice greeted her.

"I'm here," replied Amanda briskly, omitting his name and title, struggling to control herself now that she was in his presence.

He took a seat across the table from her. "Thank you so much for agreeing to see me. I almost despaired of having this opportunity until I received your message two days ago." His voice was low, musical, his eyes searching her face.

"Well, since you have taken the liberty of addressing me by my first name, what shall I call you? Not 'Dad', I hope? 'Bishop', perhaps?" Amanda asked coldly.

Stephen Marks' golden green eyes showed hurt momentarily. "Call me what you will. 'Steve' will do nicely, in the absence of a list of other epithets I'm sure you'd rather use."

"I'd use the term 'bastard', but I guess that more aptly applies to me, doesn't it?" Amanda retorted scathingly. Then suddenly contrite, she closed her eyes and bowed her head. "I'm here at your request. What do you want from me?" she whispered.

His heart broke at the sight of her. "Dear child, you have every right to hate me, and I ask for no quarter from you. However, I would be completely beyond the pale if I had not surmised that because of me your world has turned upside down. I have felt this desire to meet with you and somehow let you know how very sorry I am at—at all this," his voice trailed off.

He swallowed. "You must not let your anger at me overwhelm you and stifle what is good and kind in you, all that you were taught by your adoptive parents, and all that you inherited from Marjorie."

"You dare to even mention her name?" Amanda cried suddenly, her eyes flashing, mirrors of his own.

Marks gasped as he gazed on his daughter. "I dare, if only to save you from yourself. Marjy herself forgave me and saved me from my own self-destruction, by giving me someone else to live for."

He shifted to face her, leaning forward. "Don't you see? She could have easily let me go to my grave not knowing about you, but she knew that with her death there was only me left to repent, to stop the terrible wheels of Bill's scheme from running over and crushing you. How she knew about the conspiracy I will never know. She took a great chance, for as reprobate as I was, who knew whether I was capable of caring for someone other than myself? Whether I would turn away from the conspiracy and protect you rather than frame you?

"But God is merciful, and he did turn me around. I realize that the sins of the fathers are visited on the children, and that you are still suffering the consequences of my enormous transgressions."

"My whole life has been a lie," hissed Amanda, her rage near the surface as her hands involuntarily clenched into fists. "You can't fix that, can you? My parentage, who I was and am. How does one just shrug that off and take it in stride? In one terrible moment the truth came crashing down on me." She shuddered. "Just before I thought I was going to die. I have survived—but for what? There's still the public disclosure which will inevitably come, the shame and humiliation."

His voice was low and tender. "No, your life is not a lie. You are the product of all the people who have been close to you, loved you, nurtured you, of all the moments you have experienced. Amanda, you are young, and a lifetime full of hope and love still awaits you. Don't repeat my mistakes. You survived for a purpose. Your life has meaning. Do not throw it away as I did, on hatred, vengeance and greed."

Amanda, spent, sat there silently not looking at him, her eyes brilliant. Marks watched her apprehensively through hooded lids.

"I sit before you as the poster boy of bad decision-making and lost opportunity," Marks continued haltingly. He paused, clearly uncomfortable, his eyes pleading. "Did Marjorie ever tell you anything about—us?"

"No, you were never mentioned," Amanda stated flatly, suddenly wanting to hurt him.

She was instantly sorry, as he swallowed, pain evident in his features.

He bowed his head, his voice barely audible. "We had dated ever since junior high. I took it for granted that we would marry. I was finishing up my graduate work and was going to ask her to set a wedding date. But she was full of doubts, and had been left cold by my increasing forwardness, my attempts to force her to give herself to me.

"She had come home from college to tell me that she was breaking up with me. That night she had asked to meet with me at the park. I was so blown away by her news. I was convinced I wasn't hearing her right. Then I accused her of seeing someone else, although she denied it. She said that I was not the person she thought I was, that she realized she didn't love me, and that it was time we both grew up and moved on.

"I tried to persuade her that she was wrong, that we were meant for each other, and that she could not leave me."

Amanda stirred uncomfortably, Marks' words recalling Billy Barnes and his statement to her. She swallowed convulsively, the sound of Bill's voice and the images of his physical advances flashing through her mind. She tensed, clutching the edge of the table.

Marks continued, his eyes on his hands. "But she was adamant. She was struggling, and I would not let her go. I became angry, I lost my head, and the next thing I knew I had her down on the ground.

"Amanda, at the time I justified my actions with the belief that she belonged to me and no one else. I couldn't believe she didn't want me, that all my carefully laid plans were going awry, and that her 'no' meant 'no'. Bill, Billy's dad, had reminded me of what our uncle always said—that a coy woman just needed some manhandling into submission. Bill laughed at me for not having already had my way with her. Bill had taunted and bullied me into showing her who's boss.

"I thought I could force her to love me, that she would be mine. I was wrong, Amanda, so wrong. I lost her and her respect forever. That one moment, that one bad judgment, took me down the path that led me here."

Tears spilled down his face unchecked as he recounted his story. He looked up pleadingly at his daughter, who would not meet his eyes.

"She never spoke to me directly again, never told me about becoming pregnant or about you. She married Jerrod Witherspoon. I really thought it would be Malcolm Howells. I knew he adored her. I was livid and full of plans of vengeance for what I thought was denied me."

Amanda felt Marks' eyes on her, but was paralyzed and could not return his gaze. All time had fled, and she and Marks were locked into this room, into the past, from which she knew there was no escape. She could not even speak, could not move to ask the guard to let her out. She was almost faint with apprehension.

He continued relentlessly, "All I thought about was myself. You know, I took top marks in all my classes, even at divinity school—isn't that a joke?—but none of it touched my soul. Until her letter was delivered to me just before the memorial service I had no idea that I had a child."

"Letter?" Amanda echoed dully, finding her voice.

"Yes. I received a letter just before the funeral written by Marjorie. She entrusted it to Colin Anselm to deliver to me after her death. She told me that she had to forgive me before she died, and that she had to tell me about our daughter. She said I had to protect you now that she was gone. She did not identify you, but said I would know you when I saw you—that you had my eyes. She was right, and Malcolm Howells confirmed that he delivered you into this world, and that you were indeed Marjorie's child."

Amanda felt like she was drowning as she listened to Marks' narrative. It confirmed everything Billy had said to her that night he almost took her life. She had hoped that night was just one long lie, a nightmare from which she would eventually awaken.

Amanda dared not look at Marks. Her chest constricted in silent agony. How much more can I take? she prayed frantically. Is this what hell is like?

"I know how my selfish arrogance changed our lives forever. I can never go back and undo it, and I cannot beg her forgiveness. She could have ruined me at any time, but didn't. Why not? I'll never know. And all I can do now is try to mitigate the damage I've done to you, and perhaps counsel you to avoid the mistakes I made, if you will let me."

Amanda felt light-headed, as though she had stopped breathing, her throat choking off the oxygen. The stillness was broken only by the sound of Marks' own labored breaths.

Finally she rasped, her voice low. "Where do you get the idea I need your help?" She hid her eyes with her hand, her elbow propped on the table, as she tried to breathe deeply, choking back a sob.

"Because," he paused briefly, "I can sense the rage, the hurt in you, Amanda. Because I know what you have already endured, and that you are crushed by all this. I would like to somehow let you know how much I wish I could undo it all. And Jon Connor comes to see me about every three to four weeks. He was here two days ago, right after I received word that you were coming."

"And what has that to do with me?" she countered, trying to act nonchalant, her heart hammering in her ears. It was as though she was experiencing vertigo, and she gripped the bench tightly, her knuckles white.

"I always ask him about you, whether he's seen you, how you are, what you are doing. I can tell from Jon's responses that he cares very deeply for you and he's very guarded, protective of you. Do you return that feeling?"

"What does it matter?" she whispered despairingly.

"It matters, my dear. During this last visit, I could tell that he was preoccupied. He did not stay long. He was restless, worried, could not speak of you without pain, a deep pain in his eyes. He knew we were to meet and said I must be gentle with you, that you have suffered so much." Marks stared at her. "Something has happened between you two. What is it?"

Amanda breathed in sharply. "Number one, that is none of your concern. Number two, this case, the result of your big scheme with the Barnes, pretty much militates against a relationship between your bastard daughter and the chief case officer, don't you think? Besides, thanks to you and Barnes, I was the prime suspect initially, and Barnes' attorney intends as his defense to convict me of the crime."

"You're right—it's none of my business, and I have no right to ask. But the government has me as its witness and I know differently, that you are innocent of this conspiracy."

"Thanks for the vote of confidence," Amanda replied sarcastically, then fell silent. She knew she was lashing out, and could hear Jon's voice exhorting her not to give in to her anger. She closed her eyes and silently prayed, her body rocking back and forth in small motions as her lips moved but made no sound. Marks watched her anxiously, divining her actions and silently saying a prayer himself to the God he had failed to serve for so many years.

After several minutes of silence between them, Amanda, her eyes still closed, expelled a long breath. "Tell me about your family. Are there any living relatives out there, other than William Barnes, I should know about? Any more skeletons in my closet?" her voice shook slightly.

Marks, sensing that she was struggling to attempt some form of truce, let out a breath in relief. "Actually, yes. I have a paternal aunt, a widow. She is only ten years older than I, a late arrival to my father's family. She married into some serious Ocala horse ranching.

"Since my arrest I had avoided contact because of the shame I knew she must feel, but I recently wrote her, telling her about you. She's a lot like me, I'm afraid—crusty and supercilious. She was disappointed that I did not marry and produce an heir. I think you might like each other. Here, I had hoped to give you this. It's her address and phone number. Perhaps if you are down that way you might look her up."

Amanda, sitting quietly and trying to assess her feelings, took the slip of paper absently without comment. Marks watched her warily, afraid to say more.

They sat together silently for what seemed a small eternity. Finally Amanda broke the silence. "Jon proposed to me. He gave me a ring."

"That's wonderful news," began Marks, but Amanda cut him off.

"But I broke it off. I cannot ruin his career by allowing his name to be associated with mine when I know that I am to be the target of Barnes' defense."

"But you love this man? He loves you. I can tell that you mean a great deal to him.

"The timing will never get better, Amanda. I know you've lost your adoptive parents, your husband, and now Marjorie. You know that life does not get simpler with age. It becomes more and more convoluted. I threw happiness away for other worthless goals. I was happy to let Bill dictate my actions. I was a willing partner to his crimes." He paused, his hand shaking. "Except for the murders. Oh, God, I was completely unaware, Amanda," he whispered, his voice pleading. "I know you think that any blindness on my part was willful, but I swear I would never have condoned murder."

He stared at her, and reached out, touching her hand. "But I'll never know now if I might have won Marjorie if I hadn't demanded to have everything on my terms and on my timetable. Don't make my mistake. Don't throw it away. You will always wonder if you don't try."

Amanda turned her full gaze on him as if she was seeing him for the very first time. He covered her hand with his own. She shrank from his touch, but his gaze held her captive.

She murmured, almost unwillingly, "My life has been so full of loss. It hurts so badly. It takes all my energy right now just to keep from hating you."

Marks nodded sadly. "You have every right to hate me. But I beg you not to, not because I'm your father, but because the hate will destroy you. You must not give in to it. I too must somehow forgive Bill Barnes for expanding the conspiracy to murder, for involving me in the shedding of blood."

He paused, an unfathomable look crossing his face. "I must forgive him for the indelible pain he has inflicted on you and—and others. He has done some evil things, Amanda, things I didn't know until just recently. Unforgiveable things. However, I can't forget my own hand in his sins. Somehow I must forgive myself too. If I had been stronger, had exerted more control, had not been so full of myself and my plans for revenge, perhaps I could have changed all that. I must live with that knowledge . . . ."

He took a deep breath. "Forgiveness is also your only salvation, my dear. And it is a huge responsibility, a tall order."

Marks continued quietly, "You must accept the gifts God offers you. Love is like luggage on the baggage claim carousel. If you don't pick up the bag when it's in front of you, who is to say someone else won't snatch it up before it gets back around to you? I spent my life grabbing what belonged to other people and screwing up opportunities for myself and others.

"Forgive me," he interrupted himself, flushing with emotion. "I have no right to speak to you about God. But Amanda, you must believe that God wants you to be happy. I think you know what it would take to get you there. The bag is in front of you. Don't wait for it to go around again."

Sergeant Wolfson appeared. He spoke apologetically. "The front desk has buzzed. The priest is here to give Mr. Marks communion. I'm afraid your time is up."

Amanda was suddenly seized with an overwhelming desire to find Jon, to tell him that he was right, that she didn't want to wait any longer. Filled with a new resolve, she stood and whispered, "I really must go."

Marks stood with her. She spoke aloud, "I need to go by the office and pick up Jon's ring. I must find him. I love him."

Suddenly realizing that she had actually voiced her thoughts, she stared at Marks, bewildered and embarrassed. She stammered, "I don't know what to say...."

"Don't say anything," he replied gently. "I've kept you long enough. Do what you need to do. But think about what I said, and please consider coming back to see me."

She nodded to the guard. As she turned to leave, she murmured, "Thank you. I will try to come see you again."

He turned and flashed her a smile, his eyes a mirror of her own. Her heart caught in her throat at the uncanny resemblance.

As she followed the guard down the hallway, her mind dazed with the discovery that she wanted to find Jon right away, she barely noticed the striking woman standing at the doorway in suit and priest's collar. Suddenly at the door back into the administration section of the prison, she turned, watching the woman as she moved away from Amanda and entered the room Amanda had just left, her high heels clicking on the concrete floor. Something also clicked in Amanda's brain. She looked familiar.

"Evie?" Amanda called in amazement.

The woman did not turn or acknowledge the sound. Amanda shrugged, certain she must have been mistaken as to the woman's identity. She passed through the door the guard held open for her, a sense of mission having come over her.

Chapter 33

Amanda was handed her purse and effects by Wolfson. Impatiently she retrieved her car keys, absently thanked the guard who buzzed her out, and strode out, almost running to her car.

She maneuvered the BMW quickly out of the parking lot and spun off, her mind in turmoil. She pulled out her phone and called Connor's cell number. Reaching his voice mail, she blurted, as though afraid she might change her mind, "Jon, it's Amanda. I'm on my way to Panama City tonight to see you." She hesitated a second before adding, "No reservations. Please give me a call on my cell."

Ringing off, she found she was breathing faster with anticipation. I can't believe I'm doing this, she told herself amazedly. She looked at the speedometer and had to tell herself to slow down.

The time seemed to crawl, but eventually she pulled into the law office parking lot and jerked to a stop. Grabbing her purse and file, she practically sprinted into the office to face a surprised Sheila.

"Hi, Sheila," Amanda greeted her breathlessly.

Shocked, Sheila's mouth dropped open at the sight of Amanda's flushed face. "Amanda? What's wrong?'

"Nothing. Everything's fine. I gotta get out of here, though. Ralph gone already? That's right—he and Claire are still in Tallahassee," she answered her own question distractedly. "If he calls looking for me, just tell him I'm playing hooky this weekend. I need to make a couple phone calls. Anything I need to sign?"

At Sheila's wordless nod, Amanda rushed into her office. Noting several unopened envelopes, she pulled them toward her as she hit the speed dial on her phone. "Ken? It's Amanda. Glad I caught you. I know it's extremely late notice, but since you are home from school, I need a huge favor. Is there any way possible you could do Sunday for me? You can? I owe you big time, man. I have to run out of town. The anthems you know, and the program is on my desk. Play what you want for prelude and postlude. Thanks. I'll call you on my way home Sunday to see how it went, and I'll leave a check for you here at the office with Sheila. I'll even throw in some extra cash for its being short notice."

Hitting the disconnect button, she provided clipped instructions to Sheila regarding a check for Ken, and flipped through the rolodex as she reached into her center desk drawer fumbling for her silver letter opener, a gift from Jon. Finding a number, she reached for the phone and dialed it.

"Hello? I need an open reservation for one room, two occupants, tonight and the weekend. Do you have anything available? I'm willing to pay to hold the reservation for tonight through Sunday. Last minute cancellation? You can? Fabulous." Quickly giving out credit card information, Amanda soon replaced the phone.

As Sheila appeared in the doorway, Amanda was frantically rummaging through her desk drawer. "Sheila, have you seen my letter opener? I swear it was here this morning."

Suddenly a man stood in the doorway of her office. Astounded, she looked up into the face of Rev. Adam Brownlee, who was himself out of breath. He quickly blurted out, "I need to talk to you. It's urgent."

Sheila was clearly annoyed, and Amanda replied, "I'm in a great hurry, Reverend Brownlee. I'm sure Sheila would make you an appointment next week."

"It can't wait," he indicated wildly. "Please help me."

Amanda rubbed her neck tiredly. "Sheila, please bring me what you need signed. Reverend, you have five minutes."

As Sheila brushed past Adam Brownlee, he followed her and shut the door in her wake. Quickly he took a seat in front of Amanda's desk, sitting on the edge of the chair and leaning forward anxiously.

"What is it you think I can do for you?" Amanda asked as she continued to search on her desk for her letter opener, absently opening an envelope by tearing the flap with her fingers.

Sheila opened the door with documents in hand, which she placed in front of Amanda. Sheila looked at Brownlee intently, before walking out, leaving the door ajar.

"I need to know how one goes about getting DNA testing done," he gushed, embarrassed.

"What? I don't think I heard you correctly," Amanda exclaimed, the letter in her hand forgotten.

"DNA testing—how does one get it done?"

Amanda looked at him intently. "For what purpose do you need the testing? Some court case?"

"Paternity."

"I see," Amanda responded slowly.

Adam interrupted. "No, you don't." Leaning forward, he whispered, "I want to determine my own parentage."

"But you're an adult, so I'm assuming we're not discussing child support? What—inheritance?"

"No, nothing like that," he continued in a whisper. "I'm convinced that Stephen Marks is my real father."

Amanda pushed her chair back sharply, standing up. "What?" she raised her voice subconsciously, shocked at his words.

"Please sit down, Amanda," Brownlee pleaded in a low voice, looking toward the partially open door.

Amanda, stunned, obeyed. "Adam," she unconsciously used his first name, "what would make you think you are Stephen Marks' child?"

"He knew my mother. I never had a father, and when she died, a cousin raised us. Stephen was always there and was kind to me as a child. I know that he assisted me financially, helping me to get into college, providing me a job as his assistant, even getting me this job. He inspired me to enter the priesthood. I remember when I announced I wanted to be a priest, he told me how happy he was and that he wanted me to be all the things he never was. We've just always had this bond.

"In the last months since he has been incarcerated, he has become that kind man again, and calls me his 'son', his 'child'. Amanda, I'm convinced that he might be my father."

Amanda looked at him in pity. "Have you ever just thought to ask him? At this point, with so much else that has happened in his life, if he were your father he would really have no reason to withhold disclosure, would he?"

There was silence for several minutes, as Brownlee looked at his hands. Amanda grew uncomfortable because she felt precious time ticking away in her quest to be with Jon. But she read the distress in Brownlee's face and said nothing.

"Because of you," Brownlee finally whispered, his eyes shining with tears. "He is intent on protecting you, on doing whatever it takes to make up for the past, to exonerate you."

Amanda's eyes narrowed. She was suddenly suspicious of Brownlee's motives, although she wasn't sure why. "I don't know how I can help you, Reverend. I've not asked Marks for anything. He was part of the plot against me, not the other way around. I have no interest in what happens to him one way or the other." Her voice was cold. "I met with Marks today, but only because he had been requesting to see me and the U.S. Attorney thought it might clear the air if we met."

She saw his face fall. She continued, her conscience pricking her for being so crass, "I really don't know what to say. DNA is pretty easy nowadays, and not as expensive as it used to be. The lab tech swabs your mouth, so it's not even invasive.

"But you really should talk to Marks. If it is possible, he may agree to the testing for your sake. He may just tell you the truth."

Brownlee shifted uncomfortably, sitting back in his chair. Amanda suddenly was overcome with sympathy for him, realizing that here was a man who never had a father at all, who grew up with far less security and love that she had known as a child. Amanda felt momentary anger at Marks if he were the man's father, but stifled it.

"I realize it must have been hard growing up without a father," she said with feeling.

Brownlee started, staring at her uncomprehendingly. "But Stephen was all I ever wanted in a father."

Amanda, saddened by Brownlee's words, was at a loss.

She finally broke the silence. "I will try to see Marks again soon. What if I bring up the subject and ask him?"

"Would you?" Brownlee's face lit up. There was a ringing sound, and Brownlee suddenly reached for his waist and pulled out a cell phone, looking at the number. "I'm really sorry. This is important. Excuse me. Yes?" he said, turning in his chair.

A moment passed, then Brownlee said excitedly, "Yes, you wanted me to, didn't you?" He paused. "What are you doing?" he demanded, suddenly upset. He listened for a moment. "Now? Can't you tell me? Yes, I'm on my way now." Sighing, he hung up.

Brownlee stood up, holding his hand out to Amanda, who took it. "That would be great, Amanda, and I'd be so grateful to you," he spoke sincerely, a trace of a smile on his face. "I'm sorry I took up so much of your time, and appreciate anything you can do for me."

Amanda, bewildered, watched him leave. Turning her attention back to her desk, she heard a short exchange between Sheila and Brownlee, then Sheila returned to her doorway.

"What did you say to him?" Amanda asked Sheila absently, rapidly reviewing papers and signing them.

"Oh, nothing," Sheila bit her lip as she retrieved the papers from Amanda.

"I still can't find my letter opener," Amanda grumbled, opening her desk drawer and reaching inside for the ring box, pulling it out and opening it. "Wait a minute—where is it?"

"Where is what?" Sheila asked as she stepped outside to place the papers on her own desk.

"The ring? Oh, no, I know it was here. I placed it here so that it would be a reminder to me of Jon. I looked at it this morning before leaving for Pensacola. Damn, it's not here. And my letter opener is gone." She looked wildly around the room.

Sheila, returning, overheard her. "Are you sure?"

"My silver letter opener is gone. And Jon's ring to me. I placed it in a ring box in my desk drawer. I need it." Amanda became hysterical, her voice breaking as she wildly ransacked the drawer. "It's important. I have to have it."

Sheila, noticing Amanda's anxiety, put a hand on her shoulder. "Stop a minute. Calm down and think. Is anything else missing?"

Amanda, frantic, pulled out the side drawers and rifled through them. "I can't think of anything else. My mind is such a muddle. Did anyone unusual come into the office today?"

"No one but an air conditioning maintenance guy."

"Why?"

"He said he had been called to check the freon in the system."

"Did you call him?"

"No—I assumed maybe you or Ralph did."

"I didn't," Amanda said suspiciously. "Damn it all." She ran her fingers through her hair, distraught. "Sheila, I've got to go. It's very important. But it's possible someone may have stolen my engagement ring and letter opener." She muttered to herself, "This cannot be happening. Not now, not today." Her voice caught in a desperate sob.

She suddenly stood and grabbed Sheila by the arm. "Will you do me a favor and please check behind me? Maybe I'm just not seeing them. But we need to make sure nothing else is missing either. We might need to call Ralph, report it to Charlie Petrino and give him a description of the guy and whoever else has been here."

Sheila, amazed at Amanda's uncharacteristic frenzied and chaotic haste, stammered, "I'll take care of it right away."

Amanda looked at her watch wildly. "I've got to leave," she muttered.

"Can I ask where you are going? You're not yourself. You've got me worried."

Amanda was clearly anxious. "It's a secret. Wish me luck. Tell Ralph I have my cell phone, but call only if it's an emergency." She grabbed her purse and started out the door. "But Sheila, if you find my ring, call me immediately."

Amanda flung herself out of the office, running to her car, overwhelmed with conflicting emotions. She was disturbed that the ring, the symbol of her unconditional acceptance of Jon, was missing, but now that she had made a decision she was intent on avoiding any further obstructions until she could see Jon face to face. She could not explain the reckless urgency she felt, but she had to reduce the miles between her and him as quickly as possible before her resolve wavered.

Soon she was traveling down the two-lane highway leading south toward the Gulf of Mexico. The traffic was heavy and the sun was low in the sky as she threaded her way around spring-breakers and vacationers on their way to the beaches. Several times she berated herself for her speed and slowed down, just in time before coming upon a patrolman wafting his radar gun on the airwaves. The traffic seemed to inch along and the miles yawned before her.

Jon's last telephone message had left the address of the condominium owned by his parents where he was staying while assisting in the Panama City investigation for which he had volunteered. She knew from past experience that rush-hour traffic over the major bridge in Panama City would be crawling, if not at a dead standstill this time of year. She therefore avoided the beach route and took the long rural way into the town proper, doubling back through the airport cutoff in order to make it as quickly as possible. However, inasmuch as the cutoff was a main commercial area littered with restaurants and hotels, she was still delayed by traffic.

It was getting dark when she finally pulled up to the condo, but she spied Connor's car parked outside. Relieved to know he was probably there, because she had not received a return call from him, she let herself out of the car, strode up to the door and rang the bell.

After several tries, Amanda realized that some music was blaring inside. Trying the door, she found it unlocked. That's odd, she thought.

Opening the door she called out, "Jon? Are you home?" Hearing no response, she walked into the foyer and called again, then froze.

In the dimly lit great room two figures were writhing on the couch, intertwined, both in a state of undress. "Jon?" she gasped.

Looking up, they spied her, and the man sprang up. Reaching for his trousers, his back still to her, he rumbled irritatedly in a mellifluous voice she found intoxicatingly familiar, "Hi. We obviously weren't expecting company—"

Horrified, she heard no more, as she turned and fled, flinging the door open and racing outside to her car. As she unlocked her car door, she heard a voice calling, "Amanda? Amanda, wait."

She jumped in and turned the key in the ignition. The car sprang to life and she rammed the gear into reverse and spun out, heedless to traffic around her. As she saw the familiar figure sprinting toward her, she shifted gears and sprang forward with a roar, leaving the man calling after her.

Stunned, her breath came in short gasps. She kept driving numbly until she reached the intersection. Unthinkingly, she turned right at the red light onto the highway, intent only upon putting as much distance as possible between her and what she had just seen. She snaked her way through the heavy traffic, thankful for anything to keep her mind off the scene at the condo and prevent the thawing of her emotions. She turned on the radio to a rock music station for company.

She heard her phone ringing, but ignored its insistence. It finally ceased. Furious, she seized it out of her purse and turned it off.

After what seemed like eons to her, she had made her way mindlessly through the city and past the eastern-most suburban communities, past the air force base, and into the gathering thickness of night. The traffic dropped off to a light patter. The rain on her windshield grew heavier as she made it further away from the urban areas and through the lonely stretch of highway surrounded by sentinels of palm trees.

How stupid could I be to trust him? Why would he lead me on? What an utter fool I am. She felt the numbness slipping. No, I mustn't. Damn it, this cannot be happening. Why? I cannot take anything more. She tried taking a couple of deep breaths, fighting tears. God, please help me to hold it together. She started reciting the Nicene Creed out loud, trying to keep from thinking, feeling, telling herself, I mustn't cry, I mustn't cry.

She was oblivious to her surroundings until she saw a city limits' sign, realized where she was, then decided on her course. She already had made the reservation, so she might as well keep it.

She drove into the gathering clouds and mist, the windshield wipers intermittently keeping tempo with the blaring music. If I can just make it there, she told herself, intent on reaching the inn at the heart of St. George Island.

Chapter 34

Jon Connor watched helplessly as Amanda gunned her engine and pulled away at a high rate of speed, her tires throwing gravel. He ran back into the hallway past a protesting shirtless man looking remarkably like himself, grabbed his car keys and cell phone off the table in the foyer and sprinted to his Mercedes.

Pulling out to follow her, he could just make out her taillights ahead. Speeding up, he tried to close the distance. As he turned onto the main highway, angrily he punched his cell phone. A man answered.

"What in the name of God did you do, David?" Jon yelled into the phone, trying to keep Amanda's car in sight.

"Nothing," a voice, not unlike his own, replied. "I was just making out with this gorgeous girl who came up to the door and threw herself at me, and this other girl showed up from out of nowhere. She was pretty too, Jon. Who was she? I'd like to meet her."

In the background he could hear a woman saying, "You're not Jon? Who the hell are you?"

"Who is that?" Jon demanded hoarsely.

"This first chick that showed up asking for you," David answered sullenly. "Apparently my dropping in down here was a big mistake. I thought we would do some bizarre male bonding, and I could score a few college queens. But no, all the women are after you. What gives?"

"Amanda must have thought you were me," Jon hissed hotly.

"Who the hell is Amanda?" David wanted to know.

"No one you need to be within fifty yards of," Jon replied, hanging up.

Why was Amanda here? Jon wondered. It was so unlike her to show up unannounced, and now she believed the worst of Jon. And who was the other woman with David?

Jon had just spent an unproductive day, after his testimony in Pensacola on Thursday, driving back to Panama City in his attempt to track down any possible lead on finding Evelyn Abermarle. He and Ian had spent the rest of Thursday and all day Friday covering some of the Panama City clinics and area hospitals for leads. He had spent much of the week combing hospital employee records with Callander that day, but they had not found anyone remotely resembling the description of their suspect.

Friday afternoon he finally had to admit defeat. "She's just not here," he waved at the filing cabinets in the administration records room. "But she had to work somewhere around here."

"What now?" Callander asked.

Jon had sat a moment, deep in thought. "We're going to be reduced to taking her photograph around to regional hospitals and asking."

Callander laughed. "This is the twenty-first century. Why don't we just fax the photo around?"

"Well, unless we could ensure that the hospital administrator himself picks up his faxes, which is generally never, we don't know but what she is working in administration, would see the inquiry and be tipped off."

"I see your point," Callander concurred. "OK, then how best to pull this off?"

"Well, there's not much to do, with the weekend here," Jon answered ruefully. "All the business offices will be closed. But come Monday we can ride circuit and try all the area hospitals, meet the administrators and see what we find. There are any number of hospitals, clinics, large and small, in this region." He ran his fingers through his hair distractedly. "Unless I think of a better idea this weekend."

He had looked at the clock on the wall at the hospital, as the very pretty head of the records division walked in. "I'm sorry, Officers, but the business office is closing for the day. That is," she smiled winningly at Jon, "unless you need to burn some midnight oil."

He straightened up, smiling back. "No, we are finished here," he answered. "Thanks so much for your help."

She batted her eyelashes at him. "If there's anything else I can do . . . ."

"We'll let you know," Jon motioned for Callander to follow him.

They walked out into the overcast afternoon. "You know," Ian eyed him as they climbed into Jon's car, "if that sheila had come on to me just now, I would have handled it much differently."

"Why didn't you ask her out?" Jon queried absently, pulling on his seat belt and slipping the key into the ignition switch.

"Because she was eying you, man," Callander laughed. "You have a thing against good-looking women?"

"No. I am just interested in one in particular," Jon murmured, his mind on Amanda.

"Ah, the woman Bubba spoke of," Callander smiled. "The former suspect."

"Bubba and his mouth," Jon muttered.

Jon let Ian off at his rental car in the office parking lot, and threaded his way through traffic, finally arriving at the townhouse. As he pulled up, he saw the familiar black Jaguar parked out front. "David," he grimaced. "That's just great."

The stereo was blaring when he let himself in. Jon was so weary that he went straight to his bedroom, avoiding his brother, and encased himself in a hot shower, trying to wash the day away. He had not even checked his messages, thinking to save that for later. I need to call Amanda, to hear her voice, he thought. No, I really need to see her, touch her.

He had thrown on some Dockers and a shirt, his hair still damp, irritated at the loud music, when he heard a commotion in the foyer. Walking out, aggravated that David was as usual apparently misbehaving, he had glimpsed Amanda running out the door.

Stunned, muttering an oath, he ran after her, but she sped away, leaving him in her dust. So he grabbed his keys and phone and went after her.

Jon suddenly thought, She must have called me. I should have checked my messages.

Flipping open his phone, he quickly hit some buttons. The first voice mail was from Greg Boyer. "We won, man. Motion to suppress is denied. No word on whether Barnes still wants trial, so I'm preparing for the worst. Need to see you Tuesday am. Congratulations—steak's on me."

Next message was from Amanda. Oh, God, he thought, chilled as he heard her words: "Jon, it's Amanda. I'm on my way to Panama City tonight to see you." A breathless pause. "No reservations. Please give me a call on my cell."

"No reservations." Oh, no, he thought, horrified, what she must be thinking.

He was having trouble trying to keep her lights in sight with heavy evening traffic down the main U.S. Highway 98 thoroughfare. *I cannot lose her now. Where can she be going?*

He called her cell phone number, but it just kept ringing. She's not answering, he realized. He tried again and got an automated outgoing voice mail message. "Amanda, this is Jon. That was not me you saw. That was my brother David with some bimbo. Please call me. Please."

He panicked at the thought of losing her in traffic, but fought it down. *OK, you've tailed bad guys plenty of times. This is no different.* Picking up his phone again, he hit speed dial and called her office, hoping that someone was still there.

A female voice answered. "Hello?"

"Sheila, is that you?" Connor asked hesitantly.

"Mr. Connor?" she replied, surprise in her voice.

Relieved, he responded, "Jon, remember. Thank God you are still there. Do you have any idea where Amanda was going tonight?"

"No, sir. She came in this afternoon acting strangely and told me to tell Ralph she was 'playing hooky' this weekend. She was in an awful hurry to get away. She didn't even stop when we discovered several items missing from the office. She practically ran out of here."

Jon's heart sank. "It's really important. Sheila, I've got to find her."

"I heard her asking Ken to cover church for her Sunday, and she was making phone reservations for somewhere, but I don't know where. Wait a minute—I have an idea."

"What?"

"Let me go check her phone for 'last number dialed'. I'll have to put you on hold."

Jon, weaving in and out of traffic, strained to try to see Amanda's car through the maze of vehicles. He could no longer spot it and was cursing at himself, all the while wondering why it was taking Sheila so long.

Finally Sheila's voice was back on the line. "Jon? She made a reservation for two at the Seagull Inn on St. George Island."

Connor breathed a sigh of relief. Hopefully that was where she was going. "Sheila, please keep this between you and me for now, OK?"

"OK," Sheila replied uncertainly. "But can you tell me what is going on? Some of Amanda's personal items are missing from the office, she ran out of here like I've never seen her before, and she out of the blue got Ken to take Sunday's service. She never does that. Chief Petrino's men are here investigating the items' disappearance and he was trying to contact Amanda, but there's no response on her phone. I'm worried."

"I don't know, but if I find her I'm hoping it will be good," Connor concluded tersely. "If she calls, try to confirm where she is and please call me on my cell."

He rang off, picking his way around traffic, pointing the car east. Gradually the traffic thinned and he prayed for grace to avoid highway patrolmen as he gunned the engine and sped toward Apalachicola, the final town before the turn onto the causeway leading to the island.

On the way he cursed his brother David. *The one moment I've waited for, and he has spoiled it with his roguish ways.* Jon wondered if he could convince Amanda of the truth. She had been betrayed so much in her life, and he had despaired several times of making it past the wary shell she had wrapped around herself. With the shedding of each layer he had loved her more and more, and she had warmed to him, giving him hope to think she might reciprocate that love. And just as she was ready to throw caution to the winds, she had seemingly been deceived again.

Briefly Jon wondered about the woman with David. Why was she looking for him? Picking up his phone again, he called Bubba.

"Yo, what's up?" he heard a voice say.

"Bubba? Connor here."

"Hey, I have caller ID, or I might not have answered the phone. You are interrupting my Playboy Channel night, you know."

"Sorry about that, but I need your help."

"No can do. It's been a rough week. Gotta hot date—your brother and I are going out clubbing later. What is it?"

"Well, this has to do with my brother." Quickly Connor filled Bubba in on the events, describing what he heard the woman say on the phone. "Why would she show up looking for me and making out with my brother, thinking it was me?"

"You holding out on me?" Bubba asked wickedly.

"You know me better than that," Jon retorted sternly. "But it's awfully suspicious, don't you think? Do you mind going over and finding out if she's still there, get what information you can on her?"

"Where are you?"

"I'm trying to catch Amanda. She thinks it was me with this girl."

"You are in major trouble."

"No shit," Jon gritted his teeth. "Just do it for me, please?"

"Awright. Why can't women show up looking for me?" Bubba grumbled. "Later."

At Mexico Beach, Jon realized his gas gauge indicator showed him low on fuel, so he pulled into a convenience store. While he was pumping gas, a state trooper pulled in to the store. As Connor went in to pay for his gas and to purchase a Coke, the patrolman was talking to the cashier, eying Jon's Mercedes sedan.

Jon stuck out his hand, and the cop and he shook hands. Jon asked casually, "Have you seen a silver BMW go through this way recently?"

The trooper was wary. "Why? You Jack the Ripper? Drug dealer?"

Jon laughed, flashed his badge and decided to stretch the truth. "No. My girlfriend is meeting me down this way for the weekend, and I was just wondering if she's going to beat me to the inn. She sometimes has a lead foot."

The trooper laughed. "I'm afraid so. I had a guy stopped, giving him a ticket. She came cruising by, not speeding because I guess she could see my blue lights a mile down the road. You missed her by about fifteen minutes."

"Guess that means I buy dinner tonight," Jon joked.

"Don't be speeding on my watch. Florida speeding tickets are enormously expensive these days," the trooper warned. "And I'd give you one, Bureau or no Bureau."

Jon waved as he left the store, inwardly relieved that maybe he was on the right track. As he pulled away, his cell phone rang.

"Jon, it's Charlie. What's going on?"

"Amanda showed up at the condo this evening and found my brother David making out with some girl." His voice caught. "Charlie, Amanda thought it was me."

"Shit," he heard Petrino mutter.

"I'm tracking her right now," Jon answered. "I think I know where she's heading."

"Do you need any help?"

"No," Jon decided. "This is something I need to handle myself. I'll call you back if I don't find her. Thanks, Charlie."

As he hung up, the heavens opened up and rain blew in torrents as he followed the highway.

About thirty minutes later, Jon arrived in front of a rambling two-story structure which vaguely resembled a smaller Mount Vernon. An attic and widow's walk graced the top of the homey wooden building. Gratefully he recognized Amanda's car parked out front. As he stepped out of the car, he heard the rumble of thunder and felt the whip of the gulf breeze blowing stinging gusts of rain on his face.

Jogging the massive steps up to the large wraparound front porch, he let himself in. The front desk was empty, but a couple sat at the bar with an elderly man as bartender. Eying Connor, he asked, "May I help you, young man?"

"Yes. My fiancée made reservations here, and I believe she has made it here before me."

The man frowned. "I'm not sure," he said, excusing himself from the bar and pointing Jon back to the front desk.

"Did a woman by the name of Childs check in the last thirty minutes or so?" Jon asked quietly.

"Yes, but she changed the reservation to one," the man replied.

"She didn't think I was going to make it. I hope to surprise her if it's possible."

"I don't know," the man was skeptical. "She seemed upset."

As the man hesitated, Connor pulled out his badge. "I want to set your mind at ease. I'm not a stalker, violent boyfriend or rapist, and she's not a criminal. She really is my fiancée. She is upset. I just want to make sure she is OK and talk to her two minutes. You can be present as witness. If she refuses, I'll leave peaceably."

"OK," the man was mollified. "Come with me."

Connor walked up the stairs with the man, and he stopped in front of a door. Knocking, he called, "Ms. Childs, this is the management. Could I talk to you a minute?"

They waited, but no answer emanated from the room. The manager knocked again, but again there was no sound. Taking his master key, he opened the door and looked in. Glancing past him, Connor could see her purse on the bed, but no other sign of life.

The manager closed the door behind him. "Sorry—maybe she went for a walk or to dinner."

"But her car is outside."

"The few eating establishments are within walking distance, although a squall is stirring up out there."

Connor asked, "Then do you happen to have any other rooms available? I'll be glad to pay for a room for the night."

The man's face brightened. "Sure. The group that reserved the whole place for the weekend canceled. Got any luggage?"

Connor smiled. "No, I was in a hurry to get here."

Moments later Connor possessed a key to the room next door to Amanda. He followed the manager into the bar as the sounds of thunder could be heard from outside. "Storm's brewing," the man noted. "What can I get you?"

"Glenlivet on the rocks, please."

Connor positioned himself at the bar so that he could watch the front door of the inn, and made small talk with the manager as the latter watched the last of a basketball game and the sports news channel.

After a while Connor looked at his watch. It was after 9:30. He turned to his drowsy bartender. "Where could she go on this island?"

The man frowned. "All the businesses here close at 9:00 at night until Memorial Day. She should be back by now. I just don't know."

Connor suddenly felt uneasy. "Do you mind checking her room once more? I'll stay here. If she's not there, I'm going looking for her."

"Say, she's not in trouble, is she?"

"No, she's just got several reasons not to trust people."

"I can understand that," the manager muttered as he turned to go upstairs.

Minutes later, he returned, a worried expression on his face. "Mister, she's not there."

Connor strode quickly out the front door, into the howling wind and blowing rain burning his eyes and arms. He looked down the short street both ways, initially uncertain about where to begin looking for her. Instinctively he decided to walk down to the gulfside.

Reaching the beach, he scanned the horizon in both directions. He started walking east along the shore, the cold rain beating harder, stinging his back through his shirt.

After a few minutes he was startled to see a dark form in the distance huddled on the beach alone. Frightened, he ran to it.

It was Amanda. As he touched her shoulder, her eyes opened, and she raised her head. At first frightened at his sudden presence, she jerked away, squinted through the rain and recognized him.

"How did you find me? Get away from me," she hissed, pushing his arm away.

Her eyes aflame with anger, she opened her mouth to speak again, but he leaned over her and laid his finger over her lips.

"Amanda, that wasn't me with that woman. I swear to you. I'm afraid you've just been introduced to the black sheep of the family, my brother David."

"But—" she began hotly, but he shook his head.

"I swear it wasn't me. Many people mistake us. We look and sound a great deal alike, unfortunately for me."

Amanda looked at him mutely, doubtfully, as the heavens opened again and the rain, made horizontal by the gusting winds, pelted both of them unmercifully, the storm unleashing its pent-up fury. He pulled her to her feet and enfolded her soaked and trembling body to him.

Over the sound of the storm and raging surf he said in her ear, "I've waited so long for just one woman. You. No one else. No reservations."

He swooped her up, a wet rag doll. She echoed, "No reservations."

Looking at her shining eyes with a feeling of glad triumph, he started back to the inn with her in his arms.

Chapter 35

Oblivious to the elements, Connor carried Amanda effortlessly through the storm from the beach up the deserted roadway to the inn. The manager met them at the door, his eyes wide with concern.

"She didn't attempt suicide?" he anxiously asked Connor.

"No," Connor replied as he made his way past the man and took the stairs, Amanda wordless in his arms and clinging to him.

The innkeeper hurried after him, unlocking Amanda's door. Connor strode in and placed Amanda on the bed. She sat up, embarrassed, as the manager bustled in the room with extra towels, blankets, pillows and terry robes. Connor immediately took a large towel and wrapped it around a shivering Amanda, enveloping her. He turned to the manager, pulled out his wallet, and peeled off several large bills.

Connor spoke low. "If I know her, she probably hasn't eaten all day. If you have anything in the larder downstairs: fruit, cheese, crackers, bread, whatever, please bring it. And I need a carafe of hot coffee and a bottle of your best champagne with glasses. Just bring it in and place it over there," he authoritatively indicated a corner table.

The manager's eyes widened as he observed the bills in his hand. "Right away," he replied gallantly, as Connor thanked him and he scurried off.

Connor shut the door and knelt before Amanda. Taking another towel, he started drying her hair. Then he removed the big towel, pulled off the jacket of her suit and slowly unbuttoned her blouse. She sat passively, gazing at him as he peeled the wet fabric off her, then continued drying her skin, his eyes not leaving her face.

The cell phone on his belt buzzed. He frowned and checked the number of the caller. Bubba, he discerned. That can wait. He then pushed a button turning the phone off. She looked dazedly at him.

"Do you realize what you just did?" she whispered. "I've never seen you turn it off. Ever."

He sat on the bed beside her, engulfing her in embrace and covering her mouth with his own. She clung to him. He whispered to her, "There's nothing more important to me than right here, right now with you. The world can wait."

She smiled, melting his heart. He let her go, wrapping the large towel around her shivering form tighter. Satisfied, he murmured, "I'm going to run you a bath. We need to get you warm."

She reached out and touched his cheek. "Don't leave me," she whispered.

He caught his breath sharply, and the next thing he knew he was again beside her, pulling her down with him on the bed, holding the nape of her neck with one hand and kissing her as her hands moved over his shoulders and face. He deftly removed her bra and encased one breast with the other hand, and she moaned in pleasure.

Finally he tore himself gently away from her. "I'm not going anywhere," he told her huskily, as he walked into the bathroom.

She heard the sound of water running in the bath, but felt powerless to move. She felt her heartbeat drumming in her head, and the room held a dreamlike and timeless quality.

Connor returned and took her hands. He pulled her up to him, kissing her again as he held her next to him. She followed him docilely as he led her into the bathroom, closing the door. From the running bath a steam was rising and bubbles were forming. The room smelled of lavender.

He said, "God, you're beautiful," as he tugged the towel off her shoulders and continued slowly undressing her.

Amanda, flushed and self-conscious as he gazed upon her naked form, looked away at the inviting bubbles.

"Get in," he ordered, and she slipped into the warmth of the water. Finding a button, he pushed it, and a whirlpool began, multiplying the bubbles. She lay back, letting the warmth steal through her and closing her eyes as the bubbles mounted and the water swirled around her.

She didn't know how long she lay there, barely conscious of her surroundings, until she felt Jon lathering her with a scented soap. She opened her eyes, and Connor, shirtless, was on his knees beside the tub. He lovingly washed her face, arms and back, stroking her until she could stand it no more and grabbed his wrist.

"Join me," she commanded breathlessly.

Needing no further invitation, he stood, undid his pants, and let them fall to the floor. She stared fascinated at his naked torso as he stepped into the tub and lowered himself to her. She pulled him to her, surprising him with the ferocity of her kiss and locking him in embrace. He groaned as their bodies made contact.

They made love, urgent, frenzied, clutching each other as though drowning. He cupped her buttocks in one hand as he brought her body to meet his. Her hands ran down the length of him, marveling at the feel of him. She gasped as he stroked her, lost in sensation as her body responded.

He brought her to frenzy, as she whispered his name over and over. Then he entered her gently, and she arched against him. She matched his urgency with her own, biting her lip to keep from crying out as he pinioned her against the tub, moaning as she melted to him. Her muscles tensed around him inside her, and her breath came in short gasps as he stroked her between her thighs, awakening her sensitivities even more. Then his mouth found her breast, before he whispered her name and released it and thrust deeper.

Time and place fled, and there was nothing but the two of them in a vortex of senses as they matched each other in intensity.

When it was over, she was shaking from the force of their union. He cradled her and kissed her, and she responded in kind as they held each other.

He smiled at her, kissing the tears in her eyes.

"I wasn't too rough, was I?" he asked concernedly.

"No—it was wonderful," she whispered tremulously.

"Now for the business at hand," Jon said as he reached for the soap. She smiled shyly. He murmured, "Don't be ashamed. You are gorgeous," as he lathered her with soap. Taking his cue, she followed suit, and they bathed together, caressing each other seductively with the fragrant soap suds, laughing and spraying each other with fresh water from a spray nozzle.

Their ablutions complete, he stepped out of the tub and held out his hand. She stepped out, and he dried her thoroughly, then himself, and held out a robe for her. She slipped into it, then held out one for him.

Hand in hand they left the bathroom, and her eyes widened in astonishment. "Food?" she cried.

She sat on the bed as he uncorked the champagne, handing her the glasses and pouring. Then he sat beside her as she handed him a glass and they drank, she downing hers in one gulp and setting the glass down.

He looked at her curiously. "The rest can wait," she explained simply.

She pulled him toward her as she backed up on the bed. He hastily finished his champagne and set the glass down as he followed her, untying her robe and his. He whispered to her, "This time I want to enjoy every inch of you."

Their second lovemaking was unhurried, slow and sensuous, as each tried to prolong the other's pleasure and explore the newness of each other. She felt giddy as he tantalized her, using his tongue and building up her sensations to the point she wanted to scream, before finally entering her.

She started to move rhythmically against him, but he held her still, and in the stillness she felt the throbbing of both their heartbeats, until such time as she could control herself no more. Thrusting upward to meet him, she begged him to take her. But still he demurred, pinioning her while teasing her and caressing the sensitive point of insertion between her thighs with his fingers and with slow controlled movements of his hips, one hand at the small of her back, holding her still to him. She writhed in an agony of delight, tormenting him as she locked her legs around his waist and moved to meet him, her reason whirling out of control.

Finally they could take no more. He smothered her cries with his mouth on hers as she met him thrust for thrust, and they succumbed to the overwhelming tide of sensation as their lovemaking culminated.

They lay together, their arms and legs entwined, both satiated and tired, as he stroked her face and licked the tiny trickle of blood from where she had bit her lip to keep from crying out. She laid her hand on his chest, feeling the beat of his heart as she nuzzled his neck.

"I never thought this moment would happen," she breathed. "You've made me so happy."

"As you have me," he stroked her hair. "I have never felt for anyone the way I feel for you, Amanda. I do love you like no other."

"I love you, Jon," she told him, gazing into his eyes. "I cannot believe I waited so long."

"What changed your mind?" he queried, smiling at her.

She shook her head. "You would laugh," she demurred.

"I promise I won't," he nuzzled her ear.

"It was something Stephen Marks said to me," she mumbled timidly.

He stopped and turned to gaze at her, a huge grin beginning. She said accusatorily, "You promised not to laugh."

"I'm sorry," he apologized, still smiling, as his lips descended on hers. Finally releasing his hold on her mouth, he said, "We haven't had time for you to tell me about your visit with Marks today."

"It started out badly," she confessed. "It was really hard for me. I was pretty horrid, and still cannot bring myself to ask forgiveness for the things I said. But all of a sudden something he said turned on a lightbulb in my head. I knew I wanted you, I didn't want to wait any longer, and I couldn't wait to tell you."

She summarized her conversation with Marks, Connor listening and stroking her hair. "I don't know if I can ever bring myself to forgive him, but I know Marjorie was right."

"Yes, the key to your own salvation is to turn loose of all that anger and frustration, to forgive."

She hesitated. "I'm sorry I barged in at your place this evening. And then I saw—" she faltered.

Jon looked at her compassionately. "I'm sorry I didn't tell you about the strong resemblance between brother David and me, but the subject never really came up. I didn't know he was coming down for the week until he showed up today. It was such a hard day, with court in Pensacola yesterday, and then I had to drive back here because we have been combing the area for a murder suspect in the case I'm working.

"I had just made it to the condo and had a shower. I hadn't even checked my messages. I was going to call you. I didn't think I could stand another day without hearing your voice. I heard a noise and walked out of the bedroom to see you running out the door."

He kissed her forehead. "I died a thousand deaths tonight, seeing you run away, then hearing your message and realizing what you must think. Thank God Sheila was still at the office and did some sleuthing on her own, discovering where you had made reservations."

She replied slowly, looking away, "I was so elated and beside myself getting down here, intent only on reaching you. Then when I saw—well, I was shocked and hurt. I didn't know what to think, where to go."

Connor silenced her with his mouth on hers again. She whispered, "I'm getting addicted to being kissed by you."

He murmured against her lips, "I will make sure to feed that habit. You never have to fear about me, milady. Now, please eat something."

He raised up on the bed, and pulled her gently by the wrists to sit beside him as he pulled her robe around her shoulders and gestured toward the silver tray on the table. She went over and perused the covered dishes as he refilled their champagne glasses.

"Ooh, crackers and chicken salad, some of my favorites," she murmured, and he smiled as she dipped a cracker in the salad and plopped it into his mouth. They both seated themselves at the table, snacking and talking, their legs entangling and their hands periodically seeking out each other.

Finally their conversation lulled, as their appetites were satiated. Jon gazed at her and she fell into an embarrassed silence. Connor picked her up bodily and brought her to the bed, pulling back the covers and dumping her unceremoniously on it. "Rule number one—no clothes in bed," he announced, grabbing the neck of her robe and in one sweeping motion pulling it off her. He disrobed and jumped in beside her. He stretched out beside her, molding himself to her back as she lay on his outstretched arm. They listened to the storm outside lash and rage and the rain drum against the metal roof, as she snuggled to him and they talked desultorily, his hands stroking her body.

Turning her to face him, he kissed her as his hands stroked her breasts seductively and she stretched toward him.

"I love you so much, Amanda. Don't ever forget it," he murmured. "I want forever to be with you."

As she moved toward him, stroking him, desire stirred again, and they gave in to it, making love slowly and luxuriously, until their passions were again spent and they lay, satisfied in each other's arms, and slumber overtook them.

Petrino blew into Amanda's office. "What do we have?" he asked his officer.

"Sheila has so far found only a letter opener and an engagement ring missing," the officer replied.

"Where's Amanda?" he turned to Sheila.

"She ran out of here. She was not herself," Sheila was upset. "I feel badly because I know these items were here this morning when she was at the office. She was upset when she couldn't find them. I called Ralph, and he and Claire are on their way back to town from Tallahassee."

Petrino pulled out his cell phone and tried Amanda's number, but got no answer, only her voice mail. "Amanda, this is Charlie. Please call me about the missing items at the office." He hung up.

"Tell me who was here all day," Charlie turned to Sheila.

She relayed the information about the air conditioning repairman, and about Brownlee's appearance. Charlie's eyes narrowed as he questioned her about the meeting.

Sheila looked at him like she wanted to say something else. "Out with it," Charlie ordered.

"Mr. Connor—" she faltered, "Jon told me not to say anything," she began.

"I just want to make sure she is all right, Sheila," Petrino tried to reassure her. "You remember the last time she ran out of the office."

Sheila nodded, her face somber. "Mr. Connor, I mean, Jon, had called looking for her, said it was important that he find her. He sounded stressed. I checked her last number dialed, and she had made a reservation at the inn on St. George Island. I told him that. He was going looking for her."

Petrino punched in Jon's number on his speed dial, and waited for several minutes.

"Jon, it's Charlie. What's going on?"

Jon informed him that he was after Amanda, and turned away Charlie's offer of help, promising to call if he couldn't find her.

Charlie hung up.

"Chief, I think we're finished here," the officer announced.

Charlie nodded. His phone rang. "Petrino," he answered. He listened a moment. "That's Bruce's jurisdiction, but I'll be right there."

He turned to Sheila. "I will call the inn to see if she shows. If Jon is on her tail, he will most likely find her. At least I hope so," the last words were a whisper. "I need to check on this situation." He patted her back. "Lock up and go home, Sheila. I'll deal with Ralph."

He gave instructions to the officer to wait and leave with Sheila, then strode out. He turned his car east and headed just out of town, to the Sundown Inn. On the way he spoke briefly to Ralph by cell phone, and informed him of the status of the investigation on the theft and Amanda's precipitous leave-taking.

It was already dark outside, and he felt the old humming in his veins when a major investigation was being initiated. I miss the thrill, he smiled to himself. I hate not being in the middle of a murder investigation. It aggravates me not knowing everything that is happening.

Just as Charlie pulled in to the motel, Bruce Williams' vehicle pulled in beside him. They both got out.

"Fancy meeting you here," Bruce greeted him. "What are you doing on my turf?"

"Just sightseeing," Petrino replied. "Wanted to see if it was a local. You know me—always curious."

The manager was standing outside the door of the motel room, and EMTs were inside. One shook his head when he saw the law enforcement men. "No use calling Doc Howells on this one. He didn't make it. He's deader than a doornail."

Petrino gazed on the face of the still form on the bed. "I know that face," he muttered. He looked over at Bruce. "Chances are this guy didn't die of natural causes. You have a probable homicide investigation, sweetie."

"Why do you say that?" Bruce demanded, studying the face of the corpse.

"Because his picture is on the wall at both our offices. Unless I miss my guess, he is Bo Bronowski, the son-in-law of one of one of the most notorious crime bosses on the Atlantic seaboard." Charlie frowned. "The feds will want to know about this. Wonder what he was doing down here?"

Williams turned to the paramedics. "You guys might as well stick around and give a statement to the men in green. Call the medical examiner, get his staff rolling. Leave everything as it is for now. Let's move out of the room so as not to disturb the scene any more than it has been."

Bruce and Charlie walked out and met the manager outside the open doorway.

"Damn mess," the manager said, recognizing Charlie. "Did the guy die?"

"Yep," Charlie replied as sheriff's cars came barreling up and drew to a stop, lights flashing.

"I hadn't seen him since last night at the bar," the manager offered. "He left with some redhead. She looked familiar. Then she came in this morning and paid cash for the room for another day. Housekeeping contacted me to let me know they hadn't gotten in the room today. I went to check and found him."

"Have you touched anything?" Bruce wanted to know.

"No. I just called the ambulance and housekeeping," the manager supplied.

"They'll have to wait now," Charlie spoke grimly. "Thanks. We'll probably want to take a statement later."

The manager nodded and walked off.

Petrino turned to Bruce. "Might as well call the FBI. Better sooner than later."

Bruce nodded and walked off, his phone in hand. Petrino sat on the hood of his car as the sheriff's people milled around, an investigator taking names of witnesses and a deputy cordoning off the area.

Charlie's mind was on Amanda. Please let Jon find her, Charlie thought. Maybe I should drive to St. George Island tonight to help him. No, he rejected that idea. As long as she is safe, I need to let them work it out. He resolved to call the inn, looking at his watch. The inn's owner's name was Chuck, wasn't it? I met him when I was down there doing some charter fishing last summer. Amanda probably hasn't had time to reach the place yet. But what if something has happened? Damn it, he told himself angrily, there's nothing I can do. Jon is on the case. Maybe he's found her. I don't need to interfere unless he asks for my help.

His reverie was interrupted when Bruce walked up, hanging up his phone. "They're sending some FBI agent from Pensacola. It will take him a while to get here—there was some other murder at the federal prison. Della with FDLE and one of her colleagues are here on another case, so I asked them to help process the scene. That's them now."

Another car pulled up, and a pretty petite brunette woman and a dour-looking man with salt-and-pepper hair got out. "Howdy," she spoke to the officers. "You all seem to have a lot of serious crime in this county," she smirked, pulling a bag out of the back seat.

"We try to oblige," Bruce retorted drily, as a van pulled up with the medical examiner's investigators, and another car, a marked sheriff's unit, arrived. "I'll leave you with it."

Petrino suggested, "Let's talk to the manager again and see what we can find out about this redhead."

Bruce nodded. "He's over there."

They sauntered over to the manager, who was looking on at the crime scene. Bruce spoke. "What can you tell us about this woman you saw with him?"

"Not much," the manager admitted. "I was bartending last night, and Amy came up and said the man, who was at a table, wanted a bottle. I obliged. The next thing I noticed was him and this redhead leaving together, his bottle in hand. Like I said, she came by this morning and paid in cash for another night, then got in a red car and left. I never saw the guy or her again."

"Any description?" Petrino asked.

"I can't tell much about cars, but it was red and sporty. The woman? Really gorgeous, head full of red hair curling below her shoulders, fine looking," the manager leered. "Looked familiar. Amy was the one who acted like she knew her, got a good look."

"Where's Amy tonight?" Bruce questioned.

"She called in this afternoon with a touch of a bug, throwing up and stuff. She is always good to be here, particularly on the weekends when the tips are better. So I know when she calls in, she is really sick." He looked at them. "Unless she's at death's door, she'll be at work tomorrow afternoon."

Bruce obtained name and phone number for the waitress, and partial description of the car.

"Thanks." Petrino and Bruce moved off. He spoke to Bruce. "You gonna talk to her tonight?"

"I'd like to, but I don't want to catch anything, and I hate to interview really sick people," Bruce rejoined, smirking. "I'll give her a call."

He dialed the number given him by the manager, walking away as he talked to someone on the phone. A few minutes later he returned scowling.

"No go. Her mother answered, said she is puking her guts out and if she's not better soon, the mom is going to bundle her off to the ER."

"Well, you can put out a BOLO on what you got, which isn't much."

"Go home, Charlie," Bruce shook his head, a touch of annoyance in his voice. "Why did you teach me all this shit, if you're not going to let me do my job? Get outta here."

"Is that any way to talk to your former boss?" Charlie rejoined, grinning.

"When you become the boss again, you can send me home if you like," Bruce retorted, smiling back. "Something tells me that won't be long in coming."

"You think?" Charlie turned serious.

"Sheriff Watson is not doing well. The cancer is in its last stages," Bruce replied, his smile fading. "He won't last much longer. So go ahead and get your ducks in a row."

"You sure you don't want the job?"

"I worked for you before. I don't mind doing it again," Bruce nodded. "But until then, get off my turf. You know I'll share any juicy information with you."

Chapter 36

Saturday around noon Malcolm Howells, dressed in Dockers and casual button-down plaid shirt, stormed into the police station, his face a picture of worry. Charlie Petrino, dressed in khakis and polo shirt, saw him first, and strode out of his office to meet him.

"I didn't know if I'd find you here," Howells greeted him somberly. "But I knew to try here before your house."

"I had something come up, some calls to make. What's up?" Charlie asked unsmilingly.

"Where is she?" Howells demanded.

"Who?" Charlie asked casually, although he knew to whom Howells was referring.

"Amanda. I can't find her. I drove out to the farm, but Fred hasn't seen her. She didn't come home last night. She's not answering her phone. And Colin said that Ken was at the church this morning practicing, saying he was subbing for her at church tomorrow."

"Why are you asking me?"

Charlie glanced up, and saw that Howells was peering at him long and hard. "Because if anyone knows, you do. You're just like your daddy—you keep your finger on the pulse of this town and know everything that goes on in it." He paused. "And the last time this happened . . ." Howells started to add something, but thought better of it and fell silent.

Petrino flushed under Howells' scrutiny. He gestured for Howells to follow him. They walked into his office, and he closed the door. He motioned toward the chair facing his desk. "Sit down, Doc."

They both took a seat. Petrino took a deep breath. "Amanda has been gone since yesterday evening. Sheila called the station yesterday evening and said there was apparently a theft at the law office. I met Mack over there. No sign of break-in, but Amanda had noted several things missing." He paused. "A letter opener and the engagement ring Jon had given her."

Howells started. "The ring? Where was Amanda?"

"She had gone. Sheila said she was worried. Amanda had come in and was antsy, not herself at all. She seemed excited about something. Sheila heard her making some reservations and calling Ken to take church for her Sunday. Sheila said Mandy was mightily upset when she couldn't find the ring, asked Sheila to call me, and all but ran out the door."

Charlie sighed. "I tried her cell phone—no answer, no callback. I too contacted Fred to check on her. He'd not seen or heard from her. I called Jon last night. He said he was on her trail, and thought he knew where she was going, said he would call me if he needed help. I called him back this morning. He's not answering his cell either, which is odd, because he always keeps it on." He paused. "However, I called the owner of the inn down on St. George Island early this morning. Apparently both Amanda and Jon showed up late last night." He stared at Howells, his meaning clear.

Malcolm said slowly, "She said nothing to me Friday about any weekend plans. She generally tells me these things."

"I'm not sure this was exactly planned," Petrino turned away. "But if they are together and I haven't heard from Jon, I'm taking that as a good sign."

After a second, he turned back, his brow creased in a frown. "When did you talk to her?" Petrino wanted to know.

"Early yesterday afternoon she called me to check on Alan's condition. She told me she was going to meet with Stephen Marks. I could tell that she was nervous, reluctant. I offered to go with her, but she declined, said she needed to do this herself."

Petrino's eyes narrowed thoughtfully. "So she did go to the federal prison?"

"I am assuming she kept the appointment. She was on her way there when I talked to her. The prosecutor had suggested it and at the time I thought it was a good idea." Suddenly suspicious, Howells asked, "Why?"

Petrino leaned forward. "I take it you didn't see the papers this morning?"

"No," admitted Howells. "I had some business at the hospital early this morning, then spent a little time consulting with Bob Cardet about Alan's condition. We called in a neurologist, and are waiting to hear from him about his findings."

Petrino pawed through papers on his desk and placed the front page of the morning's area newspaper before Howells. "So you didn't see this?"

Howells picked up the paper, reading the lead article. His face paled. "Oh, my God."

Amanda awakened Saturday morning, the sun shining brightly into the room. She looked at the unfamiliar ceiling, then cautiously felt the bed beside her. Realizing she was alone, she closed her eyes, refusing to look around her, frightened that the memories of the previous evening were only a dream.

Turning, she heard the crinkling of paper. Reaching out, she found a sheet of paper on the pillow beside her. She read the note:

> I've gone to town to pick us up a few necessaries. Be right back.
> Love you madly,
> Jon

She breathed a quick prayer of thanks, grateful for evidence that the events of the last evening had actually occurred. She cautiously rose and surveyed her surroundings. Yes, the champagne bottle and glasses, the tray of food, her clothes draped over the furniture, the bathrobes, were all still present as testimony of their tryst.

Leaving the warmth of the bed, she slipped on a robe and padded to the bathroom, where she found a travel toothbrush and toothpaste Jon had laid out for her. Smiling, she brushed her teeth, then turned on the shower. Slipping inside, she reveled in the daggers of warm water on her skin, humming to herself.

Suddenly she was not alone, as Jon, also naked, entered the shower. Surprised and pleased, she leaned toward him as he kissed her and murmured, "Good morning, milady. What, taking a shower without me?"

She whispered huskily, "We have to stop meeting like this. We'll never manage to get to work on time."

"We'll figure out something," he remarked as he pinned her against the shower wall, running his hands down the length of her body. Her heart racing, they melded into each other, the warm jets of water intensifying the effect they were having on each other.

Afterward, as they showered together, Jon looked at her sheepishly. "I just can't get enough of you, Amanda."

"I don't think I'll ever grow tired of you, so keep telling me and showing me," she breathed.

Out of the shower, dried and again in robes, she turned to the dilemma at hand. "What about our clothes?" she asked, as she looked at him in the mirror and towel-dried her hair.

He shrugged. "Guess we'll just have to stay in our room. What a shame."

Then taking her hand, he led herself to the room, where she found the bed littered with shopping bags. "What is this?" she asked in wonderment.

"I picked us up a few items to tide us over—you know, underwear, some casual clothes, toiletries."

"I'm duly impressed. You are amazing." She reviewed the items as Connor unpacked them.

"I thought we might do a little sightseeing," he said as he kissed her on the ear and reached past her for a shopping bag. Reaching in, he pulled out a shirt and some boxer briefs. She pulled out some suggestive lacy underwear.

"For me?" she stammered.

"Unless you expect me to try them on," he rejoined, grinning.

Together they dressed and put away the other items, Connor in khaki knee shorts, polo shirt and boat shoes, and Amanda in denim walking shorts, cotton print shirt and sandals.

"They fit," she sighed happily. "How did you guess my size?"

"I have my ways. Ready?"

Together they walked out hand in hand, speaking to the beaming innkeeper as they made their way to Jon's Mercedes. He opened her door for her and shut her in.

"Are you hungry?" he asked her as he pulled out on the causeway leading to Apalachicola.

"Famished," replied Amanda.

"Good. I know just the place—saw it on my way back from shopping."

He sped along the causeway as the noonday sun and cloudless sky transformed the water to a silky blue, punctuated by small waves. She stared at his profile as he concentrated on the road, and she felt wonder at being with him.

He glanced over at her. "What are you thinking?" he demanded as he caught her gazing at him.

"Just how happy I am with you," she responded simply.

His eyes returned to the road, but his smile broadened as he caught her hand in his.

They were silent, content to take in the view, until he reached town and pulled up at a corner café on the main street of town. He rushed around and opened her door for her. Alighting, she was drawn by him into the busy establishment, and they were soon seated at a massive mahogany bar giving their order.

After a meal of exquisite crab cakes with a creamy horseradish sauce, fresh steamed asparagus spears, Belgian beer, key lime pie and coffee, they left the car behind, walking down to the docks to observe the boats, and strolling around the town with its clapboard houses, wraparound porches and Victorian turrets. Hand in hand they came to the old Episcopal church. Amanda tried the door and found it unlocked.

Tugging at Jon, she led him into the structure. He stared in reverence at the tall shuttered windows and the old dark stained wood-paneled walls of the chancel. She related some of the history of the building.

"I was confirmed in this church," she told him as they stood before the aisle leading to the altar railing.

"Why here?" he asked, surprised.

"I was only a de facto Episcopalian at the time I was approached to serve on the vestry. Marjorie had just been diagnosed with cancer, and it was her dream for me to be confirmed. The 'visiting bishop' who did rounds for Marks was doing his annual visitation here, and so here I came with Marjorie."

Jon stopped in front of an ancient organ. "Does this still play?" he asked.

"Yes. That is one of the few extant and playable Henry Erben organs left from the last century, only one manual. The organist here uses it regularly. The other organ is a hybrid 1920s Pilcher. They have plans of adding to it, I believe."

"Would you play the organ for me?"

She protested, "I don't like to touch other organists' instruments without their permission."

He hooted with laughter at her pun as he caught her hand and kissed it. "An excellent policy, milady. I heartily concur."

She shook her head, grinning at him slyly. Leaving the church, they retraced their steps to the car, and drove along the highway hugging the bay. Then they doubled back to St. George. As they reached the inn, he asked her, "What is there to see around the island here?"

"This is mostly residential, not appealing to the usual spring break crowd and unknown to most of the outside world. There is a swank residential development at the west end of the island, and a state park at the east end. You can charter boats to visit the smaller islands or fish. People go scalloping in the bay here or at Cape San Blas.

"If you take a left here, it will take you to the state park," she pointed. Acquiescent, he followed her directions and soon they were at the park. Leaving the car, they explored, walking along the beaches and sand bars, examining shells and talking, sharing the vistas with only a handful of other visitors.

Jon asked her, "How do you know so much about this place? Did you and Andy . . . ?" his voice trailed off.

"No," she stared off to the gulf. "We always talked about it, because he had come down here deep sea fishing a couple of times. But every time we planned it, something happened to call him away. We decided that even talking about coming here was a jinx to our being together."

She smiled sadly at him. "Marjorie brought me down here several weekends to get away. Right after it—it happened. I didn't want to leave my room. I isolated myself. It was her way of getting me out again. I could just walk the beach and look at the shells, not think, escape the demons. So I fell in love with it. It became a wonderful place to just lounge around, read, hunt for shells, and be alone."

She took his hand. "I decided I wanted to share it with you."

He put his arm around her. "I'm glad you did."

As they watched the sun losing its conquest of the sky, he suddenly said, "This would be a perfect spot to get married. Why don't we? Where's the ring I gave you?"

Amanda looked aghast as she suddenly remembered the events of the previous day. "Oh, my God, the ring! I need to call Sheila," she exclaimed, turning back.

Jon clasped her hand and swung her around to face him. "What for?" he inquired, drawing her to him.

"When I went back to the office yesterday to get it, the ring and my silver letter opener you gave me were missing. I was so distraught but determined to find my way to you. I ran out and left Sheila searching for them."

"Missing? What do you mean? You misplaced them?" Jon demanded.

"No," she insisted. "I left the ring in a small velvet box in my desk drawer to remind me of you, and of course I used my letter opener all the time. I had them both at the office yesterday morning, but couldn't find either one yesterday afternoon. Sheila was checking to see if anything else was missing before we called Charlie and made a report."

She stopped, suddenly flustered as tears sprang to her eyes. "I'm so sorry, Jon. I would not have lost your ring for anything, and I know it was there yesterday morning."

"So you're saying someone may have stolen them?"

"I am assuming so. I was so anxious to leave yesterday and I am hoping that Sheila's back-up search behind me produced them."

Jon's features softened as he saw Amanda's apparent distress. "It's all right," he comforted her, holding her to him and stroking her hair. "They'll turn up."

Amanda remained in his arms, passively enjoying the nearness of him and the warmth of his flesh through his shirt. He turned and sat down on the beach, pulling her down to him as he kissed her hair, then lifted her chin. He kissed her eyes and mouth, then looked at her, his eyes smoldering. "I can't believe you are here with me. I never want to let you go."

He pulled her on top of him, holding her and stroking her, then rolling her over on the beach and assuming the dominant position. Towering over her in the sand, his mouth devoured hers, as her hands roamed inside his shirt. As his hand slipped inside her top and cupped her breast, she purred with delight.

As he released her mouth from imprisonment, she said breathlessly, "I'm going to have to join the gym to keep up with you."

"I intend to keep you in top physical form," he rejoined, his voice ragged with emotion. "I can't help myself. I want you right here and now."

"That's probably not a good idea," she smiled up at him coyly.

"Why? There's no one around but us."

"I think there are laws against what you're thinking," she laughed, her fingers tracing the contours of his lips.

"You're probably right," he laughed with her. "Well, then, come on, woman. Let's find some oysters and beer nearby so we can watch the rest of the sunset. We need nourishment for the night ahead."

Charlie called Amanda's number again, but got no answer. Damn, he thought. He left a message. "Amanda, it's Charlie. Call me. It's important."

He called Jon's and again got no answer. He left a similar message.

As he hung up, his phone rang. "Petrino," he spoke into the phone.

"I'm on my way to the Sundown to try to see Amy," Bruce's voice came across the line. "I'm waving a truce flag at you. Wanna join me?"

"Sure," Petrino tried to quell his irritation at not being able to reach Amanda. "I'll meet you there."

He called Jill to let her know he was going to be out a little longer. I don't know why she puts up with me, Charlie thought as he hung up. I wasn't willing to just be Amanda's lover, he realized, so why should Jill be content? I've got to put all that out of my head. Jill deserves first place in my heart.

Bruce met him outside the bar. The manager nodded at the two as they walked in. He volunteered, "Amy here waited on the guy Thursday night," pointing out a young woman approaching them.

"Hi, Amy," Bruce recognized her. "How's your mom?"

"Fine, Officer Williams," the girl responded politely.

Petrino pulled out a chair at a nearby table. "Have a seat," he offered. They all sat down. "Are you feeling better?" he was solicitous.

"Yes, much," she smiled wanly. "Just weak. My son had it a couple days ago, and I must have caught it from him."

Bruce smiled engagingly at her. "Now what can you tell us?"

"Not much," she shrugged. "This guy was sitting there at that table all morose." She pointed.

"Morose?" Bruce echoed, biting back a retort.

"Yeah. He ordered a whole bottle and paid well."

"Can you describe this woman who was with him?"

"Well she wasn't with him in the beginning. She showed up later."

"Did she know him?" Bruce queried.

"I don't know," Amy frowned. "He didn't seem to know her, but she acted real chummy with him. Then the next thing I knew he and Evie were leaving with the bottle."

"Evie?" Petrino's ears picked up. "You knew the woman?"

Amy looked at him scowling. "Of course I knew her. We were in high school together up in Alabama."

"You sure?" Charlie was incredulous.

"Yeah, I'm sure. It was Evie Brown."

"Evie Brown? You mean the woman who worked as Dr. Young's nurse?" Charlie broke in excitedly.

Amy shrugged her shoulders again. "I don't know. I hadn't seen her in several years, so don't know what she's been doing. I don't think she recognized me."

"Is there any doubt in your mind?" Bruce leaned forward.

"No," Amy replied, her eyes glinting angrily. "That red-headed bitch killed my cat with Red Devil Lye, all over a boy I was dating back in high school. I won't ever forget her."

"Will you give us a statement?" Bruce inquired.

"Sure will," she smiled. "But can I do it here at work? I really need the money."

Bruce called an investigator and gave directions. "He'll be here soon. Thanks for your help."

As they stood, Petrino smirked. "Looks like you have yourself a prime suspect already."

"I need a cause of death first," Bruce lamented.

"But you can still BOLO Evie Brown as a witness, and perhaps the ME will be able to determine cause of death today. Maybe you'll solve this murder in record time," Charlie teased.

"Yeah, just in time for the feds to claim jurisdiction and take it over," Bruce suggested glumly.

PART IV

Week 4

Chapter 37

As Sunday dawned, dim, chilly and with dark clouds and rain again threatening the western horizon, Amanda and Jon slumbered in each other's arms, wrapped in blankets on the floor beside the French doors overlooking the balcony and the gulf. Jon awakened, and lay there observing Amanda as she slept beside him. She looked so young and fragile. He wondered which Amanda was the real one: the tough unyielding attorney with a feminist, almost masculine disdain and confident iciness, or the sleeping nymph with the vulnerable eyes that he glimpsed in unguarded moments.

He felt a stirring of joy. Last night she had agreed to marry him. He thought, Today we'll make arrangements, see the priest after church, call Ralph about the logistics of getting a license tomorrow. I'm not letting her get away this time.

Peering out at the incipient day, he realized that his muscles were stiff. Talk about being out of practice, he thought to himself wryly. He looked at her again, and felt his loins stirring with desire. I'm mad with lust, he thought, but knew it was much more than physical desire he felt for her. He longed to touch her, to wake her, to love her again. However, he resolved to throw on some shorts and shoes and go running instead of disturbing her sleep. Thank heavens I had my gym clothes in a duffel in the trunk, he grinned to himself.

Minutes later, he paused before the still sleeping Amanda before propping a folded note beside her. Silently letting himself out, he decided to jog along the main road leading west.

Some time later, Amanda awakened to the view of the dark overcast sky, the misting rain and the sound of distant thunder. She stretched luxuriously before realizing that she was alone. Spying the note propped up beside her, she wrapped the blanket around her as she reached for it.

Gone jogging—be back soon. Remember you said yes last night. I know a great little Episcopal church down the road. Let's go to church, meet the priest, get married. Love you madly. Jon

She sighed contentedly. Thank you, God, for bringing Jon into my life, she breathed. She wanted to bottle up her happiness and savor it drop by drop. She never dreamed that she would feel this way ever again. And we're actually going to get married, she thought happily.

She showered and dressed, choosing the sea blue cotton knit dress and sandals that Jon had bought for her the previous day. Grabbing her purse, she sauntered downstairs to the morning room, where she ordered toast, bacon, coffee and orange juice. She sat there, lost in reverie, as she munched on her toast and thought about Jon.

As she rummaged through her purse to find her lipstick, she came across the opened letter and envelope she had stuffed inside unread Friday night on her way out of the office.

The return address on the crumpled envelope showed "W. Barnes". The address was the federal prison facility in Bayview. Bayview? she wondered. Baffled as to why Barnes would be writing her, she opened the single page, typewritten single-spaced, and unsigned. Curious, she thought, that a prisoner would be sending typed correspondence, as she noted that it was addressed to 'Amanda Childs, Attorney at Law', and labeled "Legal Mail" on the envelope. She knew from long experience that prisoners many times would label their mail "legal mail" in order to claim attorney-client privilege and prevent the corrections officials from reviewing the contents.

A photograph dropped out as she looked at the page. She picked it up. It was an old photograph she remembered of Monica, Bill and her as children. However, someone had drawn a red "X" over her in thick marker pen. She stared, transfixed at the photo, as memories flooded her mind. She frowned as she continued reading:

Amanda Childs, Attorney at Law
50 West Jackson Street
Mainville

LEGAL MAIL

Dear Mrs. Childs:

I'm sure that you are keeping abreast of the developments of my case, inasmuch as you are such an integral part of it. Lest you become lulled into a false sense of security that you will soon be rid of me and my son forever and live a life of luxury with your new-found fortune and boyfriend, let me hasten to assure you that you will never rest easy. I will be hounding you as long as there is breath left in me, and haunting you long after I am gone.

I know that Bishop Marks has a sudden soft spot for you as his 'long-lost daughter' that is all very touching, but I've known him much longer than you. In the end he will not testify against me—there is too much history between us, and he has a vested interest in keeping silence that outweighs any incipient paternal instincts.

Enjoy the moment while you may, for very soon we shall be exchanging places. You will have a long opportunity to experience what imprisonment feels like. I shall ruin you and all you have touched, and you will wish that you never existed.

Very truly yours,

Williams F. Barnes, Sr.

Stunned, Amanda drew in her breath sharply, staring unseeing at the letter as the waiter asked her if she'd like more coffee. Nodding numbly, barely comprehending his presence, she re-read the letter slowly. She again noted that the letter was unsigned. Observing the postmark, she determined that it was marked for Thursday from Panama City, one of the postal service's central sorting and distribution centers for the area.

"Is this seat taken?" she heard a familiar voice asking. Looking up sharply, she saw Jon, freshly showered and dressed in herringbone trousers and blue oxford shirt, sans tie, as he took the seat beside her, a Sunday newspaper in hand.

"I just picked this up, and thought you should see it." He looked solemnly at her as he placed it open to the front page before her. The leading headline read: "Former Judge Murdered." Beside a formal photograph of Williams Barnes, Sr., was the article:

> William S. Barnes, regional attorney and former judge from Mainville, was discovered dead at the North Florida Federal Correctional Facility Friday evening. His death appears to be a homicide, but authorities have not confirmed the cause of death.

Neither have any suspects or motives been disclosed, although the investigation is continuing.

Barnes, a former county judge retired thirty years ago under undisclosed circumstances, was an inmate at the prison. He faced multiple counts of murder, fraud, racketeering and obstruction of justice charges. He maintained his innocence, and was scheduled for trial next week.

Amanda wordlessly handed Jon the letter she still clutched in her hand. She continued reading the article, turning to the inside continuation as Jon reviewed the letter. She grew pale when she read:

The witnesses against him included confessed co-conspirator Stephen Marks, Bishop of the Episcopal Diocese of the Gulf Coast, already convicted and serving a prison sentence.

Also subpoenaed was Amanda Childs, a local attorney and suspected at one time in the alleged scheme. During the investigation it was discovered that Childs was actually the illegitimate child of Marks and local millionaire Marjorie Witherspoon. Mrs. Witherspoon, recently deceased, had named Childs as her major beneficiary.

"Oh, my God," she croaked, suddenly faint.

Jon looked up from the letter. He gently grabbed her wrist. "Where did this come from?"

"It was in the mail Friday afternoon when I went by the office. I couldn't find the letter opener and tore this open, but at the same time I was making arrangements to come to you. I didn't have time to read it, and I guess I ended up stuffing this in my purse. I found it this morning."

She rose quickly, blindly pawing in her purse for her wallet, before finding a bill and laying it on the table in payment for the breakfast. Jon asked her quietly, "Where are you going?"

She did not answer him as she fled. Jon grabbed the letter, photograph and newspaper and hurried after her, as she bounded up the stairs to their room. Jon caught up to her before she shut the door, and followed her in the room.

She sat on the edge of the bed, dazed. Connor sat beside her and took her hand. She remained there passively, her mind whirring, trying to make sense of what she had just read. Jon picked up his cell phone.

"Bubba will know what's going on. He'll fill us in. Don't worry."

Amanda sat, stunned and unresponsive, as he dialed George. Almost instantly Bubba answered. "Cramer here."

"Bubba, it's Jon. What's going on?"

"Just a moment." There was a pause for a moment, then Bubba's voice returned, almost a whisper. "Good God, where are you? It's a zoo. Have you heard about Barnes' murder? The feds have laid claim over the homicide investigation, and the Bureau is calling everyone in to work. And we've got one of the mob's family members, Bo Bronowski, dead on a slab, found Friday night just outside Mainville. The sheriff's office is investigating that. Kimball is tied up at the prison on the prison murder investigation and can't get away, so he's calling for Zeke to head up that way."

"I just saw the article about Barnes in the paper," Jon's voice was urgent. "Tell me what's happening."

"It's not good," Bubba whispered. "They're looking for Amanda. You wouldn't happen to know where she is?"

"Why? She's with me," Jon remarked as he looked at Amanda, sitting woodenly beside him, looking anxiously at him.

"I'll call you right back," Bubba said quickly, and the line went dead.

Jon, anxious at Bubba's cryptic remarks, stood up and paced the floor, his mind racing. So the feds were looking for Amanda?

"Tell me," she whispered urgently.

His phone rang. "Just a moment." He quickly engaged it. "Connor here."

Bubba's voice spoke. "It's me. I had to find a secure place to call you back."

Connor sat back on the bed and demanded, "Tell me, Bubba. Why are they looking for Amanda?"

Amanda visibly flinched, her eyes widening as she heard his words. Bubba was saying, "They found Barnes dead in the prison cafeteria Friday evening, and Marks was lying on the floor unconscious about five feet away. Jon, there was a silver letter opener sticking out of his chest—slit the aorta clean through. Initials 'A.C.' on the handle. And a three-diamond engagement ring on the floor under where he lay. Looked for all the world just like the one you bought for Amanda."

"My God, are you sure?" breathed Jon sharply, as he looked over at Amanda, who at his words had stood up and was pacing nervously.

"What is it?" she demanded fearfully, her face pale.

He held up his hand to silence her as he listened to Bubba's next words.

"Marks was evacuated to the hospital, but has regained consciousness. Appears he may have had a mini-stroke. He is babbling that he killed Barnes.

"Feds aren't discounting the old guy's story, but there's some mighty convenient circumstantial evidence linking your girl with the crime, and she was signed in at the prison that afternoon."

"It just doesn't make sense," Jon said slowly, as Amanda came closer.

"You have a decision to make, man," replied Bubba. "There's a covert sweep for her as a material witness and suspect." He paused. "Jon, Simpson's already wanting a warrant for her arrest."

"No," Amanda whispered, having overheard the last words.

"I gotta go," Jon said suddenly, as Amanda placed her hand over her mouth and fled to the bathroom. "I'll call you back."

Amanda shut the bathroom door, but Jon followed her in as she knelt in front of the toilet, retching. "Amanda," he urged quietly, "talk to me."

She turned deathly white, then passed out on the floor.

Jon, galvanized into action, bodily picked up her inert form and carried her into the bedroom, laying her on the bed. He took the pillows and elevated her feet, then ran into the bathroom and wet a washcloth in cold water, wringing out the excess water. Bringing it back and placing it on her forehead, he wondered about the news he had just heard.

After a moment he felt her move and heard her moan. Tenderly wiping her forehead and face, he saw her eyes flutter open. When she saw him, she tried to sit up, but he pushed her back down against the pillows.

"Just lie back a moment," he crooned.

"They are looking for me? They think I killed Barnes?" she whispered, tears forming. "Where would they get such an idea?"

Jon watched her, his mind in turmoil. Could Amanda have killed Barnes? He recalled Amanda's words in previous conversations that she wanted to kill the man. She was there. Her ring and letter opener were found at the scene, the latter apparently the murder weapon. Sheila had said she was not herself when she was at the office Friday evening, and had run out frantically, uncharacteristic for her.

No, Jon mentally rejected that possibility. Amanda could not be guilty of murder.

"Talk to me," he pleaded. "Did you see Barnes at the prison on Friday at all?"

"At the prison?" she echoed confusedly. "I thought Barnes was incarcerated at the Escambia County Jail," she said. "The letter and newspaper article are the first indications I had that he might be at that prison. What would he even be doing at prison, and at the same prison as Marks? Boyer wouldn't allow something like that, would he?"

"Indeed," Jon murmured. Amanda was right. He had not considered that. Boyer would want his star witness protected from contact with the defendant. "So you didn't see Barnes?"

"No," she shook her head. "Only Stephen Marks."

"Was there anyone else in the room?"

"Just the guard that was standing outside the door."

"What did you take in with you?"

"Nothing—I had to leave everything behind in the prison safe. I was frisked and went through metal detectors."

"Think carefully, Amanda. Did you by any chance have the ring or letter opener with you in your purse or car that day?"

"No, why?" she was suddenly frightened.

"You weren't wearing the ring?" Jon insisted.

"No," Amanda said slowly. Her eyes widened, staring at him as she grasped the truth. "They have found my ring, haven't they? The letter opener too?" Horrified, she sat up beside him. "Where? I don't understand."

Looking into his eyes, she became rigid with panic. "At the prison? No, that can't be," she stammered, her eyes dilating. "Not—not at the murder scene? How? Barnes' letter was right. I am going to be arrested, aren't I?"

She tried to stand, but Jon grabbed her shoulders, shaking her. "But you have been with me. You couldn't have done it, could you?"

Amanda stared at him wildly. "No, I didn't kill Barnes, Jon. You have to believe me. I haven't seen him since that night, the night he and Billy—"

She started shaking, overcome by the sudden memory, and she couldn't finish the sentence. Jon held her in his arms, rocking her back and forth as she continued shivering, crying silently. She clung to him, her voice muffled through the material of his shirt. "Oh, my God, this morning when I read that letter I wished him dead. But I didn't kill him. Believe me. Oh, Jon, you have to believe me."

"You're sure you didn't read that letter before this morning?" he asked her.

"I never read it until this morning," Amanda repeated, pulling away and looking at him. "It would have made a great motive for murder."

She gasped as she realized the implications of what she said. Jon's eyes narrowed as they came to the same conclusion.

"Someone's framing me for murder," she realized aloud as she shook free from Connor and stood up, swallowing hard. "Who would do that? Why?"

Jon looked at her cautiously. "Marks has had a mini-stroke, but according to Bubba, he is maintaining that he killed Barnes. He was found unconscious about five feet from Barnes' body."

"Why would he kill Barnes?" Amanda rubbed her forehead irritably. "He had just been talking to me about forgiveness and moving on."

Amanda stared out the window at the gulf, as both of them soberly considered what they knew, their attorneys' minds individually processing, sorting and calculating. They stood there silently for some time.

Finally Jon broke the silence, insisting fervently, "They are looking for you. We need to find you somewhere to hide away, Amanda, until we can figure out what to do next."

Amanda turned and picked up a shopping bag, throwing her clothing in it. "No, you're not going to harbor a fugitive. I have to go back."

"You can't," retorted Jon impulsively. "You're a bullseye—they'll arrest you now and ask questions later."

"I can't help that," she rejoined, suddenly cold, calm, as though she had shoved her vulnerable side into the shopping bag with her other personalty. "I'm not going to hide away like a criminal, and you can't help me if you're on the run with me or under fire as an accessory."

Jon came up to her, turning her to face him, holding her head in his hands. He whispered softly, "I can't lose you now, Amanda. I love you."

Her eyes welled as she whispered, "I love you too, Jon. I'm scared. Please don't be nice to me. We have to think."

"Marry me, now," Jon pleaded.

"No, we can't do that, even if we had the license," she pulled away, resolute, not looking at him. Again she was the hard, distant Amanda. "I will never forget our time together this weekend. But I won't marry you with clouds over our future together."

Jon started to protest, but she cut him off. "Don't you see, Jon? If we hide, we have no way of investigating this for ourselves. Even if I ran away without you, they would never believe you don't know where I am. You wouldn't be able to help me for the suspicion hanging over you. I don't have a choice, damn it."

She turned from him, picking up her clothes and casting them into the shopping bag. Mechanically, she filled a second shopping bag with his clothes, folding them carefully and placing them lovingly into the bag. He watched her, hypnotized by her.

"I'll go with you," he suggested tenderly.

Her task completed, she turned to him and handed him the shopping bag with his items. "No. Jon, you need to go straight to Marks and find out what happened, and quickly, if they will even let you in. We don't need to waste time, and I of course can't get through to see him. Get word to your colleagues and tell them you've made contact with me, and they can call off the search for me. I'm on my way to turn myself in, and they can pick me up at the Mainville Police Station. I'm not going to run. I'm driving straight there. I'll ask Ralph to meet me there. I'm sure I'll need him," she smiled bitterly.

"And Jon," she continued matter-of-factly, not looking at him as she collected her bag and purse, "Stephen Marks is the key; you really need to start there." She knew she was repeating herself, but spoke slowly as if trying to make a point to a client, trying to keep her mind from shutting down. "But in order to do so you need to distance yourself from me."

She swallowed as she clutched her car keys. "And tell no one of our tryst this—this weekend. That would discredit you immediately."

He lodged an objection, but she quelled him with a look of steel. "You're the best the Bureau has. You know and I know they're probably not going to let you work this case at all, but they're damned sure not unless you prove you can put aside your personal feelings."

Jon, angered at her words, said accusingly, "You talk as if you are already condemned. Don't you have faith in the criminal justice system?" he demanded hoarsely.

She stopped still, her eyes momentarily reflecting her bitter anguish. But just as quickly it was gone. He took a step toward her, but was paralyzed by her sudden icy demeanor, warning him off. Refusing to look at him, she coolly replied, "I have faith in you. And I have to believe that God would not be so cruel to me twice, giving me this time with you only to wrench you away from me."

Walking past him out the door, Amanda faltered. She started to say something but tore herself away abruptly, saying only, "I'm counting on you to do the right thing, for both of us," as she quickly fled without a backward look.

Chapter 38

After quickly settling the account with the inn, Amanda strode out, placing her things in the trunk of her car. She noted Jon's car still parked there. Getting in the car with her purse, she pulled out her cell phone and mechanically plugged it in to charge. Knowing she could not bear to see Jon again, she sped away and waited until she had driven as far as Eastpoint to the main highway before calling Ralph.

She heard his voice. "Is that you?" he whispered.

She remembered that he had every feature on his cell phone, including caller ID. "Yes," she muttered resignedly. "Where are you?"

"I'm at the police station." His voice sounded odd. "Are you aware of the situation?"

"Yes, I just found out," she replied. "Ralph,—"

"I can't talk right now. I'm in the middle of something. Let me call you back," he interrupted.

"Are the police there? The feds?" she asked.

"Yes," he said shortly.

"Listen to me," she stated urgently. "Tell them to stop searching for me. I'm driving home to turn myself in. I didn't kill Barnes, Ralph, but I am going to need a good attorney. The best there is," she finished bitterly.

Ralph started, "Are you sure?"

She could hear a male voice in the background asking, "Is that her?"

Amanda continued. "Tell them that I'll be there in a couple hours, depending on traffic. I'm alone, no weapons, no tricks. I'm driving straight to the police station—no detours. Would you please meet me there, if you don't mind?"

She felt tears close to the surface, and willed herself to remain calm. Ralph replied, "Yes, I will be here. Is there anything else I can do?"

Her mind suddenly went cold, and she answered, "Yeah, find out who has framed me for murder."

"You're damn straight I will," he remarked huskily, as she hung up.

Her next call was to Charles Petrino. "Amanda here. I just found out about Barnes. I've spoken to Ralph. I'm on my way to the police station to turn myself in to you, Charlie. I'm about two hours or so away. I'd appreciate you doing what you can to call off the cops until I get there. And Charlie, I didn't do it, for the record."

"I believe you, baby, and I'll do what I can for you," she heard him say. "Do you want me to come to you?"

She faltered. "No," she decided. "As it is, they may think you're prejudiced. I'm sure I'm going to need your help, so I want to save up the favors."

"I'm there for you. Just name it. Give me your route and I'll alert them to let you pass. And Mandy?"

"Yes."

"You know there's little I can do to stop the feds, and they have jurisdiction, but perhaps I can persuade them to give you escort and not stop you."

Amanda quickly gave him her location and proposed route, thanked him and rang off. The calls made, she suddenly felt tired. Rain, starting as a mild patter, became harder, pelting everything with a regular rhythm. Her mind was numb, the highway a blur as she passed Port St. Joe and Mexico Beach, continuing on to the outskirts of Panama City. She had decided to bypass the beach traffic and turned up a thoroughfare leading north toward the old auxiliary highway. The rain grew harder.

Steeling herself not to think of Connor and their time of intimacy, she turned her attention to trying to collate what she knew.

She remembered that Jon had related that Marks had made a confession to committing Barnes' murder. He apparently was present at the time, so he was the logical place to start for clues.

Trying to sort it out, she came up with three possible theories. The first one: Marks did kill Barnes. But how did he get her letter opener and ring? Why would he do it? Why would he frame her? What motive could he have? What did he have to gain?

The second possibility was that Marks did not actually see the murder, but somehow concluded she had killed Barnes, and was trying to cover for her by confessing to the crime. Again she could not figure out a logical reason for that scenario. She still had trouble, despite their meeting Friday, truly believing Marks had experienced a 'Damascus Road' encounter and was concerned for her well-being. And who was the actual murderer? How did her personal property make it to the crime scene?

But a third possibility presented itself, most intriguing of all. What if Marks saw the murder, knew who the murderer was, and was covering for him?

Who would kill Barnes? Why? Why would the murderer frame Amanda? And why would Marks cover for him?

Try as she would, she could come up with no credible alternative theories, and was stumped. She wished she could somehow find a meaningful lead, for she realized, as the distance closed between her and Mainville, that she would have little or no opportunity to participate in the investigation or her own defense if arrested and incarcerated, and would be at the mercy of others' efforts on her behalf. More harrowing than the fear of being locked in a cell was the helplessness of having to depend upon someone else for her liberty and very life. She had always by necessity been self-reliant, a staunch adherent to Tom Andrews' maxim: 'if you want something done right, do it yourself.' She realized with startling clarity how helpless some of her past clients must have felt.

The rain continued. Finally making it to the intersection only a couple miles from the bridge crossing the river, she spied a state highway patrol car parked on the side of the road. As she passed him, he flashed his blue lights once, then pulled out behind her, following but making no move to stop her. Relieved, she decided to call Connor with her ideas.

Hearing his voice, she faltered momentarily. "This is Amanda. Just listen." Before he could interrupt her, she poured forth her theories quickly. "So you see," she concluded, "Marks is the key. He has to know who is behind this."

"I agree," she heard Jon say. "I'm already on my way to the hospital to see him."

"And Jon," she interrupted before he could say anything else, "I just remembered. There was a guard who took my things, escorted me in and back out again. I cannot remember his name—something about an animal. He was muscular, medium height, buzz cut." She cast about in her mind. "Wolf—Wolfson, I think. He may be able to confirm that I was alone with Marks at the time he escorted me out. In fact," she suddenly remembered, "there was a woman priest waiting to go in to give him communion. Perhaps the guard will know something."

"Got it," Jon affirmed. "Are you OK?"

"Fine," she kept her voice even. "I even have my own escort," as she crossed the bridge spanning the Choctawhatchee River and saw a county sheriff's car at the end of the bridge pulling out in front of her. "We're forming our own parade."

A picture of Jon floated unbidden in her mind, and her voice caught. "I gotta go," she choked, ringing off as he called her name.

Her eyes blurred with tears momentarily, and she blinked them away. She matched the deputy's speed, keeping the required distance, as they continued on the highway. She glanced in her rearview mirror at the trooper's vehicle behind her, then looked back in horror as her eyes met the sight of a red sports car crossing the center line behind the deputy's car ahead of her, directly into her path.

Amanda slammed on brakes and instinctively veered right. As the right tires came into contact with the grassy muddy shoulder, she felt the car slipping sideways. She tried to correct, and the car began to straighten out, but the red car then glanced the passenger side of the vehicle, just hard enough for her car to hydroplane counter-clockwise into the lane of oncoming traffic. She barely missed a pickup truck.

With no time to think, Amanda automatically steered right. Her tires grabbed the pavement momentarily and the vehicle responded, but then because of the overcorrection the front slid off the right shoulder again.

The end edge of the guardrail of a bridge over a creek, swollen with water and flooding its banks from the rains, made rude impact with the front grille and headlights on the driver's side with a terrible wrench, throwing her forward and shearing down the driver's side of the BMW as the car continued its forward momentum. The seatbelt snatched her back, the airbag deployed, and she felt the car closing in on her and sudden stabs of pain in her left wrist, shoulder and side, as the brakes refused to check her forward progress on the slick grass. The car slid at an oblique angle down the steep grassy embankment and headlong into the rushing creek.

She gasped as she felt the car rapidly sinking into the morass and muddy water started pouring into the car, but she was pinned by the seatbelt and airbag. She was having trouble catching her breath as water started filling the car, swirling around her thighs and inching toward her waist. She reached with her right hand for the seat belt release lever to free herself, also grabbing for the door knob and shoving against the jammed driver's door with her injured left arm and shoulder, crying out as she made impact. As the car lurched forward, the dark water gushed and roared over her head.

David Connor was driving his black Jaguar behind the state patrolman and cursing at the inordinate number of cops out on the road policing the heavy spring break traffic. But he kept his distance because he didn't want to be ticketed for speeding or tailgating. He didn't know why he had decided on this route to get to Destin; he had vainly hoped it might be less congested than the beach routes.

Suddenly he saw ahead of him a phalanx of brake lights, as a red Mitsubishi coupe struck the BMW sedan in front of the trooper. He watched helplessly as the BMW teetered, veered off the road and down the embankment, and the red car passed in front of the trooper and came toward him on the right shoulder. Cursing, he slammed on brakes, and the coupe veered off to his right, ploughing into a steep ditch flowing with knee-high sawgrass.

Quickly he carefully followed the trooper, pulled over on the shoulder and parked well off the road by the trooper's car, as traffic came to a halt amidst the sound of screeching brakes, screaming tires and car horns. He exited his car cautiously, praying no one else would collide with him or adjacent cars.

The red car had come to a rest about fifty feet from him, so he quickly made his way there to check on the driver. As he got about five feet from the car, the driver door flew open and a woman with flaming red hair pulled herself out. Standing, she and he stared at each other a moment.

"You!" he said, shocked, as before him stood the beautiful woman with whom he had experienced the unconsummated sexual liaison Friday night. He continued angrily. "Where the hell did you learn to drive?" Then remembering his manners, he said, "I'm sorry. Are you OK? Here, let me help you."

He proffered his hand, but before he knew what was happening, the woman pummeled him in the stomach and he doubled over. As she flew past him up the hill, he reached out and grabbed her foot, tearing off a tennis shoe as she scrambled away. She stumbled, and a highway patrolman was immediately at her side.

She raised herself and swung, catching the officer in the chin with her fist. The impact caused the cop to topple backward. As the woman sprang up again to flee, David was on top of her. The patrolman pulled himself up and reached for his handcuffs.

The officer managed to get one cuff around her right wrist, then she jerked free, the cuff becoming a weapon, swinging and hitting the officer in the face and drawing blood. By then a sheriff's deputy had arrived to help, finished cuffing the woman and led her away, struggling and cursing, to a waiting patrol car.

David, wet and muddy from the skirmish, helped the first officer to his feet, remarking, "That's going to leave a mark, sir."

"Thanks," the patrolman responded. "Don't go away. We'll need your name, address and phone number. You're now officially a witness." He grinned, wiping his face with a handkerchief and leaving David standing there scowling.

He turned around, surveying the vista of the submerged BMW in the creek. Making his way through the drizzling rain toward the trooper standing at the edge of the creek bank, his sight was suddenly arrested by a suited man striding toward the same destination.

Recognizing him, David called, "Ezekiel!"

The man turned and squinted, then said, "My God! David Connor. What are you doing here?"

"Just experiencing close encounters of the first and second kinds," David said, ruefully rubbing his abdomen where the woman had punched him. "I was on my way to Destin. We just wrestled down the cause of the accident back there. She was gorgeous, but a hellcat."

"Trust you to find some action with a woman wherever you go," Zeke rejoined as they arrived at the creek bank.

The two men looked at the car. "Looks bad," David remarked quietly.

Zeke nodded gravely. "You don't know the half of it," he replied as he pointed out a man swimming toward them and pulling an inert form. "Your brother's fiancée was in that Beemer."

"Jon's?" David was stunned. "You've got to be joking. He's engaged?"

"Yes," Zeke nodded solemnly. "Would you mind helping me out here? You're a doctor, right? An ambulance is on its way."

As if to confirm his words, they heard the screaming of a siren coming toward them. David waded out to meet the swimmer as he treaded water with the unconscious woman in his arms. David helped him bring her to the bank. Carefully the man laid her on the wet grass, then dropped to his knees and bent over her, listening for breathing. As David watched, the man, his own chest heaving, began CPR.

David knelt beside him. "I'm a doctor," he explained simply. "Let me—you're exhausted."

The man hesitated, then moved aside to let David closer. David caught his breath as he recognized the woman as the one who had barged in on him and the red head on Friday evening, and had ran out with Jon chasing after her. He noticed on quick examination that her left cheek was rapidly swelling and her left wrist appeared to be dislocated or broken.

David gingerly began mouth-to-mouth resuscitation as the EMTs moved in with equipment. After what seemed a breathless eternity, the woman coughed weakly, gurgling as she clutched her side. Her eyes fluttered open as she gasped for breath and expelled water.

The man who saved her spoke, his voice breaking, "I had to break the windshield and cut the airbag and seat belt to get her out. I was afraid I was too late."

David initiated an examination, trying to determine if he could ascertain any other immediate injuries. He felt fairly certain that she had suffered a fractured rib or two, and immediately worried about the possibility of a punctured lung, as she was having trouble breathing and her coughs ended up as weak spasms with bloody phlegm, followed by gasps as though she was still drowning.

His initial examination complete, he instructed the paramedics as they placed her on a backboard, careful to avoid the areas where he suspected the broken bones. They carefully placed her on a stretcher and started up the embankment with the woman, the men following. Reaching the roadside, they placed her inside the waiting ambulance.

"I'm a doctor. Where's the closest trauma unit?" David shouted over the din to the ambulance driver.

"There's a brand spanking new hospital in the south end of the county, a good facility," the man replied.

"Gulfside Regional? I know of it," David replied. "How far?"

"About forty minutes. I think I can get her there in thirty, maybe less, if we're lucky," the man answered.

"Make it so," David demanded as he climbed in the back of the ambulance.

Zeke and the man who pulled the woman out of the water were standing by the ambulance doors. Zeke and the man chimed simultaneously, "I'm going too."

Zeke explained, "Fred here knows Amanda personally, and I'm the officer temporarily in charge of her."

David looked at both of them, started to ask a question, then shrugged and threw his car keys to Zeke. "No room in here—take my car and meet us there," he ordered.

The ambulance doors closed as the vehicle pulled off.

Chapter 39

As the ambulance lurched forward, David Connor turned his whole attention to the woman on the stretcher. Grimacing at his bedraggled condition, he grabbed a paper gown off a shelf and slung it on over his wet clothes, grabbing some wipes and latex gloves from a shelf. Noting that she was going into shock, he gave quick orders to the paramedic. She continued to attempt a shallow cough and to gasp, pain evident with each breath.

Her eyes suddenly fluttered open, and she gazed at David. He was mesmerized by the flashing gold of her irises as she rasped painfully, "Jon, you shouldn't be—" ending in a paroxysm. He thought as he looked down compassionately at his charge, I'm doomed to be mistaken for Jon all weekend.

She struggled, her right hand free, and grasped his shirt weakly, pulling him down to her. "Jon—the woman priest with—a—a black box," she gasped. "Evie—in the car...." She collapsed from the effort of speaking, her cough shallow, her body wracked with pain, as her grip loosened.

He laid his hand over her forehead, speaking soothingly. "Don't try to talk, Amanda," he crooned, remembering that Jon had used that name, as her eyes fluttered closed again.

Her breathing became shallower. "Come on, come on, stay with me," he commanded, as he placed an oxygen pump over her and started manually pumping air. "I haven't lost a patient yet, and don't plan on starting today."

The paramedic looked at him, half-frightened. David, reading his features, divined his thoughts. "You're new at this, aren't you?"

He nodded, his eyes wide.

"Here, take over for me a second," David was quiet but authoritative. "I don't want to, but we might have to intubate her. I hate to do it in a bouncing ambulance. What's the driver's name?"

"Arthur, sir," replied the young man.

"Arthur, how much further?" David called.

The other EMT answered for Arthur. "About twenty minutes, give or take."

"Make 'em fast," David prayed, as they rounded a corner and he braced himself. Pulling out his cell phone, he punched his speed dial. Hearing a voice answer, he queried, "Silas?"

"David! Where are you? The game has started."

"Is Joey there?" David asked.

"Sure thing. Knicks are up by 6."

"Listen. I need Joey to meet me at the ER there ASAP."

"He's on vacation, man," the voice protested. "What's up?"

"I got my brother's best girl on a stretcher in the back of an ambulance. I don't know if she is going to make it." Quickly he reeled off her symptoms and his impressions. "We're twenty minutes or so from the hospital. I need the best."

"We'll be there," the voice promised. "Good thing I know the CMO."

David grunted and hung up. Silas Fleischer was the chief medical officer at the pristine hospital, open less than a year and already establishing an excellent reputation for medical care. Their colleague and long-time friend Joseph Rand, alias "Joey" from childhood days, was one of the foremost orthopedic and trauma specialists in the country. Joey was down for a visit with Silas, and David had been invited to join them for an afternoon of watching the playoffs on television.

He stared at the still form before him as he took over the oxygen pump. She was unconscious, her breathing barely perceptible. "Hang on, Amanda, whoever you are," he whispered, as he braced himself for what seemed an interminable ride.

"We're almost there—hang on," Arthur said as they took a sharp turn, then another, and screeched to a halt. The doors opened, and David stepped out as hands reached out to grab the stretcher and patient. He strode in purposefully.

"Dr. Connor?" a male nurse greeted him inside the double doors. "Drs. Fleischer and Rand are already here and suiting up." He pointed to a corner of the emergency room into which Amanda was being wheeled. As he turned, Fleischer and Rand appeared, the latter already washed up and ready.

Silas looked David up and down critically. "You been mud wrestling? Get cleaned up before you come in my ER, man." Silas gave him a quick grin as the other man nodded at David and joined the team working on the patient. Crisp and businesslike, Rand examined the patient and gave quick, precise orders as Fleischer and David looked on.

Silas put his hand around David's arm and pulled him away. "Here—too many doctors kill the patient. You can't help her now. Let's get you out of here and let Joey work his magic."

As they walked out, the ER doors opened and Zeke and Fred walked in with more EMTs, both men looking morose. Zeke stopped to wave his badge at the charge nurse trying to halt their progress, but David motioned them forward, introducing them to Fleischer. Seeing Fred's grim, tired face and disheveled appearance, David was moved at his agitation as the man scoured the room for a glimpse of Amanda.

David pointed toward the cubicle where Amanda was. "Joey Rand is one of the best surgeons I've ever known. Amanda is in excellent hands. All we can do now is wait."

Fred nodded, saying nothing, as Zeke asked anxiously, "What can you tell me? I have to report in to my superiors about her condition."

David, surprised, queried quietly, "Why your superiors? And where is Jon? Shouldn't we be notifying him and the next of kin? Her condition is critical."

Zeke replied, his voice low, "She is a suspect in a murder case. She was on her way to turn herself in."

David whistled low as Silas interjected, "Are you out of your frigging mind? Jon's girlfriend a murderer? I don't think so." He started to laugh, but his smile died as he looked at the other men.

David turned to Fred. "Tell me, didn't you say your name was Fred? How well do you know her? Does she have relatives we should be contacting? A living will? I need to know about allergies, medical history, things of that nature."

Fred patiently answered all the demographic information he knew. "Amanda Childs is a local attorney," Fred added quietly. "She has only her brother up in Pennsylvania. Her law partner Ralph Carmichael would be privy to all that information. We called him on the way here—he'll be here soon."

Silas groaned, as David quelled him with a look. David shared Silas' unspoken question: What had Jon gotten himself into? Engaged to a lawyer? And one charged with murder?

David, wanting to get Zeke alone a few minutes to pump him for information, turned to Silas. "Silas, Fred here swam out and saved Amanda, and is probably freezing. Why don't you show him some place he can clean up, maybe get him some dry clothes and a cup of coffee? It will probably be a little while before Joey gives us any news. And, Silas, find me some clean scrubs or something."

Silas, divining David's intentions, acquiesced, leading Vaughan away, as David grabbed Zeke by the arm and pulled him to an unused examining room in the ER.

"Geez, man, tell me what is going on," David demanded as he peeled off his shirt, leaned over a sink and attempted to rid himself of the bits of mud and grass still clinging to his arms. "And what is Jon's involvement in all this?"

Zeke summarized the prior case involving the investigation that brought Jon into contact with Amanda initially, then the latest series of events culminating in the homicide of Barnes. David stripped and stepped into the adjoining bathroom, which possessed a shower. David's face grew tight as he listened intently, stopping Zeke to ask questions from time to time. As Zeke related how Barnes was found Friday dead at the prison, David stopped him.

"Wait a minute. You said this murder occurred Friday. When?"

"As per the medical examiner's report, sometime between about 3:00 and 5:00, but you know they can't be too precise," Zeke confirmed.

"I saw this woman face to face Friday evening somewhere in the neighborhood of six or seven o'clock in Panama City."

"Are you sure?" Zeke stared at David.

"I won't ever forget it," David replied, turning off the shower and wrapping a hospital towel around his waist. "I try to remember all the women who have seen me naked."

"What were you doing with Amanda—" Zeke started.

But David interrupted. "No, not her. She walked in on me making out with this red-headed chick who showed up looking for Jon."

"Red-headed?"

"Yeah," David stopped. "The woman who ran into this Amanda tonight, in fact."

Zeke's jaw dropped. "This is too far-fetched."

"I'm telling you it's a small world," David insisted. "That auburn vixen came to the door asking for Jon. I said, 'Come on in.' She said, 'I hear you've been looking for me. I'm Evie.'

"Next thing I knew she was all over me, and she and I were getting busy in the living room. This Amanda walked right into the condo, calling out for Jon. I didn't even know Jon was home.

"She took one look at me and blanched. She ran off like a scared gazelle. Jon came storming out, saw her, then me and the red-haired woman, and raced after her, madder than hell. He said something about she must have thought I was him. Then Jon disappeared for the weekend, off looking for her, I guess."

"Who's the red-haired girl?" Zeke wanted to know.

"Damned if I know," David shrugged. "She was through with me as soon as she discovered I wasn't Jon, though—walked out on me. And she belted me one there at the scene of the accident. Gave the officer a couple good licks too before they handcuffed her and carted her off."

"Did Jon know her?"

"I don't guess so, because about thirty minutes after Jon and this Amanda disappeared George showed up at the condo, said Jon had sent him, and started giving me the third-degree on all I knew about this woman, who was she, what did she look like, what did she say. And he found some little purse with a syringe and vial in it that she apparently left behind when she ran out."

"But you're sure that Amanda was at the condo Friday night around seven? No doubt?" Zeke persisted.

"I'm sure," David remonstrated. "But now I want to know where is Jon?"

Zeke shook his head. "Jon hasn't answered his calls all weekend."

"That's not like him." A sudden thought hit David. "You don't think this Amanda—"

"—bumped him off? Highly unlikely. She is head over heels for him. But where is he?"

Just then, Zeke's cell phone rang. He listened for several minutes. "Thanks for telling me. Bubba, Amanda's been in an accident. She's at the hospital now. No, we don't know her condition, but it ain't good. They arrested Jon's red-head at the accident scene."

He briefly described the events leading up to the accident and Amanda's injuries. "You might want to follow up on that, sniff around and get what info you can on the redhead at the county jail. Yeah, you're right—it's too damned coincidental."

Zeke rang off, turning back to David. "Well, Jon is alive and well, because Cramer has talked to him. He was with Amanda earlier today. But they parted company. She insisted she was turning herself in, and that's why I was at the accident scene. I was already on my way up to Mainville, got there, and all the officers swarmed out of the SO. I ended up part of the escort for her back to Mainville. Jon called George from the hospital in the next county over, where he is interrogating Stephen Marks."

"Who is that?"

"The Bishop who turned state's evidence against the guy who was murdered Friday. He may have been the last person to see the guy alive, and claims to have killed him."

David muttered, "This is more convoluted than a soap opera. 'For a good time, visit Jon in Florida.'" He paused, processing the information given him, then turned as a new thought hit him. "Who is this Fred?"

"Former Special Forces guy, and Amanda's neighbor. He insisted on riding along with the deputy as escort. He and the police chief are real big buddies. He's a helluva nice guy."

Silas and Fred returned, Fred looking more refreshed, clean and dressed in dry sweats. He spoke to Silas. "Thanks so much. Have we heard anything?" he asked, turning to David and Zeke.

David shook his head and took the clean scrubs handed him by Silas. He quickly pulled on the clothes and followed the others out of the examining room into the lobby, just as the double doors opened and a well-dressed couple and a police officer came hurrying in. Zeke walked up to them. "Chief Petrino, Mr. and Mrs. Carmichael, this is Chief of Staff Silas Fleischer, and Dr. David Connor."

At Ralph's questioning look, Zeke nodded, "He is Jon's brother. He happened to see the accident and stopped to provide assistance to Amanda until the ambulance got her to the hospital."

"How is she?" Ralph demanded tensely, his face drawn, his arm around Claire, who showed signs of recent crying. Petrino looked grim.

David stepped forward. "We don't know yet. She was in and out on the trip here. Dr. Rand is with her. He's the finest in the country, and will let us know as soon as he can."

Claire took David's hand. "Thank you so much for being there."

Ralph looked gratefully at him, then asked, "Has anyone notified Jon?"

"No. Jon hasn't answered his phone yet, but he's interviewing Stephen Marks now," Zeke said quietly. "I've left a message asking him to call me."

David took Ralph aside and stated in low tones, "I really need some information from you, and it's not particularly pleasant. Most critical: does Amanda have any allergies or reactions to medications?"

Ralph told of her hypersensitivity to some medications and gave Dr. Howells' name and number as primary physician. Ralph also filled him in on Amanda's recent medical history. David asked about living wills and next of kin. Ralph looked at him with apprehension as he responded, "Yes, she has a living will in our office safe. We review and update our estate plans annually at her insistence. She has no family other than a brother and his family in Pennsylvania. I'm currently listed as her health care surrogate." Ralph swallowed. "She's not going to die, is she?"

David replied gravely, "I just want you to be prepared for the worst, and hope for the best, OK?"

Ralph, shaken, nodded wordlessly, as they rejoined the others.

It's going to be a long afternoon, David thought, looking at the solemn group.

Chapter 40

Jon arrived at the hospital where Marks was being treated about forty-five minutes after his telephone conversation with Amanda. Unknown to her, his mind had followed a similar process during the drive, trying to determine the possible scenarios that could have led to Barnes' murder and Marks' involvement.

Showing his credentials to the federal officer posted at the hospital entrance, he made his way to the cardiac care unit. Already known to the prison warden, who was present, Jon was briefed by the prison official and the attending physician regarding the patient's condition, then waved through to Marks' private room, where a guard was posted outside the door.

Entering the room, Jon nodded at the nurse as she completed her duties, then moved toward the bed as she left the room. Marks' eyes were closed, and he looked haggard. Purposeful until this point, Jon hesitated to address him and stood silently beside the bed.

Marks' eyes opened and focused on Jon. He looked suddenly wary, not unlike the look Jon had seen in Amanda's eyes before. Jon was amazed at Marks' resemblance to Amanda, something he had not noticed until that moment.

Jon opened the conversation. "How are you feeling?"

Marks responded, his tongue thick, "I've seen better days."

"So have I," Jon was momentarily sympathetic. "I guess you know why I'm here." Jon came straight to the point.

"It's open and shut," Marks coughed wearily. "I've already told the prison officials and your people."

"Humor me and start at the beginning," Jon requested, feigning patience.

"What is there to tell? I was waiting for the weekly Eucharist to be brought to me. Apparently, the prison guards decided to kill two birds with one stone, figuratively speaking, and had Bill Barnes brought in to the recreation room too. I saw my chance and killed him."

"How did you do it?"

"I stabbed him, of course—that's how he died," Marks replied, with a touch of the old imperiousness.

"Was Amanda there?"

"No," Marks shook his head vigorously. "She'd already left."

"Who else was there?"

"No one," Marks was adamant.

"What about this priest?"

"I—uh—she hadn't arrived yet," Marks stammered.

"She?" Jon echoed.

Marks looked frightened but said nothing. He was breathing heavily.

"And pray tell me how you obtained Amanda Childs' silver letter opener?" Jon demanded.

Tense, his eyes closing as he measured his words carefully, Marks recounted, "I had Adam take the silver letter opener from her office some time ago and slip it to me. I wanted something of a personal nature of my daughter's to remember her by, and I think you will agree that Amanda was not likely to willingly comply with such a request." Marks looked exhausted from the effort of talking.

"But you used an instrument to kill Barnes that could be traced directly to Amanda, the daughter you said you wanted to protect?"

Marks hesitated, a worried frown on his face, his response guarded. "I did not plan this revenge, Jon. But I kept the letter opener hidden on my person at all times. It was all I had to use on the bastard when the moment presented itself.

"Until that night I had been closely guarded and protected from contact with Bill. Suddenly there he was in the room with me. I didn't even know we were in the same facility."

Marks paused, his breathing labored. "I was surprised, to say the least. When he saw me, he was at first surprised too. But soon he started taunting me, telling me how he intended to make my offspring's life a living hell and to re-open the past with all its scandal. I cared not for myself, but should the innocent suffer for the sins of their fathers?"

"So you took the letter opener you purloined as a sentimental keepsake and used it as a lethal weapon. Tell me, how did Amanda's ring end up on the floor beneath Barnes' body?"

Marks gasped in shock, surprising Jon, whose eyes narrowed speculatively. So he didn't know about the ring? Jon wondered.

But Marks recovered quickly. "Excuse me, but I'm still having some pangs. She must have dropped it during her visit with me earlier that day."

"What if I told you she wasn't wearing it?" Jon asked casually, watching the man's face.

"How else would it get there?" the old man cried. "Are you saying Adam stole the ring too?"

"No, you did," Jon countered calmly, watching the terror which Marks unsuccessfully tried to conceal. "Stephen, I noticed that the fingers on your right hand are bandaged. What happened?"

Marks, visibly nervous now, replied, "I guess I must have cut them on the letter opener."

"But the doctor said the marks were not consistent with slash marks of a instrument like the letter opener," Jon indicated matter-of-factly. He continued. "Let me show you a letter Amanda received, and maybe you can help me with its meaning." Connor withdrew the letter from his pocket and handed it to Marks.

Marks squinted at it for some minutes, his face a careful mask, before handing it back to Jon. "I don't see where I can help you there, Jon."

"Perhaps because you don't have your reading glasses. What happened to them, Stephen?" Jon asked casually.

"I guess they were broken in the fall," Stephen stammered uneasily. "I apparently was found unconscious. I don't remember much after I stabbed Bill. He was, after all, my friend once upon a time."

"I will posit that you don't remember because you didn't kill him. Maybe you weren't even conscious when he was killed," Jon suggested.

The old man paled. "But I was—I saw it all." He stopped, realizing he had said too much.

"What did you see?" Jon pressed.

Marks didn't answer. He sat there looking away, sweat on his brow. Finally he mumbled, "I'm not feeling well. Maybe we should continue this discussion later."

"I don't know. I think we may be getting somewhere," Jon opined carefully, watching the man. "Let me read some of the letter to you, just to make sure you haven't missed something."

Marks protested weakly, but Jon insisted. "I desperately need your help to solve this matter, if you are serious about protecting Amanda and exposing the truth. Did I tell you she is on her way to surrender herself to the authorities and be charged with this murder as we speak?"

Marks, overcome, rasped, "But I tell you I did it. Please, Jon, please don't let her do that. You must stop her. I can't bear that."

"Just this one paragraph," Jon told him casually, although inside he was seething, wanting to push the man over the edge, wanting to absolve Amanda from the fate she was facing alone. He had the epiphany that but for the murder this man witnessed Jon and Amanda would be at this moment happily planning their wedding.

Jon suddenly felt an overwhelming wrath similar to what Amanda had described to him that night at the church. He quietly prayed to the God that he had spurned several years ago, after Andy's death, asking God to now deliver him from the consequences of the hatred he was feeling for those responsible for Amanda's plight.

Jon read out loud:

> I know that Bishop Marks has a sudden soft spot for you as his 'long-lost daughter' that is all very touching, but I've known him much longer than you. In the end he will not testify against me—there is too much history between us, and he has a vested interest in keeping silence that outweighs any incipient paternal instincts.

"Stephen, why would Bill Barnes call you 'Bishop'? Isn't it true he never called you that? Didn't you tell me he always addressed you by your first name, even after you attained the status of Bishop?"

"That's true," Marks agreed cautiously.

"What is the 'history between us' he speaks of? Remember—your response could mean the difference between freedom and lifetime imprisonment for Amanda," Jon interjected.

Jon, knowing he was walking a tightrope with the old man, pressed the former Bishop. "If you truly feel for Amanda the way you have represented to me these last months, you must tell me. What is this 'history'?"

"I can't tell you who wrote that," Marks blustered, his face a mask.

"So Barnes didn't write this at all?" Jon rejoined, surprised.

Marks' eyes welled with tears. "Please don't ask me that. I don't know," he pleaded, reaching for Jon's hand in an attempt to beg, to grovel for him to stop.

But Jon would not give in to any vestige of sympathy for the man. "But you see, I love this woman and must ask you this in order to save her. As you said yourself, the innocent should not suffer for the sins of their fathers.

"Stephen, I will lay it on the line. Amanda, the product of a past over which she had no control, does not deserve the purgatory she has suffered these last few years, and which is continuing as we speak. She is giving herself up to the authorities, who are going to charge her with murder one, based on a silver letter opener and a ring, both of which I gave her.

"All this because she gave in to your request to see her. You, a man who was never her father, but who brought her into the world through the shame of your wrongful and selfish act. All you have done for her is to embroil her in scandal and suspicion of murder. Marjorie Witherspoon's last act on this earth was to ask you to protect your child. Tell me I am not justified in what I ask of you."

Marks cried brokenly, "Enough! Do I not bleed every day for what I did to Marjorie? Have I not suffered reversal of fortune and reputation and even incarceration for my part in the plot against my own daughter? She obviously didn't do it. And in the name of God, I cannot ruin the life of one more person."

Jon caught his breath. "Not even if that person is the instrument by which your daughter will go to prison for the rest of her life?" Jon countered savagely.

"All I have left of my priesthood and morality is my oath to protect the priest-penitent confidentiality," Marks whispered. Connor stared at him, as a new realization occurred to him.

"Are you telling me that the murderer has confessed to you, and that you feel you cannot reveal that confidence, even if it means perpetrating a fraud upon the court and sealing the fate of an innocent girl, your only child?"

"Who said she was my only responsibility?" Marks cried, clasping his heart in agony. "I killed Barnes, whether I wielded the weapon or not."

Jon gasped. "What are you saying, Stephen? For God's sake, tell me. For Amanda's sake."

But Marks shook his head, mute, tears streaming down his face.

The doctor walked in, saw Marks' shaken condition and intervened sternly. "He's had enough. You need to leave now."

Jon, angry and defeated, noted the vibrating of his cell phone on his belt. He had ignored it since his arrival at the prison. His frustration complete, he reached for it and answered it, his voice flat. "Connor here."

His face hardened as he listened. "David? What the hell—"

He listened for several more minutes, visibly shaken. "My God, no. David, don't let her die. I should never have let her go alone. I'm on my way."

Marks saw the change in Jon's demeanor, and the sudden tears in Connor's eyes. He demanded, "What is it? You must tell me. Is Amanda OK? What has happened?"

Connor looked at him in disgust. "Maybe you need a few lessons in what love really is." Connor swallowed. "Amanda was in an accident."

Marks gasped. "Is she—?"

Connor left the question unanswered as he left the room.

Chapter 41

Jon Connor pulled into the parking lot of Gulfside Regional Hospital as the sun was setting. He did not remember anything about the trip he had just made. In his head swam only thoughts of Amanda, the memory of her laughter, her eyes and the love they had shared over the last two days.

He covered the parking lot in long strides, jogging into the ER, his face set in stone. As the double doors automatically closed behind him, he caught sight of a group huddled in the corner of the lobby. Claire saw him first and nudged Ralph.

Ralph, spying Jon, sprang up as Jon walked toward them. Jon managed to croak, "What word?"

Ralph, mute with emotion, just shook his head. Claire, standing and taking Jon's arm, responded for Ralph, "I'm afraid we don't know anything yet."

Charlie and Zeke also stood. "Jon, I'm so sorry about all this," Petrino whispered. Jon was surprised to see tears in Charlie's eyes.

Jon said flatly, to no one in particular, "I should have been with her."

Zeke replied, "Then there would have been two of you injured, or worse."

Jon addressed Zeke. "What are you doing here, man?"

"Long story. I was with the escort in the car behind her when her car left the road. Right now I'm acting as the posted guard."

Jon listened grimly as Zeke filled him in on what had happened. As the story unfolded, Fred Vaughan walked up and placed a cup of coffee in Zeke's hand, nodding at Jon solemnly. Zeke thanked him as he continued.

Jon questioned, "Has the cause of the accident been determined?"

"The day was overcast and it was sprinkling rain. It had rained hard, but every now and then the sky would brighten up. When Amanda passed by us, she had her lights on. So did everyone else except this car. I don't see how she could have missed seeing Amanda when she pulled out in Amanda's lane. Amanda did a valiant job of trying to miss her and the oncoming traffic. This car crossed in front of my driver, veered toward the car behind us, then ended up down in the ditch, thank God."

"Driver of the other car hurt?"

"Hell, no. She was arrested," Zeke sipped his coffee.

"Florida's a tough state for bad drivers," Jon remarked.

"Willful and wanton reckless driving, a misdemeanor, but then she charged David, who went to help her out of the car, beat up a sheriff's deputy pretty badly, and had to be wrestled down. I think she racked up a battery on LEO charge and resisting arrest with violence. Troopers might charge her with attempted vehicular homicide—they're not sure it was an accident. Don't know if she was on anything."

"How could it be anything but an accident?" Jon wondered aloud.

"Jon!"

Hearing his name, Jon turned as David came quickly up to him. "Hi, bro. When did you get here?"

"Just a few minutes ago," Jon replied. "Can you tell me anything?"

"Joey has just finished working on her, per the nurse," David managed with a frown. "He'll be out momentarily to talk to us."

"Joey? How did—"

"I called him. He was down here for the week with Silas, and I was on my way to Silas' house so we could watch the Knicks game together and catch up."

"How did you become involved in this?"

David explained how he was two cars behind Amanda and saw the accident. He pointed to Fred Vaughan, who was standing quietly talking to Charlie. "That man jumped into the creek and managed to extricate Amanda from the car. He swam with her to the creek bank. He saved her life."

Vaughan, overhearing David's remark, interposed, "Your brother here did the life saving. He did CPR on her and rode in the ambulance with her to the hospital."

Jon looked at his brother gratefully, murmuring, "Sir Lancelot himself."

David colored slightly. "Aw, you know I'm a sucker for a good-looking girl. I just want the chance to give her MY name and number. I'm tired of all these women mistaking me for you."

Jon sobered as he was reminded of the episode on Friday evening. "Who was that woman with you Friday night, David?"

"Hell if I know. She came to the door asking for you. She was a stunner, so I let her in. We made some small talk, did a little flirting, and the next thing I knew she was all over me. I figured it was my animal magnetism. I never imagined she thought I was you until you called and reamed me out.

"Then your Amanda walked in on us. The red-head and I were in *flagrante delicto* at that point, and Amanda saw more of me than I generally expose on a first date," David said, a flush stealing across his cheek.

Jon, his face a mask during David's remarks, allowed himself a small grin. "Don't you ever drop your drawers around my woman again," he warned sternly. "You frightened her away. I had a hell of a time catching up with her."

"But you did?" Ralph exclaimed, relief on his face.

Claire too looked relieved. "We were so worried about her all weekend. She left without telling anyone. And then the prison incident was reported, and we couldn't raise her on the phone."

"She was with me," Jon replied shortly as a man in green scrubs walked up to them. "Hi, Joey," he greeted the doctor.

"Hi there, Parsifal," Joey spoke quietly. "Long time no see."

"I hope you have good news for me," Jon's eyes remained glued to the doctor's face.

"Is that your girl in there?" Joey inquired.

"She is," Jon announced with a conviction that left no doubt to the group standing there.

"She's lucky to be alive, from what David relayed to Silas over the phone when he ordered me over here," Dr. Rand reported. "But she's come out of what could have been a truly tragic circumstance in pretty good shape, although not out of the woods yet. She was in shock and was having difficulty getting a breath when I got here. In fact, her breathing was shallow and she had lost consciousness.

"David was right—she has fractured two ribs and punctured the left lung. Her clavicle is fractured, and the area around the sternum is bruised—all probably from the seat belt or airbag. The left wrist was dislocated. She has a hairline fracture to her cheek, and sustained a concussion.

"Our scans so far disclosed no other internal bleeding, and her vitals seem to be stabilizing. I think the clavicle is realigned well. We might have to insert a pin tomorrow, but I want to observe her tonight and get some more X-rays tomorrow. We inserted a tube and inflated the lung.

He allowed a small smile. "She's badly banged up, and will feel like holy hell tomorrow. We'll also have to be diligent in combating any infection, particularly in the lungs, and of course watch for pneumonia. Tonight is critical."

"Can I see her?" Jon asked.

"She's pretty heavily sedated right now, because her body has been through hell and we need to let it rest and regroup. Her breathing is less labored. I don't want her moving around. I don't think she'll regain consciousness for a while. And I just want to make sure there's nothing wrong in there that we missed. She's going to ICU." Joey patted Jon on the back. "No promises, guys. I'm hoping she's through the worst of it."

Ralph, relieved, kissed Claire, as Vaughan muttered, "Thank God." Petrino sat down, his head in his hands.

Rand added, "You guys need to get some rest. By the time of visiting hours tomorrow she's going to need some commiseration."

"I'm not leaving," Jon remarked resolutely, causing Rand to cock his head and look at Jon in surprise.

"You've gone soft on this girl, haven't you?" he asked softly. He shook his head. "It's going to be a while yet before we get her settled, before she wakes up. Silas, why don't you take them down for a bite at that pub down the block? Have a beer for me and get the Knicks' scores, and come back, say about 8:30. I'll see about getting Jon in. I know the CMO."

Zeke stammered, "I need to stay here until a guard can be posted. Those are my orders."

Joey rolled his eyes. "As you wish, but as they say here in the Deep South, she ain't going nowheres tonight."

Claire took Jon's arm and led him out, as the other men followed. Ralph said, "Everyone can go with us."

Silas waved him off. "I'll take my vehicle. Just follow me."

David told them, "I'll ride with Silas. See you all there."

Jon was pushed into the front seat, and Claire, Vaughan and Petrino climbed into the back of the large Escalade. Ralph pulled out, following the Lexus driven by Fleischer. Ralph glared across at Jon. "So tell me what you and Amanda were doing all weekend."

Claire, shocked, cried, "Ralph! That's none of your business."

Jon held up his hand to quiet her. "Yes, it is, Claire. All of you are Amanda's family and deserve to know. Besides, it will probably all come out anyway."

He gave them a summary of the events that occurred Friday night, and how he followed her to St. George Island and found her on the beach. "And to make a long story short, we've been together all weekend."

He heard Ralph grunt as the others held their breaths. Jon continued. "We didn't know anything about Barnes until we saw the paper Sunday. Amanda had been to see Marks at the prison Friday, but swore she never saw Barnes, didn't know he was there. And I believe her.

"When we saw the paper, I called Bubba and confirmed that law enforcement was looking for her. She insisted on going back without me. She sent me to see Marks because he may have been the last person to see Barnes alive."

Jon looked across to Ralph. "She had said yes to me, and we were making arrangements to get married. I begged her to marry me today after we found out about Barnes, Ralph, but she refused. She was convinced she was going to jail."

Ralph gripped the wheel. "She called me on her way to turn herself in."

Jon stated flatly, "She didn't do it, and I've got to determine who did and clear her."

"And I'm going to try to keep her out of jail. Count me on the team," Ralph remarked darkly. "Well, looks like we're here," he added, as they pulled into a parking lot of a dimly lit place tucked in the back of a shopping center.

They walked in together, and were able to score a large table in the moderately full room. Silas waved at the bartender as they walked through. "This place isn't a tourist trap. We've kept it a local secret," he explained. "The house draft is a magical elixir straight from Ponce de Leon's spring of eternal youth."

He ordered a round and a platter of appetizers for everyone, and they sat perusing the menu. As they sat sipping beer, everyone at the table asked questions at once, and pandemonium reigned as everyone tried to get up to speed on the events of the weekend.

Jon drank his beer silently, heedless of the others as his thoughts swam. It sounded as if Amanda might pull through, but the advent of criminal charges against her still loomed large. The thought of the agony she still faced gripped him. And he was suddenly remembering his conversation with Marks and wondering what Marks had meant. Who had murdered Barnes and confessed to Marks? Why was Marks protecting this person?

Ralph, sensing Jon's disquiet, silenced everyone and raised his glass. "To our beloved Amanda. May she heal quickly."

Everyone raised his glass and drank. Silas excused himself to speak to some friends at another table.

Ralph looked at Jon intently. "Now, let's not all talk at once. What do we know and what do we need to know?"

Jon answered quietly, "Time of Barnes' death was placed at some time between three and five o'clock Friday afternoon. Amanda signed in at the prison to see Marks at 1:59 pm and left at 3:34 pm. There was no one else signed in to see either Barnes or Marks after that.

"But Marks was apparently in the room when Barnes was killed. Why? How could they allow that to happen? The feds would have warned against having the two men at the same facility, and Greg Boyer certainly would not have condoned their having contact."

Jon added, "Amanda states she didn't know Barnes was at the same prison. She said she thought William Barnes was incarcerated at the jail in Pensacola. She brought up the same question—why would the feds house Barnes there, and why the two men at the same prison? It doesn't make sense."

Petrino replied quietly, "But we know slipups like this happen all the time. The right hand doesn't know what the left hand is doing."

Ralph asked, "Why don't the police believe Marks, if he made a statement confessing to Barnes' murder?"

"Because there was no way that Marks could have been carrying around a silver letter opener in prison," Charlie answered him. "Prisoners are frisked and go through detectors from building to building. The only way Marks could have had the letter opener was if someone had slipped it in to him during visitation."

"But visitors are also searched and go through detectors," Ralph objected. "Every time I go to see an inmate I have to turn over everything but my watch. How could someone get the letter opener in to Marks?"

Jon spoke slowly, "The ring I gave Amanda was found underneath Barnes' body too."

Ralph whistled softly. "So her letter opener and ring are found at the scene, and she was obviously there because she signed in and out. That's why she is the prime suspect."

"Marks claims she was already gone, and that he was the only one there when Barnes was murdered," Jon countered. "Amanda says she never saw Barnes. But Marks said Amanda must have been wearing the ring. Amanda says she didn't have the ring."

Petrino interjected, "She didn't, or at least that's what Sheila says."

They all looked at him expectantly. "Sheila called me Friday evening. Amanda apparently kept your ring in a box in her desk drawer. Sheila had seen Amanda looking at it more than once, including Friday morning. So it was still there at that time.

"Amanda had come in Friday afternoon after her visit with Marks looking for the ring before she left, and both it and the letter opener were missing. Sheila said she became frantic and asked Sheila to call me to make a report."

Ralph frowned. "But wouldn't law enforcement think Amanda would report the items missing or stolen to throw suspicion off herself?"

"Perhaps, but Sheila was sure Amanda did not have the ring when she left the office for Pensacola Friday morning," Charlie repeated. "Amanda took it out and looked at it while signing papers for Sheila, then placed it back in the box and in the desk drawer.

"Sheila also reported that an air conditioner repairman came by Friday at lunchtime to check the system. She did not know him, but described him as small, reddish-haired, funny-sounding voice. Said he looked familiar to her, but she didn't have much dealings with him."

Ralph rejoined, "I didn't request any A/C guy to check out the system. That's mighty suspicious. Amanda put me in charge of the building plant so she wouldn't have to deal with all the traditional male chauvinist maintenance guys.

"I was gone all day Friday. My honey accompanied me to Tallahassee, where I deposed witnesses and she shopped. We didn't get home until late that night. Sheila would have scheduled any maintenance while I was there to oversee it."

Jon's eyes narrowed as he thought aloud, "Adam Brownlee has red hair."

Chapter 42

It was as though Jon had dropped a bombshell.

"Bingo," Petrino replied.

Everyone at the table stared at Charlie again. The waitress came around, and they suspended discussion and ordered their food, as Silas returned to the table.

"Out with it, Charlie," Jon commanded after the waitress had left.

"Sheila told me that Brownlee showed up in clerical collar to see Amanda right after she arrived at the office Friday afternoon. She was agitated already, signing pleadings for Sheila, making calls and in a hurry. Sheila said she had never seen Amanda upset like that."

"That's not good for the home team," Ralph whistled softly. "Looks a lot like flight after commission of a crime."

"Brownlee walked in the back door of the office and said he had something urgent to discuss with her, and it couldn't wait."

"Amanda didn't say anything about this to me," Jon was nonplussed.

"Sheila said he walked straight into Amanda's office and closed her door, but she didn't feel good about leaving him alone with Amanda. Their history is not too amiable."

"I am personally aware of that," Jon breathed, remembering.

"So Sheila kept going in and out, trying to leave the door cracked so she could intervene if necessary."

"Good girl—I trained her," Ralph said irrelevantly. "Did she find out why he was there?"

Petrino replied, "He wanted to know about the legal procedure for obtaining DNA testing."

Claire echoed, "DNA testing? What on earth for?"

"Sheila said she was not able to hear all he said, because his voice dropped to a whisper. Amanda at first tried to put him off and get him to schedule a later appointment with her, but whatever he said certainly surprised her."

"Could she tell you any more?" Ralph asked excitedly.

"No, but Brownlee kept Amanda in there for a good thirty minutes or so. Then Sheila said his phone buzzed, he answered it, and got up and left."

"Marks claimed he got Brownlee to steal the letter opener as something personal of Amanda's Marks could have to remember her by," Jon recalled.

Petrino continued. "The items were at the office when Amanda left that morning, but were already missing from the office by the time Amanda arrived that afternoon, before Brownlee even showed up. Sheila said that Amanda was searching for the letter opener when Brownlee appeared. And to examine the time line, the murder would have occurred about that time. And after he left, Amanda opened her desk and found the ring missing. Sheila said Amanda was hysterical about the ring's disappearance.

"Sheila said that when he walked in, Brownlee looked amazingly like the A/C guy from earlier in the day, but she thought she must be mistaken. She didn't get a good look at the maintenance guy, only a glance as he passed. But as Brownlee was leaving the office the uncanny resemblance struck her again, and she asked if he had a twin. She said he turned pale as a ghost and fled."

The waitress appeared with pitchers of beer and the appetizers, and left the group.

"Brownlee is a priest. Maybe he had access inside the prison without the security measures everyone else goes through," Ralph hypothesized, mentally taking them back to the scene of the crime.

David interjected, "That reminds me. Amanda was trying to tell me something in the ambulance. She said—let me think—'priest', then something about a 'black box' and a woman's name. Damn, I can't remember."

"You sure?" Jon asked him.

"No," he frowned, "but that's close. I'm trying to recall."

"Maybe she saw Brownlee earlier at the prison, and he followed her to the office," Ralph suggested. He suddenly thumped the table. "What if Brownlee killed Barnes?"

"I've been thinking the same thing," Jon's look was grim.

"Could happen, but I don't think so," Charlie countered, swallowing a mushroom. "And Adam Brownlee would have had a hard time killing the man and then getting to Amanda's office so quickly. And my question is how anyone could kill Barnes and exit the prison without detection. There would not be much time before the whole place was locked down."

"Maybe he was using Amanda as an alibi," Ralph suggested.

"Wait a minute. He's planting evidence that she did the job, then he's using her as an alibi? That doesn't make sense. Then he becomes her alibi as well, wouldn't he?" Claire interjected.

"Maybe, maybe not," Silas spoke. Silent until this point, he was suddenly aware of everyone's eyes on him.

"Well," Silas continued, looking around him, "if she could kill Barnes and get back to the office, then so could he, conceivably. He could have showed up at her office so that he could later testify as to her demeanor and help pin everything on her. But if he did it right after she left, you're right; it would take him longer to get away.

"But," Silas continued, "what if this priest guy was at Amanda's office at the behest of someone else?"

David asked, "Why do you say that?"

"He's there on an urgent matter and forces his way in to see her. He keeps her occupied for about thirty or forty-five minutes. Then suddenly his phone rings and he walks out."

They were all silent, digesting this new theory. Jon nodded contemplatively. "It doesn't make sense that he would risk being at the office twice in the same day, once dressed as a repairman and then later as a priest, and being recognized and fingered."

"Wait a minute," David suddenly sat up excitedly. "I remember. Amanda said, 'Jon—woman priest, with a black box—Evie, in the car.' That's what she said."

"What does it mean?" Jon turned to Ralph, gauging his reaction.

Ralph shook his head, frustrated. They were silent and thoughtful.

"What a mystery—kind of like my red head," David interposed glumly. "First she's making out with me, then leaves me when she finds out I'm not Jon. The next thing I know she's running Amanda off the road."

"What?" Jon, Charlie and Ralph cried in unison, their eyes locked on David.

"Yeah, haven't I already told you this? No, I guess I told Zeke. My little Miss Fire-and-Ice is cooling her heels at the jail on all those charges. She was the one in the red car that ran Amanda into the creek. She told me her name was Evie."

"My God," Charlie muttered excitedly, "Red hair. Red car. Evie Brown. The suspect in Bronowski's death."

Zeke looked at Charlie disbelievingly. "Our mafia guy?"

"Jesus, man," cried Jon. "There has to be a connection." Pulling out his cell phone, he rapidly dialed Zeke's number.

"What do you know about the girl in the other car?" he demanded.

"This is the South, man," he heard Zeke say irritably. "You're supposed to start off the conversation asking, 'How's your marm and 'em?' I sent Bubba on a detail up to the county jail to find out details about David's forelorn lover. She is in custody. In fact, the woman's car was impounded to the sheriff's department, and George is helping local law enforcement do an inventory of the car as we speak. Report at eleven, or whenever he calls me back."

"How are things there?" Jon inquired, his throat catching as his thoughts turned back to Amanda.

"They've just moved her to an intensive care bed, and Dr. Rand is in with her as we speak. No news."

"I'll bring you back something to eat," Jon promised as he hung up. He informed the others, "Bubba is up at the jail gathering information on the driver. He'll check in."

Charlie stood. "I need to get word to Bruce. If this is Evie Brown, he needs to make sure she doesn't post bond." He excused himself and walked outside with his phone.

"I'd like her number," mumbled David as Silas grinned at him.

Their food arrived, but Jon just picked at his steak and fries. Claire, sitting beside him and noting his anxiety, covered his hand with hers. "It will be OK," she assured him softly. "Amanda's tough and will pull through. She's got a lot to live for."

"Not if I can't clear her of this," Jon murmured, his voice barely audible. "Excuse me a minute, will you?"

Abruptly he stood and left the table, heading to the restroom. Ralph stood, but Claire pulled him back down to his seat. "Let him be," she whispered.

Jon washed his face and hands and stared at his reflection in the mirror. He knew that Marks held the key, but also knew that he might have to pry it from Marks by force. But how? He felt so impotent, with forces beyond him moving the pieces on a huge chessboard to cast suspicion on Amanda and keep them apart.

Who else was there for Marks to protect? Brownlee? Why? How could the murderer have slipped out of the prison undetected?

Who was this stranger, the driver of the red car, the one who in her quest for Jon had a rendezvous with his brother, and who almost killed Amanda?

Into his thoughts came unbidden a picture of Amanda as he had seen her on the beach Saturday, in their bed that night. He felt an overwhelming desire to touch her.

He left the restroom abruptly, going by the table and throwing some bills down. "I'm going to take a walk and clear my head. Order Zeke some take-out, will you, David? I'll see you back at the hospital."

Without waiting for response, he left the restaurant, running into Petrino just outside the entrance.

"Where are you going?" Petrino asked, grasping his arm.

"I can't sit still. I've got to be there with her," Jon murmured.

"What can I do to help?" Petrino's eyes met Jon's.

"I don't know," Jon closed his eyes momentarily. "I feel so helpless, Charlie. I just know I can't lose her."

Shaking loose of Petrino's grip, Jon strode purposefully back in the direction of the hospital. The clear cool air of the early spring evening felt good after the mugginess of the day. The rain had stopped and the skies were clearing. Spring break was ebbing, but the evening traffic along the boulevard was moderately brisk.

His cell phone rang. "Connor," he said tersely.

"I just heard. How is she?" an authoritative voice demanded.

Surprised, Jon recognized the voice of Thomas Whitmore. "I don't know," he answered truthfully. "She is in critical condition, Senator. The doctor is moving her into ICU. I'm on my way back now to check on her status."

There was a pause, and he heard the man clear his throat nervously. "There's no truth to—to what they're saying, is there?"

Jon replied forcefully, "No. She is innocent."

"I believe you," Whitmore said. "Jon, could you—could you let me know when you get any news on her condition? And if I can be of any help?"

Jon was surprised. *Does he really care for his daughter-in-law, a woman he just met?* he wondered.

"I promise I will do so, Senator," he responded fervently.

"It's just—she's been through so much, and now this." Jon was struck by the change in his voice. "I never got to meet her until now. I—" he paused as if he wanted to say more, "I just hope she is all right."

Jon hung up. He walked across several well-lit parking lots until he reached the hospital. Walking back into the ER, he approached the desk.

A female orderly asked him, "Are you Jon Connor?"

He nodded assent. She continued, "Dr. Rand—what a nice guy!—said for you to follow this hallway around to the left and then to the right, and you will come to the ICU. He said for you to use the phone by the door and ask for him."

Connor thanked her and followed her directions. Reaching the unit, he saw Zeke propped up against the wall, staring at the ceiling. "David's bringing you some hot grub," Jon remarked, disturbing Zeke's reverie. "Any word from Bubba?"

"Thanks, man. Nothing yet, but he promised to check in as soon as they were through. The doc said for you to call when you got here." Zeke pointed to a wall phone.

"No need—I'm here," Rand walked out the door. "Come on in, Jon, but just for a minute."

Jon followed Rand past several rooms facing and opening up on a nurses' station. In the third room, attached to a myriad of tubes and monitors, was Amanda, whose eyes were closed and breathing was shallow. Jon's heart went out to her, as she was still and pale. He walked up to the bed and touched her fingertips, then bent down and kissed her forehead. He noticed an angry looking bruise on her cheek, and she looked battered, her left side bound up in bandages.

Rand said quietly, "Hopefully she will sleep through the night. I consulted with Dr. Howells, who wanted to drive down here tonight and personally take over her care."

Jon replied softly. "He's very protective of her, like a father."

"I asked him to wait until tomorrow, and we made an appointment for early morning. I'm monitoring her closely because of her sensitivity to drugs. Howells was concerned what a morphine drip might do. We discussed options."

"I'm concerned, too. She is very special to me, Joey," murmured Jon.

"Sounds like you found your holy grail after all," Joey whispered. "Although protecting her from harm may be a full-time job." Pausing a minute, Rand asked, "Is she really a murder suspect, Jon?"

"I'm afraid so," Jon's voice cracked. "I'm doing what I can to clear her. She didn't do it, Joey."

Rand put his arm on Jon's shoulder, leading him away from her bed. "I've never seen you like this, particularly over a woman," he remarked wonderingly. "If anyone can do it, you can. And I'm going to do what I can to keep her alive and well."

"How long will she be in the hospital? I can't bear the thought of her being arrested and incarcerated."

"I don't know," Rand hesitated. "That lung and the danger of infection, plus making sure there are no other complications, are the critical points we're watching. It could be three or four days."

Rand frowned. "You know, man, I'll help you all I can. But you gotta work fast if you're going to save her before she's released from here."

Jon faced Rand. "Can't I stay with her?" he pleaded.

Joey shook his head. "No," he was firm. "But we'll find you room at Silas' place tonight. Now get out of here. I have to leave instructions and contact information for the staff."

When Connor walked out, Zeke was gone. He retraced his steps, finding Zeke in the lobby eating out of a styrofoam carryout plate. The others had arrived and were waiting expectantly.

Ralph demanded, "Can we see her?"

Jon put his arm around Ralph. "She's asleep. They're not letting us stay here. Joey thinks she is going to be OK."

Silas came up to them. "I'll put Jon up at my place tonight, so he'll be nearby. Get some rest, everyone. Amanda will need you all more later than she does right now."

Claire stated, "We'll take Fred home and be back tomorrow."

Jon kissed her and clapped Ralph on the back, shaking Vaughan's hand. They moved away toward the doorway.

Petrino stopped in front of Jon. Charlie looked at him, his face gray. "Take good care of her."

Jon, looking at him, nodded and placed his hand on Charlie's arm. "You still love her, don't you?"

Charlie didn't answer, turning away.

Ralph turned back and said, "Call us—you know we'll do what it takes to help clear Amanda." Then they were gone.

Silas took Jon by the arm and motioned to David. "I'll put you up in the attic."

David said, "I'll wait for Joey and drive him to your place. You two go on."

As they turned to leave, Zeke's phone rang. He answered with his mouth full. "Yeah?"

He listened to a minute as he chewed. "Damn it all, how could he do that?"

He listened a moment, then his face broadened into a smile. "No shit?"

He grinned. "You're kidding, right? I can't come, but I know someone who just might. You're a gem, Bubba."

Turning to Jon, who had been overhearing the conversation, Zeke beamed. "Bad news and good news. Bad news is that the judge breezed in this evening with bail bondsman in tow, and did first appearance on our driver girl. She got a $30,000 bond, and the bondsman immediately posted it and got her out."

"Hell!" Jon exclaimed. "Where is she now?"

"Gone with the wind. And the judge ordered that she get her car back *instanter.*"

"That's utterly crazy," Jon's anger was unmistakable. "The car is evidence. Who's the judge that would allow this?"

"Some guy named Kilmer. But," Zeke was smiling, "guess what Bubba and the officers found in the trunk before she pulled off?"

David breathed, "A dead body?"

"Almost as good. A duffel bag. And inside was priest garb replete with a communion kit, spotted and smeared with blood, and a whole slough of pharmaceuticals."

Jon queried excitedly, "Did they detain her?"

"No. They didn't realize they still had the duffel until she left, and then Bubba decided to open it. Still part of a valid inventory search as he saw it."

"Damn, she's got away," David swore. But Zeke kept smiling.

"Not entirely. When the hubbub occurred with the judge, Bubba slipped a GPS tracking device underneath the spare tire in the trunk of her car."

"And what's this red-head's name?" Jon asked, hardly daring to breathe.

"She gave it as Eve Brown. But they found two driver's licenses in the duffel after she left. The Australian one named her as Evelyn Abermarle."

Chapter 43

"Shit," Jon breathed.

"Yeah, Bubba was hot when he saw the Abermarle DL. That's the woman you all have been searching for in Panama City."

"Yes." Jon's mind was whirring.

"Bubba says he is calling in all his pointers to get a manhunt going. He needs another set of hands at the sheriff's department pronto, because he cannot clone himself, and is after the redhead with everything he's got."

"I'm on it," Jon assured Zeke.

Jon expelled a shaky breath as he recalled Amanda's words to David: "Woman priest—with a black box. Evie, in the car."

He realized that there was finally a connection that could lead to exonerating her. He was torn. He did not want to leave Amanda, but knew he had to take the chance.

"David, I need your help," he turned to his brother.

"Sure."

"I need for you to stay with Amanda and keep me informed of her condition," Jon pleaded. "I need to go to Mainville."

"You're leaving? Why?" David asked amazedly.

"To catch a murderer," Jon replied cryptically. "And David, take good care of her. She's important to me." He muttered as he turned to go, "And keep your damned hands off her. She's mine."

Jon left quickly, as though afraid he might change his mind. Sprinting to his car, he spun out of the hospital parking lot, heading north. He buzzed George. "Where are you?"

"Hi, Connor," Bubba responded. "Somewhere near the great state of Alabama, the land that time forgot."

"What do you need from me?" Jon asked. "I'm on my way."

"I have a trusted friend and colleague who works at the crime lab for the Florida Department of Law Enforcement, Pensacola office. She was in Mainville regarding another murder investigation. I've handed off physical possession of the duffel and its contents. She is at the sheriff's department wrangling with them over it. I need for you to pull jurisdiction, extricate her and get her back to her lab with that bag post haste. She in return has information for you on our suspect that I'm tracking."

"How will I know her?"

"She looks like my type," Bubba laughed. "Short, petite, dark curly hair, and tough as nails. She'll be expecting you. How long will it take you to get there?"

Jon looked at the dashboard clock. "I'm not sure. Forty minutes, more or less."

"I'll get her to warn them you'll be flying low. I'll call you back in a few."

Jon tried to keep his mind off Amanda as he raced toward Mainville. He kept thinking back to his interview of Marks. Could this female that Bubba was tracking really be Evie Brown, aka Evelyn Abermarle? But how and why? It was just too fantastic.

The miles seemed to drag on, but finally he made it to Mainville and the sheriff's department. As he pulled into the parking lot, he saw a uniformed officer standing outside puffing a cigarette.

Walking up to him, Connor said, "How's it going?"

The officer grunted. "Fine. Your name Connor?"

"That's me," Jon replied.

The officer pointed. "I just walked out of the line of fire. You follow around the building that way. When you get to a door, take it. They're waiting for you. Tell 'em Bubba sent you." He grinned.

Connor waved and took off around the building. As he entered the doorway, he could hear a female voice saying, "I don't give a damn if it hair-lips the whole north of Georgia . . . ."

The woman had her back to him. She was petite, about 5' 2", with short black curly hair. She was neatly dressed in a navy suit, but was giving forth, with the proficiency of a sailor, to three plain-clothes officers, all with badges and guns on hips.

"Excuse me," began Jon, "but I'm looking for someone named Della."

"That's me," she said, turning around. "Are you my fed express man?"

Jon displayed his FBI badge to her and the other three men. "Bubba sent me. What seems to be the problem?"

She motioned him over to a table. "Come see what we got here."

Jon followed her as the other men moved aside. On the table was a huge plastic bag. Inside was a black duffel. Putting a gloved hand inside she pulled out just enough for him to see a dark shirt and white priest's collar. And down the front were several large unmistakable splotches.

"Blood," she said triumphantly. "Lots of it. There's also a communion kit. Need to get this to the lab and do some comparison. Guys here seem to think that they're in trouble if the judge released the suspect and we still have the goods. Politics is thicker than thieves. But they're willing to release it to you and let you take the rap."

"Then I will be happy to take jurisdiction and relieve you of it," Connor stated to the officers.

"Consider it done," the tallest of the three said. "Please sign here," he said, pen in hand and indicating a release form on a clipboard. He was visibly relieved. "Now I can focus on my newest murder investigation."

Connor reviewed the form and signed. The man asked, "Any news about Amanda?"

Jon, surprised, remarked, "She's in critical condition, but they think she'll pull through. You know her?"

"Sure do," the man retrieved the clipboard and stuck out his hand "Bruce Williams, Chief Investigator and Acting Sheriff."

Jon shook his hand and started to introduce himself, but the man interrupted. "I know who you are." At Jon's questioning look, Bruce added, "It's a small town. I hope it all turns out well. Give Amanda my best. In the meantime, we're lending our assistance to Bubba to find our murder suspect."

"Your murder suspect?" Jon was surprised.

"Yeah, this woman is also our primary suspect in the Bronowski murder. Already had a BOLO out. Charlie called me to tell me she was being booked at the jail. But by the time I got here Judge Kilmer had let her go. I cannot believe it."

Looking at Williams, Jon could tell there was a battle brewing between Williams and the judge. Bruce continued, his temper barely under control, "And Della here says she might make a connection between her and the Shelby Young murder, as well as the assault on Dr. Young. Your Ms. Abermarle aka Evie Brown is about to be a very popular person with all the area's law enforcement, much sought after."

"I think the term is 'most wanted'. Thanks for your cooperation. Nice meeting you." Jon's smile was quick. Then he turned to the woman. "OK, Della. Need a lift?"

"Don't mind if I do." She picked up the plastic bag.

"No, please allow me," Jon insisted, taking the bag from her and escorting her out of the building. He led her to his Mercedes and opened the passenger door for her, before putting the bag carefully in the back and returning to the driver's side. Letting himself in, he quipped, "OK. Where to now?"

"Get me to Pensacola and I'll direct you from there," she smiled. "My team abandoned me here. I wasn't leaving without that bag. Then George ran off and left me for some red-head."

Jon pulled out, heading for the interstate highway. "So you know Bubba?"

"Bubba?" she was confused.

"Yeah, George got christened 'Bubba' on the last investigation we worked together," Jon smiled tightly. "He was our resident expert on Southern culture."

"That he is, so that information's good to know," she laughed. "Yep, we've been friends for a long time," she replied. "He's a lot of fun."

"Yes, but he also has a heart of gold," Jon rejoined. "So what is your involvement in all this?"

"Oh, I'm currently the custodian of the evidence collected in the Shelby Young homicide investigation. I also collected evidence on the near murder of Dr. Young, and the Bronowski homicide. I've also taken a morbid interest in this William Barnes homicide at the prison."

"Shelby Young?"

"The late wife of young Dr. Young here of Mainville. Surely you've read about it in the papers."

"Sorry, I don't know the details. I'm not from around here," Jon turned onto the interstate entrance ramp, accelerating smoothly.

"I just thought you might know something about it, inasmuch as Amanda Childs represents Dr. Young and has already saved the doctor from arrest once."

"Really?" Jon was intrigued. "No, I didn't know that. I know that Amanda and the Youngs are close friends. But Amanda is very private about her business."

"You really don't read the papers, do you? What rock have you crawled out from under the last few days? There is a connection, although it's not the one they're looking for."

"Who is looking for?"

"Jon, this is a small community and people here still judge each other and choose their dress, houses, cars, associates and mates based on the history according to the oracle of Mainville. The oral history is very strong and many times masks the truth. Those who know this can manipulate the oral history and thereby the community."

Jon couldn't hide his confusion. Della laughed. "Excuse my philosophizing. To explain, Dr. Young's wife suddenly has convulsions and ends up in the hospital. Next thing anyone knows she dies. Was this a fluke? No—it was a homicide.

"But suddenly a faction of the local caste system is anxious to put a spin on this. Agenda? Undetermined at this time. But in a soap opera or murder mystery, who's the most likely suspect? The husband doctor. Motive? Sweet young thing waiting in the wings plus insurance proceeds."

"What has this to do with my case?" Jon's curiosity was piqued.

"Similar scenario—you don't see it? Your prize suspect is about to go to trial. He is murdered, and all the evidence is pointing to Amanda Childs. It's just too convenient."

"Precisely," Jon agreed, as he looked at the agent. "But I still don't get the connection."

"Hairs and fibers," she spoke triumphantly.

"Hairs and fibers?" he echoed disbelievingly.

"The manna of crime resolution—DNA," she said. "Guess what I found when I did fiber analysis on Mrs. Dr. Young's clothing?"

"I hope you're going to tell me," Jon glanced at her, his face grave.

"Several items. Some white cat hairs, and some teeny-tiny burgundy fibers. And a couple of red hairs. Both the Youngs have dark hair, and no pets."

"OK," said Jon slowly. "Tie it up for me, Della."

"Examination of the area of Barnes' murder revealed—" she paused dramatically—"some white cat hairs, and a single strand of red hair."

Jon tried to control his excitement. "But to what degree of certainty can we trace these fibers and hairs?"

Della laughed. "Oh, ye of little faith! If I get the right pieces of the puzzle, pretty damn close. That's why I don't mind George's running off tailing our sweet young thing, and why I needed this duffel bag so desperately. It might solve my murder, and even yours too."

Jon felt his heart tighten. Could this bag be a missing link in solving the case? Amanda, hang on, he prayed silently.

As if reading his thoughts, Della spoke, breaking the momentary silence. "That Amanda Childs is one helluva lawyer."

"She is?" Connor was surprised.

"Yep. I was before her in deposition not too long ago. She was really polite, but she didn't miss a beat. Chain of custody, procedures and protocols, the different tests and pros and cons, and degrees of probability. She knew it all, and didn't let anything slip past her. I lost a pound of sweat. But I liked her. She wasn't fake. She wasn't just there playing a TV lawyer. She was sincere. And you could tell she really cared for her client."

Jon smiled grimly, saying nothing.

Another silence occurred.

Della spoke again, "You know, this could end up solving a string of area crimes. If the fibers match, I may be able to determine whether Evie Brown was the culprit in at least four major murders or near-murders."

"I certainly hope so," Jon was fervent.

They were silent, then Della broke it again. "How is she? George said she'd been in an accident, and this woman was involved."

Jon's jaw tightened. "Doctor thinks she will be OK, but she's under observation. She was injured pretty badly, and is heavily sedated."

"Hey, I'm sorry. It must be rough," Della declared sympathetically.

"Hell," Jon muttered.

They spent most of the remainder of the trip in silence, Jon still trying to sort out what he knew. They arrived in Pensacola, and she directed him downtown to the lab.

He followed her in, carrying in the plastic bag containing their precious cargo. She cut on some lights in the outer office, then pointed to a couch in a small office lit only by a desk lamp. "You might as well stretch out here and catch a few Zs. I don't want anyone tainting my evidence, you know. It will take me a little while."

Jon, looking at his watch, noted that it was already 12:15 a.m. "What about you? It's late for you too."

"Naw, I like it when there aren't all those interruptions and people running around," she smiled. "It's peaceful here at night. It's when I get most of my work done. Besides, I've already called Joe to meet me up here to help." She grinned. "Like me, he eats this stuff up. More fun than hunting Easter eggs."

She disappeared, and Jon propped himself up on the couch. The day had been long and eventful. It was hard to believe that he had started the day with Amanda in his arms. That seemed an eternity ago. The day that had held so much promise had ended in tragedy. He hoped that the duffel bag provided fulfillment to the rays of hope to which he clung.

Exhausted, he fell into a fitful sleep, jerking awake at every sound. He dreamed of Amanda calling out to him, screaming in pain, and he woke in a cold sweat. He told himself severely, You've got to get a grip. You're no good to her like this. He finally drifted into a state of semi-consciousness.

Suddenly he felt someone shaking his shoulder and calling, "Hey, Fed-Ex Man," as he stirred and suddenly became alert. Della was standing over him, wearing a white lab coat and gloves and excitedly holding a piece of paper in her hands.

"Bingo," she cried, and he sat up quickly, taking in his surroundings. She reached over, cut on the overhead light, and motioned him to follow her.

"Here, put these on," she ordered, giving him a paper gown and gloves as he followed her into the lab.

He quickly donned the gown and gloves, then followed her inside the large room full of equipment. They walked up to a long table in the center of the work area, where several items were carefully laid out. The guy named Joe was there.

"Howdy," Joe said in greeting.

"Howdy," Jon echoed, grinning.

"Guess what I found," Della exclaimed.

"Tell me," he mirrored her excitement.

"Lots of little white cat hairs in the bag," she replied, pointing with a gloved hand to the fibers meticulously lined up on a microscope slide. "They match my other two samples from Barnes and Young."

Moving down to the next item on the table, she announced. "Small burgundy colored pills from a garment. A polyester blend, a match from that found at the Young site at the hospital. And they came from—"

She walked to the next item. "Found in the duffel bag. A nurse/orderly scrub top, nice shade of burgundy, female. Generally they can be found anywhere, but these were bought through a hospital supply company, so probably by someone who worked at a hospital." She pointed to the label in the collar.

"Next," she continued, "black and white fabric pills found at the Barnes site. Came from the collar and shirt in the duffle, which are old priest issue, maybe discards."

"Priest duds? But this is too good to be true. Amanda told David she saw a woman priest go in to see Stephen Marks as she was leaving the prison. Did you take a look at the blood?" Jon asked.

"Yes. Strange—I think I can distinguish three different persons' blood. Have been able to type Barnes' blood. Not sure about the other two. However, one type O matches a drop of blood I found on the corner of the burgundy shirt, which does not match Mrs. Young's blood. What does this mean? I think the same person who wore the burgundy scrub shirt was involved with this priest shirt. Duh, you say, but this stuff proves important when defense counsel gets involved.

"We're still processing the evidence collected from the ER when Dr. Young collapsed, and from the Bronowski crime scene. But if my fibers match, it will be better than a triple word score in Scrabble.

"Of course, all this blood and DNA will have to be re-checked. But I've been closely following the Barnes murder as well—talked to Joe here assisting with the fed's crime scene processing here as well as the house where Mrs. Young collapsed. On a hunch, I twisted his arm to sign out his evidence for comparison.

"At the Barnes crime scene were some slivers of glass, with blood on them, two types. One was our type O, perfect match. I checked against his findings. The other matches one on the shirt, but is not Barnes. The slivers apparently came from this—I have saved the best for last," she said dramatically.

Reaching the end of the table, she waited for Connor to catch up, before taking a gloved hand and opening the communion box. "Broken communion flask," she pointed. "Now, one minute, please," she said, going over to another table and picking up two clear plastic evidence bags, returning.

"See this indentation?" she pointed to a crease at the corner of the box and another next to the allotted space for the cup. Carefully opening one of the baggies, she gingerly pulled out a silver letter opener. Jon recognized it as the one he gave Amanda. She placed it so that it fit perfectly into the indentation.

Next she pulled out the ring Jon had given Amanda and placed it in the other indented spot, where it nestled, a perfect fit.

Jon let out a long breath, transfixed by what he saw.

Chapter 44

Jon's phone rang. "Yes?"

"Private Bubba here, reporting in, sir."

"Where are you?"

"I'm standing guard at *la femme* Evelyn's house, at least the place she came to, which is what she listed on one driver's license, a nice place in the middle of nowhere," Bubba replied.

"Is she there?"

"It was a long two-rut trail to the house, so I hid my vehicle and trekked up on foot. Can't say for sure—all is dark, but a red Mitsubishi sits in front. By the way, did you rescue my girl?"

"She's right here with me," Jon grinned at Della. "She's really good."

"That she is, but if she's showed you her tattoo, I'll have to kill you," Bubba growled.

"I didn't know you had a jealous bone in you," Jon told him. "But she has been extremely busy analyzing evidence. Your Evelyn also known as Eve is now a major suspect. Are you in Alabama?"

"Actually, no. The road doubles back and this place is actually on the Florida side, as best I can tell and what the GPS is telling me, but over in the neighboring county to the east," Bubba replied. "Glad I'm a fed and don't have to worry as much about state jurisdictional lines."

"Bubba, do we have anyone who can take over the stakeout for you? I need you. This girl's having the stuff in her car is going to buy us probable cause for search and arrest warrants. You're our best warrants guy, and we need to pull together a task force to consolidate our affidavits, decide if we have enough to make arrests and for what, determine who will prosecute what, and track down a judge or judges, hopefully other than this Kilmer guy."

"Ahead of you. I've got permanent leg cramps from crouching in the woods all this time. Got a couple of guys out here I borrowed from the sheriff over here. Great good ole boy. I'm still trying to track down law enforcement on the Alabama side."

"That's good news. I'll put Della on and let her tell you what she has."

Jon handed the phone to Della, asking, "You've got a tattoo?" He saw her blush prettily as she took the phone and turned away, her tongue lashing the hapless George over the airwaves.

Jon looked at his watch. It was a 4:53. He knew they still had to try to place their target at the sites of the homicides and obtain known comparison samples. He stood staring unseeingly at the evidence, trying to determine the next move.

Della handed him back the phone. "George says he has something important to tell you."

Jon took the phone. "I'm back at my car," Bubba was saying, "and just on a hunch I ran the lovely Eve Brown's name in a public property records check. Guess what?"

"I'm game," Jon remarked.

"She just happens to co-own this property with someone you know."

Jon, anxious, waited. "Don't hold out on me, Bubba."

"The Rev. Adam Brownlee. And it is apparently next door to property across the state line owned by none other than William Barnes, Sr."

Jon, stunned, could only manage, "Bubba, I'd kiss you if you were here."

Bubba grumbled, "Hell, man, I got a reputation to protect."

Jon continued. "I'll hunt the Rev. Brownlee down and pay him a visit. Stay in touch."

Jon, galvanized, his mind racing, called the Mainville Police Station. Asking for the chief, he was soon on the line with Petrino.

"I knew you'd be at work already," Jon said.

"Yeah. I'm always up this time, and I couldn't sleep, thinking about Amanda and this mess."

Jon's voice was quiet. "I know, man. That's why I am calling you."

"How is she?" Jon could hear the anxiety in Charlie's voice.

"Nothing new right now. I'm trying to hold off on calling until I'm sure Joey has made rounds. David is with her."

"Where are you?"

"I am in Pensacola. I left David there with Amanda, because some new developments have occurred in the case, and I'm chasing some leads, trying to clear her."

"Yeah, Bruce filled me in on some of it."

Jon updated him on the latest regarding the FDLE analysis of the evidence.

"That's good news," Charlie enthused.

Jon asked, "Could you do some sleuthing for me?"

"You bet. What do you need?"

"I'm sure you know about the Young homicide investigation."

"I'll say I do."

Quickly Jon summarized the events of the previous night and his suspicions regarding Abermarle's involvement. "Charlie, could you check on what the Young investigation uncovered in witness interviews, to see if anyone could put this Evelyn, Evie, whoever she is, in the vicinity of Shelby Young at any time before death? That would help a great deal."

Next Jon called directory assistance for Pensacola, but could find no listing for Adam Brownlee. Overhearing Jon's request, Della stated, "Come with me. Maybe I can help you."

Connor followed her back to her office, where she sat down at her computer. "Like you guys, we have several locater services, as well as our central information systems. Let's see if I can make a hit."

She brought up several programs and punched data in. Jon watched over her shoulder as she checked several databases. Finally, she said, "Here's an address from his driver's license—1420 Conte Avenue, Milford. Just a minute; you know people don't always update their driver's licenses when they move." She pulled up another database and ran a search. "It's good—he's getting his VISA bill there."

"You know where that is?"

Della quickly gave him directions, which he jotted down on her business card. She also quickly printed out a Google map for him.

"And just one more thing," she said, squinting at the screen. "The title 'Reverend' is listed before his name. Do you know which denomination?"

"Episcopal," Jon replied.

She started punching into the internet, running another search. "He is currently rector at St. Margaret's, which happens to be next door to that address. Probably a rectory."

"Good work, Della. You and Bubba make a fine pair."

"Tell him that," Della said, staring at the screen, embarrassed.

"I will," Jon surprised her. "I'm going to grab a quick shower. I think I'll make an early morning visit to the good Reverend. Can I drop you off anywhere?"

"No. My car's here. Joe and I will be making lists, checking them twice, and doing up a supplemental report of our findings," she declined.

Jon reached down and kissed her on the cheek.

"What's that for?" she asked, surprised.

"You may have just saved my girl."

Jon left, pulling out and heading for the temporary apartment quarters he shared with the Greg Boyer. Letting himself in, he looked at the clock. 6:05 a.m. He could hear the shower running upstairs, and decided to try to intercept Joey Rand, who he knew was prone to make early rounds, to find out Amanda's condition.

Pouring himself a cup of coffee and calling the hospital number, he identified himself and asked if the doctor could be paged. After several minutes on hold, David Connor's voice came on the line.

"Jon, it's David."

"David! How is Amanda?"

"Amanda did not have a good night," David's voice was solemn. "She ripped off her monitors and IV in the night. Thankfully, the staff rushed in and kept her from doing any other damage. I stayed with her."

"Oh, no," breathed Jon. "Is she OK now?"

"She was out of it, raved for a few seconds again about a priest named Evie. You know what that's about?"

"I think I do," Jon replied grimly.

"And she kept saying she had to play on Sunday. What is that?"

"She's a church organist," Jon allowed himself a smile.

"A church organist accused of murder?" David was astounded.

"Never trust a church organist, particularly if she's a lawyer," Jon chuckled. Suddenly serious, he asked, "How is she now?"

"She's resting quietly now. Joey was worried about whether there was some internal damage from the accident, and he's planned some more tests today to rule out anything. Dr. Howells is due here any time and they're going to consult. Where are you?"

"I'm in Pensacola, but I can leave now and drive straight there."

"No," David responded firmly. "You can do nothing for Amanda here. I'm hoping that you are making more progress where you are. I promise to take good care of her."

"Thanks, bro," Jon's voice was hoarse with emotion. "I owe you big time."

"Just know this—if you decide to throw this one over I'm waiting in the wings to sweep her off her feet," David said lightly.

His remark had the intended effect, and Jon laughed. "I'm not sure it's such a good idea to entrust her to your care."

"Do what you do best, man, and I'll do what I do best," David asserted, suddenly somber.

Jon hung up as Boyer walked down the stairs, dressed in shirt and tie, his suit jacket hanging from his fingers. "Hi there, roomie," he drawled. "Long time no see. What's up?"

Jon summarized about Barnes' homicide at the prison, and Boyer's jaw dropped. "Rita and Molly flew down, and I took them to Orange Beach this weekend. No one notified me about Barnes, but I haven't checked my messages. Where have you been?"

Jon told him about the encounter with Amanda. Boyer listened intently, making no response when Jon related that he and Amanda spent the weekend together. His face paled when Jon told of the accident and Amanda's injuries.

"My God!" he cried.

Jon interjected, "There's more." He then told of Evelyn Abermarle's arrest, her release, and the finding of the duffel bag with its contents. When Jon relayed the findings of Della's analysis, Boyer's eyes grew large.

"This is really big," Boyer murmured. "How did Barnes get put in the same prison as Marks?" he asked angrily. "I told Bureau of Prisons classifications officers to make sure the two did not meet. I didn't want anything to happen to my witness. Damn! Heads will roll over this."

Jon shrugged. "I don't know, but I'm sure you'll find out."

Boyer glanced at Jon, noting his haggard look. "You look all in. You need some rest. Can I make you some breakfast?"

Jon shook his head. "No. I'll feel better after a shower. I want to try to find Adam Brownlee this morning first thing, then perhaps make another trip to the prison to visit Marks again and see if I can get anything else out of him."

"Do you think this Brownlee is involved in this?" Boyer asked.

Jon told him about the property records check, and Boyer shook his head in disbelief. Jon continued, "I've got Bubba trying to marshal the information and get a warrant for this Evelyn's place, and to try to organize a task force. I'd appreciate your help."

"Sure thing," Boyer promised. "I'll call George and see what I can do on this end. I'll be happy to line up a judge or magistrate."

"Just make sure it isn't this Kilmer fellow," Jon muttered.

As Jon turned to go upstairs, Boyer added quietly, "And Jon? I'm really sorry about Amanda. She's a great girl. You know if there's anything I can do . . ." he left the sentence unfinished.

Jon replied, "Thanks," as he took the stairs two at a time.

Minutes later, Jon stepped into the shower. As the jets of water sprayed on him, he recalled his weekend with Amanda and their shower together. He felt weak as he stood under the steaming water, his eyes closed, the feel and taste of her imprinted on his mind. God, take care of her and bring her back to me, he prayed. Help me to clear her name.

By 6:45 he was dressed and leaving the apartment. As his car pulled out of the driveway, the phone rang.

"Jon? This is Ralph," he heard a voice say. "What's going on?"

Jon quickly told him about Amanda's status. "I'm following some very promising leads right now. We have a suspect in our sights. David is at the hospital with Amanda and keeping me informed."

"Claire and I are on our way back to the hospital now. We're meeting Dr. Howells and Dr. Rand there. I'll let you know if anything new develops. And Jon? If there's anything I can do to help clear Amanda—"

"You'll be the first to know. Thanks," Jon responded as he hung up.

About twenty minutes later he was within the Milford city limits, following the directions given him by Della. Finding the location he sought, he noted a recent model Buick LeSabre in the driveway. Parking and going to the front door, he rang the doorbell.

Momentarily, the door opened and Jon found himself face to face with Adam Brownlee. "Rev. Brownlee? I would appreciate if I speak to you just one minute."

Brownlee showed surprise, but greeted Jon and stepped aside to let him in. Motioning him toward the living room, they were soon seated.

Brownlee began, "Please call me Adam. And I'm very sorry to hear about Amanda's accident. How is she?"

Jon, surprised, inquired, "How did you know about that?"

"Stephen Marks contacted me last night from the hospital. He was very distraught. He asked that I find out what I could about her condition. In fact, I was going to drive down and try to see her on his behalf because I of course could not discover anything by telephone last night. I can't believe it—I just spoke to her late Friday afternoon on a personal matter. This has been a very tragic weekend."

"Yes," echoed Connor, watching Brownlee intently. "Very tragic."

"I cannot believe that William Barnes is dead," Brownlee continued. "I went to take Stephen communion later after leaving Mrs. Childs' office, and Barnes had just been discovered. I didn't even know he was at the prison. The ambulance was taking Stephen to the hospital, and I accompanied him."

"Adam, why were you taking communion to Stephen Marks?"

Brownlee, surprised by the question, answered, "I go every Friday afternoon to take the Eucharist to Stephen. It's sort of a standing date—the chaplain made arrangements for me to make regular visitation without having to constantly clear it with the prison officials."

Jon's eyes narrowed. "Then do you have any idea why someone else might have come earlier that day to bring communion?"

Brownlee frowned. "That's weird. One of the guards mentioned to me when I arrived that he thought a priest had come earlier. I just thought he must be mistaken."

Jon paused. "Adam, what do you know about Evelyn Abermarle?"

Brownlee visibly paled. "What does Evie have to do with any of this?" he demanded, his voice quavering.

"So you do know her. I thought perhaps you could tell me," Jon replied quietly. "Did you know she was involved in the same accident that injured Amanda Childs?"

Brownlee started, surprised, a tinge of fear in his eyes. "No. Is she OK? Was she hurt?"

Jon, watching his apparent distress and confusion, responded, "No, but she was arrested and faces several charges at this time."

"Oh, no. Is she in jail? She didn't call me. What has she done now? She didn't try to kill Amanda, did she?"

Jon leaned forward, his eyes intent on Brownlee, who was clearly agitated. "Tell me, Adam. What is your relationship with Evelyn Abermarle?"

Brownlee said, standing, his voice quivering with emotion, "Evie is my twin sister."

Chapter 45

It was Jon's turn to be surprised. "Your twin sister?" he uttered, incredulous.

"Yes," whispered Brownlee anxiously. "You must tell me what she has done," he pleaded, as he clutched Jon's arm.

"Why would you think she would attempt to kill Amanda?" Jon peered intently at Brownlee.

"Because she has had this unreasonable and bitter hatred of Amanda for years now," Brownlee acknowledged as he slowly released Jon's arm. "My sister had a crush on Bill Barnes for years, but Bill was perennially in pursuit of Amanda Childs. It drove my sister mad with jealousy.

"My sister is a beautiful and intelligent woman. But she has from time to time been hospitalized for schizophrenia. She has been prescribed medication, which helps to normalize her behavior, but every now and then she quits taking the medicine and decompensates.

"She has developed a recurrent pattern of becoming infatuated with a man and having an affair with him. Generally that's when her condition deteriorates. She was released from a spate of hospitalizations just a couple years ago after a torrid relationship with a public official."

"Do you know who that official is?" Jon asked.

"I'd rather not say, for his sake," Brownlee was suddenly cautious.

Jon said solemnly, "I'm afraid this matter is too big for that at this point, and he could very well be implicated or in danger."

Brownlee paused for several moments before apparently deciding to divulge the information. "It was Judge Kilmer. I finally convinced her that it was a self-destructive relationship and sent her away to a private hospital for four months. He was understandably nervous about his standing in the community and the consequences of the information's becoming public.

"I've spent a long time trying to keep this quiet, because she agreed to treatment as long as she wouldn't lose her job. She told me she got her job back, and seemed to be doing much better.

"Then all this happened with Mr. Barnes' arrest. She was convinced that Amanda was the perpetrator, and at first I was too. I read the papers avidly, and heard word that they had confessions on tape. I began thinking about it and went to Stephen. Stephen confessed to me his and Barnes' involvement, and I realized how Mr. Barnes had been manipulating me for information and assistance all those years."

Jon was burning to ask questions, but realized that Brownlee was unburdening himself and filling in gaps, so he said nothing as Brownlee continued. "Stephen was so caught up with rectifying the mistakes of the past with his new-found daughter. He talked me into applying for St. Margaret's—the best thing that ever happened to me. I went from total distrust and resentment of Amanda, to actually understanding some of what she must have gone through.

"But Evie hated Amanda even more for Barnes' arrest. She was adamant she didn't want to go to continuing therapy with a psychologist, and was afraid that her condition would be found out. So I set it up for her to discreetly visit Stephen Marks. He has a degree in counseling, even though that and the status of his priesthood are pretty much in limbo now."

Jon countered eagerly, "Was she seeing Stephen on a regular basis before he was arrested?"

Brownlee hesitated. "No. I set this up since his arrest. She's been visiting him at the prison regularly. But she refused to listen to Stephen or me when we tried to tell her the truth about Barnes. When I tried to talk to her, she became violently angry—'Am I not good enough a sister to you? What—are you ashamed of me?'—statements like that.

"Evie imagined that Amanda had taken everything from her—her boyfriend Bill Barnes, her surrogate father Barnes, Stephen, and now her own brother. I have tried to reason with her. Then she got a new 'boyfriend'. The last few weeks she had seemed more withdrawn. That should have been a warning sign that things were not going well."

Jon breathed in sharply. "You said Evelyn had been visiting Marks regularly. The prison officials did not show her as a visitor on the sign-in sheets."

"She went *incognito*, because she didn't want anyone from the community to recognize her. That's it!" Brownlee exclaimed, his eyes wide.

"What?" asked Jon eagerly.

"That's why the guard thought a priest had been there earlier. It was her!" he cried.

"You mean—"

"—she had borrowed one of my shirts and collars," Brownlee faltered, "so that she could visit with Marks without someone in the community recognizing her and finding out that she was going to counseling. There is a separate sign-in list for clergy. She was very sensitive about her condition, and took precautions that people did not find out about it. She even borrowed one of my communion kits, just to make it look believable, she said. Stephen took me to task about it, said it was sacrilegious for her to dress as a priest, and was angry at me about giving her the communion kit. But Evie always had a way of getting what she wanted."

Jon, his excitement mounting, volunteered, "Amanda mumbled something about a woman priest and a black box. She must have seen your sister go in after her to see Marks at the prison. Amanda recognized her—'Evie'. That means—"

Brownlee looked at him in terror. "Oh, no. Oh, my God, no. You must be mistaken."

Jon rejoined quickly, "I'm sorry, Adam, but I don't think so. Tell me—why would your sister want to kill Barnes?'

"She wouldn't," Brownlee denied emphatically. "She loved William Barnes. He was the father she never had. He basically took care of us when our mother died. We were orphans—my mother died of a drug overdose when we were very small. Our mother's cousin raised us. Barnes and she were some distant kin, and he made sure that we lacked for nothing growing up. He came to visit us and brought us toys, clothes, other stuff. He gave our cousin money to help us out. He put us through school. He was especially close to my sister and spent hours with her. I developed a bond with Stephen Marks; he—" Brownlee stuttered, "—he became my mentor. But Barnes was Evie's."

Brownlee laughed, mirthlessly. "That's what I went to see Amanda Childs about on Friday. I wanted to know what one had to do to get paternity testing. I've always felt that Stephen Marks was something more to us. He knew our mother before she died, and took such an interest in us. After he got that letter from Marjorie, which I photocopied and gave to Bill Barnes, I felt such anxiety that Amanda would come between us, break the bond I had with him. And of course Evie noticed it, and it fueled her fervor against Amanda, even though she has never believed that Marks could be our father.

"But on Friday afternoon, my sister called me out of the blue and convinced me to go see Amanda Childs and ask her about how to go about getting DNA testing. I couldn't imagine why Evelyn would have me go to Amanda, or right then, but this question has been burning in my mind for so long. And Evie was rabid that I drop everything and go talk to her.

"I always worry about my sister's compulsive tendencies, so in order to placate her I did as she asked. Amanda was apparently in a hurry to get out of the office. I think I shocked her when I told her why I was asking.

"It's funny, but I felt for the first time Amanda and I actually connected and talked. Even though she was preoccupied with something, she was kind to me, even after I barged in on her. I realized while talking to her that all this about Marks being our dad might just be a pipe dream of mine. But she offered to ask him for me the next time she visited him.

"But suddenly Evie called me on my cell phone and told me she needed to meet me. She said it was an emergency—a matter of life and death, to meet her at the prison. So I left as quickly as I could. She never showed up. And I found . . ." he left the sentence hanging.

"But that wasn't your first visit to Amanda's office that day, was it?" Jon pressed the attack, suspicious.

"What?" exclaimed Brownlee, bewildered. "That was my first trip there since the day you and I visited her about Marjorie Witherspoon's will."

"What if I had a witness that put you there earlier in the day, disguised as an air conditioning repairman?"

Brownlee looked at him like he was crazy, then his expression turned to horror as he divined the truth. "Evie wouldn't," he whispered, as though to convince himself. "She wouldn't. That's why Amanda's secretary asked if I had a twin."

"Evie wouldn't what?" Jon prompted him.

Brownlee looked at him wordlessly, tormented. Jon divined his thoughts. "Your sister dressed as a repairman and stole the letter opener and ring from Amanda's desk. Then she dressed as a priest and made it into the prison."

"No," whispered Brownlee disbelievingly.

Connor decided to confide in him about the physical evidence found in the trunk of her car.

Brownlee, all color having fled from his face, looked at Connor. "If she killed Barnes, then wherever my sister is right now, she's over the edge. She's dangerous."

Brownlee's phone rang. He said, "Excuse me," as he walked over and answered it. Jon could hear an angry voice yelling over the receiver. "You've got to stop that crazy sister of yours. She's going to ruin me. She's threatening to expose me. I wish I had never met her."

He heard Brownlee ask quietly, "When did she contact you?"

"Yesterday afternoon. She was arrested for several charges, including some felonies. The law enforcement community is screaming at me for letting her out, but I had to do her first appearance and pay the bondsman myself to get her out. That's an ethics violation, Adam. And she says she has evidence of my true paternity. I'm a ruined man."

"Oh, no," Brownlee stated softly. "Do you have any idea where she might be now?"

"Hell, I don't want to know. But you have to do something, and do it quick. My whole family, my career—"

"I'll find her," Brownlee replied quietly.

Hanging up, he looked weary. His eyes beseeched Connor. Connor said quietly, "I heard. That was Kilmer?"

Adam nodded. "She's my sister, damn it. All these years we've had no one but each other. We have each spent our lives looking for a father. You must help me find her and keep her from hurting anyone else. I can't live with that."

"I must alert others to be on the lookout. Will you come with me to talk to Marks? If he has counseled her, he might be able to help us," Jon asked him.

"Yes," he acquiesced, grabbing a black blazer off the back of a chair. He picked up his phone and dialed a number. "Mrs. Anderson, I won't be in today. I have a family emergency. Please cancel my appointments. I will check in with you later."

They quickly left, climbing into Connor's Mercedes. Connor soon had them buzzing down the interstate highway toward Bayview.

Connor hit the speed dial on his phone. "Bubba? How's it coming?"

"Got the sheriff's boys interested in a state search warrant of *la femme* Evelyn. Got Della's affidavit faxed to me. I'm a little worried because my guys still haven't seen any sign of life at the place, even though the car is still there."

Jon turned to Brownlee. "Evelyn was tracked to a place out in the woods last night. The place is in both your names, so I assume you know it?"

Brownlee nodded. "That's her place."

Jon spoke into the phone. "Call you back."

Handing the phone to Brownlee, Jon advised, "Does she have a number there you can reach her to see if she is still there? You said it. We have to find her before something else happens."

Brownlee dialed a number. After several rings, he shook his head. "Let me try her cell number."

He dialed another number. "Evie? Where the hell are you? Why didn't you show up Friday?"

He listened a moment. "Are you home?"

"Evie?" he repeated, looking at Connor. "Evie, I'm worried about you. You're getting in over your head. We need to talk. Can you meet me somewhere? Anywhere? Please, Evie."

A pause. "How about we go talk to Stephen together? He's at the hospital. He could use the company. You know he can help."

Seconds later he handed the phone back to Connor, his eyes shining with unshed tears. "It's a no go. She hung up on me. She's not there, Jon. She won't tell me where she is."

"But the car?"

"Barnes owned a farm next to ours, across the state line. She has access to his place. Chances are she's in his Lexus."

Jon called Bubba back, relaying information. "I need for you to prepare and put out an all points bulletin on Evelyn Abermarle, aka Evie Brown. Do a DMV search for a black Lexus or other vehicles owned by William Barnes, Sr.—she may be in one of them. We need some back-up at the hospital checking people coming in and out, to protect Amanda. Please notify other agencies, and make sure Zeke knows, as well as the officials at the hospital where Marks is. And call Petrino and the sheriff's office. We need a team protecting Judge Kilmer and his family, and Dr. Young and his family too. Tell Charlie to make it discreet."

"Got it. You know what red-head's and Brownlee's connection is?"

"Yeah—he's her twin brother," Jon replied.

"Damn, how did you find out?" Bubba wanted to know.

"He's here with me, and we're on our way to the hospital to see Marks now. Maybe we can break his silence."

Connor summarized the information he had received from Brownlee as Brownlee looked dazedly out the window.

"Got it," Bubba said. "Are you going to be around if I need an affidavit from you for this warrant?"

"Let me know when the papers are ready."

He hung up. "Adam, do you think she might take your advice and show up at the hospital to see Marks?"

"I don't know. She said she didn't need him anymore, but I guess it could happen."

They covered the remaining miles in silence. Arriving at the hospital, Jon quickly showed his badge and pulled Adam in after him. As they headed toward Marks' hospital room, the warden caught sight of Jon and called to him. "Just a minute. I've got some info for you."

Jon halted, as the warden rushed up. "We got a guard who ushered Amanda Childs out of the prison. Wolfson's his name. He said that Barnes wasn't in the room when Childs left. He specifically remembered the woman saying something to Marks about going back to the office for a ring. She seemed in a hurry to leave. A female priest met them in the hallway going in to see Marks."

"Name?" Jon inquired, seeing Brownlee's face turn pale.

"Nothing on the sign-in sheet, but a description. Beautiful, built like a brick shit-house, with red hair and high heels. Another guard said she had called ahead, stating that she was there to do rounds for the regular priest, and that she had a special request from Barnes for communion. She wanted to do it for both of them at the same time—said she was in a hurry to get to a function."

"Thanks," Jon murmured, as he pulled a visibly shaken Brownlee with him into Stephen Marks' hospital room.

Stephen, his face pale, looked apprehensively at Jon. "How is Amanda?"

He listened intently as Connor briefed him on her injuries. "She had a reaction this morning. She is currently resting. They will be doing more tests today."

Brownlee came up to Marks and took his hand. "Stephen, we need your help."

Marks angrily interrupted. "I know why you're here. I killed Barnes," he said irritably. "Can't you just believe me? I have nothing left to lose."

Brownlee looked at him earnestly. "Evelyn ran Amanda off the road and tried to kill her."

Stephen visibly blanched at this information. Brownlee continued. "Evie is beyond the pale right now. She was arrested and blackmailed Judge Kilmer into getting her out. She is missing. We don't know what she will try next."

Jon interjected, "We know Evelyn was there when Barnes was murdered, and we're pretty sure she did it. You know the answer." Jon summarized the evidence found in Evelyn's car, and Stephen groaned.

Brownlee continued. "You cannot protect Evie by keeping the information secret. Any privilege as to your communications with her does not extend to shielding her from prosecution, and you must not allow her by your silence to commit more crimes."

Stephen squeezed Adam's hand. Piteously he demurred, "She's not the only one I've been trying to protect."

Chapter 46

That night David Connor had spent sprawled in a chair beside Amanda's hospital bed. After David convinced Silas to allow him to remain the night in the ICU, Joey had looked at him like he had gone mad. "Suit yourself, Lancelot," he shook his head disbelievingly.

"I made a promise to Jon," David insisted quietly. "Thanks for pulling her through. I'm sorry you missed the Knicks game—they won," David slapped him on the back.

"No problem, but don't thank me yet. We're not far down the road if you need us," Joey told him, yawning as Silas and he waved and left.

David had looked at his charge long and hard as she lay unconscious. Sighing, he shook his head. How and when did this vixen steal his brother's heart? A lawyer? Geez.

A nurse came in and smiled as David stretched and rubbed his neck. "Doctor, there's a bed and couch in the doctor's lounge, as well as a shower. If you're insisting on staying, Dr. Fleischer said for you to make yourself at home."

"Thanks. I'll think I'll step out to the nurse's desk and chat with Zeke."

David left the nurse and made his way to the lobby, where Zeke was talking with another nurse and perusing an old magazine. Zeke looked over at David. "You, know it's foolish for both of us to stand guard. Why don't you go catch a few Zs? I promise to call you if anything happens."

David looked dubious, but Zeke continued, "You rest a couple hours, then you can spell me. It'll be morning before I can get a relief officer."

David nodded and headed to the doctor's lounge. Stopping the nurse coming out of Amanda's cubicle, he told her where he'd be and added, "If there's any change, you get me stat."

She nodded understandingly.

David reached the lounge and took a quick shower to help work out the knots in his neck, before stretching out on the couch in the lounge. He wondered about the green-eyed woman and the story behind her. He mulled over the information shared by the group at the pub. Never a dull moment with my brother, he thought as he became drowsy. More fun than my 'nip and tuck' stories and my women adventures any day.

He fell into a light slumber, a dream overtaking him. He dreamed that he was again giving Amanda CPR, and she wasn't breathing. He was trying to bring her back, but was not able to revive her and was worried about his brother's reaction if she died.

He awoke suddenly to the sound of the intercom. "Dr. Connor to intensive care; Dr. Connor to ICU stat."

Alert, he jumped up and sprinted back to the ICU. The wall clock read 2:37. He almost ran into Zeke. Zeke said excitedly, "I was just coming for you. Amanda's gone crazy."

David flung himself into Amanda's room, where a male nurse was trying to hold her writhing form down, and a female nurse was trying to staunch the flow of blood from her arm. "She has snatched out her IV tube and portal. Jack caught her trying to get out of bed."

David went over and took over from the male nurse. "I got her," he said, placing his hands on her shoulders as she struggled and moaned loudly. "Slow down, Amanda, slow down. I don't want you to aggravate your injuries," he crooned as the nurse quickly checked her blood pressure.

"She has a sensitivity to drugs," David recalled, remembering the information Ralph had relayed. Quickly he gave instructions. "We need to reinitiate an IV," he added. Looking at them, he said quickly, "Go. I got her."

The nurses ran to comply with the orders.

Amanda struggled up. David held her next to him to immobilize her and prevent her thrashing about. She kept whispering something. David bent closer. "Evie—it's her," she kept saying.

David felt Amanda's rigid body as he held her to him and attempted to restrict her movements. "You have got to hold still, Amanda," he said next to her ear. "Otherwise we'll end up going back in, and you'll have to be immobilized."

He tried another tack. "You know, Jon will be pissed if I let anything happen to you."

"Jon?" she quavered dazedly, clutching toward her left arm and shoulder, whimpering. "Oh, my God, it hurts," she moaned. "I can't play," she cried.

"Yes, Jon," he replied, pulling back, meeting her eyes and smiling. "Let's try to lay you back against the pillow here. You know we called him Sir Parsifal when we were kids?"

"Where's he?" she whispered, her eyes unfocused. "Oh, please," she cried again as she bit her lip against the pain. "Tell him about Evie." She cried out again, clutching at her left wrist. "I have to play Sunday."

"Jon's out fighting dragons for you. You have got to calm down and get well. He'll be here soon."

The female nurse returned and quickly started another IV, as the male nurse brought in a hypodermic needle and vial. David reclined Amanda gingerly, pulled on some latex gloves, took the materials from the nurse, expertly withdrew the fluid from the vial into the hypodermic, and gave her the shot himself. Handing the needle to the nurse to throw in the hazardous waste bin, he said softly, "Pray."

"Do we need to tie her down?" the male nurse asked.

"I don't want to, but I don't want a repeat of this episode. I guess so," David answered reluctantly. "I'll stay with her a while. Zeke," he spoke to the agent, who was standing in the doorway gaping at the scene, "go stretch out on the couch in the lounge. Despite her antics, I'll make sure she doesn't get away."

Zeke watched them for a moment before disappearing. Amanda again started to sit up, but David held her several minutes longer, until he felt her relaxing against him. He gently leaned her back against the pillows and stood over her, watching her intently as the monitors showed her numbers gradually settling back into normal range. The male nurse secured her hands with restraints.

"Dr. Rand is not going to be happy that she moved that shoulder. Let's hope her vitals stay there," he told the nurses solemnly. "At least her pressure seems to be holding steady."

After a while she appeared to drift to sleep, and David sighed with relief. He pulled the chair beside her and slumped into it. He noticed that the fingers of her right hand kept moving incessantly. Intrigued, he became hypnotized by the movement of her long tapered fingers against the sheets. He dozed fitfully, waking at every sound.

"What you doing, Lancelot, my man?" Joey and Silas appeared in the room.

"Just having fun," yawned David, as he stretched. His watch showed 5:53. "What is she doing?" he asked, pointing to Amanda's still moving fingers.

Joey shrugged, but Silas looked closer. After a minute of close observations, he said, "Beethoven."

"What?" the other two men rejoined in chorus.

"Looks like 'Variations on the Duet *Nel cor piu non mi sento* from Paisiello's *La Molinara*', to be exact," Silas said, pleased with their looks of disbelief. "Fingering practice, guys, years of piano lessons, something you weaseled out of as teenagers. The patient's subconscious is definitely hard at work."

"No wonder you're CMO—you're so full of crap," David laughed softly.

"Better than you. When you two get together, you sound more like automobile mechanics than doctors," Silas retorted loftily.

"Any problems during the night?" Rand asked David, ignoring Fleischer.

David briefed them on Amanda's episode, and Rand nodded seriously. "Since then she's been resting quietly, no more spiking."

"Based on what Dr. Howells said, we could have anticipated something like this." Joey examined her, looking at her chart and the new test results the nurse was inserting in it. He bent over Amanda, probing gently around the clavicle. "Geez," he muttered, irritated. "I want another picture of this. I don't like it." He looked at David and winked. "I want to make sure I don't have any leaky valves before we go in," he remarked for Silas' benefit.

The ICU nurse interrupted, "Dr. Rand? There's a Jon Connor on the line holding."

David said, "I'll take it." Going to the phone, he spoke to his brother, summarizing Amanda's condition as Joey walked up and listened.

As David hung up and they turned back toward Amanda's room, they saw a white-haired gentleman in dark suit who had quietly slipped in past them and was standing over Amanda's hospital bed holding her hand and kissing her forehead. As they entered the room, he straightened and proffered his hand.

"Malcolm Howells," he introduced himself.

"Dr. Howells, I'm David Connor, Jon's brother, and this is Dr. Joseph Rand, who worked on Amanda yesterday. Jon has had nothing but good things to say about you," David said.

"I've heard of you, Dr. Rand, and your work," replied Howells gravely. Turning back to David, he said with a twinkle in his eye, "And Jon has told me about you as well, Dr. Connor."

"Hope it was good," muttered David. "And call me David."

"Please tell me about my girl."

Rand handed Howells the patient's chart and began briefing him, David answering questions about the accident and about Amanda's incident during the early morning hours. As the men continued their discussion, David noticed that Amanda's eyes were fluttering open, and she was looking about her uncomprehendingly. As she flexed and stretched, she moaned and gasped, coughing slightly.

The other men turned at the noise. Howells took her right hand fervently. "Amanda Katharine," he breathed.

She made a face something between a smile and grimace at him. "Where's the Mack truck?"

"What?" Joey looked at her incredulously.

"The one that ran me over," she replied faintly, catching her breath sharply at the discomfort in her shoulder area. She reached with her right hand toward it, but was brought short by the restraints around her wrists. She groaned softly.

The men grinned at her attempt at a joke, as Howells untied her right wrist restraint and grasped her hand. She feebly squeezed his hand in return. She looked over at David.

"You're not Jon," she whispered, half accusingly.

David let out a small laugh. "I'm so glad you finally noticed."

She squinted and frowned. "But I've seen you before," she mumbled groggily.

David flushed slightly.

Howells asked her, "Tell me, how are you feeling?"

"I don't know," she quavered hoarsely. "What happened?"

"What do you remember?" Rand asked her.

She frowned, trying to recall. "Evie. At the prison. And she ran me over. Water. I couldn't get out," she replied, shuddering and wincing out in pain. "Am I in jail?" she whispered confusedly.

"You're in the hospital. Your friend Fred came to your rescue," David replied. "He swam the creek, and managed to break the window and cut the seat belt. Then we revived you and got you here. Dr. Rand here put you back together."

She squinted at Dr. Rand. "Thanks," she said simply.

"My pleasure, milady," Joey answered her.

She rasped. "Jon calls me that."

David smiled at her. "Joey, Jon and I grew up together. We played together as kids. One of the games Mom devised for us was playing Knights of the Round Table. It's remained one of our oldest jokes. I'm Sir Lancelot, Joey here is Gawain, and Jon was always Parsifal."

"The Holy Grail?" she asked tremulously, trying to smile, but wincing again and catching her breath sharply.

"The same," Joey remarked. "Looks like he found it, but we got to keep you in one piece for him."

She was silent, closing her eyes, spent from the exertion of talking.

"What's the damage?" she finally asked as she grimaced and moved again, more alert and clearly uncomfortable.

Rand briefed her on her condition. "We're going to get a couple more x-rays this morning, make sure there's no hidden damage. I'm afraid you're going to need a pin at the very least."

Howells told her, "You're going to have a bit of a miserable time, child. We are limited in the painkilling drugs we can safely give you, and the next few days will be the worst. You have to be strong until your body knits itself back up."

She nodded, more focused, her eyes closed against the rising pain in her side and clavicle as it grew more insistent. "Where's Jon?" she inquired weakly. "Have you heard anything—"

David leaned over her, looking at her bruised cheek. "He's following up on some new leads, promising leads. He wants to be here, but I told him he could do you more good doing what he is doing."

Tears appeared in the corners of her eyes. "I'm in such a mess. I'm about to go to prison for the rest of my life, and I can't even defend myself," she whimpered despairingly.

Howells, alarmed, leaned over her. "Don't go there," he commanded her sternly. "That's not the Amanda I know, the 'tell the world to go to hell' battler for justice. Don't give up—we have several rounds yet to go. It will all turn out OK."

Amanda slumped, catching her breath sharply, biting her lip and crying out as her shoulder exploded in pain. "No, Doc, I can't fight anymore," she whispered dejectedly. She coughed as the pain traveled down her side, and tears formed as her right hand balled into a fist and her body tensed. "Help me, please," she coughed.

With a great deal of effort, she opened her eyes and looked at Rand, careful not to meet Howells' gaze. "Make the pain go away," she whispered brokenly. "I don't want to feel anymore."

Howells read her expression, and his heart ached for her. He squeezed her hand. "I need to talk to these good men a few minutes, and I'll be back."

Amanda nodded dejectedly, turning her head away. Howells followed the two men out of the room. The men discussed possible drug trials and dosages for her, and Rand gave orders to the nurse.

Turning to the other doctors, Joey remarked. "I think we need to have a talk. Come on, let's get breakfast at the cafeteria." Turning to the nurse, he ordered, "Page me immediately if there's any change."

Silas interrupted them. "Guys, I need to make my early department rounds. I'll see you in a bit."

Howells, Rand and David walked down the hall until they found the cafeteria. Moments later they were sitting at a table.

Howells spoke first. "I don't like this," he told the other two doctors gravely. "She's sinking into depression. She has never asked for painkillers before in her life."

Rand put his hand on Howells' arm reassuringly. "I'm sure that she is in a great deal of distress from her injuries. What we've given her is wearing off."

Howells was grave, "You don't understand. She's a fighter. That girl in there is not my Amanda. She's always refused medicine before. She's giving up."

David looked at Howells, his heart going out to the older man. "Doc, I talked to Jon a few minutes ago, and he sounded very hopeful. He had some excellent leads, but of course he didn't give me any details."

"Let's pray it's resolved soon, for her sake," Rand remarked solemnly.

They were silent as they ate. Howells excused himself for a few minutes, leaving the two alone.

David broke the silence. "Well, Joey, what do you think of the white sands of the Gulf Coast?"

"I like it down here," Joey replied. "Silas has made me an offer and has already found me an office, a house and a wife, if I want them."

David grinned. "What about Kelly?" David sipped his coffee and buttered his toast.

"Kelly? She's too tied to Colorado and your dad. I think she likes snow better than she does me. And meanwhile our biological clocks are ticking," said Rand glumly.

David hooted with laughter. "You're not serious? I didn't think either of you would ever settle down. You're both too headstrong."

Joey looked at his plate. "You're probably right. Maybe I'll take the job, and it'll force her to a decision, maybe a compromise. You got any better ideas? She is, after all, your sister."

"Kelly is as inscrutable as Jon," David shrugged.

Rand leaned back, downing his orange juice. "What do you think about this girl of Jon's? The situation? I mean, what Silas told me last night is rather incredible."

David shook his head. "Leave it to Jon. He's always seemed to land on his feet. And you know he's not one to let a woman turn his head."

"Unlike his brother," Joey added mischievously.

"Well, I have to be true to my title," David grinned smugly. "But Jon is pretty intense about this one."

They ate in silence, then chatted quietly about old times as Howells rejoined them. Looking at the clock, David noticed it was 7:01. "Better get back to my Guinevere," David smiled.

Howells volunteered to keep an eye on Amanda for a while to note any possible reactions.

"I'll accompany you back," David offered.

As the men made their way back down the hall, they met Ralph and Claire in the ICU waiting room. As Howells and Rand stopped to talk to them, David suddenly remembered Zeke.

"Guys, excuse me a minute. I need to wake Zeke up and get him some breakfast."

David hurried down the corridor, letting himself into the doctor's lounge only a few doors down. He saw Zeke lying unconscious on the couch. Laughing, he went to shake him awake, but Zeke didn't respond. David checked his pulse, and noticed that it was weak. He then saw a coffee cup with spilled contents on the floor.

"Zeke!" he shook the man urgently, trying to awaken him. "Zeke, can you hear me?"

Zeke's head rolled from side to side, and he mumbled.

David pulled Zeke up to a sitting position, but Zeke was still incoherent, and fell back against the couch, unresponsive to David's questions.

David ran to the door and called down the hall. "Joey, Dr. Howells, can you come here a minute?"

He saw the two men coming quickly toward him, followed by Ralph and Claire. David returned to Zeke's side, trying to slap him awake. "Come on, Zeke."

The party entered the room, as Rand knelt in front of the groggy man. Lifting his eyelids, Rand examined him, then picked up the coffee cup. Touching the remaining contents in the cup to his finger then his lips, he noted, "He's been drugged."

Ralph suddenly pointed to Zeke's waist. "His gun is missing."

David, his heart suddenly cold, raced out of the room.

Chapter 47

"Please don't hold back," Adam Brownlee blurted out to Stephen Marks.

"Adam, I wish you had been my son. But I'm afraid it is not so. I've tried to be a father to you and to prevent harm to you, but I found out I was not as fortunate in doing so for your sister. I've been trying to shield you from something terrible," Stephen replied, looking up at Connor, his green eyes glistening with unshed tears.

"I did not know about the hold Barnes had over Evelyn until she started opening up and talking to me during her prison visits. At first she confessed her affairs with men, but when I tried to find out the root causes for her constant liaisons, her sexual promiscuity and her jealousies, I was in for the shock of my life.

"I thought I knew Bill Barnes. He was arrogant, self-serving, conniving and cunning, but that he would molest a child, and I never suspected—"

Adam looked at him blankly for several minutes, until the import of his words sunk in. "Evie?" he breathed, disbelievingly. "No, how could that be?"

"Barnes had started early on seducing her with presents and secrets, telling her she was special, that they were soul mates with a secret that no one must ever know. She said that on her twelfth birthday she had full sexual intercourse with William Barnes, the first of a lifetime of his sexual abuse of her."

Jon was transfixed, revolted as Marks gently told the story to the amazed and disbelieving Adam Brownlee. Adam sputtered, "But that couldn't be—I would have known it. She told me everything."

"No, she didn't," Marks responded tenderly. "Barnes threatened her to silence, not to let anyone, even you, especially you, know about their 'special time together'," he said bitterly. "And if you recall, you were hanging around with me a lot in those days. She said you were so happy—she wouldn't tell you. And Barnes had threatened her, withholding favors, money, presents, and saying he would have you dragged out in the desert and abandon you to the coyotes. She believed he would do just that."

Brownlee, tears streaming down his face, spoke. "I always fantasized that you were our dad. I was always babbling to her about how great you were."

Stephen looked at him compassionately. "I wish that had been so. Maybe all this would have turned out differently.

"It took a long time for Evie to open up and start talking to me. She had faithfully kept Barnes' secret, keeping alive this dream of hers that he would marry her and make her his queen. Of course he had no intention of doing that. So she kept turning to other men.

"I was trying to get her to see that there was a life out there much different than what she had made for herself with Barnes and her fantasy lives. I had hoped that what I said was reaching her, particularly when she was faithfully taking her medication.

"About a month ago, she told me about another man she had fallen for, a doctor with a terminally ill wife that would die any day. I tried to make her see that she was repeating her old pattern. Apparently he then rejected her—she kept saying she knew that he really loved her but would not abandon his wife. I began to worry. She became more outrageous in her stories, and they didn't ring true. She said she was taking her medication, but I didn't believe her. I could see the signs."

Brownlee whispered, "Dr. Young. I knew what she was saying could not be true. It was all her own making. But then his wife did die."

Jon's eyes narrowed as he made the connection.

Stephen Marks continued. "Evelyn would come to visit me dressed as a priest, except for those ridiculous high heels she wore. I told her how inappropriate it was for her to dress like that, but she just laughed at me.

"She came in two weeks ago and said she had seen a daytime television talk show about the therapeutic benefits of confronting one's abuser. She was talking wildly that she wanted to see Barnes and stage a confrontation with him. I tried to talk her out of it. I could see no good coming from it, particularly in her state of mind.

"Somehow she managed to set up a meeting Friday in the recreation room. When Amanda left from her visit with me, the guard said for me to stay put; 'the other priest' was going to provide the Eucharist.

"Next thing I knew a guard had escorted Barnes into the room. I was in total shock. We had been kept apart, and I hadn't seen Bill since—since the day of Marjy's funeral. I had no idea he was at the same prison.

"At first we just stared at each other. Then Evelyn walked in dressed in her priest garb.

"She told Barnes that she had planned this meeting, that she had arranged for his transfer to the prison. She didn't reveal exactly how that happened. She informed him that she divulged about their 'affair' to me, and that she wanted him to confess and repent for what he had done to her.

"Barnes, stunned at first, started laughing, telling her she was crazy. He kept on, taunting her and saying she would never find anyone else like him, that they were destined to be together, and that she was nothing except what he made her.

"I could not stop him. He turned on me and told me that I would never see the light of day outside prison if I testified against him." He took a deep, shaky breath. "I didn't really care what he said to me, but I could see Evie shrinking before me, and could see the impact of his words, the power he had over her. I was truly frightened for her.

"It looked like he was winning the argument, until she suddenly pulled herself up, like a queen. I'll never forget the look in her eyes as she said, 'Oh, but I've had several other 'soul mates', William. One of them happened to be your precious son. Yes, we were quite an item. In fact, I didn't use birth control with him, because I liked him so much and wanted to bring another Barnes into the world. See the ring he gave me.'

Stephen paused, the horror of the retelling making him shiver. "A little water, please," he coughed. Jon picked up the pitcher and cup on the bedside table and filled the cup with water, giving it to Marks.

Gratefully, Marks drank the water, handing the cup back. He noted the terror on Brownlee's face. His voice became soft, gentle. "Adam, it all happened so fast. I was in total shock at what was unfolding before me. She had pulled out the communion box. I was horrified, and tried to take it away from her, breaking the flask and cutting my fingers. She tried to knock me away, and my glasses went flying.

"The next thing I knew, Barnes had turned purple with rage, and reached out toward her neck. I tried to push them away from each other. I think he would have strangled her. But suddenly she pushed me down, stepped right up to him and thrust the letter opener in him so quickly, he just deflated and dropped right in front of her.

"She stood there watching him die, and that's all I remember. When I came to I was in the hospital here."

Adam moaned, "Oh, Evie."

Stephen weakly stroked Brownlee's hair as he buried his head in the sheets beside the elder man and sobbed. "That's why I wanted so badly to take the fall. Perhaps if I had been less caught up in my own selfish ends, I could have discovered this sooner, stopped it. I felt Evie was not responsible for her mental illness, and I was ready to take the responsibility for Bill's death."

Stephen continued talking, as if to himself. "She was always so fascinated with medicine and the human body. She talked about her time spent interning with the medical examiner's office in Alabama so that she could learn all she could about forensics and pathology. She apparently knew exactly where to strike to cause the most damage, the quickest death with the least amount of blood spilling. She really could have been a doctor. She boasted to me that she was Dr. Young's best nurse—I'm sure she was."

Jon's head jerked toward Marks, as he registered Marks' last words. "Nurse? So Evelyn Abermarle is a nurse?"

"Yes, she is a registered nurse," Marks finished. "She worked for Dr. Young. He was the doctor she claimed to be involved with."

"Then she could probably get into a hospital without any trouble?" Jon said out loud to himself.

Adam looked up quickly, meeting Jon's eyes and reading Jon's train of thought. "Amanda," he said, his eyes wide. "That's where Evie is going. My God."

"Adam, I need your help," Jon blurted quickly. "Stephen, we must go. We have to get there before she does."

Adam stood up quickly, leaving Marks and following Jon as he raced out of the hospital. The prison warden was walking in the door. "Jon! What is it?" he called.

"I will need law enforcement assistance at Gulfside Regional Hospital. We think our target is heading there," Jon explained breathlessly. "One Evelyn Abermarle, aka Evie Brown, early 30s, red hair, long curly. If she's spotted, have her detained. She's dangerous, may be armed. May be posing as medical staff."

He made it outside and leaped to his car, Adam following closely. They sped off, heading in heavy morning traffic toward Gulfside Regional. Jon pulled out his phone. "Dead," he exclaimed, jerking the end of a cord from the power source and plugging into the end of his phone. He buzzed Zeke's number.

"No answer. That's odd," he mused. Calling Bubba, he asked breathlessly, "Have you heard from Zeke?"

"Not since about 3:00 this morning," Bubba answered, yawning. "He said David was spelling him a couple hours on guarding Amanda."

"Bubba, we got a Code Red. Zeke doesn't answer his phone, and we think Evelyn may be on her way to the hospital, with Amanda as her next target. We're on our way now. See what you can do for me. Get some help there now. I'll try Charlie, too. And by the way, just in case I'm wrong, please notify the sheriff's office to put a guard on Dr. Young."

Jon hung up, not meeting Brownlee's terrified stare, his own heart racing.

Chapter 48

Amanda lay motionless, her eyes closed until she was certain the men had gone. She knew that it hurt much less if she could just remain still. But then the cramping in her joints and the need to cough would become so strong she gave in to it, shifting her weight and reintroducing the shooting pain again.

She longed for oblivion. Her situation seemed so bleak and hopeless. Unless Jon was able to obtain evidence to clear her, she had no future with him. She missed him so much. She felt desolation closing in around her.

There was a commotion outside as a patient was brought in from recovery on a gurney, and the nursing staff was otherwise occupied. Amanda was alone in her thoughts, trying to shut out the memories of her weekend with Jon. I don't know if I can handle being locked away, without him, she thought, frightened.

Amanda was engulfed in searing pain, and was unconscious of the noise outside as staff rushed around treating the new arrival. She lay still and bit her lip, her mind searching for something to divert her attention. She didn't know how much time had passed. She heard someone come in, but didn't open her eyes.

"The doctor ordered something for pain," a female voice said.

"Thanks," she murmured, then stopped. That voice was familiar.

Opening her eyes, she gasped as she saw Eve Brown, dressed in nurse scrubs, standing beside her bed, a hypodermic syringe in hand. "Hello, Evie," Amanda spoke quietly. "How are you?"

Evelyn, surprised, stared at Amanda. "You recognize me?"

"But of course," Amanda responded feebly. "It's funny. I haven't seen you in a while, then all of a sudden we keep running into each other."

Evelyn, startled, countered, a sly smile on her face, "That's true."

"Are you working here now?" Amanda asked sluggishly. "I thought you were still with Dr. Young." The effort to talk tired her.

"Well, I like to stay busy," Evelyn laughed breathlessly. Looking down on Amanda, she noted her discomfort. "Does it hurt much?" she inquired, a glint in her eye.

"It was you at the prison, wasn't it?" Amanda asked tremulously.

Caught completely off guard, Evelyn dropped the syringe and it clattered to the floor. "Yes," she nodded, laughing mirthlessly. "That was a close call. I almost turned around when you called my name."

"Why did you do it?" Amanda suddenly gasped as she moved involuntarily and the pain radiated through her body.

"Because William was such a rotten bastard. He didn't deserve to live, even in prison, for what he did to me. Taking my virginity, promising to make me his wife and heir, stringing me along all these years. Killing him was such a great plan, if I do say so myself. I wrote the letter to you, and I stole the letter opener and ring to plant at the murder scene. I wanted you to go down for it as punishment because you were always coming between Billy and me."

"Billy Barnes and you?" echoed Amanda weakly, coughing and catching her breath. "I didn't know anything about Bill and you."

"You're all he talked about," hissed Evelyn, her face, contorted with hate, coming close to Amanda's. "I did everything I knew to hold on to him. But everything was 'Mandy this' and 'Mandy that'. I was so sick of you. Then Billy was killed—I lost him forever, and it was all your fault.

"Then we found out you were Stephen Marks' daughter, and I could see what it was doing to Adam, tearing him apart. He always had this foolish dream of wanting Marks to be our dad, and God damn it if you weren't in the way again. You've always been in my way. Then you had William arrested."

"So you ran me off the road?" Amanda rasped as she moved slightly and grimaced with agony, crying out weakly. She desperately looked out to the nurse's desk but could see no one else.

"Yes, it was all part of the strategy. That was tricky. I knew they'd be looking for you, but I lucked out with the police scanner. They radioed your location and route. But I didn't quite accomplish it. You're still alive. And I also planned for you to catch me in bed with your fiancée—it was a tight schedule to get there before you. Then I was going to off him right in front of you."

Amanda eyes flashed. "But you ended up with Jon's brother instead?" Amanda finished for her, her voice a little louder.

Evelyn laughed, a brittle sound. "Oh well. Bad break."

Amanda looked at Evelyn fully. "I never realized that you hated me." Amanda paused, fatigued. She attempted another breath, another cough escaping and shooting pain through her. "I thought that time in Tallahassee when I saw you and Judge Kilmer at that restaurant—"

"—that we were a thing. Well, we were," Evelyn replied, triumphant. "But what an ass he turned out to be, not leaving his wife for me, wanting to keep everything so hush-hush. Of course," she added slyly, "he's had his uses lately." She laughed again harshly. "I thought he was going to have a cow when we spied you at that restaurant. He was hoping you didn't see him."

"And you also tried to snare Alan Young, didn't you?" Amanda continued, more alert, trying to keep her engaged in conversation. "He told me you were coming on to him. Just what did you do to Shelby?"

Evelyn stared at her, her eyes narrowing to slits. "I could tell Alan wanted me—what man wouldn't?—but he had this huge sense of honor to her. He wouldn't even touch me, although I tried hard to wear him down. So I went to his house for a confrontation."

Evelyn's eyes stared off unseeingly. "She was there alone. I thought I had given her enough to kill her. Guess I miscalculated—she didn't die the first time around. So I knew I had to finish the job, and there was only one thing to do."

Amanda stared her down. "And what was that?"

As Evelyn bent down to pick up the fallen syringe, she purposefully drove her left hand down on Amanda's shoulder, slamming her weight to Amanda's bandaged collarbone. Amanda screamed, but Evelyn covered Amanda's mouth with her hand. Evelyn looked at her in mock sympathy as she straightened up, and jammed her elbow into Amanda's side into the area of her fractured ribs. Amanda, tears in her eyes at the sudden excruciating pain, doubled forward and began gasping, choking, tasting blood, not able to breathe. She tried to scream, but could not summon sound.

Evelyn said softly, "There, there, now. You just relax. I gave her the same thing I'm about to give you. A little cardiac arrest. I added a little morphine to yours. I tested it on a subject just a few days ago. It works really well. You'll just go to sleep and never wake up, that is, if you don't have a nasty reaction first. There's a note on your chart—you really shouldn't have any of this. But that's OK. After a bit, while you wish you were dead, you won't feel a thing. Ever again."

Evelyn quickly took the cap off the needle of the syringe and expertly placed it into the portal of the IV bag above Amanda's head. Amanda reached for her, but found her left arm still tied to the bed. Lunging and howling in pain, Amanda found her right hand free, and gathering force, somehow found strength, balled her hand into a fist and hit Evelyn in the jaw, knocking her away. Surprised and off balance, Evelyn fell against the window heavily.

Amanda tasted blood on her lips and struggled for breath. Seeing the needle still stuck into the portal out of reach, Amanda in panic cantilevered her body and yanked the IV tube out of her arm, feeling a searing in her side and blinding pain in her shoulder as the bone separated from the action. She screamed weakly, almost blacking out from the pain, fighting for oxygen.

Evelyn staggered against the wall and righted herself, coming back toward Amanda, a vicious look on her face as she fumbled in her pocket.

A sudden movement at the doorway made Evelyn turn around suddenly with a gun in her hand. "Stop right there," she ordered, as David Connor came toward her and stood next to the bed. He froze as she leveled the pistol at him.

"You again!" she yelled. Amanda looked on helplessly, unable to scream, coughing up a bloody phlegm.

Someone shouted, the loud report of a gun was heard, and she saw David fall to the floor as Evelyn spun around, facing her, suddenly coming toward her, gun in hand pointed at her at point-blank range.

Another shot was heard, and suddenly Evelyn's eyes turned glassy and she fell heavily across Amanda's injured body, the gun clattering to the floor.

Fantastic pain exploded throughout Amanda's body, as lights danced before her eyes. She heard someone screaming, then all was black.

David sprang up from the floor and sprinted to the bed. He rolled the fallen woman over, quickly checking for a pulse. "She's dead," he announced, as Charles Petrino stood behind him, holstering his pistol. "Help me get her off Amanda," David ordered tersely.

"Are you OK?" Petrino asked David.

"Fine, thanks for the warning." They quickly lifted the dead woman off and placed her on the floor. David went around to the other side of Amanda's bed.

Pandemonium broke forth outside her room. Joey Rand pushed his way through as law enforcement came from nowhere and swarmed the nurses' station. Staring at the body on the floor in disbelief, he was brought back to the present by David's voice. "I need you, Joey," David yelled, as he examined Amanda.

Sheriff's investigators and deputies were mingling with emergency staff milling around in chaos outside the room. Joey examined the unconscious girl. "We need to get her to surgery, stat," he directed. Turning to Petrino, he demanded, "Clear a path—we're coming through."

Charlie turned and ordered people aside as a nurse came up with a gurney. Rand, David and the nurse grabbed the ends of the sheet under Amanda and gingerly placed the girl on the gurney, wheeling her out of the room, out the side door to the surgical suite. Joey reached over and pulled a pair of surgical shears off the table. In seconds he had the bandages stripped off Amanda, and was examining her injuries. David, having grabbed a blood pressure cuff, was checking her pressure. He announced, "Pressure is dropping."

Silas walked into surgery. Rand told him, "We need to go in now. There's internal bleeding from the trauma. I'll need your very best anesthesiologist, although I don't think I can wait. I've done this before, but we've got a girl with a punctured lung and hypersensitivity to drugs. David, I need you to assist."

Meanwhile, Ralph and the others had seen David bolting toward the ICU. and only moments later heard the sound of gunshots. Ralph told the others, "Stay here," as he looked carefully out into the hallway and disappeared.

As Ralph started to enter the ICU doorway, he was stopped and grabbed by sheriff's deputies. "Whoa," he said, as one of the deputies recognized him.

"Hey, Mr. Carmichael," the deputy ordered. "I wouldn't go in there if I were you."

"But Amanda's in there," Ralph yelled excitedly, grabbing the door and defying them.

He caught a glimpse of the two doctors pushing a gurney with Amanda out the other door, as Silas entered behind him. The nurses were clamoring from behind the station. Four deputies were trying to secure the area, but Ralph pushed his way forward, finding Petrino standing in Amanda's room over the body of Evelyn Abermarle.

"Damn!" exclaimed Ralph. "What happened?" Looking at the body, he recognized her. "What's she doing here? What's happened to Amanda? Where are they taking her?"

A hulking muscular man came up to them. Ralph recognized him as the sheriff's chief investigator Bruce Williams. Nodding to Ralph, he turned to Petrino.

"OK, Charlie," Bruce growled. "Start talking. What happened here?"

Charlie cleared his throat. "I had just driven down from Mainville to check on Amanda, but had received no answer when I called on the ICU wall phone outside the door there. We had relayed the information regarding getting backup here, but I didn't see anyone outside yet. I tried the door and it opened. I walked in, and David was heading toward Amanda's room, his back to me.

"I followed him, and saw Evelyn there—the deceased—sticking a needle into Amanda's IV. Amanda tried to scream and reached over and whacked the hell out of her. As David moved forward to try to stop her, the deceased pulled a handgun and pointed it at David.

"I yelled at David to get down, and I shot her once. Then she spun around to face Amanda. I was afraid that her next move was to kill Amanda, so I shot again." He paused. "She's dead."

Turning to face the investigator, Charlie asked, "How did you guys get here so fast? My men had just gotten the call from Bubba, and I had sent someone to the hospital to check on Alan Young and Judge Kilmer. I was already on my way here, and put on the blue light to get here as fast as I could."

"We got a call from the FBI for immediate assistance and a BOLO for a woman matching that description," the investigator said, pointing toward the room where the fallen woman lay. "We were on our way in when all this apparently went down."

"What about Amanda?" Ralph demanded.

"They took her to surgery. We don't know her condition yet," Williams replied. "We'll need to take formal statements. Where's the guy who you said saw this?"

"He is prepping for surgery as we speak," a voice spoke behind Ralph. Turning, he saw that it was Silas Fleischer.

Ralph cried, "Amanda?"

"She's bleeding internally; her pressure's plummeted. They have to go in." Fleischer spoke softly to Ralph. "You said you were her surrogate? It would help if you sign the consents for us, but Dr. Rand has deemed it an emergency. I had to pull a surgical team, and will suit up myself if Joey needs me." He cleared his throat. "It doesn't look good."

Ralph reeled as if he was about to faint. Fleischer took him by the arm, steadying him. "David and Joey are in there with her. She's in excellent hands. It is best if you go and wait in the surgical waiting room. I promise to let you know the minute I get word of Amanda's status."

Williams looked at Petrino. "Charlie, why don't you go with him? Just don't leave the premises."

Charlie and Ralph walked back to the open doctor's lounge, where an officer was attempting to take a statement from a still dazed and groggy Zeke, while placing the cup and some of the sponged contents in a plastic evidence baggie. Ralph explained what he knew to Claire and Dr. Howells, as hospital personnel worked on Zeke.

Zeke was replying, still woozy, "Damn it. I knew the nurse that brought me that coffee looked familiar. I'm so stupid."

Ralph placed his hand on the man's arm. "Don't beat yourself up."

"But Amanda could die," Zeke said soberly, "and I let the perpetrator drug me and take my gun."

Petrino replied comfortingly, "Ralph's right. It's not your fault."

Claire sat, mute and numb, as Ralph stroked her hair and whispered to her. She began crying, and Ralph held her, looking grave.

Jon Connor burst in, followed by Adam Brownlee. "What's happened?" he demanded. "Where's Amanda? They won't let me in ICU, and sent me here."

Petrino stepped up and spoke lowly to him. "She's in surgery, Jon. Evie Brown tried to kill her."

Brownlee clutched at Petrino's arm. "And Evie?" he cried.

"She's dead," Charlie replied bluntly.

Brownlee collapsed into a chair. "Oh, my God."

Jon explained, "This is Evie's brother, the Rev. Adam Brownlee. We just obtained the evidence that she did in fact killed Barnes. We feared her next stop was here, and tried to get here." He looked compassionately at the stricken Brownlee. "We weren't in time."

Then turning to the group, he asked urgently, "How is Amanda? What can you tell me?"

Ralph replied, "They've taken her into emergency surgery. It's bad."

"Where's David?" Connor demanded.

"He's with her," Petrino answered.

Connor sat heavily in a chair across from the group. He held his head in his hands. "Amanda, you have to live," he muttered. "God, please let her live."

Chapter 49

As the ER nurse wheeled Zeke out, he put his hand out, touching Jon's shoulder. "I'm so sorry, Jon. I let you down."

Ralph quietly explained to Jon how Evelyn had drugged Zeke and stolen his gun.

Jon nodded quietly. He echoed, "It's not your fault, Zeke. You're a good agent."

As Zeke disappeared, Jon looked over at Brownlee, whose face was in his hands. He walked over to him.

"Adam, I'm sorry for your sake."

"No, it is I who am sorry. I should have figured it all out and stopped it, stopped her. If so, maybe none of this would have happened, and maybe Evie would still be alive, and Amanda—" he left the sentence unfinished.

Jon felt sorry for him, realizing that Adam had in the matter of a few hours suffered a series of brutal revelations regarding his only living kin, and had now lost her. Gripped in the fear of his own potential loss, Jon could think of no words of comfort. He squeezed Brownlee's shoulder.

Turning, he walked out of the waiting room, and wandered aimlessly down the halls, past the law enforcement, staff and visitors.

He almost collided with a nun. Apologizing, he stopped, looking through open double doors to a chapel. He stared for what seemed a small eternity before walking in. He walked to the front railing, watching a young girl, assisted by a woman, her mother perhaps, light a candle before a marble statue of the Virgin. He found a seat in the far corner, alone with his thoughts.

He thought about his own decline in piety. He had found it awfully convenient to turn his back on his already shallow and simplistic beliefs when he found his friend Andy brutally murdered. He had convinced himself he didn't miss the Sunday services, the friendship of the priests he had known, the glorious music of the organ and choirs, the security of believing in a God in heaven.

Then he had met Amanda during the Bureau's continuing investigation of a large embezzlement scheme. Initially a suspect, she had intrigued him. He had found himself unable to believe in her complicity, and was drawn to the complexity of her. As the case had unfolded and her innocence was confirmed, he found himself in love with her. He had found her outwardly tough, unyielding, but inwardly wary and withdrawn, reticent about approaching a relationship after the tragic loss of her husband.

He enjoyed the badinage with her, watching the layers of self-protection she had constructed around herself slowly peel away. Through her devotion to the church, its music, its children, and the fulfillment she seemed to experience, he had come to realize the dimensions of her faith in God and what he was missing.

When she had initially accepted his proposal of marriage, he felt a momentary thrill to think she was his. But just as quickly she was gone. Discouraged, he resolved to start from scratch, to prove his love to her. So her coming to him without reservation was nothing short of a miracle, and he thought they had found their paradise.

Then she walked away again, with the shadow of arrest looming large over her. He had keenly felt her anguish as she left him, had heard it in her voice moments before the accident. Now she lay on an operating table, her life at the mercy of God. A God of whom I am not worthy to ask anything. A God in whom her own faith had struggled during the last years, particularly the last months, as she fought anger, bitterness and hatred against those who had cruelly used her.

He stared ahead of him unseeing. Gradually he focused, noting a figure kneeling in prayer and lighting a candle. The figure stood, and he recognized Brownlee, who saw him.

Brownlee approached him and sat down a few feet from him. They were silent a while. The Brownlee spoke.

"You know he is God, whether we believe in him or not, whether we understand his ways or not, whether we serve him or not. Our faith actually does nothing for him, but everything for us."

Jon said nothing, but pondered his words. Brownlee went on. "Jesus said that those who are well need no physician. We go through life never caring about God except for using him as perennial justification for our actions. That is, until we really need him. But he doesn't just exist when we need him; it's just that we don't notice he's there until then."

They sat silently several minutes. Finally, Jon spoke. "I know it is hard for you, Adam. I'm sorry for your loss."

Brownlee stood up. "I'm praying for you and Amanda," he whispered, putting his hand on Jon's shoulder before walking away. Jon watched him leave, recognizing Claire a couple rows back in the tiny chapel.

Standing, he moved to where she was and sat down beside her, taking her hand.

Claire said softly, her eyes straight ahead, "You know, if it wasn't for Amanda, Ralph and I wouldn't be together right now." She paused. "I remember talking to her the Sunday we got back from our honeymoon. The strain of the decision she had made weighed heavily with her. She was afraid to admit it, but she described to me how much she loves you, Jon. She was so afraid of giving in, just to lose you."

Claire squeezed his hand. "Dr. Howells said Amanda was despondent when he saw her this morning. She actually asked for painkillers, saying she 'didn't want to feel anymore.' He was afraid she had given up, and she didn't seem to care that she had miraculously escaped death. I know what it was. She was afraid there was no future with you.

"But I believe her faith is stronger than her discouragement, Jon. She has to make it."

Jon nodded solemnly. "I also want to believe that."

After a while, Claire stood. "I'm going back—can't leave Ralph alone too long or he'll get himself into trouble."

"I'll go with you."

They walked down the hall to the waiting room. Jon sat in a corner away from the others and became lost in reverie about Amanda, his face somber as he waited.

After a while, Jon excused himself, walked out in the hallway and dialed Bubba, summarizing the events.

"Well, thanks to Boyer's help, we're already executing a search warrant at this Evelyn's house," Bubba said.

"That was fast," Jon replied, amazed.

"This place is a pharmacy. She had everything she needed to set up shop for herself. She apparently had a fetish for painkillers, particularly injectibles. And there was a white Persian cat in the house."

"The cat hair Della found," Jon exclaimed.

"Della drove up to be here and gather evidence."

"You know, I think she is sweet on you."

"Shit, you say," George whistled softly.

"No shit," Jon responded. "But you need some spit and polish. You're the consummate Southern male—more solicitous of your hunting dogs than your women. You need to woo her."

"A good hunting dog is worth his weight in gold," Bubba mumbled.

"I give up."

"Hey, Jon? Amanda will be OK, won't she?"

"I don't know. Hope springs eternal." Jon spied David, still in scrubs, coming out the door from the surgery suite. "Gotta go—the doctor has just come out."

Jon quickly followed David into the waiting room, where the others saw him and stood, crowding around him.

David looked haggard as he gazed at the group before him. "Glad we went in when we did. It was messy—had to repair the damage done to the clavicle and duct-tape the blood vessel. Joey was really worried we might lose her."

"Duct tape?" Howells echoed, incredulous.

"Relax, Doc," smiled David. "Just a figure of speech. The lung held, and we think we've patched the damage. That break is pretty bad, so Joey contrived some brace to hold it together. He's brilliant—I wouldn't have thought of it. She'll have the most beautiful little scar, a masterpiece of my own creation. Now we wait to see."

David looked into their expectant faces. "Seriously, there are no promises yet. Doc, I believe Joey wanted you to come back so we could discuss her recovery. The rest of you need to go grab a bite. It will be a while before she can see visitors." He stared at his brother. "Including you."

Jon bit his lip. "David, when she wakes up, I'd like to be there to tell her we have the evidence to clear her."

Howells murmured, "Thank God."

David replied, "And you can tell the investigators that I walked into the room in time to hear the red-head's last words to Amanda. I'll be happy to make a statement when I finish here."

As David and Howells left, Ralph and Claire kissed, and Jon collapsed into a chair, weak.

Charlie slapped Jon on the back. "You have to have a strong heart to love Mandy," Charlie murmured.

Jon looked at him gratefully. "Thank you for saving David and Amanda in there. You know, I've almost lost her three times, and you or Fred delivered her from danger."

Petrino was grave. "Maybe in some small way I'm being allowed to make up for not being there to prevent Andy's murder." He added quietly, "Amanda's special, a good friend. I just don't know what we'd all do if she wasn't there. I hope we don't have to find out."

Their eyes met, before Charlie turned away.

Ralph walked up to them, trying to smile. "Let me treat you to lunch. Jon here didn't eat last night as it was."

Chapter 50

Amanda awakened slowly. She felt something uncomfortable sticking her shoulder, but she couldn't move. She drifted along peacefully, her mind unladen.

She heard a voice calling her name. No, don't bother me, she thought irritably. I like it here.

But the voice persisted. It sounded familiar to her, painfully so, although she did not know why. "No," she whispered.

"Amanda, it's safe to come out now," the faceless voice spoke into her ear.

She opened her eyes into the blinding lights, disoriented. She felt a stab of pain in her left side, but her arms were too heavy to move. Her right hand felt another hand and squeezed it weakly.

"I'm here," Dr. Howells' voice answered, as he squeezed her hand in return. "You are driving this old man to an earlier grave. I insist that you change your lifestyle and slow down, for my sake if not yours."

Dr. Rand's face floated into view, then David Connor's. She whispered, confused as some faint memory crossed her mind, "Dragons?"

David hooted. "You're a free woman, Amanda."

She drifted to sleep again.

Some time later she opened her eyes. The light was not so bright. She looked into the brilliant eyes of Jon. He bent down and kissed her unhurt cheek.

"I love you," he whispered. He gave her a heart-stopping smile.

"I love you back," she croaked, before closing her eyes again.

After some time, she stirred again. The others, noticing she had awakened, gave a glad cry and surrounded her. She could not focus on faces, but felt bathed in a warm glow as they chattered and she listened uncomprehendingly. Gradually her senses sharpened. She saw Jon standing there, silent, gazing at her. She whispered, "Jon?"

"I'm here," he bent down to her.

She could hear Ralph's voice somewhere, but closed her eyes, still tired.

She didn't know how much time elapsed. She opened her eyes, and Jon's face floated back into focus. "We've got to stop meeting like this," he murmured, his hand on her cheek.

"'Come live with me, and be my love,'" she struggled, softly, feebly, but determinedly.

He caught his breath. Was she proposing to him? He finished the quote, "'And we will all the pleasures prove that valleys, groves, hills and fields, woods, or sleepy mountain yields.'"

"I'll take that as a yes then," she mumbled with great difficulty.

A couple of days later Jon walked into a private hospital room, to find Amanda sitting up uncomfortably in bed laughing at one of David's jokes. His eyes flashed as he met her gaze then looked over at David with jealous glints. David threw up his hands in mock surrender.

"OK, OK, so I'm flirting with your girl," he confessed, a wicked grin on his face.

Jon's eyes smoldered momentarily, until he saw Amanda's look. His heart melted at the sight of her liquid golden eyes on him. He asked her quietly, "How are you feeling this morning?"

She turned her smile upon him, mesmerizing him. "Better, now that you're here. Your brother is insufferable with his bag of lawyer jokes." She grimaced. "It hurts to laugh."

Jon grinned at her predicament. "He and Dad trade them like baseball cards. You can never win with them."

"I have questions," she suddenly sobered, taking a painful breath. "How did you end up at the accident with me?"

"That was me," David interjected. "I just happened to be on my way to Destin, saw the accident, and was there when Fred pulled you out of the water. I rode with you in the ambulance to the hospital. I told Jon here later about what you said in the ambulance."

"I knew the priest looked familiar," Amanda divulged, "but when I glimpsed the driver of the car that forced me off the road, I thought I was crazy."

"It was Evelyn Abermarle, probably known to you as Evie Brown," Jon confirmed. "She was Adam Brownlee's twin sister."

"Twin?" Amanda echoed disbelievingly. "I have known her from the time she was one of Alan's nurses. I never put together that she and Adam were kin, much less twins."

Jon nodded. "She killed Dr. Young's wife, and William Barnes, Sr. She almost killed Alan Young and you. Not only that, she took out a major henchman for the mob. She apparently left other victims back in Australia."

David intervened excitedly. "How in the world did you muster the energy to knock her away, Amanda?"

"I don't know," Amanda responded somberly. "Suddenly in a cold moment of clarity I was angrier than I think I'd ever been in my life. I just couldn't let her get away with snuffing me out without a fight. Ralph would say the bad cop asserted itself."

The two men laughed heartily. She added breathlessly, "Besides, she said she had wanted me to catch her making love to my boyfriend. That was the final straw. And she meant to kill Jon afterward, right in front of me."

"So she really was after Jon that night?" David expelled his breath angrily. "What a sick woman."

"Yes," agreed Jon softly, "she was a very sick woman, with a terrible childhood secret. Thanks to Fred, David and Joey for saving your life."

"And Charlie," Amanda breathed.

"Particularly Charlie," Jon said fervently. "He has rescued you so much, I'm afraid I'll never be equal to him." He looked at her penetratingly.

"That's true," Amanda agreed, biting her lip to keep from smirking. Jon caught it and flushed with jealousy.

"But you're the one who followed the clues and cleared me," Amanda added, her voice almost a whisper. "Otherwise, even if I survived, I would be on my way to a jail cell."

She shivered, and Jon squeezed her hand. "It was more Bubba and his girl Della. Her hair and fiber analysis is what clinched the matter."

"Della? The FDLE crime lab woman?" Amanda queried. "Really? I never thought any law enforcement would come to my aid, after all the grief I've given them over the years."

"And again justice has prevailed," a booming voice spoke behind Jon. Turning, he saw Ralph and Claire coming through the door, a large bouquet of yellow roses in Ralph's hands.

"How beautiful," smiled Amanda. "I'm glad to see you two."

"We're glad to see you too," Claire replied affectionately, kissing her on the cheek as Ralph placed the flowers on her bedside table and grabbed her hand.

"And I have good news. Can't wait for Dr. Howells to tell you. Alan is out of his coma, and Dr. Cardet thinks he is going to be OK. The kids are ecstatic. We took them to see him yesterday, and he is rallying."

Ralph sobered. "It may take some time to determine whether there will be any long-lasting effects. Dr. Cardet is hopeful."

"That is great news," Amanda breathed.

"And Senator Whitmore's aide Richard Dover was arrested and charged with racketeering and murder," Jon provided quietly. "The Bureau laid a trap for him by setting up a meeting between Whitmore and Knox. I don't know all the details, but apparently Dover and several crime bosses were netted in the sting."

"Oh," Amanda's eyes grew wide. "So the senator had nothing to do with the attempts on Knox's life?"

"No. He had to play along for a while so that the Bureau could gather the evidence against Dover. Your father-in-law gave an exclusive interview to your buddy Michael Knox, disclosing all about his fathering Andrew." He smiled. "Knox was pretty gentle, relatively speaking, given his history of 'balls to the walls' reporting."

She looked at Jon sadly. "How is the senator taking all this?"

"He says he feels younger, now that the burden of carrying that secret is gone. He is surprised at the positive responses from his constituents and the general public from the disclosure, and he is gratified that the FBI managed to catch Dover and his compatriots." Jon gazed at her. "He wants to see you, has been calling me every day to check on you."

"You haven't been propositioning anyone today, have you?" Ralph demanded, his eyes twinkling.

"Actually," she mumbled, "I'm grateful for the visit by the clerk of court. I didn't know she provided house calls, or I guess 'hospital calls'."

Jon grinned. "Your law partner has some real political clout, getting an elected official to make a personal visit to assist with an application for marriage license."

Ralph hooted with laughter. "She owed me for some legal advice I gave her a few years ago, and I finally called in the favor. She said she'd take care of it personally. So now you owe me."

"Thanks, man," Jon clapped him on the back.

Ralph grinned. "Oh, by the way, Charlie sends his love. He's up to his neck in alligators, helping Bruce Williams and the Bureau try to tie up the loose ends on all these cases. Fred said he would be by later to see you.

"Oh, and Alan asked about you. His short-term memory is cloudy, and he's still quite weak. But he wanted you to know he is grateful that he is cleared of wrongdoing. Guess we'll have to return that retainer," he sighed melodramatically. "Trust Amanda to solve the case and lose the client."

"Oh, hush," exclaimed Claire as she pinched Ralph's arm good-naturedly.

"Adam Brownlee made an early morning visit this morning," Amanda informed Jon. "I feel for him. He has no other family now."

"Let's give him David," Jon rejoined wickedly, casting a sidelong glance at his brother.

Amanda quelled him with a look. "I have great plans for David," she announced loftily. "You leave him alone."

Robert Kimball, FBI Bureau Chief, walked into the room. Connor introduced him all around. "Congratulations on your promotion and relocation," he told Kimball. "Pensacola is a nice town, just the right size. And you'll get along well with Greg Boyer, who has decided he likes the area as well."

"So what about you?" Kimball asked. "I didn't appreciate the sheaf of papers you left on my desk, particularly that letter of resignation."

Amanda looked at Jon questioningly. "I'm relocating in a sense also," Jon explained. "I left my notes, final reports and affidavits on the ongoing investigation, plus a request for one month's sick leave, followed by one month of annual leave. The Bureau can cut a check for the rest. Oh, yeah, and my notice that I'll be leaving the Bureau," Jon added.

Kimball cleared his voice, addressing Amanda. "You know the Bureau doesn't want to lose him, and I sure as hell could use him."

"But I'm sure," Jon nodded, smiling. "It feels righter than rain."

Kimball grinned at Jon. "You're beginning to sound more and more like Bubba. This Southern dialect is rubbing off on you."

Connor smiled. "Amanda and I are getting married."

"Congratulations!" Kimball cried, pumping Jon's hand. "All you guys must have been bitten at the same time. Bubba is going steady with Della at FDLE, and Zeke's sweet on some nurse he met here in the hospital."

"We just need to find my brother David someone. He's hanging around my woman way too much for my comfort," Jon smiled, looking at David slyly. "I admit I'm a little jealous. He's been talking of moving somewhere around here and buying a house."

Kimball laughed. "Wonders never cease." His smiled died as he turned to business again. "Two questions about the case, if you don't mind filling me in. How did this Abermarle woman set up the kill on Dr. Young's wife?"

"Petrino found out about that," Jon replied. "When law enforcement was doing interviews at the hospital, they could not locate the intensive care nurse on duty. She was signed in, but was nowhere to be found.

"Petrino knew this woman, and he and Bruce Williams located her at home. She had been called and told an old annual leave request had been approved. She was confused, but took the time off.

"Then Charlie showed a picture of Abermarle around the hospital, and an orderly recognized her, had known her from when she worked there before. He said she was there that night, and told him she was filling in for the charge nurse. He didn't see her after that, and never thought any more about it until he saw the picture.

"Toxicology showed amounts of lidocaine in the blood, way higher than normal therapeutic levels, and the Young woman had not been prescribed any. Della found a couple boxes of lidocaine vials tucked into a pocket of the duffel bag. It's amazing how someone could just slip into a hospital, commit the deed and slip back out.

"That was apparently the game plan for Alan Young. It seems he spied Abermarle at the hospital, and wanted to tell Amanda his findings, hopefully before she got away. This Evie got to him before Amanda got there.

"But why did she off Bo Bronowski?" Jon asked.

"We haven't figured that out, but we got DNA that matches her there, and the autopsy showed the same levels, with some morphine."

"Amanda was slated for the same treatment. Thank God Amanda was alert enough to knock Evelyn away and snatch the IV tube out, or she wouldn't be here."

"You're a lucky man, Jon," Kimball murmured.

"Don't I know it," breathed Jon, his hand reaching for and squeezing Amanda's. "But why did this Judge Kilmer let Evelyn out of jail?"

"That's pretty interesting," Kimball responded. "We have gotten a voluntary statement from him. There's enough there for a judicial qualifications commission inquiry, and possible criminal charges. His wife is suing him for divorce, so he's already having a taste of hell.

"Kilmer had an affair with Abermarle a few years back, and ever so often she reappeared. But he was nervous about his wife's discovering his indiscretions.

"Turns out Evelyn had done some sleuthing on her own, and discovered and actually proved that the judge's father was not Kilmer at all. Kilmer's mother had an affair with Dr. Young's father before she married Kilmer, who couldn't have children, and the judge is the son of Young, Sr., and therefore Alan Young's half-brother. The senior Kilmer knew, but raised him as his own.

"Evelyn had a huge file at her home, which Bubba found when the search warrant was executed. And apparently Kilmer's mother had been quietly paying her hush money for a couple years."

"My heavens," whispered Amanda, and Ralph and Claire looked shocked.

"Evelyn threatened to expose all about the affair and Kilmer's true parentage unless he helped her. When Shelby Young died he was convinced that the doctor killed her so that he and Evelyn could be together. He had the State Attorney do up the arrest warrants. He had decided he wasn't going to let the doctor get away with murder, and at the same time he would have leverage against Evelyn to keep her quiet, with her lover in jail on murder charges and him as the presiding judge."

Amanda spoke up. "Truth is that Evelyn threw herself at Dr. Young, and he said no. He felt so badly, thinking that perhaps through kindness to her he had led Evelyn to believe he was interested in her romantically. He was aware of her emotional problem, although apparently not the extent of it or her diagnosis, else he would not have hired her. But Evelyn apparently thought that if she eliminated the wife, his feelings would change."

"That was one sick woman," Ralph said quietly.

"But the frightening thing is that she got away with it for so long, and almost succeeded again," David replied gravely.

"How did she know where Amanda was in order to run her off the road?" Kimball asked.

"Police scanner," Jon responded. "She knew law enforcement would be looking for Amanda, after the evidence Evelyn planted at Barnes' murder. She just waited alongside the road until she saw Amanda's car coming."

"But she could have been killed too," David interjected.

"We'll never know what was going through her mind—whether she didn't care if she survived a crash, or thought she was indestructible. She was almost successful."

"Man," murmured Kimball. "Man, oh man. Are you sure you want to leave the Bureau? Life could get boring for you."

Jon laughed. "Not around Mainville, apparently. And Amanda and I have decided we could use a little boredom in our lives, although I cannot imagine ever being bored with Amanda."

Amanda gazed at him. "Not so far," she confirmed. "But I hope the relationship gets safer. I'm tired of hospital beds."

They all laughed. "How are you doing?" Kimball asked Amanda.

Amanda replied, "Getting stronger every day."

Connor added, "I get to take her home day after tomorrow if all goes well. I want to be there for her, because it will take her several weeks to recover, and she'll need help. Dr. Howells has already warned that I have my work cut out for me trying to slow her down. I'm going to help Ralph out at the office a little, then I'm accepting that position in Destin."

"You look happy, and I'm happy for you," Kimball said wistfully.

"I am happy," Jon replied. "Love has a way of rearranging your life like that. I wrote down a phone number in case you need to reach me—just leave a message."

"Where are you staying?" Kimball asked, curious.

"My place," Amanda responded, a flush stealing across her cheeks.

Jon kissed her fingers lovingly. "I'm not giving her a chance to back out this time. The next hurdle—meet my parents."

Kimball crossed himself, grinning at Connor. "Poor girl. Or," he paused dramatically, "is it poor parents?"

They all laughed, as Amanda rolled her eyes. "I get no respect," she told David in mock disgust.

Kimball said, "Well, I gotta get on to work—someone has to run this show. I feel I already know you, so I'm so glad to finally meet you, Amanda."

He shook hands with them and took his leave, David following him out. Jon turned serious and looked around at the room's occupants, nodding toward the door. Ralph suddenly blurted out, "Claire, we need to find a vase for these flowers. Let's check the gift shop."

As quickly as they had come, they all left, leaving Jon and Amanda alone. He asked her, "Do you feel like sitting up?"

"Of course," she assented, curious at his request.

At the moment her feet dangled from the bed, Jon knelt in front of her. She looked at him in wonder. "I know this is the wrong hand, but it will have to do for now," he murmured as he slipped a ring on the finger of her right hand.

She was shocked. "My ring!"

"I managed to get it released from evidence and cleaned for a very important occasion," he said softly.

She smiled tremulously. "It's been through so much, just like us."

Jon remained kneeling. "I want to marry you, Amanda."

"I want to marry you too, Jon. But where's Fred?"

"Why do we need Fred?" Jon smiled, confused.

"Because every time I accept a proposal from you something traumatic happens. Fred has saved my life twice, so . . . ."

He laughed at her as she squeezed his hand. She whispered, "So let's get this done as soon as possible."

He looked deep into her eyes. "I'm so glad you said that. I don't know how you feel about long engagements, but I know how you feel about 'living in sin' and that you want to set an example for your kids at the church. I'm not letting you get away from me again. I wondered if you might feel up to tying the knot at St. Catherine's when you get out of the hospital, on your way home?"

Amanda's eyes misted. "Oh," she breathed. "That would be great. You wouldn't mind doing it there?"

"No, I'd do it right here and now if Florida law would allow us," he kissed her. "That three-day waiting period is a pain," he grinned. "Ralph says he thinks he can get it waived. I would really like to have a church wedding. But are you sure you won't be disappointed with a small private service? And St. Catherine's won't dredge up bad memories, will it?"

"It's home to me. I would like that, if you don't mind," she murmured, her face glowing. "I'll be happy just to be finally married to you. But," she faltered, "do you think we can get Father Anselm to marry us on such short notice? I mean, there's the license, and Father requires a counseling session."

The door burst open and Doctor Howells, Ralph and Claire came tumbling in. "It's all arranged," Howells boomed. "We were counting on your saying yes."

Amanda laughed heartily. "Were you listening in at the door?" She turned to Jon, who was smiling broadly. "We have really got to get out of here soon. The privacy sucks."

Chapter 51

That day and the next were a whirlwind of activity. Drs. Rand and Howells showed up early the next morning. Rand examined her carefully.

"You had a touch of fever last night, but it appears to be gone. You still have a bit of cough, but the lungs sound clear today. I want you to complete those IV antibiotics today, then we'll see," he was all seriousness. He probed her shoulder gingerly, and she winced as he checked the wrist. "That's all looking good."

He straightened up and glanced at Howells, his eyes twinkling. "I don't think you need to be getting married, and certainly no sex, for the next six months."

"Well, that ain't happening," Amanda replied vehemently. "You're fired." She met his eyes, her own dancing with devilment.

Howells asked, "How are you feeling?"

"I'm anxious," she said truthfully. "There's much to do, and I'm so excited. I don't want anything to impede our plans, now that we're so close. I've been at this point with Jon twice already."

Joey squeezed her right hand. "You really need to take it slow for awhile, Amanda. I don't want you overexcited or careless. Those injuries are nothing to sneeze at, and I don't want any complications." He grinned. "I have a reputation to maintain, particularly if I'm going to relocate down here."

"You are?" Amanda exclaimed.

"Thinking hard about it," he smiled. He glanced at Howells. "I'll leave you two. Later."

Howells sat down beside the bed, taking her hand. "Jon said he'd be here as soon as he could. Ralph and he had a couple of appointments this morning."

"Appointments?" she echoed. "We have to see Father Anselm this afternoon. The application for the marriage license is complete. Ralph is working on waiving the three-day waiting period. Arnold said that if necessary he would provide the statutory counseling for us this evening."

Howells squeezed her hand. "Just calm down, Amanda. It will all work out."

The door opened, and a short man in suit came striding in. Amanda's eyes widened in shock. "Judge Moore?" she was astounded.

"Good morning, Amanda," he came up to the bed, as Howells moved aside. "We have a bit of business to discuss," he replied gravely.

"I'm honored that you would visit me, sir. What can I do for you, Your Honor?" she cleared her throat nervously.

"I think it's more what I can do for you," he smiled, as Ralph and Jon entered the room. "These men came waltzing into my office early this morning demanding that I waive the three-day waiting period for you to get married to this stranger here," he jerked his head toward Jon. "They maintained that you were not able to make the request in person. I had to confirm their story and see for myself if there is good cause."

She blushed. "I'm so sorry to trouble you, sir . . . ."

He took her hand. "Are you sure you want to marry this guy?" he smiled down at her. "As many divorces as you've handled over the years, do you think it advisable for me to allow you to marry without a reminder course, counseling and all that jazz?" his eyes were twinkling.

"I'm sure," she looked over at Jon, and her tone left no doubt.

"He threatened that if I didn't grant the waiver you two were going to live in sin until he could marry you," the judge laughed, as Jon flushed.

"That is true," she confirmed, blushing too.

"Well, we can't have that, or Tom Andrews and Marjorie Witherspoon would both be haunting me," the judge chuckled. He turned to Ralph. "I'll get with Paula when I get back to the courthouse and sign the waiver. You can have your wedding."

"Thank you so much, Judge Moore," Amanda smiled.

"Just remember this next time you clobber me over the head with one of your impassioned arguments," the judge called over his shoulder.

Jon shook his hand. "You don't know how much this means to us."

"Just take care of her. She's the best attorney in town, much better than her partner there," he winked at Ralph. "And you came with high references. Seems Charlie Petrino thinks you're the right stuff for Amanda." At the question in Jon's eyes, he nodded. "Yeah, I got a call from him last night."

"Take care, and thanks," Ralph spoke to the judge, shaking his hand.

Ralph looked at Jon and Amanda and remarked gruffly, "Gotta go. Lots of work to be done. I leave my partner alone to handle the office while I go on a honeymoon, and what a mess when I get back."

"Bull," Amanda retorted. "You know that office was in better shape than you've ever seen it."

"Yeah, yeah," he waved at her and walked out.

Howells looked at them. "I need to be on my way as well," he said.

"Me too," Jon countered.

"Where are you going? You just got here," Amanda exclaimed.

"I'm getting married in the morning. There are a lot of preparations, and my bride is lounging around in bed, so somebody has to do it," Jon smiled broadly at her.

He leaned over and kissed her. "I'll be back with Father Anselm soon for our counseling session. I have to run pick up Ken at the airport. He finished his final exams, and is coming in to cover for you at church until you are recovered. He said he would play something you'd like for our wedding tomorrow."

"That will be nice," Amanda glowed, as she pulled Jon down and kissed him again.

"I have been given permission to spend a little time alone with you this evening, before being banned so that you girls can do whatever it is you do to get ready," he murmured against her lips.

"Maybe you can recite some poetry for me," she whispered.

The morning of Amanda's discharge from the hospital Claire showed up at the hospital early with Jill in tow, both dressed to kill in matching pale blue sheath dresses of raw silk, Claire carrying a garment bag over her arm and Jill an overnight case. Within the bag was a beautiful creamy yellow tea-length organza confection.

Amanda was ecstatic. "For me? Oh, this is too much," as she felt the folds of the dress lovingly. "This is too good to be true."

"Jon ordered the color and approved our selection," Claire explained. "He said he lost all control when he first saw you in yellow."

Laughingly, the women prepared Amanda for her big day. Claire called in the owner of a local salon to help with Amanda's toilette. "Dr. Howells ordered no overexertion by the bride," she warned Amanda good-naturedly.

The hospital staff all greeted Amanda with warm wishes as she emerged from her room, dressed in her bridal finery, her arm in a sling.

She was wheeled out to Ralph's Escalade, Fred there to tuck her in. His eyes shone with admiration as he let out a low whistle. "Wow! You are a knockout!

"Ralph is in charge of Jon, or maybe it's the other way around. Ralph is a basket case." At the unspoken question in her eyes, he added, "Jon is solid, just fine, and waiting at the altar. I'm your sworn protector today. Jon has charged me with getting you married without incident." They both smiled.

"Andy would be glad to see you so happy," Fred's voice was gruff. "He thought the world of Jon, and always wanted you two to meet. If he couldn't be here with you, I know he wouldn't have it any other way."

Amanda's eyes misted, as she nodded. Fred handed her a velvet case. Inside were Marjorie's pearls, and a small velvet box. Amanda, surprised, opened the box to find two large yellow diamond studs.

"Petrino made arrangements as you requested to obtain the pearls from Marjorie's safety deposit box. The earrings are a wedding gift from Jon. He wanted to give them to you himself this morning, but Ralph vetoed his seeing you before the service."

Amanda was overwhelmed. Claire laughed from the back seat. "Don't get teary and mess up that wonderful make-up!"

Amanda laughed with them as Claire helped her clasp the pearls around her throat and put her earrings on for her.

They made the trip to the church quicker than she expected, as they kept up a cheerful chatter. When they arrived, Charlie and the twin boys were there to greet her. As the vehicle door opened, she could hear an organ prelude in the background. Charlie gently helped her out of the car.

She bent down awkwardly and hugged the boys, all dressed up in matching suits. "I'm so happy that Dad is better."

"Gosh, you're pretty," Caleb gushed.

"Thank you," she beamed, as Pamela squeezed her hand and pulled the boys away to go into the church.

"You're much prettier today than that night at the prom," Charlie joked.

Jill turned to Fred and Claire. "Let's give them a minute," she said quietly. Suddenly Amanda and Charlie were alone.

She reached up and kissed him on the lips quickly, grimacing from the pain in her arm. He put his arm around her to steady her and kissed her back.

"Are you happy?" he whispered.

"Yes, Pete, I am," she smiled. "Charlie," she whispered, "I can never repay—"

He put a finger over her lips. "Remember to take your own advice. There's nothing to repay."

"You're still the best sex in seven states," she teased him.

"Only seven?" he laughed with her. "I must be slipping."

He kept beaming at her, and she looked at him suspiciously. "What is it?"

"Jill is pregnant."

"Oh, my God, Charlie," she flung her good arm around his neck. "I am so happy for you. This is such wonderful news, baby."

"That's my line," he chuckled, as Jill walked up to them.

"He told you my news," she looked at him crossly, then smiled as Charlie tucked an arm around her and drew her to him.

Amanda kissed Jill on the cheek. "I have no words to tell you how happy I am for you . . . ."

"It is you who have made us happy, by introducing us. For you to have done that when you yourself were in such pain that day . . ." Jill's eyes glistened with tears. Charlie nodded smilingly as he hugged his wife closer.

"You told her?" Amanda smiled at Charlie.

"Yes. She asked me why you were so sad that evening, and why I sent the flowers every year on that date."

"And now I can only hope that the love between you and Jon can match ours," Jill smiled warmly at Amanda.

"Me too," Amanda squeezed her hand. "But I have a good feeling about it. And now that date represents a happy event."

Dr. Howells in tailored gray suit walked up to them. "It's time," he announced, as Charlie kissed her cheek and disappeared into the church, and Jill went to join Claire heading down the aisle.

Howells led Amanda to the narthex and took her arm. She expected the ceremony to be small and simple. However, as she looked into the church, she was in for a surprise. A large contingent of friends was in attendance, more than she expected with no advance notice. Her eyes widened as she noted that Ken had secured a choir ensemble, much to Amanda's delight.

"Marjorie and Andrew would be so happy," Howells spoke hoarsely, as the organ went silent and the choir sang *O taste and see* by Ralph Vaughan Williams. Their clear voices wafted an ethereal welcome to her as Jon, decked in tailored gray as well, stood at the altar and caught sight of her. His heart caught in his throat, as she approached him with her eyes shining with unshed tears. Ralph and Claire, along with Petrino and Jill, stood as their witnesses.

After their vows, Jon took her hand and gently pulled her to face him. His eyes locked on hers, he quoted 'When you are old', by William Butler Yeats. When he reached the line, "But one man loved the pilgrim soul in you," tears glistened in her eyes.

"I do love you," she whispered.

"I'll do my best to make you as happy as Andy did," he promised.

After being pronounced as husband and wife, Jon whispered in her ear, "I have a surprise for you."

"Another?" she breathed. "I'm not sure whether I can take any more. This is all too wonderful."

She heard the strains of the piano, and turned. Claire and Ken performed *O! Quand je dors* by Franz Liszt, Claire's fine soprano voice adding a lovely benediction over their union. Amanda clutched Jon's arm tighter. "I would never have guessed," she whispered.

After the homily, during which Father Anselm expressed his personal pleasure and blessing, the congregation stood and sang 'Praise, my soul, the King of heaven'. Healey Willan's anthem *Rise up, my love* was sung by the choir as the couple took Eucharist, Jon gently assisting Amanda as they knelt together.

After the service, Jon made her sit so that she could greet all their friends, including David and Joseph Rand. She was surprised when the crowd parted, and there stood Senator Thomas Whitmore. He took her hand and kissed it.

"My dear, I am so happy for you," he spoke clearly. "I brought another fan with me." Beside him appeared Mike Knox, beaming.

She glowed. But her eyes grew cloudy. "I'm so sorry to hear about the scandal with your staff."

"I too am sorry. I rather liked Walter Norton. He was a fine reporter, and a good man." Whitmore's face featured anger briefly, then he looked at her, apology in his eyes. "But you need to focus on making your future with this man," he added, changing the subject. "And I still want that date."

"Yes, sir," she squeezed his hand.

She spoke to all their guests, until Rand turned to Jon and said half-sternly, "That's all the merry-making she gets today."

Jon, nodding assent, smilingly led her out amid the organ's pealing of Mendelssohn's *Sonata No. 3*. She hung back, reluctant to leave the room swirling with music and friends crowding around wishing them well. Jon, however, noticing her flagging strength, urged her on, one arm around her waist, another holding her arm.

Leaving the church, Jon led her to his Mercedes at the front door and assisted her in, sprinting around to the driver's side as people surrounded them wishing them well. As he got in, she laughed, "No huge reception?"

He feigned a severe look. "The bride has just been released from the hospital. Doctor's orders are that I get her home immediately and attend to all her needs." He smiled broadly, reaching over to kiss her.

"Besides, I'm planning an extravagant honeymoon for my wife once you have fully recovered, and we're going to have a shindig, a big party to celebrate," he added as he turned the key in the ignition. He turned and looked at her, concern showing on his face. "Is that OK? Was the service all right? I wanted it to be as special as possible."

"I could not have asked for a more beautiful wedding, Husband," Amanda exclaimed, her face aglow with pleasure. "Thank you."

"Husband? I like that," Jon beamed. "Claire was the brains behind the service, and the fact that you're so well-loved by the community didn't hurt in getting what we needed," Jon demurred.

They were mostly silent during the trip to the farm, Jon gingerly holding her injured left hand and she contentedly clutching his arm with her right.

When they pulled up to the house, he jumped out of the car, running around to Amanda's door. Amanda weakly smiled at his chivalric gesture. As she protested in vain he picked her up and carried her up the steps and into the house.

As they entered, she could smell the delicious aroma of food. "What have you done?" she asked as he gently maneuvered with her in his arms through the house and up the stairs and lowered her onto her bed.

"Not me," he confessed wryly as he straightened up. "I believe the church ladies are guilty."

He paused, sudden apprehension written on his face. Amanda, alarmed, asked, "Jon, what is it?"

Jon hesitated. "I hate to bring it up right now, but don't want it eating away at me on our wedding day."

Amanda blinked, surprised. "Out with it, then."

"My folks are coming down to the condo for a visit next week. David has told Mom all about you, and she is insisting on meeting you. They couldn't get away in time to fly down for the wedding, and I was frankly afraid of overwhelming you with them."

"Your parents?" Amanda echoed, dismayed. "Next week?"

Noting the reluctance in her voice, Jon was suddenly defensive. "Yeah, but don't worry. They won't barge in or anything. We can say no."

"No, it—it's not that. I'm anxious to meet your family, but I'm a little nervous. I mean—" she stammered, her eyes on the floor, "what do they know about—me? Everything that has happened, my past? Will they approve?"

Jon studied the anxiety in her features, as it dawned on him what she meant. Since the revelation about her true parentage, Amanda had confided in him her great apprehension about how to deal with disclosure. She had ignored and hoped to avoid the moment, being reticent and ashamed of the truth about her origins, but Jon knew that her personal ethics made her concerned about not lying or hiding the truth when the subject presented itself. In anticipation of the Barnes trial, she had already braved disclosure to her fellow church members, but was still anxious about the subject.

He sat down on the bed beside her. "It's all up to you," Jon smoothed her tresses as he sought to set her mind at ease. "You can tell them however much or little as you want, Amanda. It's your life. I hope you married me, not my family."

She regarded him with huge eyes. "I would rather they found out from me than from some other source." She awkwardly pulled him toward her. Lovingly he enfolded her to him. "I just feel so unequal to your family."

He laughed out loud. "Amanda, we all have skeletons in our closet. Dad actually smoked weed as a teenager, and inhaled. Mom and Dad conceived me out of wedlock. They almost divorced over one of David's girlfriends at a high school reunion—Mom accused Dad of looking at her lasciviously.

"Kelly had a short and disastrous marriage with her high school sweetheart, running away from home and eloping. We had a hell of a time with her until she came to her senses, and I had to track her down all the way to Scotland to bring her home." He kissed her lips lightly. "That's why I missed your and Andy's wedding, and why the case of Glenlivet.

"My marriage was a short-lived failure, and David has never settled down, still a different girl each week."

He looked at her and shook his head. "Mandy, you had nothing to do with your past. It was all out of your control. People of good sense are not going to think differently of you for it. My family will love you because you love me, and they won't be able to keep from loving you for yourself.

"But," he paused significantly, "they are going to want to meet you, sooner or later."

"How about having them for dinner next week?" Amanda inquired, glancing at him with hooded eyes.

"You're sure?" Jon stared at her in amazement.

She nodded. "I would like that. Of course, you'll have to do all the cooking and cleaning," she baited him slyly. "I'm still recovering, you know."

He captured her chin with his hand. "You're truly a vixen," he told her as his mouth lowered to hers.

"It's going to be hard to keep you on task, I can see," she softly taunted him as he released her mouth. "I really need to assess the level of household skills you possess now that we're married," she scoffed good-naturedly.

"Oh, I'm very, very good," he whispered as he tenderly claimed her, molding her to him. "I aim to please. And I want the job something awful."

"You really are beginning to sound like Bubba," she teased him as he lowered her to the bed, grabbing a pillow to cradle her shoulder. "Could you quote some more Yeats to me?"

"You liked that?" a smile played around his lips, as he nuzzled her neck.

"Yeah, but right now a little more of 'Leda and the Swan' would be appropriate, don't you think?" she murmured against his mouth, pulling him closer.

LaVergne, TN USA
07 December 2009
166142LV00001B/58/P